THE
EMPIRE'S
GHOST

For my parents

ACKNOWLEDGMENTS

Without the encouragement of Emily DeLeonardo, who has been spending entire afternoons letting me all but act out my stories for her since we were fifteen, I could never have believed my writing would be of interest to anyone. Without the efforts of Thomas Flannery Jr., David Vigliano, and Pete Wolverton, this book would be a dormant manuscript, its indulgences uncurtailed and its sharp edges not yet sharp enough. And without my brother's craftsmanship, I could never have sat at my desk through multiple rounds of revisions without succumbing to the pain of irritatingly persistent injuries. If the computer he built makes it that much easier to play games instead of working, the fault is mine alone.

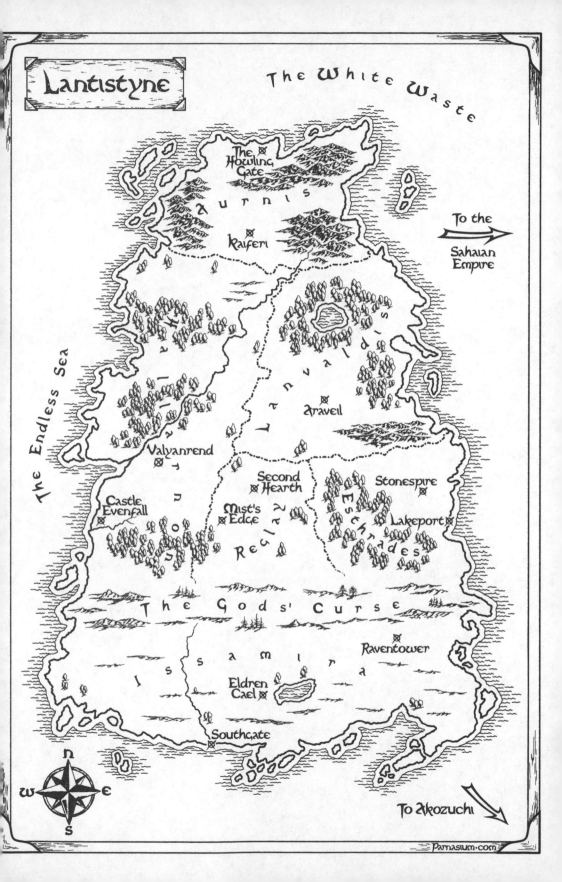

THE
EMPIRE'S
GHOST

PROLOGUE

The last time it snowed, Roger took a bundle of firewood and some biscuits to the Dragon's Head.

The streets of Sheath Alleys were perpetually dank, as narrow and twisting as a guilty thought—and they inspired many, as Roger knew all too well. It was as if Valyanrend itself fled to Sheath to escape its past, to disappear into the shadows as so many of its citizens had done. For the city, at least, it was a lost cause. A stray motif here, a crumbling cathedral there—all pointed to the capital's storied history, its follies and its fall. Even the cobbles of the streets were suspect—you could fancy you saw dried flecks of red in the mortar, the remnants of countless uprisings and revolts. As a boy, Roger himself found what he convinced himself was a bone from a human finger in a crack between two pieces of brick in an alleyway; now he admitted it was as likely a fragment of chicken picked clean by a dog, but it *could* have been the lost remains of a dethroned emperor. Who was anyone to say?

But now the jagged streets of Sheath looked almost peaceful, all the grime covered by cold, cloying white. Roger pulled off his cap before he'd gotten halfway, feeling the snow settle behind his ears and catch in his hair. Whenever he stepped into the shadows—there were always shadows to spare in Sheath—he watched his breath, pale and smoky in the dark. The moon was high and full, but even if every star had been snuffed out, he could have found his way by less than a candle flame.

His ears had gone numb by the time the old tavern came into sight, but he didn't mind. He stood before it for a few breaths, feeling the cold so fresh and sharp in his lungs that it seemed almost to have bitten him, left a pain gentle enough to cleanse. Too bad ale'd soon ruin all that, he thought, and rapped three times.

Little Seth, Morgan's only hired hand, opened the door for him, his pale face brightening at the sight of what Roger held. "Miss Imrick!" he called through teeth that were slightly chattering. "Mister Halfen's here!"

Morgan Imrick came out from the back room, shaking her head. "Gods' sakes, you two, pull the *door* closed!" She grabbed a fistful of Roger's coat, dragging him inside and shutting the offending object on its hinges—the wood was old and scarred, and the hinges were so loose that you didn't so much open the door as send it hurtling toward the wall. But it was so tightly fitted to the frame that when she slammed it, you'd believe even death couldn't slip past. Only then did she turn to him. "Good to see you, Roger. Get that wood to the fireplace, all right? Braddock!" she called to the tavern's only other occupant, snapping her head in the direction of the far corner. "Help Roger with the firewood, would you please?"

As far as Roger had been able to tell, Braddock never went anywhere without three things: a shabby brown coat, three-day-old stubble, and a surpassingly gruff demeanor. Roger usually tried to keep clear of anyone with a large assortment of weapons and a small sense of humor, but Braddock had earned Morgan's trust somehow. And Roger had never known him to be disorderly in her tavern, no matter how drunk he got. He'd been sitting in his accustomed spot by the window, but he stood up and plunked his tankard down when Morgan spoke, with a vague grunt that could not possibly have been an honest attempt at a word. "Right then," Roger said, dropping the bag of biscuits on the bar and passing Braddock half the wood. "Where are Lucius and Deinol?" he asked Morgan over his shoulder.

She clicked her tongue. "Out," she said flatly, pouring some ale into another tankard. "Here." She slid it down the counter toward him as if the movement signaled an end to the discussion.

But Roger couldn't have a drink until he got the wood settled, and with his reward secure, he figured he could keep talking a bit. "Those two are on the ups, eh?" he asked. "Big job going down tonight?"

"I don't know what you mean," Morgan said, so primly that he knew there were secrets to be ferreted out.

He grinned. "Well, I *hear* that old merchant Lorrin's planning on moving house tonight, and their best route takes them right through Ebon Corners. Rotten luck, that—everyone knows Ebon's crawling with brigands of the worst sort. Be pretty hard to find the culprits if anything were to go missing, eh?"

"I suppose it would be," Morgan said, as if she couldn't care less. "Try your drink."

"Don't mind if I do!" He raised his tankard to the room at large. "And a hearty gods' grace to you all."

"Grace," Seth said, with a timid smile. The other two were silent.

Roger laid claim to his favorite stool, placing the tankard back on the bar and draping himself beside it. You couldn't say much for the decoration in the Dragon's Head—Morgan refused to hang anything on the walls, and Seth's attempts to brighten up the mantel over the fireplace were more well intentioned than effective. Roger supposed he understood flowers, even if he held no personal attachment to them, but the boy had found much more than that: oddly shaped stones, bits of colored glass, four-fifths of a porcelain dish he'd pulled out of some rubbish heap. Morgan complained about nearly every new addition, but she'd outright refused him only the pigeon feathers—if Seth wanted to catch diseases, she had said, there were plenty of poorer districts that could accommodate him. In fact, as far as Roger was concerned, Morgan's fastidiousness more than made up for her lack of aesthetic sense: he didn't doubt that the Dragon's Head was the cleanest establishment in Sheath, despite the best efforts of some of its patrons. How she got the wood of that bar to gleam like that was beyond him.

"So," he said after polishing off the alc, wiping his mouth contentedly with his sleeve, "can a fellow get another swallow or so? It is mighty cold out there."

Morgan rolled her eyes. "*You're* just the same as ever, aren't you, Roger?"

"And why should I be otherwise, my dear?" He aimed a cheeky smile at Seth, who started to grin back, though the expression immediately disappeared when Morgan turned on him.

"Seth," she said, "if you have time to flirt with Roger, you have time to stoke the fire. I suggest you get to it."

"R-right away, Miss Imrick!" Seth squeaked, nearly throwing himself at the hearth. One of the Dragon's Head's best features, it was large enough for the boy to curl up in, but the resulting fire never seemed to bother him—it was the cold he couldn't handle.

"You needn't shrink from her so," Roger said, laughing. "When has she ever laid a hand on you?"

"I hit far too hard for one so delicate," Morgan—quite rightly—pointed out. She turned to Roger with her arms folded, but he caught the wry smile tugging at one side of her mouth. "I *do* appreciate the supplies, Roger—and the company, believe it or not—but this is a tavern, not a home for the destitute. And tavern means business, and *business,* as I know you're not too familiar with the term, means standards."

Morgan had been saying that since she'd first taken over the Dragon's Head, and, well, she did *mean* it, but her tavern didn't attract the types it did for nothing. A thief had to choose his haunts carefully, after all, and the Dragon's Head had become Roger's because Morgan was one of the precious few people he both trusted and liked—which, given his profession, meant trusting her discretion as much as her honesty. Her standards, if she had them, were a good sight stranger than everyone else's.

"There's something doing in the streets," Braddock said suddenly, peering outside. "I don't think I like the look of it."

The Dragon's Head had two walls open to the street, both generously studded with windows. But the glass was cheap and milky, and all Morgan's attempts to clean it couldn't change that. The light that filtered in always had a muted quality, and you had to get up close to the windows in order to get a detailed view of the other side—no doubt that was why Braddock always chose to sit there. Morgan strode over to stand by Braddock's stool, following his gaze. "Soldiers passing through," she said for Roger's and Seth's sakes. "More than I'd like. Were there supposed to be military maneuvers tonight?"

Roger scratched his head, trying to remember. "I want to say no, but I don't recall, honestly. Course, the usual channels aren't infallible."

"This is bad," Seth said, his voice skidding high on the last syllable. "What if Lucius and Deinol—"

"Hush," Morgan said, with an abortive wave of her hand. "If anything had happened to Lucius and Deinol, there'd be no reason for soldiers to show up *here*, would there?" But her face was drawn, and Roger knew what she was thinking: if Lucius and Deinol were doing what Roger was almost certain they were doing, there was a chance they'd bring the loot back here—and they couldn't do *that* with a bunch of soldiers making the rounds.

It was Braddock, surprisingly, who broke the silence. "Doesn't look like a patrol to me," he said. "Strange for little pests like those to be passing through so far from their fellows, though."

"It *is* strange," Morgan said—but she only looked puzzled now, not anxious, and Roger would have flashed Braddock a grateful smile if he'd thought for a moment it would have been accepted. "It didn't seem like they were responding to a crime—"

"Pah," Braddock spat. "Whenever there's *real* trouble, those dogs are nowhere to be found. I'd say they've caught the scent of a profit, but there's slim chance of that down here."

"And we'd've heard if there were some sort of plot about," Seth added.

Morgan looked to Roger. "You're sure there's been nothing?"

He shook his head. "Quiet as a Ninist vestry—for the last fortnight, no less. Nothing doing in all Sheath Alleys, I warrant you."

As their imperator's war with Lanvaldis had dragged on, he'd started pulling more and more soldiers out of the capital, either to join the front lines directly or to replace men he'd taken from other strategic locations across the country. Perhaps that was why it felt so strange to see them now, though Roger had always known them to give Sheath a wide berth regardless. It was probably good for him that their presence was reduced in his city, but thinking about the war always made him uneasy, for reasons he'd never been able to determine. It wasn't that he feared for himself: every battle so far had taken place on Lanvaldian soil, and the vast majority of them had ended in victory for Hallarnon, especially of late. Better still, a month ago Imperator Elgar himself had left Valyanrend to join his troops on the front lines as they inched ever closer to the Lanvaldian capital of Araveil. Most of the people Roger trusted to understand military matters had even claimed that the Lanvalds' defeat, at this point, was practically inevitable. So then why did seeing those soldiers give him such a bad feeling? Surely it wasn't pity for people he'd never seen?

Morgan frowned, drawing her fingers absentmindedly across the windowsill. "I suppose," she said at last, "that if the soldiers are only passing through, there's no sense in getting worked up over it. Isolated little groups like that one probably make many inconsequential movements over the course of a single day, and we'd think nothing of it if we weren't . . . on edge." *Waiting,* Roger thought, was the word she was looking for—waiting on a couple of brigands, no less.

"I could go," Seth offered suddenly, trying to draw himself up to his full height—which wasn't much. "I could go ask—"

Morgan shook her head with surprising gentleness. "They'll be all right," she said. "They always are. You'll just have to trust in them, Seth."

"They're fond of flash," Braddock added, "and they talk a good game, but they've skill to back it up—we all know it. And even if Deinol sometimes lacks the sense to be discreet, Lucius always makes him mind in the end. They won't go courting danger tonight."

"I think," Roger said, "we could all use another round. And nobody's so much as touched these biscuits yet. I guarantee they're fresh enough—fully half delicious, in fact. Allow me to demonstrate." He strode over to where he'd left the biscuits atop the bar, fished in the bag until he found one, and then took a huge bite, chewing merrily. "You see? Perfectly edible, and not half hard. I spoil the lot of you, swear on the gods I do."

Seth smiled at him, and Morgan said, "I'll take one—pass them here." Even Braddock raised his head and looked at him. Roger grinned at them all and then tossed another biscuit across the room to Morgan, then held the bag teasingly over Seth's head when the boy asked for one too.

When they were all supplied with biscuits, Morgan passed out the tankards: stout for Braddock, another ale for Roger, and the same for Seth, albeit it was one-third water. Morgan herself didn't drink during business hours, though she wasn't overfond of the stuff in the first place, having as she did to kick out passels of drunkards nearly every evening. Roger and Seth stoked the fire, and once his ears had forgotten what it felt like to be cold, Roger said, "End of the year's approaching, isn't it? Good time for aspirations, I'd say."

"Aspirations?" Morgan asked, her elbows resting on the bar.

"I mean," Roger said, "look to the future, and say what you'd like to see. Why not?"

Morgan shook her head, casting free a brief laugh that wasn't quite bitter. "What aspirations, Roger? We're all stuck down here, and you know it."

"Nothing's permanent," Roger said, but somehow it didn't sound as forceful as it had in his mind.

Lacking a tankard, Morgan raised one fist in a mock-salute. "I suppose we shan't see you around here much longer, then. No *aspirations,* I'm sure, ever thrived long in the Dragon's Head. And you'll be wanting bigger and better things, won't you?"

"Things are always changing," Roger said, because saying nothing was tantamount to sulking. "There's another year about to go by, and . . . and perhaps it'll snow again tomorrow, and perhaps it won't."

Seth looked about to speak, but Braddock's grunt silenced him. "Thinks he's a bard," he said, "thinks he's—"

But Roger was not destined to find out what he thought he was, for at that moment the door leaped nearly off its hinges, banging with such force against the opposite wall that all four of them were stunned into silence. And into that sudden absence the two interlopers poured enough commotion for all of them, nearly dancing into the room, hands full and lips brimming with merriment. "Shut the *door*!" Morgan yelled over the tumult, and Lucius Aquila cast the cloth bag he was carrying to the floor, pausing only a moment to make sure the entrance was well and truly closed. Then he looked up in triumph, the customary enigmatic smile smoothing his face.

Deinol had already bounded into the center of the room, dropping his own sack and throwing an arm around Seth's shoulders. "And there's my boy!" he said in full jubilation, mussing Seth's pale hair. "And he'll come with us one of these days, won't he?"

"He certainly will *not,*" Morgan replied, as unamused as only she could look. "No hired hand of mine is going gallivanting off for a night of pilfering, I warrant you that for certain."

"Ah, Morgan, the boy'll grow up as dull as one of Roger's fake flints if you don't loose your hold on him."

Morgan arched a single eyebrow. "I seem to recall that *someone* was entirely convinced the boy wouldn't get the chance to grow up at all if I didn't take him in."

"You did say something of the sort," Lucius said, clapping a hand on Deinol's shoulder. "Besides, Seth's a right proper boy, isn't he? He's an honest living to put us both to shame, and Roger, too."

"Hey there," Roger said, "don't lump me in with *your* sort. There're leagues of difference between us—for one thing, I'm a coward, the way a true swindler ought to be—"

"As much as I love being made privy to confessions of dishonesty and criminal acts in my own establishment," Morgan interrupted, "I don't believe I gave you two *any* impression—any at all—that this was the proper place to stash your spoils."

Deinol looked genuinely puzzled. "But, Morgan, where did you *think* we were going to stash it? These days we do everything here."

"Isn't that the truth?" She sighed. "Well, let's see it then. What've you got?" Then, as she saw what he was about to do, she tried to grab his arm. "No, no, *don't*—"

But Deinol, of course, had already upended the bag, pouring its contents onto the floor. In spite of himself, Roger peered at the lumps eagerly: he saw jewelry, good silver, and several odd little trinkets, as well as more than a few coins. "You godsforsaken *idiot*," Morgan hissed. "How are we going to hide all this if someone comes in?"

"Morgan," Deinol said, "it's the darkest hour of the night on one of the coldest days of the year. No honest man is going to come *this* way—they're all in their beds."

"If only there were any honest men in Sheath, then," Morgan replied, and Braddock barked out a laugh. "Well, Lucius?" she asked. "I suppose you'll be wanting to show us your treasures as well."

He smiled gently, picking his own sack back up and fishing around inside. "It's mostly the same as Deinol's lot. We grabbed whatever we could get our hands on, once we'd gotten the wagons in disarray. But I did find this." He pulled out a small figurine: a dragon with outspread wings and a pensive gaze, looking down on them as if from a lofty height. Its scales looked blue in the shade, but when Lucius turned the figure in the firelight, they glinted a perfect green. Roger stared at it, thinking on deep caverns, pathless forests—a different, stranger sort of adventure than his city's twisting alleyways, and one he had never seen.

"It's beautiful," Seth said at Deinol's elbow, his little voice shrouded in awe.

"Isn't it? It seems I can't bring myself to sell it." Lucius's smile turned inward as he spoke, as if he amused himself.

"It is lovely," Morgan agreed. "But I hope you didn't think I could display it at the bar. A stolen trinket—there's no way I—"

"Oh no, I understand," Lucius said. "It has nothing to do with the Dragon's Head, really, except that I—well, I like dragons. Always have."

"I suppose it's lucky you're not likely to ever meet one, then," Roger said. "I expect that would take the romance right out of it."

"I'll tell you what," Morgan said—at her words, Lucius shut his mouth, concealing whatever response he would have made—"how about we get all this safely stashed away, and I'll serve everyone another round? I *ought* to charge you two double, but you did a damned good job with the roof, so I'll let it go this time."

"I'll take that bargain, Morgan," Deinol said, and scooped his treasure back into the sack—all except one coin, which he proffered to Seth with a wink. (Morgan pretended not to notice.) Lucius passed over his own sack, and Deinol disappeared into the cellar to hide them. He left the little dragon, but Lucius promised he'd make sure it stayed hidden securely enough not to cause trouble for anyone. Deinol had just returned, and Morgan had just started her sigh of relief, when the door banged open once again, admitting a tousled, wild-eyed young man it took Roger a few seconds to place. He finally recognized Harvey Wapps, an apprentice tinker and one of Morgan's occasional patrons.

"It's fallen!" he cried, before any of them could react. "The news is spreading through the city—Lanvaldis has fallen!"

Morgan shook her head vaguely, as if she thought she disagreed. "What?"

"How do they know that?" Roger asked at the same time. "Elgar can't have reached Araveil already, can he?"

"By now he might well have," Wapps said, "though I don't expect *that* news will reach us for some time. But King Eira's army is finished, they say—crushed so decisively that it'll never recover. If that's so, even Araveil won't hold out for long."

"We've won, then?" Deinol asked.

Wapps nodded darkly. "Aye, we've won, all right—another kingdom, reduced to a mere jewel in Elgar's crown. He has the whole north now, and most of the east—he has half the *continent*."

"Better a win than a loss, though, isn't it?" Roger said, but he couldn't grin, not with Wapps's face so pale. "Our boys'll come back home—your own brother, Wapps—"

"And what of the conquered?" Lucius asked suddenly, with uncustomary harshness, his face drawn and grim. "I don't want to think of the kind of mercy that man will extend to them."

That put them all to silence for a few moments, as well it might: Lucius was originally from Aurnis, the country to the far north that Elgar had crushed more than two years ago. He had said very little about how he had come from there to here, but Roger doubted that it had been a pleasant journey, or that he had been able to salvage much of what his life had been before Elgar's forces had come. But Lanvaldis was far larger than Aurnis—it was as large as Hallarnon, mirroring the territory in the east that Hallarnon held in the west. With them both under his control, and Aurnis above them . . . Wapps hadn't exaggerated. Elgar really did rule half the continent.

Finally Morgan spoke. "There's nothing *we* can do for the conquered, Lucius. And what's Lanvaldis to us, anyway? I'm just as glad I don't have to wonder what kind of mercy *they're* going to serve *me*."

"I'll drink to that," Roger said, but his mouth was dry.

"You're welcome to a drink as well, Wapps, if you'd like," Morgan said, but the apprentice shook his head, snow fluttering about his ears.

"I'm spreading the word. Everyone ought to know about this."

"Then shut the damn door," Morgan said, without any bite.

After Wapps had gone, Deinol looked to Lucius, who was still casting dark looks at the empty air. "Are you all right?"

"I'm fine," Lucius said. "Morgan's right; I'm glad it isn't me."

But something more than cold had sharpened the air, and Roger's eyes were stinging with it. He traced the rim of his tankard with one finger, shifting uncomfortably under the weight of the deepening silence.

The snow was falling thick throughout Araveil, and for just a moment Shinsei let himself imagine that it was snowing everywhere, that the world was fully blanketed in white, stifled into perfect stillness. It would be beautiful, he thought—quiet and peaceful, untouched by grossness and irregularity. He would walk through the streets, and the falling snowflakes would erase his footsteps behind him, like a slow, bittersweet forgetting. That was what memory should always be like.

But tonight his presence was stark and incisive, unyielding as a knife's edge, brazen as a firebrand. He left a bitter trail behind him—it was the blood he scattered through the streets.

It was unfortunate; it was not how he would wish it. But it was what his master willed.

The streets of Araveil were beautifully formed, sprawling and yet somehow orderly, like a daydream shaped into verse. It was a shame to mar them with carnage, but his work was nearly done. King Eira's famed army had been in ruins since the battle at Blackridge, and now even the soldiers left guarding the capital were decimated. There was but one objective remaining, and it lay here, beyond these palace doors.

A handful of men—Shinsei counted them: seven—guarded the great hall.

They were panting and frayed, nearly staggering toward him. They were too tired to hide their fear.

Shinsei removed them quickly—it was growing late, and his master wanted the city before the sun rose—and passed into the inner chamber. It was white and silver and pale blue—it reminded him of the snow.

"Your Grace," he said.

The aging man before him started back, his grimness touched with surprise. "They would send such a one as you?" he asked.

"I am the best they have," Shinsei informed him. "I have killed the most tonight of anyone."

King Eira made an expression Shinsei did not understand—eyes narrowed, lip slightly curling. "That is evident," he said.

Shinsei followed the king's gaze to his own bloodstained garments, his arms darkened past the elbows—the red dripping in his footsteps, marring the marble and soft carpet at his feet. "I am sorry," Shinsei said. "This is a beautiful chamber, and I have ruined it."

The man's eyes were level and steady, his shoulders shifting slightly with his breath. "This was a beautiful city, once," he said. "I wonder you do not apologize for that."

"It will be beautiful again," Shinsei told him. It would be better than it ever was, because his master would rule it.

The king shook his head. "I do not think so. But then, I don't suppose I will ever know."

"No," Shinsei agreed. "You will not."

King Eira let free a soft sigh. "I have committed sins enough," he said. "If I must die for them now, I suppose I cannot complain. But do not think"—he was already charging, his blade half free of its scabbard—"I will go without a fight—"

Shinsei calculated the distance, took a careful sidestep. The Lanvaldian king overreached, almost stumbled, and was just whipping himself back around to try again when Shinsei's weapon struck him through the spine. The crunch of bone boded well.

After he freed his sword from the body of the king (unfortunately, he had to brace his foot against the man's back to yank it out, which made an even bigger mess of the chamber), Shinsei crouched beside him, listened for his breath, heard nothing. Good.

This was a man with excellent taste, he thought, casting one last look back at the once-immaculate room before shutting the door behind him.

———

The messenger had been covered in wet, from all the snow that melted as he rode, but he had not brought it home with him to Stonespire. It wasn't just the area around the capital, either—he claimed that even northern Esthrades was clear, with little more than a flurry after he'd crossed the border from Lanvaldis. Well, that was something, Gravis thought. Winter hung lightly, as yet, about this land he loved, leaving only the ghost of a chill in the air, silent overnight frosts that faded after a few hours of sun. Perhaps the gods favored Esthrades still, or perhaps the cold merely lay coiled, waiting to strike.

His feet weighed heavier than the stone they trod as he trudged back up the long steps and passed under the gate. He touched the double doors of Stonespire Hall, his hands weak against the wood, trembling like a coward's. The doors opened at last, and he strode a silent passage to Stonespire's great hall—still warm and lit, even in the depths of this winter's night. There were no sconces on the walls—they were hung floor to ceiling with heavy tapestries, each depicting some triumph of one of Esthrades's past rulers. Instead the light came from candleholders planted the length of the hall, each nearly the height of a man. They were set some distance from the walls so that the smoke would not ruin the tapestries, and formed a sort of avenue down which potential supplicants could approach the throne. But the room lay deserted, empty of servants and guards, of subjects of any kind. He raised his head, staring at the most painful absence of all: the great oaken throne of Esthrades, standing cold and empty.

He sank to one knee—it seemed the old patterns of obeisance were too deeply etched in him to die. "My lord," he whispered, only half aware he spoke aloud, "my lord, this is no time to be abed! Where is the strength I saw in you of old?"

Grief, perhaps, would have mastered him then, but for a croaking voice: "Is that you, Gravis?" He leaped to his feet, but it was only Verrane, Lord Caius's elderly nurse, shutting the tower door softly behind her. Age and care had lined her face, but they had not stooped her shoulders, had inspired no trembling in her limbs. Her pale gray eyes were intent on his. "What troubles you so? I thought you a man of action, not oratory."

"A weaker man than I might weep, confronted with such news as this," he told her. "Lanvaldis has fallen."

Verrane's sharp intake of breath only made Gravis realize just how deathly silent it had been in the hall. "When?" she asked, darting glances into every corner of the room, as if Gravis had said they'd been the ones invaded.

He shook his head. "It's difficult to say. Elgar's men shattered their army at Blackridge some time ago—that's when the signal fires started, when birds and horsemen began to carry messages. King Eira's reinforcements are heading south from Helba Fortress, but they'll never reach the capital in time. Once Elgar has taken Araveil, he can pick them off at his leisure—if they do not surrender out-right."

"Lanvaldis is twice the size of Esthrades," she said. Her voice was strong—she might almost have been making a casual observation, save that she was as still as stone.

"That's hardly the worst of it," Gravis said. "Lanvaldis has a standing army—the best on the continent, or so Eira boasted. If Hallarnon can crush *them,* what chance do we have?"

Verrane was pale, her fingers fumbling absently at the air. "But . . . but will Hallarnon's army come *here*?"

He shrugged hopelessly. "It's surely only a matter of time."

"You can't truly believe that."

"Why not? Why should Elgar stop until he's grasped the whole continent? Esthrades is an easy target."

She brought her fingers together and clasped her hands as if to steady them. "What should we do?"

"What *can* we do? We have not even a master to guide us." He glanced at Verrane. "His lordship is no better?"

She shook her head. "No better."

Gravis started to pace, darting another look at the empty throne. "Has he his wits about him? I can manage things in the capital well enough, but he needs a proper general to maintain the borders. If he would but name a commander to succeed him—"

"Lord Caius has an heir," Verrane said, a note of genuine surprise in her voice. "What other successor does he need?"

"What he has," Gravis retorted, "is a snake at his heels—a daughter only, and a daughter who loves him not. I wish, at the least, he'd give her a husband."

Verrane actually smiled. "You say that as if he had not tried."

"*Tried?*" Gravis scoffed. "The marquis is her father, and sworn lord of his realm—he had every right to *make* her mind. I wonder how he did not."

"In truth it is no wonder at all," came the reply, and this time Gravis's hackles were raised before he even turned, because there was no mistaking *that* voice.

Though her bearing belied it, Arianrod Margraine was still young—it had been twenty-two summers since, but he could still remember the ill-fated day of her birth. Lord Caius was broad and dark-bearded, but his daughter looked like the winter that waited to engulf Esthrades: tall and fair-haired, with blue eyes fading into gray and skin that stayed ever pale—no blush of modesty, Gravis was sure, had ever darkened *that* face. Though she had the sleek vivacity of the young and prosperous, there was something in her slender frame and quick, searching eyes that hungered perpetually.

"Your ladyship," Gravis growled.

"My father," she continued, unperturbed, "is in love with the legacy of his blood, and there is none left to carry it but I. That is why he will name no other successor, and why, no matter how many ways I may devise to vex him, he would never harm my person or position." She smiled. "Did you think it was out of affection for me? I am sorry to disillusion you."

"I wonder, then, that he never doubted the blood in your veins was his," Gravis dared. Verrane shot him a panicked look, but his master's daughter did not flinch.

"Oh, I don't doubt it," she said carelessly. "I may not like it, but I don't doubt it. Who could doubt my lady mother? Everyone tells me how unendurably devoted she was to him. So much the worse for her."

"My lady, do not speak of your poor mother so, I beg you," Verrane said.

The marquis's daughter eyed Verrane with some amusement. "She is long dead. What harm can words do her now?"

"Some would say," Gravis said, trying for Verrane's sake to curb his tongue at least a little, "you have no right to speak of her at all. You killed her with your birth."

At least the woman had enough grace not to smile openly, but the expression seemed to lurk somewhere in her eyes. "Yes, well, I am hardly the first child to have done so. I am sure I would have behaved myself better, could I have helped it."

Gravis did not trust his tongue, so he said nothing.

His expression must have revealed something, however, for she turned serious for the briefest of moments: "Come, Gravis, don't you think I would wish the woman alive again, if wishes could help her?" But then she smiled, irreverent once more. "They tell me she never wished harm on another soul, not as long as she lived. I would have liked to see so rare a creature; I cannot claim ever to have had the good fortune to meet one."

"I don't believe your ladyship would have any use for one such as your mother was," Gravis said.

Arianrod Margraine did not answer that; she gave a thoughtful pause instead, glancing about the empty hall. Though all else in the room was pristine, the steps to the oaken throne were covered in an unaccustomed layer of dust, a testament to how long it had been since Lord Caius had taken his seat there. "I must admit," she said, "I did not come here to talk about my mother. Before I entered this discussion, Gravis, I heard you speak of Lanvaldis's defeat, of Esthrades's future. Will you not continue?"

She was listening in, then. Of course she was. He scoffed. "I extended *you* no part in this discussion."

"Yet you would speak of strategy to Verrane? Surely you admit I know more of military matters than she, at least."

"You know a great deal, your ladyship, there's no denying it," Gravis said. "Indeed, I don't doubt you are skilled in matters no mortal ought to think on." He would have said more, but Verrane bit her lip, looking anxious. Gravis remembered that she, like so many women, possessed an all-enduring propensity to dote on the child she had raised, and so he fell silent.

Yet he had not spoken out of turn. All of Stonespire, all of *Esthrades* whispered of it—that the marquis's daughter was that most forbidden thing, a sorceress.

It wasn't just the way she seemed to know things—she'd been clever since she was born, reading before Lord Caius had even dreamed of calling a tutor for her, and flustering said tutor entirely by the age of seven. Many of her ancestors had been scholars; the Margraines had made a grand tradition of it. But Gravis had seen his share of scholars, and he knew enough to know that there was clever and there was strange. She didn't just *seek* knowledge; she devoured it; she hoarded it. She sharpened it like a weapon, and who could say where she meant to aim it? Gravis had always suspected that she knew far more than books, more than the dry tomes and treatises of her father's library. She knew things about the world that were best forgotten, and things about people she had no call to know, as if she could read every thought in their heads before they could themselves.

She turned her gaze on him as if to prove his point, smug and serene despite the severity of her father's illness. Or, for all he knew, perhaps because of it. That seemed somehow more likely, where she was concerned.

"That's what I like about you, Gravis," she said. "You shun everything fair, everything alluring, and cleave always to what is simple and stark, what can be laid bare at a glance. Even your wife is plain."

Gravis ought to strike her one for *that*, but everything she said was true. "I'm in no mood for jibes, your ladyship," he said instead, like a sullen young subordinate.

"Then I'll be brief," she replied. "Esthrades is in crisis. I think it is time for you to convene your men in the hall."

"Only my lord the marquis can give such an order," Gravis said immediately.

The look she gave him was indulgent; he wanted to spit at the sight of it. "You well know he is indisposed. He has difficulty commanding his own four limbs, let alone more distant vassals."

"And so I should countenance a usurper to stand in his place? Lady, not while I live."

What irritated him most of all was how genuine the woman's good humor was. There were some who smiled to hide the rage that stuck in their throats, the gall that roiled their stomachs. But *her* amusement, the wry delight she could find even in intended insults, rang true every single time. "Gravis," she said, "I know you value a candid tongue."

"I'd rather know the heart behind it," he said, "but yes, I do."

"Then let me speak plainly." She let her smile fade, and gazed brazenly on him, with one flick of her eyes toward Verrane to show the old woman she was not forgotten. "I know the great respect you have for my father. However, I must confess that I have never shared it. I find him and have ever found him neither a wise ruler nor a worthy man, and my life with him has been naught but one quarrel after another. I doubt we were meant to coexist." She paused. "I assume this is not news to you."

"Indeed it is not," Gravis let himself growl.

"Then when I tell you, Gravis, that the illness that now has him in its grip causes him so much suffering that even I would grant him peace if I could—if you will not believe for mercy's sake, at least believe that he is too far gone now to answer for anything—when I tell you this, Gravis, for it is the gods' plain truth, I trust you will understand the full import of my words." She paused again, drew in a breath. "If not, then I'll be plainer still. The man you call your lord is in his last illness. He lives still, but he will nevermore rise from his bed. He will leave his chamber only in a coffin. That is all I can say for him."

Gravis could not bring himself to look at her, nor at the empty throne, the ancient tapestries. His gaze found purchase somewhere near his feet, on the tiled stone floor, gray upon gray. "Then Esthrades is lost," he said quietly.

She let another smile flick across her face, swift and fleeting. "Why do you say that?"

Gravis gritted his teeth. "Because, my lady, I will take orders from none but my sworn lord, and that dying man is he."

"And when he is dead?"

"He is not dead," Gravis said. "I do not *like* hypotheticals."

She sighed as if indulging a simple child, but there was nothing of indulgence in her eyes, which had gone coldly, dangerously hard; Gravis could almost have wished for the smirk again. "And *I*, sir, cannot and will not abide a lack of wit. Believe that I respect the abilities that allow you to execute your office, but *do not* play the fool with me or I will treat you as a fool deserves. Whether you admit the fact or no, I will *imminently* have your life in my hands, and you are not the only man in Esthrades capable of being captain of the guard."

Gravis's pride burned strong in him—pride driven by encroaching despair, but pride nonetheless. "You speak as if it matters," he said. "What is it to me what you do with my life? Hallarnon's imperator will have it soon enough, and yours as well."

She shook her head. "I don't blame you for believing it, Gravis, but you're wrong."

"And why is that, your ladyship, if I may ask?"

She strode idly to the nearest tapestry, running a finger along its edge. Gravis had forgotten what ancestor it depicted—a man standing on a promontory looking out to sea—but he didn't doubt she knew all their stories by heart. "How do you imagine Imperator Elgar is feeling at this moment?"

"I have heard he is a man of solemn humor," Gravis said, "but even such a man would not be blamed for dancing upon the Lanvaldian cobbles at such a juncture."

She smiled. "And I would bet you twice the contents of my father's treasury that he is in a fury."

That got his attention. "What could *he* possibly have to be angry about?"

"The messenger to whom you spoke was not the only one to arrive at the hall tonight, Gravis," she said, pacing back toward the throne. "I heard something very interesting from one of them—even though their supply lines remained unbroken, when Hallarnon's forces broke the Lanvaldian army, they had nearly run out of the foodstuffs Elgar had set aside. In another two weeks they would've had to forage among the populace."

Gravis shrugged. "So Elgar and his men won't starve. Good for them."

"If my father had been leading the invasion, Gravis, I would have said the same. But Imperator Elgar is not my father. His every maneuver bespeaks a cautious, nearly paranoid man. Such a man does not attack another country if he thinks victory is *probable;* he would not move without being *certain,* several times over, of success. He would plan for every pitfall, every possible thorn in his path, until victory was not a question of if but of when. He would calculate the time it would take him to wage his war, and then he would provision his men for that length of time and half again. But the war between Hallarnon and Lanvaldis has lasted just over six months, and he wins his victory with only two weeks' worth of rations remaining? It isn't like him."

"He must have thought it would take him five months," Gravis realized. "Perhaps even four."

She grinned at him. "Precisely. So what Imperator Elgar sees, when he looks at his army, is not the unstoppable force that won him a new country, but the band of fools he overestimated by nearly two months."

Gravis's thoughts raced, hurrying to catch up with hers. "His figures were all wrong. He does not know his own strength as he thought he did, and that worries and infuriates him. He must take stock of his forces; he must redraw his plans again and again, incorporating the weaknesses he has discovered into his strategies."

"It will be a long time indeed," she finished, "before he gains the confidence to attack again. There is no hope for Lanvaldis, but for us there is very much hope indeed, provided we use our time wisely." She shot Gravis a level stare. "First of all, you'll need to learn to obey me."

Gravis shook his head. "My lady—"

"We do not and will never agree on the subject of my father," she interrupted. "But there is at least one thing more important to you than your service to him, and that is Esthrades itself. You love this land, Gravis, and I know it."

Gravis wanted to say that a woman like her had no business speaking of service, or of love. Instead he gave the slightest of nods.

"So save Esthrades," she said—it was not quite a command, and yet there was nothing about it of entreaty. "Summon your men to the hall."

"But I"—Gravis seemed to have grown hoarse—"my lady, how can I trust you? Do you expect me to believe *you* love Esthrades?" *Or anything at all, save your own person,* he did not add.

She seemed to consider the question. "I suspect I shall love it, once it belongs to me," she said. "And even if not, you need not fear on that account. I wish to rule, not to be ruled, and to that end no one will fight harder for Esthrades than I." She regarded him calmly, smiling once more. "Well, Gravis?"

Where did she learn to speak so well? It was not from her father; that was certain. She made him feel—or perhaps it was really true—that he had no choice. And so he looked away, at the empty throne, and said quietly, "It is done. I will call my men."

He turned his back on her as he left, grateful not to have to look on those mocking eyes. Such a wretch of a woman knew nothing of a soldier's pain, he told himself, but in thinking it, he only felt like a mongrel cur licking its wounds.

———

The capital had grown relatively quiet, and Shinsei found he was able to relax. With the Lanvaldian army ravaged, the Hallern soldiers had thought to command the city unopposed, but some unexpected civilian resistance had flared up in the streets. Fortunately, Shinsei was there to take care of it, and the damage to Hallarnon's army was negligible. But his master, sour enough to begin with, was displeased at having to enter his new city to such a welcome. He had given Shinsei one more task: he was to scour the remaining districts for agitators before reporting to the palace. Shinsei was looking forward to getting some sleep, but a mission was a mission, and this one would not be difficult.

There was a bloody lock of hair stuck to his knee; the hair was not his. Shinsei frowned, then bent to remove it, and when he straightened again, there was a girl standing before him.

The girl was slightly built, a bit small for one who had fully grown. Her hair shone pale in the moonlight, though it was golden against the snow. She was dressed like an ordinary citizen, in heavy linen and white wool, the ends of her pale blue scarf flapping slightly in the wind. But she carried a sword, as thin and quick as she was. They faced each other in the darkened street, and Shinsei stopped, puzzled. She was not fleeing.

"Did you kill all these people?" Her voice, in the cold air, came very clear. It had a pleasant ring to it, not quite musical but reminiscent of it.

"Yes," Shinsei answered.

Her eyes were bright and vibrant; he thought they were green. "Why?"

"We are invading," Shinsei informed her—did she not know? "I was ordered to dispense with any resistance."

She gestured at the corpses. "But these were no soldiers."

"Yes," Shinsei said patiently. "They were resisting me."

She looked at the items strewn on the ground. "With brooms and shovels? These people were no threat. Why did you not press them to surrender?"

"I believe some of them attempted to," Shinsei said. "But I am tired, and it was quicker to dispose of them."

Her eyes were angry; her sword seemed somehow naked, gleaming and stripped bare. "It is a cowardly thing you have done," she said.

Shinsei did not understand. "Why is that?"

"You slaughtered the weak," she said, as if it were obvious. Shinsei thought, not for the first time, that there was something about her that made her seem very young indeed.

He tried to explain. "It is always the strong who win. That's *why* they win."

"Just because you have the brute strength of arms—"

"My will is strong enough too," Shinsei said. "It must have been, or they would have defeated me."

She was very quiet, very still. It made her like the snow. People must find her very beautiful, Shinsei thought. "And what is your will?" she asked. "Your strength is proven. But what do you wish for?"

"My will is my master's will," Shinsei said.

"And what does your master want?"

"He wants many things," Shinsei said. "Today he wants your country."

"Well," she said quietly, "I guess he has it now."

"He does," Shinsei agreed.

"Then why are you still here?"

"Your people have angered him with their resistance," Shinsei explained. "Before I can rejoin him, I must destroy any who seem capable of causing further unrest."

For a moment the girl looked away from him, down the deserted street, and Shinsei thought she was uncertain. "Those who seem . . . capable?"

"It would not be you," Shinsei said, wondering if that was what she feared. "You are only one girl. Soldiers, or mobs of civilians . . . those are my targets. You do not concern me."

For some reason, she looked at him not with relief but anger, curling her fingers into a fist. "If my brother were here, you'd see what a truly capable person looks like. If he could fight, you'd never—*none* of you would get away with any of this! But even I—even I can be more than you think. I can stand between you and him." She raised her sword. "I challenge you, soldier of Hallarnon, whoever you are. Let us see which is stronger—your will or mine."

"Do not be foolish," Shinsei said. "You cannot defeat me. My swordsmanship is perfect."

"A battle is not over before it is fought," she said stubbornly.

"You are capable of fleeing. You ought to flee," Shinsei told her. "There is no reason for you to die."

"There was no reason for any of these people to die," she said, motioning again to the corpses. "And yet you killed them."

"They were resisting me—"

"*I* am resisting you!" Her voice was loud; her gaze was level, proud and determined and clear. "So fight me."

"I do not understand the reason for this waste," Shinsei said slowly. "But if you truly intend to resist, I shall indeed kill you here."

"You can try," she said. "But I . . . I will protect him, no matter what. I do not fear you."

In the seconds before they closed in combat, he examined her carefully. Her movements were quick, but she was very light, very slender, very young. She was incorrect; this fight was over before it began.

He shifted his grip on his sword, and struck.

———

It never snowed in Hallarnon anymore. The cold was just as bitter; some said it had even *more* bite. Some days the sky was so gray with clouds that you could swear the snow was caught up there, swirling perpetually, unable to fall. Three years since the fall of Lanvaldis, and Roger had walked the streets on many a cold winter's night, but he couldn't claim to have seen so much as a single flake. It was a pity—he'd always loved the snow.

Conflicting theories abounded; there was never a shortage of gossip in Sheath. Some said that, after conquering Lanvaldis, Imperator Elgar had found some hidden magic that stopped the snow from falling; some said it was the gods that had stopped it, as punishment for his atrocities. Some said it was the result of malevolent substances seeping into the earth and air, and some said it was just one of nature's moods. One idea sounded as good as the next, as far as Roger was concerned, and he'd stopped thinking about it overmuch. But he did miss it, sometimes—the old winters, the way they used to be.

It still snowed in the north, in the country that used to be Aurnis; it had snowed in Lanvaldis as Elgar tightened his hold on it, parceling it out to administrators and filling its old castles with his soldiers. It still snowed in Reglay and Esthrades to the east, as their people waited anxiously to find out which of them Elgar would attack next—and then waited longer, as the months turned to years with only occasional border skirmishes to show for it. It did not snow in temperate Issamira to the south, but then it never had, so its residents could hardly be expected to worry about it. But the people of Hallarnon worried—about the snow, and about Elgar's wars, and which would return first.

But Roger wasn't one to wear himself out with worrying, and he settled for turning his eyes up to the cloudy sky, drinking in the chill fog of early morning. He'd look, and he'd muse for a bit, and then he'd put away that too-seductive word, *adventure,* and saunter off down the nearest alley, letting the day begin. Sometimes he thought of Lucius's dragon—the one he had brought home that night, with its outspread wings and beautiful eyes. Lucius still treasured it, and sometimes, during late nights at the Dragon's Head, when all those who didn't know the trinket's history had left, he'd bring it downstairs with him, set it down on the edge of the bar. He'd let it perch there as the night marched on, keeping watch over them as they remembered. And Roger would sit by the fire with Seth, setting embers a-twirl with a stray twig.

He should have been a bard, Roger thought. He and Lucius both.

CHAPTER ONE

Y ou're not feeding those birds again, are you?" Morgan called, and Seth
started. He hadn't realized she was awake. He tried to kick the crusts
out of sight, but Morgan was already opening the door, squinting into the sun.

Valyanrend's districts tended to be jumbled and haphazard more often than
not, but the streets of Sheath seemed especially capricious, as if they'd been
designed to make no sense. The slender lane that ran along the left side of the
Dragon's Head abruptly bent to cross in front of it, widening out as it continued east; on the tavern's other side was what looked like a perfectly respectable
cross street, but was in fact a blind alley culminating in an unforgiving brick
wall nearly ten feet high. It was too narrow to admit much sun, but the birds
seemed to like it anyway, and Seth could sweep the crusts that way to keep them
out of the street. Morgan kept saying she'd find a use for the alley one day, but
so far none of her plans had come to fruition.

She sighed. "Seth, you're just teaching them to hang about. Let them fend
for themselves, like everyone else."

He turned to her. "Don't you wish they could talk? The things they must
have seen . . ."

Morgan laughed. "Well, they must not have been *too* impressed—wouldn't
have come back here if they had, would they? Of course, that's presuming pi-
geons have any sense." She reached out slowly, resting a hand on his shoulder.
"*Don't* feed them, all right? Gods know you need all the food you can spare for
yourself."

"All right," Seth agreed. He leaned on his broom. "I'll just let them have
this one last meal."

"Fair enough," Morgan said. "Remind me to give you some money when
you come inside; I'll be wanting you to run down to Halvard's later on."

"I won't forget," Seth assured her as she disappeared through the doorway.
Once she was gone, he turned to the birds. "Sorry, fellows," he told them, "but
rules are rules. You'll have to find your bread somewhere else from now on." In
truth, the birds reminded him of himself—he'd been hardly better than a beg-
gar when Deinol found him.

He went back inside, giving the room a cursory glance as he headed for the stairs. Roger was here this morning, putting in a drink and a chat before he started his day, as he often did. He was just the same as always: bright red hair, scrupulously clean-shaven face, and an endless appetite for talk. He might have no skills with a blade to speak of (Seth barely did, either, and Roger was always kind to him on that account), but he could talk his way out of just about anything. He smiled at Seth as he passed by, gave a customary wink. "Not too sleepy, I hope?" he asked.

"Not hardly, thanks," Seth said, and couldn't help smiling; Roger knew how many times Morgan'd had to yank him from his bed. "Early morning's the ripest time for work, don't you always say that?"

"And it's a fact," Roger said, nodding. "If a man's trying to get anything of import done in the dark of night, you can be sure he doesn't half know what he's about. What'll he do if his neighbor can't sleep? But even murderers retire when the sun starts to rise." He turned back to the bar. "Speaking of sleep, Morgan, you ought to try it sometime."

"How funny you are, Roger," she replied, barely looking up from polishing the bar.

"Funny? What's funny about it? Sleep does wonders for the temperament— just ask your boy here."

"Hey," Seth said, "leave me out of it."

Roger laughed. "Clever lad."

"You swept the cellar, didn't you?" Morgan asked, picking at an imaginary splinter in the wood.

"Aye," Seth said. "Yesterday, like you asked."

"But you'll need to do the upstairs," she said.

He nodded. "I'm on my way. You can give me whatever I'll need for Halvard's when I come back down."

Morgan was still young, though Roger often said she acted like an old lady. She was lean and tough, but soft in certain places, if you knew how to look. And Seth had always thought she was pretty, with long dark hair and dark eyes to match. Roger said it was because he was fond of her, and Deinol said it was because he had more sweetness than sense, but Seth didn't have to force it—it was just there, whenever he looked at her.

He had the day half planned out already: if he got the upstairs swept quick enough, Morgan wouldn't mind if he dawdled a bit on the way back from the shop. Deinol would be up by then for sure, and he was never a hard man to find—not if you weren't a guardsman. Maybe Lucius would be with him, and he could watch them spar, but Seth also liked it when it was just the two of them.

It was Deinol he loved best. Deinol had convinced Morgan to take him in in the first place. He never had a harsh word for him, and Seth could always come find him and talk to him, no matter when or where, and know that Deinol would be happy to see him. He never felt in the way, as he did so often otherwise.

But he'd hardly reached the landing when he heard Morgan calling for him again. "Seth, get back down here, would you? I've changed my mind."

It wasn't like Morgan to change her mind, so Seth ran back down quickly, settling the broom over one shoulder. He found her peering into a pot, wrinkling her nose contemplatively.

"The stew's almost out, but it seems a shame to get rid of this last bit," Morgan said. "It's not enough to make much of a profit, but perhaps Braddock and those bandits would be interested." She smiled at him. "More for us if not, eh?"

Seth smiled back. "I can go get them if you'd like."

"Would you? Braddock never strays far, and the others are probably just loafing about somewhere, as usual." She shook her head. "Ill at the thought of honest work, yet they can rob a caravan like professionals. Sometimes I'd swear mine's the only honest business in all of Sheath."

"I'd back you on that wager, Morgan," Roger called, holding his tankard high.

———

Seth darted through the alleyways, his feet finding the way almost by reflex. When he first came to Sheath, he'd gotten lost at least a dozen times in succession; he'd thought he'd never learn his way around. And now here he was, traversing with ease what a stranger would call a maze. The thought made him smile.

It hadn't taken but three people asked to hear the story: Lucius and Deinol had gone to practice as usual, but this time Braddock was with them. Seth knew where they'd be: there was a nice wide alley that hit a dead end behind the ruins of a Ninist vestry. He arrived just in time to see Lucius strike Braddock so hard with the flat of his blade that Braddock lost his footing, falling forward onto the cobbles as Lucius stepped back.

Deinol watched with evident amusement from where he leaned against the wall, well out of the fray. But then he saw Seth, and his eyes brightened. "Got away from Morgan, have you? Come and watch. Lucius is having the best of it."

"So far," Lucius said, but Seth could tell he was pleased.

Braddock spat the dust from his mouth, bracing his weight against his weapon as he struggled to his feet. He was fighting with a sword today, and no doubt that didn't help him: Braddock preferred axes, but even though the three of them had always practiced with live steel, his favorite ax was still far too dangerous to spar with. "You damned cocky bastard," he hissed, his teeth gritted.

Deinol laughed. "*I'm* a damned cocky bastard, Braddock. Lucius is just *good*."

The man in question loosed an easy smile, lowering his blade. "You'll go again, then, Braddock? You don't look licked just yet."

"And it's a look you'll never see on me; bet your throat on that," Braddock replied, rolling his shoulders to work the kinks out. "Try me."

"With pleasure." Seth was always struck by just how *fast* Lucius was; he darted forward on the balls of his feet, seeming scarcely to touch the ground, or to flash from point to point as if by magic. Combining that speed with the surprising reach of that slender Aurnian blade he always favored, Lucius could bring a fight to you before you so much as had time to set your stance.

Braddock scowled, met the blow hard, but he was a born brawler, and strong enough to absorb the impact without breaking his block. He turned at the point of disengagement, flinging Lucius back with what seemed a mere flick of his wrist. But Lucius had reflexes such as Seth had never seen, and he refused to lose his balance, skidding only slightly.

"Not bad," Deinol offered.

"Wasn't asking you," Braddock grunted, hefting his sword aloft for a mighty swing.

Lucius knew better than to take *that* head on, and the opposing blade hissed by his left shoulder. Braddock turned gamely at the end of the stroke, trying not to overreach, but Lucius swept his blade under and up, aiming right for Braddock's chin. Braddock pushed back off his heels, then doubled back for a charge after the sword point passed him by. Lucius ducked as quickly as he could, just tearing the cloth at his elbow. They all paused a moment, squinted, but there was no blood.

"I daresay you're getting angry with me, Braddock," Lucius said with a slow grin.

Braddock shook his head. "Don't like to lose, that's all. Especially not to you."

"And if I say you shall?"

Braddock didn't bother answering in words, just brought his sword over and down with such force that Seth was tempted to close his eyes. But Lucius dodged easily, sending his sword's edge skidding across the alley wall before clipping Braddock's wrist almost gently.

With a muttered curse, Braddock wheeled after him to strike again, but then Seth, with a sudden start, remembered why he was there. "Er," he mumbled, "you see, Morgan says . . . Morgan says you're to come right away if you hope to get what's left of the stew—"

"Not *now,* boy," Braddock snapped, and Seth's voice died in his throat.

But Deinol came to his rescue, as always. "Now, fellows," he said, "this fighting's been getting a little too heated anyw—" But at that instant, Braddock caught Lucius square in the stomach with his flat, and Lucius, swept back with the force of it, nearly rammed right into Deinol. He caught himself before he could fall, though he swayed dangerously on his feet.

"Get you—for that," he panted, with a determined smirk. Then he leaped into the air.

Braddock managed to get his sword up just in time to block, but Lucius wouldn't be deterred, snapping one foot under their blades as he landed and catching Braddock in the ribs. When Braddock shifted to favor his wounded side, Lucius turned his sword sharply, connecting with Braddock's cheek. The skin turned instantly red from the sting of the impact, but thankfully Lucius had struck with the flat, and there was no cut.

"Bastard—" But as Braddock tried to bring his weapon around and down, and Lucius set his stance in preparation, Deinol stepped between them, his own sword drawn, blocking Braddock's blow. "That's *enough,*" he said, trying to see behind him. "Lucius—"

"Don't you interfere," Braddock spat, shoving Deinol sprawling to the ground.

"Ow!" Deinol clutched at his sword. "You damn idiot—"

"—not your fight—"

"—just making him madder, Deinol—"

"I'm not *finished* with him—"

"You think *I'm* finished with you? Just trying to get you to calm—"

"—out of my blasted *way*—"

"If *that's* how you want to play, you oaf, allow me to—"

"Er," Seth tried, "you really shouldn't—not all at once like—oh dear."

Somewhere along the way the duel had turned into a brawl, and now all three of them were giving as good as they got. But just as Seth was turning to go fetch help, he was brought up short, hiccupping his heart out of his throat. Morgan was standing at the mouth of the alley, and she did *not* look pleased.

He ducked his head. "Morgan, I *told* them, but—"

"Never mind, Seth," Morgan said quietly. "I'll handle this." She finished tugging on her gloves—thick leather, only slightly worn despite all the use they'd seen—curled her fingers once to check the joints, and strode nonchalantly into the fray.

They were so focused on one another that they didn't even see her until it was too late. Her first blow caught Deinol right below the eye, and he recoiled, staggering back with an oath. Lucius, the most even-tempered of them all even on his worst day, retreated immediately, dropping his sword in favor of holding both hands before him in a gesture of surrender. But Braddock was still plunging after him, oblivious to all else, and Morgan half turned, giving him what could most properly be called a box on the ear. His head whipped around, just in time for her free fist to connect with his jaw. It took him more than a few moments to recover himself after that.

Morgan stood in their midst, nodding slightly in grim satisfaction. "Now then," she said. "I suppose what stew we have left will be reserved for Seth and me. There *may*, however, be some bowls of soup available, provided there'll be no more fighting today."

They said nothing. It was probably wise, Seth thought.

———

When the lot of them trooped into the Dragon's Head, Roger couldn't help but burst out laughing.

Morgan was at their head, looking a little more miffed than usual, but also, to Roger's trained eye, slightly remorseful. It was easy to see why: Deinol was massaging his cheek with the back of his hand, and while Braddock was too proud to show his hurts, the streak of red along his jaw was evidence enough. Seth trailed after them, and Lucius brought up the rear, trying his best to assume a sufficiently grave expression—*he'd* gotten off without a scratch, no doubt, but Roger wouldn't have expected any less from him.

"Well, now," he drawled. "Been brawling again, have we?"

"Go to hell," Braddock said succinctly, heading toward his usual corner.

Roger beamed at the rest of them, but even Deinol seemed subdued. "It's not a good day for jests, Roger," he moaned, collapsing onto a barstool. "Gods, Morgan, you don't play around, do you?"

Roger sighed. "No sense of humor—none at all. Is it any wonder her life's so devoid of romance?"

"Will someone plug up that *monkey*," Braddock growled, "or I'll have to break my word and have just one more fight today."

"Best to keep quiet, I think," Lucius said, clapping him on the shoulder. "Plenty of time for ragging when your life's not in danger."

This was very true.

"Ah, well," Roger said, "I suppose I prize my own skin as highly as the next man. Speaking of, Morgan, did I hear something about stew?"

The looks he got could have pierced steel.

Morgan closed the Dragon's Head at midday—so she could take a quick rest before nightfall, she said, though Seth wondered if she'd actually be able to sleep. She left him to himself until sunset—even going to Halvard's shop could wait until the morrow, she'd decided—but before he could even begin to think of what he wanted to do, Roger caught him by the sleeve as he headed out the door. "Say there, boy," he said softly, with another of his winks, "how'd you like to feast your eyes on a secret?"

Seth hesitated, looking up at him. "If it's such a secret, why would you show me?"

Roger grinned. "Because it's too delicious a find to keep to myself, and telling someone now makes it less likely I'll blurt it out when I'm in my cups. Besides, you're a discreet lad, and we share an appreciation for forgotten things, don't we?"

He was right about that—Roger knew Seth had a weakness for his stories. He rocked back on his heels, considering it. "It's not . . . unlawful, is it? Because Morgan will—"

Roger waved a hand at him. "Gods, boy, no. I'll dream up plenty of unlawful ways to make use of it, I'm sure, but I'll not make an accomplice of you. I can respect honesty in a man—not enough to want any of it for myself, but there you have it." He cocked his head. "So? Will you be seeing it, or won't you?"

Seth finally smiled. "I'll come," he said.

He thought *he* knew the streets, but he'd no doubt Roger could walk them backward with his eyes closed. He never once looked about him to check the way, just strode forward confidently on his longer legs and left it to Seth to scramble after him. Seth counted every turn they made, checking each intersection to make sure he still knew where he was, and to his surprise found they were soon leaving Sheath entirely. The narrow jumble of streets straightened, but didn't widen, into the long lanes of the Wilting Roses, the largest cluster of cheap brothels in the city. The air was awash with conflicting perfumes and experimental oils, sold as often as applied, and washing lines crisscrossed overhead like flags at a festival. Seth was mildly terrified they might be mistaken for customers, but Roger moved through the chaos with singular purpose, and it seemed that Seth could remain unnoticed in his wake. But as the streets sloped upward and finally widened out, the buildings got shorter, grayer, and older, and the strong scent of perfume gave way to the faint whiff of soot. There could be no doubt about it: they were passing into Wallward Heights.

"Roger," he finally whispered, "are you sure this is a good idea?"

Roger looked back at him, surprised. "What's the matter? Haven't been any

patrols based in Wallward since Elgar built them that new garrison in Edge-
wise. Moved them right out of the place I want to show you, in fact."

"Aye," Seth said, even though he hadn't known that, "but you're . . . not
exactly popular in Wallward, are you?"

Roger scratched his head a moment, then burst out laughing. "Oh, *that*? That
bit about the southern plague? That was more than a year ago; nobody remembers that. Besides, even if they did, it's not like they could prove anything. They
want to forget it ever happened—trust me."

Since it was agreed upon (though not always followed) that thieves didn't
cheat thieves, Roger kept his swindling schemes out of Sheath, foisting them
instead on unsuspecting residential neighborhoods. Wallward Heights had been
privy to a particularly lucrative one concerning the southern plague, and a cure
that, Roger had assured him, really did work, for all he knew. The trouble was that
no one had actually come down with the southern plague for the better part of
a hundred years.

"You see, lad," Roger continued, "while cheating a man by selling him something that doesn't work is all well and fine, you'll do your best when you sell
him something that *does* work, but that he doesn't need. The world is crammed
to bursting with things that people don't need, and you can get most of them
for practically nothing until *you* decide to set the price. That cure, for instance.
Now, remedies are good business to start with, because all you have to do is
describe an ailment in enough detail and you'll convince *someone* in your audience that he has it. And that's all anyone can *prove* I did. So they couldn't come
charging up to me, demanding I return their coin just because I sold them something they only thought they needed—it was their mistake, not mine. But between you and me . . ." He hesitated, then lowered his voice. "*Just* between you
and me, it was the symptoms of the southern plague that gave me the idea. It
starts with a tingling in the hands, right? And then the fingers or feet go numb?
Well, hypothetically speaking, apply a bit of snow's down and you can get much
the same result, can't you? So I go around the neighborhood, explaining about
the plague, detailing the very official nature of my cure, shaking a few hands—
just a few, mind; don't want to overdo it—and . . . well. Between my natural
charm, a few cold fingers, and mankind's tendency toward overactive imagination, they didn't stand a chance."

Seth shook his head. "Morgan *knew* you'd done something. She always
said so."

"Aye, but she never figured out what, did she? And you're not going to tell
her. It's between us, I said." He grinned suddenly. "Ah, here we are."

They'd stepped out into a close, dilapidated circle, ringed all about with sagging dwellings, that had probably once been open and airy. Seth stared at the

building in the center—made entirely of stone, it was narrow and angular in front, wide and curved in back, with the sharp pointed spire he had seen in so many other places. He slumped a little. "Another Ninist vestry? But they're all over the city."

Roger wagged a finger at him. "Wait before you judge. The best discoveries are those that look simple, eh? Or I'm no true Halfen. Now come on."

The door was heavy wood, but it was half rotted; Roger could probably just have kicked it in, but instead he opened it slowly and carefully, easing around the edge and inside before he'd even gotten it halfway. Seth slipped in after him, and Roger closed the door behind them, then folded his arms behind his head, craning his neck to take a look at the room. Seth looked too, with more curiosity than he wanted to admit; as many Ninist vestries as he'd seen, he'd never actually been inside one.

If there had been tapestries or other decorations in the vestry, they'd long since been stripped or stolen; only the wooden rows of seats remained, here and there slightly crooked. The back of the vestry was more stone, curved into the shape of a semicircle, but the statues set into the circle were made of marble. Their size was more or less true to life, but they stood on great pedestals, so they would tower over any man who stood near them. Seth looked at the first one on his left, a boy about his age, dressed in fancy robes a bit too big for him, with a stack of books under one arm and several scrolls in the crook of the other. His hair was long and loose, as if he hadn't time to tend to it, and his eyes tilted slightly off to the side, as if something over Seth's shoulder had caught his interest. The sculptor had been no amateur; the details stood out even after so much time, down to the keen look in the boy's eyes, the lock of hair that had fallen down into his face. But then Seth darted a glance around the rest of the circle, and frowned. "This *was* supposed to be a Ninist vestry, wasn't it?"

"And so it is," Roger said, looking over at him. "Why wouldn't it be?"

Seth waved a hand at the statues. "It's called Ninism because they have nine gods, right? But there're only seven statues."

Roger laughed, scratching the back of his neck. "Not to worry; that's as it should be. I forget only swindlers and thieves have cause to know about Ninist traditions nowadays." He thumbed at his chin. "They're not strictly gods, but there *are* nine—nine of them, and nine statues." He gestured to a low doorway at the center of the circle, with steps leading down. "The other two are down here. Come on—I'll show you."

But Seth lingered, looking up at the marble faces. After the boy came a man and woman in fine robes, with crowns upon their heads, and then a tall, imposing man hefting his unsheathed greatsword high. On his other side was a mild, retreating woman in plain dress, and then a man in full armor, his head bared to show an earnest, youthful face. On the far right was what looked to be a holy man, garbed in flowing, ornate robes, his long hair pulled back and tied at the base of his neck. But Seth still liked the boy best, with his clever face and abstracted air. "Who are they, then?" he asked Roger. "Who are they supposed to be?"

Roger screwed up his face. "Hmm, let me see . . . That one you're eyeing there's the Magician—I remember that—and then the King and the Queen are easy, and then—the Knight? No, that's wrong, the Knight comes later. . . ." He frowned and then suddenly snapped his fingers. "The Warrior! That's it. Don't know why you need a Knight *and* a Warrior, but nobody asked me. So that would make this young lady the . . . Maiden, I believe." He smirked at Seth. "Or so they say, at least."

Seth tried to ignore that as implacably as Morgan would have. "All right. Then . . . maybe this is the Knight?"

Roger followed his gaze. "Aye, that's right, and then the fellow at the other end's the Apostle. Which leaves two to go, as I was saying."

Seth still couldn't stop looking at the statues. "So they . . . they founded Elesthene?"

"That's the story." Roger paced around the circle. "The greatest earthly kingdom that ever was, with this very city as its beating heart. But they all went on to win a much better one—the kingdom of eternity. And after that, they never died—or so they say."

"So what happened to them, if they never died?"

"Well, they just . . . stayed on, didn't they? You couldn't *pray* to the Ninists' god—he was far too important to care about *you*—but his favorite servants were always about, in one sense or another. If you followed one of them faithfully, perhaps he or she'd intercede for you."

"What if they didn't?"

Roger shrugged. "Then it was hellfire for you—until the day the Ninists' god raised up the penitent and cast down the soulless forever, at least. Don't ask me when *that* was supposed to be—always *one day, one day.*"

Seth frowned. "That's all they were for? You spent all your time praying to them, and *maybe* they'd say something nice about you to their god?"

Roger laughed. "Well, they might've been immortal, but they weren't all-powerful—they had their own problems, some more than others. The *Niniad* tells all about their lives when they were human, and you'd almost feel sorry for some of them, if you didn't know they found eternity in the end."

"Eternity," Seth repeated, staring into the Magician's face.

"Hmm." Roger twitched his nose. "Well, not for your boy there. Not quite, anyway. You'll understand in a moment, if you'll just follow along." He pointed to the doorway again. "Come on, this way."

They descended the steps at last, single file, Seth close behind Roger. They came out into a small circular chamber, like a miniature of the one upstairs, with a low, stifling ceiling. They were belowground, but light filtered in through holes in the ceiling—which was funny, because Seth hadn't noticed any holes in the floor above. Perhaps they were set behind the statues.

Roger had spoken true: the last two statues were here. It seemed a crime to hide them underground—these were the most beautiful of the lot, a woman so fair it made your heart hurt and a man nearly as handsome, both endowed with a dignity of bearing and expression that couldn't help but command respect. Seth took a step forward almost without realizing it, then turned to Roger in bewilderment. "Why do they pick *these* to hide?"

"Because nobody calls on these two," Roger said. "Not now, and not then, not even at Ninism's height. These were always to be feared, and warded away. But they had to be recognized all the same, so they were always given their place down below."

"But why did nobody pray to them?" Seth asked.

Roger was clearly enjoying this. "Because nobody would ever want to pray to two such bad ones as these, my boy."

Seth started back. "They're . . . bad?"

Roger faced the statues, grinning his slender grin. "The Traitor," he said, jerking his chin at the man, "and the Whore. Enemies to the seven, and to all of us, besides."

Seth looked at them again, but he couldn't see anything about them that was so bad as Roger said. The man held his chin a little too high, perhaps, and an imperious frown sat on his lips, but his eyes, marble though they were, were not haughty or cold, and they looked you right in the face. And the woman . . . Seth had seen whores enough, though few were either shrewd or simple enough to try to do business in Sheath. Some looked . . . properly lascivious, as Roger might say, but most just looked tired, and more anxious than Morgan. But this woman was entirely different. She didn't beckon—didn't even seem to know she was being looked at, and though she looked up, her gaze seemed turned somehow inward. Her clothes were simple enough, and her finest ornament was her long loose hair. She had a sweet face, gentle eyes, and a beautiful, beautiful smile.

"I don't understand," Seth said. "If we're supposed to think these are the bad ones, why make them so beautiful?"

Roger shrugged. "They're lust and ambition, my boy, and you'd be hard-pressed to find two things that call more strongly to most men. Easy to resist something that turns your stomach, but when a thing is beautiful, who's going to stop to ask whether it's good or bad? You clutch at it either way, don't you? Just as your boy up there did."

"He did?" Seth asked.

Roger knelt, poking at the stone between the Traitor's feet. "Oh, he did. He might have been a prodigy, but he was also a boy, just as you are." He flicked his gaze to the woman. "All his magic couldn't save him from one of *her* smiles, and soon he cast his spells only on her word, neglecting even the king who had been his friend. That's the story, anyway." He finished whatever he was doing, and smiled. "Course, lust and ambition have been friends to my kind for as long as men have breathed, so we like to leave messages for one another in places like this. If there's a Ninist vestry still standing, it's more than likely there's a smuggler or thief knows it better than its faithful ever did. Have a look." He stepped back and let Seth see what he had done.

There had been a thin layer of dust on the stone, but Roger had smoothed it away, revealing a set of shallow, etched markings. Seth knelt to make them out: there was a circle, and within it, five lines, one that ran diagonally from the left edge of the circle to the bottom, and four longer ones that extended from the top down.

"It's a hand," Roger said, laying his thumb along the diagonal line and his fingers atop the others. "See?"

"I see," Seth said, cocking his head. "What's it mean?"

Roger patted the mark affectionately, then took Seth's hand, placing his fingers against the raised front of the pedestal the statue perched on. "Just apply a bit of pressure there, and maybe you'll find out."

Seth pushed, and realized something was moving: the part of the pedestal between the statue's feet could slide away, revealing a hollow cavity underneath. There was a box inside, a plain rectangle of unvarnished wood.

Seth reached out, pulling the box free. It wasn't locked, only held closed with a simple latch. And when he opened the lid, he found . . . nothing. It was empty.

He let the box fall from his hands, listening to the soft clatter as it hit the floor, inches away. "That's it? An empty box?"

Roger grinned. "It's only been empty for the past day and a half or so," he said. "Before that, it held this."

He reached into his pocket and pulled out a cut ruby bigger than a man's eye. It sparkled in the low light, richer than blood.

Seth lurched back on the heels of his hands. "Gods," he said breathlessly. "Sweet *gods,* Roger, why didn't you just show that to start with?"

"And tell the tale out of order? Come on, boy; that wouldn't have done at all." He tossed the gem aloft, then caught it out of the air with an easy flick of his wrist. "Besides, what's the point if you don't understand where it came from?"

"But I don't, really," Seth pointed out. "I thought you were going to tell me what that symbol meant?"

Roger pocketed the ruby again, then tapped his chin. "Eh, was I?"

"Isn't that why you brought me here?"

"I brought you here so you'd make that face when I pulled out the stone. And you didn't disappoint me, that's for sure."

Seth groaned. "Come on. You told the story this far, now finish it. Or I won't follow you around again, *or* listen to your stories."

Roger held up his hands. "All right, all right, this once . . . Don't tell anyone, though, you hear? I'm only supposed to tell my apprentice."

"But you're always saying how you don't want an apprentice and you'll never have one."

"Aye, I *know* that. Why do you think I settle for showing off to you instead?" He sighed. "That's a finger-sign—one of our ways of leaving messages for one another. I suppose that one best means *take what you will.*"

Seth raised an eyebrow. "Some thief gets away with a gem like that and just leaves it for anyone to take?"

"Did I say it was that simple?" Roger laughed. "We thieves are notorious for . . . forgetting to mention things, after all. When a fellow leaves a mark like this, it means he's pulled something off, but it's too hot for him to fence—he's being watched, perhaps, or else there isn't a half-wit in the sewers who wouldn't recognize it if he tried to sell it, or the hunt to reclaim it is so fierce, he daren't pull it out of his pocket even in his own chambers. So he stashes it instead. The mark is to say he's decided the damned thing is more trouble than it's worth, and he hereby washes his hands of it, and invites you to have better luck, if you can." He tapped his fingertips together, staring at the mark. "Perhaps it's better to say it means, *Take what you will, and don't say you weren't forewarned.*"

Seth picked up the box again, turning it over in his hands. "If it were me, I'd just hide it without making any marks on it at all. Then I could just come back for it."

Roger winked at him. "That proves you're no true thief, my boy—it proves you're not thinking to the future. There was so much dust on that thing when I found it, I reckon it's decades old—whoever stole it in the first place is probably dead. But even so, it's like he's speaking to me, saying, *Well, my man, here's a story for you: once there was a fellow so clever, he got his hands on a treasure like this and never got caught, and that fellow was I myself. See if you're ever so lucky.* And here I am in awe of this mysterious fellow, who might've died before I was ever born. But if he'd just hidden it away like you wanted . . . Well, it was still here, so we know he wasn't able to come back for it. And then his legacy would've died with him. What's the fun if nobody *knows* how clever you are?"

"I'd rather be clever enough to sell it," Seth said, wrinkling his nose. "How are *you* going to?"

"If it's as old as it looks, it should be safe enough—no doubt everyone's forgotten about it by now." He grinned. "And don't forget I'm a swindler, not a burglar. *We* could sell a man's own piss back to him without him so much as smelling anything funny." He took the jewel out again, turning it over in his hand. "First step, though, I want to figure out what it is—where it came from, if I can. That means I'd best head to Kratchet's, ask him if he knows of any fine gems that went missing ten or twenty years ago. Gods know he's a dodgy little rat, but if anyone can tell me, it'll be him." He cocked his head at Seth. "Want to come?"

Seth shook his head. "Kratchet'll be even less inclined to talk to you if I'm around—as far as he's concerned, saying anything to me's as bad as saying it to Morgan." And the man made him nervous, but he didn't need to tell Roger that. "Besides, Marceline hates me."

Roger laughed. "What, the monkey? Don't tell me you're afraid of her."

"I'm not *afraid*," Seth said. "I just . . . should probably get back to Morgan, that's all."

"As you like." Roger shrugged, putting the ruby back into his pocket. "Doubt *she'll* have any secrets to share with you, though."

CHAPTER TWO

It wasn't that Marceline didn't feel *any* guilt about stealing from her own sister, but Cerise did work at a grocer's, and that meant she ate a sight better than anyone of her means had a right to. Halvard was always giving her scraps, some choice bit or other he hadn't been able to sell that day. *He* said it was because it was useless to let it go to waste, and because his books had never been kept in better order, but Marceline was willing to bet it had more than a little to do with the fact that Cerise was pretty, and people liked to give pretty people things. But Marceline had never been pretty, so she'd had to find other ways of getting her hands on things.

There were *five* fresh eggs—those must've been from Halvard—and they were tempting, but Marceline knew from experience that she'd only break them, no matter how careful she tried to be. She reached for the rolls instead, tucking several into the sack she'd brought from Tom's. They were so soft, and still faintly warm, and it was an effort not to stuff one into her mouth right then, but she forced herself to finish her pilfering first. She fingered the grapes longingly but decided to leave them be—they'd just get squished on the way back to Sheath. She took the two apples she found instead, and some strips of salted beef, and she was just about to reach for a wedge of cheese when she heard a very familiar sigh, wrought out of only the finest world-weary exasperation.

"I can't *believe* you," Cerise said, hands on her hips, as if this weren't a common enough occurrence. "Will you *never* learn?"

"I don't know what it is I'm supposed to learn," Marceline said, resisting the urge to stick out her tongue.

"Not to steal from your own flesh and blood, perhaps? You can *start* there."

Half my flesh and blood, Marceline didn't say. "If I am your blood, then you ought to be more openhanded with me."

There was that sigh again. "I have told you, half a hundred times if I've told you once, that you're welcome to *sit down* and eat with me anytime you please. But when you slink in here and empty my stores so you can feed it all to that thieving old man without so much as a *by-your-leave . . .*"

"Tom's got to eat same as anyone, and he'd be a mess if I didn't help him," Marceline insisted. "And I give back to you, don't I? I pay you back when we have money." She and Tom, like most Sheathers, generally went through dry spells followed by windfalls when their schemes panned out, and Marceline didn't see anything wrong with taking a little extra from her sister when times were lean, as long as she shared the spoils, too.

But Cerise sniffed. "That's a fine way to pay me back, offering me coin you got unlawfully."

"What's unlawful about it? We sell things just like everybody else." She *had* gotten to be a pretty accomplished pickpocket, but Cerise didn't need to know that, and Marceline hadn't lied—she didn't offer her sister *that* money.

Cerise shook her head. "How is it always *we*? You and that old man! Gods, Marceline, you're lucky he hasn't killed you already—or worse."

Marceline wasn't sure how anything was supposed to be *worse* than being dead, but she was used to people being afraid of Tom. Everyone she met, it seemed, was afraid of Tom, even other Sheathers. But it wasn't themselves they feared for; it was always Marceline herself. Even Morgan Imrick at the Dragon's Head, who was one of the few people Marceline actually liked, was always saying,

Listen here, monkey: if that old rat ever gives you any trouble, you come tell me, all right?

She rolled her eyes. "Would you come off it about Tom? He's harmless."

"He carries a knife," Cerise said—how on earth did she manage to make her voice that shrill? "Didn't you tell me he carries a knife?"

Had she? Not one of her brighter decisions, that. "*I* carry a knife," Marceline pointed out. She'd been practicing with it too, aiming throws at the back of the door—at Tom's, naturally, because Cerise'd pitch a fit if she did it here. She was getting better—she'd gotten it to stick, most times, although just *where* it stuck was anyone's guess. Even when she couldn't take the knife out, she'd practice the motion during dull times, flicking her wrist over and over.

"There's no reason for me to be afraid of Tom, and I'm *not* afraid of him," she added for good measure. "I can run faster than him, I can pick locks *almost* as well as he can, *and* I can hold my liquor better." When Cerise raised an eyebrow at her, she blushed and muttered, "Well, I can hold it better because I don't drink any."

"Thank the gods for that, at least," Cerise said, throwing up her hands. She let them drop in a moment, though, falling defeated to her sides. "Listen, Marceline, I can't stay and argue with you; I'm expected at the shop before the hour's out." She jerked her chin at the shelves. "If I leave you here, are you going to be content with what you have, or are you going to clean me out and leave me to starve?"

Marceline scowled. "You're not going to bloody *starve.*"

"*Language,* Marceline—"

"I said you're not going to bloody well starve," she insisted, gripping her spoils more tightly. "It was never *you* who got thrown out."

Her sister fell silent, biting her lip, and Marceline immediately felt guilty. That had been low of her, lower than Cerise deserved. She knew Cerise had tried to get her father to let Marceline live with them when he was alive. She knew he'd hardly been cold in the grave, and the house newly Cerise's, when her sister had come to find her at Tom's, even though she must have known how dangerous it was for an ordinary person to venture into Sheath. It wasn't her fault that their mother had been such a little fool, that she'd told her husband that Marceline was her lover's child, that she was going to run away and live with him. The lover himself had had other plans, of course, and then Marceline and her mother had nowhere to go. Cerise had just been caught in the middle.

"I know you never threw anybody out, either," she finally said, because she had to say something. "I'm not . . . blaming you for what your father did. I'm just saying . . ."

"He might've been your father too, you know," Cerise said quietly. "Mother said you weren't his, but she wanted to believe that so badly . . . I wonder if even she knew the truth." She squinted at Marceline. "We do look alike, here and there, though maybe that's just from her."

Marceline didn't think they looked alike. Cerise's nose was straight and elegant, but hers was small and stunted and ever so slightly turned up. Marceline's hair was the color of dried blood and just about as silky, but her sister's was gold licked with red, soft and glossy every day of her life. They'd both been given fancy names—they could thank their mother for that—but Cerise's seemed to suit her. Marceline didn't feel like a Marceline, and most people seemed to agree; the only people who used her given name were the insufferable ones, like Cerise and that boy Seth from Morgan's tavern, who was fully sixteen but acted like a boy of twelve. "I might've been," she said at last. "I might've been his. That'd be funny, wouldn't it? Man throws out his own child because he thinks it's someone else's?"

Cerise looked horrified. "*Funny?* For him to have torn our whole family apart for nothing? I told him so many times how much he'd regret it, if it ever came to light that you were really—"

"Well, he's dead now," Marceline said, "so he doesn't have to worry about that, does he?"

Cerise bit her lip again, and for a moment Marceline thought she was going to pursue it, but she only said, "Listen, I wouldn't leave you here, but I wasn't joking about the shop. Just . . . take things, if you're going to. And lock my door."

And that made her feel guilty again, to remember the weight of the spare key in her pocket, which Cerise had given her even when Marceline refused to come live with her. She almost wanted to pick the lock next time, just on principle.

———

For a moment the light filtering through her bedroom window looked almost pretty—muted, soft, faintly blue, the way light often looks in dreams. Morgan stretched slowly, curling and uncurling her fingers as if grasping at it. It had been, all things considered, a decent afternoon.

"Getting restless already?" Braddock asked, and she was sprawled against him enough that she could feel his voice as well as hear it, resonating and immediate, with that slight amiable lilt he never used when they were in company.

She sat up slowly, brushing the hair away from her face. "Mm . . . I'd better start setting up for this evening. Customers won't wait."

"Fair enough," he said, rolling out of bed and to his feet in a single motion, then casting urgently about for his clothes.

She smiled—he got so uneasy over appearing naked in front of her, as if he worried she'd compare him to someone else. "I didn't mean I would *race* you," she said.

He stopped, looked over at her, only one leg in his pants. "Oh," he said. "Right, then. My mistake."

The light drifted along his jaw, and Morgan had to hold back a wince as she looked at the still-forming bruise. "Does that hurt?"

"Not as much as you think, I'm sure." He shook his head. "If I'd seen you, you never would've landed that punch. Not a chance."

"But you didn't see me," Morgan said.

He snorted. "Aye, aye. Teach me to turn my back on you."

He still stood awkwardly by the window, though, and Morgan asked, "Is something bothering you?"

"Agh, it's"—he scratched at his stubble—"stupid worries, old worries, but . . . I heard something today. Imperator's men've been poking around, asking about . . . deserters."

Morgan grabbed her clothes from the floor, shaking them out before she started to put them on. "If they are, it's some recent affair, no doubt. Nobody's going to care about what happened years ago."

Braddock snorted. "Elgar cares about whatever he's decided to care about, and that can be anything from what the witch-queen's plotting over in Esthrades to what you and I ate for breakfast this morning. If they start offering gold . . ."

Morgan tried not to smile. "Well, who else knows about it?"

He looked startled. "What, besides you? No one I know of."

"And I'm not one to gossip—nor to take anything Elgar's creatures have to offer. So there you have it."

That wrung a chuckle out of him. "I know it's a foolish thing to fret over. I said it was, didn't I?"

"You did." She reached over, gripping his shoulder gently. "Sheath isn't the place for their kind. It's not a place to order or sift through—you can't pick one piece of information out of a hundred thousand others. Roger's family has a history too convoluted and ancient for anyone but him to make sense of, and Deinol's father could be a king for all we know, and Lucius—I'm afraid to wonder what on earth Lucius's secret might be. And I own a tavern, and you were in the army once, a long time ago. And nobody cares about any of it." She released him, carding fingers through her hair to try to straighten it. "We're all not quite right, and we're all running from something. That's why we're here."

He craned his neck to get a better look at her, and almost smiled. "What're you running from, then?"

She smiled back. "These days? Nothing more exciting than the poorhouse,

I'm afraid." She patted his back, half amazed he let her get away with it. "Speaking of, will you help me set up? I'd certainly appreciate it."

"I suppose I could see my way to doing that," Braddock said, after only a slight pause. "Might as well get the place looking nice before the usual lot roughs it up again."

"Now you're thinking like me," Morgan said, and followed him downstairs.

———

"Afternoon, monkey—or evening, rather, I suppose," Morgan said, a damp rag wrapped around one hand. "It can't be a drink you're after, can it? Or did that old goat send you to fetch something for him?"

It was too early for the Dragon's Head to be full, but there was a decent crowd, especially at the tables: a group of regulars laying claim to their usual spot and enjoying a more or less quiet dinner; what looked like a passel of apprentices shirking work, giggling over somebody's last trip to the Roses; and about a half dozen fellows in the far corner who had decided to get drunk earlier than normal and were stumbling their way through a chorus of "The Rose's Thorn and the Bloody Boar." Morgan winced at every wrong note, but her rule was that you could be as loud as you pleased as long as you kept the peace, so she said nothing. There were only a couple of people at the bar, both nursing tankards and sulking, so Marceline had plenty of space. And that mercenary, Braddock, was sitting by the window as usual, though he was only drinking water.

Seth ducked into the room, winced and stiffened the way he always did when he saw her, as if he thought she were going to hit him. "Er, Marceline," he said. "Hello."

Seth wasn't precisely an idiot, but he *was* irritating, so Marceline ignored him and turned back to Morgan. "No, Tom doesn't need anything. I just dropped some supplies at his place, but he wasn't in, and I don't feel like going back to my sister's."

"Well, pull up a stool," Morgan said. "How is Cerise these days?"

"Cerise? Cerise is always the same—always *annoying*," she added, for good measure.

Morgan smiled. "Probably good I never had a sister."

"You wouldn't want one. They never do you any favors, and they always complain."

She was going to say more, but then the door banged open, and Roger Halfen strode in, breaking out into a grin when he saw her. "Ah, that's where the monkey's got to! I just dropped in on your old man."

"He *isn't* my father," Marceline said, just as she always did.

"Didn't say that, did I? He's certainly as grubby as ever—I'd recommend getting him to clean his fingernails once or twice a decade if I were you."

Marceline ignored that. "What did you want from him, then?"

He wagged a finger at her. "Now, now, monkey, that'd be telling." He turned to Morgan. "Can't stay long, my dear, but I thought I'd down some ale before I set off." He set two copper coins on the counter, and Morgan slid a full tankard across to him.

Tom hated Roger Halfen, and Marceline tried, out of some halfhearted sense of loyalty, to agree with him, but she'd never quite been able to manage it. Roger could be self-satisfied, certainly, and he talked far too much about the line of legendary thieves he was supposedly descended from, but he *was* talented, whether or not Tom was willing to admit it. He preferred swindling to outright stealing, usually, but his schemes were so clever his fellow Sheathers were all in a rush to imitate him—at which point he always exposed his own deception and moved on to the next one, of course.

"Where are you going?" Marceline asked him. "Is it a new trick?"

"If it were, monkey, I wouldn't tell you. Nothing personal against you, of course, but I'm not about to pass my inventions on to Tom Kratchet." He set down the empty tankard, then wiped his mouth and stood up again. "Thanks, Morgan. I'll be back tomorrow for another round, if all goes well."

Marceline wasn't about to be put off so easily, though, and she followed him into the street. The sun had set while she'd been inside, and the two of them stuck to the shadows easily, falling into step. "Roger, come on. *Are* you going to work?"

He sighed. "Not hardly, all right? I'm just on the trail of something."

"On the trail of what?"

"I'm not going to *tell* you, my dear. Either run off to Kratchet's or head back inside."

Marceline sniffed at that. "I can go where I like."

Roger threw up his hands. "So do that, if it pleases you. Just leave me to my business. I've no need for an apprentice."

"An apprentice?" Marceline scowled. "I wouldn't be *your* apprentice even if you asked."

"Monkey, you would be even if I didn't, and we both know it. Even you must know you couldn't find anyone better."

She did know that, but that didn't mean she had to admit it. Besides, what would Tom say? "If you won't have any apprentices, then what's the point in asking?"

He chuckled. "Well, you'd best be someone's, if you hope to go far in the craft. Tom hasn't obliged you?"

She shook her head. "*He* thinks he might as well be my father, even though he *isn't,* and he says it's bad luck for a thief to apprentice his own children."

Roger nodded. "He's right about that, at least. My own father refused to take me on, as talented as we both were—I suspect that had more to do with his promise to my mother that he'd go straight than with any old superstitions, but he always claimed that was the reason." He laughed again. "Gran *hated* that. 'If I'd wanted you honest, I'd've *raised* you honest, you bleeding ninny. Are you really going to let some woman order you around like that?' Course, he just pointed out that he'd been letting *her* do it for years. I think she liked my mother for all that, though."

Marceline huffed. "You're ready to talk everybody's ears off about *boring* things, but you keep all the interesting bits to yourself."

"And what about old Tom, eh? He *sells* his information. Least I'm not that greedy."

"Well," Marceline said, "well, he's better at it than you, anyway."

Roger laughed. "I wouldn't need to pay him if he weren't."

Marceline looked out over the tops of the buildings, to where the Citadel's shadow loomed vaguely through the dusk, obscure behind its black walls. "Roger," she said, "is Elgar bad?"

Roger scratched his cheek. "Well, I never met the man myself, monkey. I think he probably is, though." He smiled slightly. "Course, if you asked me the same question about your old man, I expect I'd say the same thing."

Marceline didn't know what to say to that, so she ignored it. "If he's so bad, then why do so many people like him?"

"It's not *him* they like," Roger said. "It's his dream."

"His dream?"

"Aye," Roger said. "Elesthene."

———

That night, after even the last customers had gotten turned out and been sent stumbling on their way, Seth stopped Morgan before she went upstairs. "Can I ask you a question?"

Morgan turned, leaning against the edge of the bar. "Another one, you mean? Go ahead."

Seth shuffled his feet. "Why is it . . . Why does no one ever go to the Ninist vestries anymore?"

Whatever she'd been expecting, it clearly wasn't that. "Because Ninism is dead."

"Yes, I know," Seth said, "but *why*?"

"Because it's a stupid religion," Morgan replied. "You need me to tell you that?"

"But what makes it stupid? All religions are . . . fanciful, aren't they?"

Morgan sighed, shutting her eyes for a moment. "You don't talk about where you came from, Seth, and I don't ask. But for those of us who grew up here, who've lived in the shadow of the Citadel our whole lives . . . we could never get away from the stories. Our parents were always telling us the stories, but it wasn't really their fault—*their* parents had never stopped telling *them*. And the stories were always the same: Elesthene, Elesthene, Elesthene. An empire that covered the whole continent, from the White Waste beyond the Howling Gate to the red cliffs at Issamira's southern edge. All of it was ours, and all of it was glorious, and this city was the best of it all. It wasn't just the Citadel—the very streets used to sparkle, or so they said. And back then everyone was a Ninist." She laughed. "You had to be, or it would be your head. Ninism had more rules than even Elgar could dream up, and the citizens of Elesthene had to follow every one. But it didn't matter, because Ninism was God, and Elesthene was God, and the glory of the one would increase the glory of the other, until the earth had become a heaven fit for even God to walk."

Her lips drew together, and she scratched at the bar. "What do you see of that empire now? It ate itself from the inside—those fools who came before us fucked it all to nothing and left us with this. They made us what we are, and we have to scrabble for our bread in the ruins they left. So it's not so surprising that nobody wants anything to do with their god anymore." She shook her head at him. "Go to bed, Seth, all right? There'll be time enough to turn to religion when you're old, and then maybe you can pick a better one."

He hadn't meant *he* wanted to be a Ninist, Seth wanted to tell her, even after she had gone. He just didn't understand how people could care about a thing so much and then just *stop*.

He knew his wasn't the most exciting kind of life, spending his days with a broom in his hand—especially in a place like Sheath, where most everyone was up to some reckless scheme. But he found himself almost happy at times—or maybe this *was* happiness, this lack of dismay at the passing days, this knowing you would see the people you loved again and again, so that there was never any need to feel sadness at parting. Whether it was or not, he didn't want it to change; he knew it was better than the life he'd had before.

But if he could be content with no more than this, what had plagued the citizens of the fallen empire, who had lived with wonders as if they were ordinary things? What did they suffer from, that they commissioned artists to build things of such beauty just so they could forbid themselves to look upon them?

––––––––

"I knew it was shaping up to be a bad night. Roger damned *Halfen* was here earlier, asking about things that were obscure fifteen years ago and bloating everything he said with his usual damned nonsense about this or that—did I know about his great-uncle on his grandmother's side, there was a fine story involving a barrel of wine and a stray horse—and so on until I was about to beat his nose back into his face. If I had a piece of gold for every time that swindler talked my ears to bleeding, I'd— Are you *listening* to me, girl?"

"Aye, Tom," Marceline said, drumming her fingers against the table. "I'm always listening."

"Then stop slouching, why don't you, and look like you've got a head on you. Even my charity only goes so far."

Marceline sat up, incensed. "Your *charity*? Whose thanks is it you could eat today?"

He screwed up his face. "That don't count."

"Doesn't," Marceline said. "That *doesn't* count."

"Well, why *doesn't* you let me speak the way I like, eh?"

He only did it to be obstinate, Marceline was certain. Seth had come from the countryside too, or at least he'd spoken as if he did, but he wasn't in Sheath half a year before you couldn't tell his speech from anybody else's. And if *he* could do it, Marceline had no doubt that Tom could too. He just *wouldn't*.

"What did Roger want?" she asked, finally.

"Halfen? What's it to you? That bastard never pays me enough, no matter what he's after." He sat down heavily, drawing a hand through his long, matted hair and getting it tangled halfway. "Get me a bottle from the back room, will you?"

Marceline folded her arms. "Get it yourself."

"Get it for me, girl, and I'll tell you what I found today."

Marceline got to her feet in spite of herself. "It better've been good, old man." But she'd only just pushed past the tattered curtain dividing the two rooms when someone started thumping on the door. She decided to pay it no mind—if Tom thought she was going to answer his door *and* fetch his wine, he was *already* drunk.

The banging continued, and she heard Tom lurch to his feet. "All right, all right, don't break your fingers." Under his breath, he muttered, "Or do."

Marceline's hand closed around the neck of the closest bottle, but then she heard the door swing open, the stumbling of feet as someone hurried inside. She stepped sideways so she could see through the doorway, and caught her breath. Luckily for her, Tom had done the same thing, and much more noisily.

Full plate was prodigiously expensive—and, common wisdom held, not always worth the added weight, given the current state of weaponry—so only a very few of Elgar's elite guard wore it. The lower officers wore boiled leather and the occasional brigandine, and the common soldiers whatever protection ordinary leather or thick wool could afford. But all wore the deep blue-black that marked them out as Elgar's creatures. Those in plate trailed the color behind them with thick capes, and the others, like this one, wore plain tunics, devoid of a single ornamental stitch.

This guardsman was a guardswoman, with tight, brittle brown curls and a nose that looked like it had seen a break or two. There was a small vertical scar along the side of her face, just shy of her left ear, but Marceline's gaze moved quickly from her face to the sword in her hand, drawn and pointed right at Tom's upper lip. "Tom Kratchet?"

Tom raised his palms, taking a step back. "Now, now. No need for that, is there?"

"Are you Tom Kratchet or aren't you?"

Tom chuckled nervously. "Eh, well, that depends what you want him for."

"I'm a customer," the woman said, but she moved the sword point closer. "You sell information down here, don't you? I'm buying."

Marceline saw the way Tom's throat worked as he swallowed, but he didn't flinch. "Well enough. What do you want to know?"

The woman drew the sword back just an inch. "Deserters."

Tom frowned. "Deserters? Like from the army?"

"Is there another kind?"

He laughed. "See here, I don't know what you've heard, or how you found this place, but I don't deal in *gossip,* for you or anyone. If you want to know something ancient, something forgotten, something that's truly a mystery, I'm your man. If you want to know about the last brawl at the Dragon's Head or who your fellow's fucking while you're down here wasting your time, I don't know no more than anyone else."

Any more, Marceline thought reflexively. *You don't know* any *more than anyone else.*

The woman didn't gut him immediately, and Marceline supposed that was something. "We are prepared to pay you fairly for good information, but also to kill you for any attempt at subterfuge."

Tom didn't blink. "Well, I wish I *had* good information, as I dearly like being paid. Truth is, I don't."

"Not a word?" Her eyes narrowed. "Not even down here?"

Tom waved a hand at her. "It's as I said. What more do you want from me? *I'm* no deserter."

They looked at each other for a long moment, and the guardswoman finally shrugged, sheathing her sword. "Well, if you do get your hands on something, any one of us can pay you." She ducked out the door, but turned back at the last moment, curling her fingers around the edge of the doorframe. "Take care," she said, and then she was finally gone.

Tom waited a few moments before he shut the door, but it was only after he'd latched it that he looked in Marceline's direction. "Well?" he asked, slumping back into his chair. "Were you just going to stand there gaping and watch her slice me up?"

"She had a *sword*," Marceline pointed out.

He threw up his hands. "This is the thanks I get. *This* is my reward for offering shelter to some scrawny orphan out of nothing more than my own goodness—*this* is the loyalty I'm owed, eh? Don't know why I ever bothered with *you*."

Marceline scowled. "She had a *sword*, Tom."

"Aye, and I thought you were so fearless."

"Not against *guards*."

"Well, you sure proved that." He sighed, rubbing a hand over his face. "You'd better bring that bottle, girl. And so help me, you'd better bloody *pour*."

CHAPTER THREE

Varalen struggled through yet another interminable corridor, trying to arrange his robes into some semblance of order without slowing down. Not for the first time, he cursed the architects of the Citadel, whoever they were—he didn't doubt there was something to be said for magnificence in a palace, but did there have to be so *much* of everything? Four libraries, half a dozen kitchens, sixteen armories, five floors of dungeons, surely more state-rooms than there were dignitaries on the entire continent, and enough damned *corridors* to line the road to hell. You practically needed a horse to get from one place to another on time. And he hated horses.

He finally skidded to a stop before the heavy double doors of his destination, and took a deep breath before pushing his way through. The room might have been large and airy, with a row of windows in the far wall that looked out onto the Citadel courtyard, but it always felt like a prison to him.

Imperator Elgar looked so small whenever he sat at his strategy table, his thin shoulders hunched over, his sleeves rolled up to reveal his slender wrists and long, spindly fingers. It didn't help that the room had been designed to seat a council—had sat *the* Council, in the days of Elesthene—with a high vaulted ceiling and so many extra chairs that they'd been shoved against the far wall to gather dust. "You're late," he said when Varalen walked in, barely looking up. "This is the *third* time you have been late in as many weeks. Tell me, do you do this on purpose?"

If only I had so much courage, Varalen thought. Out loud, he said, "My apologies." His own accustomed chair was not dusty, but it sat a foot or two farther away from the table than it should have been; had Elgar vented his frustrations on it in its owner's absence? Varalen corrected the chair's position without commenting on it. "I will do my best to keep it from happening again."

"It's on account of those robes he wears," came a voice from the only other occupied chair, and Varalen turned with extreme reluctance to face Captain Nathaniel Wyles, who was—gods, who was actually eating a leg of chicken during a damned strategy meeting. As Varalen watched in disbelief, the captain tore off a strip with his teeth that was so long, he had to jam it into his mouth with two fingers. After licking them clean with a noise that surely didn't need to be half as loud as it was, he continued, "Too fancy by half, those things. One of these days he's going to trip on the steps and break his neck." His cheerful tone indicated just how broken up he would be if that ever came to pass. "Besides, robes went out of fashion with magicians, eh? That makes you . . . what, centuries out of date?"

"Robes, Captain Wyles," Varalen said, tugging at the sleeve of his own, "have long been customary in advisors, and since I serve the imperator as such, I hardly find them inappropriate. You cannot seriously expect me to dress as you do." *That is, like a thug,* he added mentally. Wyles was not uncommonly tall or uncommonly broad-shouldered, but he had fingers like overstuffed sausages and a jaw like a marble slab; Varalen wouldn't have been surprised to see him unhinge it, like a python. He also had the imperturbable calm and cold-eyed smile of a veteran torturer, which, not coincidentally, was the position he had held before Elgar promoted him. Varalen didn't doubt that he could hurl the inhabitants of the nearest orphanage over a cliff and retire to bed untroubled by anything worse than indigestion.

At least his verbal sparring with Wyles helped him hide his disappointment that the captain was present at all; Elgar set far too much store by his brutish opinions. Captain of the city guard was admittedly a prestigious position, but that hardly meant Wyles had anything worthwhile to contribute on the subject of actual warfare. He was meant to keep the streets in order—what did he know about the movements of entire armies?

Elgar scowled, but decided to hurl a roll of parchment into Varalen's lap instead of making whatever curt remark was running through his mind. "The latest report from the southeast," he said. "You're going to tell me how to fix it."

Jevran had the southeast, and he was no fool. A surprising number of Elgar's commanders were—or had been, when Varalen first arrived—but Jevran was one of the ones he had kept on. Besides being able to tell a battle formation from the inside of his own ass, he knew how to write reports. Varalen finished reading and set the parchment down with a shrug. "It's nothing so bad. Nothing I hadn't warned you about, certainly."

"Not so," Elgar replied. "You said the border between Esthrades and Reglay would be clear."

"I said it would be *relatively* clear, in the *north*. Commander Gerd apparently decided that meant ordering Jevran to charge down the border like a madman was a good idea, and he was predictably caught between outlying patrols on both sides—it's to his credit he managed to withdraw at all. And *now* the border *won't* be clear, since both countries know we're thinking of pressing forward that way."

Elgar ran a hand through his hair—still thick, and mostly black, though it was starting to gray right above his ears. "Then how *should* we press forward?"

Varalen gave another shrug, a much unhappier one. "My lord, you're like a man who's just been disarmed asking whom he should stab next. Jevran would have been your best choice to lead the charge into Reglay, but with so many wounded—"

"The charge into Reglay?" Elgar looked up sharply. "You have already decided so much?"

"You asked me to tell you where we should attack, my lord, and I am telling you. We were fortunate that Eira and Caius Margraine fought each other while they lived, because it allowed us to continue poking at Esthrades's northern border on the pretense of claiming land that rightly belonged to Lanvaldis. But we have failed to secure any kind of victory, and this state of affairs simply cannot continue. It is a waste of men."

Elgar shook his head fiercely, curling his fingers around the edge of the table. The wood was faded ebony, doubtless older than both of them put together. The table could easily have seated twenty, but it was otherwise plain. Varalen wondered idly what had happened to the table the Council had used, made for seven and only seven. "When I first called you into my service, you nearly begged me, despite my many misgivings, to move against Esthrades at once. And now you would have me simply abandon the campaign?"

"I don't wish you to *abandon* it—just to set it aside for the moment," Varalen insisted. "Reglay is an easier target. They have less land, and fewer men in a less-disciplined army. King Kelken is not hated, but he is not loved, and he is certainly no great commander. The harvest has been bad—the common folk are malnourished and discontent—"

"And they're all cravens," Wyles put in, still chomping away at his chicken.

"Which is why I know they won't come to Esthrades's aid, if we attack there instead," Elgar finished. "But if I move to take Reglay, I expose my flank to that bitch in the Fellspire—and who's to say she won't join the fight just to spite me?" He wrinkled his nose, the snuffling sound he made as he inhaled somehow dismissive. "If it's a choice between Esthrades alone or Reglay and quite possibly Esthrades anyway, the correct course of action seems clear enough to me."

Wyles wiped his mouth. "It seems to me, Varalen, that you should want Esthrades down quickly more than anyone. The little marquise has been giving you quite the run for it, hasn't she? But even you could tie up Reglay into a nice enough present for His Eminence without much trouble. What threat could possibly come from that quarter? That weak-kneed cuckold King Kelken?" He laughed. "Or rather, I suppose it's that son of his who's got the weak knees, eh? The little cripple? Is it either of *them* who's got you so concerned?"

It took all of Varalen's restraint to ignore him, but he knew that was the wisest choice. He turned to Elgar instead. "My lord, let us agree Esthrades is the greater threat. You are right that, as much as I would urge caution, the time to attack"—*since you insist on doing so,* he thought to himself—"must be soon; the situation in Issamira will most likely never be as favorable as it is now, and it cannot last forever." To emphasize his point, he swept a finger around Issamira on the map, a wide arc that encompassed the entire south. It was the largest country on the continent that Elgar had not conquered, and King Jotun had left it in a state of financial and military prosperity. Varalen was not looking forward to the day when Jotun's children finally decided which one of them was going to rule it. "We both likewise agree that a conquest of Reglay would be simple, provided we would *only* be attacking Reglay, and not Esthrades, Issamira, or, gods forbid, all three together." Another sweep, this one including a sizable chunk of the east—all the territory Elgar had left to conquer, and all he was determined to. "But I *assure* you that Lady Margraine will not follow you to Reglay—I am sure she would like nothing better than to snap at your heels as you charge, but she simply does not have the men. And she will not have them, if you attack now."

Elgar scratched at his beard—short, black, and impeccably maintained; Varalen had never so much as seen his whiskers glisten when he drank. "Yet she has enough men to defeat us?"

"I didn't say that."

"Well, if she *doesn't* have the men to defeat us, why should we not take Esthrades and be done with it?"

"My *lord,* you are being—" *Petulant* or *childish* would try Elgar's patience needlessly, and even *deliberately combative* wasn't safe enough to risk. "I cannot convince you of the wisdom of a plan you are determined to disdain," he said at last. "Reglay is weak *now.* We know, beyond a doubt, that it is weak, and you can take it with little trouble—and without anyone else attempting to stop you. Why not simply take what is within your grasp, rather than risking more on something harder to obtain?"

"You seemed to think it would be easy enough before."

"Because I knew the Esthradian army as it was, not as it is. I never dreamed that woman would be able to do so much with it, and *never* so quickly. They say she hasn't so much as *seen* a battlefield."

"So you're afraid of her, then," Elgar said.

It was probably best not to answer that. Instead Varalen spread his hands along the table, brushing at the edge of the nearest map. Elgar had an ancient one, he knew, one that still depicted the Empire of Elesthene. He never took that one out when they discussed strategy, but it was among the piles of other documents heaped upon the smaller table on his far side, and Varalen had often seen him close his thumb and forefinger around the rolled-up parchment, as if he could encompass the world he wished to make just so easily.

"My lord," he said at last, "I am not sure of her. I am not sure of what she might do, and that . . . unnerves me. I am sure of King Kelken, and I am sure of Reglay."

Elgar stared hard at him, as if the correct answer lay in the lines of Varalen's face instead of in his words. "I mislike this," he said. "You say she does not have the men to harry me in Reglay. Yet in her own land we send enough men to outnumber her three to one, and she routs us five to one. If she can do so much with so little, how many men does she *need* to be a nuisance?" He bit his lip, and it turned white against his teeth. "And what if it is more than *men* we must concern ourselves with?"

Varalen wasn't sure whether to laugh or to bang his head against the table, but he wisely decided against both. "If not men, my lord, then what? Women? Babes? Feral dogs?"

"Magic," Elgar spat passionately, a reverence and a curse at once.

"Magic," Varalen repeated, pinching the bridge of his nose. The word sounded flat and plain when he said it. "My lord, Arianrod Margraine can no more use magic than I can. And I assure you I am quite without any gifts in that regard." *As is everyone who breathes,* he didn't add.

"I hear rumors that say differently," Elgar insisted.

Varalen tried not to smile. "Of course you do. And where do you think they come from? Her ladyship knows as well as I do that the most important question is not whether she possesses magic but whether she can get her enemies to believe she does. Do not do her that favor, my lord."

Elgar drew one long finger down the tabletop, tracing patterns in the wood. "Leave that for now." He looked over at Wyles, who was licking his fingers and trying not to seem like he was smirking at Varalen. "Nathaniel, fetch Quentin and meet me in my study. I want to discuss changes in the guard rotations." That wouldn't go over well, Varalen knew. Quentin Gardener was the captain of the *Citadel* guard—a less prestigious position than Wyles's, but one that put him closer to Elgar. And since he was a generally decent person, all things considered, he and Wyles disagreed about nearly everything.

None of this showed in Wyles's expression; he merely nodded, bowed, and, with a muttered "Your Eminence," showed himself out, thankfully taking the sad remains of his chicken leg with him.

But before Varalen had so much as a chance to feel relief, Elgar asked, "What progress have you made on the matter of Hornoak?"

He wanted to simply drop the issue of what to do with his army so they could discuss empty superstitions and impossible demands? Varalen wanted to drive the heels of his hands into his eyes, but instead he merely folded his arms. "It is . . . a difficult task you have set me, my lord."

"I know it's difficult. That's why I gave it to *you,* not whichever guardsman was closest to hand. What have you decided?"

Varalen swallowed. "My lord, you are a ruler, and I a mere servant. If *you* cannot find yourself a man who is incorruptible, what success can I hope to have?"

"I do not need a man who is incorruptible," Elgar said, waving a hand at him impatiently. "I need a man whose obedience to me cannot be undone by any temptation, and who is strong and capable enough to make the journey and return."

What's the difference? Varalen thought. Out loud, he said, "I cannot claim ever to have met a man, weak or strong, who could not be undone by temptation."

Elgar surprised him by smiling, but there was no warmth in it, no mirth, and it did not reassure him in the slightest. "This is the sum of your advice for me. I cannot do as I wish, and . . . I cannot do as I wish. What I want is simply impossible, and so I should sigh, throw up my hands, and give up."

"That's not what I—"

Elgar sat back in his chair, pressing his fingertips together. "Remind me again why I have not killed your son."

He felt his spine stiffen, but he kept his hands under the table so Elgar could not see them twist. "Because I have been right before," he said, once he could trust his voice, "and I will be again."

"Let us hope so," Elgar replied, turning his gaze back to his maps.

CHAPTER FOUR

In his dreams, he flew far above Second Hearth, both the castle and the city at its foot. He skirted the city's edges, the uneven sprawl, without proper walls or fortifications, that he'd traced on his father's maps so many times but had never been able to walk for himself. He raced up the walls of Second Hearth's highest tower—not very high, as towers went, or so he had been told, but in his dreams it always touched the clouds. In his dreams there was no dirt or dust, no beggars in the streets, no air of hopelessness drifting down to weigh on the shoulders of the people. There was only open space and fresh air and the feeling of possibility.

Kel woke to his sister's hand on his shoulder, her voice so soft, it drifted into his dreams. "Kel. Kel, His Grace has asked for you. You must go to him."

Kel mumbled something even he wasn't sure of, gripping her hand to pull himself up. "Mm . . . Father? What time is—"

"The sun's been up an hour," Alessa said. "The king wishes for you and Eirnwin to attend him in his chambers. Eirnwin's come to help you get dressed."

Kel tried his best to rub the sleep from his eyes. The room was just as it always was: cold and spare, without any unnecessary furnishings. He didn't want anything in it that he could not personally use, so the mirror was built into and above his writing desk—that way he could stay to fix his hair without having to stand. The washbasin was by his bed for the same reason, and the bed itself was built low, so he never had to feel like he was climbing into or out of it. The armchair, upholstered in faded blue silk, was the one exception: it was so saggy that he couldn't sit in it without pain, but Lessa liked to cocoon herself there to read, so it stayed. "You won't be there?" he asked her.

His sister hesitated, then shook her head. "His Grace gave orders only for his advisor and his heir."

He'd come to some decision, then. When his father was mulling an issue, he spoke only to Eirnwin; he honored Kel by calling him into his presence, according to the rules of court, but it only ever meant he was informing Kel of something, not asking for his opinion.

As if sensing his thoughts, Alessa patted his hand, smiling at him reassuringly. Or perhaps she did it only because she couldn't seem to help smiling at him, no more than Kel could help smiling back. "Are you ready?" she asked. "Shall I call Eirnwin in?"

He nodded, and she withdrew, holding the door open so Eirnwin could walk past her. Bald and beardless, all he had for hair was the gray stubble that passed for eyebrows. But his voice and hands were strong and steady, and he was still able to carry Kel about the castle without much effort, even though he was nearly twelve. That was not to say it was often required—Kel had stopped needing to be carried years ago.

Eirnwin's bow was solemn enough, but he couldn't stop his eyes from crinkling at the corners. "Good morning, my lord. What shall I fetch for you today?"

Kel could wear shirts and tunics that would fit any boy roughly his stature, but his pants were all specially made, much wider than the usual fashion. This was to avoid chafing, to accommodate swelling, and, he suspected, to obscure the abnormal shape of his legs. "Give me the blacks," he told Eirnwin, "and my new tunic, and a cloak. It's cold today."

While Eirnwin got the clothes out, Kel used his arms to help move his legs over the side of the bed—bending and turning were what they were worst at. They felt better when he got them into position—like this, the soles of his feet just resting against the floor, they scarcely felt deficient. They felt like they could carry him.

His legs weren't *weak,* he liked to say, just stupid—they didn't understand what they were supposed to do. They hadn't understood the way they were supposed to grow, either, so they were crooked and stiff, perpetually swollen at the joints and prone to random spurts of pain when he put his weight on them the wrong way. That was why he had the crutches. Eirnwin had made him the first set when he was very small, then kept enlarging and refining them as he grew, so that he must have gone through more than a half dozen sets by now. At first Eirnwin had tried to make them beautiful, getting woodworkers to carve them with all sorts of fantastic shapes, but Kel had refused that, even when he was little. They were what they were; he preferred to be as little aware of them as possible, to acknowledge them no more than he had to.

While Kel pulled his tunic on, Eirnwin knelt on the floor, guiding his legs into the trousers. He had to have special shoes, too, to accommodate the gnarls and high arches of his feet, and Eirnwin slipped those on for him as well, to spare him the pain of drawing his knees up. Then he passed Kel his crutches, and they left for his father's study.

Everything about Second Hearth testified to the faded glory of the Rayls: the curtains were moth-eaten, the rugs stained and threadbare, the halls drafty and the mortar crumbling. Kel was fairly certain that if it weren't for Lessa's lungs, no one would even bother to dust. He was always searching for it, squinting into shafts of sunlight to see if the servants had missed a spot. He didn't mind any of the rest—who else in the kingdom even had faded silk, anyway?— though he knew it caused his father pain. But Lessa's health couldn't be trifled with, no matter what other corners they had to cut.

King Kelken was pacing before the window when they entered, his goblet of wine barely touched. He was not truly bald, but the coat of chain he wore left only his high forehead and receded hairline visible, so that he seemed as hairless as Eirnwin. His nose was sharp, his eyebrows thick and severe, but his delicate chin allowed vulnerability to slip into his expression from time to time, as if through a crack in his defenses. "My son," he said.

Kel could not truly bow, not with the crutches, but he bent his head. "Father," he replied, wondering at the formality. "Did you . . . want to tell us something?"

His father gestured to a nearby chair, and Eirnwin helped Kel settle himself into it, arranging his legs so they bent with minimal pain. His father looked away while they moved, his gaze flitting out the window, and he did not glance back at them until Eirnwin had stepped away. "Kelken," his father said, "I have never condescended to lie to you, and I will not start now. I have done all I could think to do, yet we are still too weak. If Hallarnon attacks us, Reglay will fall. And our only hope—that Elgar will choose not to attack—grows slimmer every day. Can you understand what this means?"

Kel suppressed a twitch of irritation—of course he knew what it meant. His father could hardly have spoken more plainly. "I understand that we're all in danger," he said instead. "I understand that just fighting won't work."

His father bowed his head. "Yes." He looked out the window again, drawing the fingers of one hand over the knuckles of the other. "Our only hope is to secure strong allies," he said at last. "I have considered the matter carefully, and have made a decision to that end."

Why was his father drawing things out like this? Why was he avoiding Kel's gaze? "What is it?" he asked.

His father's weak chin trembled, his throat working as he swallowed. "Your sister," he said slowly, "is of a decent age to be married, but I have not wanted to be hasty with her. I would have preferred to give her more time, but I can no longer delay. She will be married, if the gods do not spite me."

Icy fingers worked their way into Kel's gut. "She'll be married to *whom*?"

"I had only one choice," his father said. "Issamira is the only power on the continent that can possibly repel Hallarnon now, and we cannot send ships we do not possess out of a port we do not have to cross the sea and beg for help from foreigners who care nothing for our struggles." He swiped his goblet off the desk, taking a sip he appeared not to taste. "Even before all this, it had been my hope to marry her to Prince Landon, but he has not been found, and at this late hour he likely never will be. So I must appeal to Prince Hephestion. If a marriage can be struck between them, as I believe it can, then Issamira will surely aid us."

His father only sent for him when he had already made a decision—Kel knew that. That meant he was determined to take this course, however nervous he might seem. So to buy time as much as to hear the answer, Kel asked, "Why have you not called Lessa here? This concerns her much more than me."

His father's eyes flicked to the bottom of his goblet. "I have already informed her."

"What did she say?"

That finally drew his father's gaze to his. "Why, that the choice was mine to make, of course. And so it is, and I have made it."

Kel's arms were prickling, but he cleared his throat. "No." Beside him, he felt Eirnwin flinch.

His father's jaw clenched, stilling any last quivering of his chin, and his heavy brows drew together. "Alessa does not refuse, yet you seek to answer on her behalf?"

"You can't marry her to Hephestion," Kel insisted. "Don't you know what they say about him?"

"Kelken, I do not base my decisions on rumors I hear from servants about a foreign prince they have never seen. I would have thought you had the judgment not to pay them any heed either."

"They say women have been coming from all over the continent to try to marry him," Kel said. "They say he likes a different one every day—and then he gets bored of them and casts them aside."

"They also say he is handsome and gentle-humored and beloved by his people," his father said. "If you insist on giving voice to rumors, you must admit those as well."

Kel had heard that, it was true. But what did it matter whether the lordling treating Lessa as he pleased was *handsome* or not? "You don't see, Father. You don't want to see."

"Don't I?" his father said, his fingers clenched tight around his cup. "What don't I see?"

Kel shook his head. "Lessa will never make it to Issamira anyway. She can't cross the border; you know that. The air there is foul; even people who have never had trouble breathing go into coughing fits, or choke outright during dust storms. She'll never make it. She'll get sick."

His father frowned, but the tension in his fingers eased, and he set the cup down. "If she stays here, she'll be worse than sick when Elgar finds her. This journey is the only thing that can save us, Kelken."

Somehow it was harder to argue with his father when he looked sad than when he stormed and scowled, though Kel had never been able to figure out why. "Please don't send Lessa away." It wasn't what he'd been expecting to say, and he hated the way his voice trembled as he said it. "Please."

"Kelken, she must marry eventually—she can't simply stay here forever." He sighed. "You must understand: I'm not *punishing* her—I want only what is best for her, no less than I want what is best for you. Though you are so young, you show a thoughtfulness and determination that would put grown men to shame; you have never preoccupied yourself with childish things, so it would be wrong to tell you that childishness prevents you from seeing the truth. But only experience can teach you how bitter a king's choices must sometimes be. One day you will have that experience, and the wisdom that comes only with time. You will know then that a king cannot flinch from a decision, even one that pains him to his soul." King Kelken turned away. "A choice was presented to me, and I have made it. Your sister has already accepted it, and so must you."

———

"What did *you* say?" Kel asked Eirnwin as soon as they had gotten him settled back into a chair in his own chambers.

Eirnwin blinked at him. "Beg pardon, my lord? I rather thought you were about to chastise me for *not* speaking, not for speaking."

Kel shook his head. "My father never listens to anything I say, but he'll listen to you—that's why he tells you everything first. He called for me today because he'd decided, but you were in his chambers for so long yesterday because

it was difficult. That means you must have argued against him. So what did
you say?"

Eirnwin sank heavily into a chair. "That holds no importance now, my lord.
The king has decided."

"Even so, I want to hear it."

Eirnwin sighed. "I reminded him of truths he does not like to think on. That
is why we spoke for so long a time."

"You reminded him of *what*?"

Eirnwin's hands twisted in his lap, as if they were trying to speak for him.
Finally he said, "Alessa is a beautiful girl, my lord, and kind enough to delight
anyone with even the slightest notion of what is good. She will make a fine wife,
and one day, gods willing, she will be sister to a king. But her blood . . ." His
mouth worked as if he would finish the sentence, but ultimately he could not.
"I need not say the rest."

He didn't have to, because Kel knew it all too well. Alessa's blood would
never be royal, because his father was not hers. "My father always honored
her—"

"Yes, my lord, but that doesn't mean that Prince Hephestion and his family
will. The king sees this proposal as a mark of his regard—they may very well
see it as a slight. What sort of man offers a bastard to a prince?" His hands chafed
against each other. "If Prince Landon still lived, I would have counseled your
father to proceed with the match. But as it stands . . ."

Kel had met Prince Landon only once, many years ago, when he came to
Reglay on his father's behalf. He had stayed inside while his soldiers hunted with
Kel's father's, preferring to sit at the high table with Kel and spin tales of Issamiri heroes. He never averted his gaze from Kel's legs, or wasted time saying
how *sorry* he was. It was so strange to think of him as dead. "Are you sure?" he
asked Eirnwin.

"Well, not entirely—there is no way of knowing how much Prince Landon
would have been influenced by his family. But—"

"No, not about Lessa," Kel said. "Are you sure Prince Landon is—that he
really died?"

Eirnwin shrugged helplessly. "I cannot claim to know Prince Landon's fate
for certain, my lord, but his father is certainly dead, and his country certainly
needs a ruler. I have read many a tale in my life, and I know that important
personages who mysteriously disappear tend to reappear just as mysteriously.
But Issamira has spared no resource searching for him. If he is lost, how have
they not found him? If he is held captive somewhere, why have his jailers made
no demands? If he does not return because he *will* not, what could he possibly
be doing that is more important than ruling his country?" He spread his hands.

"In the end, the reason for his absence makes little difference—the result is the same. Issamira must have a monarch, even if it is only until Prince Landon returns. But I doubt we will ever see him again."

Kel could not well remember how Prince Landon had looked, but he remembered his soft voice, the mildness in his eyes. His shoulders had hunched slightly whenever Kel's father complimented him, but he was not a shy man, and if his smiles were melancholy, they were also frequent. He and Lessa might have liked each other, Kel thought. But there was no way to know now.

"If Prince Landon won't come back . . . that means you agree with me, then," he said to Eirnwin. "You agree Lessa can't marry Hephestion, so she shouldn't go to Issamira."

Eirnwin shook his head. "I informed your father of my concerns, but he made his decision regardless. It is up to both of us to abide by it."

"But Hephestion is—"

"My lord, all you know of Hephestion you know from rumors; your father was correct in that, at least."

Kel scowled. "Why would everyone say those things about him if they weren't true?"

Eirnwin touched his lips, and his fingers obscured his expression, leaving only his earnest eyes. "Do you know what the rumors say about you, my lord?"

That he was half one thing and half the other, waist up a normal boy, but with the twisted legs of a demon. That he was the result of a sinful mother and a weak father, and a judgment on them both. "I've heard them," he told Eirnwin. "I know."

Eirnwin sighed. "People often say things, my lord, simply for the pleasure of saying them. The most delightful secrets are the ones everybody knows and no one can substantiate. In truth, we cannot know what kind of man Prince Hephestion is—he has never ventured here, and I know no one who has ever seen him."

Kel shook his head. "I don't understand Father at all. In one breath he praises me, and in the next he dismisses anything I might say, just because I'm not king yet. But I don't need to be king to know that it isn't fair to risk Lessa on a prince none of us have met—to give up a member of our own family just because the rest of us are desperate." He folded his arms. "And I'd still feel that way, even if I *were* king."

Eirnwin looked at him carefully, and the smile he wore was sad, like one of Prince Landon's from long ago. "You are not king, my lord," he said. "Your father is merely trying to ensure that one day you will be."

CHAPTER FIVE

T he day dawned dark and overcast, and Roger wasn't halfway to the Dragon's Head when he told himself it was going to be a bad morning. He wasn't as surprised as he should've been, then, when Morgan seized him by the arm the moment he arrived, her face a mess of anger and worry. "That good-for-nothing *bandit*," she hissed, squeezing tight enough to leave marks. "Roger, you find him, and you tell him not to run off with *my* kitchen boy before sunup and leave me without any help to speak of."

"Deinol's gone somewhere with Seth?" Roger asked.

"The gods know the truth of it," Morgan said. "All I know is he's not here, and whom would he go off with but Deinol? Who else would even take the trouble to lure him away?"

Seth was as earnest and dutiful a boy as Roger had ever known, but he also had the misfortune to feel a sense of loyalty to *Deinol,* who was neither of those things. Roger couldn't exactly blame the boy—Deinol was the one who had gotten him both a home and a job with Morgan, out of nothing more than whatever drops of goodness he'd been able to wring out of his bandit's heart—but he felt sorry for Seth all the same. "The crime sure fits our Deinol," he agreed. "Well, Morgan, you do something about that sour expression, and I'll see what I can do to get your boy back."

It didn't take but three people asked to find Deinol, lazing about behind Halvard's shop eating his breakfast. "Well, now," Roger said, looking down at him sprawled out on the cobbles, "you're one to have at trouble with both hands if ever I saw the like."

Deinol tipped his head back so he could look up at him. "Why, what's the story now?"

"The story, my friend, is you tell me what mischief you sent Seth on, we retrieve said lad, and I intercede before Morgan can break your neck."

Deinol frowned. "Seth? I haven't seen him since yesterday."

Roger laughed. "Come off it, will you? Morgan says the boy's gone from his bed, and we all know you're the only one who could tempt him to shirk his duties.

So just tell me where you've stashed him, all right? I've got a day's work to see to same as anyone."

But Deinol just looked more confused. "Roger, I mean it. I haven't seen Seth at all today. I haven't been up for hardly an hour, and I thought he was working."

Neither one of them wanted to say it, but Roger was sure the growing worry on Deinol's face was mirrored on his own. "We've got to tell Morgan," he said at last. "It might be nothing, but I'd rather we knew where he was."

"I'm with you," Deinol said, springing to his feet more quickly than Roger would've believed possible. "Just give me a moment."

Leaving Roger to follow after him, he ducked around the corner and poked his head back into Halvard's shop. "Sorry about this, Hal, but could you send a runner down to Iron's Den to fetch Lucius? I've got to head back to Sheath straightaway—tell him Morgan's boy's gone missing." Well, that wasn't as bad as it could have been—Iron's Den, where most of the smiths set up shop, wasn't too far a run from Sheath. If Lucius had been in the richer districts sniffing out a new target, they'd have had to chase him to the other side of the city.

Halvard looked up, one hand still plunged elbow-deep in a barrel of salt pork. "What, the little one? You go on—the boys aren't up to much right now anyway." He looked over his shoulder at the girl who kept his books, who was scribbling something in a ledger. "Cerise, fetch one of the boys in here, would you? Whichever's looking lazier."

Once they were confident the message would find its way to Lucius, Roger and Deinol nearly ran back to the Dragon's Head. When they got there, they found Braddock with Morgan, who was pacing the length of the room, jaw tight and fingers clenched. Braddock was sitting in his usual corner, and Roger assumed that scowl meant he was thinking. "Well?" she asked when she saw Deinol, but her face fell at seeing him alone, and Roger thought she'd already guessed. "What have you done with him?"

"Nothing at all," Deinol said, "but I'll help you find him. It's not like him to do this; he's an honest boy."

"The most honest I've met," Morgan agreed. "But if you haven't taken him, where is he?"

"Did you search his room?" Deinol asked. "Was there . . . I don't know, anything strange?"

Morgan shook her head. "It's all in order. It's just as it looks every day."

The door opened, and Deinol turned to it eagerly. "Luciu—" he started, but it wasn't. Instead, Tom's monkey blinked at him, then turned her gaze to Morgan.

"Morgan," she said, "Tom told me to— What?" She looked around at the rest of them. "What is it?"

Morgan tapped her on the shoulder. "Tavern's closed right now, monkey. I can't help you till I've gotten my boy back."

She frowned. "What, Seth? You can't find him?"

"I'm afraid not."

"Did you ask at the Night Market?"

Morgan stared at her. "The—the Night Market? In Draven's Square?"

"Aye, I saw him there a time or so. I thought he was there on errands for you."

"I've never sent him there," Morgan said. She leaned on the edge of the bar. "But it's past sunup—the Night Market's closed."

Marceline shrugged. "Might be he got delayed on his way back. I can go ask if you like."

Morgan pressed a hand to her forehead. "Hold a moment, monkey. I need to . . . think on this. Why would he have gone to the Night Market?"

"I told you, I've seen him there before. I couldn't say why, though—he never bought a thing, just hung about and looked. *I* think he just liked to be there, but I'll not claim to know him."

"I liked the Night Market well enough when I was a boy," Roger said. "It needn't be something sinister, Morgan. Besides, if he's gone there before, he's also gotten back all right before, and none of us the wiser. It's where he went after that concerns me."

"After?" Morgan asked.

Roger nodded at Marceline. "The monkey thinks he's been delayed, but I can think of only a handful of things that could detain him for this long, and none of them are good."

"He might not even have been there—"

"Aye," Marceline said, with another shrug. "It was an idle guess, that's all. I'll run and ask, though, if you like; Tom told me not to come back until I'd gotten your scraps, and as the tavern's closed . . ."

Roger laughed. "That old skinflint would buy three-day-old rat off you, Morgan, so long as he could get it cheap."

Morgan bit her lip. "I am sorry for the trouble, monkey, but would you go? If he was there, we can start to trace his path, perhaps. I'll give you something for Tom when you get back—I won't even balk at the pittance he must've given you to pay me. You have my word."

But Marceline had no sooner opened the door than she started back from it, nearly knocking Deinol onto the floor. Lucius slipped through easily, as if the disturbance had nothing to do with him, and shut the door firmly before he spoke. "I've gone a bit ahead of you, it seems," he said, though Roger wasn't quite sure whom he meant. "Halvard's boy caught up with me in Draven's Square—you sent him, I think? But I was already looking by then. I heard a rumor in Iron's Den that gave me a bad feeling, so I started asking questions."

Morgan curled her fingers into a fist. "Well?"

Lucius set his jaw, swallowed hard, and began again. "The last time anyone saw him was at the Night Market—"

"*See?*" Marceline said.

"*Quiet,* monkey, please." Morgan turned back to Lucius. "What was he doing there?"

"I couldn't tell you. But the story is . . ." He swallowed again. "When I asked at Draven's Square, they said there was a woman there—a guard. She seemed to know him, and, well . . . she took him in. She . . . arrested him, they said."

There was a silence.

Roger spoke first, because someone had to. "What the hell do we know about this woman? What could she want with him?"

"I don't know," Lucius said. "And I couldn't find out. I tried, but . . ."

"You're sure she arrested him?" Morgan asked.

"Well, I wasn't there. . . . That's what the ones I talked to seemed to think, though."

Marceline had been biting her lip very assiduously, but finally she spoke up. "This guardswoman—did she have a scar on her face?"

"I don't know," Lucius said again. "I didn't ask."

Morgan turned to her. "What's the significance of the scar, monkey?"

"Maybe nothing, it's just . . . a woman like that dropped in on me and Tom in the middle of the night—not a very friendly one, but none of that lot are. She was asking about deserters, but we try not to get involved in things like that, so we put her off."

Morgan clutched one hand in the other, and pressed both to her heart. When she stayed silent, Deinol spoke up instead. "Well, look, he can't be a deserter, can he? He's just a boy. He's been *here* for more than three years, and before that . . . before that he was so young, he—" He gritted his teeth and broke off, shaking his head.

Lucius took his time replying, his face grim. "If we're all perfectly honest, we've got to admit we don't know a thing about Seth's life before he came here."

"And yours neither," Braddock said. "And same for countless folk who drink here every day. That's the way of things in Sheath."

"And I'll defend it as fiercely as you," Lucius said. "But that doesn't mean Elgar's men haven't a score of reasons for wanting our boy."

Deinol slammed his hand down on the bar. "Who cares why they want him? They can't have him." He glared at them all, as if practicing his defiance for the soldiers. "Can they?"

Morgan was slightly hunched over, one hand pressed to her forehead. "What can we *do,* Deinol? If I knew where he was . . ." She covered her eyes, slumping over the bar.

"Well, we've got to do *something*—" Deinol started, but Lucius put a hand on his shoulder.

"Morgan's right," he said. "The first thing to do is find out where he is. I think we're all pretty sure we know, but in a situation like this we've got to know for certain. We can't take any action until we do." He turned to Roger. "I've tried to avoid Elgar's men as much as possible, but in Kaiferi there was always a jailer or—what do you call them?—warden you could bribe if you wanted to know the contents of the castle dungeons. I expect things aren't so very different here?"

Lucius almost never talked about his life in Aurnis, and he almost never stumbled over his words, so to hear him do both at once was enough to leave Roger speechless for a moment. "Aye," he said at last. "I imagine they're twice as crooked here as they were in Aurnis." He found himself grinning. "So you were up to the same tricks even back home, eh?"

Lucius laughed. "I was on the other side, actually—I was supposed to help put a stop to all that."

"What, Lucius, you can't tell me you were a guardsman? I'll never believe it."

If it had been any other man, his smile would've grown tight, but Lucius's mouth stayed just the same. It was only the slightest disengagement, a faraway look about the eyes, that showed he had no wish to continue the conversation. "Not quite," he said, and brushed a hand absently against his sword. "Either way, if there *are* such men as I've said, I'm sure you know them."

"And so I do," Roger said.

"Then let's go and ask them. I have enough coin—"

"*I'll* go and ask them," Roger said. "They won't take kindly to the sight of you, whether you were ever a guardsman or not. And gods know I've got coin enough to spend on my own endeavors."

Morgan raised her head. "Roger . . ."

"I don't want to hear it," Roger said. "This is a job for me, and I like the boy as much as any of you. I'll accept your thanks later, but only if they come in the form of a lot of ale."

He hadn't taken ten steps outside before he realized he had a shadow. "Go back inside, monkey," he said. "Didn't you have to fetch something for Tom?"

"I haven't the heart to ask it of Morgan. Not now. He can bargain for scraps somewhere else." She scuffed her feet against the cobbles, but she was looking off and away, over his shoulder. "Roger," she said, "what's going to happen now?"

Roger followed her gaze and stared at the dark mass of the Citadel looming in the distance. "I think I know, monkey. But I wish I didn't."

———

"Third floor." Every word Roger spoke was another weight hanging on him. "Third floor, since this morning."

He was almost afraid to look at their faces, but he already knew what he'd see there. Deinol had that fierce look again—he'd scarce taken it off all day. Lucius's face was settled, but his fingers drifted to his sword. Morgan nodded slowly, though no one was speaking. And Braddock was scowling, but that just meant he had a pulse.

"Now listen here—" Roger started, but Deinol cut him off.

"You all said we should find out where he was," he said, jerking his chin at nothing in particular. "Well, we know. Now what are we going to do about it?"

"I know what you want to do about it," Morgan said.

"And?"

She sighed, cracking her knuckles absently. "And I'm with you, mad though it may be. As far as I'm concerned, those dogs stole my kitchen boy, and I'll take that theft about as well as I'd take any other."

"You ought to consider—"

"Save your breath, Roger," Deinol said. "I've defied Elgar's men before, for things that were worth a lot less. You'll not turn me from this."

"It's not as if it's never been done before," Morgan added more kindly. "And these louts are sharper than they look."

"That's all very well," Roger said, "or rather I'm forced to say that, since you won't listen to reason—and I almost don't want you to, for the boy's sake. You know, of course, that I . . . that I'll help in such ways as are . . . suited to my talents, let's say. But you see, ah, it's gold that's my metal, not steel." He grinned sheepishly. "I'll gladly take silver or copper as well. Just . . . not steel. I'm sure you understand."

"Didn't expect anything more from you," Braddock said, shifting only slightly from his ponderous slouch.

"It's more than *you're* offering," Roger retorted.

"And who says so, swindler?" Braddock finally stood up, stretching to his considerable height. "I don't normally go in for fools' errands, but as I can't talk you lot out of it"—his eyes flicked to Morgan—"I suppose I might do my part to make sure I can keep drinking here. And, well . . . I like the boy. Never gave offense, that one didn't, and that's more than I can say for most men." He nodded vaguely, as if that settled it. Morgan met his gaze, but she said nothing.

Deinol looked to Lucius. "And you, Lucius?"

Lucius looked almost surprised. "You have to ask? I'm with you all, no question." He smiled. "What on earth would you do without me?"

It would have been like Deinol just to grin, but instead he stayed solemn. "It'll be dangerous, you know."

Lucius shook his head. "Danger's none of my concern."

"If only we could all say that," Roger muttered.

Morgan leaned against the bar. "You will help us, though, Roger, won't you? You'll help us get in."

At first Roger attempted not to look surprised, but then it occurred to him, too late, that looking surprised might actually have helped. "What, ah, what do you mean?"

"I mean," Morgan said, "that you can get us inside the Citadel, one way or another."

"Look, even if I could—"

"You can," Morgan said. "I want to know whether you *will*."

Gods, and he'd been *saving* that one. "You're lucky I'm not about to have that boy on my conscience," he said at last. "I'll do what I can do."

"Good." She leaned her forehead on the heel of her hand, squeezing her eyes shut. "I swear, that boy's going to be paying me back for *years*."

———

The ceiling of the cell was so low, there wasn't more than a hand's breadth between it and the top of Seth's head. The back wall was slanted, so his upper body leaned back where his wrists were chained to the stone, but his legs were forced forward, so he always felt like he was about to fall. Something dripped unsteadily from the stone above him, seeping into the cloth between his shoulder and his neck.

The woman at his side shifted, casting one eye up to look at him. "Don't fret so, boy," she muttered. "You'll rile the guards."

Until she spoke, Seth hadn't realized he'd been shaking. "S-sorry," he said, but she didn't react one way or the other, just looked straight ahead again.

The woman was what Roger would've called an odd bird, though Seth couldn't have said exactly why. She was young, probably of an age with Lucius and Deinol, and thin, but there was nothing weak about her; instead she was wiry and lean, as if everything inessential about her had been boiled away. Even though she wasn't unusually tall, she was still taller than he was, and that meant she couldn't stand upright in such a tiny cell. Their jailers had had to content themselves with fastening manacles to her wrists and leaving her to crouch on the stone floor, but her predicament didn't seem to bother her; she sat there almost lazily, with one leg bent and the other straight, her chained wrists resting on her knees. Her tangled hair was the color of new copper; he hadn't been able to see her eyes very well in the torchlight, but he thought they were blue.

She had already been there when they locked Seth in, and she'd barely moved since, not even a fidget. He wanted to ask her why she was there, but he'd been too afraid; there was something in her manner that discouraged questions.

When she wasn't shooting the occasional glance over at him, she mostly kept her eyes closed, as if willing her thoughts to wander. Seth couldn't blame her: if he could have found a way to distract himself from all this, he would have. Instead all his senses seemed heightened, so that even the sound of the dripping ceiling was almost unbearable.

"Stop *fidgeting*," the woman said again, her eyes snapping open, and again Seth was startled to realize that he was. But how had she even noticed, if her eyes had been closed like that? "Nothing will happen to you if you just stay calm, all right?"

"Beg pardon if I'm not convinced of that," he replied, trying to keep his voice from cracking. "Things are looking pretty bad for us, if you hadn't noticed."

The woman shook her head, but he couldn't tell what it meant—if she disagreed with him, or if she were merely trying to wave his words away.

He pitched his voice lower. "Do you think—do you think they'll let us out? Eventually, I mean. Or are they—are they just going to—"

The woman snorted. "If it's favors you're counting on, boy, you'll grow old in here."

"But I— It isn't *fair*. I didn't—I don't even know what I *did*—"

"It doesn't seem like your imperator is in the habit of requiring a reason for this sort of thing," the woman said. "Or am I wrong?"

That was true enough, Seth admitted to himself. And it wasn't quite true he didn't know his offense—he knew what he'd *done,* he just didn't know why they *cared*. If they arrested everyone in his position, there'd hardly be anyone left to walk the streets. Of course, Palla had been able to arrest him only because she'd been there at Westcross, and presumably knew the whole story. But surely someone higher up than she was had taken an interest in him, or else he'd just have been fined or whipped and sent home. That was how these things worked, right?

He squirmed, trying to avoid the slimy water—he hoped it was water—but it was useless. "Well, if it was so much better where you're from, I wonder why you didn't stay there."

Her nose twitched, her expression going opaque. "I imagine there are scores of places more hospitable than this one, but their existence isn't going to be much help to either of us."

Seth shook his leg out, trying to keep it from stiffening. "I don't know that anything will help us."

"Your silence," the woman said, "will do wonders. Just wait and see."

Seth waited, but before he'd seen anything, he heard the shuffle of feet coming down the hall. Palla stopped in front of their cell, the torch she carried making her pale skin look sallow. Seth had forgotten the color of her hair and the shape of her face, but he never would've forgotten that scar; he was just surprised she'd remembered him. He supposed that his attempt to bolt when he saw her might have aided her memory, but it wasn't as if he'd been thinking clearly at the time. "Well, now," she said, much more self-satisfied than he ever remembered seeing her back then. "Enjoying your new quarters, boy?"

What did she expect him to say to that? What wouldn't make her angry? "Am I . . . going to be here a long time?"

"That depends on what you have to say, doesn't it? Your memory hasn't been very good so far. We have ways to help that along, though, if you'd prefer."

Seth quailed where he stood, but the woman just snorted, hiding an ironic smile behind her hair. Palla cocked her head. "You think that's funny, do you?"

"Not particularly," the woman replied, flat and toneless.

"That's good. You won't be doing much laughing when you get called to answer."

"I don't do much laughing anyway," the woman said, just as before.

Palla curled her fingers against the bars. "And screaming? Are you used to much of that?"

The woman's nose twitched again. "I'm not some child you can frighten. If you truly think your kind can break me, you'll be disappointed. But I know you wouldn't dare try."

"Wouldn't *dare*?" Palla snapped. "Orders are simple enough."

"Yes, and I can guess what yours were," the woman replied, tilting her chin so she could catch Palla's eyes. "If your master thought torturing us would get him whatever information he's after, you'd already have done it. He's not known for letting his prisons get too full, after all. My guess is he knows the boy's fragile—any fool can see that—and he doesn't want any of you getting carried away and killing him by accident. As for me, I suppose I've been deemed too valuable to damage just yet—or else too worthless, but the result is the same."

Palla scowled, but her silence was enough. "Might be if you push me, I'll get tired of following those orders."

The woman shrugged. "Might be I'll kill you. Doesn't much matter to me."

Palla snorted, then shot a glance back at Seth. "If you remember anything more about that trinket you stole, boy, we'd love to hear it. Otherwise you can count on a very long stay in here . . . or a very short one, depending on His Eminence's mood."

Seth looked at his feet. "I already *told* you everything I remember."

"Mm, perhaps. But long confinement can sometimes . . . unearth forgotten memories, or so I've been told." She raked a hand through her curls. "You can always give a shout if your answer becomes more favorable. Think on it." She turned and left, her footsteps slowly fading away. The woman made a soft but audible scoffing noise, but she said nothing more.

"Do you . . . really think they're not going to torture us?" Seth finally ventured.

The woman just shrugged again. "What they intend to do with us is not my concern."

"I'll respectfully disagree with you on that—it very much matters to me whether I'm tortured or not. I don't know what you think's going to happen here, but—"

She sighed. "Boy, will nothing convince you to be quiet? You're not helping your chances."

"If I wanted to help my chances, I'd think of some story to—"

"Not your chances with *them,*" the woman interrupted. "You have none. I mean your chances with me."

She extended one arm, and when she flexed it, something shifted, the glint of metal peeking out over the edge of her sleeve. Seth squinted at it, confused at first, but finally he realized what it was.

The woman met his gaze. "It might be I'm feeling generous today. But first I need to know that silence is a concept you understand. Have I made myself sufficiently clear?"

Seth didn't even squeak.

CHAPTER SIX

So where exactly are we going to—"
"*Will you be quiet?*" Morgan hissed.

Roger laughed. "There's no cause to worry about that yet, Morgan—it's not as if they can hear us from here." To underscore his point, he tapped on the thick stone wall of the tunnel, producing a blunt, weak sound that didn't even echo. Perhaps it would have been more appropriate to tap on the ceiling, since they were underground, but it was far too high for him to reach. He hoped Morgan was reassured anyway.

"Thank you, Roger," Deinol said, so smug that even Roger wanted to groan. "Now, as I was saying, where exactly does this passage of yours come out?"

Roger tapped his chin. "Well, I don't have a map of the Citadel, mind, but this tunnel'll put you in among the kitchen stores—it's a false floor, just push up on the panel when you get to the end; you'll see it. That's ground level, and below that you've got five levels of dungeon, and we know Seth's on the third. So . . . it could be worse, all told."

He couldn't help but feel a twinge of regret—this passage was one of the few secrets valuable enough for him to keep, valuable enough even to outweigh his inclination to brag. There were many times he'd been tempted just to let a slight hint slip, but he'd always shut his mouth just in time. And now here he was, leading four people right to the spot. It *was* a pity, no denying it. "Don't say I never did anything for you," he muttered. "I'm damned proud of this thing, you know."

Deinol peered down the passage, squinting into the dark as if it were sunlight. "How long have you known about this?"

"Oh, year and a half, maybe two—would've sat on it for a lot longer if I'd had my way. Do you know how many people would kill for a direct route into the Citadel?"

"How did you even find it?" Morgan asked.

Roger felt himself beginning to grin; if he had to give up the secret, at least now he got to boast about it. "Folks've been whispering about hidden routes into the Citadel for as long as I can remember—story is, they're as old as the empire, or even older than that. Gran used to talk of a whole tangled web of tunnels right in the dungeons themselves—more false walls than true ones down there, she always said. She was never able to find any of those tunnels herself, though, and I never knew of anybody else who had, either. I'm fairly certain this is as close as anyone alive's going to get you."

Braddock shook his head, holding the torch well away from himself so he didn't singe his hair. "Swindler, you expect us to believe this precious little passageway has been here all this time and the only one wise to it was *you*?"

Roger had no idea how many other people might've stumbled upon the passage as well, but he wasn't about to say that. "And why not?" he asked. "You know more of my exploits than most, and you're still surprised? I was *born* for this sort of thing. Gran always said I was the smartest Halfen in the family—well, 'cept for Cousin Len, but he wasn't a *real* Halfen anyway. 'Roger,' she'd say, 'one of these days you're going to—'"

"Yes, Roger, that's wonderful, thank you," Morgan said, clapping him on the shoulder. "I'll be happy to hear all about your family once we're back at the Dragon's Head, but at the moment there's a kitchen boy who requires our attention."

They didn't think there was any sense in his stories, and they had absolutely no respect for Gran. But Roger was used to that by now. "All right," he said. "I've brought you to it in any case, haven't I? What're you waiting for?"

Morgan peered dubiously down the length of the passageway. "You're sure this goes where you say it does?"

"No doubt of *that*. Nearly stumbled right into a guardsman the day I first discovered it—lucky he was drunk off his ass, or I'd have been spotted for sure."

Lucius cleared his throat. "Speaking of guardsmen, Morgan, I really think it's better that you stay here."

She sighed. "Not this again. I'm not defenseless, Lucius; you know that."

"Aye, but these are killers, not brawlers. They—"

"Do you think I've never had anyone draw a sword on me before? If this were solely a matter of stealth, you'd have to bring Roger along, and you wouldn't let Braddock or Deinol anywhere near. As it isn't, you'll need as many pairs of hands as you can get, and I know how to use mine. Let's say no more about it."

"Well, you tried," Roger said to Lucius. He shook his head, unsmiling, but said nothing more.

This was where Roger had chosen to leave them, so he faced the four of them, searching for any last scraps of advice he could give. "I . . . Well, be as quick as you can." He leaned against the wall. "I'll wait out here for the first hour or so."

Lucius looked surprised. "Why not just head back? Safer that way."

"Aye, well, maybe I'd rather know if you've hit trouble or not. Wondering about it would just ruin my concentration, anyway."

Morgan smiled slightly. "As you like." Then, to the others, "We all ready?"

They looked at one another with vague grins, but Roger knew it couldn't have been easy. As far as he knew, Morgan had never killed anyone before, and though Deinol and Braddock had talent, they were only two men. Lucius was special—anyone who knew two bits about swordplay could see that—but even he couldn't take on every guardsman in the Citadel. Roger tried to remind himself of all Gran's tales of daring prison escapes through the years, the grand majority coming off without so much as an exchange of blows. And no matter what anyone else thought, Gran had always known what she was about; she had always told him such tunnels existed, and here one was.

He pressed his fingertips together, then clasped his hands. "Well, good luck."

"We'll need it," Lucius said quietly. "Thanks."

"We'll be fine," Deinol insisted. "Come on." He started off down the passage, going on his way with at least the appearance of confidence. Lucius hurried after him—no doubt to make sure he didn't trip on his own feet, as Braddock was the one with the torch—and Braddock exchanged a glance with Morgan before following suit. She gave Roger a lingering look as the torchlight faded ahead of them.

"If we're delayed," she said at last, "you make sure nothing happens to my bar, you hear?"

Roger nodded, and then she was gone.

He waited until he couldn't hear so much as the whisper of a footfall on the stone, then walked back out of the tunnel and pulled the door shut behind him, leaving it indistinguishable from the rest of the wood paneling. That left him— where else?—in the lower chamber of a Ninist vestry. He sat himself down to wait, tucking himself into a corner of the room and looking up at the still faces of the Traitor and the Whore. These had been done in granite, not marble, but he'd know them anywhere. *Always a Ninist vestry,* he thought, and wondered if Seth would have been disappointed or impressed.

———

Perhaps it was a rather childish method, but at this point Varalen was prepared to try anything. At the top of a new sheet of parchment, well away from the eyes of the guardswoman, he wrote: *Problem the First: the Woman Prisoner.* Then he glanced at her over the tip of his quill. "He didn't ask for her to be tortured?"

The guardswoman—Palla?—pursed her lips. "His Eminence did not deign to answer, milord. He said only that he was not to be bothered, and that we should direct our questions to you until such time as he is better disposed to answer them."

Lovely. "Well, I have rather an aversion to torture myself, so if we're leaving it to me, I'd just as soon not." He brushed the tip of the quill against his cheek. "Tell me truly, now—your fellows arrested the wrong person, didn't they? I'll make sure no harm comes to them from the mistake, I promise you, but I can't afford to waste my time chasing shadows."

She stayed tight-lipped, and her eyes gave him nothing. "She matched the description we were given."

The description Elgar's esteemed guardsmen had been given amounted to nothing more than this: every several nights or so, claimed their informant, a woman involved in the very highest orders of the resistance bought rumors off a trader at the Night Market named Six-Fingered Peck (who, it seemed, had ten fingers, five on each hand, just like everybody else). And the woman herself? Why, she was tall and cloaked and carried a sword. So, naturally, instead of waiting to overhear any suspicious conversation between Six-Fingered Peck and any of his female customers, Elgar's guards had simply arrested the first armed woman who approached him. But Varalen couldn't tell Palla outright that he thought her brothers-in-arms had behaved like proper imbeciles, so instead he rubbed his temples and considered his words.

"Captain Gardener told me he'd swear to her innocence," he said at last. Unfortunately, since Quentin Gardener was only captain of the Citadel guard, he lacked the authority to reprimand anyone who'd been involved in the woman's arrest—it had been entirely carried out by members of the *city* guard. What a surprise that Wyles's people had made a mess of things. "And he's been interrogating prisoners for years, so I imagine he knows what he's about." Of course, Wyles had interrogated prisoners for many years as well, but although he had many preferred instruments, words were not among them. Thank the gods Elgar hadn't left *him* to deal with the prisoners.

"She won't give her name," Palla muttered, and now she looked almost sulky.

Varalen laughed. "That's insolence, not secrecy. If she really didn't want us to know, she'd just make up a name—how would we know the difference?" He tapped his chin, looking down at the parchment again. "Where the boy's concerned, though, I'm told you know more?" That was *Problem the Second,* and he marked it down as such: *the Boy Prisoner.*

"Aye," Palla said. "I was at Westcross with him, more than three years ago now. He's a tick or two bigger, but it's the same boy—and he knew me on sight, no doubt of that."

He nodded. "But he was never actually a soldier, isn't that right? So he can't be a deserter, either."

She shook her head. "He ran off, to be sure, but that's not why I took him in." She hesitated. "This all happened before you came here, milord. . . ."

Would they really insist on calling him that? "That's all right," Varalen said. "I'll do my best to follow it regardless."

She fidgeted, tugging at her glove. "Well, there was a soldier at Westcross, Ben Ginn, who ended up running afoul of His Eminence right after the boy ran off. Seems Ben swiped some bit of jewelry off a prisoner bound for the capital, and His Eminence heard of it and wanted it back. But Ben could never turn it up, and he always swore it was the boy who took it. So I thought—"

"I see." Why on earth had Elgar cared whether his guards stole from their captives or not? "Has the boy been able to produce this trinket?"

She shuffled her feet. "He claims he sold it."

"An entirely likely course of action, given how many years have passed." He dipped the quill in the inkwell again. "Is there anything else?"

Palla bit her lip. "I think they know each other."

"You think that who know each other?"

"Her and the boy. The ones we brought in." She still fidgeted a little, but she met his eyes. "I . . . had an idea, milord. I thought it was funny, picking up two people an hour apart in nearly the same spot—I thought I saw the boy talking to Peck too, but he ran for it as soon as he laid eyes on me. So I put him in the same cell with her, just to see what they'd do. Prisoners aren't usually ones for talking, but I keep hearing those two whispering to each other, and they clap their mouths right shut whenever I get near. Might be they meant to be at the Night Market at the same time—might be they were up to something there."

And by *something* she undoubtedly meant *resistance business*. Varalen left the quill in the inkwell while he thought it over. "Well, it's not impossible, especially if they frequent the same areas. But even if they do know each other, that's not necessarily significant. I grew up in the capital myself—not too far from Draven's Square, actually—and I can assure you that big cities often feel smaller than they have any right to." That wasn't the answer she needed, though, and he sighed. "Leave them where they are for now. If you happen to overhear anything of interest pass between them, be sure to report it."

She bowed. "Milord."

Varalen waited for the door to shut behind her before he let himself slump forward over the table, but a moment later he was reaching for his quill again. *Problem the Third: the Resistance,* he wrote. If the soldiers had indeed apprehended the wrong woman, as he was almost certain they had, that meant there was a real member of the resistance out there somewhere—well, assuming their little weasel had told the truth. Varalen didn't doubt a resistance movement existed in some form—there were *always* resistance movements, no matter who ruled. The question was, did it have any substance after its members had left the tavern and sobered up? Elgar certainly thought so, but Elgar gave as much weight to ancient legends as scouting reports, so perhaps his opinion wasn't the most reliable. Either way, Varalen had no idea how they were supposed to go about finding this woman now; if she had the slightest pinch of sense, she'd stay far away from Six-Fingered Peck in the future, and he'd been all they had.

Problem the Fourth, possibly his least favorite of the lot, was *Hornoak.* It was like a bad joke, or some sort of demented riddle game: What did it mean to find someone who couldn't be tempted? Elgar was no more naïve about human nature than Varalen was himself, and yet he had demanded such an impossible creature in all seriousness, as if he felt Varalen ought to have it sorted out in an evening. He'd finally offered to go himself, but Elgar refused to allow it; he'd suggested *Elgar* go himself, but the imperator would have none of that, either: "If there's danger in it," he'd said, "I'll not be the one to suffer it." Asked what sort of danger he meant, of course, he'd refused to answer.

Pinching the bridge of his nose, Varalen finished his list: *Problem the Fifth: the War.* As to that, the lines of his maps were starting to blur before his eyes, and he still didn't feel as if he'd made any progress.

An easy victory against the Esthradian army used to be the one thing he could count on. He'd made his name in the east, helping the Lanvaldian army drive Caius Margraine's men back across the border when the marquis had decided he'd like to have some more territory. Caius Margraine was built like a bull, all tough muscle and hard head; he led the van of every brigade he ever commanded, ever since he was a boy, yet he bore surprisingly few scars—easy to spot but damned hard to kill, as his men liked to boast. They loved him for his bravery, and perhaps he deserved it, but as a strategist, he was worse than useless—the only order he seemed to know was *charge*. And charge he did, over and over and over. Varalen broke him every single time, so easily that by the end he fiddled with his strategies solely for variety's sake.

He'd viewed those battles as a necessary annoyance, a stepping-stone on the road to his larger ambitions. But now they seemed positively idyllic—now that Caius Margraine was dead and Varalen's talents had served only to catch the eye of a man who wouldn't take no for an answer.

After he'd conquered Lanvaldis, Elgar had been able to pick at the Esthradian forces near the border, under the pretense of continuing the territorial dispute the former marquis had started. But these skirmishes were nothing like the old ones. Lord Margraine had died just after the fall of Lanvaldis, of an illness that had run approximately six weeks. It was a long time to die, certainly, but precious little time to organize an army when your father had never let you command so much as a single soldier before, and such was the position Arianrod Margraine found herself in after assuming her father's throne. Perhaps if, as he had advised, Elgar had attacked Esthrades immediately, they might still have caught her half prepared. But Elgar was displeased with the unexpected difficulty with which his army had taken Lanvaldis, and refused to so much as consider another campaign until he had reorganized and retested his soldiers in every conceivable fashion. By the time he finally agreed to send them to Esthrades, it was too late.

If Caius Margraine had been a charging bull, his daughter was a silken noose; she slipped around and around Varalen's men, and by the time she tightened her grip, it was too late to escape. She sent her soldiers to seek him across mountains and through forests, while Varalen's own swore the cliffs were sheer and every tree looked the same. He knew it was no magic, as Elgar feared—the woman was simply a formidable intellect, and that, to him, was far more threatening. Magic, he supposed, could be overcome by superior skill just like any other military advantage, but if she was actually *smarter* than he was . . . that was not something he liked to think about.

He massaged his temples, tracing the lines of the map again. He *could* win this, he knew he could. Issamira was as good as paralyzed until the succession was sorted out, Reglay was toothless and had been so for years, and Hallarnon's own borders were secure. He had run every scenario he could think of through his head, and the conclusion he came to was always the same: Esthrades's marquise might hold them off for some time yet, but without Issamira at her back, she simply could not hope to mount a counteroffensive. And if that were true, which it *was,* then his best course of action, and Elgar's, would be to snap Reglay up quickly and attack Esthrades from two sides, leaving her trapped between them, the eastern sea, and the Gods' Curse to the south. Even *she* couldn't hope to withstand that.

But if he'd already decided, why was he still poring over his maps at this time of night? Why couldn't he seem to sleep?

He reached for his quill again, even though he hardly knew what he meant to write, but the door opened so abruptly, he nearly knocked over his inkwell. He was half expecting Palla again, but it was Quentin Gardener he saw, his face gone pale behind his long side-whiskers. "My lord," he said, head still respectfully bowed despite his agitation, "if it's not too much of an imposition, please remain here for the present. You may want to lock your door. The commander's having a bad night."

Elgar had many commanders, but there was no need to ask which one the captain meant. "I see," he said, trying to imitate Quentin's steadfastness. "I think I will lock my door, thank you."

Quentin nodded and hurried out, and, true to his word, Varalen got up to close the latch. He stood aimlessly before the door, wondering if he shouldn't add *Problem the Sixth: Shinsei* to his list. Whatever Elgar said, whatever any of the other officers or soldiers said, the commander was clearly mad, and had been for some time, if not from birth. He had been years in Elgar's service before Varalen ever met him, but rumor had it that Shinsei had been different, once: still quiet and removed, still shrinking from all company save Elgar's, but . . . composed, or at least restrained. Now he skulked through his quarters like a man who saw ghosts. One moment he seemed to sleepwalk; the next, he'd be too full of nerves to speak. Varalen could not stay more than several minutes in his company without feeling the hairs rise on the back of his neck, and he did not understand how someone as cautious as Elgar could put such absolute trust in a man who seemed as if he might come unhinged at any moment.

It was Lanvaldis, men whispered, that had changed the commander so; something had happened in the final battle, some unhappy accident that festered in his mind, and Shinsei had never been the same since. But Lanvaldis had been before Varalen's time, and no one he asked was willing or able to enlighten him further.

If Shinsei was, as it seemed, in another of his moods, he'd have to be forcibly removed to his own chambers; this generally required at least half a dozen men, if they were lucky and he kept his sword sheathed. Yet Elgar always spoke with him alone, with no more nervousness than he might have shown before an interview with his own reflection. How could he be so unyieldingly particular about some things and so nonchalant about others?

Varalen finally returned to his seat, and glanced at the map again. This time, he planted his index finger squarely on Hornoak. He'd suggested sending Shinsei as well—there was no one Elgar seemed to trust more—but Elgar had refused that idea more stridently than any of the others. And that left Varalen here, with nothing but a list of problems, and no answers in sight.

It was Ryam's life that swung tremulously behind his eyes whenever he closed them; if not for that, he could almost be at peace with the idea of his own execution. There were days when he began to think a quick death preferable to the interminable sentence of serving a man he could not respect, who challenged him only with trivialities.

———

It was soft, but Seth could hear the commotion clearly—the clatter of metal on stone, the ghost of a shout. He looked down at the woman, thinking to warn her, but she already had her head cocked toward the noise, her eyes contemplative slits.

"Well," she muttered at last, turning to him, "I suppose this is as good a time as any."

Seth tried not to shiver. "Do you . . . What do you think that is?"

"Does it matter? It's a distraction, and we're not like to get another. Are you coming or not?"

He didn't have to think about that one. "I'm with you."

"Good." He tried to watch her carefully, but he couldn't seem to follow the movements of her wrists, the way she managed to draw the pick from her sleeve and turn it so it slid into place. She did it as smoothly as if she broke out of prison every day of her life, the click as the manacles released her so soft he might almost have dreamed it. Then she stood, or as near to it as she could get with the ceiling so low, and went over to him.

He hadn't realized how much the shackles had been holding him up, and when she unlocked them he staggered suddenly forward, nearly falling into her arms. She caught him easily, holding him by the shoulders and easing him back onto his feet. She held his gaze, and he knew it was the same question again: Could he do this quietly? He nodded.

It took her a bit longer to get the cell door open; she crouched in front of it for more than a minute, twisting the pick back and forth until she found the right angle. She caught the door before it could creak open, sliding it slowly inch by inch until she could slip by, then nodded to him. He followed her out into the corridor, hoping he didn't look as petrified as he felt.

The hallway looked the same to him in either direction, a long unbroken line of cells stretching endlessly into the darkness. The guards had lit a torch in the brazier before his own cell, but beyond that there were only a handful of torches visible along the entire corridor. He hadn't the slightest idea which way to go, but the woman started striding to the left as confidently as Roger walked through Sheath, and Seth had to hurry to catch up.

In the dim light he couldn't always tell which cells held prisoners and which didn't, or if those prisoners were awake. If they were spotted, mightn't some of the others rouse the guards? He took hold of the woman's sleeve, trying to question her as discreetly as possible, but she turned about immediately and grabbed his wrist, fixing him with a look so fierce that any inquiry died in his throat. She loosened her grip a little, then, but still kept hold of him, so he had to shuffle along twice as fast to keep pace.

The passage grew dimmer the farther they walked, and eventually the woman put her free hand before her, feeling along the wall so she didn't lose her way. A queasy feeling started up in the pit of Seth's stomach, and he wondered if she wasn't just making it up as she went along after all, but then he realized the corridor was getting lighter again. He soon discovered why: a couple dozen steps more and they were around a corner, a flight of steps ahead of them, another torch flickering halfway up. The woman kept climbing past the first landing, but when she reached the second, there were no more stairs, so they had to walk down another hallway. There were still cells lining this one, but the only other torch Seth could see was all the way at the other end of the corridor, leaving heavy shadow in between. The woman tugged on Seth's wrist, pressed one finger to her lips, and starting creeping down the hall more silently than Seth could ever have managed. He did the best he could, wincing every time his feet made a scuffling noise against the stone.

It seemed to take forever to reach the far end of the hall, but when they turned the corner, there were no stairs, just another corridor running perpendicular to the first. There were no cells here, though, and he supposed that was something. The woman seemed encouraged too—she walked with more purpose now, as if her goal were in sight. They were about halfway down when she stiffened and paused, her fingers pressing sharply into the back of Seth's hand. She kept motionless like that for less than an instant, then released him altogether. She ran the fingers of her right hand along her left wrist—smoothly, as if she'd made the movement a hundred times before. And then she caught her breath and leaped backward, just as an indistinct figure flung itself at her from the other side of a shadowy archway Seth hadn't even seen, missing her by inches.

The other person hit the floor hard, grunting softly at the impact before rising to his knees. The woman didn't give him the chance to recover further, kicking him in the gut and then in the side when he doubled over. She aimed the third kick at his head, but he grabbed her leg and pulled her down. They scuffled on the floor, and Seth backed up so they wouldn't knock him over too. He wanted to help her, somehow, but he didn't know how to hit the other person without hitting her.

Then there was yet another figure, taller and slimmer, appearing as if out of nowhere; it grabbed the first interloper by the back of the neck, hauling him off the woman, who jumped immediately to her feet. "Wait," the new figure whispered, and Seth started, because he knew that voice.

"Lucius?" he asked.

The man in question released his companion in favor of brushing his long hair back from his face, then smiled calmly. "Evening, Seth. Fancy meeting you here."

"Then—wait, *Deinol*?"

"The very same," Deinol agreed, wincing. "I'm not acquainted with your lovely friend there, though—just know I'd rather wrestle with a wildcat. Gods, my *face*."

"It's no more than you deserved," the woman muttered, leaning against the wall. "What did you think you were doing?"

Deinol ignored her, turning back to Seth. "We heard it was a woman with the guard who brought you in—thought this was her."

"Does everyone here think there's only one woman in the whole damned city?" the woman asked, rolling her eyes. "Am I dressed like a guard to you?"

"*Is* she your friend, then?" Lucius asked Seth, still smiling faintly.

Seth nodded. "Close enough."

The woman seemed to regard Deinol as lacking the intelligence necessary for conversation, so she directed her next words at Lucius. "Did any guards see you?"

"Only one," Lucius said. "We knocked him out—stole his keys just in case, though Deinol's decent with a lockpick."

"And do you know how you'll get out?"

He nodded, pointing down the hall. "Up the stairs at the end there, and then through the kitchen stores, right nearby."

If she was surprised, she didn't show it. "Good, let's go."

Deinol scowled. "No one said *you* were—"

"Not now," the woman snapped, but as she passed the archway, she came to an abrupt stop. "Oh, you're *joking*."

"Afraid not," Morgan said from the darkness—had even she come to rescue him? "Lucius, what should we do with her?"

Lucius shrugged. "Seth likes her well enough. She'll come with us."

"Are you sure that—"

"There's no time," Lucius said. "I think I hear them."

The woman cocked her head, her eyes fluttering slightly as she listened. "You're right. I'll follow you."

In answer, Lucius brushed past the woman and down the darkened corridor, leaving her to fall in behind him. Deinol nodded to Seth, and as they drew abreast with Morgan, Braddock appeared, hefting an ax in one hand. Seth couldn't believe his eyes—had they *all* come in after him? That had to be why they were here, didn't it?

"Roger's playing the coward back in Sheath, as he's wont to do," Lucius said, as if reading his thoughts. "But he showed us the way."

"How did Roger know how to get inside a prison? I thought he was so proud of never having been in one."

"Let him tell you himself," Lucius said. "Come on—we're close."

They made it up the stairs, and around one more turn. On the other side, a wall of swords met them, before even Lucius had time to draw his blade.

The man who looked to be in charge of the soldiers scratched his side-whiskers almost sheepishly. "I did think I heard a disturbance from down below, but I can safely say this is not what I was expecting."

At Seth's elbow, Braddock's fingers knuckled white around the shaft of his ax, but he kept it hanging limply at his side. "Well, shit."

CHAPTER SEVEN

There was a girl," Shinsei said—again? Yes, he could remember saying it before. "In the snow. I saw her. She had golden hair. I *saw* her."

His master's voice came out of the dark beside him, measured and calm as always, but it did not soothe Shinsei as it usually did. "That's true enough. You did see her."

"But she's gone now," Shinsei said, "and I wanted—I wanted—I *want* to ask her something, I just can't—"

"You cannot ask her," his master said. "That's true as well, I'm afraid."

"No, I meant—" He meant to say that he couldn't remember the question. But what his master had said was true too; there was a reason Shinsei could not ask her, and it wasn't just that she wasn't here.

Coward, she had said; he remembered that. She had called him that. He understood, in a purely definitional way, what a coward was, but it was as if a sheet of glass separated him from the word; he could not put his hands on it, to grasp its meaning. He could not say what it was about a coward that set him apart from other men.

"I think there is something wrong with my mind," he said to his master.

His master smiled wearily. "It is true you are different, Shinsei, but that does not mean something is wrong with you."

He didn't *want* there to be something wrong with him, but there it was. He sensed the way others could move from thought to thought, in a strong, unbroken chain, but Shinsei would reach a conclusion only to realize he could not recall the thoughts that had led to it. It was like walking through snow, and turning back to see your footsteps erased behind you. That could not be permissible—could it? That was . . . a dangerous way to be.

Wasn't it? Or hadn't he loved it, once?

"I *want* to remember," he said to his master. "Or . . . this time I do, anyway. But I can't seem to hold on to it. I keep remembering there's something I want to ask her, but never what."

His master sighed. "Does it truly matter, Shinsei? It was years ago. You remember that, don't you?"

Had it really been years? But yes, that was right. Years. She had been so young when he saw her—was she older now? No, he reminded himself: she wasn't any older. She would never be any older than she was, because . . . something had happened. He remembered his head hurting, and . . . yes, that was the first time his head had hurt like that. Is that what he wanted to ask her? Why his head kept hurting? No, that wasn't it. Was it?

"She had golden hair," he said again, and then wondered why. Was that important? Not in itself, he was fairly certain, but only because the color of her hair had reminded him of something else. Of *someone* else. But it hadn't reminded him until afterward, when his head started hurting. That was right, wasn't it? That was right. "She had golden hair, and she said that I was . . ." *A coward.* "Wrong. She said that I was wrong." He cocked his head, looking at his master. "But I wasn't, was I?"

"No," his master said.

"No," Shinsei agreed. "So then she must have been wrong, and why would I want to look for guidance from someone I knew was wrong? Yet I'm sure it was important. There was something I—"

"Shinsei," his master said, very quietly, very patiently. "We have discussed this before. We have discussed this girl, and what happened to her. Do you remember?"

He remembered that they had discussed it, yes. His master was always having to discuss things with him over and over, and for that Shinsei was sorry. But try as he might, he could not seem to remember anything they had said about the girl. His master knew that Shinsei wanted to ask her something, yes, and—

"The girl was from Lanvaldis, Shinsei," his master said. "From Araveil, the old capital, before we conquered it. She got caught up in the civilian resistance. Do you remember that?"

She'd had a sword. He remembered that. She'd been armed. "Did we . . . fight?" he asked.

"Did you and the girl fight? I'm afraid so."

That was right—he remembered seeing her naked sword, the way it had gleamed under the moon. He remembered the look of determination on her face. He remembered how he had watched her, how he had judged her—he remembered how he had shifted his grip on his sword, and—

"She should not have fought me," he said; it tasted like an excuse. "My swordsmanship is perfect. I'm *supposed* to be perfect, I—" He reached for the hilt of his sword, brushing his fingertips across it. The others always drew back in alarm when he did that, and he never knew what to say to them. But his master never looked frightened. "I was only doing what I was supposed to do," he whispered.

"I know," his master said, resting a hand on his shoulder. "I know, Shinsei. And it's all right. I don't mean to cause you any more pain. But you keep asking me what happened, and the answer's never going to change. It was years ago." He took a deep breath. "You meant no harm, Shinsei, but what's done is done. She got in your way, and you had your orders, and she is no longer in any pain."

He remembered blood against golden hair. He shut his eyes, but nothing changed.

His master leaned back in his chair, folding his hands in his lap. "I know you never intended for it to happen that way, but that's how it happened. It's *all right*. You can let it go. Torturing yourself like this accomplishes nothing."

Was this torturing himself? It was another concept Shinsei couldn't fully understand. Sometimes the memory of her was like that, was a weight that wanted to crush him, but sometimes it seemed as if he held on to it because he *needed* to, as if letting go of it completely would only ensure he was lost forever.

He met his master's eyes. "I'm sorry," he said. "I'm sorry I frightened the guards. I'm sorry if I—if I frightened you."

His master smiled. "You never frighten me, Shinsei." And that was true. His master never looked frightened, no matter what Shinsei did.

"Why?" he asked.

"I know your heart is true," his master said.

Was his heart true? It had to be. His master had never lied to him.

The man the guards called Lord Oswhent was of average height, about as physically imposing as Roger, with brown hair that fell to his shoulders and a clean-shaven face. He was not yet old, thirty or a bit over, though at the moment he looked very tired indeed. "You must be having me on," he said to the guardsman, passing a hand over his face. "Why would anyone want to break *into* the dungeons?"

All six of them had been unceremoniously shoved back into a cell—a bigger one, on the highest floor, but that didn't mean it wasn't cramped. It was true they could all stand up in it, but that wasn't much of a comfort to Seth at the moment, and he doubted the others were cheered by it either. The sheepish captain with the side-whiskers had been called away, leaving in his place a pale, slightly hunched man with a pockmarked face, and it was he who answered Lord Oswhent's question. "Sad to say, milord, it's true. These two here were in the cells right enough, but the rest of 'em . . ." He shrugged. "We've no idea how they even got in, but it's clear they meant to spring their friends."

"It's clear, is it?" Lord Oswhent asked, but the irony in his voice seemed to breeze right by the guardsman. Then he turned to the cell. "Well?" he asked, mouth quirking in what might even have been amusement. "*You've* got nothing to say for yourselves, I assume."

When their silence bore him out, he stepped closer, peering through the bars. Braddock and Deinol stared him down readily enough, though Lucius hung slightly back, looking at him sideways. Morgan barely bothered looking at all; the woman from the cell didn't even acknowledge she'd been spoken to. At last, Lord Oswhent sighed. "I may live to regret this, but I've an idea." Before Seth could figure out whom he'd been talking to, Lord Oswhent turned back to the guard. "Fetch Elgar. He'll want to be part of this." When the man gaped at him, Lord Oswhent waved a hand at him impatiently. "Oh, *Imperator* Elgar, His Eminence, whatever you like, just go *get* him, will you? And be quick about it."

The guardsman fidgeted, scratching the side of his face. "I don't think it's wise to leave you alone with 'em, milord."

"And why is that?" Lord Oswhent asked. "Did you fail to secure the chains properly?"

"Er . . . no, milord."

"Is the cell door unlocked?"

"No, milord."

"Well, then I should be fine, shouldn't I?" He smiled dryly. "I assure you that if I find myself being attacked, I shall yell at my very loudest; you won't possibly be able to miss it. Now *fetch me your master.*"

The guardsman frowned, but he left quickly enough, throwing half a glance over his shoulder as he went. When they were alone, Lord Oswhent started pacing back and forth in front of the cell, flicking his gaze to each of them in turn. "I assume you used some rather impressive tricks to get in here, but I wouldn't try any of them just yet. I *will* call the guards back, and I assure you that you don't want that—not until I've said my piece."

Braddock spat between the bars, but Seth was fairly certain that was his way of assenting.

Lord Oswhent let it pass with another of his dry smiles. "Excellent. Now. First things first. My name is Varalen Oswhent, and no matter what any of these half-wits tell you, I'm not a lord. They just have to take orders from me, so it confuses them if I don't have some title or other. Wouldn't want you to misunderstand."

Seth looked at Morgan, but she just shrugged.

"So now it's your turn," Lord Oswhent continued—or rather, he'd said he wasn't a lord, so Seth supposed he was just Oswhent, then. "Names?"

"Go fuck yourself," Braddock said. Morgan smiled as if in spite of herself, but she said nothing.

Seth didn't see the point in saying anything—they already knew who he was, didn't they? But just when he thought no one else was going to speak, Deinol swung a fist through the air in irritation. "Shit, what's it matter? He knows Seth, and it's not as if the rest of us are so very hard to find. Deinol. There you go."

"Deinol what?" Oswhent asked.

"Deinol *what*? Deinol's all there is. Deinol son of who knows, and a very illustrious man he was."

"Fair enough," Oswhent replied. "I happened to know my father, but that's about all I can say of him."

Seth thought Lucius was going to stay quiet too, but finally he moved slightly, lips twitching as if he would smile, then pressing flat just before he spoke. "Lucius Aquila."

"Hmm," Oswhent said. "I'd half expected an Aurnian name."

"Half is about right," Lucius said, but offered nothing more on the subject. Then he did smile. "What's the point of all these niceties?"

"I'm trying to build trust," Oswhent said nonchalantly. "Is it working?"

"No," everyone except Seth answered, at more or less the same time.

Oswhent seemed to have expected that; his sigh smacked of the theatrical. "Either way, you will have to answer some of my questions, I'm afraid. There's nothing I can do for you otherwise."

"What is it you can do for us?" Lucius asked.

"Oh, you'd be surprised." He pressed his hands together, and his gaze drifted to Seth and the woman. "Is it really true you broke in here just to spring those two? Palla was convinced they knew each other, but I have to admit, I didn't lend much credence to her theory."

It took Seth only an instant to have the idea, and he was speaking before he'd even had time to consider what he was going to say. "That's the truth of it, milor—ah, sir." He nodded at the woman. "It was only chance we got put together—"

"It wasn't," Oswhent said. "It was Palla's plotting."

"Oh," Seth said, but that was fine—it didn't change the story he could tell. "Well, I didn't know that. But either way, it worked out, because it meant they could spring both of us at once." He looked around him. "I mean, it *would've* worked out. It almost did."

He'd been praying Deinol would just keep his mouth shut, but when had that ever happened? "Seth, what're you—"

"Don't bother, Deinol," Lucius interrupted, and Seth held back his sigh of relief. "What are we going to gain from lying now? It's not as if we can tell him we all got lost on a walk." He faced Oswhent. "The boy's told you true, but neither of them knew we were coming for them. We planned it all ourselves."

Deinol, thankfully, was long used to the fact that Lucius both fought and thought faster than he did, and he didn't object again. Seth looked over at the woman, but her face hadn't so much as twitched.

Oswhent just smiled again. "So they're innocent, is that it? If it turns out you are all in the resistance . . . well, this little escapade is nothing compared to treason."

Deinol's blank stare probably did them more good than the most eloquent denials could have. "The *resistance*? Who the hell said *that*?"

Oswhent nodded at the woman. "She and the boy were both seen in conversation with . . . well, I still don't know why they call him Six-Fingered Peck, but he seems to have offered the supposed rebels aid in the past."

The woman finally spoke up. "Merchants at the Night Market offer a lot of things to a lot of people; that's why so many people go there. From what I know of Peck—which is admittedly little—he's a good sight too cowardly to resist anything, but even if he *is* with your resistance, I'm surely not."

"Then what did you have to see him for?"

She scowled. "Scavengers like him pick up all the gossip. I needed to find someone."

"You'll have to give me a name."

"Really."

"Yes, really," Oswhent said. "On my honor, I am *trying* to secure leniency for you, but you're not making it easy for me."

Her scowl etched itself deeper into her face, but she finally spat out a name. "Whit Norse. He's a soldier in your bloody army. Don't tell me *he's* a member of the resistance too."

Oswhent frowned. "Whitford Norse, isn't it? That sounds familiar." He tapped his chin. "I'm fairly certain he's one of our recent deserters."

She shrugged. "I don't know about that. I haven't seen him in weeks. And I don't know if Peck saw him either, because your bloody guards had their hands on me before I'd gotten three words out."

Oswhent thought that over, still smoothing his thumb over his chin absently. It must have satisfied him in the end, however, because he turned to Seth instead. "And you? Were you looking for Whitford Norse as well?"

"No," Seth said. "I wasn't looking for anyone."

"Then why talk to Peck?"

Seth blushed. "It's like she said—he knows things. He knows things people pay for, usually, but I never have much coin to speak of. So sometimes he'll tell me things that aren't worth paying for. Stories and things, what happened to people in Goldhalls or the Glassway or somewhere else in the city where I could never go. That's all."

Oswhent pinched the bridge of his nose. "This just gets more and more embarrassing on our part. And this trinket or whatever it is you stole? What of that?"

Seth set his jaw as stubbornly as he could. "I already *told* them, I *sold* it. Years ago, when I first came to Valyanrend. I haven't even thought about it since then. How was I supposed to know it was special?"

"I can't say it was, to be honest," Oswhent said. "Sometimes the imperator fixates on the strangest—" He shut his mouth when a soldier appeared, but this one was the captain with the side-whiskers again. "Yes, Quentin, what is it? Is he coming?"

The captain inclined his head, looking even more sheepish than Seth remembered. "He'll have you come up, my lord."

Oswhent raised an eyebrow. "Come up? What for? I need him here."

"Yes, my lord, I understand, but . . ." He shrugged helplessly. "He won't come down. He said to fetch you up."

"Gods' sakes, I swear he's doing this just to spite me," Oswhent muttered, but he turned on his heel and started back down the hall. "Stay with them," he said over his shoulder before he left, and the captain nodded.

There wasn't much they could talk about with the guard standing there, so they settled into a glum silence. Deinol kept throwing furious looks back and forth between Seth, Lucius, and the woman, as if demanding an explanation, but it wasn't as if any of them could answer him. Finally Oswhent returned to them; Seth didn't know how long he'd been gone, but he looked as if he'd aged a year.

"All right," he said, and cleared his throat. "Well. The imperator has decided . . ." He trailed off. "Quentin, maybe you'd better . . . Oh, never mind. I'll need you in a minute." He took a deep breath, then let it out again without saying a word; next he paced the floor before their cell for a few turns, unable to look them in the eyes. Then at last he wrung his hands once or twice and said, "I don't enjoy saying this, but it's like this: Elgar reckons you lot didn't precisely mean to commit treason, but as far as he's concerned, it's been committed anyway. So in light of the circumstances, he's decided that only one life will suffice, rather than all your lives. He leaves it, ah . . . He leaves it to you to choose."

Seth gasped aloud at that—even the captain caught his breath sharply and bit his lip. The rest of them made no noise, but they still hesitated, the strain telling on even the woman's implacable face. Only Lucius did not hesitate, but faced Oswhent calmly, his voice soft but steady.

"If that's the case," he said, "this can all be resolved very easily, and I thank you for that. I will offer my life to satisfy the imperator's demands, so I hope you will not hinder my friends any further."

Oswhent's sigh was conspicuously relieved. "Well, that was a lot easier than I imagined. Good." He nodded to the captain. "Quentin, I'll need you to help bring him up."

Deinol had been opening and shutting his mouth ineffectually since Lucius spoke, but as soon as the captain moved, he finally shook off his silence. "Absolutely *not*," he snapped, trying to stand in front of Lucius. "Lucius—"

"We should at least discuss this," Morgan added, but Lucius shook his head.

"Discussion won't change my mind," he said. "I'm set on this." He looked ahead of him again, to where Deinol was blocking his way. "Don't get in their way, Deinol. You're only making it worse." How could he be so calm about this? Seth wondered.

"Damned right I'll make it worse," Deinol said. "They try to do this and I'll—"

"You won't, actually," Oswhent said. "We can do this with Quentin alone and you can stand still and behave yourself, or we can do it with half a dozen other guards and they can beat you into the floor. They won't be shy about using their weapons, either, and you have none—unless you count those chains, and I wouldn't." When Deinol only glared at him, he stepped forward, a rougher edge in his voice. "Look, you idiot, Elgar isn't going to kill him *now*. He told me to bring up the one who offered to die, so that's what I'm going to do, whether I have to have you killed in the process or not. If you want to fight us all to the death, wait until we're actually hauling him off to the chopping block, will you?"

"*Deinol*," Lucius said, suddenly sharp. "I'll swing at you myself if you don't move. Stay *back*." Deinol wasn't any good at hiding his emotions at the best of times, and the fury on his face was stark, but he finally stepped back. The captain unlocked the cell door, then curled his fingers almost gently around the length of chain between Lucius's wrists. He didn't need to tug; Lucius walked forward easily, his calm restored. Deinol didn't look up from the floor once, not even when the cell was locked again and Lucius turned to walk down the hall.

───────

It wasn't that Varalen disagreed with the plan—he had suggested it, if not the melodramatic manner of its carrying out. He simply wished he could've known more about the prisoners first, this Lucius Aquila not least among them.

It wasn't an Aurnian name, but some Aurnians had been known to change theirs, or to give their children names that belonged to the land they lived in now, rather than whatever land it was their ancestors had come from. The nose was admittedly wrong—Aurnians' tended to be flatter, but Aquila's nose was so long and sharp he could've put out someone's eye with it. His skin was just the right shade, though, and the hair, thick and blue-black, was right as well. The eyes were more ambiguous, narrow for a Hallern but perhaps a bit wide for an Aurnian. *Half is about right,* he had said—did he mean that literally?

If Aquila's name had led Elgar to expect anything different, he didn't show it. He was seated when Varalen and Quentin escorted their prisoner into his study, and he looked up for only a moment, mouth quirking in a vague expression Varalen couldn't read. "Thank you, Quentin," he said. "That'll do. I don't think he's going anywhere."

Varalen was always struck by how genuine Quentin's deference to Elgar was—it made a stark contrast to his own, no doubt. The captain's bow was elegant in its simplicity, and he left them with a quiet, "Your Eminence."

Varalen couldn't have said why Elgar chose his study for this conversation—it was a small corner room, with stark stone walls and a bare wooden floor. It was also usually cold, though at the moment having three people in it made the air feel thick. The bookshelves lining each side wall jutted out too far into the room, so he and Aquila had to watch their elbows as they walked side by side to Elgar's desk. The desk was the only ornate thing in the room, a wide and heavy piece whose dark wood was lacquered with some ancient scene from a bit of history even Varalen didn't know. First empire, maybe, from what he could see of it that wasn't covered by neat stacks of paper. Elgar gestured to the chair across from him—the only other chair in the room—and Varalen stepped back from it, leaning against the wall. "Go ahead. Those chains must be weighing you down."

Aquila did not say thank you—did not say anything—but simply lowered himself into the chair, keeping his eyes trained on Elgar's face.

"Your name is Lucius Aquila?" Elgar began.

"Yes."

"And what is it you do?"

Aquila did not hesitate. "I rob wealthy men in the streets and fence their goods."

Elgar smiled. "You're very forthcoming."

"There's no reason not to be. I'm going to die, aren't I?"

Elgar pressed his fingertips together. "You've guessed, I assume, that that was a bit of a ruse."

Aquila's expression did not change. "Not when your man announced it, but when you had me brought here, I began to suspect something was afoot."

"You'll have to forgive the rather unsubtle nature of it," Elgar said. "It was necessary, you understand."

"I do understand that," Aquila said. "What I don't understand is why."

Elgar didn't answer right away. "Are you an Aurnian?" he asked at last.

"I was born there," Aquila said.

"The guards tell me the weapon they took from you was an Aurnian sword—one of those long and slender blades your people favor. What are they called again?"

Aquila's voice remained calm; he did not lean forward, but Varalen saw his fists clench atop his knees. "You know what they're called. You trained your men for months to fight against them—perhaps for years. You know what they're called."

Elgar smiled. "And that answers my next question. Very good."

Varalen was not sure himself what the question was, and Aquila didn't seem to know either; his posture loosened, and he cocked his head slightly. "If you don't want to kill me, what *do* you want with me? More importantly, what do you want with my friends?"

Again Elgar paused, and Varalen could feel the deliberateness of it, the pacing. "I'm very curious, Lucius Aquila, about the kind of man who agrees to surrender his life so readily for the sake of others."

Aquila shrugged. "Do your soldiers not do the same for you?"

Elgar laughed. "Hardly. They venture into the *threat* of death, not its certainty, and if they succeed, the benefit is far from wholly mine. You would die tonight, this moment, for the sake of five people in a prison cell."

"I would," Aquila said. "We've established that's not what you want. What *do* you want?"

Elgar finally answered him, looking straight into his eyes. "I want you to perform a task for me."

"You want to hire a criminal and a traitor?" Aquila asked.

Elgar raised an eyebrow. "Does that seem strange to you?"

"Not in itself," Aquila said, "but if that's what you were after, you needn't have waited for chance to drop one in your lap. Just go out into the city and wave your arms about—you'll hit one in less than a minute."

"Ah," Elgar said, unruffled. "But I need a certain *kind* of criminal and traitor, you see."

Aquila pursed his lips. "If you mean the kind, as my friend might put it, who will bend over for you just because you ask, you're wasting your time."

"Not at all," Elgar said. "I mean the kind who will bend over for me because I hold something they care about."

Aquila shrugged. "I care about a lot of things."

"No," Elgar said. "I don't think you do."

That gave Aquila pause, and for several long moments no one spoke. Elgar's smile took its time unfolding, spreading across his face like something dangerous. "I know you're not inclined to trust me, but there was no question of trust when you offered to die at my command, and I might just as easily have been lying then. So if you were willing to pay such a steep price, I can't imagine you'd balk at a lesser one: one errand for me, and all six of you are free to go."

Aquila frowned, but though it was grim, it was thoughtful. He curled and uncurled his fingers in his lap. "What is it you want done?"

"Do you know Hornoak?" Elgar asked.

"I've never been there," Aquila said, "but I know about where it is."

"There's an old shrine there—not a Ninist vestry, just some ancient building that was allowed to become holy again after Elesthene fell. Inside it is something of mine, and I want it brought back here."

Aquila's eyebrows rose. "That's it? Any handful of your guards could do that for you."

"They could try," Elgar said. "Perhaps they might even succeed. But then again, as I am sure you noticed, they are not always as . . . apt as I could wish. I would prefer to send you."

Aquila's frown only deepened. "I just . . . It's a simple thing, isn't it? Go to Hornoak, get this thing of yours, and come back? You'll pardon treason for *that*?"

"Treason is whatever I decide it is," Elgar said, "so pardoning it is no very great matter." Then, as if the thought had just occurred to him, he added, "I should also mention I have heard there is a man who guards what I wish you to recover—a priest or holy brother or some such. He may be . . . disinclined to part with it."

Aquila smiled. "Ah, so when you say it belongs to you . . ."

"I mean it belongs to me because everything in my realm belongs to me, should I require it." He pressed his fingertips together again. "And I require this object absolutely, make no mistake about that. I worry any of my servants might decide he had a right to it, simply because I allowed him to put his hands on it for a moment. But you won't make that mistake, will you, Lucius Aquila? If your own life is not worth the lives of your friends, then surely no mere object could be."

Aquila hesitated, the chains clinking softly as he twisted his hands about. "It should be simple enough," he said slowly, "but I am only one man, and I have not left Valyanrend in many years. Perhaps my success would be better assured if others came with me."

Elgar smiled. "I thought you might say that, and I'm inclined to agree with you. By all means, let your companions go with you—you all risked your lives to come here together, after all."

Aquila blinked. "My companions?"

"I can't let you have all of them, of course," Elgar said. "Then what would I bargain with? But it seems a waste to leave them all idle, especially when they showed such ingenuity in getting in here. I will be reasonable: we started with two, so we shall keep two, just in case one or the other causes problems. The other four will go to Hornoak for me—I don't care which four, so long as you're among them. Decide it among yourselves as you like."

Aquila's fingers were digging into his palms. "I don't believe," he finally said, "that you wouldn't just kill us upon our return."

Elgar shrugged. "Why? What are you to me?"

"Exactly," Aquila said. "Why not just kill us and have done with it?"

"Why not just run away, as soon as I let you go?" When Aquila did not answer, he continued, "Because you have more to gain by coming back. And I have more to gain by keeping my word, so I intend to keep it." He tapped his fingertips together. "Besides, last I checked, it takes only one man to actually *deliver* a thing—the rest of you will have your freedom, and you need never see me again. Even if I do decide to kill the one who returns, along with the captive two, that still leaves half of you free, and if I keep my word, you're *all* free. Decent odds, wouldn't you say?"

Still Aquila hesitated. "What exactly is it you want us to get?"

Elgar pursed his lips, his brow furrowing. "I've never laid eyes on it myself, so I cannot tell you what it looks like, only what it might look like. It will be made out of some stone or ore—not metal, but perhaps a kind of quartz. Its surface will be rough, worn and uneven, full of etchings like scars. It will not look natural, but like a thing crafted, shaped by man."

It was more than he'd ever said to Varalen about it, and if Aquila didn't like the answer, Varalen couldn't say he did either. "And what does it do?" Aquila asked.

Varalen would have expected Elgar to be irritated by such impertinence, but he actually laughed. "Very much indeed, in the hands of one who knows how to make use of it. In my hands, I expect it will bring a satisfying end to all my wars—and that's only the beginning. But in *your* hands . . . well, perhaps nothing. Either way, it is none of your concern. I wish to have it, and I will have it, one way or another."

Aquila's frown was more melancholy than angered, and Varalen folded his arms uncomfortably, trying not to think about how many times he must have worn the same expression. Elgar had that effect on people, it seemed.

———

It felt strange to discuss it with Oswhent and the captain there, but beyond lowering their voices, there wasn't much they could do about it. Seth wondered why Imperator Elgar didn't come down himself, why he'd wanted to talk only to Lucius, but he didn't suppose he could ask, and Lucius didn't look like he wanted to talk about it much, either. He'd somehow managed to say even less than usual, despite being the one who had to explain everything.

Braddock was against it from the start, but that was to be expected—for a mercenary, he sure had trouble following orders. Morgan had stayed mostly silent while Deinol talked too much, swerving from one opinion to another. And the woman had stayed in her corner, slouching against the wall, her eyes half closed, as if all this had nothing whatsoever to do with her.

"Here's the worst of it," Deinol said at last. "How're we to decide who stays and who goes? If we *are* doing it, I suppose it makes sense to have the strongest ones go, but to leave Seth here . . ."

"It's more dangerous to leave anyone here, I think," Lucius said. "I'd have offered to stay myself, but Elgar wouldn't allow it."

"Well, there's always . . ." Deinol jerked his head toward the far corner, lowering his voice. "*Her.* Why not have her stay, eh?"

Lucius shook his head, but Seth couldn't tell what that meant. *Drop it,* most likely. But Deinol had a point—what *were* they going to do with her?

"I—I don't mind staying, if you all think that's best," Seth said. That was only fair, wasn't it? This whole thing was his fault if it was anyone's. "If you want to just leave us as you found us, and the four of you go . . ."

"We haven't decided that *anyone*'ll go," Braddock said, curling his lip. "I don't trust any of this lot for a moment."

"I can't say I do either," Lucius said, "but having some of us out has got to be better than the alternative."

Morgan nodded. "He's right." It was the first substantial thing she'd said in what seemed like ages. "I think you should do it."

Lucius cocked his head. " 'You'? Not 'we'?"

"No," Morgan agreed. "I'm staying here."

Deinol blinked. "Why on earth would you want to do that?"

Morgan took a deep breath. "The boy can't stay here," she said. "He's too delicate, and he doesn't know how to take care of himself. Out there I'll hardly be more help than he would—I've never left Valyanrend in my life, and even if Deinol hasn't either, at least he can use a sword. As for the rest of it . . . well, I wouldn't mind a rest, even if the accommodations aren't what I'd have chosen."

Seth felt something twist in his gut. "No, listen, I—I'm not a *child*. I can—"

"You can't," Morgan said. "I've decided, and I'm more stubborn than you. Leave it be."

Braddock shook his head. "Fuck *that*. You stay, and so do I."

That made her look weary but not surprised. "Braddock, you'd be more help to them than anyone."

"I'd be more help to *Elgar* than anyone, you mean," Braddock said. "And

I've no desire to be his little errand boy. Let the rest of them run about on his orders." He twitched his broad shoulders. "Besides . . . who knows whether they'll even keep us in the same place, but if my presence could do any good, I'd rather be there to do it than stuck outside somewhere wondering about it."

"I don't need looking after," Morgan insisted.

He scratched his cheek. "That's as it may be, but it doesn't change my mind."

Lucius hesitated. "Well, if you're both truly certain . . . that would give us our four and two."

"I am certain," Morgan said, and Braddock nodded.

Deinol rolled his eyes so violently at the woman, it was a wonder they didn't pop out of his skull. "I can't *believe* we're going to—"

"Hush," Lucius said. "Wouldn't be courteous of us to leave the women behind while we made our escape, would it?"

Deinol sniffed. "Those two want for *courtesy* as much as a stone wants bread."

Lucius glanced at the woman, and she looked up for the first time, meeting his gaze halfway. "Is this all right with you?" he asked.

She shrugged. "You can settle it whatever way you like."

"You see?" Deinol hissed, but Lucius just shook his head again. He looked to Morgan and Braddock.

"If this goes wrong," Lucius said, "it's all on my head. But I don't imagine that'll be any comfort to you."

"Leave off the sentiment and tell him we've decided, will you?" Braddock growled. "If I have to rot in a cell, I'd at least like an emptier one."

CHAPTER EIGHT

The woman stayed quiet when she was fetched out of the cell with Seth, Lucius, and Deinol, and when their weapons were returned to them and they were escorted, by a dozen guards, out the massive double doors of the Citadel. She looked at the worn paving stones as the group made its way down the path that led from the castle to the walls surrounding it, entirely made of the strange, pitch-black stone that had so awed Seth when he first came to Valyanrend. He'd never been on the other side of them before. As the guards shouted commands to the men on the walls, ordering the gate raised and the drawbridge lowered, he couldn't resist glancing behind him, even though the dim predawn light made it hard to see. The Citadel itself was the largest castle he had ever seen, studded with more than a dozen tapering towers. The entire edifice was made out of marble that might have been white once, long ago. What Seth could see was a melancholy gray, insubstantial and ghostly beside the dark outer walls. And then he was being shoved forward, a guardsman forcing him through the gate and over the bridge. The guards left them on the other side, retreating back behind the black walls, and they were free to go on their way.

They weren't ten steps out of sight of the Citadel when the woman tried to make a run for it, but even Seth had been expecting that. He'd never have caught her himself, but Lucius slipped his fingers around her wrist easily, pulling her up short. She didn't even try to shake him off; perhaps she'd been expecting that, too.

"Not so nice of you," Lucius said, still holding her fast. "The boy did you quite a good turn, as I recall."

"I did him one first," she replied, but when she looked at Seth, her eyes were mild.

Seth scratched the back of his neck. "I'm sorry. I know I should've asked you before I—"

"Why apologize to her?" Deinol asked. "She's the one who got helped out of it."

"I didn't *ask* for any help, and I certainly didn't need it," the woman snapped. "I have *you* to thank only for your unwanted interference, and you have yourself to thank for any misfortune that came of it."

"That's a sour attitude to take, considering we just saved your life," Deinol protested.

The woman glared at him. "Don't be an idiot. If you lot had just stayed wherever you came from, I could've had myself out and the boy, too. This is far from the first prison I've seen the wrong side of—they never hold me for long."

Deinol made her a low, sweeping bow, twirling his wrists outward. "Well, I *do* beg your pardon. It's not a mistake I'll make twice, I assure you."

"Easy," Lucius said. "Don't forget we've far more unfortunate decisions to weigh."

"Oh, Morgan's going to kill us all," Deinol moaned, clutching his head. "Even if she has to do it from beyond the grave, she won't let that stop her. Gods, but they'll never let her out, or Braddock, either."

"If they don't," Lucius said, "we'll just have to find some other way."

"Hard to do that if they kill you on your return," the woman said. "And they have every reason to do just that."

Lucius glanced over at her. "Did you say you'd bested many prisons, miss? Well, many men have tried to kill me, for more reasons than I care to count. I'm still here."

The woman shrugged. "Please yourself. It's not my business to dissuade people from seeking their deaths."

Lucius hardly seemed to be listening, staring at some point beyond her. But finally he turned to her again. "You should come with us," he said.

Deinol nearly choked on a mouthful of air. *"What?"*

"I rather agree with that sentiment," the woman said. "I don't have the time or the inclination for such a jaunt, and I'm surprised you'd even want me."

"Why?" Lucius asked. "You're skilled, aren't you?"

She frowned. "What makes you say that? You don't know anything about me."

"I know you got out of that cell on your own. I know that the guards didn't disarm you when they took that sword away, no matter what they might have thought." He nodded at the sturdy one-hander she had received when Lucius and Deinol got their own swords back. "You had a knife up your sleeve the whole time—and more than that, I think, if I had to wager on it."

Seth remembered that little movement he'd seen her make in the hall, sliding one hand to the opposite wrist. That made sense, if she'd been reaching for a knife. He watched her face, but her continuing frown told him nothing.

"I don't doubt you have a smattering of skill yourself," she said at last, "and I won't claim to be entirely without some of my own. But I'm not what you would call trustworthy, and I think you know it. Even if you're fool enough to seek my help, I'm not fool enough to offer it. I told you, I don't owe you anything."

"But we would owe you," Lucius said.

"And what use is that to me? I'm not one to go about collecting debts." She tried to flick her eyes away, but Lucius turned about, keeping himself in her view.

"Listen," he said, "I'm not too proud to know my own limits. Deinol and I are good, but the city's our territory, and out there . . . I think we're going to need help, and I *know* you can provide it. So help us, and any business you're on, any task you need done . . ." He stopped, struck by a sudden thought. "Weren't you looking for someone? A soldier?"

She shook her head. "If you're going to offer to help me look for Norse, there's no need. I know where he is—or at least where he was, and I've no need to inquire further."

"Then—"

"Yes," she said. "I lied. I'm sorry if you're shocked, but I felt it was the most sensible thing to do, under the circumstances."

Deinol started forward. "Then you really *are* in the—"

She curled her fingers as if she wished they'd been around his throat. "No, for the gods' sakes, I'd never even heard of your blasted resistance until they told me I was apparently part of it. I've half a mind to join, though, after all this."

Lucius spread his hands. "Fine. Forget that. Forget Norse and the resistance and all of it. I won't ask why you're here, or what you were doing at the Night Market. But you *could* get us to Hornoak, couldn't you? If you were so inclined."

"I could, aye," she said, after only a moment's hesitation. "I've been there before, and to many more dangerous places. But as I'm *not* so inclined—"

"Then what would it take to change your mind?"

She was quiet for a while, her jaw clenching tight as she looked up at the sky. "Any task, you said?" she asked at last. "Even something . . . dishonorable?"

Lucius laughed, but it was brittle. "I dishonored myself a long time ago. Another stain or two won't make much difference."

The woman cocked her head, looking back over at him, but this time Lucius avoided her eyes. She shifted her gaze to the ground instead, scuffing the cobbles with the toe of one boot. "I'll help you find this thing Elgar wants, and then you'll do something for me. Is that the deal?"

He frowned. "You won't tell us what it is?"

"No, I won't, because *I* don't trust *you,* no matter what *you* have decided about *me.* I'm not going to ask you to kill anyone, and you won't *get* killed unless you're stupid—which is as much of a risk as I take going to Hornoak. Beyond that, you'll have to wait."

"Wait until when?" Deinol asked.

She considered it. "I'll take you to Hornoak, and if this rock or whatever it is really is there, I'll help you get it. That should be enough time to make up my mind, one way or another. I'll either tell you then, or else I'll decide you're useless, and we need have no more to do with one another."

Lucius hesitated. "We'll need to bring it back here first to get Morgan and Braddock freed."

She shook her head. "*My* business is in the east. If you think I'm going to stroll to Hornoak and back before I get to it, you greatly underestimate the value of my time. I'm late enough as it is."

"Late for what?" Deinol asked, but she ignored him.

Lucius tapped his palms together, then faced her again. "All right. You help us find it, and then I'll help you. I don't suppose Morgan and Braddock will be going anywhere." When she made no further protest, he continued, "One last thing—if we're going to be traveling together, shouldn't we know what to—"

"Seren," she said. "Almasy." Then, when the three of them blinked at her, "My name. That's what you wanted, right?"

"It was," Lucius admitted, "but I'm . . . surprised. When Oswhent asked—"

"He had no right to it," she said. "That's all." She walked away from them, moving farther down the street. "There's something I have to fetch beyond the city walls, but I will not move on from there. I'll meet you just outside the east gate—you have until then to change your minds."

"Are you sure *that* wasn't stupid?" Deinol asked, once she was gone. "Because it sure seemed that way from where I was standing."

Lucius shrugged. "You've never even been outside the city, and I haven't left it in years. I could wish for a less enigmatic traveling companion, but we're not like to get one."

Deinol rubbed at his face. "I should just let Morgan kill me and be done with it."

———

Roger tapped his chin. "You know, I knew an Oswhent once—incredibly dull man, that one was. Married my aunt Rheila after her first husband died, but we never really considered him part of the family—Halfens've always lived by their wits, Gran said, and that one couldn't make up a story if you gave him the words and forged an official document affirming it—"

"That's wonderful, Roger," Lucius said, "and you have successfully proven, once again, that there is no event you cannot tie back to your illustrious family in some way. But I think Morgan would be quite irritated if she were to hear you going on like this while she's locked up, so let's try to use some of those Halfen wits, shall we?"

The Dragon's Head seemed all wrong without Morgan in it, the space behind the bar dreary and stale instead of welcoming. It was closed until her return, not that that stopped them—it was still the best place for the rest of them to meet, whether Morgan was there or not.

Roger slouched forward on the bar, resting his chin in his hands. He was acting cheery enough, but Seth thought he must have been worried. They had taken so long that he'd given up waiting for them in the vestry, and they'd had to track him down back in Sheath. Who could say what troubles he must've thought had befallen them in that time? "Fine, fine, back to this business about Hornoak. No, I haven't heard a word about anything of value there. What's it matter? We'll find another way to spring them."

Lucius shook his head. "Better to follow the rules this once, Roger. I think Elgar means to keep his end of the bargain."

"You aren't even curious about what this object is?"

"No," Lucius said. "I figure the less we know about it, the better. Elgar was counting on our not being tempted, and the best way not to be tempted is not to hear anything that might tempt us. I'm not about to play around with Morgan's and Braddock's lives."

Roger waved him off. "All right, all right. It's no harm done to me if you go. Just keep your wits about you." He looked over at Seth. "And as for *you*, I had no idea you'd pulled off a bit of pilfering of your own! You act like such an upstanding young fellow that even I'd never have suspected. A pity I couldn't have examined that trinket you nicked."

Seth grinned. "You can, if you like."

Deinol stared at him. "You said—"

"That I sold it," Seth finished. "I lied."

That made them *all* stare at him, until finally Roger broke the silence by laughing. "My boy, I take it all back! Perhaps you'd make a decent apprentice after all. Who knew you had it in you to lie so brazenly to Elgar's guard?"

"Not me, I'm sure," Seth said. "But . . . well, I couldn't lead them back to the Dragon's Head, could I?"

He fetched the pendant from the little pile that contained all his worldly possessions—it was buried at the bottom, stuffed inside a sock. He still couldn't figure out what was so special about it—it was just a bit of silver set with a dull gem that might have been an emerald, though it was so small as to hardly matter. It was barely even *pretty;* he couldn't imagine it'd be valuable.

Roger said much the same thing, once he'd gotten a chance to examine it. "My boy, I hate to tell you, but folks've dropped more expensive pieces than this in the street and hardly considered it a loss." He turned it over, running his thumb along the edge. "How did you ever get it in the first place?"

Seth clasped his hands out in front of him, feeling his shoulders draw together. "It's from back when I was with the army."

"Then that was true too?" Deinol asked, leaning toward him over the bar. "You're a deserter?"

Seth shook his head. "No, I wasn't a soldier; I just hung around the camp because I didn't know where else to go. They were willing to feed me if I ran messages and things, that's all. I thought they'd let me fight eventually, when I got older, but I only wanted that at first. I didn't . . . realize what it would be like. I thought they'd actually *teach* us to fight, for one thing, and I haven't learned anything about that to this day. I never saw any battles or anything, but I saw men killed, bandits and the like, and our own men sometimes, and . . . well, it wasn't very long before I'd had enough of that.

"There was this man there who . . . I don't know if he liked me or liked taunting me, but he wanted to have me around, and sometimes he'd make me sit with him while he got drunk and played whatever game of chance he liked best that night. *He's* the one who stole it—or else he got it from the one who did; I don't know. But he never said anything about taking it from Elgar's men; he just looked hard at me, and talked about how there had been a boy about my age 'who won't be needing *this* anymore,' he said, and pulled it from his pocket to make sure I could see. That was the night I ran for it—he drank so much he passed out, and I was used to running errands for him, so nobody minded me on his horse until I was well away."

Roger gave him a teasing rap on the top of the head. "And here you always said you were no pickpocket."

Seth blushed. "I wasn't. He left it on the table."

They all laughed at that, and Seth hardly minded. "So you just kept it all this time?" Lucius asked.

"I figured I'd save it for a pinch," Seth said. "I was about to try it when Deinol first found me. When I started working for Morgan I offered it to her, as thanks for taking me in, but she just told me it wasn't charity, that she intended to work me damned hard, and I should save the thing until I found someone else to give it to. So I meant to do that, but, ah, mostly I just forgot about it."

Deinol whistled. "Then Morgan knew you had it the whole time? She never even blinked when you told Oswhent you'd sold it."

"She's a better liar than Seth," Roger said—this was true. "If *he* could pull it off, I'm not surprised she could follow."

Seth took the pendant from Roger's open palm, turning it in the light, then set it back down on the bar. "I think . . . if it's not too much trouble, I think you should keep it for now, Roger. We shouldn't bring valuables where we're going, and maybe you can find out what it is, or why they wanted it so much." He grinned. "And if it gets too hot for you, I know you know what to do with it."

Roger grinned back at him, but Lucius looked pensive. "I won't stop you from going with us, Seth, but maybe it'd be better if you stayed with Roger. We don't know what we'll find out there."

Seth shook his head. "I've spent more time outside the city walls than Deinol ever did—my whole life, save the last handful of years of it. I haven't been to Hornoak proper, but I've been near it, and much else besides. I may not be able to help *much*, but I can help."

"I don't see the harm in it," Deinol said, ruffling Seth's hair. "If the boy ran with soldiers, a bandit or two on the road shouldn't scare him."

"There's a bandit or two right in front of me," Seth pointed out, "and I'm not scared."

"True, true." He yawned. "Gods, I'd love to sleep, but I'd hear Morgan

scolding me even in my dreams. Besides, I don't trust that woman to wait long—
what was it, Almasy? Seren Almasy? Don't trust her to do much of anything,
truth be told, but especially not that."

"She's all right," Seth said. "She *did* try to help me, and I would only have
been more trouble for her."

Deinol laughed. "It must've been your lovely face that won her over, my
boy. Next thing you know, she'll be sweet on you."

Seth hid his red face in his hands, but he doubted any of them were fooled.

————

Elgar traced a circle around Hornoak with one long finger, pursing his lips
absently. "They took the boy?"

"Aye," Varalen said. "The two swordsmen, the woman we held first, and the
boy."

"The swordsmen are useless to me," Elgar said, stroking beneath his chin
with the pad of his thumb. "I do wish we could've kept the other two a bit longer, though I doubt we'd have gotten anything more from either of them." He
sighed. "I wonder how the lords of the Fellspire have managed to safeguard *their*
treasures for so many years—another thing I shall have to ask Lady Margraine
once I've conquered it."

"But not yet," Varalen said, hoping he sounded uncertain enough that it
might pass for a question, and not a command.

Elgar furrowed his brow. "No, not yet, much as I'd like to. I won't risk moving against Esthrades with so many matters still unsettled. When our little
search party comes back, and when Shinsei returns, then I will move the army—
not a moment before."

Unease settled in the pit of Varalen's stomach. "The commander is . . . gone
from the city, my lord?"

"He is," Elgar said, without looking up from his maps.

"But so soon after his—"

"After his what?" Elgar snapped, and Varalen did not dare answer. "After
nothing. After nothing of significance. Shinsei will serve me well in this, as he
has in everything. And that's more than I can say for you."

Varalen swallowed. "I am sorry if you disapprove of my plans, my lord, but
you seemed to agree with my—"

"Oh, never mind about *that*," Elgar said, waving a hand impatiently. "I am
pleased enough with your plans, especially of late."

"You . . . you are?"

Elgar actually smiled, a thin, pointed little thing. "Your idea to use the prisoners was a better one even than you knew. If anyone is to retrieve it for us, I believe those four will do it—especially with that Lucius Aquila leading them. He seemed such a strong man, and yet he aspires to so little—it's his own kindness that will betray him in the end." He tapped his fingertips together. "It isn't often one encounters people so simple, and what would I have done without them?"

Varalen scoffed. "If all it took were concern about the welfare of someone under your control, you could've just sent me to retrieve it."

Elgar laughed. "Of course that's not *all* it takes. Besides, you want much more than your son, whatever you claim to the contrary. There's nothing simple about you, Varalen, and much that is ambitious. And for a person like that, what I have sent our friends to fetch would prove very dangerous." His continued smile was unnerving. "Of course, I can't promise that it won't prove dangerous anyway, but that's why I prefer to send others to lay hands on it first."

Varalen shrugged, though he couldn't help feeling a bit relieved. "Well, I didn't fancy a trip to Hornoak anyway." He followed Elgar's gaze back to the maps. "So then, about . . . the second matter I mentioned . . ."

"Oh yes, I haven't forgotten that. In fact, it is my hope it will turn out to please me even more than the first." Elgar swept his finger down the border, then pulled it back in toward the capital. "Tell me more about this little bird who's been singing for you," he said.

———

Deinol claimed it'd be a shock to rival the fall of Elesthene if they ever saw Seren again, but Seth didn't doubt her—she wouldn't have spent all that time hammering out terms with them if she just meant to slip away. Sure enough, she met them outside the city gates as promised. It was somewhat intimidating for Seth to look at the walls from the outside—it had been years since he'd left Valyanrend, and he'd nearly forgotten how terrifying they looked from this vantage point. Perhaps someone else wouldn't have found them frightening at all: they were only made of stone, without any barbs or spikes to be seen, and no traps more elaborate than cover for archers. But they were so high and so thick and so old that they seemed to him as immovable a reality as time, or death itself. When he was new to the city, he had asked Deinol and Morgan and Roger how the walls had been built, but they had had no answers for him. Valyanrend, they told him, was a city older than the written word itself, and no history book could attest to its founding. The city walls, like the Citadel itself, had the mysteries of their construction lost to time. But however old those walls might be, they had never once been breached—Valyanrend had been taken before, but always from the inside.

You had to walk nearly a hundred yards from the walls before you'd find any trees, and they were mostly crooked and skinny, like weary travelers aching for a rest. It was at the edge of these trees that they found Seren, rifling idly through the contents of a leather satchel. She closed it when she saw them and then stepped away from the tree she'd been leaning against. "That's all you're bringing?" she asked.

They'd given Seth the cloth sack containing all the food they'd been able to scrape together; as he wouldn't be doing any of the fighting, it was only fair for him to take the first turn with it, although the others had promised to relieve him in due course. Beyond that, Lucius and Deinol had little more than their swords. Deinol shrugged. "It isn't all *that* far, is it? And it's not as if there's nowhere to stop along the way."

"It'll seem long enough to you, I don't doubt," Seren said. "But have it as you like."

He nodded at the satchel. "How'd you put all that together so quickly?"

"It was easy enough." She slung the satchel over one shoulder. "I had it all beforehand—I just never brought it into the city. I wasn't about to risk it in a place like that. It was a good thing, too—if I had brought it, those blasted soldiers would *still* be pawing through it."

Deinol was frowning. "A place like that? A place like *what*?"

"A place with its own army of pickpockets, of course. Gods, you Hallerns really are touchy about your precious capital, aren't you?"

"You Hallerns?" Lucius asked.

"That's what I said."

"No, I mean—you aren't from Hallarnon?"

"No more than you are, unless I'm much mistaken. And I'll thank the gods for that after what I've had to contend with here." Her smile was biting and dry rather than warm, one side of her mouth tugging crookedly upward. "I assume you wanted to leave straightaway? I don't need a map to get us to Hornoak, but there's something I wanted to ask you first."

That made Lucius give a smile of his own. "Finally managed to stir your curiosity, eh? I bet I know what it is, but you're free to ask."

She dropped her gaze to his sword. "Are you a *shinrian*?"

Lucius's eyebrows rose. "I take it back—that wasn't in the slightest what I was expecting. I don't mind answering it, but you first. Where do you come from?"

Seren hesitated, but it wasn't out of reluctance; she seemed to be trying to pick the right words. "I was born in Esthrades," she said at last, "so if I 'come from' anywhere, I suppose it's there."

"But . . ." Lucius said.

"But I left Esthrades when I was very young, and . . ."

"What, you never went back?" Deinol asked.

"I went back," Seren said. "It just took a long time. Many, many years." She didn't say more, but Seth thought he understood, and maybe the others did too.

Deinol cocked his head. "Why so long?"

She shrugged. "I wanted to make sure the person who came back was different from the person who left, I suppose."

"And was she?" Lucius asked.

"Yes and no—not so much the same as I'd feared, yet not as different as I'd hoped." She sighed. "I suppose that's always the answer, isn't it?"

"Not always. Not in my experience, at least." Lucius folded his arms, tapping his fingers against his elbows. "I am a *shinrian,* though that title means less than you've probably heard. I did live in Aurnis, for as long as it existed. But my reason for staying away is the opposite of yours—neither Aurnis nor I can return to the way we were, so I've chosen to make my home somewhere else." He tightened his fingers against his arms, pressing his lips together. "Someplace better suited to the person I am now."

CHAPTER NINE

The Gods' Curse was an easy thing to find on any map: an empty, colorless ribbon that stretched from coast to coast, dividing Issamira from the rest of the world. On the maps it was easily spanned, less than half an inch thick on all but the very largest ones, but Eirnwin had told him it stretched on for leagues. It took a full day to ride through it, and that was if your horse was fast and you knew the way. To the Issamiri, who sent their youth to learn it as a rite of passage, it was a boon, a natural line of defense against invaders. But its name bespoke what the rest of the world thought of it.

There was a saying about Issamira and the Curse—most deserts had oases, it went, but Issamira was an oasis with its own desert. Yet the Curse was no true desert, for though it was made entirely of dust and sand on weathered stone, it was not especially hot, just barren and dead. No crops would grow there, and the sun barely ever shone, obscured by the intermittent sandstorms that were as common as sunsets.

When Prince Landon had been alive, his father had made the Curse his responsibility; he spent half the year ranging it and the lands beyond, and the other half at the palace in Eldren Cael, learning the ways of government. Whenever Reglian outriders had come across him and his men, they brought back tales of how he seemed to know every inch of the Curse, how he went his way unimpeded by even the thickest sandstorm. But Prince Hephestion, it was said, had only ever visited the Curse once, for his coming-of-age; he had lost his horse almost immediately and had to wander back in disgrace, and his mother had forbidden him from ever venturing so far again.

It was the Curse that Alessa would have to cross, if she were ever to reach Issamira at all.

Kel pushed his chair back from the desk and reached for his crutches, easing his weight onto them and turning his steps out into the hallway. Alessa was in her room as usual, but although there was a book open on her lap, her face was turned up and away, not out the window but sideways toward a blank spot on the wall.

Kel might've learned to walk quickly, but he'd probably never be able to walk quietly, and Alessa turned as he crossed the threshold, smiling at him. "Kel, there you are. I was just thinking about you."

"You were?" She had looked so distracted, whatever it was. "What about me?"

She looked down at the book on her lap as if noticing it for the first time, and nudged it shut. "I was looking out the window—not now, earlier, in the small hall. There were children playing in the streets, and one of them had crutches a little like yours."

"He did?" He sidled over to her, showing off how smooth and facile he could make the movement. "Was he fast like me?"

She shook her head, and it was as if she were shaking something off, finally turning her full attention to him. "Not at all. It seemed terribly hard for him to keep up with the others, I'm sorry to say. But he made me think of you, and of how much you've accomplished."

Kel settled into the chair next to hers. "Remember when I took the stairs to the great hall for the first time?"

She laughed, lilting and genuine. "How could I forget? Eirnwin was convinced you were going to kill yourself, but he didn't dare stop you once you'd started."

"Father was worried too," Kel remembered, "though he tried not to show it. But not you. You knew I could do it."

"Mm." She leaned back in the chair, gaze flicking slightly away as if she were seeing it again. "I was worried for you . . . other times. But not that day."

"And what about you?" Kel asked. "No one ever worries about you."

She looked sharply back at him again, her eyes going wide. "You do. Too much, I'm afraid."

He shook his head. "I've been coddled always. If I ever wanted to do anything for myself—even walking!—I had to make it known. If I'd just done nothing, if I hadn't ever told people to leave me be, they'd just have . . . taken care of everything. That was natural for them. But where you were concerned, everyone always just left you to yourself."

"That isn't true," Alessa said. "Just look around us."

Kel looked at the room that was always kept so painstakingly clean, the servants instructed not to allow so much as a single speck of dust. "That may be so—"

"It isn't only that," his sister said. "I wouldn't be in any sort of health today without a healer. It's just that there's only so much he can do. You don't say that people have been inattentive to you because they've been unable to fix your legs—it's the same with me. I have an impediment, and I've just got to live with it; being fussed over all the time isn't going to help, and I don't like it any better than you do."

"But the pain—"

"Oh, Kel, I'm not blind," she said. "There are days when your legs hurt you; I've seen it. There are days when you ought to let Eirnwin carry you, but you never do. You suffer through it, because that's what you've decided." She smiled, a tad reproachfully. "You could allow me that much pride, at least."

"But when my legs do hurt," Kel said, "or even when they don't, everyone's always like to smother me. They offer me help whether or not I ask for it. But if you don't *ask,* they ignore you altogether."

Alessa considered it, stroking the side of her jaw with one finger. "Perhaps it's because they can see where you must hurt, so they're always reminded of it. But on the outside I look the same as everyone else." She stretched slowly, straightening her back. "Or perhaps it's because you'll be king one day, and they know you'll need to be strong. They just don't realize you are already, so they're too eager to prop you up—for their own peace of mind as much as anything. But for me . . . I don't suppose it matters whether I'm strong or not, so they don't mind that I'm weak."

I mind, Kel thought, but he knew she'd only smile sympathetically at him if he said it. "It matters if you can't cross the Curse," he said instead. "And you can't."

Her lips drew together. "No one knows that I can't."

"They *must* know you'd put yourself in great danger to make that journey. *You* must know it."

She sighed. "We're all in danger, Kel. Even you and I are, even at this very moment."

"So what if we are? Why does that mean *you* have to do something to rescue us? If it's so important for me to be strong, why isn't anyone asking me to do something?"

"Because you'll—"

"Because I'll be king, yes. Does that make you disposable?"

"Yes," Alessa said, without a trace of hesitation.

Kel picked up his right crutch and slammed it back down onto the floor, and Alessa bit her lip to hide her smile. "Well, you've made your opinion on the matter plain enough. That doesn't change the truth of it." He was still wondering how to respond in words when she spoke again, her gaze half turned away as before. "You know, I've never heard you complain about your legs? Not even when you were such a young child that you might simply have asked *why* you were different, out of puzzlement more than anguish. But you never did, not once. Yet here I am about to be married—a common enough occurrence for someone my age, I'm sure—and you act like it's the cruelest injustice you ever heard of. It's quite perplexing."

"You know what else I never asked?" Kel said. "I never asked why I was a prince, and other boys weren't. From the moment I could understand anything, people told me that I would be king one day. Only me, of everyone in Reglay. So who can say whether I've really been fortunate or unfortunate? There are far more cripples in the world than princes."

She smiled at that, and reached out to ruffle his hair. Kel almost forgot that he was angry, but then he remembered.

"You asked why I wasn't a princess, though," Alessa said. "I remember that."

"I did ask that." He curled his fingers loosely around the crutch. "Alessa, do you *want* to go?"

She touched his hand. "I *want* to help. If going is the best way for me to do that, then so be it."

Kel scowled. "Why is it the best way? Just because my father's decided it is?"

"You say that like it's a strange idea," she said. "He's the king. Of course his decisions are final. One day yours will be too."

And that *was* a strange idea. What would happen if he ever made a mistake?

"I don't want you to go," he said. "Please."

His sister shook her head. "It's already been settled, Kel. This is how it has to be."

"You don't deserve—"

"I deserved much worse," she said, very quietly. "Few bring more shame to a house, especially a *royal* house, than bastards. Yet His Grace has treated me as his own daughter."

Kel clenched his fists. "Would he send his own daughter away like this, do you think?"

"Yes," Alessa said, meeting his gaze easily; Kel was the one who had to struggle not to look away. "I believe he would."

Kel was fully prepared to slam his door as hard as he could the moment he returned to his chambers. But as soon as he crossed the threshold, he found Eirnwin sitting in the armchair, a musty book open in front of him, and surprise drew him up short. Eirnwin, unlike Alessa, was actually reading, but he looked up when Kel walked in. "Something amiss, my lord?" he asked.

Kel took hold of the door, but he shut it carefully, making no more noise than the scraping of the latch. Then he flung himself down onto his bed, letting his crutches clatter to the floor. "Don't act like you don't know, Eirnwin."

"Alessa," Eirnwin said, and moved the book to the nearby desk. He kept it open, though, to mark his place.

"Yes, *Lessa*." He paused. "*And* Father."

Eirnwin stretched his legs out in front of him. "And me, I suppose."

"Yes," Kel said. Why not? "You could've kept arguing with him."

"To what purpose, my lord? His Grace has decided."

"What if he *decided* something you knew was stupid?" Kel asked, turning his head so his voice wasn't muffled in the heavy cloth of the coverlet. "Would you just go along with it anyway?"

"I am an old man, my lord, much older than your father. I may have strength and health for my age, but I was never trained in arms like His Grace was, and I have no soldiers to call my own. If I disapproved, how would I stop him? Do you wish me to cling to his arm like a child, making him drag me around after him wherever he goes? I doubt even you would go so far, as angry as you may be."

"I wouldn't keep insisting if it weren't worth it," Kel said. "I don't stay angry about everything; you know I don't. But this is Lessa we're talking about! We hardly know anything about why she gets sick, but if she nearly chokes on dust, on *air,* what'll happen to her in a sandstorm? Father says we're all in danger, but the only one he's gambling on is her. It isn't fair."

"His Grace has shown nothing but kindness to Alessa all her life," Eirnwin said. "He might have—"

If Kel's crutches weren't out of reach on the floor, he would have thrown them across the room. "Why does everyone always say that? Oh, Father's so wonderful and kind just because he didn't kill Lessa when she was born! What Mother did wasn't *Lessa's* fault, and it wasn't mine! And yet all everyone says is that we should never have been born—Father should've killed her to preserve his honor, and I—" He gritted his teeth. "It would have been *kinder* if I had never existed at all, just because my legs don't work like everyone else's! What if I don't *care* about my stupid legs?"

Eirnwin sat back in his chair, threading his fingers together. "*I* have never said such things, I am sure, and I am certainly part of everyone."

Kel knew he was sulking, but he was too angry to think up an answer.

"When you were three years old," Eirnwin said, "I told your father myself that you would never walk, not as long as you lived. And I believed every word I said. His Grace raged and grieved at my words, but he believed them too. Only Alessa shook her head at them, and said she was sure you would walk one day. When we asked her why, she said it was because you had told her you would."

Kel frowned. "I don't remember that. You never told me that."

"I know that, my lord. I am telling you now." Eirnwin looked down at his clasped hands, then back to Kel's face. "By the time you were five, you had already proven me wrong. The first time I ever saw you hobbling about your chambers, I thought the shock would hobble *me*." He chuckled faintly. "Your joints swelled so badly from that little excursion that you couldn't get out of bed for three days. But you'd made your point, and I had work started on your crutches immediately. And I swore to myself that I would never again presume to tell you what you could and could not do."

Eirnwin leaned forward again, his hands tightening in his lap. "I have given all the counsel I know how, my lord, and your father has expressed no desire to discuss the matter further. Alessa herself has acquiesced to the king's proposal. If there is another way to be found, I am afraid you must find it yourself."

CHAPTER TEN

The first time Lucius had talked about being a *shinrian* had been in the dead of winter—only Seth's second with Morgan, but she'd already taught him to stop calling her *miss*. It was after the fall of Lanvaldis, so there was no snow, but that didn't stop the cold from creeping in, threatening to swallow the Dragon's Head whole.

They were accustomed, by that point, to being just the six of them—Seth still wasn't brave enough to start a conversation with Braddock of his own volition, and he hadn't quite learned to trust Roger with much more than a smile, but he didn't find the grouping odd or out of place. Braddock was staring out the window, and Morgan was behind the bar, and Seth was sprawled near the fire with Roger and Deinol, basking in the heat of the flames. Lucius was sitting back a bit, in a chair some feet away; Roger had invited him closer several times, but Lucius just said he was plenty warm enough, and stayed put.

Seth was half asleep by the time Roger's story touched on Aurnis, but he knew enough to follow along. Aurnis had been the country far to the north, that stretched all the way up past the Howling Gate to the shores of the White Waste. The Aurnians had come from across the sea a hundred years ago, before the northern waters had become blocked by ice year-round, and they had carved out a home for themselves up there, pushing the Hallerns and Lanvalds away to the south and building their city of Kaiferi upon the frozen plains. The Aurnians were relatively few in number, but the warriors they called *shinrian* were said to be among the greatest swordsmen in the world—worth ten of any normal man, the Aurnians boasted. Every heir to the Aurnian throne chose five of them for his personal guard, and these, his *kaishinrian,* were the most lauded of all, their names and deeds given to immortality. Yet Aurnis was the first country Elgar had attacked, and it fell before Seth had even arrived in Valyanrend. The *kaishinrian* had all perished defending their liege, and Elgar had executed every *shinrian* he could find, to keep them from seeking revenge for the fall of their country.

"My great-uncle Bosric always said he ran jobs with a *shinrian,* back in the day," Roger had said, off on another of his interminable digressions. "There were a good sight more of them back then, of course, but the Aurnians were never very fond of leaving Aurnis, so you hardly ever saw one this far south. The fellow sounded like a proper drunkard, though—just another down-on-his-luck swordsman who happened to know which end of a blade was up, not some great man."

Lucius bestirred himself at that, throwing an arm over the back of his chair. "To be called *shinrian* is a designation of skill—not rank or distinction, and certainly not greatness," he said. "To earn it, all you have to do is learn to wield the proper blade, then win one match against one who already carries the title—in the sight of judges, of course, so you can't slit a *shinrian's* throat in his sleep and claim you dueled him in some back alley. But once you win, you're *shinrian* for life; nothing you do afterward can erase it, no matter how cowardly or cruel. Even if you lost half a hundred battles to orphan boys wielding sticks, the title remains." He reached for his drink. "Of course, in practice, those *shinrian* who cared overmuch about the honor of the order often tried to track and kill the members who had become particularly disgraceful, but they weren't always successful."

The rest of them had regarded Lucius with surprise; it was rare indeed to hear him speak about anything to do with Aurnis. "Were there a lot of *shinrian,* then?" Seth asked, when it seemed as if the others weren't going to speak.

Lucius laughed shortly. "Not so many as you might think. *Shinrian* tend to like to lose even less than ordinary warriors—losing means making your opponent a *shinrian,* and the more you let in, the less special you are. So many of them refused to duel unless they were sure they'd win. More than one aspiring *shinrian* found himself—or especially *her*self—without anyone to fight, or else with only a choice of the best warriors in all of Aurnis. No one remembers this now, but the prince himself was a *shinrian,* and *that* was quite a bother—no one wanted to lose to him, but no one wanted to risk doing him harm, either. In the end, he defeated one of his own *kaishinrian* to win the title." He tilted his head back as he drank, frowning vaguely at the tankard when he'd finished. "Perhaps that should've shown him he needed more than five swordsmen to defend him, no matter how skilled." He reached for his sword, flicking his thumb against the hilt so it popped half an inch out of the sheath, then sliding it back in again. "I happened to be a *shinrian* too. Don't think I ever mentioned it, but . . . there you are." When no one said anything, he looked up, frowning at them all. "You don't look overly surprised."

"Well," Roger said sheepishly, brushing the back of his neck, "truth is, we always figured you for a *shinrian.*"

They had just a second to watch the surprise flicker across Lucius's face before he veiled it, smoothing his features before he addressed them. "Did you? What gave me away?"

Morgan raised an eyebrow. "Gave you away? Your skill did that well enough. You're not exactly a common swordsman, Lucius."

"And that sword did the rest," Braddock spoke up. "Don't find many of them this far south, but I know a *tsunshin* when I see one."

Lucius looked down at it again, as if pondering it. "Deinol, you guessed as well?"

Deinol laughed. "Well, it's like you said: not everybody who deserves to be a *shinrian* ends up becoming one. But even though you're easygoing enough, I can't see you being satisfied before you were the best at something you'd decided to do. So I was . . . moderately sure."

Lucius smiled. "It seems you've all found me out. And here I thought I was being so mysterious."

"Oh, there's still mystery enough," Roger said. "Just because we know your title doesn't mean we know anything about the rest of it." He cocked his head. "Don't suppose you'd care to enlighten us, eh?"

Lucius shook his head. "There's nothing much to say—certainly nothing I'm particularly proud of."

"How did you become a *shinrian*?" Seth asked, so quietly he almost wondered if it had been audible, but they all turned to look. "Who did you fight?"

Lucius laughed. "You still think there's something in that, even after everything I've said about it?" He looked at his sword again. "For a while I thought I'd never earn the title—a man much greater than I was the first to accept a duel with me. The way *I* remember it, he defeated me handily, but the onlookers seemed to think I held up well against him, and after that no one else wanted to challenge me. But I had a second match eventually, and that was that." He shrugged. "I spent so much time training, trying to win that title. . . . Back then, it was everything to me. I thought that if I could win it, I'd have proven something—I'd be worthy of something. And everything I'd ever known seemed to bear me out. And then to rise higher than I'd ever dreamed . . . even now I can hardly imagine it. I thought I had come so unfathomably far." He raised his eyes to the flames. "But then Elgar attacked my home, and I ran. So it seems I was wrong about that, after all."

———

"You're not supposed to be here," Roger said—uncharacteristically few words, coming from him.

"Neither are you, without Morgan," Marceline said. "It's her I want to see, not you. So where is she?"

"Not here." Had Roger ever answered a question with two words in his life? Something was definitely afoot. "Won't be back for a while, perhaps. I'm looking after the place in the meantime, but I can't possibly run it at the moment. So it's closed. And it'll be closed until Morgan decides otherwise, no matter how long you spend banging at the door."

"You can't just *close* it," Marceline said. "It's a *tavern*—what about the lodgers?"

Roger leaned one elbow on the bar. "The only close to regular lodgers we have are Lucius and Braddock, and they're both gone too. Any new arrivals will have to sleep somewhere else." He pulled a morose face. "I don't like it any better than you do, monkey, but there you have it."

"What about Seth?"

"Also out."

Two words again. "Well, where's everybody got to, then? It's hardly like them to just up and leave."

Roger tapped the bar. "I expect that's their business, not mine or yours."

"Oh, come on, Roger. You think *everyone's* business is your business. If you really didn't know where they'd gone, you'd be doing everything you could to find out."

"I never said I didn't know where they'd gone." He leaned on his arms, releasing a heavy, put-upon sigh that was almost like one of Cerise's. "It's too early in the morning for this, monkey, don't you know that?"

"And it'll be all over Sheath before midday, whatever it is, so you might as well—"

"I sincerely doubt that." He pulled another face at her, but it looked like his heart wasn't in this one. "What'd you want with Morgan, anyway? If it's just liquor for Tom, it's easy enough to get that elsewhere."

"It isn't *that*." As if she were just Tom's serving wench. "I just wanted to see if she'd found Seth all right."

"She found him." But Roger's face was about as grim as it ever got, so she doubted it had been as simple as he made it sound.

She hesitated, but finally asked, "He isn't . . . dead or something, is he?"

Roger drew back as if she'd hit him. "Gods, of course not. What are you thinking?"

"Well, *something* must have happened! He goes missing one morning, and the next the whole tavern's practically been cleaned out!" She narrowed her eyes at him. "Does this have anything to do with that business about deserters?"

Roger snorted. "Who do you think's a deserter? Morgan? Seth?"

She had to admit it was unlikely. It wasn't as if people knew everything there was to know about Morgan, but she'd been a fixture in Sheath for many years, even before she'd taken over the Dragon's Head. And she couldn't picture Seth wielding any weapon more lethal than a broom. "It must be something about what happened in the Night Market, then."

His lips twitched slightly. "Why must it?"

Damn it, but he could be so annoying. "Fine, it *mustn't,* then. But whatever happened to Seth is obviously *still* happening to him, and it seems like whatever happened at the Night Market isn't over, either."

Roger's amusement abruptly faded. "Wait, there's more to this Night Market business, too? What happened?"

Marceline tried to make her shrug every bit as irritating as one of his smirks.

He just sighed. "No need to get in a snit about it. Just tell me already, and I'll play with you some other time."

Marceline resisted the urge to stamp her feet—Cerise was always saying it was childish, and perhaps Cerise was right about this one thing. "You never want to tell me even the slightest bit of news, and yet you act like I'll tell you anything you like just because you ask for it." She sniffed. "Well, fair is fair. You'll get nothing out of me."

He laughed, undeterred. "Come on, monkey. You can hardly blame me if I don't want Tom catching wind of this or that."

"And you can hardly blame *me* if he feels the same way about you, can you?"

"That's why I'm not asking after something Tom knows; I'm asking after something you know." She must have looked unconvinced, because he sighed again, running a hand through his hair. "Listen, monkey, this is more than idle curiosity. If you know something about Seth, I want to hear it."

Marceline scowled. "What do you always care so much about him for?"

"Ah, it's jealousy now, is it?"

She should've kept her mouth shut, but she couldn't help it. "If you're thinking of making *him* your apprentice, you're daft."

"Because you'd be so very much better, you mean?"

"Better than *him*!" Marceline snapped. "And better than anyone *you* know, I bet. Seth isn't even a thief, and if he were, he'd be terrible. But *I* have the talent, whether you want to admit it or not."

"And so modest," Roger said.

"Please. Are you going to tell me *you* value modesty?"

He laughed. "I've gotten men to trust things you wouldn't believe, but even I'd have trouble with that one, I admit it." He leaned forward, resting his elbows on the bar. "I'll tell you this for nothing, monkey, since you care so much: I wasn't ever thinking of taking Seth as an apprentice. He isn't above you, and neither is anyone else, for the simple reason that I don't want anyone as an apprentice, and I doubt I ever will."

It was rare for him to be so direct with her, and she tried not to let her disappointment show on her face. "But why?"

"Why don't you ask your old man the same question? He never took an apprentice either, and unlike me, he's about out of time to do it."

Marceline shrugged again, because she didn't like talking about Tom's affairs with Roger.

He just kept on laughing. "Well, then don't bother me about it, either. I'm surprised you'd even want to apprentice with someone he hates so much."

"*I* don't hate you," Marceline said. "You're just annoying."

"And you're not the first one to say so, either." He stood up, brushing his hands off on his trousers. "So. This business at the Night Market. You didn't think I'd forgotten it, did you?"

She hadn't. "I'll tell you when I know for sure," she said, and paused. "Maybe."

Roger clapped a hand to his heart in mock resignation. "It's about as generous an offer as I should expect from a monkey, I suppose."

———————

Roger talked a good game about adventure, once he was tucked into a barstool, a tankard of ale in front of him. But Roger wasn't here now, to see how the pristine wilds of his tales were choked with blood-colored nettles and infuriatingly vibrant weeds, how pathless forests were more of an annoyance than a wonder when you actually had somewhere to go. Deinol stumbled onto a rosebush—no flowers, all thorns, naturally—and swore, longing for nothing so much as a return to the grimy back alleys he knew so well.

He'd announced his intention to cover the rear in hopes of obscuring the fact that he was falling behind. Seth, who as the frailest of them had every right to be the slowest, was holding up surprisingly well. He seemed to have two distinct advantages: his ability to slip by brambles and between trees and his desire to keep pace with Seren Almasy, who forged mercilessly ahead as if all terrain were the same to her. Lucius hung about in the middle; even though it was his turn to shoulder the pack, Deinol was sure he could have stayed abreast of the other two if he'd wanted, but no doubt he was showing some measure of solidarity.

Sure enough, once Deinol made an effort to close the gap between them, Lucius dropped back, falling into step with him. He didn't speak, just kept a companionable distance away, not quite shoulder to shoulder with him.

"*He's* rather smitten, isn't he?" Deinol asked at last, jerking his chin in Seth's direction.

Lucius chuckled. "No need to be jealous. He's just impressed; you have to admit she's something of a novelty."

"That's one way of putting it," Deinol said, aiming a glare at the back of Almasy's neck. "What do *you* make of her?"

Lucius shifted evasively. "I don't know."

"Do you trust her?" Deinol pursued.

Lucius hesitated. "I want to," he said at last, "and perhaps that means I shouldn't. It clouds my judgment, in any case." He grinned. "She'd make a hell of an ally, though, eh? I'd love to have someone like her at my back."

"Why, so she can stick a knife in it? No thanks." He turned his eyes back to Almasy, watched the way she moved. He still hadn't managed to figure out precisely how many weapons she carried; that protrusion at her back as she turned could be the shift of her shoulder blade or the edge of something much deadlier.

"What makes you think she's so impressive, anyway?" he asked Lucius. "So she can hide a knife or three, and she's traveled a bit. We've never seen her fight."

"You can already tell she's quick on her feet," Lucius said, "and the way the world is now, you won't get very far traveling if you can't defend yourself. But that's not what intrigues me most."

"Are you going to tell me what does?" Deinol asked when Lucius fell silent again.

He nodded at Almasy's back. "Look at the way she's dressed."

Deinol looked, but he didn't think he'd ever seen clothing more nondescript in his life. It was all simple and sturdy, layers of cloth and leather in various shades of brown and gray. "I don't think I'm seeing whatever you're seeing," he said at last.

Lucius smiled. "Do you see any holes? Any tears, any patches, any irregular seams? Look at her boots. Do they seem worn out to you, or fresh and fine? When you and I wear through our boots, we have them patched. When she wears through hers, it appears she buys new boots."

Deinol began to see. "So either her father's a cobbler, or . . ."

"Or she has coin to spare." He squinted at the back of Almasy's head. "So either someone is paying her *very* well, she has a decent fortune to call her own, or she's even better at divesting others of *their* fortunes than we are. No matter which theory proves true, they all raise a few more interesting questions of their own, wouldn't you say?"

"I would." He followed Lucius's gaze, staring at her profile as she turned. She seemed not to mind Seth's presence, nor the constant stream of questions he asked. The thought made Deinol smile—that was his boy for you, sweet enough to melt even the hardest heart. Not that he thought Almasy especially hard—just ruthlessly pragmatic, which, in its way, was even worse.

"Watch her," he said, not harshly. "All right?"

Lucius nodded. "Of course."

Deinol was just as glad to let Almasy lead; he could read, but he'd never been one for maps, and the one Oswhent had given them only confused him. He knew Lucius must've had quite the journey from Aurnis, but he hadn't left the city since he arrived, and he winced at the sight of the map just as surely as Deinol did. Even if they couldn't trust her, he figured she wouldn't waste any of her supposedly precious time leading them in the wrong direction; if she'd wanted to lose them, she needn't have agreed to come along in the first place.

As soon as they crossed a stream deep enough for her to bury her hands in, Almasy stopped to drink, and Deinol drew abreast of her, trying not to reveal how out of breath he was. "What kind of resistance do you think we'll have to face?" he asked her. "Elgar didn't mention anything of note, but he might have been hiding something."

Almasy shook her head. "He does want us to succeed in this, so I doubt he'd have neglected to mention anything that could help us prepare. It's the nature of the prize itself I wonder about—he lied about that if he lied about anything."

That earned her a quizzical stare from Lucius. "What makes you say that?"

"The most curious piece of it," Almasy said, "was Elgar's reluctance to send his own soldiers. It has nothing to do with not wanting to draw attention to himself—strip half a dozen of your best men of their uniforms and send them off, and who'd be the wiser? No, he doesn't want to send his soldiers—not one, not a hundred—because there's no one he trusts enough not to run off with the thing instead of bringing it back. And that means it must *look* so obviously valuable that there's no way he could try to hide it, no way to convince the men they're handling something routine instead of something precious. But you say he told you it was just some rock, and that can't be. Either he lied outright, or there's something he's leaving out."

Lucius was staring at the water; when he finally spoke, it was as if he had to drag the words out. "He seemed to think . . . He said that it would turn the tide of all his wars, though what he meant by that, I couldn't say. But he also said that to me—to us—it would be worthless." He frowned. "Or I suppose he said *perhaps* it would be worthless. What could that mean?"

"Too many things," Almasy said, wiping her mouth. "Depending on what it really is, he could derive all manner of things from it: knowledge, influence . . . some arcane power, if you believe in that sort of thing."

"Do you?" Lucius asked.

She shrugged, but she looked uncomfortable. "We know Elgar does. Perhaps . . . perhaps it's something that held power in the past, when magic thrived in this world. If Elgar believes that studying it could help him bring magic back—that he could possess it—might that not be enough to win his wars?"

"But even if magic really did exist once, that was hundreds and hundreds of years ago," Lucius said. "Bringing it back couldn't possibly be that easy."

"Perhaps Elgar thinks it is."

"What makes you say that?"

Almasy leaned down to take another drink. "Nothing. I'm speculating, that's all."

"Might you speculate on how much farther we have to go today?" Deinol asked, drying his hands on his shirt.

One side of her mouth twitched, curving ever so slightly upward. "Yes, I noticed you struggling back there. It all depends on how quickly you want to reach Hornoak—no matter how much ground we cover, we're not going to reach a safe haven tonight, and I suppose one clearing's as good as another."

"I wasn't *struggling*—" Deinol started, but Lucius waved a hand to cut him off. He tried again. "Are there really no towns anywhere in the area?"

"Not *safe* ones, and not that we'll reach tonight," Almasy said. "If you don't mind that there's no inn, and you're in the mood to have your throat cut and your belongings stolen, Swine's End is another hour to the southeast—out of our way, but have it as you like."

"Swine's End?" Deinol asked. "There's really a town called Swine's End?"

"I found it an accurate enough name," Almasy replied. "Shall we go?"

"Sure, sure, I just . . . would've thought the road out of the capital would be more populated, that's all." It would make it the second night they'd spent sleeping in the open, but they hadn't traveled very far the first day, and he'd assumed inns would be more frequent once they were out of the shadow of Valyanrend's walls.

"We're not on the road," Almasy reminded him, "though that's about what I'd expect to hear from someone who's spent his whole life in the capital. You can't blame people if they don't want to settle down around here—as I understand it, the best harvests in Hallarnon are found everywhere else."

"It's true," Seth piped up. "The most fertile farms are to the south, though you can find some in every other direction, as long as you go far enough. But the land right around Valyanrend's been stinting with its harvest for as long as anyone I knew could remember."

Deinol frowned. "The trees seem to grow well enough."

"Trees are stubborn, especially this sort—beggar-elms, we used to call them. Corn and wheat are less so. My mother always said it's the weeds you don't want

that'll follow you anywhere." He shook his head. "I sure didn't miss seeing this area again."

"It's not a place I like to linger," Almasy said, and looked almost as if she would touch his hair. "Come on."

Deinol let her take the lead again, with Seth scrambling to keep up. Then he exchanged a look with Lucius, who nodded slowly, his eyes grimly fixed on Almasy's back.

CHAPTER ELEVEN

It was the third time they'd changed cells in what was probably as many days. Once again they examined it as best they could once the guards were out of earshot—Morgan even leaned on the wall for good measure just as in some silly story—but once again they found nothing. If there really were more false walls than true ones down here, as Roger had claimed, they were faking it very convincingly.

The cell they were in now was, as far as they could tell, on the lowest floor of the dungeons, and it looked more like a cave than anything. The ceiling, the back wall, and the one to their left were made of stone blocks and mortar, but the other wall was solid rock, and some of the cells across from them were natural on all three sides, as if the builders had only had to add bars. At first the guards had always taken all the torches with them when they left, no doubt to try to frighten their prisoners, but then they'd inevitably grown suspicious, scurrying back to light up the cell after too long without hearing any noise from within. Now they left one torch burning in the sconce on the opposite wall, though Morgan wasn't sure what they thought it would help them see. She was no hand with a lockpick, and Braddock was much more likely to knock a door down than tease it open.

"We should start keeping a tally, like in one of Roger's gran's tales," she muttered to him, trying not to think about what she'd give to be able to rub her wrists.

"Of what, the days? How would we tell down here?"

She shook her head. "Not the days. Say . . . the number of times the guards have been annoying."

That made him laugh. "It'd fill half the wall already."

It wasn't only the matter of where to put them or how much light to give them—the guards couldn't even seem to figure out the proper way to restrain them. At first they'd simply chained them to the back wall, but they quickly realized that meant either unchaining them every time they ate or sticking the food directly in their mouths. Next they'd tried chaining one of each of their legs to the bars, but then one of their jailers had almost tripped on the chain. (He'd blamed Braddock, though Braddock had been half asleep at the time.) So now they were stuck with the traditional two chains apiece, ankle to ankle and wrist to wrist. It was certainly more comfortable than the wall, but the chains were heavy enough to discourage standing up.

Morgan leaned back, resting her hands between her knees. "I expected to be more . . . impressed by Elgar's men. Isn't he supposed to have the greatest fighting force on the continent?"

"He has the *biggest* fighting force on the continent," Braddock corrected her. "Which is the kind of thing that means just enough to make people complacent."

"*Elgar,* complacent? I can't picture it."

Braddock shook his head. "Not him. His soldiers."

"Maybe he just stashed all the half-wits in the dungeons because there's hardly anybody down here," Morgan suggested.

"Hmm . . . he isn't known for keeping many prisoners. Maybe they're just not used to having actual work to do."

He lapsed into silence after that, but Morgan couldn't help pressing him on one thing. "You haven't grumbled at me for deciding to stay behind yet."

Braddock scratched his cheek, the chains making the movement slow and ungainly. "I figure you know how foolhardy it was without me telling you. Besides, I stayed too, didn't I? Couldn't very well grumble at you without giving myself the same treatment, and I've got enough people to be angry at as it is."

"Well, if you hadn't, I'd probably be in here with . . . whoever that strange woman was." She didn't precisely want to tell him how much better it was to endure this with him rather than a stranger, but she thought he probably knew.

"Mm," Braddock mumbled. "I hope she's feeling properly grateful to me, wherever she is."

"I wouldn't bet on it," Morgan said.

"I wouldn't either." He gave a low chuckle. "Could you ever have imagined it? You and me in here while those two bandits have their freedom?"

"Gods, and my *tavern*. If Roger's neglecting it, I swear . . ."

"Oh, the little swindler wouldn't dare. A man may be dishonest, but you can always trust a coward to act like a coward."

Morgan shifted awkwardly backward, wriggling up to the wall so she could lean against it. It was rough and cold against her back, but at least she could stretch her neck out some. "I can't decide whether I wish I'd listened to him or not. It's not clear whether we're in a better or worse position now than we were before we ventured here." She stretched her arms out next, wincing as the chains chafed her wrists again. "Have you ever been in a prison before?"

"What kind of question is that?" He laughed. "Not exactly—not a proper prison, anyway. Had a couple captains administer what they thought was discipline once or twice, but I don't suppose that really counts." He brushed a hand against her arm. "It'll work out, Morgan. Between Lucius's skill and the swindler's cunning, they'll get us out of here however they have to, no matter what Elgar decides. They won't give up until they do."

"I'd like to believe that, but . . ." She trailed off only as long as it took her to squint at the wall near the far corner, and then she finished—for the guards' sake, on the small chance any were listening—"we can't be sure of anything, I suppose." With that done, and before Braddock could start another sentence she'd have to answer, she jerked her head sideways, hoping he could read in the urgency a need for discretion.

He nodded slightly, then scuttled over to her, his voice as soft as she'd ever heard it. "What is it?"

Morgan's pointing wasn't very precise with the manacles on, so she stared at the spot as well, hoping he could follow her gaze. She kept her voice a whisper too: "What do you think that is?"

———

"Shit," Almasy muttered, tugging at her sleeve absently.

Lucius, naturally, had tensed before she'd even spoken. "Well, at least we spotted them before they could do the same."

She snorted. "They aren't exactly making it difficult."

"What about this one, eh?" one of the men in the clearing practically yelled. "That's an emerald at least!"

"It's a bit of colored glass, idiot," another called back to him. "Not worth the effort to foist it off—better give it to some dim-witted girl for a favor."

"Like you got anything better."

"Shows how much you know—that farmer had more tucked away than he let on. Have a look."

Deinol looked at Lucius. "Three?"

"Four," Lucius whispered back, nodding at a skinny, silent man brooding near the far edge of the clearing. He had a knife out, and he was idly carving into a piece of wood while his companions babbled. The other three carried a spear, a saber, and a two-handed ax, but they were preoccupied in stripping the corpses that littered the clearing. If the fresh blood bothered them, they didn't show it, though Deinol supposed they bore enough of it on their blades and clothes already.

Almasy shrugged. "Irritating, but easily dealt with. If we're lucky, we'll have it over with before they even realize we're here."

Lucius hesitated. "You want to kill them?"

She rolled her eyes. "They're *looters,* and they're in our way." Deinol had a sinking feeling that the second reason was really all she needed.

"We can go around them," Lucius persisted.

"Did they go around those farmers?" She jerked her chin at Seth. "They certainly won't go around your boy, if they catch sight of him. They'll kill him first."

Seth looked absurdly guilty, as if this were all somehow his fault. Lucius glanced back at him, paused a moment more, fingers against his sword hilt, and then nodded. "Fine. Strategy?"

She gestured at the one on the far side, who'd dropped the wood and was now sharpening his knife against a whetstone. "Can you take care of that one? The rest should be easy enough."

Lucius nodded again. "Done. Deinol, try for the big one. Seth, stay back." He laid his hands on his sword—not pulling it from its sheath, just gripping the hilt with one hand and the sheath with the other. Deinol reached for the hilt of his two-hander, easing it carefully free so he didn't strike a branch or rustle a leaf. Seth drew back into the trees as ordered, but Almasy didn't unsheathe her sword as he'd expected. Instead she drew the fingers of one hand along the opposite wrist, and Deinol understood—she was going for the knife she had up her sleeve.

Almasy looked to Lucius. "You should move first." He nodded once more, then glanced back out at the men. They were still scavenging their prey, and even the man with the knife wasn't looking their way. Lucius gathered himself and leaped into the clearing.

He was as good as his word, making straight for the man Almasy had pointed out, who tossed away his whetstone and had his knife up in an instant. Deinol charged the big man with the ax; he was slower than his companion, but he still spun away at the last moment, slipping back with only a minor slash to his arm. Deinol turned to chase him, but before he could close, another man stepped in his way—the one with the saber. The big one had his ax in position by then, and Deinol hesitated, unsure which to strike at first. He risked a look at Lucius, but the man with the knife kept dodging away from his strikes, no doubt hoping he could hold Lucius off until one of his friends could assist him. Since Lucius couldn't help him out, Deinol blocked a sword stroke, spun away from a swing of the ax that set the air singing, and then looked the other way, at Almasy.

The last man was the one with the spear, and it was taller than he was; he stabbed at her again and again, but Almasy danced away from each thrust as if he were moving through water. As Deinol parried a stroke of his own, she finally planted her feet, seeming to slow for one moment, and the spearman set all his weight behind his next blow, lunging as far as he could. The reach was impressive, but it didn't matter, since Almasy was no longer in front of him. She was at his side, within his reach and too quick for him to pull the spear back in. The knife snapped out as if it were part of her arm, so fast his eyes couldn't even follow the movement; he hadn't even seen her draw it. And then the spearman was falling, throat opened in a harsh red line.

She moved immediately back toward Deinol, forcing the swordsman to step away from him to engage her, and he surprised himself by feeling grateful. The one with the knife, seeing his comrade fall, moved to help the other man attack Almasy, but Lucius whirled and planted himself once again in his way, scoring a brutal cut across the man's shoulder. Deinol was half embarrassed by how far the lout with the ax had been able to press him, but the man was bigger than he'd looked from back among the trees, and not half as slow as he ought to have been.

The swordsman tried to strike Almasy through the shoulder, but she had already moved, as if she'd known it was coming. While he was still frowning in puzzlement as he stabbed through air, her arm shot out again, the knife piercing leather and skin once, twice, three times. He groaned but didn't immediately go down, just staggered back a few steps. Her fourth strike buried the knife to the hilt in the hollow of his throat, and this time she twisted it so savagely that Deinol was glad to look away.

Lucius and the man with the knife both turned, distracted by the swordsman's fall. But Lucius recovered first, and that was all the opening he needed. His next stroke sliced under the other man's arm and took him in the side, cutting almost halfway through his chest. Deinol's axman was the only one left, and Lucius and Almasy both turned in his direction, but Deinol was damned if he wasn't going to take at least one on his own. He parried the man's next swing with as much force as he could, driving him back just enough to make room for the stroke he wanted. It cut the axman's leg clean out from under him, and then Deinol planted his sword through the man's chest, wrinkling his nose at the blood spatter.

Once they were sure none of the looters would be getting up again, Lucius glanced around the clearing. "You can come out now, Seth."

Deinol winced. "Not with all the—"

"We don't have time to bury them," Lucius insisted. "What's he going to do, close his eyes?"

Seth took a long look at the bodies, but he made no noise, just drew close to Lucius and Deinol again. "A-are we . . . Can we get moving now?"

"Aye," Lucius said, and touched his shoulder. "Good hiding."

Seth shook his head, but he didn't brush off Lucius's hand, just stood there for a moment, his shoulders slightly hunched.

Almasy was looking almost contemplatively at Lucius, her brow furrowed. "That was the second school, wasn't it?"

Deinol didn't think he'd ever seen Lucius's eyebrows shoot up so fast. "Ah. Yes, it was. I'm surprised you know of it."

"I certainly don't know of it," Deinol broke in. "What the hell is it?"

Lucius pursed his lips, but Almasy spoke up. "As I understand it, those who learn to wield a *tsunshin* may be taught in one of two schools. Many of the techniques are similar, but the most important difference is the starting position of the sword before combat. The first school, so called because it is more commonly taught, uses techniques that rely upon a drawn sword. But in the second school—"

"—you begin combat with the sword still in its sheath," Lucius finished. "That's correct, yes."

"Oh," Deinol said. "You never told me there were *schools*. I thought all *shinrian* fought like that."

"Hardly," Almasy said. "They say the second school is the more difficult of the two by far—even most *shinrian* never master it."

Lucius shrugged. "I heard that, too, but this always felt more natural to me. Did you have a point in mentioning it?"

It was Almasy's turn to shrug. "Not particularly. It's simply that you're not an ordinary swordsman—or even an ordinary *shinrian*."

"I wouldn't call you ordinary either," Lucius said, "but I'm afraid that when it comes to knife techniques, I am sadly ignorant."

Almasy's face was expressionless. "Even if you weren't, you would not have seen mine."

Neither one said anything more, but Deinol didn't feel any anger between them; they just stood there, staring at each other. Almasy finally broke the stillness, striding forward without so much as a *follow me,* and Seth broke away from them, hurrying to catch up with her.

Deinol hung back once again, and again Lucius waited for him, walking by his side. Once he was certain Almasy was no longer paying attention to them, he said, "She's good."

"She's *very* good," Lucius replied.

"She's . . . better than me, I think."

"Yes," Lucius said. "I think so too."

It was one thing to guess that she was talented—quite another to actually see her skill for himself. She wasn't just better than he'd imagined; she was better than he was comfortable with. Whatever else she might have been or done in her life, it was clear fighting—killing—was a significant part of it. You didn't get to be that good at it without a formidable amount of practice.

He kept his voice low. "Could you beat her, if you had to?"

Lucius hesitated. "I don't know," he said at last.

———

Not standing watch was out of the question after their encounter earlier in the day, but even though Seren had offered to go first, Seth found he couldn't sleep. It wasn't because of the bloodshed—whatever the others thought, he'd seen men killed before, though admittedly not for a long time. He'd forgotten just how messy it could be, but he doubted it would haunt his dreams. It was something else that weighed on him—he couldn't say exactly what, but he felt it had something to do with Seren, and the way she had approached the fight.

She surprised him by turning to face him, her mouth unsmiling but not unduly stern. "You want to say something, boy, then say it. You're not in prison any longer."

Seth picked at the grass at his feet. Lucius and Deinol seemed deeply asleep, but he watched them for several more moments to be sure. Finally he said, "What happened today . . . what you said about those looters . . ."

"I wanted to kill them from the beginning," Seren said. "It wasn't a difficult decision for me—I didn't hesitate. And that bothers you."

"Yes."

She laid her arms atop her knees, nodding at Lucius and Deinol. "You must know that those two have killed plenty of their own."

"Yes, and I have other friends who've done the same. I know." He paused. "But it's different with you. Lucius and Deinol live by robbing people, not killing them—they *do* kill people sometimes, but only when it can't be helped. And they never steal from people like those farmers—people with nothing to spare. You wanted to kill those men because—because it was *convenient*."

"Yes, I did," Seren said. "And Lucius and the other one helped me. And you didn't make any objections—not while it was happening, anyway. That's all true."

It was, but he didn't like it when she put it like that. "Lucius and Deinol didn't want to, not at first."

"But they still did it."

"Because those men were murderers! But if they'd been innocents—"

She shook her head. "Boy, there's no such thing as innocent people. If they'd been *harmless,* it wouldn't have been, as you say, *convenient* to have killed them, so I wouldn't have suggested it."

Seth frowned. No such thing as innocent people?

She sighed. "Listen. The kind of business your friends do, they're not naïve about it. They don't think that if they do their job well enough, no one has to get hurt. They *know* people will get hurt—people will get *killed,* and it'll be their fault. And they go ahead with it anyway, because that's how they live. I can tell they think they're different from me, just like you do. But it's an illusion. It rings hollow."

Seth rested his chin on his knees. "I'm not angry at you for what happened—I don't think you did anything that was so terrible. That's not what I'm trying to say. I just want to understand . . . the way you think about it."

"The way I think about it?" But it wasn't scornful; her expression was open, thoughtful. "It's not some taste for battle or anything like that. It's just . . . something that happens sometimes."

"Wouldn't you rather fix it so that it didn't have to happen?"

"No," Seren said. "I'd rather live the way I choose, without leaving anything I want undone because I'm too weak or scrupulous to accomplish it." That sardonic half smile crossed her face again, just for a moment. "I doubt I'm someone you want to take advice from, boy, but if I were, I'd tell you this—if you find yourself thinking you'd rather anything be different, you're going about things the wrong way. You ought to correct it, if you can."

Seth thought about it for a moment, just to be sure, but he already knew what his answer would be. "No, I didn't want to change anything. I was happy, before all this happened."

Seren stared at the grass, and this time her expression was closed, unreadable. "Perhaps you will be happy again."

———

"All clear?" Morgan whispered over her shoulder.

Braddock nodded. "All clear."

She turned back to the wall, poking at the cracks between the stones. The strange mark they'd found was a circle split into fourths by two slender diamonds, one horizontal and one vertical, with a smaller circle inscribed where they cut across each other. She and Braddock had no idea what it meant, but it had been deliberately done, and too carefully to be the design of a madman. They'd started examining the wall around it, when they were sure the guards weren't around, but it hadn't yielded much. There was nothing promising near the mark itself, so Morgan had started looking at other parts of the wall, following the cracks where the mortar had worn away.

"Hmm," she muttered, half to herself. "It *is* loose—that is, it ought to come loose. The cracks are small, but there's nothing to fill them, nothing to hold the stones in place. Just wiggle it enough, and it should move. I know it'll move."

"Aye, but *is* it moving?"

Morgan bit her lip. "If I push too hard, part of the wall might cave in."

"Right," Braddock said. "Isn't that what we want?"

"Not if it collapses just enough to draw attention but not enough to crawl through. You're not tiny, you know."

Braddock sighed. "Fair enough. What now, then?"

"Now I . . . hmm." She traced the widest crack with her fingertip, following it up and around. "I think someone had the same thought—the stones in this specific area are meant to come out, but then we should be able to put them back in. It's the entrance to a passage, and the way to hide it."

"Aye," Braddock said, "but that's assuming there *is* a passage. It's assuming we can get to the other side of that wall in the first place."

"Why would anyone go to the trouble of fixing the wall like this if it didn't lead anywhere?"

He shrugged. "I was surprised enough to find *one* passage out of the Citadel. You really think we're lucky enough to get two, and the second right at our feet?"

"I don't know about luck," Morgan said, "but this is either the most poorly built wall I've ever seen, or it's meant to hide something. Roger *is* occasionally right, and he was right about this. The Citadel is centuries old; it's lived through the collapse of Elesthene and who knows how many other corrupt regimes before then. People escaped all the time back then; we've all heard the stories. There had to be many passages—probably far more than two."

"They wouldn't still use the dungeons if that were true."

Morgan shook her head. "Little people remember when the bigger ones forget." She squinted at the wall again. "Remind me to thank Roger's gran, if we ever get out of this."

Braddock chuckled softly. "I'm starting to think maybe she was half as sharp as the swindler always says."

"There's truth in Roger's stories; you just have to sift for it." She scraped at the highest and thickest crack she could see, but the blocks still wouldn't move.

Morgan gritted her teeth and tried the next one down, and the next, and the next—and it moved. She pressed on it again, and heard the scraping of stone. "And there we are."

"Well?" Braddock asked.

"We're going to need time," Morgan said. "We're going to need a lot of time. I have to make sure I can get more than just one block loose. Even then, they're heavy, and they'll move slowly, and I don't know what kind of a hole we're going to get in the end. But it's like I said: there's nothing holding them in place, and I think there's something on the other side."

Braddock was silent for a while, but then he finally asked, "You don't suppose there's any way to get my ax back before we leave, do you?"

"Don't test your luck," Morgan said.

CHAPTER TWELVE

So you've never actually been to the shrine," Deinol said, for the third time.

Seth was surprised Seren was still answering him at this point. "Once again, I've passed through the town before. But I never stayed there, and I never had any cause to visit the shrine. So no, I can't tell you what sort of tapestries they have hanging in there."

Lucius snorted, and Deinol sulked in his general direction. But then Seren brushed her hair out of her face, catching the ends between her fingers and frowning at the length, and Deinol turned to her again. "Why don't you just cut it, if it bothers you so much? We've got more than enough blades between us."

Seren didn't even look at him. "No."

Lucius laughed lightly. "A bit of vanity after all, eh?"

Him she looked at, but her expression stayed the same. "No," she said again. But then she seemed to bestir herself, and added, "*Your* hair's even longer than mine, but I don't see you in a hurry to cut it."

Lucius just laughed again. "Ah, well, *that* is because of vanity, I assure you." Seth could swear to the truth of that; Lucius took so much trouble about his hair, you'd think he was attending a ball every evening.

"To be honest," Deinol said, striding quickly forward so as to minimize the distance between him and Seren, "I'm surprised you didn't dye it. Unless that *is* dye."

"It isn't," Seren said. "What on earth would I want to dye my hair for?"

Deinol shrugged, but he was watching her carefully; Lucius was watching both of them. "Hair that color's going to make you stand out—more likely you'll stick in people's minds, maybe. I figured that was the last thing an assassin would want."

Of course he was hoping for a reaction, but Seren didn't give him much; she finally turned to look at him, but she didn't flinch, and her mouth stayed a thin line. "I'm not an assassin," she said, calmly and clearly.

"Is that so?" Deinol said, his mouth twisting wryly. "And I suppose if you were, you'd tell me, would you?"

"Of course not," Seren said.

"Of course not," he echoed. "So you'll forgive me if I don't believe you."

"I don't care whether you believe me," Seren said. "You're only making a fool of yourself."

"What are you, then, if you're not an assassin?"

Seren rolled her eyes. "You certainly love to ask the same questions over and over. Why don't you tell me what *you* are?"

"That's easy enough—I'm a common bandit, I suppose, and a Sheather, and a bastard. You see, I ask so much because normal folk don't balk at the question."

"Perhaps I can't name myself as easily as you," Seren said. "Or perhaps I merely prefer to keep the answer to myself. It makes sense for us to work together for the present; that doesn't mean we will always have the same goals, and it *certainly* doesn't mean that I owe you any explanations."

"So, what, you're not answering because you don't like me?"

"I didn't say that."

"Well, what *do* you say? Can I be blamed if I'd prefer to talk?"

Seren sighed. "I am not accustomed to talk overmuch, so I suppose I am not very adept at it."

That seemed to surprise him, but Seth couldn't have said why. "You might get better at it if you practiced."

"I might," Seren agreed. "I just don't see the point."

"You'd earn a lot more friends that way," Lucius offered. "What happens if you need someone's help again in the future?"

"I don't need your help this time," Seren said. "It's just more convenient this way. And it would get you to stop bothering me—or so I thought at the time."

"You still won't tell us what you're having us do for you, though, eh?" Deinol asked. "Helping out on one of your contracts, maybe?"

"I am *not* an assassin," Seren repeated. "And even if I were, you would make the worst assassin's accomplice I could think of." She moved to avoid a low-hanging branch, then added, "It doesn't involve killing anyone. Or . . . I should say it's rather like the kind of undertaking you're used to: no one needs to die, but it might inadvertently become necessary. I doubt that, though."

Lucius frowned thoughtfully. "But it's still . . . something dishonorable?"

Seren looked straight ahead. "You may find it so."

"So when are you going to tell us what it is?" Deinol asked.

"After we finish *your* errand."

"You mean, so we can't back out of it?"

"No, because I am properly *cautious*." She sighed. "I've heard Valyanrenders think their concerns are the world's concerns, but I never knew how true it was until now."

Deinol scowled. "What does that mean?"

She gave him a long look. "I've already told you I'm not a Hallern, but you don't seem to understand what that means. I have no loyalty to Elgar, conflicted or otherwise. None of you seem especially fond of him, but it's not as if you actually want him to lose the war, do you? Your city would be overrun, your way of life disrupted. I, on the other hand, would not care in the slightest if your precious Valyanrend fell into the sea, but I *would* care if Elgar conquered this continent. That means, as I keep saying, that while our present goal is the same, our larger goals are very different. Why is it such a surprise that I want you to know as little about me and my affairs as possible?"

There was a long silence, in which Seth was fairly certain Lucius and Deinol were thinking the same thing he was. It was . . . uncomfortable, to have their predicament pointed out to them so clearly. Seth didn't like Elgar, and he knew Lucius and Deinol didn't either—Lucius especially seemed to despise him, but that was understandable, given what Elgar had done to Aurnis. None of them wanted to think of themselves as on Elgar's *side* in this conflict, but in a way they were, weren't they? Seren was right—they'd never want to see a foreign power conquer Hallarnon. So didn't that mean they didn't care whether Elgar won, as long as he didn't lose?

Deinol recovered himself first, which was hardly surprising. "So, what, you're saying . . . that we're natural enemies, then? We've got to support Hallarnon, and you've got to support Esthrades, and it's as simple as that?"

Seren shook her head, and when she spoke, there was a sharper edge in her voice Seth hadn't heard before. "I don't *have* to support Esthrades—it isn't *about* Esthrades. I told you, I hardly even consider myself Esthradian. I don't feel any sense of loyalty to a *place*, whether I happened to be born there or not. If things had been just a little different, I might not even have gone back."

"What are you loyal to, then?" Lucius asked.

She scowled. "You wouldn't understand."

"No?"

"No." She poked at the grass with the toe of one boot. "What about you, then? Didn't you choose Hallarnon over Aurnis, if protecting Valyanrend is more important? Wouldn't a loyal Aurnian seek revenge?"

Lucius put a hand to his heart in mock injury, but the pain in his eyes could not be dismissed so easily. "You've hit upon it, I'm afraid. I am, all things considered, a rather embarrassing excuse for an Aurnian. But it comes down to loyalty, as you said—loyalty to people, not places. There are people I love in Valyanrend. But all those I loved in Aurnis are dead. Even if I could defeat Elgar, it wouldn't restore our prince to his throne, or reunite me with . . . with any of the people I have lost. Why should I give my life for a country that no longer exists?" He clenched his fist; Seth had never heard him speak so passionately before. "It doesn't mean I don't feel the injustice of it! Elgar destroyed the only world I had ever known, out of nothing more than a lust for conquest, and for that I will hate him forever. But I . . . I have no right to speak as a loyal Aurnian. I have gone a different way."

"You could help bring Aurnis back," Seren said quietly.

"That isn't possible."

"Why isn't it? Elgar conquered the Aurnian people; he didn't exterminate them. Most Aurnians still live in their old lands—how loyal do you think they are to their new administrators? Do you think they would all agree that Aurnis is dead, just because of what the maps say?" When he didn't answer, she continued, "If Elgar were defeated, and Hallarnon thrown into chaos, the lands Elgar conquered could break free. They could—"

"Yes," Lucius said, squeezing his eyes shut. "Yes, I *know*. I have thought all these things."

"And yet you're still content to help tip the balance in Elgar's favor?" She shook her head. "You have more power than you know. Helping Elgar, or not helping him, could make a difference in—"

"Helping him *how*?" Lucius asked. "Do you truly believe those things you said about bringing magic back—that this thing we're looking for could help Elgar do it? Do you really think that's possible?"

The question struck some subtle change in Seren; she grew more subdued, more distant, and only then did Seth realize how unusual it was for her to talk so much. "About magic . . . about magic I would assume nothing. It holds no allure for me, and never has. But in the course of my life I have seen things I could never explain—things I still can't explain, even now. I would not presume to know the truth behind them."

Lucius frowned. "What is it that you saw?"

"I do not wish to speak of it." The way she said it made plain that there was no use protesting. "I will only say . . . that it was something impossible, something I *knew* to be impossible, but it seemed so wondrous, so beautiful, that I could not bring myself to question it. I wonder if I will ever know the truth behind it." She curled the fingers of one hand around the other, almost as if she were unaware she was doing it. "And so I will not venture to say what may or may not exist in this world, when even I, who consider myself a traveler, can be so surprised by it. But perhaps magic is closer to us than we know, and restoring it a simpler matter than we could ever have imagined."

Though she said nothing more about it, Seth couldn't forget her words, and he turned them over and over in his mind as the sun sank lower in the sky. But there was something else he wanted to know even more, that nagged at him long after nightfall. So when it was time for Seren to take her watch, and he was sure they were the only ones awake, he whispered, "Seren?"

"Can't sleep again?" she asked, but she didn't seem cross.

"Guess not. I was . . . thinking."

"About what?" She paused. "I mean, if you care to tell me."

The hesitation seemed so unfamiliar on her that Seth smiled. "Just that I've seen a fair amount of fighting—even though Lucius and Deinol like to pretend I haven't. And I've seen *you* fight, and . . . you're strong."

Seren seemed to consider it. "I suppose it's fair to agree to that. What of it?"

Seth scuffed his feet in the grass. "I was just wondering about it, because you seem just like anybody. So looking at you, I almost feel like anybody could fight like you. But I know that's not true. I've never been able to fight—I've never been strong at all. But you—"

"Where do you think strength comes from?" Seren asked.

Seth hesitated. "What do you mean? Either a thing is strong, or it isn't. A bad sword'll shatter under a blow, but a fine one will hold good. A strong man can fend another off, but weak ones like me just crumple."

"I did not ask you what strength *is,* I asked you where it *comes from.*"

"Well, it's . . . it's in the way things are made, isn't it? If you don't know how to make swords, they'll come out weak."

"But people aren't swords." She spread her hands and stared at the gaps between her fingers. "Were you always this way? Weak like this?"

"Always," Seth said. "I was small since I was born."

"So was I," Seren said. "A small infant, and a small, weak child. Do I seem weak to you now?"

"Of course not."

"Yet I was once as weak as you. Probably weaker."

Seth felt his face growing hot. "Well, good for you."

"Yes," Seren said sharply, "very good for me. I was *made* weak, but I decided not to be. *You* were made weak, and you choose to complain about it."

Seth kept silent for a few moments. "All right," he said at last, "where did *your* strength come from?"

"I created it," Seren said. "Bit by bit by bit. I earned it."

"How?" he asked. "Why?"

"By struggling. By practicing. By testing myself." She paused, curling her fingers again. "And because I know what happens to weak people, and I refused to let it happen to me."

"What happens to weak people?" Seth asked, but he thought he already knew.

"They die, more often than not," Seren said. "But even when they live, their will is not their own. They can't make choices for themselves. They have no say in the shape of the world." She looked at him fiercely. "I decided long ago that that would never be my fate. I do only what I wish to do—no less, and no more."

Seth picked up a stray stick, twirling it between his thumb and forefinger. "What do you wish to do, then?"

She smiled—it was still wry, but he was growing used to that by now. "Never run short on questions, do you?"

"Does that mean you're not going to answer it?"

"It means I don't know an easy way to answer it." She threaded her fingers together, rubbing her palms absently. "For a long time I wasn't sure—I had been so focused on becoming strong that I hadn't thought about what I would do afterward. Then I thought I wanted to settle things—to make my peace with the person I had been. But that wasn't enough either. And now I want . . . It's complicated. I want to prove myself, I suppose—though that means something far different to me now than it did when I was younger."

"In what way?" Seth asked.

She sighed. "That's a difficult question." When he kept looking at her, waiting for her response, she shook her head. "That means I'm not going to answer it. Not today, anyway."

Seth wanted to press her, but the way she'd said it didn't invite further argument. But then she asked, "What is it *you* want?"

"I want to save Morgan and Braddock," he said immediately. "None of this would have happened if I hadn't stolen that stupid necklace."

"I always thought that was odd," Seren said. "Was it very valuable, do you think?"

"Hardly. It wasn't even worth the trouble to take it, and taking it was easy enough—it's what happened after I took it that brought the trouble, I suppose."

"Hmm." She turned her hands over and back again. "Elgar seems to be a man who has a fervent desire for worthless things. And yet I doubt it's folly; you don't seize control of Hallarnon and win two wars by being an idiot. There must be some value to that trinket, whether or not it's apparent."

Seth had a sudden uneasy feeling about leaving the pendant with Roger. But if anyone could hide something, Roger could. And it wasn't like anyone would know Elgar was looking for it, would they?

"I'll make it right," he said, as firmly as he could. "Even if I can't help you and Lucius and Deinol—even if I can't fight—I'll do whatever I can. I'll make sure we put things right again."

Seren looked away from him, stroking her fingers through the grass. "Don't make promises you can't keep," she said.

———

It took far longer than she was proud of, and long enough for Braddock to start insisting she was crazy, but Morgan finally discovered the trick behind the stones, though by then she was far too exhausted to rub his nose in it. If she felt anything at all, it was a sort of awe: whoever built this passage had been a genius. How were they ever able to build it in the first place? she wondered.

She was right about the cracks: they *did* show how the stones were supposed to come out of the wall. The trick was getting them to move. The key, as it turned out, was the first stone she'd managed to work loose—it was in the center, almost all the way down. She'd no idea how she was supposed to find it, as the strange scratch marks on the wall weren't pointing to it in any way she could figure out. But she had found it, and it had helped her realize what they were supposed to do.

She and Braddock had waited as long as they could, done everything they could think of to make sure the guards were out of earshot, but there was no helping the risk. The first stone was very low to the ground, but if she was right, and there was a passage behind the wall, it would still make a noise as it hit the floor on the other side. How loud the noise would be depended on what that floor was made of, and there was no way to know that. Morgan tried her best to ease the block over the edge, but when it finally fell beyond her grasp, she winced, already closing her eyes. But the sound was surprisingly muted—dirt, then, most likely—and when she looked over at Braddock, he nodded.

It made more sense to let him do the next part—he hadn't studied the wall as she had, but he was far stronger, and it was easy enough to show him what to do. He crouched down and stuck one hand through the hole, shoving it in as far as the chains allowed. Then he clutched the wall from the far side, and *pulled*.

It was just as she'd thought—the lower section of the wall moved as a single piece, coming out from the back of the cell along the lines of the large crack she'd found. And behind the wall, on the other side of a space just large enough for Braddock to crawl through, was empty blackness.

Braddock sat back heavily, panting just a bit. "That looks like the passage to hell."

"Does it look like a prison cell?" Morgan asked. "Because that's where we are right now, in case you've forgotten."

He shook his head, but he was smiling. "Didn't say I wasn't coming. Let me just do one last thing."

Morgan regarded him curiously, but he didn't say anything more, just reached into his coat and pulled out a single coin. He stuck his hand through the bars to the other side, then pitched the coin as far as he could down the hall.

"Oh, *clever*," Morgan said, and he grinned at her.

"It's only clever if the noise doesn't alert them," he said. "Let's go."

Morgan crawled through first, making her way around the fallen block and into the tunnel. She couldn't have gone more than ten feet before she noticed two things: the dirt floor had given way to stone, and the passage was tall enough to stand up in. As Braddock crawled in after her, she whispered, "You can stand if you get this far."

He nodded. "Let me fix the wall."

As he began to pull the larger section back into place behind him, he frowned. "Well, that was well done."

"What was?"

He pointed to a lip of rock hanging down from their side. "This blocks the loose part of the wall, see? So if you're in the cell, you have to pull it out, like I did—you can't push it, because it's stuck. So if any guards tried to push on the wall to see if it was loose, it wouldn't work—not unless they hit that one block you found."

"Gods, I wonder who made this thing."

"I'd like to know that myself." Braddock grunted as he tugged the wall the last few inches. "Don't suppose you've any idea how we can see our way down the corridor?"

Morgan bit her lip. "You wouldn't happen to still have that torch you were carrying on our way in, would you?"

"No such luck. They snatched it from me after the lot of us got caught in the hall. Along with my ax," he added pointedly.

"I've got a spare flint," Morgan said, ignoring that last bit. "Course, I got it from Roger, so it might not work. And I know you've got at least one striker somewhere in that coat. Isn't there anything here we can light?"

Braddock rested one hand on the last loose block, unwilling to close off their only source of light just yet. "Seems like these fellows thought of everything—they had to figure they'd need some light. Is there anything lying about?"

Morgan peered down the passage, waiting for her eyes to grow accustomed to an even deeper darkness than had filled the dungeons. "There's nothing set into the walls . . . no braziers or anything like that." She crouched down on the floor, following the shadowy edges where it met the wall, and finally her fingers brushed against something that wasn't stone. "They really did think of everything," Morgan said, and pulled a decently sized torch from an impressive pile of them.

Braddock passed her his striker, then glanced regretfully behind him. "Now if they could just have devised a way to help me get my ax back."

Morgan rolled her eyes. "Are you still going on about that?"

"I *liked* that ax. It was a good ax!"

"If we get out of here alive, I'll buy you a new ax."

"I don't want a new ax, I want . . ." He paused as the torch finally caught, then hurried to replace the last stone so the light wouldn't flicker into the hall. Then he finally got up, moving to stand at her side.

The corridor was hardly cramped; they could walk comfortably side by side, and the floor was remarkably smooth and even beneath their feet. The chains still hampered them—if the mysterious builders had *really* thought of everything, they would've left a file, but unfortunately the torch turned out to be the extent of their generosity. But even though it was admittedly slow going, the corridor was unmistakably long, sloping up and down and up once more, turning again and again. Before long Morgan had no idea in which direction they were headed, or where under the city they might be. At least they hardly worried about getting lost, because there was nowhere else to go.

When they finally did come to a split, Morgan held the torch close to the wall where the paths diverged, squinting at the scratches on the stone. "There's something etched here, but it's different from what we found in the cell."

The first mark they'd seen had been light, but deliberate and sure, the circle and diamonds carefully inscribed. This one was haphazard and lopsided, as if the etcher had been drunk or didn't know what he was doing. It looked like a straight double line, with smaller, curved lines extending from the sides. Whatever it was supposed to be, it was decidedly on the right side of the split, so Morgan nodded in that direction. "Maybe it means we should head this way?"

"Or maybe it means there's something incredibly dangerous down that way," Braddock said. Then, when she looked at him: "What? It's just as likely."

"Well, we have to pick one," Morgan said. "I'll go left instead if you like, just as long as we go."

Braddock shook his head. "Those damned signs have helped us out so far. We may as well follow this one too."

So they went to the right, following that path for another indeterminable amount of time until they reached the second split. There was another etching on the right wall again, just the same as the last one they'd found, and again they followed it. When they stumbled upon a third one, with the same symbol on the right wall as before, Braddock turned to her uneasily. "We can't be going around in circles, can we?"

"That's not possible," Morgan said firmly. "There's no room to get turned around—there's only been one path so far."

"If you say so." He looked dubiously at the mark, then peered down the hall. "Right again?"

Morgan shrugged. "Why not?"

This time the path went on straight for so long that Morgan was sure they'd come out again at the Howling Gate, but finally Braddock said, "It's a bit lighter, don't you think?"

"Hmm," Morgan said as they turned a corner. "I think—" And then she stopped, because they were in front of a wall with a hole in the center that looked large enough to crawl through. She handed the torch to Braddock. "Hold this."

"Are you sure you should—" But Morgan was already halfway through the hole, and once she'd reached the other side, she turned to murmur back to him.

"It's all right," she said. "But put out the torch; you won't need it."

She didn't stand up until Braddock joined her, and then they stood there together, as if frozen in place. The moon was shining down on them, and beneath their feet was grass. "We're outside the city," Morgan realized.

"Just," Braddock agreed. "Look there."

They'd come out of the side of a hill, with a riverbank within reach and surrounded by clumps of scraggly trees. Perhaps a hundred and a quarter yards away lay the towering city walls, casting hardly any shadow by moonlight. Morgan looked up at them in disbelief. "That's one way to escape, I suppose," she said.

CHAPTER THIRTEEN

Roger sat slumped behind the bar in the empty Dragon's Head, spinning the ruby between his fingers on the counter top. He'd had to be careful making inquiries about it—a prize this valuable would only attract the worst sort of attention—but he hadn't turned up a single thread to follow. Even Tom's information had been woefully sparse on ancient jewel thefts, and if *he* didn't know, it was doubtful anyone would. How many hundreds of years had the thing been sitting in its hiding place, anyway? It might've been there as long as the statues themselves, or been put there generations later—there was no way for him to tell.

Seth's pendant, at least, he could be freer with, since it was practically worthless—a judgment that was only confirmed when he had it appraised. "The stone's a real emerald, small as it is," the man had said, "but the setting is clumsily done, far more amateurish than it deserves. If you ask me, it looks like an apprentice's vanity piece, something to cut your teeth on. There's no worth in the thing beyond the materials themselves."

But that couldn't be true, or why would Elgar have cared that it was stolen? It couldn't just be the principle of the bloody thing. He wished he knew more about the pendant's original owner—"a boy who won't be needing this anymore," according to what Seth had remembered, but that was far too narrow even for him to chase.

He groaned, setting the ruby to spinning again. Most thieves would puff themselves up at merely having found a treasure like this, and wouldn't give another thought to where it had come from. But Roger had far more ambition than that, just as Gran had had. She was the one who had told him about Valyanrend's secret past, the things hidden underneath that even the scholars had forgotten. It all went back to the Ninists, she always said, but it hadn't *started* there; it was the Ninists who had put an end to what came before, in order to build their vestries and spread their teachings. There had been some older, stranger religion, some secret sect, that the Ninists had taken over and destroyed, obliterating it so utterly that even their own faithful eventually forgot the truth. It was only their people, the thieves and swindlers, who took pains to remember, Gran had said, because they remembered that secrets held power, and that it was very dangerous to lie when you didn't know the truth. Someone ought to have told the Ninists that.

That was how he was going to make his name—by finding those secrets, and making them his own. He was as fine a swindler and schemer as Sheath had ever seen; there was no point in honing those skills any further. But stealing whatever truth his city had kept hidden for so many centuries—*that* was what would make him a thief of legend, worthy of the Halfen name. Gran had known he could do it, too; he was sure of it. "Roger," she'd always said, "you're the cleverest Halfen among us, and don't you forget it." But then she inevitably paused, and added, "Except for your cousin Len, but that boy's no true Halfen, and an awful prig besides."

But *Len,* Roger thought, spinning the ruby savagely, had hated being a Halfen, and had hated living in Sheath, and had hated what he called Gran's *silly stories.* Len had left Valyanrend to make his fortune *honestly*—anathema to any true Halfen—and that meant Roger was his family's only chance. He had to figure out Valyanrend's secrets, for their legacy as much as for his own. What had been so dangerous about this city that the Ninists didn't even want their own faithful to discover it, and yet so vital that others sought any means to preserve the knowledge of it?

He watched the ruby as it slowed its spin, trembling toward where the pendant lay flat on the counter top. He wasn't expecting anything more remarkable than the sight of the ruby wobbling as it struck the pendant. But as the two objects crashed into each other, in the moment before the ruby spun away, he thought he saw it catch the light in an odd way, reflecting a flash from no source that he could see.

Roger sat up straighter, stilling the ruby with one hand and snatching up the pendant in the other. He let it dangle from its chain, then swung it like a pendulum at the ruby in his other hand.

The first time it struck the ruby, the flash, if there truly was one, was too faint for him to be certain of it. But the second time there could be no mistaking it—it glowed, just for a moment, when the pendant hit it.

Next, Roger pinched the pendant between thumb and forefinger, pressing it against the ruby directly. Again, the reaction was so slight, he couldn't truly tell if he was imagining it, but then a thought struck him: he was pressing the edge of the pendant's setting to the ruby, not the emerald in its center. He shifted his grip on it and tried again, this time pressing the two gems directly together. And there was the flash again, momentary but unmistakable.

Now that he knew the trick of it, he found he could reproduce the same results endlessly: every time he touched emerald and ruby together, the ruby gave off that flash, and the pendant failed to change or react in any way he could see. When he'd exhausted his attempts at further experimentation, he laid both objects on the bar, staring at them in bewilderment. This was certainly a secret, but what did it mean? Was it the ruby that was exceptional, or the pendant, or both? Were they connected somehow? Had they been—

"Roger!" Morgan whispered from somewhere above him, and he nearly fell over the bar.

"What the hell?" He peered up the stairs, but it was undoubtedly her, albeit clad in chains and a lot more grime than he was used to seeing on her. She didn't seem to have seen what he was doing, and he quickly swept both objects off the bar, setting each in a separate pocket for good measure. "Morgan, what are you doing here?"

"It's my tavern, isn't it? Now fetch a pick and help us get these chains off."

"You escaped, then?"

She rolled her eyes. "No, they decided to let us go for a song, but we kept the chains out of sentiment. Will you fetch a pick or won't you?"

"What kind of thief needs to *fetch* a lockpick?" Roger asked, rolling his own eyes. "Come here into the light. Is Braddock upstairs?"

Morgan nodded. "Sleeping. We figured you'd probably come by."

"Aye, told Lucius and them I'd see to it—and you, before."

"I owe you for it," Morgan said, "and I'm not like to forget it. The pick?"

Roger wasn't some trembly fingered novice, so he had Morgan and Braddock freed before you could tell the story of Cousin Ayne and the fishwife—though he tried. Then, once he'd given them time to rub at their wrists and Braddock had poured a tankard high with ale, he asked, "You won't be insulted, I hope, if I ask how in all the hells you managed to get out?"

Morgan smiled. "You got in, didn't you? Why is it so hard to imagine someone else could get out?"

"Because *someone else* isn't me," Roger said, "and you and Braddock, no offense meant, are *definitely* not me. You yourself are always trumpeting your own honesty, and I'm sure you're right, but honest people tend to be terrible at escaping prisons."

"Well," Morgan said, "we had . . . help, of a sort. Someone else figured it out first, I think, and we just . . . followed along."

"It's going to sound crazy," Braddock added, nursing his ale, "and if we weren't standing here now, I'd swear we *were* crazy. But somebody cracked that dungeon even better than you, swindler."

"Maybe not *better*," Morgan objected, and Roger had to smile. "What would we have done if they'd put us in a different cell?"

Braddock shrugged. "For all we know, there are passages all over the damn place. Maybe there was one three cells over that came out right under where I'm standing."

"Let's hope not," Morgan said.

Roger tried to contain his impatience, and failed. "So you found a passage? To where? From where?"

"From our cell," Morgan said, "and . . . well, it goes a lot of places."

Roger knew he must've looked bright-eyed by then, feverishly eager, struggling to keep still. "How many other places?"

Braddock laughed. "Look at him, would you? We've beaten him at his own game. Bet with all your searching you never found a place like this."

Morgan was more solemn. "Roger, listen. The tunnels are very old—far older than the one you took us through under the vestry. We think they're dangerous. So I'll tell you, if you like, but don't go poking around too much down there. Besides, we tried to hide our escape, but we can't say whether the guards won't find it and come after us."

"Yes, yes, all *right,* just tell me, will you?"

She sighed. "It forks enough to make me dizzy, but we discovered three ways out. The first one we tried took us outside the city, but that was no good—how were we supposed to make it through the gates with these chains on? So we went back in. The next one came out in the upper Bowels, right next to Rat's Tail, but that's bad territory to be in, so we thought we'd see if the next one was closer. And the next one . . ." Morgan hesitated. "The next one was right where Sheath runs into the Fades, at the end of that alley down a ways from where that uncle of yours used to live, across from where they had that fire however many years ago."

"My Halfen uncle or my Varsten uncle?" Roger asked.

Morgan blinked at him. "Eh?"

Roger tried again. "I'm not sure which uncle you're talking about. My father only had one brother, so he's my Halfen uncle. The other was my aunt's husband, and his name was Varsten—Irius Varsten. Gran was always skeptical of that one, because he—"

"All right, I understand," Morgan said. "It wasn't Irius, so it must've been the other one."

"Uncle Tarben?"

"Hmm . . . no."

"Maybe you mean one of my cousins," Roger said. "Haften? Nall?"

Morgan snapped her fingers. "Darry. Darry Halfen, that was it."

"Oh *him,*" Roger said. "Aye, he was a cousin—distant, Gran liked to say, because he was a *terrible* thief, and with all that Gerrin blood—"

"Yes, Roger, that's lovely. Anyway, it was down from where he used to live, back when Irius was alive."

"Aye, I think I know the spot."

"I wish you wouldn't go looking, though, Roger. Things are about to get a sight more dangerous around here, I'm afraid."

Roger nodded. "If Elgar was really keeping you two as hostages in exchange for whatever it is he's after, they won't just let you go. Normally this city is large enough to allow people to disappear, but if they offer coin . . . Sheath takes care of its own, but only up to a point. We are largely thieves and swindlers here, after all."

"There's no way of knowing if anyone saw us make our way here," Morgan added. "It wasn't far, but chains are fairly remarkable, I'd say. Braddock and I'll have to leave the city; I don't see any other way."

"What about the rest of them?" Braddock asked. "Shouldn't we go fetch them back? There's no need for them to do any favors for Elgar now."

Roger shook his head. "They may already be at Hornoak by now; you'd probably just pass each other by on the way. No, I can't imagine they'll report to Elgar's men without coming to me first, and I can tell them what happened. Who knows? If they manage to get their hands on the thing, it might be we can turn it into a profit, or at least make use of it ourselves."

"I'll be pleased enough if they all get back safe," Morgan said. "Where do you think we should go? Esthrades?"

Roger considered it. "Esthrades is generally safe these days, but Reglay isn't, and going around will take you too long. No, I'd head south, near the Issamiri border. Wherever you settle, try to get word to me, and I'll try to get it back to you once this thing's blown over—and I'm sure it will. Then you can come back and have the rest of us waiting for you, and we'll be able to get drunk and tell tales about this whole thing."

Morgan glanced around the room; he couldn't tell if she believed him. He couldn't tell if he believed it himself. "We'll see," she said.

———

Their first sight of Hornoak consisted of a couple of sagging huts with wispy thatched roofs. There was an older man leaning on a pitchfork in front of one of them, and Lucius waved to him. Seth couldn't help tensing up a little, and he saw Deinol frown. "Is that wise?"

"Trust me," Lucius said, and even if they hadn't, it was too late: the man was already walking toward them.

He was callused and squinty-eyed, but his mouth was mild. "If it's an inn you want," he said, his voice low and scratchy, "you'll not find one. Used to be travelers could kit up in the old shrine, but no more."

"Is that so?" Lucius said smoothly, raising his eyebrows. "May I ask why?"

The man shrugged. "Sure, what's it to me? We had a pack of fellows come in—acquaintances of Bergen's, I think, or at least they were up to something at his place. But it's no bigger than mine, so he had Marten house 'em in the shrine for some days. Nobody much liked them, but they kept to themselves, and we've seen worse." He frowned, staring back off into the village. "Then all of a sudden they decided they wanted Marten's altar stone."

"They wanted whose what?" Lucius asked.

"Marten, he's the closest thing to a priest we've got here, takes care of the shrine with that boy of his. 'Altar stone' is what he calls this hunk of rubbish that he found in the shrine somewhere—he's convinced the thing's some kind of talisman, but I can assure you it's a bloody rock. Either way, these fellows must've heard Marten babbling about it, and they decided they had to have the thing, and they somehow convinced *Bergen* that *he* had to have it too, even though he's no stranger to it. Anyone else would've let them have the damned rock, but Marten was ready to defend his altar stone with his life. Lucky for him, Bergen convinced the others to just beat him and run him off—I bet they wouldn't have hesitated to kill him, and they've been shaking their damn swords at anyone who comes near the shrine ever since. No one knows why they haven't just cleared out with the thing, but they don't leave—don't even come out of the shrine unless they're sending somebody to fetch food. It's right odd, to be sure, but I don't know how we're supposed to get to the bottom of it."

Lucius fiddled with the hilt of his sword. "Say we were searching for a place to sleep and wouldn't mind a fight, either. Would that ruffle any feathers?"

The man shrugged again. "Bergen's got no other kin that we know of, and those others have been nothing but trouble since they showed up. I hope you're not expecting a reward for clearing them out, but I imagine most folks'll be glad of it, if you can manage it."

"I see," Lucius said. "Perhaps we'll head toward this shrine, then."

The man leaned heavily on his pitchfork, pointing with his free arm. "It's over that way, to the northeast. Big thing on the hill—tallest building around by far. You'll see it."

"Thanks," Lucius said. When the man nodded and went back to pitching hay, the rest of them moved on, though they didn't continue up the hill toward Hornoak. Instead, as if by unspoken agreement, they moved off to one side, into the trees.

"We'll have to leave as soon as we get our hands on it," Seren muttered.

Lucius nodded. "This Marten'll be wanting his altar stone back, and we don't want to explain why we won't be giving it to him. The fact that we want it at all might make us as bad as these brigands in the villagers' eyes."

"The sun's almost set—maybe we should wait for dark before we move," Deinol suggested. "With any luck, the rest of the village needn't know we were ever here."

"That would be best," Lucius agreed. He looked over at Seren and Seth. "If you have any preparations to make, now would be the time."

Seth didn't, so he just fidgeted and watched the others. He wasn't sure how long they all stood there until Seren finally wandered away, drifting off between the trees. Deinol shot an anxious glance after her, but Lucius shook his head before reaching into the pack he carried, probably in search of food. He didn't react when Seth moved to follow her, though, so he figured that was all right.

He found her leaning against a tree not far away, eating with slow, methodical bites what looked like slices of dried apple. She nodded at him as he approached, but didn't say anything.

"Are you nervous?" Seth asked.

She took another bite, and he felt a little envious; there had been no fruit to be had at the last village Seren had let them pass through. She must have had it with her since before they met in Valyanrend. Seth supposed she traveled often, so no doubt she was used to stocking up for long journeys. "Say wary, rather," she said. "It's only natural when you approach an uncertain situation."

"Do you think something bad's going to happen with those men at the shrine?"

Seren regarded the next slice of apple before taking a bite. "I think we're going to have to kill them. Whether you think of that as something bad is up to you."

Seth didn't know what he thought of it. Those men had already done bad enough things themselves, if the farmer could be believed. No, he was worried about something bad happening to one of them, not at the thought of anyone they might have to face.

"I wish I could help fight," he said, and Seren smiled.

"I understand that well enough, boy, but those friends of yours are talented—the one more than the other, of course, but they're both good enough, and they're used to fighting together. I think we'll be all right."

"This must be more than you bargained for," Seth said. "You agreed to help us fetch something, not to risk your life—or fight anyone."

Seren shook her head. "From the moment I first heard about that stone, I knew there'd be blood in the getting of it. It's not the first time I've done something like this, either. Don't worry about me."

Seth watched her take another bite of apple, and then he asked, "Could I have a piece of that?"

She smiled again—wider, but still same dry, one-sided expression. "You won't like it," she said, but she handed him a piece anyway.

He studied it, wondering what she'd meant. It looked just like an ordinary piece of dried apple, slightly browned but still with a deep red rind. He shrugged and took a bite—and then he understood. It was *tart*—so tart he almost choked. It tasted more like a green apple, or one that wasn't quite ripe, with none of the sweetness he'd come to expect from red ones.

Seren watched with vague amusement as he spluttered. "I told you. Not quite as sweet as you thought, eh?"

"That's one way of putting it," Seth said. "What sort of apple *was* that?"

"I don't think anyone likes it at the first taste," Seren said. "It's like particularly potent spirits—you choke on them at first, until you get used to them. Now I find other apples too sweet, so I don't much care for them." She glanced at the piece still left in Seth's hand. "If you're not going to eat that, then give it back."

But Seth took another stubborn bite, and managed to swallow it without any fuss this time. He finished the last bite as well, and looked up at Seren with a sheepish grin.

She shook her head at him. "I don't know why you're looking so pleased with yourself. You don't get any reward for finishing it."

She almost looked as if she might ruffle his hair, the way Deinol did so often and so unconsciously, but then Deinol himself called to them, making his way through the trees. "Seth, tell the assassin it's time we were off."

Seren rolled her eyes, retreating into herself again. "Sweet gods, I am *not* an assassin. How many times do I have to say it?"

"Come off it, Deinol," Lucius agreed, and Seth nearly jumped—where had he come from?

"Oh, *you* come off it—like hell she isn't. How many people do you know who can kill like that?" Lucius opened his mouth, but before he could speak, Deinol continued, "And don't talk to me about *talent;* gods know you're as *talented* as she is, but the way she fights . . ."

"The *point* of fighting is to kill people as quickly and efficiently as possible," Seren snapped. "If you've forgotten that in the course of all your petty looting and ridiculous duels, that isn't my fault."

"See, that's something an assassin would say."

Seren threw up her hands. "If by *assassin* you just mean *murderer,* I expect we're all that, except for the boy. And if you mean someone who kills for coin, well, I don't, and I never have. So you're wrong either way."

"I believe you," Lucius said, and Deinol sulked.

"I don't much care," Seren replied, "but thanks, I suppose."

Deinol had been right about one thing—the sun had all but set, and it was time to make for the shrine. As they moved off out of the trees, Lucius asked, "So after we get through this . . . that's when you'll tell us what job it is we owe you?"

"If I still think it's worth it after that," Seren said, "then yes. But I imagine at this point I might as well follow things through—I came this far with you, after all."

Deinol cocked his head at her. "You're not worried you'll be . . . late, was it? Your precious time and all that?"

Seren hesitated. "It isn't actually like that—nothing bad will happen if I'm late, I'll just be late. And that irks me, so I try to avoid it when I can. That's all." She jerked her chin forward. "See there? That'll be the shrine."

They got a few more curious looks as they passed through the village, but it was small, and most people were already inside now that night had fallen. The shrine was still clearly visible, though. A squatter building than most Ninist vestries, without the high pointed spire that always marked them out, it was still tall and long, with an arched roof and two heavy wooden doors.

Lucius stopped first. "Seth," he said.

"What is it?" Seth asked, though he could guess what he was about to hear.

"You can't do any fighting," Lucius said. "Go on past the shrine, and stay out of sight. We'll fetch you on our way out."

"But—"

"We won't fight as well if we have to keep an eye on you," Lucius said, "and we haven't time to argue. Do it."

Seth nodded. "All right." But he stayed a moment longer. "Good luck in there."

Lucius smiled. "Oh, I expect we won't need too much of that. But thanks, all the same."

CHAPTER FOURTEEN

The shrine's windows were long and narrow, made of dirty, blue-stained glass. It was hardly picturesque, but Deinol hoped the grime would be thick enough to keep anyone from noticing what was going on inside. They'd killed all the men there easily enough—Almasy had been especially helpful, he had to admit—but the last one got in a lucky slice to Lucius's forearm, and he wanted to wrap it up before they set out.

Deinol caught his eye, and he grinned weakly. "All right?"

"I should be asking you that," Deinol said. "Are you badly hurt?"

Lucius shook his head. "Eh, it's a scratch. Wash and dress it and I'll be fine. I'm embarrassed more than anything; that lout didn't have *half* my skill."

"He was a better swordsman than he looked," Almasy said from farther away. "And even the best of us make mistakes now and then." Deinol followed her voice, and found her at the far end of the shrine, plucking something from atop the altar. "And this is it, I assume." She squinted at whatever was in her hand. "How odd."

"What is it?" Deinol asked.

She tossed it to him. "I think there's something written on it? It's not anything I can read, but the marks don't seem random."

The stone itself wasn't what Deinol had expected—it was glossy, slightly transparent, its surface covered in etchings that followed a spiral pattern. Almasy was right: they did look somewhat uniform, like they could be letters, but there was nothing there he could understand. "You were wrong, you know," he said to her, hefting the stone in one hand. It was much lighter than he would have guessed, given its size, and he wondered what it was made of—no common rock had that weight and texture.

She blinked. "What?"

"What you said when we left the city—that Elgar didn't send his guards because whatever he was after was too obviously valuable. There's nothing *valuable* about this that I can see—I'm not even sure I would pick it up if I saw it lying in the street."

"You're right," Almasy said, and frowned. "But that doesn't make sense. If this is all it is, what was the harm of sending soldiers?"

Lucius nodded at the bodies around them. "Maybe the soldiers might've become like this lot—heard the priest's ravings and gotten convinced there was something to the stone."

Almasy shrugged. "Maybe he was right, for all we know."

Lucius grimaced at that. "Gods, this is going to bother me just enough to make me uneasy, isn't it?"

"It's a long enough journey back to the capital," Deinol said. "If the thing has aught extraordinary about it, we'll have plenty of time to find it."

"But we're not going back yet," Lucius reminded him. He looked at Almasy. "You helped us, like we agreed, and I do try to keep my word when I can help it. What is it we can do for you?"

But Almasy shook her head. "Not now. Let's take care of it tomorrow; it's too late to travel much farther anyway."

"As you like," Lucius said. "We should get clear of the village, at least."

"And hope Seth's where he told us he would be," Deinol added. "I'm surprised the boy didn't follow us into the shrine."

———

Seth supposed they didn't exactly have a direction—*away from the village* was good enough—but Seren walked confidently ahead, and as she was the only one who knew where they were going next, he was content to follow her. He was glad when they finally decided it was safe to stop for the night, though; they'd done even more walking than they were used to, and the others had had to fight a battle besides. Seth was probably the least tired among them, so he agreed to take first watch, and it was doubtless a testament to their own exhaustion that the others didn't argue. Lucius and Deinol went to sleep almost immediately, but Seth looked up after some indeterminate amount of time to find Seren staring at him.

"Aren't you going to sleep?" he asked.

"Think I'm getting there," she mumbled, but her face was drawn, her brow vaguely furrowed.

"Did you have any trouble?" Seth asked. "Getting it, I mean?"

She shook her head. "Easy enough. Easier than I'd thought. The hard part comes now."

"What do you mean?"

She looked at the stone, lying in the grass in front of Seth's crossed ankles— he had to keep watch over it as well. "What do you think, boy? Is it just a rock, or is it something else?"

Seth considered it, reaching for the stone and turning it over in his hands. "I think it doesn't matter," he said at last. "It's what we need to free Morgan and Braddock. Even if it's a weapon . . . well, Elgar has many weapons already."

"Yet, weapon or not, this was important to him."

Seth put the stone down again, careful not to drop it. "I can't say I know Elgar personally, but word is he believes all sorts of outlandish things. They say he thinks the marquise of Esthrades is using magic to defeat his men in battle."

Seren smiled. "I'd heard that one, yes. And that he won't keep men to occupy Mist's Edge because he thinks it's haunted."

"By vengeful ghosts," Seth said, and laughed. "I wish it were—then maybe they could take care of him for us. I guess he'd just get replaced by someone even worse, though."

"Quite a bit of history is bad people being replaced by worse people, it seems," Seren said. "Sometimes they get replaced by slightly less bad people instead, and then that's really something. Everyone writes a book about it."

"My stepfather used to talk about what it was like when Gerde Selte ruled Hallarnon. Elgar was like a bleating lamb compared to her, he always said."

Seren tapped her chin. "From what I've heard, Gerde was worse—more talented than Elgar, probably, but worse. They say she liked to leech some of her enemies, and burn the rest alive. Elgar may be just as merciless, but he isn't half so fond of terror—he kills to accomplish things, not for the sheer spectacle of it." She smiled again, even more dryly than usual. "The problem is that the things he wants to accomplish aren't so lovely, of course. At least he's further from his goal than Gerde ever was."

"Is that really true?" Seth asked. "They like to talk about how she killed all her rivals, but if that's so, who was left to assassinate her?"

Seren waved a hand at him. "It wasn't an assassination; that's just a story. She was unchallenged in Hallarnon, and when she died, your precious city was in chaos for months. It was sickness that felled her, not some arcane poison—just bad luck. Or good, depending on how you see it."

"Hmm," Seth said. "I guess it's too much to hope for to have Elgar choke on his breakfast in the morning, eh?"

"You can always hope," Seren replied, staring off into the trees.

Seth woke so suddenly that his head nearly snapped back off his neck, his eyes frantically blinking in the dark. For just a moment he didn't know why he'd woken, and then he did—his watch hadn't ended, had it?

He tried to remember. Seren had had the watch after his, but she'd been awake at first, and they'd been talking. They'd stopped eventually, and he thought she'd dozed after that, but had he woken her before falling asleep himself or hadn't he? "Seren?" he whispered, but no one answered, and he kept blinking, trying to see through the darkness of the forest. He stared at where she had been sleeping, but he could make out nothing but grass.

Then he heard a rustle from beyond the edge of the clearing, and a horrible certainty made the pit of his stomach drop out.

He dove headlong after the noise, sprinting as fast as he could, tearing past trees as their branches snatched at his eyes. He could see just enough to keep from slamming into anything, but he hardly cared—all he cared about was finding her, and if that brought every creature that lurked in this forest snarling out of the darkness, it didn't matter.

It felt like he'd been running for half a moment and half an hour when she caught him, but it was probably closer to the former. She threw one arm across his waist, trapping his arms at his sides; the other hand was at his throat, and he didn't have to see it to know it held a knife.

"You're going to want to do something very stupid right about now," Seren said, right against his ear. "Don't."

Seth started to squirm, but then the edge of the knife kissed his throat and he went still. "You took it," he said, hardly able to breathe.

For a moment she was silent, and almost as frozen as he was. "Aye," she said. "And I'm going to leave with it."

"*That's* what your errand was," he hissed, clenching his fists so he wouldn't struggle. "You were already looking for it, even back in the prison."

"That's right."

"Why?" he insisted. "What's it to you?"

"To me? Nothing. It's a rock."

He wanted to spit, but his mouth was dry. "Liar."

He'd thought that would wound her, but she didn't even flinch, didn't tighten her hold on him. "I said I'd help you find it, and I did. And now you're going to do something for me, just like you said. Believe me, that's the way we both want this to go."

"Like hell it is," Seth snapped, but *that* made her grip tighten, the knife coming so close that it was an effort not to whimper.

"Boy," Seren whispered, holding so still, "listen to me, because I mean what I am telling you: I don't *want* to kill you, but I will."

Seth scoffed—or as close as he could get to it with the fear bearing down on him. "I thought you only did what you wanted to do—no less, and no more."

He felt Seren hesitate, though she didn't move. "Aye," she said again. "And this *is* what I want—make no mistake about that. One day, if you're lucky, you'll kill for something too."

Seth said nothing. He could think of nothing to say. She was going to get away, and it was going to be his fault.

"I'm going to let you go," Seren said, "and I'm going to walk away. If you scream, or if you take *one step* to follow me, I will end you. You can shout if you like once I'm gone—I expect it's the only way the others will find you again."

"We'll come after you," Seth insisted. "We'll get it back, and they'll kill you."

"You won't catch me before I get where I'm going," Seren said. "And by then it won't matter."

"You couldn't take them both," Seth said; he couldn't seem to stop himself. "*I'm* nothing, but against Lucius and Deinol both, you'd be—"

He felt the knife prick at his throat, and for a moment he thought she'd killed him, but then he realized the pain was slight, and he was still breathing. Seren shifted her hand just a bit, and he felt something sticky slide against his neck and the underside of his jaw. "Do you feel that? That's your blood, boy, do you understand? Don't make me spill any more of it."

Seth took a deep breath, suddenly light-headed. "Fine. Go."

"If you—"

"I *won't*. Get the hell out of here."

She released him so suddenly, it was almost as if she'd vanished. Seth was afraid to turn—he didn't think she was bluffing, and what if she counted that movement as a step?—so he stood where she'd left him until he could no longer hear her. Then he released a breath, trying to steady himself against the dizzying pounding at his temples. He had to call for Lucius and Deinol now, or the shame would overtake him. He'd curl up in a ball amidst the fallen leaves, and they would never find him.

He shouted their names until they stood before him, and by then he was out of breath. Deinol looked bewildered enough, but Lucius looked as if he only wished he were. "Do I need to ask where Seren's gone or don't I?" he said.

Seth bit his lip and felt absurdly like crying. "You don't."

Deinol still blinked at them. "Why, what's she done now?"

Seth couldn't speak, and Lucius sighed into the silence. "She stole it after all. I should've guessed."

"Then what the hell are you standing around for?" Deinol nearly roared. "We've got to go after her! Which way did she go?"

"I don't know," Seth said.

"Deinol—"

He ignored both of them. "She was as tired as we were—more, probably. She can't have gotten far. We—"

"—move far more clumsily than she does," Lucius finished. "Even me. If we go looking for her now, in the dark, we'll be lucky if we don't find her—then we also won't find the point of that knife. And by the time morning comes, she'll be so far away she might as well be across the sea. She knows where she's going and how to get there; we barely know where we are."

Deinol stared at him. "Is it so simple for you? Can you just give up on Morgan and Braddock like that?"

"I haven't *once* said I'm giving up." Lucius leaned against the nearest tree, stroking the hilt of his sword. "I'm just saying that chasing after her is hopeless."

"That's the same thing!"

"No, Deinol, it isn't." He ran a hand through his hair. "That damned stone is worth nothing to us in itself, remember? It's just a means to an end. We need to find another way, that's all."

Deinol kicked at the grass. "What other way is there?"

"Well, we've got to try some, haven't we? What we need to do now is go back to Sheath and find Roger, and then we can come up with a plan. Even if trying to spring them again is a bad idea, maybe we can gain an audience with that Oswhent—"

"Because he'll be so happy to hear how we failed, I'm sure."

"Look, Deinol, it wasn't unlikely Elgar would have tried to kill us whether we succeeded or not. Even if we had gotten the stone, it wasn't a safe or certain thing, and you know it."

"Aye, I *do* know it. That's not what gets to me." He paced along the line of the trees, pausing every other step to scuff the grass. "She *tricked* us. We had it, and she stole it from us."

Lucius smiled. "We've certainly stolen enough from other people."

"That's not what I mean!" He threw up his hands, then let them fall to his sides again. "She played us for fools."

Lucius sighed. "Well, it worked."

"Not if we find her—"

"Deinol, I'm sorry to have to remind you of this, but every day we waste looking for her is another day Elgar has to grow impatient and decide Morgan and Braddock are better dead. We've spent enough time away. We need to go back."

Deinol rubbed at his face, then looked to Seth. "You've been awfully quiet. What do *you* think?"

Lucius turned to him too, and Seth fidgeted under the sudden scrutiny. What could he say? The truth was he couldn't even think about what Seren had done without feeling anger rise in him, and he would've been willing to chase her to the ends of the earth, if he only knew he'd find her there. But Lucius was right— she was long gone by now, and there was no way they were going to hunt her down. If only he'd been able to fight like Lucius and Deinol, to challenge her instead of standing there helpless while she walked away . . .

"I think Lucius is right," he said at last. "Revenge may be sweet, but it won't do much for Morgan and Braddock, and we have to put them first." He stared at the ground. "Look, this was—this was my fault. I bargained for her freedom, I let her get loose—"

"And I was the one who wanted her to come with us in the first place," Lucius said. "Hell, it seems the only blameless one here is Deinol, eh? You never liked her."

"Oh, I deserve my fair share of blame," Deinol said. "I could've tried harder to get you two idiots to listen to reason, and I didn't. Besides, we'd never have gotten this far without her—you think the two of us alone could've taken on five brigands in that shrine, or even those looters? You figured her blade would be useful, and you were right—you just didn't think about what would come afterward."

Lucius rubbed at his arm. "My skills really do need sharpening if five against two is a problem for me. Remember when we did seven at once on the Rat's Tail job?"

"Remember? I'm not like to forget that. I saved your hide at the end there."

"Aye, but four of the kills were mine."

Deinol laughed. "You *would* remember that."

Lucius shuffled his feet. "So . . ."

"So, fine," Deinol said. "We'll go back to Sheath, and we'll find Roger. But if the gods are ever good enough to cross my path with that woman's again . . ."

"The gods are rarely that good," Lucius said. "But if they are, I suppose we'll deal with it then."

CHAPTER FIFTEEN

A daring prison break from the very heart of the Citadel, and you've turned up *no* news about it?" Captain Wyles smirked. "Isn't information your job?"

"*Information,* yes." Varalen spread his hands along the edge of the table. "There's always information to be found when you're willing to pay for it. But will it actually help? I doubt it."

"And the cell yielded nothing," Elgar said. It wasn't a question.

"Nothing," Varalen answered anyway. "The only clue we have is the coin that was found in the corridor, though I suppose that could as easily have been dropped by one of our men while he was making his rounds."

"It seems to me that my men don't make very many rounds, if they're this inept at keeping prisoners in their cells," Elgar said, smoothing his beard. His breath came a bit short, and his eyes were still bloodshot, but he looked much better than he had the day before. He had walked the walls in the predawn hours, and seemed to have caught a bit of a chill. Varalen knew better than to ask after his health: all men, no matter how great, took sick from time to time, but Elgar scowled ferociously at even the barest suggestion he might be ill, as if it were some grave insult. "By now," he continued, "there is little hope of finding them still in the city."

"Unfortunately," Varalen agreed.

"Then perhaps it is time we stopped paying for information about them."

"We needn't have paid for it to start with," Wyles said. "Given a longer leash, my men could—"

"Your men could round people up at random and terrorize them into feeding us a thousand lies," Varalen finished for him.

"And have you turned up aught but lies, for all His Eminence's coin? Even you admit—"

"I understand if you lack the finesse to see it, Captain Wyles," Varalen snapped, "but this city is the imperator's home, as much as yours or mine, and he has enough reason not to wish to stir up a panic among its citizens." He silently prayed that this was true.

But Elgar nodded easily, and Varalen suppressed a sigh of relief. "He has the right of it in this instance, Nathaniel. I wish the streets to remain as calm as possible for the present."

Wyles scowled. "Your Eminence—"

"*Enough,*" Elgar said, with a harshness that surprised Wyles and Varalen both. "I have not forgotten what happened the last time you assured me of the superiority of your *methods,* Nathaniel, and I trust you have not either. You do your job well enough on the streets, but you are not equipped for more subtle matters, and you forget that at your own peril."

Wyles clearly knew what Elgar meant, though Varalen had far less of an idea. There was something Quentin Gardener had told him once, about an incident that happened before Varalen had come to Elgar's service, when Wyles was still chief among Elgar's torturers. Even Quentin had never known all the details, but it seemed some of Wyles's subordinates had been *interrogating* a prisoner who turned out to have an unexpectedly weak constitution, and the boy had died in the midst of their ministrations. This mistake had sent Elgar into an unparalleled rage—something the loyal Quentin had taken as evidence of his master's moral character. But Varalen had never had reason to suspect their master of any moral character whatsoever, and he often wondered at the truth of it, though he knew better than to ask.

Either way, Wyles had clearly overstepped, and Varalen wasn't about to let that opening go to waste. "My lord, I must entreat you again to let me—"

Elgar waved his words away. "I know well enough what you want, Varalen, and I've already told you no. Stopping and searching everyone who tries to enter the city will, at best, wreak havoc on every trade or enterprise in the area, and at worst it will frighten Aquila and his friends away when they would otherwise have returned."

"My lord, if they return to the city and learn their friends are free—"

"We must endeavor to make sure they do not learn of it."

Varalen shook his head. "We spread enough rumors making our own inquiries. It is not possible to keep them ignorant: if they stay in Sheath for more than a quarter of an hour, they *will* hear of it. And then why would they come anywhere near us again?"

"All I need," Elgar insisted, "is to get them within the city walls without incident. Once they are in Valyanrend, I can take the stone from them at my leisure. But if they take it and flee . . . no. That is what we must prevent above all."

What on earth did he mean, at his leisure? It was difficult enough to find someone in Valyanrend who *wanted* to be found; did he think it would be so easy to capture a group of thieves who had every reason to hide? "I don't understand," he said, as mildly as he could, "just how it is you propose to know when they're in the city at all, let alone how you propose to hunt them down once they're here."

"I know you don't understand. It is not necessary for you to understand. I am telling you that if that stone passes into Valyanrend, I shall know of it, one way or another. You can disbelieve me if you choose, but I will hear no more on the subject."

Well, it wasn't as if it mattered to him whether Elgar obtained the thing or not, so why should he care if he wasn't making any sense about it? "Understood, my lord."

"Good." He turned to Wyles. "Nathaniel, you may consider anything more on this matter outside your purview. Return to your post, and when next we speak, I'll want to hear that you've made *some* discoveries about this resistance."

Wyles bowed, but said nothing more as he left.

Varalen would have been happy to take his leave as well, but he doubted it would be that simple. "Was there something more you wanted to discuss with me, my lord?"

"There was," Elgar said. "This little bird you found for me . . . he appears very promising, but I think you should continue corresponding with him in my stead. He took my assurances well enough, but you seem to make him feel more comfortable." He smiled. "Perhaps he finds you more trustworthy, or simply more palatable. Either way, we cannot allow him to reconsider our arrangement."

"He won't," Varalen said. "He's come too far to turn back now; what he's done for us already damns him a hundred times over. His only hope lies with us, and he knows it."

"That may be so. Men have still been known to develop consciences at the least opportune moments."

Varalen laughed. "Oh, he has a conscience already. That's precisely why I'm so sure of him."

Elgar raised an eyebrow. "Really."

"Undoubtedly. It's the ones without consciences that cause all the trouble."

"Hmm." Elgar folded his hands, leaning calmly back in his chair. "Which are you, I wonder?"

Varalen bit his lip. "I wouldn't presume to say, my lord."

"Yes," Elgar agreed. "That's just what I thought you'd say."

He *had* told Morgan he'd be careful, yes, but wasn't a coward always careful? She was the one who'd gone in for all the damned heroics back in the Citadel. All Roger wanted to do was explore a tunnel or two—that hardly mattered by comparison, did it?

He passed the torch to his left hand so he could mark the wall. If he'd been retracing Morgan and Braddock's steps correctly, to his left was the passage that came out near Rat's Tail, and to his right was farther back toward the dungeons. Rat's Tail wasn't the most destitute of the districts—that was the Bowels—but it was the most dangerous, because the inhabitants of the Bowels were already too ill or starved to do much of anything besides die slowly. In Rat's Tail, so the saying went, they'd steal the clothes off your back, and then they'd eat the skin off your bones. He figured it was best to prevent any fellow thieves from wandering out that way unawares, so he fished in his pocket for the key Morgan had given him and used it to cut as deeply as he could into the stone on his left side. Most thieves were cowards by nature, so perhaps the finger-sign for *danger* was so intuitive because it was the one they least wanted to forget: a circle divided in fourths by an X—so simple, you barely had to be taught it to understand what it meant.

Morgan had drawn the mark she'd found in the cell for him, and that was a finger-sign too—the one that marked a hidden escape route, naturally. But the second mark, the one she and Braddock had seen three times as they traveled down the right-hand passageway, had not stuck in their memories, and they could only vaguely describe it to him. Even then, it was decidedly not a finger-sign, and had no meaning Roger could determine. That, if he was honest, was the main reason he was here right now, not to explore the tunnels. Once within them, he had seen that Morgan's concerns were justified—these passages were indeed far older than any he had traversed in the city before, and he wasn't entirely certain they weren't about to come crashing down around his ears. Worse, sometimes he thought he heard shuffling noises echo off the stone—rats, perhaps, or perhaps guards searching for their lost prisoners.

The next fork was the one he wanted, and, sure enough, the wall bore a series of strange, rambling lines. Roger tilted his head this way and that, trying to figure out what it was supposed to be. Was it a sort of map? Perhaps the branching lines were meant to be the forks in the path—but no, he had it. *Branching.* The longest line was the branch of a tree, the smaller ones were offshoots from the central stem, and the heavy marks at their tails were the leaves. He nodded, confirming it—then caught himself, and almost laughed. Even if he were right, what would be the significance of drawing a tree branch on a cavern wall?

The answer that came to him first was that the branches were meant to communicate that the route they marked led outside the city walls. That made sense enough, but somehow it didn't seem right to him. According to Morgan, the finger-sign in the cell had been painstakingly carved, but what good was this drawing if you could barely figure out what it was supposed to be? It suggested that the one who had drawn it didn't care whether anyone else understood it or not—so it probably hadn't been meant to communicate anything at all. The etcher had meant it for his own benefit, so he could tell which pathways he had tried. But that just brought Roger back to the same question: Why draw this tree branch, when an arrow or an X would have worked just as well?

Roger wasn't sure how long he stood there pondering it, but eventually that shuffling noise brought him back to his senses. He would have had a hell of a time trying to copy the marks and hold the torch at the same time, so instead he stared at it as intently as he could, hoping he could remember enough of it to produce a workable sketch once he got back outside.

But he hadn't retraced his steps very far when he felt something strange, a mild heat spreading into his hip. He reached into his pocket, and his fingers closed around the ruby—it was radiating an inexplicable warmth.

He pulled it out, half expecting to see it start flashing again, and for a moment he almost thought it did. But he couldn't have said for sure, and then it was certainly dim, and maybe even slightly cooler. He waved it around, then pulled out the emerald and started waving *that* around, but neither gemstone reacted any further. And when he touched them together, he just got the same flash from the ruby as always—it was even starting to grow mundane to him.

In the end he decided to go back for the day, after another look at the symbol to make sure he'd memorized its lines enough to sketch it when he got back into daylight. It was best to tackle one problem at a time, and at least this one had a potential lead. But he'd be taking the ruby with him the next time he explored the tunnels, that was for sure.

CHAPTER SIXTEEN

His father looked up from his desk, the firelight flickering in the hollows under his eyes. "Kelken. Eirnwin said you had something to discuss with me."

"I do." Kel eased himself into the opposite chair, propping his crutches up next to him.

His father grimaced. "Something else about Alessa, no doubt."

"Yes."

His father's fingers curled around the edge of the desk, but his expression smoothed out. "I've made my decision. You know that."

"I know, but if you'd just listen to my idea—"

For a moment he thought he'd only be dismissed, but then his father sighed. "Very well. Tell me."

Kel took a deep breath, trying to steady himself. It wouldn't do to capture his father's attention only to muck everything up because he was nervous. He *knew* this was a good plan, and he'd rehearsed it. He just had to get his father to see what he saw.

"It's not that I mind about Lessa getting married," he said at last. "Not really, anyway. It's just the journey—the Curse. I know—we *both* know there's a good chance she won't survive it. So I thought of another way." He took another breath, resting his hands on the arms of the chair. "I could be the one. I could go in Lessa's stead."

His father's eyebrows rose. "You? Whatever for?"

"To arrange a marriage," Kel said. "That's what you want, isn't it?"

"You think you're equipped to go to a foreign land and convince its rulers to entertain a betrothal with a girl of uncertain blood whom they've never seen?"

"I don't mean I'd arrange a marriage for her," Kel said. "I mean I'd arrange one for me."

His father's brow furrowed, but he was confused for only a moment. "You mean with Princess Adora."

"Yes."

King Kelken sighed again. "I don't object to it in theory, but the princess will not possibly accept you."

"Why not?" Kel asked.

"For a hundred reasons. The children of kings aren't used to marrying for love, it's true, but they're also used to having their marriages *arranged*. However, King Jotun never so much as entertained a proposal for any of his children's hands while he was alive, and with him and Landon dead, Adora is free to do as she pleases. Even if she were somehow inclined to do away with her newfound freedom by rushing into marriage with you, it would not be the excellent political stratagem you seem to think it is. The Issamiri throne is in a state of terrible uncertainty, and the best way for Adora to tighten her hold on it would be to marry someone who can get her with child immediately. Even if you did possess that ability, I doubt Adora would relish the prospect of a child husband."

"She might not," Kel agreed, "but if it's tightening her hold she wants, that's all the more reason she should be interested in what I have to say."

His father glanced at him swiftly, as if he'd somehow guessed. "And why is that?"

"We could have two marriages," Kel explained. "I'd go to her, and she could marry me, and then Prince Hephestion could come here, and marry Lessa. So he wouldn't even be around to contest her claim, because he'd—"

"Because he'd be *here*, sitting on *your* throne," his father snapped. "Absolutely not."

"Why not? I'd lose Reglay, but I'd gain Issamira—a much bigger country, a much more powerful country. Your grandchildren would be kings in Issamira one day—"

"And some stranger's children would be kings in my country."

Kel glared at him. "*Lessa's* children."

His father shook his head. "Alessa is not my child."

"Does that matter so much?"

"In this it does." His chin quivered. "My son, you are very young. You don't understand what you'd be giving up."

"I *do* understand!" He clenched his fist to strike the desk, but then he considered that that wouldn't help prove his point, and let it fall back to his side instead. "I don't want to give up the throne, but I don't care about it more than Lessa's life."

"It is not yours to give to her," his father said, slowly and clearly. "I will not allow it."

"Why is it so bad that Lessa should have it?" Kel asked. "Do you resent her that much?"

His father glared back at him, his fingers closing on the edge of the table.

"You think I resent her? There were those in my court who would have had me cut that child from her mother's belly with no tool more refined than the edge of my sword. If it had been caught earlier, no doubt the herbalists could have brewed a draft to end the pregnancy, but your mother concealed her condition for as long as she could. By the time it was discovered, everyone knew it was too late. Then, on the day Alessa was born, the man who once held Eirnwin's post came to me in my chambers.

"It would be a kindness, he said. The babe was so weak that it was likely she would not live long, and it would be no mercy to let her grow up scorned and reviled. The damage and dissension she would cause, he said, would affect countless lives—the lives of everyone in Reglay. Compared to that, was not one life a very small thing?

"I told him I would think on it, and I dismissed him. And then I went to see the babe. She was such a tiny thing—it was the first time I had ever seen a newborn. I expected her to cry, but she did not—she had no teeth to worry at her lip, but otherwise she fretted as mildly and composedly as she does today. I held her in my arms as we took the measure of each other, and I thought about what I could do and what I could not do. I do not know how long I stood there thinking, but when I had done, I swore to her that I would never harm her, nor would I suffer any other to raise a hand against her while I lived. They had told me none would love her, so I decided to love her myself." He traced a circle on his desk with one fingertip. "And the next day I took up my sword, and I cut out my advisor's tongue, for no man deserves a voice who would give his king such counsel." He shook his head. "You may lay many things against me, my son, but never tell me I did not love that child."

"But if you love her, doesn't that make it easier?" Kel asked. "Am I so much better than she is?"

His father smiled. "The day *you* were born, you can believe no one counseled the sword—for one thing, Eirnwin had come into his position by then, and for another, you were our true heir, the one we'd all waited so many years for. But there was . . . murmuring. Sad looks, and whispered condolences—tears in the eyes of the midwives. I myself . . . I was not sure what I felt. To know one has a son is an indescribable feeling; to know that son is maimed is just as indescribable, though far different. And once again my advisor came to me in my chambers.

"I expected Eirnwin to commiserate with me, but he did not. He told me instead that—that I should be proud of you, and look forward to what you might accomplish. 'If your son is to thrive,' he said, 'he must first live with hardships that would overwhelm lesser men. If he triumphs over them, he will have learned resolve in the face of suffering, and the countless lessons that come with weakness and pain. Such a man will make a better king than one who as a boy knew only smiles.'" His father stopped fiddling with the desk and looked at him. "And I believe that he was right."

Kel was at a loss for what to say. "Eirnwin never said anything like that to me," he mumbled at last. But then he remembered how Eirnwin had talked to him about how he'd decided to walk when he was young, and he wondered if that had been what Eirnwin was trying to say.

"I know . . . I know I could never look at them," his father said. "I know I always left Eirnwin to look after you. *He* could always look at them. Alessa could look at them."

Prince Landon, Kel wanted to say. Prince Landon had glanced but never stared, and he had asked Kel about the pain that came with walking but never sought to dissuade him from doing it. *It seems to me that you are very brave,* he had said—Prince Landon always formed his opinions like that, as if he were afraid that you would disagree with him.

"I have tried to do right by Alessa," his father said, "as I have tried to do right by you. Doubtless I have failed in many ways. But I cannot give you what you want, Kelken. Alessa is a sweet child, a worthy child, but she is not *my* child. The throne is not hers by right, and I will never, never consent for her to sit it."

"Then don't send her to Issamira!"

"Who else can I send?" his father asked. "What else will move them to help us?"

"I . . ." Kel bit his lip. "You won't let me go? Not for marriage, just . . . to try?"

His father sighed. "Why should they listen to you?"

"I'm the prince—"

"Of a country they've scoffed at for decades. Make no mistake, Kelken, the Issamiri are not patrons of virtue simply because their country is bigger and more powerful than ours. They won't help us fight Elgar simply because that would be kind; they'll move against him if and when they perceive a threat to themselves, and not before."

Kel frowned. "But how can they not see the threat? Elgar wants the whole continent; it's obvious."

"It is obvious to us, because denial is no longer an option. But the Issamiri can offer themselves a whole range of excuses: Elgar will never attack them because they are too powerful, because the Curse protects them from invaders, because he'll never be able to sustain an empire stretched so thin, because he fears making the same mistakes Vespasian Darrow made . . . There are plenty of arguments that sound reasonable. But none of them change the truth."

Kel's leg started to throb, and he shifted, trying to straighten it out. His father hesitated. "Are you all right?"

"Fine," Kel said. "I understand what you're saying, I just . . . Ow, I think I should stand up, I have to get it straight. . . ."

His father stood up too, and while he didn't ask if Kel needed help, he came around his desk, hovering close by. Kel reached for his crutches, then eased himself out of the chair, straightening his legs out at the knee. The change in posture did help, and he released the breath he'd been holding, letting himself sag against the crutches.

His father was still watching him closely. "Everything in order?"

Kel smiled at him. "Yes, I feel—" But then he caught sight of something over his father's shoulder, some shift in the darkness at the edge of the room, near the balcony. "Father, what's—"

His father turned before he had time to ask the question, and as he moved, the patch of darkness moved too, flinging itself at him. His father stepped back and sideways, and as the thing slammed into the desk, the sudden arrest revealed it as a person, covered up by a hooded cloak but revealing the glint of steel in one fist.

His father had no blade of his own, but that didn't stop him from lunging at the figure immediately; he was taller and heavier, and they grappled without any clear winner, the knife pinned away from their bodies. "Run, Kelken!" he yelled. "Get away from here! Get the guards!"

Kel barely thought about what he was doing; he tightened his grip on his crutches and rushed from the room.

He couldn't run as a normal boy could, but practice had made him faster with the crutches than many would have believed possible. He hurried down the hall, passing door after closed door, and he was more than halfway to the other side before he realized he was running the wrong way. He was going past the bedrooms, and he wanted the opposite end, where the stairs went down and the guards had their stations. He whirled around, drawing in a breath to call out for help, but then he heard the soft, rapid patter of footsteps, and he knew it was too late to head back the other way. Perhaps he ought to have yelled, but no one might hear, and then he'd just have alerted the footsteps in the dark. Instead he turned again—and his crutches caught on something, tilting sideways and sending him tumbling to the floor.

It seems to me that you are very brave, Prince Landon had said, before he died.

I'm not, he thought. *I never was.*

The door beside and behind him opened, and Alessa peered out at him, her surprise giving way to concern. "Kel? Are you all right?"

She stepped out into the hall, but Kel could still hear the footsteps. "No! No, Lessa, don't come out!"

"What?" she asked, but she was already turning to look back down the hall, toward the ever-closer footsteps. She sucked in a sharp breath, but she did not run; she stepped in front of him, and raised her arms.

The figure in the cloak stopped dead in front of her, recoiling at the edge of what would have been a lunge. It stood there for a moment, hunched, slightly quivering. From his position on the floor, Kel could make out the curve of a chin, a mouth opening and shutting without any sound.

"No," the figure said at last, and ran away.

Alessa crouched at his side, reaching for the crutches. "Did you hurt yourself?"

"No—" Kel started, but then he remembered. "Lessa—Lessa, help me up. We've got to get to the study. . . ."

Alessa passed him the crutches, and he shifted his weight to them after she helped him to his feet. They walked side by side down the hall, but he could not have said which one of them slowed down for the other. The study door was halfway open, and Kel pushed it wider as he entered, Alessa at his heels. He did not see his father at first, and then he did.

King Kelken was lying on his back on the floor, the blood pooling around him already lapping at the tips of his fingers. His eyes were open, and so was his throat, in a brutal gash that stretched from ear to ear.

CHAPTER SEVENTEEN

W*hat?"* Deinol said. *"Free?"*

Roger scratched the back of his neck. "Look, we wanted to tell you, but we couldn't think of a likely way to reach you. There was no sense in sending Morgan and Braddock off after you and getting the whole lot of you lost or killed at once."

The three of them had certainly gotten lost enough on their way back. Luckily, they'd eventually wandered into a village Seth remembered from the days before he'd come to Valyanrend. His memories, added to the villagers' directions, had proven enough to get them home again, but their bumbling wasted more than a day, and even when they had been on course, they went far slower than when Seren was with them.

Whatever else it might have done, the return journey certainly hadn't improved Deinol's mood. "So we did all that for nothing? Some godsforsaken Esthradian assassin made a fool of me for nothing?" He leaned against the bar, letting out a slow breath. "Do you know where they've gone? Can we fetch them back?"

"They said they'd send word once they got settled somewhere, but they haven't yet," Roger said. "It's probably not a good idea to call them back in any case—best to wait until the heat dies down."

Lucius frowned. "Heat?"

"Sheath protects its own at the best of times," Roger said, "which, I suppose, is why it helps to live among people who are mostly as crooked as you are. But Elgar's people may exert more pressure than usual to get people to talk—and they may offer rewards. There's also the fact that . . . well, Morgan and Braddock aren't actually crooked, remember? Morgan never cheated a soul that I can think of, and mercenary work isn't pretty, but it's honest. There are some who'll take that as an affront—those two always acted like they were better than the rest of Sheath, and now they'll get what's coming to them, or something like that."

"That's ridiculous," Deinol said.

"Of course it is. Doesn't mean it won't happen." He looked to Lucius. "Whatever you're going to do now, I think you should leave the boy with me. He's seen quite enough danger already."

The cut on Seth's neck had almost healed, but it still itched whenever he remembered it. "No," he said. "I want to help. I'm as much a part of this as anyone."

"Aye, I'm a part of it too, and I can't fight much better than you can," Roger said. "I'm just realistic about what I can do and what I can't."

Seth hesitated. "Well . . . fine. Maybe. It depends what Lucius and Deinol decide to do."

Lucius stroked his chin. "There's something I need to be sure of first. We certainly took enough time returning—Elgar has to have people looking for us. I want to know who, and how."

Roger nodded. "There was a whole flock of his men fluttering about Sheath, but then they suddenly dispersed—no guardsmen have bothered us for nearly two days." He shrugged. "It might be he's given up on you."

"On us, maybe, or on Morgan and Braddock, but he wanted that stone," Lucius said. "I doubt he'll just let us have it."

"Eh, well, but you *don't* have it," Roger said. "Will he care about you without it?"

"That depends on . . . well, on several things." He frowned. "Do you think there's any danger that someone will tell him we've returned?"

Roger snorted. "Now that they've stopped offering a reward? Not a chance. You and Deinol are no Braddock and Morgan, and even Morgan has friends here. Perhaps they'd sell you for coin, but not for spite."

"Good," Lucius said. "That makes things much simpler." He stirred, stretching out his arms. "Well, if I am free to walk the city as I please, I'm going to go to Iron's Den. My sword wasn't half as sharp as I would've liked on the road."

Lucius was even more fastidious about his sword than he was about his hair, but Seth and the others knew better than to remark on it. "Don't go too far today," Deinol called. "Best to be safe until we know more."

Lucius waved to show he'd heard. "Take care of these two, Roger."

"Gods, why is it always me who's got to look after things?" Roger muttered as Lucius swept out. "I'm a swindler, not a guardsman."

"Speaking of your particular talents," Deinol said, taking his seat again, "there's something I wanted to ask you."

"Without Lucius hearing, I take it."

Deinol winced. "It's not *that,* it's just . . . he would've made that face at me, that's all. He never said I couldn't ask."

"You want to know how we can find Seren," Seth said. "That's what I want to know too."

"What, the woman who stole Elgar's rock? I thought you lot said there was no way to know where she'd gone."

"There was no way for *us* to know," Deinol said. "But you've got a good head for these things, Roger—might be you'd pick up on something we missed."

"Might be," Roger said, easing the words out slowly. "What're you going to do if I do?"

Deinol shrugged. "Maybe nothing."

"Oh, I don't believe that for a moment."

"Come on, Roger, you like to know things, don't you? And I'm curious. The boy's curious. I bet Lucius is curious too, he just won't admit it."

"I don't know that *curious* is the word for it," Roger said, and sighed. "All right. I don't honestly expect I'll know anything, but tell me what you can remember."

"She said she was born in Esthrades," Deinol started.

Roger yawned. "Easy enough for a person to be born somewhere and go somewhere else—Lucius can vouch for that."

"I *know* that. I haven't finished." Deinol tilted his head, thinking. "She had at least two blades, but she only used the knife. She carried a sword, but she never drew it."

Roger shook his head. "I do know more than people think, but most of it's odd, so the things you tell me've got to be odd too. It's quirks that'll give it away—the things that don't seem to make sense."

"Oh, she had *quirks* aplenty," Deinol said, his words starting to come faster. "She could never answer a question straight, or even *smile* normally. She swore she wasn't an assassin, but she acted more like one than anyone I've ever seen."

"I don't think she was," Seth said, and Deinol looked at him sharply.

"What makes you say that?"

"I don't think she liked to lie," Seth said, "or else she wasn't very good at it. If there was a question she didn't want to answer, she just wouldn't answer it, rather than make something up. Even the bargain she struck with us—it was as if she arranged it like that so she'd have been telling the truth, in a way."

Roger slapped him on the back. "Looks like the boy's doing my job for me, eh, Deinol? Go on, Seth—what else about the way she spoke?"

Seth considered it. "I don't think she was highborn herself—from some of the things she talked about, it sounded like she didn't have much as a child— but she spoke well. Among lords, but not of them, perhaps."

Deinol frowned. "I don't know about that—she hardly spoke better than Lucius, and I doubt if he's ever gotten close enough to a lord to spit in his whole life."

"All right," Seth agreed, "but you think I'm right about the rest, Roger?"

"Aye, I do," Roger said. "I'm just not sure what I can make of it, that's all. I'm still thinking."

Deinol slumped. "Well, we knew it wasn't likely."

"Wait," Seth said, "there's one thing more." As soon as they looked at him, he felt embarrassed to mention it, but still he pressed on. "It's probably not important, but . . . she brought her own food. It was mostly hardtack, but she had this apple. . . . It was so tart, like no apple I've ever tasted. It was all I could do not to spit it out."

Roger's eyes narrowed, and he jerked to his feet, planting his hands on the table. "But it was red? As if it ought to have been sweet?"

"Yes, exactly," Seth said, taken aback. "Why, do you know it?"

Roger struck the table with his fist; the noise he caught in his teeth could have been excitement or exasperation. "Know it? I'm surprised you idiots *don't* know it. If Gran told me one story about them, she told me a hundred. Red and ripe enough to make your mouth water, but so sour at the first bite you might well imagine it's not meant to be eaten—those are blood apples, and they've baffled history's finest thieves for generations." He grinned. "Of course, any thief worth his pick might steal an apple from a tree, no matter how high the wall. But a single blood apple is worthless—it's the *orchard* that's beyond price. And how do you steal an orchard?" He sat back down again, idly tapping the table with two fingers. "I might not know where your assassin comes from, or where she's going. But if you think something's better than nothing, I can tell you where she got that apple."

The throne of Esthrades was seven feet high from foot to tip, and more than half as wide. It was built so large, it was said, so that even the fattest man might occupy it comfortably, if it was his right to sit in it.

Caius Margraine had not been a fat man, but he was six and a half feet tall himself, broad-shouldered and burly—Gravis could not have said how much he weighed when fully armored, but it had taken half a dozen men to lift him into his coffin. He had filled out the throne well, reaching both armrests with only a bit of a stretch. It had always seemed shrunken without him, somehow lacking, as if it were missing a piece.

His daughter was not a short woman, but the throne still swallowed her up, towering above the top of her head. It could have fit three of her abreast, and she did not even try to use both armrests at the same time. Even so many years after her injury, Gravis still caught her sitting with self-conscious stiffness at times, but in *that* seat she was always at her ease. When she was especially bored, she would sometimes slip sideways, slinging her legs over one of the arms and propping her elbow up on the other; today, thankfully, she only leaned slightly to one side, the better to be comfortable. But no matter her posture, she had never dozed, as the lords of old were said to have done (including her own grandfather). And despite her most ardent protestations of boredom, even Gravis would have been hard-pressed to catch her at inattention.

Even before Esthrades broke away from the empire, it had been the custom of its lord to sit in judgment six out of every seven days, with the last set aside. Primacy was given to any members of the guard or militia who brought forth criminals or other reports of lawbreaking. But then the hall was opened to the common folk, that they might air any grievance they pleased in their lord's hearing.

Lord Caius had never dozed either, though sometimes his attention had drifted during some long and mundane complaint; Gravis, he was ashamed to admit, had often done the same. But unless she had some cause to cut a complainant off entirely, the marquise merely leaned her cheek upon her hand, that faint, cold smile always playing about her lips, and listened.

The man before her was skinny and small, a wisp of a thing, his hair going gray and wrinkles lining his face. He held his hat in one hand as he gestured, his eyes wide and beseeching. It irked Gravis, as it always did, to see such earnestness answered only with insolence, but he knew better than to tell Lady Margraine that. She would only laugh.

"So he showed me a paper, milady, though he knows I can't read, and he said the paper explained everything. But I said it had always been six, never eight, and to change it all of a sudden—"

"Did he offer to read it to you?" the marquise asked.

"The paper? No, milady, not that I recall."

"I see. And did he explain himself through any other methods?"

The man looked at her helplessly. "He said when you took how much land there was, and the crops you could hope to get from one plot, and how many people usually lived on one plot, and you . . . did something to the numbers, eight per was the right number, not six. But that's not . . . That's not right. That's not how it was."

Lady Margraine tapped the fingers of her free hand against the edge of her seat. "If I had this paper, I could check the numbers myself, but as I do not . . ." Her eye fell on Gravis, and he straightened up, tensing under her gaze. "Gravis, are there two members of our esteemed guard whom you trust to pass judgment in our stead, and who can also read and do basic arithmetic?"

"There are, my lady."

She smirked at him. "I should certainly hope so. Choose whichever two you like, and send them back to Woodhearth with this gentleman. If his rentholder is, as he claims, cheating him, remove the rentholder's head. If this gentleman is lying, remove *his* head. It may also be that everyone is telling the truth, and this rentholder is simply hopeless at arithmetic and too proud to allow his tenants to correct him. If it should come to that, remove no heads, but fine the rentholder five pieces of silver for making me send my guards all that way just to help him with his sums. That will be all."

The next man was red-faced and somewhat portly, and claimed to be a messenger. "I come from Renfred Dutton," he said, "who sends the following proclamation through me, if it please milady."

The marquise sighed. "If I know Dutton, it will not, but go ahead."

The messenger cleared his throat, then launched into his prepared speech. "The Honorable Renfred Dutton, Grand Rentholder of the East, declares through me—"

Lady Margraine laughed, and he shut his mouth uncertainly. "I beg your pardon; it appears I spoke too hastily. Grand Rentholder of the East—that's marvelous. Grandiose enough to sate his hunger for a title, but *just* on the proper side of legal. How it must have taxed his poor intellect to come up with it." When the messenger still hesitated, she waved a hand at him. "Well, continue."

The man cleared his throat again. "—declares through me that all proper gentlemen of the east are resolved to have satisfaction for the great and grievous wrongs done them by House Margraine and its present marquise. As of this writing, we have compiled a list of twenty-two offenses, all carried out by her ladyship against the merchant's guild of Esthrades—"

Several people gasped, though most looked as perplexed as the messenger, who stopped and looked around him. Gravis did not gasp, but he felt himself wince, and looked to the throne.

Into the silence, Lady Margraine's voice came very clear. "Against the what?"

The messenger swallowed hard. "The . . . the merchants' guild of Esthrades, milady. That's . . . that's what I was told."

"Were you also told, sir, that any man who refers to a merchant's guild in any part of this country will have his tongue cut out?" The man paled, but she continued on, unperturbed. "No such thing exists, you see, nor ever shall so long as I sit this throne. To suggest otherwise is . . . well, it's treasonous, I suppose, though I hate to sound so melodramatic."

The messenger's hands were clenched, his knuckles white. "I . . . milady, I did not—I never—"

"Yes, I expect you did not know—the common folk either know no such thing exists or cannot imagine why they should ever wish to talk about it. Dutton and his ilk are the only ones who fussed over it, because they yearn for any influence beyond their grasp." She smiled at him. "Tell me, how much did he pay you to deliver such a grievous message? Grievous in more ways than one, I should say: his composition is atrocious."

"Milady, please, I—"

The marquise did not raise her voice or straighten her posture in the slightest; her words came as smoothly as if she were savoring them. "Are you aware I asked you a question, sir?"

"Y-yes—yes, milady—your pardons—it was t-ten. Ten silver."

Lady Margraine's eyebrows rose with supreme delicacy. "Ten silver for your tongue? That doesn't seem like a very fair price, does it?" She shrugged. "And he fancies himself part of a merchants' guild."

"Milady, I wasn't s-selling my tongue—I mean, I was, just not in such a l-literal—"

"Yes, I follow you," Lady Margraine said. "The Honorable Rentholder Dutton sent you to speak with his voice, because he is too lazy or cowardly to come himself." She tilted her head, considering—or, more likely, pretending to. "*I* am certainly not afraid of Renfred Dutton, but that pile of three moss-covered bricks he calls a castle smells like pig shit, and I am loath to leave my other duties to attend to him. But perhaps you might consent to speak with *my* voice instead?" She smiled. "You will find I am not half so miserly as our friend Dutton."

The messenger straightened up, his eyes fever-bright. "Say—milady, I'll *say* anything, anything, I—"

"And not only to him, I think," the marquise said. "I'm sure you'll agree that everyone in the area should hear my reply—that'll make it much less likely that Dutton will have you killed and claim you never arrived, after all." When the man only kept nodding, she continued, "Very well. Go back to that shack of his—what does he call it? Sweet Sow? Hogsmother?"

"S-Skyhaven, milady."

The marquise frowned. "Hmm. Not the name I would've chosen—he must be referring to the holes in the roof. Anyway, go back to the Leaky Roof and inform Grand Rentholder Dutton that he owes me one tongue, and I expect him to come here in person to render it. If he defies my ruling, either by fleeing or through armed resistance, I shall kill him, as I abhor loose ends."

It was unlikely Dutton would resist, Gravis thought—what few men he'd bought would no doubt turn on him before they'd commit suicide by treason. He might flee, but he must know he would not get far—he was hardly beloved among the populace, and no one would shelter him for fear of meeting a similar fate. He had no doubt Lady Margraine hoped Dutton would run, however; then she would get to kill him, and she did, as she said, mislike loose ends.

The messenger bowed so low his forehead nearly scraped the floor. "Everyone I meet from here to Skyhaven will hear of it, milady, I promise you."

"Oh, I don't doubt it," Lady Margraine said, but her smile was for the empty air; perhaps she was already picturing Renfred Dutton's face when he heard of his punishment. "For this you will be paid twenty silver—oh, make it twenty-five. That awful smell alone is worth five silver at least."

The next man to step up was old and stooped, stroking the few white whiskers he had left. Gravis could almost hear his bones creak as he bowed. He had come to offer a gift, a rectangular object meticulously wrapped in sackcloth. But he halted before the throne, wincing at the steps leading up to it. Gravis moved forward instead and took the parcel, nodding at the man's murmured thanks.

He could not say he was surprised when the marquise unwrapped it to reveal an old and heavy book, the once-bright colors on its cover faded to various shades of brown. The title still appeared legible, though Gravis couldn't make it out from this distance. Lady Margraine opened it carefully, turning the first several pages and scanning their contents. Gravis hardly knew why the hall was so quiet, except that she was.

Her ladyship's love of books was well known—her first few weeks on the throne had made sure of that. She had been used to keeping a book beside her while she sat in judgment and taking it up between one grievance and the next. However, before too long she became so absorbed in her reading that she failed to notice the next complainant had arrived. They all stood there helplessly for nearly twenty minutes as she read, each one afraid to interrupt her. Finally Gravis had cleared his throat about as loudly as he could, and she had looked up only reluctantly. "*What,* Gravis, can't you see that I'm—" Then she had finally noticed the man before her, the long line stretching out behind him, and blinked, more at a loss than Gravis had ever seen her. "Ah," she finally said, as if that explained everything. After that, whenever her ladyship sat in judgment, her books remained in her study.

She did not repeat that performance now; she looked up from the old man's book soon enough, shutting it gently. "This is a treasure," she said. "What is it you hope to gain in return?"

The old man released a heavy breath. "I leave no children behind me, my lady, and I have given my farm to my neighbor's second son because I am too old to work it. I do not wish to stay there and become a burden to them. So I would ask . . . I would ask for a quiet place, where I might sit in the sun without being disturbed."

The marquise shrugged. "Not what I would've chosen, but it's up to you, I suppose. I do know of a seminary two days outside of Stonespire full of scholars older than you; House Margraine ensures they live reasonably well, in return for whatever meager illuminations they can provide. You could rest easily enough there, if you like."

The man bowed again, just as creakily as before. "I should be heartily grateful, my lady."

While the marquise drew up the parchment detailing the old man's right to remain at the seminary as long as he wished, Gravis drew nearer to the book on the pretense of stretching his legs. The title became slightly clearer; he could make out *Traditions of* . . . something, a word that was probably *Before,* and *the* something *Empire.* The Elesthenian Empire, perhaps?

Lady Margraine rearranged herself in her seat in preparation for the next complainant, and Gravis straightened up again, casting his gaze down the hall. Before the man at the head of the line could speak, however, someone started yelling at the back of the hall, her voice floating up to the high vaulted ceiling and crashing back down. "I'll not be silenced!" she cried. "Do what you will, I'll not be silenced!"

The marquise turned to Gravis, her usual smile untouched. "Well, she appears to be right about that at least, doesn't she?"

Gravis knew Dent was one of the guards on the door today, so he stayed where he was, waiting to see how Dent would handle the disruption. Sure enough, he heard his friend's voice rising above the agitated woman's: "Madam, there will be no time to see to you! I told you, the line ends here for today!"

"Do you think my children can wait another day? I'll stand here all night, but the witch will hear me!"

The marquise looked at Gravis again. "She certainly sounds serious. This should be interesting." Then she raised her voice. "That won't be necessary," she called. "The witch can already hear you, much as she might wish it otherwise. Dent, bring whoever that is up here—at the very least, we'll spare everyone's ears."

Dent came reluctantly, dragging along a woman all in black. Though she seemed to have aged prematurely, as if life had ground her down, she displayed none of the weariness Gravis often saw in complainants. Dent let her stand before the marquise, but he didn't let go of her arm. "She came at the back of the line," he said.

"Yes, I know, but I didn't fancy listening to that all night, did you?" The marquise shrugged. "I suppose we could always just kill her. Would you prefer that?"

Dent bit his lip. "Not especially, my lady."

"Well, I've already demanded one tongue today, and repeating oneself is so dull. If she wants me to have her tongue out too, she's going to have to work a bit harder to earn it." She turned to the woman. "Go on, expostulate and so forth."

The woman took a deep breath. "I come here on account of my—"

Lady Margraine put a hand to her ear. "Gods' sakes, I'm sitting right in front of you. There's no need to shriek like that."

The woman scowled but controlled her voice more carefully. "I come here on account of my children, who're starving. I come to get back what you took from me."

Lady Margraine looked her over skeptically. "Well, I for one cannot imagine anything of yours I could possibly want."

"My husband's life," the woman snapped.

Lady Margraine sighed, as if disappointed. "I presume you mean that in some sort of metaphorical sense, as I don't require a husband myself and certainly have no use for yours."

"You had your use of him, all right," the woman said. "He died at the border, nearly a month ago now. He was killed in the fighting."

"And so?" the marquise asked, with so little regard that Gravis gritted his teeth.

"And so his children are starving," the woman said. "His children are starving, and he can't provide for them, because he died for Esthrades."

"Ah," Lady Margraine said. "Now I follow you. If you've come to beg, you might have said so from the beginning."

The woman's jaw clenched, but she didn't deny it. "It may seem so, to one such as you," she said.

Lady Margraine leaned backward, tapping her fingers together. "You put me in a rather difficult position," she said slowly. "I find you very annoying, but also very boring. Annoying people are usually the ones one wants to kill, but boring people are almost always not worth the killing. It would certainly not be worth the lecture I'd undoubtedly get from Gravis, who, despite occasional flashes of brilliance, remains the most boring person I have ever met. So I must confess, I'm not at all certain what to do."

"Easy for you to be hard-hearted!" the woman spat, her composure cracking. "Easy for *you,* who've never known hunger or cold or fear—who've never known love, and never will!"

Gravis winced with the rest, waiting for the punishment. But the marquise continued to smile even at that; if anything, she only looked more amused. "You see, that's just what perplexes me," she said. "I am quite ignorant when it comes to love, it's true, yet everyone tells me it knows no price—*nor gold nor jewels can match my dear one's eyes,* and so forth. Then were it not the gravest insult I could bestow to *pay* you for your loss? If you truly loved this man, would you not spit at even a mountain of diamonds?" When the woman remained silent, she tilted her head quizzically. "What, do I misunderstand something? Tell me, I entreat you. Is love not thus?"

Still the woman said nothing. She stared at the floor, her face slowly reddening.

"Oh yes, this I like much better," the marquise said. "I do believe I've found the answer." She put a hand to her throat.

The Margraines were accustomed to wear few jewels, just as they were accustomed to wear no crowns, but the marquise had worn a necklace that day, an opal set in silver. She did not bother to unclasp it, just snapped the chain and tossed it to Dent, who caught it reflexively. "You should be able to sell that for more than a little. Consider it thanks for teaching one with a heart such as mine about the true nature of love."

The woman stared at the jewel Dent handed her, blinking furiously at it as if she couldn't decide if it was real. Then she looked at Lady Margraine as if struck with the same dilemma. "I do not know whether to thank you or curse you," she finally said.

"Good," said the marquise. "That was the effect I intended."

———

Once the hours of judgment had passed and the hall was quiet again, Lady Margraine turned to Gravis. "You disagreed with me, did you?"

Gravis sighed. "About what, my lady?"

"You know, that affair with the old man. The one with the book? Your face became even more pinched than usual."

Gravis shook his head. "It was not anything especially important. I simply found his request a wise one, and you seemed not to."

"What, sun and silence?"

"Peace, I thought, was what he meant."

The marquise tossed her hair back from her face. "Then why didn't he just ask for peace? Either way, I can't think of anything more boring."

"You are fond of saying that," Gravis agreed, and bit his tongue before he could say more.

She laughed anyway, of course. "Oh well, perhaps when I am old I shall see the value in sun and silence as well. If I ever live so long, of course."

Gravis did not doubt that she would outlive them all. "Is there anything else you require of me, my lady?"

She stood, tucking the old man's book under her arm. "Not today, but we should discuss the situation at the border before too long. I think we may be in for something of a reprieve, but I want to look over the reports before I decide anything." She took a few steps, then stopped. "I'll be in my study. See that I am not disturbed by anything but the direst circumstances."

He should have just let her leave, but instead he said, "You like quiet enough in your study, my lady, do you not? And I always thought it had quite a bit of light."

She half turned to him, still infernally smiling. "There is light so that I may read, and silence to keep me from being interrupted. But books themselves are not quiet, though reading may appear to be." She tapped her chin. "If that old man merely wanted a suitable environment for *reading*, then I misjudged him. But if that were so, I doubt he would have given away his books."

After she was gone, Gravis sat on the edge of the steps, resting his elbows on his knees. The rest of the hall was empty—Dent had gone to man his post outside, and the servants wouldn't be down for another hour or so. These silences had been easy enough to bear when his lordship was alive, but now they were a torment as much as a relief.

He didn't need to wait for the morrow to know Lady Margraine meant to disagree with him about strategy once more. And he would have no arguments to fall back on; she would simply ask him who had been right the last time, and who had been wrong. That was the part that stung most of all: she had never taken part in a single battle, and yet her strategies were better than his and her father's put together. Did experience count for no more than sincerity? She possessed neither, and yet it never seemed to matter.

He might've sat there all afternoon, staring down the length of the hall without seeing it, but then he realized he was not alone. He had not heard the doors open or close, but a familiar shape moved into his line of sight. He blinked, bringing his vision back into focus, and saw Seren Almasy making her nonchalant way down the hall, brisk but somehow unhurried, just as usual.

Gravis got carefully to his feet, and Almasy gradually slowed as she neared him; for a moment he thought she was going to pass him by altogether, but she finally stopped, raising her eyes to his expectantly. "I hardly thought to see you back here," he said. "Have you actually found it?"

"I wouldn't *be* back here if I hadn't," Almasy replied. "Where is Lady Margraine?"

Gravis took a closer look at her. Her clothes bore more dust than blood, but the blood was still there. "You weren't sent to kill anyone," he said, "but I suppose you couldn't resist?"

"There aren't many valuable things that don't require you to kill someone or other to get them," Almasy said. "But you knew that. Where is her ladyship?"

"You don't really mean to tell me that—"

"I mean to tell you absolutely nothing," Almasy said. "Where is your lady?"

He snorted. "Yours as much as mine." Almasy inclined her head, accepting that, and before she could ask again, Gravis answered her. "She's in her study. She didn't wish to be disturbed, but I don't doubt *you* can go up, especially if you're carrying what you say you are."

Almasy patted her satchel, as close to smug as he'd ever seen her, and passed him, heading for the stairs.

———

Arianrod's study was built at the back of Stonespire, above and opposite the great hall. Its north wall formed a slight semicircle, set with windows that looked out onto the orchard. But Arianrod's chair faced away from the windows, because she did not want the sun to blind her as she read. Instead she either stayed bent over the desk, or else, like today, she pushed her chair out and to the side, holding the book open on her lap. She did not look up when Seren crossed the threshold, and for a few moments Seren stood there, thrown off balance by the persistent nervousness that never seemed to go away. She had to say something, but the appropriate words escaped her. "I—"

But Arianrod looked up before she could say any more, her smile as instantaneous and meaningless as ever. "And here I thought today was going to be dull," she said, letting the book fall across her knees. "Well?"

In answer, Seren slung the satchel down off her shoulder and held it out. "Here."

Arianrod stared avidly enough at the satchel, but she made no move to take it. "You really found it?"

"I told you I would," Seren said. "I don't leave things half-done."

"No, you certainly don't." She seemed to find that funny, but there were few things Arianrod *didn't* find funny, so Seren let it pass. "And you had no . . . trouble with the thing itself?"

Seren frowned. "No. It's just a stone. It's not even particularly heavy."

Arianrod smiled again. "I was fairly certain, but . . . ah well." She stuck a stray sheet of paper in the book to mark her place, then closed it and set it on her desk. "Let's see it, then."

Seren drew the stone from the satchel and offered it to Arianrod, but Arianrod shook her head, jerking her chin at the desk instead. Seren set it down, and Arianrod leaned over it, finally picking it up so she could turn it about in her hands. For several moments she just kept twisting it between her fingers, squinting at the marks that covered its surface. Then she laughed. "Well, I certainly wasn't expecting *that*."

"Does that mean you can read it?" Seren asked.

"Of course. It's Old Lantian."

"What does it say?"

"Hmm," Arianrod said. "Roughly translated, it would go something like this: 'My desires are vengeance, and many lives I having taken. Grant power me, and despair all others.'"

Seren stared at the stone in disbelief, as if she could translate it for herself with nothing more than the power of her own incredulity. *"What?"*

"Yes, I'm afraid whoever wrote this wasn't quite as firm in his linguistic studies as he was in his ambitions," Arianrod said. "I bet the *wardrenholt* itself winced at the grammar."

"The what?"

"The *wardrenholt*," Arianrod said. "That's what it is. Did I neglect to mention that?"

"And what's a . . . vordren . . ."

Arianrod tapped one finger against her lips. "How shall I explain it? A *wardrenholt* is . . . well, it's most properly a container meant to hold magic, I suppose."

Seren had heard people speak of magic before, had noted the excited little shiver that ran through them as they wondered at its possibilities. But whenever she tried to think of magic, there was only an emotionless blank—a failure of imagination, she supposed. She could not think of what she would do with it even if she possessed it. There was only that one time . . . but that couldn't possibly have been magic, could it? "But then—does that mean . . ."

"That magic exists? No, nothing so monumental as that, I'm afraid. It proves magic *existed,* but most historians worth their inkwells admit *that* much. Think of it this way: let's say that once, long ago, the fields were full of wheat, and you harvested some and made flour, and you hid the flour away somewhere. Then say a terrible blight came along, and all the wheat in the world died out. Just because someone eventually found your hidden sack of flour, that alone wouldn't prove that wheat had started growing again, would it? That's what a *wardrenholt* is like." She smiled. "The ironic thing is, when magic was plentiful, *wardrenholt* were worthless. Less than worthless, even—the refuge of the weak. How funny that a device invented by failed mages turned out to be the only way magic survived to the present day."

"Failed mages?" Seren asked.

Arianrod laughed. "Well, Seren, you're no Gravis, so I don't imagine you lend much credence to superstition. But perhaps you've heard tales of the mages of old—how they cast their spells with this special staff or that enchanted amulet or some such?"

"Something like that," Seren agreed.

"Such are the stories that stick in the minds of the common people, but any decent history of magic will tell you the truth: mages of any worth needed nothing but their own selves to cast their spells. The truly bad mages, however, lacked the power for all but the most rudimentary spells on their own, so instead they stored their magic in stones or crystals or glass over time, the way you might bleed yourself day by day until you could fill a keg with it. That's where *wardrenholt* came from, originally."

Seren shrugged. "It seems a useful enough trick to me."

"Yes, the same way setting the grass on fire seems a useful trick, until you've burnt the forest down. Magic that comes from inside yourself can never betray you—my arm will snap if I force it to attempt a task beyond its strength, but it can never take it upon itself to strangle me. If you take your magic out of yourself, if you make it separate, it warps into something different, something capricious. That's why this little rock has likely been the death of many people who tried to use it. I don't intend to make the same mistake." She stared hard at it, and finally sighed. "I so dislike bringing pageantry into this, but it's best to take no chances. Let's see . . . I suppose blood would have the best effect."

Seren did feel something at that—a shiver not of excitement but of distrust. "Blood?"

"Blood is very much like magic—in so many ways. Perhaps that's why it's so often used for these things." She rolled up her sleeve, extending the bare curve of her arm to Seren. "If you would?"

Her smile was even more pointed than usual, and she wore that look Seren had seen so often: the intent but detached appraisal of a child pulling the wings off a butterfly, not out of anything so intimate as cruelty, but merely to see what will happen. It was a test, and Seren did not know whether she'd succeeded or failed when she looked away, pressing her lips tightly together. "I have no stomach for that," she said.

Arianrod raised her eyebrows slightly, but only shrugged. "As you like. Give me a knife, then."

Seren considered a moment, then reached into her boot; that knife was small, and very sharp, and she hadn't used it yet. "You don't have to press down hard—that'll do most of the work itself."

"Seren, I know I haven't had weapons training, but I do know what a knife is."

Seren was not entirely convinced. "When was the last time you held a blade?"

Arianrod laughed. "Why, several hours ago, when I cut my cheese. It was a valiant battle, but I assure you the cheese came out the worse for it."

She sliced into the soft part of her arm, just a couple inches shy of the crook of her elbow. She did not wince, just drew the knife away and held her arm out over the stone, letting the blood drip onto it. When she was done, she bent her arm and lifted it, casting about for something to press against the cut. Seren reached into her satchel. "Here."

Arianrod took the offered cloth, pressed it to her arm for several moments, then turned her gaze back to the stone. "I'm sure my grasp of Old Lantian is much better than our mysterious friend's, but I do want to make sure I get this right. Something short and to the point is best—you leave any kind of loophole in the language, and the damn thing'll find a way to fuck you with it."

She pondered a few moments more, then finally pressed her fingers into the blood, tracing something against the surface of the stone. She could not possibly have used enough to write whole sentences in it, but that didn't seem to bother her; she just kept tracing letters until she was through. Finally she set the stone down and nodded once, turning slightly to press the cloth against her arm again. "Good. We'd best get this done now, while . . . well, while it's on my mind. Fetch a shovel, and meet me in the orchard."

Seren nodded, but when Arianrod made to leave the room, she did not take the stone. Seren looked over at it, confused. "Won't you be bringing that?"

Arianrod stared at it for a moment, then turned away. "I think it would be best if . . . well, you've carried it this long, haven't you?"

After she had gone, Seren walked over to the desk and examined the stone. The blood had already dried, but the inscriptions that covered its surface were just as impenetrable as before; she couldn't even tell if they had changed.

The Margraines were wont to keep guards patrolling the orchard, but when she arrived, she found that Arianrod was alone, staring out distractedly at the trees. The sun was starting to set, bronzing the edge of a wisp of cloud. "Any spot will serve," Arianrod said. "We don't need a large hole, just one big enough to bury it in."

Seren raised her eyebrows, but she began to dig. She was no master with a shovel, but thankfully the stone was not large. When she finally finished, leaning on the shovel with a grateful sigh, Arianrod laughed. "Remind me to assign future burial duties to someone else."

Actually burying the stone took less time, and the sun had barely moved when Seren patted the last heap of dirt back into place. Arianrod knelt then, pressing her palm flat against the dirt, as if she wanted to make sure the stone wouldn't come bursting out of the ground again. She nodded, satisfied, and got back to her feet. "Well," she said, on the heels of a surprisingly shaky breath, "that's that."

Seren frowned. "We're . . . hiding it in the orchard? That doesn't seem unsafe to you? I know you normally have men on patrol, but—"

Arianrod smiled. "Is it theft you're worried about? You're free to try to steal it if you like—I'd even let you keep it. But I for one am going back inside. You can play around out here until you're satisfied, but then come back to the study; I'm not quite finished with you yet."

Seren didn't relish picking up the shovel again, but her curiosity got the better of her; she disturbed the dirt once more, wondering if Arianrod had really meant for her to keep it. But it seemed to her it was taking a lot longer to hit the stone than it should have, and finally she knelt by the hole, sticking her arm in to see how deep it was. There was no way they'd buried it even that far down, yet she was sure this was the spot. She sifted about in the dirt, looking for fragments of stone, but there wasn't even any dust.

Once again, Seren filled in the hole she had dug and got to her feet. She brushed off her hands and slung the shovel over one shoulder. And then she walked over to the trees, plucking a single blood apple from the nearest branch before heading back inside.

CHAPTER EIGHTEEN

They say that before Stonespire was the seat of the Margraines—before it was a city at all, or even a castle—there was only the spire and the orchard, high up on that hill. They say that was why the very first Daven Margraine chose that spot, because he'd learned the apples' secret." Roger nodded, surpassingly pleased with himself. "And thieves have been plotting to make their fortunes off those same apples nearly ever since."

Lucius frowned. "What, so she was really the marquise of Esthrades? That can't be right."

"I doubt it is," Roger said, and laughed. "If Arianrod Margraine were really wandering about stabbing people instead of sitting on her throne, I expect we'd have heard about it."

"But if the apples only grow in the orchard at Stonespire Hall, and they can't be stolen, and the Margraines won't sell them, how did Seren obtain one?"

"I didn't at all say they *couldn't* be stolen," Roger said. "I told these two already: the trouble isn't stealing one, it's that one alone isn't worth anything. Nor two, nor five, nor even ten, and I'm certain no one's ever stolen so many as that at once."

"Why aren't they worth anything?"

Deinol answered that one, waving his hand absently. "Because the value's in the orchard, or something like that."

Lucius's frown didn't soften. "So why not just take the seeds from the apples you stole and plant your own orchard?"

"Wouldn't work," Seth said. "If you want the same kind of apples you started with, you've got to graft the branches onto rootstock. Though I suppose a thief might steal a branch as well, if he was clever enough."

"Even I can't say whether *that* ever happened," Roger admitted. "All I know is that the second Daven used to hand out branches for grafting to his very particular friends—for a while, at least. But what do you think happened to all those grafts?"

"They wouldn't grow," Seth guessed, because he couldn't see where else this might be going.

Roger beamed. "Right you are. No one, in fact, has been able to get blood apples to grow anywhere other than that orchard." He scratched his neck. "Not that many people have been able to try—it isn't as if the Margraines are eager to share them."

"Yes, but *why*?" Lucius asked. "Are they some delicacy?"

"You really don't know?" Roger asked, but he was grinning—he knew they didn't. "Gran told me any thief worth his pick had heard of them."

Deinol struck the bar with his open palm. "Yes, well, I may be a thief of sorts, but not every thief happens to share your family's peculiar taste in stories, all right? Stop preening, and just tell us about the bloody apples."

Roger pursed his lips, but he obliged. "The Margraines have been eating them in everything since the orchard first came to be," he said. "But they never share them. Whenever the lords and ladies of Stonespire dine alone, it's apple-stuffed pork, mutton in applesauce, apple pie, apple pudding, apples dipped in molasses or dusted with sugar. But whenever they have company, apples are never served—they can't eat normal ones, Gran said, because they don't like the taste, and they don't want to waste blood apples on guests. And *because* they eat blood apples . . . you can't poison them."

Deinol rolled his eyes. "Oh, come on, Roger."

"*You* come on, it's the truth! Or it's probably the truth, anyway. It's just . . . well, no one knows precisely how or why the apples have that effect, and the Margraines aren't telling. But folks have been trying to poison the rulers of Stonespire for generations, and if you check the history books, you'll not find one recorded success. The sixth Daven lived through three attempts—the last one was the stranger's red, the deadliest poison this side of the eastern sea. They say he shat blood for three days afterward, but three drops of the stuff should've turned his insides to paste. And Gran told me a story about old Berius Margraine, who was so fat, even the throne of Esthrades squeezed him. One of his rentholders feasted him for his birthday, and served an entire suckling pig stuffed with as much evenflower as he could fit. Berius had the place of honor, so of course the pig went to him first. The rentholder watched his supposed victim eat the ribs, the belly, the rump, and two legs, after which he merely retired for an after-supper nap and woke up in time to arrest his host for treason."

"And your gran told you all this," Deinol said. "Did she also tell you about how Elgar has two cocks and I'm the son of an emperor?"

"Laugh if you like, but Gran knew what she was about. The fact is, the Margraines are unpoisonable, and those blood apples are the reason. That's why they'll sell every trinket in Stonespire Hall before they let those apples go: they don't want anyone to get the chance to study them, to figure out if maybe there's some poison they can't guard against."

"Wait a moment," Seth said. "I had some of that apple myself. Does that mean I—"

Roger laughed. "I'm afraid not, boy. I told you, didn't I? One is worthless. You have to keep eating them over time—I couldn't tell you precisely how long, but the Margraines start their whelps on 'em as soon as they can take solid food."

Seth frowned. "So if Seren had one . . ."

"Then it's likely she had the promise of more, yes—especially if she let *you* eat part of the one she had."

Lucius held up a hand. "I don't care if she has one apple or a hundred—*how* does she have them? She's not a Margraine herself, and if you're right, there's no point to stealing them."

"It's got to be the stone," Deinol said. "Elgar wanted it, and it seems like the marquise did too. They must know something about it we don't, and that makes it worth any price."

Lucius's brow furrowed at that. "So blood apples were Seren's price? That doesn't make sense."

"Why not?"

"First of all, Roger just said the Margraines wouldn't—"

"Maybe for this they would. Maybe it's just that important."

Lucius shook his head. "If those apples really do protect you against poison, then I'm sure that's useful. But if you can name your price, why ask for that in particular? It makes sense to value them if you're a Margraine; people try to assassinate rulers all the time. But whom did Seren think was going to poison her? She didn't seem overly paranoid to me, and why else would you be willing to do so much for those apples?"

One day, if you're lucky, you'll kill for something too, Seren had told him. But she had shared the apple with him as if it was just food to her. Lucius was right; it didn't make sense. Surely she wouldn't have been so passionate about an antitoxin, no matter how effective it was?

"Maybe we're thinking about this the wrong way," Seth said at last. "Maybe the apples weren't the reward at all."

Lucius shook his head again. "I doubt Lady Margraine would just give them away."

"Maybe she—"

"Oh, what does it matter?" Deinol asked. "No matter how she got them, no matter why she wants them, she has to be at Stonespire, doesn't she? That's where we'll find her."

"That's where we *would* find her," Lucius said quietly, "if we were going in search of her. But we aren't."

"Well, why the hell not?"

"Because we have no reason to," Lucius said.

"No reason? Lucius, she stole from us. She *betrayed* us. What more reason do we need?"

"Even if she did, we're no worse off for it, are we? So your pride took a blow—all of ours did. We'll get over it."

"Aye, we could do that," Deinol said. "Or we could get even."

"Oh, and how do we do that? By marching up to Stonespire and ordering the marquise to give us Seren and the stone back?"

"You were willing to take on Elgar and his guards, weren't you?"

"In order to free Morgan and Braddock, not just for the hell of it!" Lucius snapped. "But they're free now, so who cares about the rest of it? In a way, Seren almost did us a favor. I didn't relish handing Elgar anything of value, no matter how slight."

Deinol sighed, staring at his boots. "Is giving it to Arianrod Margraine really any better?"

"Yes," Lucius said, without hesitation. "Arianrod Margraine didn't destroy Aurnis. Arianrod Margraine didn't kill Prince Ryo and his *kaishinrian*. That might not matter to you, but it matters to me. If not for that man, I . . ." He clenched his fist around empty air. "The only gift I should be giving him is a sword in the belly."

Deinol's scoff came out half choked, almost guilty, but Seth knew his pride wouldn't let him back down. "If you believe that so strongly, what are you doing here? Why don't you join the Issamiri army, or start your very own rebellion in the streets of Sheath?"

Lucius laughed without any mirth. "Because I'm a coward, that's why. But a coward can still have convictions."

Deinol blinked at him, stunned. "What in the gods' name do you mean? *Roger's* a coward. You—why, if any other man called you that, I'd knock him flat."

Lucius smiled. "I know you would." But then he dropped his eyes, crossing the room to rest his hand against the doorframe. "I'm going round to Halvard's for a bit," he said at last. "I won't be long."

He'd barely left before Deinol started to fidget, reaching for the hilt of his sword. "I'd, ah . . . I'd best be gone as well. Errands. Mind the shop, you two."

After he had gone, Roger leaned heavily on the bar. "That's hardly what I like to see from those two, especially now."

"No," Seth agreed. And it wasn't over yet, he knew. Neither one of them was prepared to concede the point, but Deinol didn't want to go without Lucius, and Lucius clearly didn't relish the thought of letting him go alone. "We'll have to wait for them to settle it, I guess."

Roger propped his chin on his hand. "Well, maybe not. What do *you* think?"

Seth started. "Me? I . . . Well, what do *you* think?"

Roger laughed. "I think I'd dearly love to see Stonespire Hall one day, but not as an unwelcome interloper, much less a prisoner. And my, ah, expertise only works in this city, I'm afraid, so I'd be no help in *those* prisons." He grinned at Seth from over his clasped hands. "All right, now it's your turn."

Seth bit his lip. What *did* he think? Lucius was right, of course; he always was. The only thing they'd find at Stonespire was trouble, in one shape or another. And they didn't *need* to go—all they had to do was lie low and get word to Morgan and Braddock once the whole affair had blown over, and they could go on just as before. He'd have everything he loved back again, just as he had wanted. Deinol was stubborn, but with Seth, Lucius, and Roger all entreating him together, surely they could get him to see reason. He was angry, but he'd been angry before. It would pass.

He remembered Seren's knife at his throat, the feel of his blood against her fingers. And he remembered before that: *What happens to weak people?* he had asked.

They die, more often than not, Seren had said. *But even when they live, their will is not their own.*

"I don't know, Roger," he said. "Does it even matter what I think?"

Roger spread his hands along the bar. "You were there, boy. You were part of it, just as much as they were. If anyone else's opinion matters now, yours does. So you'd best figure out what it is, and quickly."

In the days of old, the rulers of Reglay had been buried beneath Mist's Edge, in a maze of crypts hollowed out under the stone. But it had been generations since Mist's Edge had belonged to the Rayls, and the second Kelken, whose father had died losing the castle, had decreed that he would be buried in the tomb at Mist's Edge or not at all. And according to his tradition, all the succeeding kings and queens of Reglay had burned.

His father's ashes were scattered from the tallest tower of Second Hearth, in the hope that the wind might carry them to Mist's Edge. It fell to Kel to do the scattering, standing beside the great urn with Eirnwin and Lessa, an honor guard around them. He dipped his hand in again and again, trying not to think of how this dust had once been his father. It took longer than he would have thought to scatter it all, and by the time he was done, his legs were stiff and sore from so much standing in the same position, leaning on one crutch so he could keep the other arm free. Eirnwin helped him soak his legs, and dressed them in snow's down to ease the swelling. He demanded that Kel stay abed until his legs were back to normal—or what passed for normal with them, anyway—but Kel knew their plans could not wait. So Eirnwin and Lessa pulled up chairs beside his bed, and Kel propped himself up against his pillows, his crutches resting nearby.

"My lord," Eirnwin started, bowing his head, and then abruptly stopped. "No—Your Grace. You must know, first of all, that if you wish to name a new advisor, there are—"

"Don't be silly, Eirnwin," Kel said. "Come on, we don't have time for formalities."

Eirnwin's eyes remained grave, but the set of his mouth eased just slightly. "If that is so, Your Grace, my first suggestion regards your coronation. It must be held sooner rather than later—immediately, dare I say it, would be best."

"It will be done as soon as I can manage it, given the circumstances," Kel said. "I'll have more to say about that soon. Right now I wish to speak of my— of my lord father's plans, and of what mine shall be."

Eirnwin nodded. "Of course." Lessa said nothing, but looked at him expectantly.

Kel took a deep breath. "Before my father—before—" He bit his lip, and started again. "You all know what he wanted. But I told him there was another way. I could go to Issamira in Lessa's stead, and offer Princess Adora my hand. Lessa could still marry Hephestion, but the marriage would take place here, not in Issamira. And if the princess agreed, I would stay in Issamira with her."

Alessa started up in her chair. "But, Kel, that would mean—"

"Giving up the throne, yes," Eirnwin said, his face expressionless. "But I expect His Grace realized that." He hesitated, then spoke more slowly, choosing his words with care. "While I understand your father's concerns, Your Grace, it is not my place to ensure that the succession follows any particular bloodline. I am merely here to advise the current king as best I can, and in that capacity . . . your plan might work as well as your father's. Perhaps better. The alliance with Issamira would be much more secure—you'd be offering Hephestion a kingdom, not a bastard, and removing a potential thorn from Adora's side. It would not be ideal to leave Reglay without a sitting king while you go to negotiate, but on the other hand, you should be able to complete the journey with no problems, while for Alessa the risks would be . . . considerably greater. And recent events have proven that Second Hearth is not so safe a place for its king as we might wish."

Kel thought back to the assassin, to his thin fingers and trembling mouth. Kel suspected he was a man, from what he'd heard of the assassin's voice and seen of his face when he'd looked up at him from the floor. But other than that, neither Kel nor Lessa could remember anything of note, and if his father had seen the man's face, that knowledge had died with him. As much as it infuriated Kel to admit it, he could think of no way to find his father's killer.

He remembered how the man had stopped so suddenly, the way he had shuddered as if he was afraid. But why had he been afraid of Lessa? Why had he run when he saw her?

His father had told him to run, and he had. But he had told Lessa to run, and she'd stood her ground. He had run, and she had stayed. And now his father was dead, and he and Lessa were alive.

"Your Grace?" Eirnwin asked mildly.

Kel started forward, wincing as his legs shifted. "Yes. Sorry, I'm . . . surprised you like my plan so much."

"It is not a matter of liking it or not, Your Grace. It is simply a matter of what might work, and what might not." He clasped his hands. "Do you mean to tell us you have decided to pursue this course?"

Kel hesitated, but he already knew what his answer would be. "I . . . No, I can't."

Eirnwin frowned. "You can't?"

"You know what happened," Kel said, looking at Eirnwin and Lessa both. "My father . . . died for me. He died to save me. And before he died, he told me what he wanted. The throne . . . it's barely real to me, but what my father wanted most was to see me sit it after him. Even if my plan could work, I can't throw away everything he wanted, not after what he did for me. I just . . . I can't."

Eirnwin worked his tongue against his teeth. "If you can't, Your Grace, then you can't," he said at last. "Does that mean you will be doing as your father wished after all?"

"No," Kel said. "I owe him a debt, but the throne is mine now. Lessa stays with me."

"But then—"

"We won't be sending anyone to Issamira," Kel finished. "That's right."

His sister finally spoke up. "Kel, if we don't get the Issamiri to help us—"

"We may still get them to help us," Kel said. "But I won't send anyone there just now. There's something else I need to do first." He paused, gathered himself, kept going. "You're the one who said Second Hearth isn't safe, Eirnwin, and you're the one who said I need to hold my coronation. You're right, and that's why . . . that's why I've decided to hold my coronation at Mist's Edge."

For a moment they simply stared at him, and then Eirnwin sucked in an audible breath. "And how do you propose to do that, Your Grace?"

"I propose to walk to Mist's Edge and put the crown on my head," Kel replied. "Elgar hasn't kept soldiers there for more than two years; it's deserted. My father could have taken it back at any time, but he was afraid of giving Elgar cause to attack us."

"And does that fear not still stand?" Eirnwin asked.

"Elgar's going to attack us no matter what we do," Kel said. "He wants Reglay, so he'll find some reason to try to take it. Mist's Edge is *our* castle—who can fault us for taking back what's ours? I should think they'd be impressed. They'll think we have some fight left in us, and we do."

"So you mean to make Mist's Edge the home of the king, as it was of old?"

"That's right," Kel said. "That assassin got in so easily. . . . We can't ignore the possibility that someone was helping him. Even if they weren't, if he could get into Second Hearth once, he can again. There's a good chance Mist's Edge will be safer." He swallowed. "There's another thing. I'd like to invite the other rulers to my coronation."

Eirnwin nearly choked. "I beg your pardon?"

"Imperator Elgar," Kel said, "Lady Margraine, and . . . whoever wants to come from Issamira. They shall all be allowed to pass through Reglay to Mist's Edge unharmed, as long as they don't try to bring an army. And as long as they are at Mist's Edge, they shall be our guests."

Eirnwin shook his head. "Your Grace, they will never come. They would be fools to come."

"They wouldn't be," Kel said, "because I don't intend to kill them, and I probably couldn't if I wanted to. But I guess you mean they can't be expected to know that." He saw Eirnwin nod, but continued before he could speak. "It's a risk for them, I know—it's a risk for *us*. But I think they'll come anyway. I think we can make it worth their while to come."

"Well, I'd certainly like to know how," Eirnwin said.

Kel smiled. "Lady Margraine will be the easiest, I think. They say . . . well, they say many things about her, but I meant that I've heard what she'll pay for even *one* rare book. Mist's Edge holds the library of kings, easily the equal of what she inherited at Stonespire. If I offer her free rein of it, I think she'll agree to come. And if she does, Elgar will have to come too."

"He won't be able to bear the thought of his two foes in conversation with each other," Eirnwin agreed, a thoughtful cast to his expression. "What might you be plotting behind his back? What if you are forming an alliance? And if the Issamiri come as well . . ."

"The three of us joining together—that's got to be what he fears most of all," Kel finished. "He's got to come, if only to disrupt our plans."

"And if he decides to disrupt them by killing you?"

"He won't," Kel said. "If he's afraid to even set foot in Mist's Edge because of the ghosts, if he won't even keep *soldiers* there, how would he dare try to murder me there, in the home of my ancestors, while he's a guest under my roof? He'd piss himself at the thought."

"Are you not afraid of the ghosts?" Eirnwin asked, but he did not seem to be joking.

"I don't believe in ghosts," Kel said. "And even if they do exist, why should the ghosts of my ancestors hurt *me*? I'm trying to set their legacy to rights."

Eirnwin stroked his chin, but then he sighed. "Even so, Your Grace, the Issamiri will not come."

"Why not?"

"Well, they are safe enough on the other side of the Curse, for one thing, and I doubt they will want to venture beyond it. But even if they did, neither Adora nor Hephestion can afford to leave Issamira just now, not until the succession is decided. If one of them is crowned before your coronation, perhaps one or the other of them will indeed attend. But until they are, do not expect to see them."

Kel considered it, trying to ignore the sinking feeling in his stomach. He had been so sure that he'd thought of everything. "Even without Issamira," he said at last, "I will still have Mist's Edge. I will still intimidate him, before he knows what to make of me. I will be strong the way a cripple knows how to be strong; I will show him that I am more determined than he is. It seems to me that makes it worth the doing."

Eirnwin inclined his head. "To me as well, Your Grace."

"You mean you agree?"

Eirnwin smiled. "It is a risky plan, certainly, but as I think your lord father said to both of us, there is nothing we can do now that does not involve risk. I would caution that we cannot hope to survive long without help of some sort, but the prospect of retaking Mist's Edge is an enticing one."

"I'm glad you think so," Kel said. "I'm going to need your help to get there."

———

Her ladyship sent Almasy out again early; she was gone before Gravis had finished his breakfast, and the knowledge of her leaving made the food churn in his stomach. It was never good news that sent Almasy from Stonespire, and he did not doubt that soon men would die.

Though the day's judgment had concluded, he was surprised to find her ladyship seated once more on the throne, propping a book open upon her lap as she read. "Don't be alarmed, Gravis," she said, looking up when she felt his eyes on her. "I just desired a change of scenery, that's all."

He watched her carefully. She seemed a bit paler than usual, and somewhat drawn about the eyes, but if anything, her mood was better, not worse. He couldn't say that was unexpected. "I never thought Almasy would return," he said. "I was so sure that damned deserter was lying."

She chuckled lightly, keeping her eyes on her book. "And yet you believe in curses and demons and all sorts of superstitious rubbish. I'll tell you what your problem is, Gravis: too much listening, not enough reading. Not every story your mother told you was true, but there are many strange things out there she never mentioned."

Gravis snorted. "I don't doubt it. And I don't doubt you'll find a way to put that thing to some nefarious use, whatever it truly is."

She smiled. "Are you afraid of that, Gravis?"

"Should I be?"

"As it happens, no," she said, leaning back against the throne. "As much as I love putting things to nefarious uses, this time it simply wasn't worth the trouble."

Gravis frowned. "What does that mean?"

"Well, if your demons existed, I'd say it means I won't be turning into one at present, but as they don't . . ." She shrugged. "I suppose it means you can stop looking at me as if I'm about to burst into flames."

"Do those books of yours tell you demons don't exist?" Gravis asked.

She tapped the spine of the one she held, still smiling. "They do, in fact, though common sense could serve as well."

"Just because a man decides to write a book about something *he's* never seen doesn't mean it isn't real."

For a moment he thought he saw a flicker of annoyance in her eyes. "Actually, Gravis, sometimes people who write books prefer to study the subjects of their inquiries, rather than simply trading stories around campfires. I could offer you several works of exquisite scholarship disproving the existence of demons, ghosts, spirit transference, instantaneous transportation, resurrection, divination, and the goat-pig hybrids my farmers love to gossip about, but I'm sure you'd fall asleep just from the unaccustomed exertion of opening the front cover."

Lord Caius had disdained books all his life, and never willingly set foot in Stonespire's library. After his father's death, he would've been perfectly willing to leave its volumes to gather dust, but his daughter had found her way there before they'd even thought her old enough to need a tutor. After that they'd see her dragging a tome or three after her no matter where she went. When she was a child, she would read at the dinner table, stealing a bite of food here and there if she remembered. Her father always watched her with what might have been jealousy, though of whom or what Gravis couldn't have said, and the books soon became the target of his irritation. "Put that down while we're at table, Arianrod," Gravis remembered him saying once, his voice carrying effortlessly throughout the high spare room.

His daughter barely looked up, a sliver of pale blue peeking over the book's spine and then back down again. "Don't worry, Father, the big scary words aren't going to hurt you."

Lord Caius learned very quickly not to try any verbal sparring with her—she could out-insult him before she was ten, and his favorite rebuttals were littered with words that were not suitable to use before a young lady, however trying she might be. Instead he resorted to what *he* was best at, and thumped the table with one enormous fist, sending a tremor down its length. His daughter gave a startled yelp as she lost her grip on her book; a hasty catch just barely saved it from tumbling into her soup. "You made me lose my *place*," she complained, all prim disapproval, but she did not touch the book again until supper had concluded.

When she grew older, Lady Margraine no longer took her meals with her father, and alone in her chambers she was free to read as much as she desired, waving away trays of cold porridge and half-eaten roasts. And though he'd always loved to eat, Lord Caius had picked at his food, listlessly muttering to his servants that he was not hungry this evening.

"I don't doubt that some books tell the truth," Gravis said at last. "And some lie, just as men do. So just as with men, I believe the ones I trust and doubt the rest. I put most faith in what I've seen with my own eyes." *And that's enough to know you aren't like ordinary people,* he didn't add.

Yet she seemed to guess at his thoughts. "You know, it's funny, but when Esthrades first rebelled from the empire, they told my ancestors the people would never fear us, because we claimed no crowns, and no title grander than we'd had before. Back then, that was what passed for common wisdom. Men had to *see* power, we were told, to believe in it."

If only that were true, Gravis thought, wondering what she meant by it. "I should've thought that way myself," he admitted.

"And you would've been as wrong as the rest. It doesn't matter if you sit on a throne, a chair, or a cold stone floor, so long as you can rule from there." She propped her chin on her hand. "Men fear the splendor of the crown, they said; men fear the grandeur of throne and title. My ancestors knew this was nonsense. Men fear what they are taught to fear, Gravis, and if they do not fear you, that only means that you have failed to make the lesson stick. The people of Esthrades have never ceased to understand what the title of marquis means, no matter how many hundreds of years have passed. And look at yourself—you were raised on superstition, and so it dogs your steps. You see witches in the walls, and simply because you and I have our disagreements, you cling to the conviction that I am some demon from your mother's tales. If I truly *were,* you'd probably fear me less."

"Pity there are no demons, then," Gravis said.

"There are no demons, Gravis, because if there were, we should have outstripped them ages ago. Why look to shadows for the violence and greed you can find all around you? I should think that, of all people, the captain of the guard would have learned this by now."

Gravis shook his head. "Men are good by nature, else they would not submit themselves to justice. It is only that it is too easy to turn them from what they are."

She laughed. "Do you truly believe that? I would never have expected it of you. Does that mean you think *I* had some original goodness in me? Where would it have gone, I wonder?"

Gravis stared hard at her, then shook his head again, more slowly. "I don't think there was ever any good in you, my lady. That is why you are something out of the common way of mortals."

She leaned back in her seat again, smiling faintly. "Now how shall I take that? I don't know whether to be complimented or simply unimpressed." But then her gaze turned almost serious. "You are wrong, though, Gravis, to think of me so. I may be out of the common way, as you put it, and glad I am to be so, but I'm as mortal as you are. I would not have you forget that." She laughed again. "My enemies, to be sure, are free to forget it—in fact, I hope they will. But as it is your job to defend me, I would prefer for you to remember I may one day need defending."

Gravis bowed. It was stiff, but it was a bow. "I have not forgotten my oath," he said.

Lady Margraine had already turned back to her book. "No, if nothing else, I am certain you will remember *that.*" She turned a page. "Tell me, do you still think my father deserved such an oath?"

The question brought back far too many memories: Lord Caius's bloodstained hands, the silence that had fallen over Stonespire, and the screams. But if she thought the remembrance would make him uncertain, she was mistaken. "I do."

She smirked, stroking the following page but not quite turning it yet. "Yet now your oath brings no benefit to him, and only binds you to serve me. It hardly seems fair."

Gravis kept himself very straight, looking down the length of the hall toward the doors. "It isn't," he said.

"What are you doing?" Seth yawned, rubbing the sleep from his eyes. "Nobody's here but me. Even Roger's left."

"I know," Deinol said, propping himself up against the doorframe. "It's you I want. I'm leaving a message."

"A message?" Seth asked, his stomach dropping out sharply. "Are you going somewhere?"

"Aye," Deinol said, with a smirk that didn't quite reach his eyes. "To Esthrades. That's what you can tell them, if they ask."

If they ask. As if they would all simply fail to notice that Deinol wasn't where he'd been every day since they'd ever known him. "You're leaving *now*?"

"I've waited long enough, I think." He was trying to sound nonchalant, but Seth could see how stiff his posture was, how he clenched and unclenched his hands. "I don't want to wait any longer."

"Not even long enough to tell Lucius yourself?" Seth leaned against the nearest table. "It'll hurt him, you know."

Deinol shook his head, not saying no, just giving vent to his frustration. "I gave him enough chances to come around, didn't I? He knew what I wanted; I never made a secret of it."

He hadn't, and neither had Lucius. It seemed that Seth was the only uncertain one. "Do you have a plan?"

"I'll make it up as I go."

"That means no," Seth said, and couldn't help a smile.

"I've tried to forget about it." Deinol finally curled one hand into a proper fist, bringing it up to his chin. "It's not that I care so much about the stone's value—Lucius is right about *that*. If we wanted riches, there are plenty of other ways to debase ourselves getting them. I don't want to do what Elgar wants, or what he or Oswhent or anyone else expects. But I *do* want to get even with her. We helped her—*you* helped her, more than any of us. So I want to look her in the face and see what she has to say for herself."

Seth could go get Lucius. Deinol wouldn't run away, if he did that. He could convince Deinol just to talk to Lucius one last time, and then Lucius would convince him not to go. That was how it worked: Deinol was always saying he was going to do one crazy thing or another, and Lucius was always talking him out of it.

"I want to go with you," he said.

Deinol's eyebrows rose a little, but he wasn't really surprised; Seth wondered if that was part of the reason he had come. "I won't lie, I'd be glad of the company," he said. "But it's going to be dangerous, much more dangerous than before, and we're going to be doing it without Lucius. Are you sure you're all right with that?"

Are you sure you are? Seth thought. But he smiled. "If it's going to be that dangerous, then I'd *better* come along. Someone's got to make sure you don't do anything stupid." He shook his head. "Anything stupider than this, anyway."

CHAPTER NINETEEN

Elgar's fingers curled into the parchment, but he didn't crumple it; he knew, no doubt, that he'd just have to smooth it out when he inevitably went over it again. "You're sure this is right? The old king is dead, but the boy lives?"

Rumors had been pouring into Valyanrend for days, and it had been nearly impossible to separate truth from falsehood. Varalen had heard all manner of stories: both Kelkens were dead, or only the father, or only the son; father and son were alive, but the old queen's bastard daughter had been slain; the assassin had been captured, or he had escaped; he had been young or old or fat or thin or male or female; he had appeared in a puff of black smoke and vanished the same way; he had grown wings and flown; he had scaled the walls with hands like claws. But over time he had managed to discard the wildest tales, marking which details were repeated again and again in each day's gossip. "As far as I can ascertain, my lord, that information is accurate. The boy Kelken is the new king of Reglay."

"Lot of good it'll do him," Wyles muttered, snickering, but Elgar appeared not to hear him.

He stood up, bracing his weight against the table with both hands. "He is young enough, but still . . . this is not how I would have had it. His father was mature but predictable; we knew all his tricks, had counters for all his strategies. This boy is an unknown. He could be a genius or an idiot, and we won't know until he makes his move." He glanced at Varalen. "Yet your report claims he has hardly moved at all. He has made no announcements, no changes. He burned his father, the way they do, and then he retreated into Second Hearth. He has not even held a coronation ceremony."

"Considering what happened to his father, perhaps he is afraid."

"Perhaps," Elgar said, but he did not look convinced. He stroked the parchment. "They say he is a cripple."

Varalen raised his eyebrows. "They . . . do say that, my lord, yes."

Elgar shook his head. "And yet the father fell to the assassin's blade while the son lived? How bizarre. Unless it was pity, I suppose."

"I doubt that," Varalen said carefully.

Wyles snorted. "A pitying assassin's in the wrong business." Had they actually just agreed on something?

Elgar finally released the parchment, sinking back into his chair. "It does not please me, but what's done is done. If I could resurrect old foes, Caius Margraine would still be sitting the Esthradian throne, and I'd have many fewer headaches."

So would I, Varalen thought. Out loud, he said, "What does this mean for your plans for Reglay?"

"What are you getting at?"

Varalen took a deep breath, choosing his words as painstakingly as he could. It would make sense for a man to be willing to share his plans with his strategist, but Elgar was absurdly secretive about more than just his meetings with Shinsei; sometimes he remained tight-lipped even about things that had already happened. Whether or not he had, as Varalen suspected, been the one to hire the assassin who killed King Kelken and failed to kill his son, Elgar might still take offense to Varalen's suggesting so. "If . . . if both Kelkens had died, the throne of Reglay would have no clear successor, and it would be . . . a near-perfect opportunity for us. But since that does not seem to be what happened . . . how do you wish me to proceed?"

"How indeed." Elgar sighed. "If you still insist that Arianrod Margraine will stay put if we move into Reglay, I see no reason why we shouldn't move. I will give the order as soon as Shinsei returns."

But that was the question: When *would* Shinsei return? Varalen had known him to disappear on Elgar's orders once or twice before, but not often, and certainly not for this long. Where on earth had he gone, and what was he doing? Varalen didn't imagine that someone as obviously troubled as Shinsei could avoid notice for long, even among people who did not know him by sight, and yet the common folk spread no rumors of him—most did not even seem to know Shinsei had left the capital. Had Elgar sent him very far away? Why would he do that, with such an important battle looming on the horizon?

"Do you . . . have an inkling of when that might be, my lord?" he asked.

"He will return when he returns," Elgar snapped, his composure suddenly gone. "You will be informed of it *then,* and not before. Now, shall we move on to the subject of your newest catastrophe?" He paused, seeming to remember just then that Wyles was still there. "You're dismissed, Nathaniel."

The captain hesitated, and for a moment Varalen thought he was hoping to hear more about the failure Elgar had alluded to, no doubt so he could gloat. But instead he said, "Your Eminence, I thought you intended to discuss—"

"I do intend to discuss it," Elgar said quickly, "but not at this time. You're *dismissed*."

Wyles stared at him another moment, then shrugged easily and bowed, showing himself out with his usual calm. Varalen himself was hardly calm about it, however. What had the two of them been plotting, that Elgar clearly wasn't prepared for Varalen to know about?

He started out of his reverie when he felt Elgar's eyes on him. "Now, where were we? Your various inadequacies, I believe?"

Varalen winced, but he was not so frightened as he might have been. No matter what Elgar said, his failure with the stone was hardly *new*, and had it been enough to damn him, he didn't doubt both he and Ryam would already be dead. Since they were not, Elgar must have decided he was worth keeping around, whether or not he was prepared to admit that right away. "I . . . I can only apologize. But you did, ah, agree with me right up until the end, and if those two in the dungeons hadn't gotten free—"

"*Another* disaster on your part—"

"With respect, my lord, *that* was a disaster on your *guards'* part. The safeguarding of prisoners is not among my responsibilities." He shot a significant look at the door Wyles had just left through, in case Elgar had forgotten whose responsibility it actually was.

"Let's thank the gods for that," Elgar said. He didn't even look peeved, just distracted, one hand moving up to stroke his beard. "However they learned of their friends' escape, they must have learned of it—I'm certain they would have returned otherwise."

"They might've *returned*, only—"

"Hmm." Elgar's fingers kept probing his chin. "Only neglected to inform us, eh? Perhaps they never even found the stone to begin with."

Why did he seem so oddly nonchalant about that possibility? "Could someone else have taken it first?"

Elgar tilted his head to the side, his lips pursing faintly. "It's possible, of course. I wonder what such a thief would have wanted with it."

What do you *want with it?* Varalen thought. "You did say it wasn't valuable."

"I said it was only valuable to me, which was only half a lie. To you, Varalen, I expect it would be entirely useless."

"Why to me in particular?"

"Because you believe in less than any man I know," Elgar said.

Varalen tried not to roll his eyes. "Ah, so it's a *magic* stone."

Of all things, Elgar laughed. "To think you consider yourself so clever. If I didn't need your battle strategies, I could dress you in motley and hardly notice a difference."

Stepstone was the fourth town they passed through, and only the third one they stopped at; Eirnwin preferred to lead them away from crowds when he could, and Kel didn't blame him, despite the attentions his legs required. They could not march to Mist's Edge with an army: there would be no way to keep such a thing secret, and if Elgar heard, he'd simply send his own men to block them, superstitious or not. Their only chance was to get Kel into the castle before Elgar got wind of anything—sending an army to kill the heir to Mist's Edge in his own ancestral hall, once he'd claimed it in the very names of those so long dead, was quite another matter, and one they had every reason to believe Elgar would balk at. So the fewer people who even knew he'd left Second Hearth, the better.

He needed Eirnwin with him at Mist's Edge—what good was an advisor when he was in another castle?—and Lessa had wanted to be left behind even less than he wanted to leave her. It might not have been *her* ancestral home, but she was his family, and if she wanted to see this through at his side, that was her right. Eirnwin still clung to the suspicion that a traitor might have let the assassin in, so they'd brought only the three guardsmen Eirnwin trusted most, and dressed them as sellswords. Grizzled Herren had served at Second Hearth for twenty years, and had been a favorite of Kel's father; the other two deferred to him as if by some unspoken agreement. Dark-haired Hayne had failed to catch anyone's notice until the only other time an assassin had infiltrated Second Hearth, an attempt on the royal children during a banquet when Kel was five. The long scar on her arm was covered up by her clothing, but it marked a blow that had been intended for him. And Dirk was the youngest of the three; he had been assigned to Kel for the past two years, and if Eirnwin had frowned at the familiar tone he took with Kel sometimes, he never had cause to complain of Dirk's dedication to his duty. As for the rest of them, Eirnwin played the part of a trader, and Kel and Lessa were his children. If the new King Kelken was known to be a cripple, well, so were many boys, though they still tried to draw as little attention as they could. Kel was doubly glad, now, that he'd insisted on making his crutches so plain; he could leave the rest of his finery behind, but those he could hardly do without.

A healthy boy his age might have made it to Mist's Edge in three days, even less if he knew how to ride. But Kel had tried both horse and cart before, and the pain all the bumping and jostling caused his legs was so great he couldn't endure it for any length of time. So he walked for as long as he could walk, and when the exhaustion and the swelling became too much, he took to the cart, and when he couldn't abide that any longer, it was time to stop for the night.

Eirnwin said if he could be strong tomorrow, they might reach Mist's Edge by nightfall, or early the following morning. Kel wanted to think he had that well in hand, but he had to admit he wasn't used to distances like this, to the uneven ground and the endlessly jostling cart. But he had made it this far, hadn't he? He had walked like this for so many years, when no one had thought he'd be able to walk at all.

Nevertheless, he couldn't suppress his relief at the thought of any kind of bed. None of them had ever been to Stepstone, but a villager pointed out an inn to Eirnwin easily enough. Hayne and Dirk took the cart around to the stables to feed the horses, and Herren went with the three of them into the inn.

The room they entered was dim and spare, with roughhewn tables and a roughhewn woman behind the counter pouring the ale. Kel squinted toward the back of the room, but he could barely make out more than the outlines of people. Eirnwin approached the woman while Kel hung back with Lessa.

"I'd like two rooms for the night, if you please," Eirnwin said. "One will serve for me and my children, with another for my hired hands."

"Sounds cramped," someone said—the voice felt like it was right at Kel's elbow. "Don't worry, old man, your children can kit up with me. Well, the girl can, anyway—might even let the cripple watch, if he behaves himself."

If he heard, Eirnwin gave no indication of it, but Herren's fingers inched toward the hilt of his sword. Lessa was looking firmly at the floor, her lips pale and pressed together. Kel turned toward the voice, but the nearest table seated three grinning men, and he couldn't tell which one had spoken; it half seemed as if the words had come out of the air above them. The woman behind the counter barely blinked. "Upstairs, back end of the hall," she said. "You want food as well?"

"Certainly—just name your price. And we'll need hay for the horses."

The woman jerked her thumb out the door. "As for that, you've got to talk with my boy out by the stables."

Eirnwin frowned. "I didn't give Dirk and Hayne any coin," he said to Kel. He looked at Herren, then at the group of men around the table, and hesitated. "I'd better go myself," he said at last. "Herren, you stay here." Herren gave a barely perceptible nod, and Eirnwin left.

Kel fidgeted, trying to resist the urge to inch closer to Herren; Lessa was still looking at the floor. Herren shifted from one foot to the other, keeping his eyes on the three men at the table. The woman behind the counter was looking ahead and slightly down, her eyes focusing on nothing.

Then, so suddenly that Kel nearly lost his balance, the voice spoke again. "You look mighty cold over there, sweetling," it said, and this time Kel looked over quickly enough to see the speaker, the man in the center. "I'd be happy to warm you up, if you'd like. Better than sharing a room with the old man, surely."

Lessa didn't move, but Herren hissed low in his throat, and the man's head snapped in his direction. "And what do you think you're growling at, dog? Bet you'd do the same if you had the balls. Or are you trying to lay claim to her?"

Herren took a step forward, his sword half out. Lessa choked back her gasp, but Kel said, "Herren, stop," before he really knew what he was saying. They couldn't draw attention to themselves. They couldn't cause any trouble. There were too many men at that table, let alone in the room.

Otherwise, he'd never let anyone talk to Lessa like that. He *wouldn't*.

The man in the center laughed, his lips stretching wide. "Aye, listen to the cripple, dog. You'd be worse off than him after crossing blades with me."

Herren's eyes darkened, but he sheathed his sword again, keeping his eyes on the far wall.

Then the man in the center got to his feet, and Kel's blood ran cold. He took a step around the table, and then Herren was right in his way. The man spat at the floor. "Move aside, dog, I just want to talk to the lady. We can't see each other so fine from all that distance away."

"You have no business with her," Herren said, his hand on his sword hilt again. "Keep your distance."

"I think I'll say who I do and don't have business with, thanks. I *certainly* don't have business with you, though, so you can get well enough away from me."

Herren took two steps back. Then he drew his sword.

The other two men were up in a heartbeat, and suddenly there were four swords out, the steel glinting in the dim light. The man near Herren smiled, and his teeth glinted too.

Kel tightened his grip on his crutches, hoisting himself up to his full height. "Herren—"

The man in front of Herren took a step forward, as if he meant to shove him with his shoulder, and Herren turned and lunged, his blade sliding just wide of the man's neck. Before he could retreat, one of the other two stabbed him in the side, and the third's sword went right through his thigh. Faster than Kel could think, the man in the center stabbed Herren in the chest, twisting the blade with a grin before drawing it out. Herren slumped to the floor, bleeding so heavily that Kel took an involuntary step back, and the man stabbed him again. This time he didn't remove his blade until Herren had stopped moving altogether. Out of the corner of his eye, Kel saw Lessa bite her lip, but she didn't gasp, and she didn't cry out.

Kel waited for anyone else in the tavern to do something, but no one did. All the other drinkers just kept drinking, and the woman behind the counter kept looking at nothing with her pale distant eyes. "You killed him," Kel said, because someone had to say something.

The man stepped toward them, his eyes sliding from Kel to Lessa and back again. "Eh, there are plenty of dogs in this world, boy. I'm sure your father'll buy you another one." There was still blood on his sword. It was *dripping*.

My father is dead, Kel thought, and then, *I wish I could kill you*. Out loud he said, "Go away," and his voice was a frightened boy's.

The man heard it, and laughed. "Don't worry, little bit, I don't care about you. Just quiet down so your sister and me can have some words, eh?"

"No," Kel said.

The man looked unconcerned. "No?"

Kel's legs were screaming at him from all the walking, but he still pushed himself forward, moving in front of Lessa. He shifted his weight carefully to one leg, preparing the other crutch. "*No*. She doesn't want to talk to you. Leave us alone."

Lessa laid a hand on his arm, but it was the one he was leaning on, not the one he was keeping free. "Kel, maybe we should—"

Kel shook his head. "He's not going to have his way."

The man grinned. "And if I say I shall?"

Kel lifted his crutch and hit him.

The man didn't quite try to dodge; he probably thought he'd just shrug off the blow to show how weak Kel was. But Kel's arms were stronger than they looked, because they'd spent so much time supporting his weight, and his crutch fell across the man's chest with a satisfying thud, making him stagger backward with a curse.

The man behind him giggled. "The little cripple hit you."

The one who'd killed Herren was no longer grinning, his face dark and grim instead. "You're not going to want to try that again, boy."

"I *will*," Kel insisted. "If you don't go away, I'll—I'll—" His voice kept skidding higher and higher, as if about to break, but he stayed where he was. He'd run before, and Lessa had stayed. He might sound frightened—he might *be* frightened—but his legs weren't shaking, and he wasn't going to run. Not because he was a cripple who *couldn't* run, but because he was going to stand here, and look at the man who'd killed Herren.

The man lifted his sword, and one last drop of blood fell from it to splatter onto the floor. He held it in front of Kel's face, keeping the point right between his eyes. Kel swallowed hard, but he didn't step back, and he didn't tremble, and he raised his crutch again, laying it against the man's blade as if they were crossing swords.

The man's scowl deepened, but before he could speak, a hand tightened on his shoulder, dragging him backward. Kel sighed in relief, expecting Hayne or Dirk, but the interloper was a man he did not know. "That's enough out of you," he said to the one who'd killed Herren. "I don't make a habit of interfering in other people's business, but you've defied all my attempts to ignore you. You're irritating me."

The man spun away and raised his sword again, pointing it at the stranger this time. "Easy enough to settle that." Then he lunged.

The stranger sidestepped easily, drawing his sword as if he had all day to do it. It was a one-and-a-half-hander, the steel gleaming and immaculate, and he swung it in a smooth, beautiful arc, beheading his opponent in one clean stroke. His lips pressed together where another person might have smiled. "Yes," he said. "It certainly was."

Kel gaped at him. So did the other two men, who flinched back when the stranger turned to them. "I don't have any particular desire to kill you," he said, "so if you'd like to live, sit down and stay there." They couldn't follow his advice fast enough.

The stranger nodded to Lessa and Kel, and turned to walk back into the shadows of the room.

Kel was about to start after him, but Lessa's grip tightened on his arm. "Come on," she said. "We've got to find Eirnwin and the others before anything else happens."

Kel followed her out to the stables, where they found Eirnwin and Hayne in furious conversation with a young man who must have been the boy the innkeeper mentioned. Dirk was leaning against a wooden post, but he stood upright when he saw Kel and Lessa, walking over to them. "Damned boy can't open his mouth without telling a bloody lie," he muttered. "If our cart broke that pissing gate, I'm Elgar's handmaiden. Er, begging your pardons." He squinted at them. "Is everything all right?"

"No," Kel said. He thought of Herren, and his throat closed up. "Is—I— when will Eirnwin be finished? We need to—tell him something."

Dirk frowned. "Eirnwin," he called, "can you get away?"

Eirnwin sighed, half turning, but then he saw Kel and Lessa and hurried over. "Dirk, help Hayne get some sense into that boy for me, will you? And you two—what's happened? Where's Herren?"

Kel swallowed, but Lessa spoke up. "Herren's been slain, Eirnwin," she said, and her hands shook, but her voice was steady—the opposite of the way Kel had been, inside. "There was a fight in the tavern—Kel might've been hurt too, but a stranger stepped in and saved us."

Eirnwin paled. "Your Grace, I should never have left you for so—"

"Don't call me that out here," Kel said, "and don't blame yourself. You couldn't have stopped him even if you'd been there." At least the man was dead, he thought to himself, and then wondered if it was all right to think that.

Eirnwin pressed a hand to his mouth, as if keeping something in. "We'll have to . . . see to him. We'll have to bury him."

"*That* man?" Kel asked. "What for?"

"No, Your Gr—I meant Herren."

"Oh." He shuddered. "Of course. Should we sleep somewhere else?"

Eirnwin shook his head. "There *is* nowhere else. Not in Stepstone, anyway, and the next village is too far away. Besides, we've already paid for the horses. The best thing would be to go back inside, if you can."

Kel nodded. It was better that way; there was something he wanted to do.

He peered once more into the depths of the room when they all walked in, after Hayne and Dirk finally got the stableboy to cease his accusations. The stranger was still there, drinking alone in the back corner, but the dead man's two companions had left, and their table was still empty.

"Wait here," Kel said to the others, and headed toward the back of the room. They hurried after him anyway, of course, but he was too tired to try to stop them.

The stranger looked up when he heard the creak of Kel's crutches, but just barely. He did not say anything, just waited to see if Kel would speak.

The light was even dimmer this far back in the room, but Kel could easily see that he was handsome, with glossy brown hair, a smooth, clean-shaven face, and eyes a pure, pale blue. His nose was straight, his brow unfurrowed, his cheekbones elegantly defined. There was only one flaw in his face: a long slender scar, starting in the middle of his forehead, almost at his hairline, and running halfway down the bridge of his nose. Even that was oddly perfect, so smooth and straight that Kel could only imagine the sharpness of the blade that had made it, or the skill of the hand that had held the blade.

"I wanted to thank you," Kel said. "Um. Sir. For helping us."

"You don't have to call me that," the man said, leaning back in his chair. "I'm no *sir* by anyone's reckoning. And you don't have to thank me."

"Well," Kel said, "maybe not, but . . . I wanted to."

The man nodded, then took a long sip of his drink.

From behind Kel, Alessa said, "I—I should thank you as well."

The stranger looked over at her, and though he stared for a moment, it was only for a moment, and whatever he saw only seemed to make him sad. By the time he spoke again, his gaze had already slid back to Kel. "You're welcome."

Kel knew he should walk away, but he wanted an indefinable something more from the man, some confidence or concession he could name. "Why did you help us?" he asked at last; perhaps it was impolite, but it was all he could think of to say. "You didn't get up when Herren was killed, but you helped me."

"People get killed all the time," the stranger said. "I usually leave them to it—it's none of my business, and I'm usually better at killing people than saving them anyway. But with you . . ." He looked at Lessa again. "She's your sister?"

"Yes," Kel said. There wasn't much he could say of himself that was true, not out here. But that, at least, wasn't a lie.

"I had a sister once," the stranger said. "I wasn't any good at saving her, either. You were doing a better job of protecting yours than I ever did with mine, so I helped you out. That's why."

"Oh," Kel said. Did that mean the man's sister had died?

Eirnwin cleared his throat, and the man raised an eyebrow at him. "And who are you?"

"I would thank you for saving my children," Eirnwin said—a lie that couldn't be helped, Kel reminded himself—"but I seem to be out a sellsword." Another lie—Herren had been a royal guard. "I wonder if we might ask for your help a little longer."

"I'm not a sellsword," the man said flatly.

"Yes," Eirnwin said, "but you don't need to be one to come to an arrangement with me. Our destination is near Mist's Edge—not far at all now, and I'm willing to pay you whatever you deem fair. It might not even be out of your way."

The man scratched his neck. "I don't know if it's out of my way. I haven't figured out where I'm going yet." But that wasn't *no,* and Kel waited. The man seemed to struggle with himself, but he finally said, "I suppose a couple days' march west won't take me any farther from where I need to be. All right, I'll make sure you and your children get where you're going, and you can pay me whatever you were going to give the dead man." He looked down at the table. "Now let me finish my drink."

"Wait," Kel said. "What's your name?" When the man hesitated, he added, "I'm Kel."

The man wrinkled his nose, then ran one finger down his scar. "You can call me Cadfael," he said.

CHAPTER TWENTY

Almasy was bloodstained, which in itself was anything but unusual. A swath of it had dried on her cheek, and the cloth at her hip was soaked with red; her fingers bore haphazard stains. He doubted any of it was hers.

"Your hunting went well, I trust," Gravis said.

She regarded him coolly. "I have returned. That should tell you all you need to know."

Indeed it did. "Lady Margraine is still upstairs—I don't suppose you'll clean up before you see her?"

Almasy shrugged. "I have never known her to care about such things." That was true enough; if the marquise were capable of squeamishness in anything, Gravis had never seen it. Perhaps it even amused her to see Almasy in all that blood. He wouldn't be surprised.

He was going to let her go, but then it occurred to him to ask, "Why did she require them killed?"

"It is not for me to question her," Almasy said.

"So you're just a dog to be kept on a leash? I thought you of all people wouldn't accept that."

Some of the men had taken to calling her Lady Margraine's dog—sometimes even to her face—but Gravis had never been among them. It was enough to make her pause, if not, it seemed, to rattle her. "We're both dogs, Gravis, but you're the only one on a leash. And just because I come when I'm called and you have to be dragged, you think *you're* the free one."

She walked past him. He wished he could think of something, even just a taunt, to detain her, but his mind was blank, and soon she vanished up the stairs.

How could someone who claimed to value her independence so highly be as content to follow orders as Almasy was? Gravis had been beholden to one master or another nearly his entire life, and even he choked on a command every now and then. Yet if Almasy had ever refused a task Lady Margraine had set for her, Gravis did not know of it.

With *him* there was no mystery. He had sworn an oath years and years ago to serve Lord Caius and his heirs for as long as he should live, and he did not intend to break it, no matter how infuriating Caius's actual heir had turned out to be. But what had Almasy sworn, or what had she been offered? He could not make it out.

Lady Margraine had made it clear from the beginning that Almasy was to receive anything she asked for, that her commands were to be followed as if they were the marquise's own. But Almasy asked for nothing, ordered nothing and no one; she accepted coin when she needed a blade sharpened or an article of clothing replaced, and she took her meals at the hall when she had not been ordered elsewhere, but that was the extent of her demands. And so she was both the most exalted member of the marquise's guard and the least—possessed of great power in theory, but only in theory. Indeed, the more Gravis pondered it, the more certain he became that Lady Margraine had bestowed that power only for the sake of her own amusement, because she knew Almasy would never make use of it.

He had no ideas about the blood apples, either. It was against every tradition for anyone but a Margraine to eat them regularly, and even though Lady Margraine laughed as easily at most traditions as she did at everything else, she'd seemed content enough to keep *that* one until Almasy came along. He'd asked Almasy once if they were her reward, but she denied it. "She believes it will be some irony against her father if I eat them," she said, and nothing more.

Lady Margraine could never resist an opportunity to slight her father, it seemed. Why didn't she just retrieve Lord Caius's corpse and spit on it? Gravis wondered.

He found the man he'd hoped to see idling outside the kitchens. Denton Halley had just taken an enormous bite of his bread and butter, but he swallowed it quickly when Gravis caught his eye. "Gods, you look sour. Something I can do for you?"

Gravis might have responded that there was hardly any reason to be cheerful, but Dent never seemed to need one. "Almasy," he said.

"What, again?"

"I'm not going to stop thinking on it until I'm satisfied, Dent."

"Aye, but there's only so much you can ask me that you haven't asked before. I knew her, what, a day before you did? Two?"

Gravis had been on an errand south of Stonespire when Almasy first arrived there; it seemed an unfortunate tradition that he should find himself away from the hall on the days he could most have wished he were present. But Dent had been there, and Gravis knew he hardly gave him any peace because of it. "I didn't intend to ask you about that." He wished he could have, but Dent was right—every potential question that flickered through his mind was one he had asked countless times before. "I only meant that I wonder if we should let this continue."

"This? You mean Seren?" Dent laughed. "Gravis, I hope she *does* stay here. I don't think her ladyship's ever been so safe as she is with that woman prowling about her chambers."

"Does that mean you trust her?"

Dent took another bite of bread, chewing this one more thoughtfully. "I wouldn't trust Seren with *my* life, but I'd certainly trust her with her ladyship's. I think she's proven that well enough."

"How has she proven it?"

"You really have to ask that? Gods, Gravis, she's been here long enough, and served as well as you or I ever did. If she wanted to play us false, she could've done so a year ago with no greater trouble." He tapped his chin. "More than that—I've known her ladyship as long as you, which is longer than she's known herself, and the day she trusts someone without cause is the day I sprout wings and fly across the sea. Whatever it is she knows about Seren, it's enough."

But what did she know about Almasy? What did she know that they didn't? Gravis shook his head; he'd followed these thoughts countless times before, with no results. "There's another thing—I thought she looked a bit ill the other day."

That drew Dent's concern. "Her ladyship did? You mean . . . as in the old days?"

"No . . ." Gravis started, but then he paused. Was he sure of that? Despite general good health, as a child Lady Margraine had occasionally been plagued by the oddest symptoms. She would grow pale and exhausted all of a sudden, or fall short of breath after no activity more strenuous than reading, or find herself unable to eat though she claimed to be starving. Once Verrane had found her in a dead faint on the floor of her room, and no one could get her to say how it had happened or what she had been doing beforehand. No healer they consulted could find a satisfactory reason; the prevailing theory was that her blood was thin. The symptoms seemed to lessen as she grew older, so in time they all let the matter drop; Lady Margraine herself, who ought to have been the most concerned about it of anyone, simply waved it away, saying she disliked being fussed over.

Gravis had his own theories, of course. He'd heard about how contracts were struck, how demons and spirits would take blood and bone in trade, sometimes even the years off a man's life. She'd been a child, certainly, but a precocious child; everyone had said so. He wouldn't have put it past her to come across some dark ritual somewhere in all those books she read. There was very little he would have put past Lady Margraine, in fact. "Perhaps I'd better keep a closer eye on her," he said, without thinking.

Dent sighed—had he been so transparent? "Gravis, these superstitions would befit Verrane much more than you, and even she doesn't entertain them. It would better suit you to be concerned for her ladyship's health, not . . . whatever strange doings you suspect her of."

Dent and Verrane, for reasons Gravis could not fathom, persisted in taking Lady Margraine's side, and had done so since she was a child. Verrane possessed a mother's affection for her, perhaps, but Dent was harder to understand. It was true that he and Lord Caius had often clashed, but that in itself wasn't enough of a reason, was it? Sometimes Gravis tried to let the knowledge comfort him, that someone he trusted as much as Dent had such faith in her. Yet he knew, despite what anyone else said, that there was something out of the ordinary about Lady Margraine. You could feel it, sometimes, in the rare moments she allowed anger to grip her—Gravis had seen it only a handful of times in all the years he had lived with her, but it was enough. Her looks came all from her mother, with none of her father's size or strength; she was slender and soft, not even lean and toned like Almasy. And yet when she turned on someone in anger, there was this intimidation she made you feel, as if there were something immensely powerful lurking beneath her skin. Even her father had shrunk from it, who'd never shied from a fight any day of his life.

"That's what I meant," he lied. "If she is ill, we ought to know."

Dent nodded slowly, but his usual cheer had gone.

———

"And they wouldn't admit that Eurig had paid them?"

Seren wondered at the most accurate way to answer that. "Well, they *did* admit it, but . . . only to tell me they never would. I couldn't prove it, they said, and the common people would never believe it, and so forth. I didn't see the value in discussing it further."

Arianrod ran a hand through her hair, drawing it back from her face. "That's because there wasn't any—I never required you to *talk* to them to begin with. It would've been especially convenient if I'd been able to sully his reputation a bit, though."

"I could just kill him," Seren offered.

Arianrod smiled. "You could, but Eurig is a coward who thinks he's twice as smart as he is, and those are exactly the people one wants in his position. He's been even easier to handle than Dutton, who got about a day's ride from Pigshit Castle before he was apprehended. By peasants!" She laughed, striking the edge of the desk for emphasis. "I do wish I could have overseen his execution myself, but there simply wasn't time. Besides, those peasants had to put up with him far more than I ever did; I suppose it would've been wrong to deprive them of the enjoyment of watching him brought low."

"What does that mean for this guild of merchants he's been trying to form?"

"Oh, rich men in Esthrades will be trying to form one of those until the end of time," Arianrod said, rolling her eyes. "They want so desperately to be nobility that they'll never stop trying to approximate it, no matter how harshly the throne punishes them for the attempt." She smiled. "But that's not what you really want to ask me, is it? Go on."

Seren shuffled her feet. It *had* been bothering her, even after she'd left Stonespire, and her unease hadn't lessened now that she'd returned. "The stone— the . . . *wardrenholt,* you called it? Did you move it somehow? Did you . . . Is it gone?"

"It can't return to the way it was," Arianrod said, "so I suppose in that sense it's gone, yes."

"But then where did it go?"

"Destroying it would have been easy," Arianrod started, but then she caught herself. "Well, perhaps it would have been easy. Perhaps if I'd inscribed *destroy yourself* on it instead, it would have taken me with it and gotten its revenge that way. It's hard to say." She sighed. "It's a pity I couldn't have studied it more, but in the end it simply wasn't worth the risk."

"You never intended to use it? Then why have me—"

"Well, I couldn't let anyone else use it, could I? Especially not Elgar."

The mention of Elgar made Seren hesitate, fiddling with her sleeve. She'd already told Arianrod about her brief time in the Citadel dungeons, but the memory of it still rankled. "Speaking of Elgar . . . are you sure it doesn't matter that this Oswhent fellow saw me?"

"Why should it?" Arianrod asked. "Even if he finds out who you are—even if he guesses you brought me the stone—there's no way he or Elgar can steal it from me now. Why should I care if they know I have it?"

"I may not be able to move anonymously in Valyanrend anymore," Seren pointed out.

Arianrod frowned thoughtfully. "Perhaps. It's a big city, though, and you'd hardly be the first person to roam it freely against the wishes of those in the Citadel."

Seren knew it would still bother her; she wasn't used to making mistakes, even if this one had probably turned out for the best. After all, if she hadn't been caught, it might have taken her much longer to learn where the stone was hidden. But that put her in mind of another question: "Do you have any idea what Elgar planned to do with it?"

"Nothing good, I'm sure." But she wasn't smiling; she passed a hand through her hair again, twirled a lock of it around one finger. "I can guess why he wanted it, but does it matter? The thing held pure power in it, pure potential. He could have done whatever he pleased with it—until the magic ran dry, anyway."

"But you didn't want to do the same," Seren said.

"Of course I wanted to use it," Arianrod said. "That's why I didn't."

"I don't understand."

"I told you, didn't I? Those things were made by *failed* mages—the worst of the lot, the greatest incompetents of their age. Many people would still gladly accept one, because it's as close to magic as they'll ever come. Even I— even I couldn't help but imagine things when I touched it, things I'd dreamed of as a child and banished from my mind as impossibilities. But why should I put my trust in something I know was made by a talentless fool? I wish to rule, not to be ruled—not by Elgar, and certainly not by a stone." She didn't lift her hand from the edge of the table, but her fingers curled absently into a fist. "I knew two things for certain: that I could not possibly use it, and that I could not keep it here and resist the temptation to do so. So I had to put it beyond everyone's reach, including my own."

Seren remembered how loath Arianrod had been to touch the stone, how relieved she had looked once it was in the ground. But Seren herself had never felt a thing from it, not even a ripple of power. "I don't think that I—"

Arianrod smiled. "No," she agreed, "to you it was nothing, as I thought it probably would be. You'll ask me why, I suppose, and, well, I'd like to know for certain too. Perhaps the answer is as simple as this: either you already have the things you want, or even magic could not give them to you."

That left a bitter taste in Seren's mouth, but it was true, wasn't it? Was that why Elgar had chosen Lucius and Deinol and Seth—because what they wanted most was the release of their friends, and not any kind of power? "But you didn't destroy it," she said, because she didn't think Arianrod expected to be enlightened on the subject of her wants. "You said you didn't, right?"

"I thought it would be a waste, to be honest," Arianrod said. "There had to be some way to make use of all that power without damning myself; I just had to find it. And then it finally occurred to me." She leaned back in her chair. "If I compelled the magic to cover a very large area at once, I guessed the stone might lose its physical form. So I put it in the ground—in the soil itself. I used the stone's magic to ensure that this land will remain fertile, that we will be free of blights and famines. It was something I did thoughtfully, not out of the strong passions that tend to drive these things awry. With any luck, we shall enjoy fruitful harvests until there is no longer any magic left—which may be quite a while indeed."

Seren wasn't sure if she ought to look as surprised as she was. "Well, that's . . . that's good. That's . . . wonderful, even."

Arianrod rolled her eyes. "I wouldn't go that far. But it's a trick that has its uses, to be sure."

Seren might have left the matter there, but then a new thought struck her. "But if you can't use the *wardrenholt,* what *are* you going to do?"

"What, about Elgar?" Arianrod asked, stretching lazily. "I'm going to proceed just as usual, of course. What kind of ruler would I be if I needed a magical artifact to help me keep a fool from my lands?"

———

It would take another night to reach Mist's Edge, thanks to the pace Kel was forcing the rest of them to set, but Eirnwin didn't want to risk setting foot in another small-town tavern. No one was particularly happy about lighting a fire in the middle of a clearing and trying to catch a few hours' sleep, but at least *wolves* wouldn't care whether Lessa was pretty. They'd agreed to set out a few hours before dawn; they were so close at this point that Kel wasn't the only one getting impatient.

The lumpy ground did nothing to help his legs, of course. He twisted and squirmed, scrunching them up and stretching them out, but nothing eased the ache. There was no way he was going to get to sleep like this, and he needed the rest. Instead he turned over, and looked up at Cadfael.

He was feeding twigs to the fire, looking into the flames without seeming to see them. His face was smooth, but his scar showed dark and red in the light, somehow angry. "Are you sure it's all right to keep that going?" Kel asked.

Cadfael did not smile; Kel had quickly learned that either he did not like it, or else it wasn't something he could do easily. "That's why you have me," he said. "Go to sleep. No one will bother you."

"I would if I could," Kel said. "My legs won't leave me alone."

"Well, I can't help you there. Doesn't your father carry anything you could use?"

Why hadn't they come up with another story about what Eirnwin was to him? Kel flinched every time he heard the word. "We didn't bring enough snow's down for me to use it frivolously, and even if we did, it always makes my legs go numb. I couldn't get up again in a few hours if I used it now."

Cadfael released the end of the twig. "You've had to live with a lot, I imagine."

Kel shook his head. "Just my legs. People like to look at them and feel pity for me, but there are so many other misfortunes I could've had instead, and didn't."

"Fair enough." He shifted back from the fire a bit, reaching into his pack, and pulled out a flask and what looked like a whetstone. He took a sip from the flask, then poured more of its contents—just water, it looked like—onto the stone. Then he drew his sword, and soon established a practiced rhythm, easing it over the surface of the stone.

Kel squinted at it. It was a beautiful blade, he could see that clearly: long and gleaming and perfectly straight, with a fine edge and a simple hilt made of darker steel than the rest of the sword. As for the blade itself, it was unmarred by any scratch or stain, and so clear and bright it seemed more like mirrorglass than metal. "What is it made out of?" he asked. "I've never seen a sword that looked like that."

"It's rare enough," Cadfael said, never pausing in his task. "It's known as vardrath steel—the hardest there is, without getting too brittle. No other steel could ever shatter it—or so my father told me, anyway."

"Was he a blacksmith?"

Cadfael smiled; it was crooked, but he was trying. "No, no blacksmith. It was his sword first. Well, not like this—it was a different sword when it was his, but the steel was the same." He tapped the whetstone. "He was the one who taught us to use waterstones, too—he never sharpened it with anything else. Of course, one of the benefits of vardrath is how well it holds an edge, but he was always vain about his sword, and he taught us that, too."

Kel cocked his head. "Us?"

Cadfael's smile disappeared instantly. "My sister and me. My father had a two-handed greatsword made of vardrath steel—he'd owned it as long as I'd known him, since before we were born. He never made any great fortune, but even though vardrath's so rare these days that you can pretty much name your price, he'd never sell it. He told us it was our birthright, and when he died, he wanted us to take it and melt it down, and forge a sword for each of us. I wouldn't have wanted to wield it as it was anyway—those over-the-shoulder types were always too heavy for my tastes. I made this instead, and gave my sister the rest."

Kel propped himself up on one hand, rubbing his legs with the other. "What was your sister like?"

Cadfael did not smile again. "It's a bit funny; she wasn't like your sister at all, though when I first saw her, she did remind me, somewhat . . . just in the hair, and a little in the shape of the face. But my sister was a scrapper if ever I saw one—she'd go at trouble with both hands, and never think to hold back. She always had this . . . this fierce sort of certainty—she knew exactly what she wanted from the world, and what she wanted to be in it, and there was nothing she wouldn't dare, for the sake of that dream. I felt that was true nobility, if it existed in anyone at all. I was never anything like that." He looked down again, resuming his sharpening. "Well, it didn't save her, and neither could I. Even the sword our father left her wasn't enough in the end."

Kel wondered if he was allowed to ask how she died. "Someone I cared about died once," he said instead, while he was thinking it over. "He was—he was killed, just like Herren. I couldn't do anything for either of them. But Lessa protected me, once."

"And you did your best to protect her," Cadfael said. "She's still here, isn't she? So you must be doing something right."

Maybe, Kel thought. *Maybe.* Who was that assassin, and how had Lessa stopped him? Or had it been about Lessa at all? Did that mean he was going to attack them again?

"Do you know how your sister died?" he finally asked Cadfael.

Cadfael's face grew stony, his brows drawing together. "Do I know who killed her, you mean. Aye, I know of him, though not so much as I'd like."

"What does that mean?"

"It means I haven't killed him yet," Cadfael said, "and that's an omission I can't let stand. I have a name, and a vague idea of a man. I don't know what he looks like, or how he fights, or where he is now, or how I might get to him." He held the sword still. "I don't know if he remembers her. But I'll *make* him remember. I'll make him tell me how and why, and whether he laughed to kill a girl with a sword. I'll make him regret it, before I end him."

"Maybe he regrets it already," Kel said, and didn't know why.

Cadfael's expression did not change. "I hope he does. I hope he feels me closing in on him—if only I *were*! But I'm no closer than when I started."

"Can you not find him?"

"Sometimes I can," Cadfael said, "or nearly. Sometimes I hear of him, but only ever when he is surrounded by his men, locked in a tower beyond my reach. You must understand, it is not enough for me to die *attempting* to kill him—I am content to die, but only once I have seen him breathe his last. So I cannot blithely charge into the midst of his army, no matter how I might wish to. Then there are times I hear he has set out alone, but never precisely where; there are times I could swear I must have passed him on the road or in the forest, but he always seems to slip through my grasp. Even in Stepstone I was on his trail, but by then I had started to lose hope—the rumor I had put him two days' ride from the Hallern border and heading east, but that was more than a week ago on the night we met. He's got to be gone again."

"An *army*?" Kel asked. "Just what sort of man is it you're looking for?"

"A man who's destroyed much more than just my sister," Cadfael answered. "They call him Shinsei."

CHAPTER TWENTY-ONE

Kel saw Mist's Edge for the first time just as the sun was rising. The castle was both wide and tall, sprawling along the ridge and jutting sharply up into the sky. The whole of Second Hearth would not have filled half the space within its walls, and those walls, so high that Kel had to tilt his head near to popping off to see the top of them, were unbreached, stretching around the fortress in an uncompromising square.

The walls and towers looked faded in the sun, more like the mist of their namesake than stone. There *was* mist too, drifting in wisps about the ramparts, but it burned off quickly as they approached. Kel wondered how thick it got at night, whether it could seep through the windows and wend its way down the halls. This was the home of his ancestors, he reminded himself. The very first Kelken had lived here, had most likely stared out the window of the very same tower Kel was staring into now.

Cadfael drew warily closer, laying a hand on his sword that he probably wasn't even aware of. "Where is it exactly that you intend to go?" he asked Eirnwin. "There's nothing of note outside these walls, not for leagues around."

"It's what's inside them that interests us," Eirnwin said. "We're going to enter the castle."

"What? What do you want to do that for? It's deserted." But then he frowned. "This isn't some kind of looting expedition, is it?"

"No," Eirnwin said simply, and approached the gate.

It was standing open—there was no one left inside to close it. Kel wondered how long it had stood like that, free and open to anyone who might pass by. He was a bit nervous about passing under it, but the chains looked sturdy enough, and in the end they all managed to clear the threshold without so much as a pebble falling loose.

Surprisingly, the courtyard was hardly overgrown, with only vague tufts of grass poking through the well-trampled dirt here and there—perhaps even seeds had trouble blowing over the walls, or else two years hadn't been enough time for nature to conquer the fortress. Kel had steeled himself to see a crumbling ruin, but it seemed Elgar's soldiers had taken good care of the place until they finally abandoned it; there were some loose stones here and there, but no egregious gaps anywhere. He didn't imagine they'd be so lucky about the inside, though.

He turned to Eirnwin. "What do you know about this place?"

"About as much as you—only what I've read in books," Eirnwin replied. He squinted at the far tower. "I can't help but wish it had been arranged in a way that made more sense; I can already tell I'm going to get lost, and more than once."

Cadfael's frown had deepened. "How long do you plan on staying here?"

"For quite some time, if things go according to plan," Eirnwin told him, just as calmly as before. "But don't worry, you'll get your payment now, as agreed."

"That's not what worries me," Cadfael said, but he didn't add anything further.

The throne room at Second Hearth was hardly grand, but here it was dizzyingly huge, in a long hall with windows lining each side, so that shaft after shaft of light pierced through the gray. The room itself was full of cobwebs and dust, fallen so thick on the throne that Kel could scarcely see what color it was supposed to be. The throne at Second Hearth had been carved from wood and painted red and gold, but this throne was cast in steel, heavy and somehow threatening, even under all the dust.

He touched the arm of the throne, and then hesitated. "Lessa, do you think . . . should you wait outside?"

She shrugged. "There's dust everywhere. I'll just have to hope for the best, I suppose."

"They don't seem to have stolen anything, or let the place fall into disorder," Hayne called from the other end of the hall. "Perhaps they thought they'd be returning again shortly."

Dirk grinned at her. "See any ghosts yet?"

"Ha, very funny."

"Wouldn't be if you'd seen one," Dirk said, but he couldn't keep the smile off his face. "I hear they're prodigiously hard to kill."

"There are no ghosts here, or anywhere," Kel said firmly. "And even if there were, they wouldn't hurt me."

Dirk looked askance at him. "*You,* sure. But what about us, eh?"

"Why wouldn't they hurt him?" Cadfael asked. He'd been agitated the whole time they'd been in the throne room, pacing up and down, biting the corner of his mouth absently.

Dirk and Hayne looked at each other, and then looked at Kel; Lessa was looking away. But Kel looked at Eirnwin, and then they both nodded.

"Because I'm supposed to be here," Kel told Cadfael. "This is my place."

"Your place?" Cadfael said. "But this isn't anyone's place, not now. It was abandoned by Elgar, and by the kings of Reglay before that."

"It's the place the Rayls come from, and where they lived," Kel said. "And I'm one of them, just as my father was."

"The Rayls?" Cadfael caught his breath, his face growing dark. "Then . . . you're the prince of Reglay?"

"Well," Kel said, "strictly speaking, I'm the king now, but I haven't been—"

But Cadfael's fingers clenched hard on his sword hilt, and he stepped away. "I liked you much better as a merchant's son." He nodded at Eirnwin. "I take it this isn't your father? And—"

"Lessa *is* my sister," Kel said, before he could get any further. "But Eirnwin is my advisor, and my friend."

"Hmph," Cadfael said. "Do kings have friends?"

"Why shouldn't they?" Kel asked, and thought, suddenly, of Prince Landon.

"So you've come to claim Mist's Edge," Cadfael said, beginning to pace the length of the hall again. "I understand it now. Well, you're welcome to it as far as I'm concerned, though Elgar no doubt thinks differently." He walked up to Eirnwin. "I'll take that payment you promised, and I'll be on my way."

Eirnwin held up a hand. "Wait. You're welcome to the money, of course, but—"

"If I'm welcome to it, I'll have it, and I'll leave. If I'm not welcome to it, I'll just leave. Either way, good-bye."

Eirnwin reached for his purse but paused before he drew it out. "You weren't so quick to be rid of our company before. What changed?"

"Too much," Cadfael said. "I would like to be gone, before you and the boy and the girl make me the offer I know you're going to make. I like you well enough, and the younger ones better, and I don't want to seem a hard man. So let me go."

"Why don't you want to be in my service?" Kel asked. "Is it because of your quest for Shinsei? Or is it because you think I'll make a bad king?"

Cadfael shook his head. "It isn't like that." He finally released his sword hilt, tracing his scar with one finger. "I followed a king's orders once, to my greatest sorrow. I cannot do so again."

"Why?" Kel asked. "What happened?"

"The same thing that happens to all men who follow orders too well," Cadfael said. He turned to go. "I wish you only good fortune, boy—or king, if such you are—but I had best return to my pursuit of Shinsei. I will not find him here."

"Wait." This time it was Lessa who spoke, and Cadfael turned to her abruptly.

Kel wondered if she sounded like his sister too, even if their personalities were as different as Cadfael had claimed. "This Shinsei you're after—do you mean Elgar's commander? He might come here, if you're willing to wait for him."

He squinted at her, his jaw tightening. "Explain yourself."

"My brother reclaimed this castle so he might hold his coronation here," Lessa said. "He means to invite the rulers of all the surrounding countries: Issamira, Esthrades, and Hallarnon. If Elgar comes, and he must come without an army, will he not wish his most trusted general at his side?"

Cadfael was still staring at her, stony-faced. "You're mad to invite him. Elgar will never come *here*."

"He will," Kel insisted. "Or, well, we think he will. He won't want to be left out, and his superstitions will—" He sighed. "Look, it doesn't matter. We think he'll come, and Lessa's right—if he does, it'd make sense for him to bring Shinsei with him."

Cadfael looked at him now, but blankly, his focus fading out. "He could fit quite a lot of men in this fortress, but only a handful compared to those he houses in the Citadel. He wouldn't be able to care about Shinsei's protection— he'd be too busy worrying about his own. And within the confines of this place . . ." He nestled one fist inside the other, gripping it so hard his fingers shook. "This way, I could . . ."

Eirnwin stared at him for a long moment before speaking. "This quest of yours . . . you wish to kill the commander?"

"Aye," Cadfael said. "And I will, one way or another."

Eirnwin turned to Kel. "Your Grace, assassinating Elgar's favorite would be . . ."

Kel shrugged. "What, it would make him angry? He won't leave us in peace no matter how nice we are to him, so why should we care whether he likes us or not? He can't threaten us with anything worse than he's already plotting— our destruction, and the destruction of Reglay."

"Your Grace, I am sure I have taught you that murdering a guest under one's roof is considered one of the highest forms of treachery? It might seem a clever stratagem, but the damage to your reputation—"

"It wouldn't have anything to do with *me*," Kel said. "He'd be my guest, true, but he wouldn't be Cadfael's. And Cadfael won't follow my orders, he said so himself."

"If Elgar demands my head for it, that's fine," Cadfael said. "As long as I can kill Shinsei, I don't care about the rest."

"Very well," Eirnwin said, throwing up his hands. "Very well, Your Grace. I will not argue the point further." He rounded on Cadfael. "And you? If we allow you to do this thing, you will pledge your fealty to the king?"

Cadfael hesitated, tracing the line of his scar up and down. "I cannot pledge my obedience," he said at last, to Kel instead of Eirnwin. "It is too dangerous for a man like me to make such a promise. But I will remain at your side, and make sure you never come to harm. However, if Elgar does not come to this castle, or if he comes without Shinsei, then after your coronation, I wish to leave, and ask that you not trouble me again."

Kel bowed his head. "That's fair. We'll settle it after my coronation, one way or another."

"Good." He turned on his heel. "I should see whether there are any rooms fit to sleep in in this place."

But he did not leave right away, and then Alessa said, "Do you really wish to die after you get your revenge?"

He did not turn to look at her. "I don't *wish* to die. I just don't care."

"You have nothing to live for?"

"I did," he said. "One thing, and nothing else. Revenge is all I can give her now, but after that, what can I do for her? If it were possible for me to live as she would have, I would do that. But I have none of that fire in me."

After he had gone, Kel took Lessa's hand. "What do you think? Do you not trust him?"

She squeezed his fingers, then let him go so he could adjust his grip on the crutches. "I trust him. I just . . . I don't know if I quite like him."

"What do you mean?" Kel asked. "He's so strong, and he's always been direct with us. . . ."

"He has," Lessa agreed. "He just seems so . . . empty, as if he rings hollow. He saved us, certainly, but he let Herren die dispassionately enough. I suppose I don't know what to make of a man with so few convictions of his own."

That was right, Kel realized: Cadfael didn't seem to believe in anything, one way or the other. His sister had probably done the believing for both of them. Kel wished he could have met her.

"I don't think he'll harm us, at least," Eirnwin said. "It was lucky he took a liking to the two of you."

It was Lessa's resemblance he took a liking to, Kel didn't say, *and my being a brother who wanted to protect her.* But his being a king had displeased Cadfael, and he wondered if there were any other pitfalls to the man's regard.

"Come on," he said. "We've got a lot of work to do before this place'll be fit for guests, and Eirnwin *did* say he wanted to hold my coronation as soon as possible. We'll need to send word back to Second Hearth, and in the meantime we can start tidying up ourselves."

"I doubt you'll make a particularly apt chambermaid, Your Grace." Eirnwin smiled. "Though I would dearly love to see you try."

Had they been back in Sheath, the arrival of a message that made Braddock's face darken so severely would have been cause for worry. But they were *not* in Sheath, and the truth, no matter how Morgan tried to hide it, was that she doubted she could stay here another week, no matter how hospitable Braddock's old friend had been. Perhaps Roger and the others would've imagined she'd be eager for the chance to rest, after her incessant labors at the Dragon's Head— perhaps she herself would even have thought so, before. But sitting here idle day after day while their coin slowly dwindled was more than she could stand. She needed a change, and if this mysterious message portended such, she couldn't regret its arrival.

The message had come for Vash, not Braddock, yet the two of them had been discussing it for what must surely have been an hour by now, leaving Morgan to fend for herself. She walked a vague circle around the house, peering southward every time she made another turn; Vash had told her that the Gods' Curse was a mere handful of leagues away, but though the ground was fairly flat, the horizon was too indistinct for her to make anything out. It was warmer this far south, despite the persistent clouds that hovered overhead, but not unpleasantly so. The view, however, couldn't help but be discouraging, what with the dim light and the dusty plains covered with scrubby, faded grass.

Braddock came out at last, looking even more disgruntled than usual. "Sorry about that," he said, scratching the back of his neck. "And sorry about, ah, what I'm about to say."

"Well, you haven't said it yet," Morgan replied. "Why don't you start by telling me what Vash's correspondence has to do with you?"

He nodded slowly. "I know the man who sent that message—he was my friend as well as Vash's, from our mercenary days."

Morgan raised an eyebrow. "I thought you always said the mercenary business wasn't the right place to make friends. Here are two of yours in as many weeks."

Braddock scowled at that, but at the ground, not at her. "Well, I can promise you that's all you'll meet. The rest are dead."

"The rest of your friends?"

"The rest of that company." He finally looked up. "We made sure of that."

Morgan wasn't sure what to say to that. Were congratulations appropriate, or condolences?

Before she could do more than draw a breath, Braddock spoke again. "It was, ah . . . We didn't plan it like that. I suppose the best way to explain it is to say that after so much time spent routing bandits and suchlike, the rest of our fellows began to act far too much like them for our tastes. Then one day we liberated this tiny little settlement, like we'd done dozens of times before. Only the rest of 'em decided they'd rather have it for themselves—and all its coin, and all its women. You don't *reason* with men when their blood's up like that, not unless you want to get yourself killed. So . . . Vash and Nasser and I struck first. That's why . . . well, that's why I never had quite the same taste for sell-swording after that."

At first she could only stare at him. "That's . . . You ought to've said."

"Well, I didn't. It's not something I like to talk about."

Morgan shook her head. "I mean it was . . . noble, or something like it."

He laughed. "Or something is right."

She could tell he wanted her to change the subject, so she asked, "It's this Nasser who sent the message, then?"

"Aye, from Issamira."

"But you and Vash don't agree on what's to be done about it."

"Aye. Nasser's in trouble, is about the gist of it, and he thought to call on someone he could trust. Vash may live on the wrong side of the Curse now, but he's Issamiri born and bred—no doubt Nasser thought his experience would be welcome. Problem is, Vash's experience is just the issue—he ran afoul of the law back home all those years ago, and he's afraid to go back lest somebody recognize him. I told him no one's going to mind about it now, but he won't listen."

"So he's not going to go help Nasser," Morgan guessed.

Braddock scowled. "I did all I could think of to convince him. I told him he owed Nasser, but he just figures Nasser owes *him* just as much, and filled my ears with how he was already doing enough for *me*." He rubbed at his face. "Vash is all right, but Nasser's a good man—or as close to one as I've ever known, and there aren't many would get me to say that. I've never known him to be a man who needs help—and certainly not one to ask for it. So the fact that he *is* asking for it has me more than a little worried. He has a family, and the letter wasn't clear about where they are . . . there are so many things that could . . ." He cleared his throat. "So, ah . . . fact of it is, I told Vash I'd go instead. Wouldn't be able to live with myself if I didn't."

"All right," Morgan said.

That clearly hadn't been what he was expecting. "Oh. Well. So Vash has already said he doesn't mind if you stay here—"

"Oh, no, no, no," Morgan said, before he could get any further. "I've stayed here quite long enough, thank you. I miss Sheath, and I miss my damned tavern, but even if I can't get back to them yet, there is quite simply no chance in hell that I will lie about here on the godsforsaken backside of the continent with

Vash while you run right into the middle of whatever trouble is waiting in Issamira." When he still looked confused, she added, "I'm going with you, you idiot."

He shook his head. "I don't think that's wise."

"I don't care whether it's wise or not. I am *not* staying here without you—I can hardly stand to stay here *with* you. And I'm tired of just waiting for something to happen. If there's something you have to do, then at least I can help you, and that's something."

Braddock looked like he was going to continue the argument, but then he abruptly gave up, and for a moment she almost thought he would smile. "I ought to've known you were going to say something like that."

"Yes, you really should have," Morgan agreed. "Now perhaps you ought to tell me what exactly this friend of yours needs us to do?"

CHAPTER TWENTY-TWO

Tom said every good thief had a sense for things, without ever having to be told. They could hear trouble coming from leagues away, or sniff out treasure in the deepest and dirtiest pit. Marceline had wanted proof she'd had such a talent all her life, but now for the first time she wished she didn't. For if it *were* her thief's sense that was to blame, the fact that she'd been driven to do nothing but practice knife-throwing for the past three days couldn't be good.

She'd thought things had quieted down: the rumors flowing through Sheath had become a sight less fantastical, and even Tom seemed calmer, if as stubborn as ever. But all she had to do was take one look at Roger's face and she felt her spirits sink again—if anyone had a thief's sense, Roger did, and he looked as low as she'd ever seen him.

He'd taken to haunting the Dragon's Head like it was his new home, but he never told her anything about when Morgan was coming back. There were rumors about that she and Braddock had run afoul of the law at last, and had to flee Sheath for good. Although Roger always scoffed at that, he never offered anything in its place. Marceline had to admit she found it unlikely—she'd scarcely ever seen someone more dedicated to the straight and narrow than

Morgan. But she also knew Morgan loved the Dragon's Head, no matter how she might complain. What could compel her to leave it for so long, if not just the kind of trouble everyone whispered about?

She hadn't expected any enlightenment from Roger, and it was just as well—he wasn't providing any. "Go away, monkey," he said wearily, resting his chin atop his crossed hands, which in turn were resting on the bar. "There's nothing here for you."

Marceline scowled at him. "You look like a child."

"And you look like something that crawled out of the gutter, but at least *I've* seen better days."

She was about to snap out a retort when she caught sight of a scrap of parchment pinned beneath his elbow. "What's that?" she asked, tilting her head to try for a better look at it. There wasn't any writing on it, but she could just make out the edge of something—a drawing or symbol, perhaps?

Roger, naturally, started back, snatching up the parchment and shoving it into his pocket. "None of your business and none of your business, thank you. Have any other questions I can refrain from answering?"

Marceline gritted her teeth, trying to keep her voice from growing shrill. "What is *wrong* with you? I haven't seen you in a sulk like this since . . . well, since *ever*." She considered it. "Maybe since the last time you lost a bet with Tom."

He groaned. "Monkey, that is *not* what I need to be thinking about right now."

"Whatever you *are* thinking about, it's clearly not helping your mood any better."

"Can you blame me? Here I am, minding my own like always, just hoping to do a turn or two for a friend here and there, and the whole blasted lot of them are running about like chickens with their heads hacked off, getting into one scrape after another before I've even had time to look round. This could all be so much simpler than they're making it, but they just won't see that." He dragged a hand down his face. "Deinol I expect to have no sense, but to drag the *boy* into his madness! And now Lucius is gone too, the gods only know what Morgan and Braddock are doing or when they'll decide to come back, and I can't even solve one bloody mystery! At this point I've half a mind to shut myself up with a case of liquor and act like your old man."

She ignored that. "A mystery? Is that what that paper's about?"

The way he scowled was proof of how important it was. Roger loved to dangle his secrets just out of reach, lest anyone forget how clever he was. If he didn't want to even tease her about that scrap of parchment, it was because it was a lot more important, and he was a lot further from solving it, than he'd ever let her know.

"You see," she said, "it's times like these when you could use an apprentice."

He snorted. "Don't be ridiculous. What could *you* ever do?"

"Well, how can I know that when I don't even know what it is? Give it here a moment, and then we'll see."

He didn't move. "Monkey, don't make a fool of yourself. There's nothing worth doing you could do that I can't, and that's a fact."

"Oh, is that right?" She was angry enough to stamp her foot right through the floor; she was angry enough to tear half his hair out. But he'd never take her seriously if she raged at him, so she did her best to keep her voice level. And if her fists were clenched, well, it wasn't as if he could see them. "I bet you I could," she said. "I bet you I could find out something you never dreamed of, and you'd be left begging me to tell you."

He laughed, but it was harder than normal, with an edge of bitterness. "I wish you could! I'm in the mood to hear something fantastical these days."

"I'll do it," Marceline insisted. "I will. And then you'll *have* to take me as your apprentice, because you'll be afraid I'll get better than you all on my own."

"Maybe I would, at that," Roger said, slumping over the bar. "But you'll never manage it." There was no grin, so she knew he wasn't trying to bait her; he was just saying what he thought was true. That made it even worse.

"You'll see soon enough," she snapped, though he barely even looked up. She stalked over to the door, about to slam it as hard as she could and get his attention that way. But then she remembered that it wasn't Roger's tavern; it was Morgan's, and wherever she was, she still loved it. So she shut the door as carefully as she could, the hinges barely creaking as she slipped it closed.

———

Tom set his tankard down on the table with an audible clunk and a sloshing sound—which was notable in itself, as he never liked to stop when there was any left. "Well, girl," he said, "I expect you'd better come out with it. It's ruining my evening, and any chance I have to drink in peace."

Marceline sniffed. "You'd finish that ale if Elgar had his whole guard charging through here. And I have nothing to say to you."

"You do, or you'd be off elsewhere with your sulking. Out with it, I say. What's got you in such a snit?"

It wasn't a *snit*. Ugh, he was such an impossible old louse. "You wouldn't understand," Marceline said, folding her arms.

He slung an arm over the back of his chair. "Give an old man his due, at least. I've been putting up with your moods for quite some time now."

"If you want to talk about *moods*—" Marceline bit her tongue, and only barely resisted the urge to slam her hands down on the table. "I'm angry because . . . I want to know things," she said. "I'm as good a pickpocket as there is in this city—even you admit that. My lockpicking's fine enough, and even if my knife skills need . . . more practice, the point of proper thieving is that it shouldn't come to blows in the first place. So that's all fine, and I can hold my head up all right among my own kind. But it's different with you and Roger, because you can find things out that nobody else can—sometimes it seems like you can pluck secrets out of the air. And *that's* what I want to do, because lately I've been feeling like all those secrets are just rushing past me all the time, and I can never grab hold of them."

Tom kept drinking for several moments in silence, but she knew he was considering it. "Well," he said, "you know you'd be welcome to anything I know, if you ever really had need of it. You just couldn't go bandying it about everywhere, but I expect you've learned how to keep your mouth shut by now."

"I know," Marceline said, "but . . . it's not the same thing, is it? It's not the same thing as being able to find out for myself."

Tom ran his thumb along the edge of his tankard. "If you want to find something out for yourself, girl, you've got to start with *what* you want to know. That'll at least narrow it down some."

She'd already had time to think about that. "The Night Market," she said. "That place is odd enough to begin with, but something special's been going on there lately, hasn't it?"

Tom snorted. "Aye, resistance business, and that's the last thing that should concern people like us."

"The resistance?" Marceline asked. "You mean there really is one?"

"Its members'd like you to think so, but there's not enough resistance in the resistance to ruffle a sparrow. It's all talk—that and incompetence, and wishful thinking."

"But it exists," Marceline said. "That's what you're saying, isn't it?"

Tom wrinkled his nose, scratching idly at the rough stubble of one cheek, and it took Marceline a few moments to realize he wasn't sure how to answer her. "Listen, girl," he finally said. "A *resistance* is most truly an idea—a word. Anyone can claim to be such a thing, just by speaking of it, and there are those who've done so—*that* is true. But whether they're a *real* resistance . . ." He shrugged. "I'm not expecting any liberation to come from that quarter. Why, were you thinking of joining?"

Marceline laughed. "Not for my weight in gold. I'm no idiot." She leaned her cheek on her hand. "Do you know who it is, though? Do you know what they're like?"

"You have to ask? They're fools, of course." He took a last great gulp of ale, plunking down the empty tankard. "From what I've been able to turn up, there's not a trained soldier among them. That's not to say that soldiers are the only ones who know how to wield blades, but here it most properly means that our resistance possesses too much in the way of pretty words, and not enough in the way of actual skill." Leaning back in his chair, he added, "You know the one who calls himself their leader is some sort of peasant historian? A book reader from Iron's Den, younger than Halfen. That's the story, anyway."

Damn it, this was sounding worse with every word. Maybe Roger didn't know about this yet, but would he even care? Would he even count it as something she knew that he didn't if the knowledge itself was worthless?

"You're sulking again," Tom said. "Don't tell me you're disappointed?"

"I'm annoyed," Marceline told him. "If they're going to be so useless, why the hell do they have to exist at all? Why can't they just leave all of us alone?"

"I can't help you with that one. Some folk are born to meddle, hopeless or not."

Marceline scratched at the table with one fingernail. "How widely known do you figure this is?"

"In a word, not. I could learn of it, but I do, as you say, have something of a talent for such things. I doubt Elgar's people know, or even common Valyanrenders. Most of Sheath's in the dark too, though I expect that's more to do with the fact that most of us don't care. The merchants at the Night Market know more than they ought, but I think that's about it."

"So that's where the connection to the Night Market is, then? Through the merchants?" Then another thought struck her: "Is that why Seth was arrested? Because he was at the Night Market?"

Tom frowned. "Who's Seth?"

"Morgan Imrick's boy."

"Oh, that whelp at the Dragon's Head? Aye, but that was a mistake. *He* never had any dealings with the resistance."

"Are you sure about that?" Marceline asked. True, Seth was timid and soft, and usually had enough sense to stay out of things that could bring trouble down on him. But Seth had disappeared from the Dragon's Head, hadn't he? If the arrest had truly been a mistake, wouldn't he have come back by now?

But Tom shook his head. "No, that trail's cold, girl. I'd wager there's quite a story behind the current whereabouts of the Dragon's Head's proprietress and her kitchen boy—not least because I haven't been able to find it out. But wherever they are, they aren't in the city. Besides, while the resistance might be made up of poor fighters, I'll admit they've done well to hide themselves for as long as they have. They at least know how to keep secrets, and that boy couldn't conspire his way out of bed in the morning. He's not involved."

"Fine," Marceline said. "Then tell me this: If they're a true resistance, then what exactly are they doing to resist?"

Tom hesitated at that, contemplating the inside of his tankard. "I figure at first all they needed to do was exist. Having pulled that off, they tried to increase their numbers in secret, something it seems they've been able to do well. But now . . . I wonder." He tapped the table with one finger. "There are things even I can't find out for sure. But it seems two of Elgar's most bloodthirsty butchers have met mysterious ends in the past fortnight, and no ready culprits to be found. I wouldn't swear that this resistance is behind it, but I wouldn't swear they weren't."

Marceline kept scratching her edge of the table. "Mysterious ends?"

"Aye. One hanged with a curtain, and the second took an arrow in the throat. Both killed indoors, and no one to say who'd done it. But at two separate times, and in two unrelated places. I suppose it's impressive, after a fashion—I certainly wouldn't be able to do as much. But if that's all they do, it won't make much difference. Elgar pays well to keep his streets the way he likes 'em—I'm sure those two have already been replaced by another lot just as bad, or worse. Their little assassinations might make those overgrown children giggle in whatever lair they've hidden themselves away in, or earn them a handful more recruits to the cause. But it won't change the state of things. That's just a fact."

And that depressed her more than it ought to have done. She didn't doubt Tom was right, and she *didn't* care about any resistance, but it seemed sad to imagine all those people come together, full of rosy ideals and big plans, only to have it all come to nothing in the end. Did some of them know that, too?

She shifted restlessly in her seat. "You said some Night Market merchants had ties to the resistance?"

Tom hesitated again. "The Night Market's gone cold by now, for all I know. There was a man called Peck who had dealings with the resistance, but that mess with Morgan Imrick's boy will have put them on edge. If they've wits at all—and I expect they have at least that much—they'll have cut all ties with him long since."

"Peck," Marceline repeated.

"Aye, Six-Fingered Peck. Though as for fingers, I failed to note that he has any more or less than usual." He squinted at her. "Are you really going to chase him down? You *aren't* thinking of joining, are you?"

"I'm thinking nothing of the sort," Marceline said, "but . . . well, I might see what I can find out there, from Peck or anyone else."

"Nothing that'll do you any good."

"We won't know that until I try, Tom."

He held her gaze, more solemn than she was used to seeing him. "I know I've told you the most important thing about secrets."

"You've got to be able to tell which to latch on to, and which were best let go," Marceline recited. "I haven't forgotten."

CHAPTER TWENTY-THREE

Varalen looked up from the letter. "Well, shit."

"Precisely," Elgar muttered, not moving from his position by the window.

"When did he even get there?"

"The bloody gods know. I don't." Elgar turned sharply on his heel, started pacing the length of the room. "She *would* go, too. She would go all that way just to spite me, instead of staying in the Fellspire like a sensible—"

"We don't know whether she's actually going," Varalen objected. "The boy could've said so as a bluff, to lure you—"

"I know her," Elgar said. "She's going. She wouldn't miss it for all the gold across the sea."

Varalen scratched his cheek. "Well, perhaps. I doubt the boy means to kill *her,* unless he's crazy. Which he may well be, I suppose, to attempt such a thing."

Elgar stopped at the wall, pressing his clenched fist against the stone. He was pale, paler than usual, dark circles standing out starkly under his eyes. "He was cunning enough to devise this scheme to begin with; he'll certainly be cunning enough to know killing her will only hurt him. It's her allegiance he wants, not her death."

"No doubt," Varalen said. "That doesn't mean he'll get it."

"That doesn't mean *I* can allow them to negotiate at all."

"That's just what he wants you to think."

"That doesn't mean he's wrong." His voice was strangely tremulous, not uncertain but breathless, as if he'd run a great distance. Was he unwell again? Varalen half wondered.

"It doesn't mean you should go, either. How can anyone protect you in a place like that, away from your armies?"

"I won't be away from my armies," Elgar said. "The boy may have effectively reclaimed Mist's Edge"—*without spilling a single drop of blood,* Varalen thought bitterly—"but that's all he's reclaimed. Mist's Edge is so close to the border it's practically in Hallarnon; we can march nearly up to his doorstep."

Varalen sighed. "If that's so, my lord, why not just oust him from the castle altogether?"

Elgar did not answer right away; perhaps he felt at least a little shame at claiming *ghosts* as a reason. Perhaps. "It does not matter so much if the boy has reclaimed it," he said at last.

"Doesn't *matter*? Mist's Edge is a fortress! Second Hearth is a lump in the sand by comparison. Kelken is no doubt moving more of his men into it by the day, and now that they've got a foothold there—"

"If it's already going to be difficult to remove them, then why are we even discussing it?" Elgar flattened his palm against the stone. "It's a waste of time."

"My lord, if you'd only kept men there to start with—"

"It's a *waste of time,* I said."

"As you wish." Varalen prodded the map in front of him. "Why not have the boy taken care of while you're there, at least? You might even be able to get rid of Lady Margraine as well." He knew Elgar would say no; he just wanted to hear him justify it.

Elgar scowled. "I'm not fool enough to murder my host in his own halls."

"Why, will the gods strike you down?"

"Mind your tongue." He curled his fingers back into a fist, but stayed by the window, eyes fixed on his hand. "*I* do not need to explain to *you* why I will or will not do a thing."

And I don't have to like it, Varalen thought. "My lord, you're telling me that you actually intend to go, that you intend to simply follow the path this *boy* has laid out for you and put yourself in danger without any real hope of—"

"Benefit?" Elgar laid his free hand atop his fist. "There will be benefits. I have wanted to lay eyes on Arianrod Margraine for some time, and this way I can take the measure of the boy as well."

And that paltry advantage was worth such a risk? Well, Varalen supposed it wasn't his neck at stake. "If you think that is worth the trouble, my lord, the choice is yours to make."

"Indeed it is." Elgar smiled thinly. "There's no need to look so put out, Varalen. I wouldn't dream of leaving you behind."

Varalen tried not to visibly start up in his chair. "What?"

Elgar's smile did not fade. "How could I attempt such a journey without my trusted strategist by my side? I'd be woefully unprepared."

You just want to make sure I don't have the pleasure of escaping any fate that ensnares you. "Will you . . . will you not be taking Shinsei, my lord?"

Elgar's face darkened. "No."

Varalen might have pressed the issue, but he didn't think that was wise at the moment. One thing he was becoming more and more certain of, though—Shinsei wasn't supposed to have been away this long. Elgar was certainly used to sending the man off on strange errands, but he was eager to start his advance into Reglay, and he was becoming ever more distressed and evasive whenever Varalen brought Shinsei into the conversation. Varalen didn't know if Shinsei had rebelled or if whatever task he'd been sent to accomplish was just taking longer than usual, but either way, it was clear things were not going according to plan.

"If you are determined to go without him," he said, "how are we to defend ourselves? Strategist or not, I can hardly help you if we're attacked outright."

Elgar waved the question away. "Don't worry about that. I'll choose enough of my men."

Easy enough to *say* not to worry about it, wasn't it? Gods, what a bloody disaster. "I hope you know what you're doing, my lord."

Elgar stroked his beard. "Yes, you had better."

———

"No," Gravis said. "This is unacceptable."

The marquise smirked at him. "My, that sounds serious."

"My lady, going at all is the highest folly—"

"I have explained to you, several times in fact, why that is an erroneous—"

"But I did not object," Gravis persisted, running over her words, "because I knew you could not be persuaded otherwise. But to expect me to stay behind while you rush headlong into danger—did you ever truly think I would heed such an order? I refuse."

As usual, his agitation only amused her. "You refuse? What about your oath?"

"I swore to *protect* you, not to obey you," Gravis said. "I am the greatest of my men, as you well know. Almasy is talented, to be sure—more talented than I am, I admit—"

Lady Margraine rolled her eyes. "You needn't remind me of your deficiencies, Gravis. I am fully aware that there is no command Seren could not carry out more excellently than you—except, perhaps, for *bore me*."

Gravis ignored that. "She is competent, and she has defended you well in the past. But she is only one person, and the rest of your guard lack my skill. I must go with you, for your own safety."

The marquise raised her eyebrows, though her voice showed no trace of surprise. "You're so concerned for my welfare, Gravis? I've half a mind to be touched. And here I was under the impression you didn't care for me."

Gravis gritted his teeth. "My lady, I am sure I need not explain to you that personal likings and dislikings have nothing to do with it. My oath is my oath, and even without it, your death would be an unmitigated disaster for Esthrades. As you *insist* on not marrying—"

"I do insist on it," the marquise agreed. "Marriage means boredom, and *I* have sworn never to be bored."

"As you insist on not marrying," Gravis continued, "you are all that stands between this kingdom and utter chaos." *Though you hardly act like it,* he didn't add.

"Believe me, Gravis, I'm far less eager to die than you are. But I cannot leave Esthrades's administration to fools while I'm gone. You may be boring, but you are also dependable, and I can trust you to make generally competent decisions without trying to seize anything for yourself."

"Why not do as your father did on his campaigns, and"—too late, Gravis realized he should not have introduced the idea in such a way, but he kept on— "and set up the customary quarter-court?" The quarter-court, according to tradition, was made up of one scholar to read the law, two marquis-appointed judges to interpret it, and one scribe to record all facts and decisions; all judgments made during its tenure were then subject to review and amendment upon the marquis's return.

Lady Margraine propped her chin on her hand somewhat wearily, but she did not look dismissive. "I could do that, but that just means I have to go through it all when I get back."

Gravis tried not to smile—when had more *reading* ever been a problem for her? "My lady, you'd want to look it over yourself even if you had me take care of it." She prized her control far too much not to, but he didn't say that.

"Hmm. That's true." She tapped her jaw. "And the judges?"

Gravis did smile then. "My men have returned from Woodhearth by now, but even if they had not, I would be able to provide you with *two* honest men, at least."

Lady Margraine let out a little huff of breath, but she was sitting up now, pressing her fingertips together. "Well, Gravis," she said, after only a slight pause, "I'm as surprised as you are, but you may actually have convinced me. If you truly want to defend me so much, I suppose I can grant your wish."

Gravis bowed his head. "Thank you, my lady."

She waved him off. "I do hope you don't require much on the road, as I don't intend to delay our departure on your account. And give me the names for the quarter-court so I can draw up the writ."

"Dent will do it fairly," Gravis said, "and Kern—hmm, no, Kern's maybe a bit too eager. You wouldn't want to find the wrong person had been executed when you got back. Benwick's not as sharp, but he's more solid."

"Fair enough." She had already started writing, but she looked up. "Gravis, I was not being metaphorical when I said I was leaving in two hours, so put your affairs in order or I will literally leave you on the steps of Stonespire."

Gravis bowed again, and quickly withdrew to head for the barracks. He didn't need much in the way of supplies, but if he hurried, he could get in a quick word to Dent and Benwick before he left.

He didn't find either of them in the barracks, or in the kitchens, but Kern was there, wolfing down the last of his breakfast. He looked up expectantly when Gravis caught his eye. "Captain Ingret? Is there something I can do for you, sir?"

Had Kern been five years older, Gravis really would have recommended him for the quarter-court—he was quick-witted and thorough, with a dedication to duty uncommon in one so young. But fire could not always stand in for experience, as Gravis well knew, and in situations where quills, not swords, were called for, it was best to let cooler, grayer heads take the lead. "I can't stay long," he said, "but since you're here, there's something I wish to tell you: her ladyship has allowed a quarter-court to be appointed in her stead for the duration of her journey to Reglay."

Kern nodded, but he seemed disappointed. "Then . . . you won't be serving as steward yourself, sir?"

"Certainly not," Gravis said. "My place is with her ladyship."

"Of course, sir, but . . . who will lead us while you're gone?"

"That's what I wanted to speak with you about." He lowered his voice. "There's no finer man than Dent for a task like this, and Benwick will follow him well. I'm going to tell them now, but I want you to watch them closely— it'll be you with Dent in the future, I don't doubt, and I want you to see how it's done."

Kern's eyes nearly doubled in size at that. "A quarter-court? Me? Sir, I—"

Gravis held up a hand. "I didn't say *now,* or even in the *near* future. But you and I both know the value of being prepared in advance."

Kern nodded, vigorously this time. "Of course, sir. Absolutely. I—I'll learn all I can from them."

"Good." He would have said more, but circumstances prevented it. "While we're on the subject, I really don't have much time. Do you know where I can find them?"

"Well, I don't know about Benwick, but I'm fairly certain I saw Guardsman Halley headed for patrol in the orchard."

If it had been up to him, he would have collided with Almasy as he rounded the turn at the bottom of the stairs, but she moved adeptly to the side, not even seeming startled. "Gravis."

"Almasy." He should've said nothing more, but he couldn't resist adding, "It seems I'll be joining you this afternoon."

Her eyebrows rose. "To Mist's Edge? Did her ladyship—"

"Aye, she's allowed it. We'll be leaving a quarter-court."

He'd expected Almasy to be irked—he was fairly sure she didn't like his company—but she only nodded; she almost looked approving. "I had hoped you would take it upon yourself to convince her."

Gravis frowned. "You did? Why?"

"For the same reason you did, I'm sure. None of the others are up to it, and if Elgar decides he feels like being an obstreperous guest—"

"She seems to think he won't."

"She is usually right," Almasy said. "But it's our job to assume she won't be." And there was her self-deprecating smile again, like a blade turned on herself. "Do you think we can find it within ourselves to put aside any grudges that may be between us for the duration? I wouldn't like to give Elgar the pleasure of thinking he sees dissension in our ranks."

"If it comes to *that*," Gravis said, "neither would I."

CHAPTER TWENTY-FOUR

According to Vash, it was impossible to cross the Curse without a guide. But since it was a full day's journey even when you knew where you were going, there wasn't a soul who'd agree to take you if you showed up in the middle of the day. It was just before dawn, then, when they arrived at the waypost he had told them about, a squat, square structure of wood and stone, with stables running alongside it and a loose cluster of people milling about in front. Morgan had watched in disbelief as more and more color seeped out of the land the farther south they went, but the ground beyond the waypost was hardly to be believed. An empty shade between brown and gray, it was devoid of all but rock and dust, without even a single blade of grass to be seen. Here and there on the unvaryingly flat landscape you could spot the gnarled skeleton of a dead tree, always standing alone, always bleached the same dead gray. The ground itself was parched, crumbling underfoot, and she and Braddock kicked up clouds of dust as they walked that were nearly high enough to choke on. The clouds overhead were thick, packed so closely together she wasn't entirely certain whether the sun had risen or not.

Braddock had been anxious and fidgety all morning, and the early hour probably wasn't helping. He had sent a reply to Nasser to let him know they'd be coming in Vash's place, but he didn't want to waste precious time waiting for a reply. So they had no idea if Nasser was expecting them—or even if he was still in a position to receive any letters. "Come on," he mumbled. "Damned if I'm looking forward to this, but we'd best get it over with."

They eventually found their way to the woman in command of the post; she was forty or fifty and just a bit plump, with short, curly hair and slightly crooked teeth. They had to wait to speak with her until the handful of travelers ahead of them had moved off, and she regarded them with a somewhat bored expression. "Ten each in silver," she said, "unless you'll be wanting extra provisions on the journey."

Morgan winced at that number, but Braddock looked unconcerned. "We won't," he said. "And I'll pay for us both."

She watched him count out the coins, then nodded her approval and turned to scan the yard. "Irjan!" she called. "These two are yours."

The young man she'd addressed was sitting cross-legged in the dirt not too far away, bare to the waist except for his long and shaggy hair. He got to his feet before she'd even finished speaking, and buckled on the longsword that had been resting across his knees. Then, without so much as a word, he walked to the side of the building to dig through a pile of what seemed to be clothing.

The woman nodded at them again. "You'll give the cloaks back to him once you've made the crossing."

"Cloaks?" Morgan repeated.

"Aye. You'll be glad enough to have them if a dust storm catches you while you're out there."

By that time the young man had joined them. Up close he appeared about Morgan's own age, graceful and smooth-faced, and with a much milder expression than she'd thought at first glance. He bowed slightly, then held the cloaks out to them, saving the last for himself. "I am Irjan Tal. Well met."

"Likewise," Braddock said.

Morgan gave him a few moments to say more, then sighed. "He means to say that he's Braddock, and my name's Morgan. Don't go looking for his manners; he's never had any."

Irjan smiled gently. "I confess that we've no need for manners where we're going, but what I do need is your obedience. The Curse is a very confusing place, and I've known many a traveler who became convinced *I* had lost my way, and *he* had the right of it. Such thoughts will only waste your time and mine, and quite possibly put our lives at risk. I can assure you I've not gotten lost on the Curse since before I came of age, and I have made the crossing more times than I care to count."

Morgan nodded. "You won't see me arguing with you."

"Aye," Braddock said. "I've no talent for direction, and no wish to claim otherwise."

"If I can hold you to that," Irjan said, "the crossing will be simple. The horses are this way." He wrapped his cloak about himself as he walked, and Morgan and Braddock did the same.

They had to wait for everyone ahead of them to leave before Irjan would move his horse, and even then he led them in a different direction; he explained that the horses had a greater tendency to spook if they clustered close together, so it was better to make the crossing in smaller groups. "They say animals are sensitive to certain undercurrents that humans miss," he offered. "Perhaps the Curse is even more forsaken a place than we know."

"It's certainly bad enough for me," Braddock said, looking about him. The waypost was fast fading into the dust, leaving only that empty color in its wake. "Having to see this landscape every day really doesn't wear on you?"

Irjan shrugged. "At the moment, the Curse is the most convenient place for me to be. From here it is easy enough for me to decide whether I wish to be inside Issamira or outside it, and I can change my mind very quickly, if that becomes necessary."

"Ah," Braddock said. "So if there's any trouble, you can stay well out of it, eh?"

Morgan rolled her eyes at him, but Irjan's chuckle was genuine. "Actually, the opposite is true. I should very much like to travel the continent—perhaps the world itself, one day. But if any misfortune or strife should befall Issamira, I would feel it my duty to come to her aid."

Well, that didn't sound promising. Morgan tried to choose her response carefully. "And do you anticipate very much, ah, strife in the future?"

He grimaced. "Not precisely, but I've been hearing more foolish talk lately than I could ever have imagined. The succession should be a simple matter, but . . ." He shook his head. "A few days ago I caught two of my fellow rangers saying the prince and princess should just have it out on the battlefield. Have you ever heard anything so preposterous? When men talk so glibly about such things, certain fears are warranted."

Braddock's scowl matched his. "Civil war is nothing to scoff at."

"There will be no civil war," Irjan said firmly. "Adora is the rightful queen of this realm, and her brother knows it as well as I do. He is not so craven as to deny it." He pulled up short, scanning the scene before them. To Morgan everything looked the same, but Irjan soon made up his mind, turning his horse just slightly to the left.

"It's that easy, is it?" Braddock asked.

"Why shouldn't it be? It's not as if they are twins. Adora is Hephestion's elder, and that is all she needs to be, to have the law on her side."

"Er, no." He scratched his cheek. "I meant . . . knowing where you're going."

"Ah." Irjan looked surprised only for a moment, then chuckled again. "One gets used to everything, I suppose. I've spent more time on the Curse than anyplace else, I think; perhaps even the incomprehensible becomes comprehensible once it's familiar."

"That's true enough," Morgan said to Braddock. "In Sheath we'd have to guide him."

"Aye, but in Sheath things look different, at least."

"Where is Sheath?" Irjan asked.

"Oh . . . it's part of Valyanrend," Morgan said. "It's where we come from."

"Valyanrend?" He considered it. "I should like to see that place someday. They say it was once the greatest city in the world."

Morgan laughed. "If it ever was, that must have been a long time ago."

He raised an eyebrow at her. "You don't care for it, then?"

"I love it," Morgan said, "but . . . well, let me put it like this: Did you ever know a man who kept a really ugly dog?" Braddock laughed so hard at that, he nearly fell off his horse, but Irjan just kept looking at her politely, only the barest suggestion of a smile tugging at the corner of his mouth. Well, that was understandable; he'd never seen Valyanrend, after all. "I suppose what I mean to say is sometimes you love a thing more when it seems as if you shouldn't, or when other people don't. It's like . . . if you don't love it, who will?"

"Hmm." Irjan still hadn't laughed. "Is Valyanrend an ugly city, then?"

"No, it's—or it mostly isn't, anyway. It's easy to see how it could have been beautiful, once. But beauty doesn't mean very much, in the end—it's the character of a place people love, if they love anything, and Valyanrend's is . . . stubborn, and uncompromising, and always persistent. It won't ever give up, and you have to be like that too, if you live there." The wind blew a cloud of dust into her face, and she blinked. "But it can be surprisingly flexible, too—there are many different ways to get to the same place, even if none of it seems to make sense at first."

She would have blushed by then, if she were at all the blushing sort, but Irjan actually looked as if he understood. "Interesting," he said. "Eldren Cael isn't like that at all."

"Well, what's Eldren Cael like?"

He took only a moment to think on it. "Fierce and proud—and surprisingly hot-blooded, beneath the veneer of stateliness. *It* won't ever consent to be caged, but it demands that you follow its rules, all the same." He looked vaguely ahead of him as he spoke, and at first Morgan couldn't tell if he was speaking in praise of the city or not. But then he smiled. "It is difficult, but worthwhile, as many difficult things are." He glanced over his shoulder at her. "Will you be heading there?"

Morgan, in her turn, looked at Braddock, who shifted in his saddle uneasily. "Hard to say. I doubt we'll find ourselves that far south, but . . ."

Irjan took his evasiveness easily enough. "Well, if you do find yourselves there, I hope you enjoy it. But be on the watch for bandits; I hear they've been especially bold of late."

From what Morgan had heard, the street bandits in Eldren Cael made Lucius and Deinol look like infants. Well, they made *Deinol* look like an infant, anyway. "We'll keep that in mind."

He nodded. "There's another thing: if you're heading south at all, you should make for Ibb's Rest. It's a traveler's haven, so it'll serve you well." He could see he'd only confused them, so he added, "I expect you don't care to know the details, but travelers are honored in Issamira for . . . religious reasons. At a traveler's haven you may stay at no cost, so long as you are on a journey."

Braddock raised his eyebrows. "Well, that sounds convenient. Who *does* pay them, then?"

"The crown," Irjan replied, "though how *much* it pays them depends on the monarch. King Jotun was a religious man, so he lavished them with riches; his eldest son was . . . not, but that matters little now. As to what Queen Adora will decide to do with them, I cannot say, but they must have coin enough for the present. If you're passing anywhere near it, you'll not want to stay anywhere else, I promise you."

"I'm sure you're right," Morgan said. "Thank you."

"Of course." He turned his eyes to the sky, and frowned. "Hmm. We'll want to move a bit faster. And"—he turned his horse's head—"just a touch more this way."

Braddock shook his head. "I've still got no idea how you do that."

Irjan chuckled again. "Well, if you did, I wouldn't be taking your coin, would I?"

The hills north of Reglay were lumpy and low, covered with stunted grass slowly fading to yellow. They hadn't seen the sun for three days, but at least it hadn't rained, and they'd made impressive progress for two city rats who had to get directions at every inn. Seth had been born southeast of the capital, and their trip to Hornoak had already taken him farther afield than he'd ever traveled. But Deinol had finally announced that they were farther east even than that, though *he* only knew because he'd asked a traveling carpenter.

They hadn't run into any battalions yet, but the chance of that grew likelier as they approached the border. "I still think we ought to have gone south," Seth said, though it was far too late for that now.

Deinol shook his head. "Trust me, with the way things are now, five minutes in Reglay is too long. And if we tried to cross the Curse and then cut back across, we'd both be graybeards by the time we got to Esthrades—if we made it at all."

"But what if we can't cross the border? We'll have come all this way for nothing."

"Seth," Deinol said with a laugh, "even if Elgar *didn't* keep old Lanvaldis so clear of soldiers on the pretext of not actually wanting to conquer the whole continent, there are always ways around these things. We'll slip through one way or another."

"I wonder what it's like," Seth said. "Stonespire Hall, I mean, or the Fellspire, or whatever it is. Are we really going to go all the way there?"

"If we have to, to find Almasy," Deinol replied. "Though I'm personally more interested in seeing old Lanvaldis."

"Why?"

"Why? Well, because they used to say it was the most beautiful country, back when it still was one. I expect the landscapes are much the same, even if the ruler's different." He adjusted his pack on his shoulder. "You holding up all right?"

"I might like to sit down fairly soon," Seth admitted.

Deinol jerked his chin at the horizon, where they could see a tiny settlement sprawled out across several hills. "Let's see if we can make it that far. We can make sure we're still going the right way, maybe get a couple drinks or a meal."

"All right." Seth focused his eyes on the little buildings and tried not to look as weary as he felt.

By the time they finally reached the village, Seth's legs were starting to ache something fierce, and it was all he could do not to beg Deinol to let him sit down. Luckily, Deinol had developed quite a thirst, and they soon found their

way to a tavern by the settlement's single road, just a narrow dirt track that me-
andered off into the hills. Seth looked at the red painted rooster over the doorway and thought of the Dragon's Head. It would be lonely there with only Roger
to take care of it.

Seth didn't care about getting the barkeep's attention, so he just slumped
into the nearest empty chair, hanging on to the back of it gratefully. Deinol un-
slung his pack and left it in the adjacent chair, then hesitated before passing
Seth on his way to the bar. "Get you anything?"

"We can look for a well once I feel like moving," Seth said, "but not ale,
no." Deinol nodded, and Seth followed him with his eyes as he approached the
barkeep, a portly man with receding ginger hair who couldn't have looked less
like Morgan.

"A full tankard," Deinol said. "And some directions, if you don't mind."

"I don't," the man said, pouring it. "Where're you headed?"

"The Fellspire."

The barkeep scratched at his stubble. "Well, you've got a long way to go yet.
Planning to cross from old Lanvaldis?"

"That's right."

"Well, if you make for Stone's Throw, you can head straight south from
there—Cutter's Vale is usually pretty clear. Things've been quiet most everywhere lately . . . perhaps too quiet, given what happened in Reglay."

"What happened in Reglay?" Seth called from his table.

The barkeep spat. "Old Kelken's dead. Long live the new Kelken, or some
such. Though I suppose he's not likely to, if those legs are as twisted up as people
say."

"Was the old king killed?" Deinol asked.

The barkeep shrugged. "That's the rumor. It's not as if I was there."

"Fair enough," Deinol said. He took the ale, then slapped some coins down.
"How do you like that?" he asked Seth once he'd taken his seat, gulping his
drink down with relish.

"What, the king's death? Do you think it was Elgar?"

"Who else would it be? None of the other rulers have anything to gain from
killing him." He scowled. "I suppose it's only a matter of time before the war
starts up again in earnest—a full assault against Reglay, just like with Lanvaldis
or Aurnis all those years ago. Only Reglay will hardly take as long to conquer—
it's the smallest country on the continent, and it has no defenders to recommend
it. Aurnis had the *shinrian,* Lanvaldis had its lauded army, and they still fell in
the end. What does Reglay have? The ghosts of Mist's Edge? A great help they've
been so far."

Seth scratched at his neck, trying not to look too longingly at Deinol's drink—it was water he wanted, and ale would just make him thirstier. Instead he looked toward the doorway, watching people trickle in and out. There was hardly anyone around, but he supposed that wasn't unusual in the middle of the afternoon.

A man who'd just walked in aimed a laugh in the barkeep's direction. "You look even more sour than usual, Nott. Lose out on business yesterday?"

"You know I did," the barkeep growled, "and as it wasn't you who profited from it, you can stop smirking."

The man held up his hands, still laughing. "Hey, if you scowl any more severely, you'll crack your jaw. Is it my fault the louts in this town would rather gossip than drink?"

The barkeep spat. "If it's *novelties* they want, they can find murderers twelve for a bit on the road."

"Aye, Nott, but you didn't *see* this one, did you? I wouldn't have thought he could cut up a corpse."

"Has there been a murder?" Deinol called lazily, taking another gulp of his drink.

The man turned to him. "Aye, stranger. Neighbor of mine got himself done in—member of the *watch,* I suppose I should call him, but this place is too small to really have any such thing. Some Aurnian swordsman cut him down in the middle of the night—claims he was provoked, but no one else was around to say different, were they? It's a damned mess. Nobody knows what to do with him."

Deinol and Seth stared at each other. "It—it *couldn't* be," Deinol said at last.

"Couldn't it?" Seth whispered. "What if he came looking for us?"

"Well, he wouldn't be able to *find* us, would he? Besides, how could he possibly have beaten us here?"

"Lucius traveled all over before he came to the capital," Seth insisted. "He wouldn't need to blunder around like we've been doing. And he's efficient. He might have been able to overtake us."

Deinol shook his head. "It's not possible. It'd be the strangest coincidence I ever heard of." But he called back to the stranger nonetheless. "Do you know anything else about this swordsman?"

"They say he's brilliant," the man said, with an easy shrug. "That's why they're so wary about letting him go—if he's lying, and he *did* murder for some unsavory reason, they don't want a fellow like that running free with a sword. He's been mostly calm about it, though—won't say much, or talk about where he's from or where he's going. Quiet sort, I guess, but you should've seen the body he left." He jerked his thumb out the door. "He's gotten quite a lot of visitors already, so go and see him if you like. We don't have what you'd call a jail, but they're keeping watch over him down by the big house to the east."

Seth exchanged another glance with Deinol. "We ought to just go look. It can't hurt to know for sure it's not him."

"Aye, aye," Deinol said, throwing back the last of his ale and getting to his feet. "Right you are. We'll go see this Aurnian wonder."

They didn't have to ask directions again: there was a small crowd gathered outside one of the bigger houses, around what looked like a stable. A couple of men in boiled leather were standing guard next to one of the stalls, but several people were staring into it heedlessly, and Seth and Deinol drew up alongside them.

Whoever the swordsman was, he certainly wasn't Lucius. He was a bit short and very thin, with dark hair cut closely but unevenly about his face. But what struck Seth most about him was how young he looked—younger than Deinol, perhaps only two or three years older than Seth himself.

The young man—or boy, or whatever he was—had been sitting listlessly in a patch of straw, his chained wrists resting on his knees, but then he looked up at Seth, his eyes widening and then focusing. "Sebastian?" he asked.

Everyone turned to stare at Seth then, even Deinol, and he shrank under their gaze, too stunned to say anything at first. "You know this one?" one of the men standing guard asked.

"Um," he said. "No, I'm Seth. I don't . . . I don't think I know him."

They looked unconvinced. The prisoner was looking about him, his eyes darting from face to face. "Did I say something strange again?" he asked.

The man who'd spoken before rested one hand atop the stall door. "Did you say this boy was a friend of yours?"

The prisoner stared at Seth again, cocking his head. "No," he said. "He looked a bit like Sebastian, but I was mistaken."

"That's more words than we've got him to say in the past six hours," the guard muttered to Seth.

"What are you going to do with him?" Seth asked.

"What can we do, if he won't talk?"

"I *did* talk," the prisoner pointed out mildly. "They asked me to explain what happened, and I did. But then they said I was lying. I wasn't, but they said I was. After that, there was nothing left to do."

"You wouldn't answer questions."

"I did," the prisoner repeated. "They said I was lying. Then they asked me more questions. I didn't see the point of answering. How is it that anyone should ask a man to say more after they've already decided he's a liar?"

"A man?" the guard retorted. "I see a boy."

The prisoner shook his head. "I am older than I look, I think. I haven't been a boy for a long time."

"Oh? And how long is that?"

"Since Aurnis fell," the prisoner said, and leaned his head back against the wood.

Seth touched his mouth. "I don't think he's lying," he said to the guard, although doubtless that would sound ridiculous.

The man shrugged. "*I* know. Doesn't seem like he'd be a good liar, does he? But I swear this is more than he's talked in days. *I've* been coaxing him since my watch started." He looked at the prisoner, then nodded at Seth. "You like this one, eh? Even if he's not your friend?"

"I don't know this one," the prisoner said, not unkindly. "But he put me in mind of Sebastian, and I liked Sebastian."

"Where is this Sebastian now?"

The prisoner had seemed animated enough before, but now he slumped, as if collapsing in on himself. "I don't know."

"Is it him you were looking for?"

"No."

"But you *were* looking for someone."

The prisoner hesitated. "Yes. Or . . . no. I don't know."

"You don't know?"

The prisoner shook his head, burying his face in his hands. "I . . . there's someone I'd like to find, but I don't know where to look. So I wasn't *actually* looking. I wasn't doing much of anything."

"I see," the man said, but he didn't look like it. "That's . . . illuminating."

"Might be he's a simpleton, Geoff," the other man standing guard said.

Geoff sighed, scratching his stubble. "Gods know." If the prisoner minded being talked of like that, he didn't show it.

Deinol tugged on his sleeve, but Seth kept looking at Geoff. "They're not going to hurt him, are they?"

He twitched his shoulders uncomfortably. "I don't think he deserves that, but . . . well, a man's dead."

"Many men are dead," the prisoner said. "I killed some of them, but not all."

Geoff threw up his hands. "There, you see? What am I supposed to do about that?"

Seth peered down at the prisoner. "Listen," he said. "You don't want them to hurt you, do you?"

"No," the prisoner agreed. "Why would I?"

"So then you have to explain what happened."

"I did."

"Well . . . explain it again. Explain it to Geoff."

The prisoner tucked his chin between his knees. "The man they want to know about asked me why I was there. I said I was still figuring it out, which was true. He got angry—maybe because he was drunk, but I don't know—and asked if I mocked him. I said I wasn't, which was also true. He asked me where I came from, and I said I wasn't going to tell him. He said he was a member of the watch, and I didn't say anything because I had nothing to say. He asked if I mocked him again, and I said no again. Then he said I had to answer his questions, and I said I didn't and wouldn't, which was true. Then he drew his sword, and he started to say something else, but I killed him before he could finish it."

Geoff winced, tugging at his forelock. "You don't think you might've heard him out before you offed him?"

The prisoner shrugged. "He drew his sword on me. Clearly he had decided that words were insufficient."

"He might've just been trying to threaten you."

"He had no business threatening a better swordsman than he was." He looked at Seth. "That's an explanation, isn't it?"

"Er," Seth said. "Did you say it like that the first time?"

"I said I killed him because he drew his sword on me."

"Well, but you don't always try to kill people who do that, do you? Or else you wouldn't be here."

"I surrendered," the prisoner said. "At that point I could see why they were upset." He stared glumly at the straw at his feet. "I didn't *want* to kill him. I probably wouldn't have, if I'd thought better of it. But I was taught to strike quickly, and without hesitating."

"Who taught you that?" Geoff demanded.

The prisoner fidgeted. "Many people," he said, finally.

"Do you like talking in riddles?"

"They are not riddles to me," the prisoner said.

Deinol shook his head. "Seth, he's daft. What do you want with him?"

"He isn't," Seth insisted. "There's nothing wrong with what he said. And he . . . he shouldn't have killed that man, but the man shouldn't have drawn on him. He might've been killed himself, if he hadn't struck first."

Geoff pressed the heel of his hand into his forehead. "Well, I don't suppose I can let them punish him too harshly after that, can I? But to just let him go . . ." He stared helplessly at the prisoner. "You've got a strange sense of things, friend, that's for sure."

"Are we friends?" the prisoner asked; he looked almost embarrassed. "I . . . rather thought you didn't like me."

If it had been anyone else, Seth would've suspected irony in the words, but the prisoner looked so earnest that he couldn't. Geoff clearly didn't know what to make of him either, and finally turned to Seth. "Listen, you there," he said. "Boy. You've got to stay on until he can repeat that to Haytham. He never started answering my questions until you came along." He nodded to his companion. "Jem, fetch Haytham. Tell him the prisoner's got more to say."

After Jem left, Deinol stepped out awkwardly from behind Seth. "Now, look here. This really has nothing to do with us. We were just passing through, and we can't stop to dawdle, anyway."

Geoff didn't look impressed. "The boy seems to want to make sure justice is done. Don't you, lad?"

Seth nodded. "I do."

Deinol smacked his forehead. "Not this again. Remember what happened the last time you decided to help a stranger?"

What happens to weak people? Seth had asked Seren. He tried to put it out of his mind, to ignore the itch at his neck. "You're stubborn, too, aren't you?" he asked. "You don't quit something just because it doesn't turn out the way you hoped the first time. If I can help straighten this out, why shouldn't I?" *At least it's something I can do,* he didn't add.

Deinol threw up his hands. "Gods, have it your way. Never say I hindered any friend of mine from his noble undertakings."

Haytham was an older man with a thick white beard and a heavy gait. "Are you in charge here, then?" Deinol asked when he saw him.

Haytham laughed. "We're not important enough to warrant any lordlings or officials here, I'm afraid. People have liked the way I handled things in the past, so sometimes they call on me to take care of 'em again. Especially for things like this—nobody wanted to be the one to have to pass judgment on this poor fellow." He looked down at the prisoner. "Well? Jem tells me he's decided to talk."

"And how," Geoff agreed. He nodded at Seth. "It's this one got him to speak."

"Ah, I don't think it was me exactly," Seth said, blushing under Haytham's intense scrutiny. "It was more like he . . . saw me, and then felt like talking."

"Do you, then?" Haytham asked the prisoner. "Got more helpful things to say than last time, I hope?"

"You should tell him what you told me," Seth said, when the prisoner hesitated. "Just say it the same way you said it before."

The prisoner was thankfully able to repeat most of what he'd said, and Haytham listened faithfully, pursing his lips every so often. "Why did you not tell it like this from the first?" he asked once the other man had finished.

"I am . . . not used to speaking to large groups of people at once," the prisoner said. "It fatigued me."

"But the boy didn't fatigue you?"

The prisoner considered it. "I liked his face. He reminded me of Sebastian."

"Sebastian?"

The prisoner sighed. "My friend. You all ask so many questions—or else you ask the same ones endlessly."

"We're trying to help you," Haytham said.

"It would help me to be unchained, and to be allowed to go. And to get my sword back," he added, almost as an afterthought.

"Yes, well, before we go *that* far, we've got to make sure you won't harm anyone else."

"I have told you I have no intention of harming anyone else," the prisoner said.

Haytham shook his head. "You said if they didn't impede you. But when we asked what it was they might impede, you wouldn't answer. When we asked you what you intended and where you were going, you wouldn't answer."

The prisoner did not dispute his words; he frowned, looking at the straw. "I suppose I do not know what I might wish to do," he said at last. "I do not know where I should go."

"You can't go home?" Haytham asked.

The prisoner hesitated again. "Perhaps I can," he said, "but I do not wish to. Not now."

Haytham stroked his beard. "Well, I don't think you can stay *here*. That's the thing."

The prisoner shrugged. "Then I'll leave."

"And go where?"

"I don't know. But I don't need to be here any more than I need to be anywhere else."

Haytham stepped back from the stall. "Well, Geoff?"

But Geoff was looking at Seth and Deinol. "You two. You're passing through?"

"Oh no," Deinol said. "Oh no, I don't think I like where this is going."

Seth ignored him. "Aye. Headed through Cutter's Vale, most likely."

Geoff nodded at the prisoner. "So just make sure he goes with you."

"Make sure the *murderer* goes with *us*?" Deinol repeated.

"Well, you don't have to give him his sword back," Geoff pointed out. "You're a much bigger man than he is, and you've got the boy, haven't you? What's he going to do to you? Just take him a day or two away from here, and then you can let him go where he likes." He paused, remembering Haytham's presence. "That sound all right?"

Haytham sighed. "I suppose."

"Gods, but you folk have strange ideas of justice," Deinol said. "I assume *you're* happy, Seth? Now that you've gotten us involved with yet another eccentric killer. Are you drawn to them?"

"It won't matter much to us," Seth said. "And this way they don't have to hurt him."

"You can even keep the shackles on if you like," Geoff added. "But I'm with the boy; I don't think he plans you harm."

Deinol waved him away. "Come on, I'm not heartless. You can take the bloody chains off, and the fellow can come with us." He peered at the prisoner. "Speaking of, what's your name?"

The prisoner bit his lip.

Deinol rolled his eyes. "Come on. Am I going to have to get Seth to ask you?"

The prisoner shook his head. "Ritsu," he said. "Ritsu Hanae is my name."

CHAPTER TWENTY-FIVE

The worst thing about people with a talent, Roger, Gran had said once, is when they're damned stupid at everything else. And the second worst thing is when they love money too much. She'd paused, scrunching up her face. Wait, maybe I've got that backward. Let me think on it.

Either way, Gran had been right in the main, as she always was. And the worst thing about Tom Kratchet was that he was precisely one of those people. So Roger just kept spinning the coin between his fingers, watching the way Tom's eyes followed it, as he knew they would. Tom rubbed the back of his hand over his mouth. "That's not even real, Halfen, and you know it."

Roger tossed the coin and caught it again, brought it to his mouth and bit down. "Oh, I don't know, Tom. Tastes pretty real to me."

"And what if it is? I've seen its like before."

"Aye, in other people's pockets." He leaned forward, hiding the coin in his fist. "Look here, Tom. There's just one thing I've got to know."

Tom sniffed. "There's always *just one thing* with you, Halfen—'cept you come armed with ten of 'em at a time, and you reckon that means you can buy 'em cheap. This business don't work that way."

Roger smiled. "All right, there's just one thing *today*. But I can be reasonable; I know I'm always coming around to bother you, and you're a busy man. There are bound to be things you don't know, after all. So I'm prepared to give you this coin regardless, just for making an honest effort." He tossed it up again, then caught it easily out of the air. "Thing is, this lovely's got a twin, and they sure would hate to be parted. And I figure they'd be just as happy in your pocket as in mine, so . . ."

There was the glint in Tom's eyes, the reflection of silver that he'd been looking for. "Eh," he said, and scratched his chin. "Eh, well, I could hear you out. I'll hear you out."

"Delighted," Roger said, "but I don't need you to listen so much as look. Here." He drew the parchment from his pocket and unfolded it on the table so Tom could see.

Roger was a decent sketch, so it looked more or less the way the mark in the passage had; trouble was, *that* mark was clearly supposed to be a copy of something else, and he didn't know how accurate the original artist had been. It wasn't as if he remotely *enjoyed* asking Tom for help, but he wasn't about to let pride get in the way of finding an answer, and he'd exhausted every idea he was able to come up with on his own. Tom did have a way with such things, and these days Roger could spare the coin.

Tom blinked at the parchment, wrinkling up his nose. "Looks like some old lord's sigil."

"Yes," Roger said. "That's what I thought too."

"Been no sigils since the end of the empire."

"Yes, I *know* that, Tom. Why don't you tell me something I *don't* know."

Tom grunted. "All right, all right, let me see what I've got." He turned away from Roger to a trunk in the far corner, his thin, knobby hands sifting through its contents expertly.

That was his one talent, or maybe it counted as two—he found ways to collect bits of information that slipped through everyone else's fingers, and he could recall where he'd stashed them with surprising accuracy. Roger would've given much to learn how Tom had amassed his hoard, but he supposed a man could have only so many talents at once.

Tom came up for air, a tattered old piece of parchment in one fist, and frowned. "Nope, that's *two* branches. . . . Hold a tick." He descended back into the mess, but before long he was out again, and this time he let out a rusty giggle. "Ah, *here* it is. You owe me two silvers, Halfen."

"Let's see," Roger said, leaning forward as Tom tugged an entire book free of the clutter. Or no, it wasn't an *entire* book—it was a fragmentary ruin of one, the spine torn down the middle and pages ripped out of the surviving half in chunks. "Well, it doesn't . . . er. What is it?"

"Heraldry," Tom said, cracking the book open—well, more open. "I'm sure I saw that damned branch in here somewhere, I just have to find it."

Roger watched him flip the pages, barely glancing at the centuries of history he was passing by, all the houses that had scrabbled for glory and fought one another and risen up from nothing and collapsed into dust. That was the end of every story in the capital: *and then it fell, never to rise again.* There were no more knights, and men who called themselves lords now had only names, where once there had been all this color, all this intricacy. The famous ones he knew, the ones from the tales, like Eglantine's red-green hummingbird and the melancholy moon of House Valerian; he did not see the single white feather of House Darrow, but it flickered behind his eyes anyway. When Tom came to a bloody sword, Roger made him stop, peering curiously at the name written there. "Wait, House Radcliffe? As in *the* House Radcliffe?"

"Don't know that there was ever more than one," Tom muttered. "The Palindors always claimed they were once Radcliffes, but they don't count."

The gods only knew where he'd learned *that*. "What about Trevelyan? Is Trevelyan in there?"

"Ought to be." He flicked through a dozen more pages and suddenly stopped; Roger whistled, staring at the page. House Trevelyan's sigil was a single golden branch on a field of green—brighter colors than in Roger's sketch, perhaps, or than had been etched onto a dusty stone wall, but the design was the same.

Tom peered from the book to the parchment and back again, stringing his words together slowly. "Say, Halfen, where'd you find that mark in the first place, anyway?"

Roger grinned. "That wasn't part of the deal, was it?"

"Maybe not, but I sure as hell remember what was." He held out his hand. "I'll take both, as promised, and thanks much for your business."

"As promised," Roger agreed, reaching for the second coin. He didn't even feel particularly bad about handing them over, despite Tom's smug expression.

Tom bit both coins, and appeared satisfied with them (as well he might be— they were perfectly genuine). "Do you want the page?" he asked, in a surprising show of generosity.

Roger looked down at it, and laughed. "No, no, I don't need any proof. I just wanted to know what it was for . . . personal reasons. And now I do." He folded the parchment and stood up to go, tossing one last glance over his shoulder. "Pleasure as always, Tom. I'll call on you again, I'm sure."

"Mmph," Tom replied, still focused on the coins.

It had been all Roger could do inside not to allow his face to give him away; it was all he could do outside not to run through the streets with a whoop. He felt the old elation rise in him, the anxious joy of knowing a secret that was *just too good* to keep to yourself. He wanted to yell it from the rooftops.

Instead he returned to the Dragon's Head, trusting the enforced isolation to keep him from blurting it out. He might've told Seth—easily impressed and faultlessly trustworthy, the boy was his favorite audience. He might've told Morgan, too; she wouldn't have cared, but she'd at least have pretended to listen, and she wouldn't have told anyone. He might even have told Braddock; he wouldn't have listened *or* cared, but he would've provided an excuse for Roger to say *something* about it. But none of them were here. (Here or not, Lucius and Deinol were never any good, Deinol because he was the biggest blabbermouth Roger knew, and Lucius because he always eventually told everything to Deinol.) And if this secret was too good to keep to himself, it was too good twice over to let just anyone have a piece of it.

The lack of an audience was torturous, but Roger was forced to endure. Hell, he'd even have told Lucius's little dragon statue about it, just for the pleasure of saying the words aloud. Instead he slumped into a barstool, stretching his hands out along the top of the bar. "Friend," he murmured to the darkness, "be it known that today I, Roger Halfen, have single-handedly uncovered the truth behind one of our land's greatest mysteries—well, all right, I guess Morgan *did* help a little. She . . . found the passage and whatnot. And Braddock was there too. But I *mostly* single-handedly uncovered the truth behind one of our— nay, the *world's* greatest mysteries. I have trod in the footsteps of Radcliffe and Trevelyan—double-crossers both, and of a height to which we poor swindlers can only aspire. I have trod in their footsteps, and I know their story. And I am the *only* one who knows it."

The words sent a pleasant little shiver down his spine, and he realized that at some point during the speech he'd sat up again, leaning forward over the bar. He laughed at himself, relaxing again and propping his chin against his hand.

Radcliffe and Trevelyan, the two treasonous councilors, had been jailed by Vespasian Darrow in the last days of the empire. They had escaped together, and had gone on to help lead one of the most impressive military offensives in recorded history. Their battles were well documented; what had never been clear was how they had managed to escape in the first place. People had been known to escape from the Citadel before, of course, though such occurrences were not common in the days of Elesthene. But to escape not just the dungeons but also the *city,* at a time when it was at its most closely guarded . . . no one had been able to figure it out.

But the marks on the tunnel walls were clear. Trevelyan had used them to mark which passages he and Radcliffe had tried—and they led to the first pathway Morgan and Braddock had used, the one that ended outside the city walls.

Roger helped himself to a tankard of ale, laughing once more. Before he drank, he raised it in a toast, holding it aloft in the darkness of the room.

"Not to worry, milords," he said, taking a hearty swig. "Your secret's safe with me."

———

When the rich folk were tucked up in their manses in Goldhalls, telling their little ones stories of the thieves and gutter-dwellers that crawled about them like so many rats, they said the Night Market was a dark and dangerous place, buzzing with treachery and corruption, where any commodity on earth could be bought and sold, no matter its nature. The truth, of course, was that no one liked the notion that everything was for sale more than the rich themselves, and that if such a site of commerce had existed, its merchants would hardly set it up at a time and place known to all.

It was a market for the strange, certainly, so perhaps it was fitting that it had sprung up in a strange place. Everyone knew Draven's Square, but nobody knew who Draven actually was, though that didn't stop them from making up stories. Some said he was a hero who had held the square during a rebellion, others that he was a notorious brigand who had been hanged in it. Many claimed that he was actually *Daven,* one of the Daven Margraines, and that the name had been changed after the sixth Daven Margraine rebelled against the capital. But no one could say which of the five previous Davens might have given his name to the square, or what cause the marquis of Esthrades might have had for lingering in such a place to begin with.

Marceline had asked Roger about it, once, because that was exactly the kind of thing Roger cared to know and Tom didn't. But he had only sulked. "Spent months on that one when I was a boy, monkey, and never turned up so much as a whisper. Even Gran couldn't help me—if she ever had the memory, it must've gotten lost. Don't remind me of my failures."

The square was a rough circle, and easy to pass through by day. But after dark it quickly became clogged with stall upon stall, crammed close together in concentric rings. Some merchants hawked their wares to the crowd, but most preferred to let an air of mystery settle over whatever they had to sell, some strange trinket looming half in shadow in the corner of a stall or glinting vaguely in the torchlight.

What *did* the Night Market sell? Things you couldn't get anywhere else—or so its merchants would have you believe. Tom liked to say that was because if you *tried* to sell them anywhere else, no one would buy them, and Marceline didn't doubt that was true of more than a few stalls. But even Tom himself was known to browse his way through the Night Market every turn of the moon or so, and he hated to waste his time, let alone his coin.

Marceline ducked around a stack of supposed spell books, their covers marked with strange letters she couldn't read, and circled behind a skinny man in a blacksmith's apron who claimed to be selling a dagger of vardrath steel. A sweet-sharp tangle of scents waylaid her for a moment, and she lingered in the shadow of a stall while its owner showed a wandering couple an array of strange flowers and fruits. But she wasn't here to buy, even if she could easily have turned up the coin for it in a crowd like this. Instead she pushed her way past the gawkers and toward one of the inner circles, looking, as she'd been told, for a dark-skinned merchant with a missing tooth and the ordinary number of fingers, selling an assortment of glass bottles filled with mysterious substances, powders and oils and liquids of all colors.

When she finally found the man, Marceline peered at him through the torch-light, looking for the missing tooth. "Are you Peck?"

"I've been called that."

"What do you sell here?"

He smiled, and there it was. "Why come here if you don't know?"

"How do you expect to sell anything if you won't answer a simple question?"

"I never said I wouldn't answer it." He indicated the bottles with one sweeping motion. "They're medicines—for any ailment you can think of, and many more you can't. Does that interest you?"

On a different evening, Marceline would've informed him that she highly doubted that, and probably would have proceeded to rattle off as many diseases as she could, trying to catch him out. But she didn't have time for that tonight. "Do you know they call you Six-Fingered Peck? Or did you come up with that name yourself?"

He shrugged. "It's not of my design, but I don't care who uses it."

"But you don't have six fingers."

He smiled. "You're a very strange child."

"I'm not a *child*," Marceline said. "And I can guess why people call you that. It's because you're a thief."

"How little you know." He brushed his thumb idly against the cork of one of his bottles. "The name is simple, but it befits a man who comes by knowledge from different sources—many fingers in many matters, as they say."

It was the kind of opening she'd been waiting for, and she doubted she'd get a better one. "I don't doubt that's true," she said. "I've heard that you know more than you should about—"

He waved a hand to cut her off. "I know more than nothing about many things, but more than I *should*? Never. I'm quite careful about that."

"Well, you weren't careful enough." Marceline folded her arms. "You know more than you ought—and more than most people do—about the resistance."

His expression didn't change. "I certainly don't know about *that*. Does such a thing even exist?"

"You know it does," Marceline said.

"Perhaps you know it does, young lady, but if I were you, I'd keep that knowledge to myself. We can continue on in this fashion for as long as you like, but unless you wish to hear more about medicines, I will tell you nothing I have not already told you."

Marceline was unmoved. "I can change your mind."

His expression approximated surprise, but she couldn't tell if it was genuine. "Can you?"

"I can," Marceline said, "or you wouldn't still be talking to me—baiting me, even, if I'm not mistaken. How much coin do you want?"

He smiled. "From the look of you, far more than you have."

"Maybe," Marceline said, "but not more than I *will* have, in a handful of minutes, if that's what you want."

His eyebrows lifted. "You claim more than a little skill, then. You'll forgive an honest man for being . . . both cautious and skeptical, shall we say?"

She rolled her eyes. "All right, how's this: I'll do what I do best, and when I'm done, you can decide for yourself how much of my spoils you want to earn. *Honestly,* of course."

Roger was a skilled pickpocket; Tom had been, in the past, but these days he mostly left that portion of his business to her. Every pickpocket needed to be quick and nimble, to be able to size up marks accurately and disappear at the first hint of danger. It took more than that to be brilliant. Tom was brilliant because he had a nose for gold like a wolf's after blood, tempered with enough cowardice to keep his natural greed in check. Roger was brilliant because he was a born dissembler, a showman and tale-teller, diverting your attention in twenty different directions, and not a single one of them to his hand in your pocket. But Marceline was brilliant because she had, better than anyone she knew, perfected the art of not being noticed. No one could suspect her of any mischief when her very presence stirred them less than a shadow, and many a time her marks had helped her disappear by jostling her into the crowd, unaware they'd dislodged their purses into the bargain. It didn't take her long to earn more coin than she was willing to give Peck, damn however much he asked for. At least she'd be taking something of value back to Sheath with her tonight, even if it wasn't what she'd sought.

She was half surprised to find Peck still in his place when she returned, but that assured her beyond a doubt he was persuadable; he'd surely have bolted otherwise. "All right," she said, laying one silver coin in the empty space between two bottles, "there's a start."

He made no move to pick it up. "A meager one at that." Marceline jingled the coins in her pocket, and he laughed. "How many of those are made of copper?"

Marceline pulled out a fistful of coins and laid another piece of silver beside the first, and then another. Then she opened her hand and showed him how much she had left in her palm.

She had learned Peck could control his face well, but she thought she saw a hint of true surprise at last. But then his face settled, and he smiled again. "It seems you have a talent."

"Aye, and you're not the first to say so." She closed her hand again, slipped the coins back into her pocket. "Well?"

He sighed. "Well, I think you're likely to be disappointed—" Marceline made to snatch the coins from in front of him, but he covered them with his hand, sparing her a forlornly reproving look. "I wasn't finished. You're likely to be disappointed, *but* I will tell you what I can."

"Then tell," Marceline said.

He leaned forward. "I was never anything so exalted as their comrade, but I knew one or two of them from . . . before their involvement, let's say. My medicines, though you seem to have naught but scorn for them, have many uses, and I was happy to continue selling them to my old friends. If we gossiped to pass the time, who could blame us?"

"So they came here regularly—or a couple of their members did."

"Not according to any schedule, certainly. But I do sell my wares in finite quantities, so when they run out . . ."

"They come back for more. Fine. Who are the ones you knew from before?"

He shook his head, and when Marceline reached in her pocket again, he only repeated the gesture more fervently. "Enough trouble came down on me and them in this place, but we managed to elude the worst of it. I am not so greedy as to tempt fate a second time."

There was only one thing Marceline could think of that he might have been referring to. "You mean when they arrested that boy here, don't you?"

"Aye, *that* whole mess. Haven't had a fright like that in years, I promise you."

"So how did it happen?"

"If I knew that . . . well, perhaps I'd sleep easier and perhaps I wouldn't. I caught the eye of *someone,* though I can't say who, or how. I must've lost it, though—believe me, I wouldn't be talking to you now if I thought I was still being watched. The tales rustling through the low places of this city have been of a different sort lately, so perhaps Elgar's shifted his gaze to other concerns. Perhaps whoever watched me before assumed it wasn't worth a second try. Perhaps they were merely perceptive enough to notice I have naught to do with my old friends anymore."

Marceline frowned. "Nothing to do with them?"

"Aye, who could blame them after what happened? I wasn't eager to have them come round again anyway, so I was just as glad they had the sense not to."

If he was telling the truth, that didn't bode well for what she might learn from him. "What do you know about the rest of them—the ones who aren't your friends? Or about what they've got planned?"

He shrugged. "Enterprising rats can burrow surprisingly far, you know. Iron's Den is positively infested, and I *hear* . . . well. They have more coin than a group of layabout commoners ought, and I wouldn't be surprised if the purse strings stretched east. Even as far as a place they once called Lanvaldis."

"There are Lanvalds financing the resistance?" If that was so, they had to be more powerful than Tom and the rest believed. Even though the Lanvalds had plenty of reason to hate Elgar, you didn't empty your pockets *and* risk treason unless you were fairly certain you'd see some return on your investment.

"Who knows?" Peck said, his face infuriatingly calm. "All I can say for certain is that there were many nobles in Lanvaldis when Elgar conquered it, and there are few creatures more determined to have their way—whatever the cost."

"But what would make Lanvaldian nobles have such faith in a group of common Valyanrenders?"

After a few moments of silence, Peck smiled. "Did you really expect me to answer that? *That* would be a very dangerous thing for me to know indeed. And really, the less I know about them, the better. For them, but above all for me."

Perhaps he was lying, and perhaps he wasn't. But Marceline had done enough bartering to know he wasn't going to tell her any more, whether he had anything worth telling or not. She could empty her pockets before him, and it wouldn't do her a bit of good.

"One more question," she said, "and then I'll leave you be. Can you buy candles here?"

Peck looked confused, but she didn't need him to understand why she was asking—in fact, it was probably better that he didn't. "They're a bit too mundane to sell here," he said, "but there's a chandler's shop right off the square where you can buy them—it's on the Ashencourt side."

"Thanks," Marceline said, giving him her best attempt at a disarming smile, and cast a departing glance at the coins she had given him. "Glad to do business with you."

"I hope we will both remain so," Peck replied, keeping his eyes on her as she turned to walk away.

CHAPTER TWENTY-SIX

T he last of the mist had burned away by early afternoon, so Kel could stand on the battlements and watch Elgar's retinue make its leisurely way forward, small and struggling against the trees so far below. The gate was open to receive them, but it would be as long as half an hour, perhaps, before they all passed through it, and still longer before they were settled in their temporary accommodations. Lady Margraine, who'd left earlier but had farther to travel, would probably arrive at nightfall, or perhaps the day after.

Eirnwin had told him much of the numbers game that would ensue; if this was to work at all, everyone had to have enough guards inside the walls of Mist's Edge so that they felt secure, but not so many that they threatened anyone else's security. Fortunately or unfortunately, Mist's Edge was a large fortress, capable of housing hundreds of men comfortably, and there was no way they could convince a man as distrustful as Elgar that they did not in fact have hundreds of men lying in wait for him. The easiest thing to do was to allow him to bring a hundred men of his own and try to accommodate them as best they could, but that meant *they* had to have at least a hundred men in case *Elgar* tried any foul play once he arrived. If Lady Margraine had been similarly paranoid, mathematicians and philosophers alike might have despaired at ever finding a balance of numbers acceptable to all three sides, but luckily for them, she seemed as easygoing as Elgar was uptight. She'd accepted the contingent of soldiers Kel had sent to escort her to Mist's Edge from the border, and she had brought, if reports could be believed, fewer than a dozen soldiers of her own. "Foolhardiness," Eirnwin had muttered, but they both knew Lady Margraine was no fool. And, well, she wasn't wrong—they *weren't* planning to kill her. There were few people it was in Reglay's better interest to keep alive, and she doubtlessly knew it.

They had done all they could to clean and order Mist's Edge, but there were still entire towers that hadn't been seen to, and no one seemed capable of navigating the fortress for long without getting lost. No matter how many people they brought to occupy it or how many rooms they cleared out, however, the gloomy, grave character of the castle remained unchanged. Kel did not believe in ghosts, and probably still wouldn't if one popped out of his morning porridge and bit him on the nose. But it was easy to see how someone might come to believe in them, if he had to spend any length of time alone here. Every evening the mist descended, like a plague from some ancient tale, and every morning it lingered after sunrise, sometimes smothering the castle all the way through the following dawn.

Kel believed what he'd said to Eirnwin: this was *his* place, his rightful place, and no part of it could ever mean him harm. Even if he hadn't believed it, though, it was important that Elgar believe it, and so he had to play his role. He'd allowed Eirnwin to deck him out in finer clothes today, a black silk doublet and trousers with elaborate whorls traced in silver thread. He had a short cape, also black, but no crown—not yet. That final piece must wait for the coronation, when it would come to rest on his head under the eyes of all.

Well, he reminded himself, not *all*—Issamira, as they'd feared but somewhat expected, had rebuffed him. He'd received a pleasant enough letter from Princess Adora—or perhaps Queen Adora, he still wasn't quite clear about that. *Please accept my deepest condolences about your father,* she had written in a neat but unremarkable hand; *it was not so very long ago that I lost my own. I am afraid, however, that we will not be able to grant your wish. I must not leave my people at this time, and while I would normally send my brother Hephestion in my stead, he received a superficial wound while out on patrol, which he then aggravated by refusing to rest. He is currently remaining in bed only at the repeated urging of myself, our mother, and our captain of the guard.* In closing, she had written simply, *May the crown rest lightly on your brow all the days that you wear it, and may those days be long.*

Kel knew that she had written it only to be polite, that it was foolish to set too much store by her words, but there was a melancholy in them that reminded him of her lost brother. He was left with the feeling that the crown did not rest lightly on *her* brow, and never had. Reading the rest of the letter, he'd tried to picture what remained of their family: the mother and the elder sister clucking over the wayward youngest. "Who *is* the captain of the guard in Eldren Cael?" he'd asked Eirnwin.

Eirnwin had frowned, his eyebrows lifting. "Do you know, I have no idea. It was Ohrun Girt when King Jotun was alive, but I think he was killed trying to find Prince Landon."

Cadfael, from where he leaned against the windowsill, had snorted. "Probably some hardened graybeard with a half-decent swordarm and a carrying voice. That's the kind they usually like, in Issamira as much as anywhere else."

He'd kept his word, sticking by Kel's side in the days leading up to the coronation. There was no way to ascertain whether Elgar was bringing Commander Shinsei along with him or not, so that was yet another wrinkle to worry about. If he *was* there, Kel had no doubt that Cadfael would try to kill him, no matter the cost to himself or anyone else. But that was his right, and the deal they'd struck; if it did come to pass, Kel would just have to suffer the repercussions then. If Shinsei did not come . . . well, then Cadfael would leave, and that would be that.

Elgar's party had reached the edge of the forest by now, and Kel leaned forward against the stone, wondering which one of them was Elgar himself. He couldn't see much more than the tops of a bunch of heads, though, and none of them seemed especially noteworthy. He'd heard that Elgar wore no crown, not even in his own halls. Apparently the people of Hallarnon had stopped setting any store by such things long ago, and its past several rulers hadn't bothered or dared to claim the title of king; Elgar's "Imperator," of course, was his own invention. Though she didn't wear a crown either, the opposite was true of Lady Margraine: *marquise* was the supposed title, but *queen* was the reality.

Then Lessa was at his elbow, her long hair fluttering in the wind that skirted the edges of the tall towers. "Eirnwin wants you to come downstairs. You have to be ready to greet Elgar and his men when they arrive in the courtyard."

Kel hummed softly, some vague pitch he could hardly hear himself. "I know."

"Will you be all right getting down there on your own? It's a lot of stairs. More than you're used to."

He would've frowned if anyone else had asked him that, but with Lessa he only smirked. "Stairs are the least of my worries today."

He hadn't really thought it would succeed in reassuring her, but it seemed to have the opposite effect. She bit her lip. "We're inviting the snakes to supper—wasn't there an old story like that?"

That sounded familiar; Eirnwin had probably told it to them. "I think I'd almost rather have real snakes. Then at least I wouldn't have to be polite." He cocked his head at her. "Make sure you stay close to Cadfael, all right? He's the best of our men; I know he'll keep you safe if anything happens."

"If anything happens, his first priority is keeping *you* safe," Lessa reminded him.

Kel grimaced. "Let's hope it doesn't, then. I'm a bit tired of being protected, and it doesn't look good in a king." He touched her hand. "We'll go together?"

Lessa smiled at him. "Together," she agreed.

Kel allowed himself one last look over the battlements, and then he propped himself up on one arm, reaching for his crutches. Lessa trusted him enough not to try to help, or to grab on to him as he walked, but she kept pace, staying at his side.

Eirnwin met them in the hall; Cadfael was idling by the door, leaning against the frame and wearing as dour an expression as usual. "There are quite a few of them in the courtyard already, but Elgar hasn't made himself known yet," Eirnwin said. "You can wait here until he arrives if you wish; it would not look amiss."

Kel shrugged, trying to feel as nonchalant as the gesture would indicate. "I have to get out there sooner or later. Might as well be sooner." He turned to look at his sister. "Lessa, you stay inside with Eirnwin."

She hesitated. "But—"

Cadfael pushed off the wall, his gaze alert. "Your brother's right, my lady. Those soldiers filling the courtyard right now are common gawkers and lickspittles; it's no place for one such as you." He nodded to Kel. "His Grace and I'll see to it."

Kel nodded back, and then once to Eirnwin and Lessa. He adjusted his grip on his crutches. "Here I go," he said.

He blinked when the doors first swung open, but more out of habit than anything else; the glare wasn't unduly harsh. There must've already been thirty or forty unknown soldiers in the courtyard, ambling awkwardly among Kel's own men. They all wore the same blue-black uniforms, with nary a bit of silver or gold to be seen. They caught sight of him in twos and threes; some bent their heads respectfully, and some merely stared. Several started sniggering to one another, but their whispers grew muted when Cadfael glared at them.

Kel could not have said how he knew the next man to pass through the gate was Elgar; he wore no ostentatious garb or air of command. He had no uniform, true, although his clothes were the same blue-black as his soldiers'. The color matched well with his hair, itself a deep black, except for a few strands of gray above his ears. His beard was small and neat, his eyes narrow and colorless, his body slim and unremarkable. Most of his soldiers hadn't even seen him yet; they were too busy looking at Kel. And yet Kel did not need to see them bow to this man to understand who he was.

At Elgar's side rode the only person not wearing that mournful color; his robes were red, and they picked out the hints of red in his long brown hair. He was younger than Elgar, though he looked a bit worse for wear. That couldn't be Shinsei, could it? He carried no weapon, and he certainly didn't look like a warrior. All the same, Kel felt Cadfael tense beside him; perhaps he was wondering the same thing.

As they watched, Elgar and his companion dismounted, handing their horses off to the waiting attendants. His soldiers had begun to notice him by now, and their deep bows would have eliminated the last of Kel's uncertainty, had he had any left. Elgar walked right up to him, his steps measured and calm; it felt like it took an eternity for him to get within speaking distance. Then he inclined his head, holding out one thin, pale hand to Kel.

"Your Grace," he said. "I thank you for extending your hospitality to so many at such a momentous time."

He did not smile, so Kel felt no need to smile back. He leaned on one crutch, freeing the opposite hand so he could shake Elgar's. The imperator's hand was dry, smooth, not overly cold. It felt just like anyone else's. "Imperator Elgar. The thanks must be all on our part, I'm afraid. We have asked you to come rather a long way."

Elgar looked about him, blinking up at the towers. "I had wanted to see Mist's Edge with my own eyes," he said quietly. "Now it seems I have been given the chance."

Was he serious? If Elgar had truly wanted to see the castle, he'd had plenty of time to do so before he ordered it abandoned. Kel decided not to press the issue further. "We had thought to house you in the northwest tower, if such would be acceptable."

Elgar pursed his lips, examining the tower Kel had indicated. "My men can all be contained in such a space?"

"The tower connects to the rest of the castle at its east and south ends; you may place some of your men along those corridors, if you please, or else leave them to guard the ramparts."

Elgar pressed one finger to his chin. "As you wish." He turned suddenly, as if he'd only just become aware of the man beside him. "Allow me to present Lord Varalen Oswhent, my strategist and advisor."

The man in the red robes was palpably nervous, but that didn't keep him from rolling his eyes slightly at the title. Kel nodded to him. "My lord." Not Shinsei, then, but Kel couldn't honestly claim to be surprised; the man looked an academic in every particular.

Lord Oswhent bowed. "Your Grace. Quite a . . . er, pleasure."

"My sister waits to receive us inside," Kel said. "If you would follow me?"

Elgar had been looking at the towers again, but when Kel spoke, he nodded vaguely and fell into step with him. His legs were much longer, but he kept to Kel's pace as easily as Lessa ever had; how strange, to receive such courtesy from an enemy. "Has Lady Margraine arrived yet?" he muttered as they walked.

Kel shook his head. "My men sent word ahead once they'd reached Second Hearth; she should arrive this evening if they meet with no trouble on the road."

Elgar nodded, accepting that, and before he could say more, they were over the threshold. Kel moved to Lessa's side, and she stepped forward with a curtsey. "My sister, Alessa," Kel told Elgar, "and Eirnwin, my advisor, who will be the one to crown me on the morrow."

Elgar bowed his head to them both, but his eyes lingered on Alessa for a few moments—not in anything remotely resembling lust, but almost in bemusement, as if he couldn't understand why she was there. "I would prefer an hour or two in my chambers, if it please Your Grace," he said, lifting his eyes again, this time to the rafters. Was there a reason his gaze always seemed drawn upward? "Our journey was somewhat more tiring than I had anticipated."

Kel could not bow, but he inclined his upper body as best he could. "Of course. I'll have the servants show you to your rooms. Shall I call you to dinner, or would you prefer us to . . . bring you something?"

The expression on Elgar's face could almost have been called a smile. "Oh, I certainly wouldn't want to miss dinner. I hope you won't take it amiss if I don't eat much, however; I am not in the habit of it."

Well, that was a . . . somewhat odd thing to say, but Kel was starting to think Elgar was a somewhat odd man. Perhaps that was only to be expected.

Varalen Oswhent, however, seemed surpassingly normal; he scurried dutifully along after Elgar, his stride quickly easing as he came back into step with him. Kel waited to assert himself until after they had gone, calling Lessa, Eirnwin, and Cadfael to his own chambers.

Once they were alone, Eirnwin murmured, "To think we managed that with so little trouble! Elgar is supposed to be such a nervous man, and yet . . ."

"I know," Kel said. "If anyone *looked* nervous, it was that Lord Oswhent."

Cadfael cleared his throat. "Well, it doesn't look like he brought Shinsei, anyway."

Kel started. He'd almost forgotten about that. "I'm sorry," he said. "I truly did think he would be coming."

Cadfael shrugged. "It was a good guess, sure enough. I don't hold it against you, and I won't leave until the rest of them do; it wouldn't be wise to depart in the middle of things." His lips pressed together. "But I *will* be leaving. That was our agreement, wasn't it?"

"It was," Kel agreed. "I won't stop you."

"There's naught but good between us, then." Cadfael's face relaxed, and his gaze shifted, moving to the window. "It makes me wonder, though: if Shinsei's not guarding Elgar, then where is he, and what on earth is he doing? What could be more important than ensuring his master's safety in such an uncertain situation?"

Eirnwin frowned. "I can't help but worry about the same thing. Could Shinsei be carrying out some plot while Elgar keeps us occupied here?"

Lessa shook her head. "A man like Elgar using himself as a decoy? I can't picture it. Imagine if we got word of anything—we could clap the gate shut on him, and he'd have to fight his way out on more or less even terms."

"And Elgar hates even terms," Cadfael said, nodding slowly. "That's why he makes sure never to face them."

Eirnwin was less convinced. "Perhaps. That doesn't make me feel any easier about Shinsei's absence."

Cadfael laughed mirthlessly. "Easier? You ought to be glad of it, old man. It means you'll be spared the headache of my killing him in your halls."

Eirnwin didn't bother to hide his scowl. "It also means we'll be out your service as soon as this is over."

"True enough." He went to the window, resting on the sill and pulling his legs up after him.

"Didn't you hear a rumor about Shinsei?" Kel asked him. "Wasn't that what you were chasing when we met you?"

Cadfael hesitated. "Aye, but it didn't come to anything. I lost him somewhere near the border—if that even *was* him. They said he was heading east, but he could be anywhere by now."

"East," Kel repeated. "To Esthrades, maybe."

"Maybe, but I doubt it. Your sister's got the right of it, I think—there's no need to be *worried* yet, but we might be curious."

"I certainly am," Eirnwin said, "but curiosity alone never accomplished anything."

Their windows faced out across the forest, not down into the courtyard; that was probably intentional. But Elgar and Varalen had both given the men strict orders, and the way this soldier was panting suggested they had been adhered to.

Elgar looked up casually enough from the book he had been reading, but Varalen saw the way his spine had stiffened. "She's here, then?"

The man nodded, still gasping slightly. "Just spotted by the men on watch, Your Eminence."

"Good." He turned his gaze away from the man without so much as a dismissal, looking over at Varalen instead. "Well? Shall we meet this viper at last?"

"It would be wise," Varalen said. "And I suppose I'm a bit curious."

Elgar got to his feet. "You knew the father?"

"I met him once, at a parley. It was many years ago now." He'd had Caius Margraine well enough in hand even then, though; he never thought he could miss an enemy so much. "They said he could twist a man's head off with his bare hands, and looking at him, I believed it. How much more frightening could his daughter be?"

"If only power always showed itself so obviously . . ." Elgar began, turning slightly away. "Is what I *would* say, but . . . well."

Well enough. Elgar and Varalen were both men who preferred to hide their strengths, and he expected Lady Margraine was no different. It would be like a game of blind man's chase, each one grasping sightlessly at the weaknesses of the other. It was not a game he personally preferred, but it was one Varalen knew how to play, if it came to that.

Since they'd arrived at Mist's Edge, Elgar had seemed tranquil enough so long as he stayed in one place, but whenever he moved about, his eyes became searching and overeager, flicking anxiously every which way as he walked. Though the fortress was certainly imposing, Varalen couldn't say it held much fascination for him personally; there was none of the history or aesthetic of the Citadel, just a whole lot of sturdy gray stone.

They arrived in the courtyard before Lady Margraine did. King Kelken and his retainers were already there; they glanced at Elgar and Varalen when they came into view, but did not seem surprised to see them there. The men entering the courtyard were still all Reglians, by the looks of them, and Varalen peered around them, trying to catch sight of where Lady Margraine's personal party might be.

She was getting off her horse almost before he could see her at all, so his first impression was of a slender frame and a mass of pale blond hair that had gotten tangled in the wind. As soon as her feet were on solid ground again, she pulled it back out of her face, giving the group before her a cursory glance. She dressed simply but elegantly, in a blue-gray color that matched her eyes. One who had not spent months being frustrated by her might have called her fair, but Varalen's pride could hardly allow him to pay her that compliment. The smirk that gently twisted her mouth was just as he might have expected, if somewhat more vivid in the flesh.

She did not curtsy to Kelken, but inclined her crownless head, tilting it slightly even after she had finished, the better to regard him. "My dear young king, how delightful to meet you at last." There was no flattery in the words, just enough dryness to make the Gods' Curse feel damp.

The prince returned the gesture, his face as solemn as it had been since they'd arrived. Varalen thought, rather uncomfortably, of Ryam, of the concentration that wreathed his face when he worked through a difficult sentence in some book. Oh, everyone was someone's father or someone's son, he knew that. That did not mean he wished to pit himself against a boy.

Then Lady Margraine's eyes met Elgar's for the first time, and even Varalen had to catch his breath. They were so different, in every particular he could think of, but in that moment the look they gave each other was exactly the same.

A stranger drops a gold coin in the street, and two urchins snatch at it as it rolls; with it out of sight, they glare, wary and bewildered, at each other, each seeking the coin in the guilty, eager gaze of the other. *You have it, don't you? I know you have it. Give it to me.*

It was, undoubtedly, a question, asked a thousand times in the space of a moment, but Varalen did not think either of them could answer it. And then, before he had time to wonder what they had been asking *for,* he caught sight of the woman at the marquise's elbow, and his breath stuck in his throat.

The woman from the dungeons met his eyes coolly; she did not appear startled, and she did not *seem* to recognize him, but he had little doubt she did. Varalen himself could hardly have failed to recognize her: even without that mass of copper hair, he remembered her stoically flat expression all too well. Questions tore at him: What on earth was he to do now? Should he tell Elgar, or would the knowledge that Varalen had helped put that damnable stone into the hands of Lady Margraine herself only assure his own death, and Ryam's?

Lady Margraine had already introduced the man on her other side, though Varalen had missed his name. The woman she did not introduce, but she clearly must have been someone of consequence—she stuck to Lady Margraine's side like a shadow, while the remainder of her party kept a slight, respectful distance.

When Elgar introduced *him,* he found himself bearing the full brunt of the marquise's smirk; it was not precisely pleasant. "I believe we know more than a little of each other, Lord Oswhent, if indirectly." That was certainly one way of putting it.

Varalen settled on a jaunty bow. "I don't know half so much of you as I'd like, Your Grace, to be sure."

Her smile widened at that; perhaps she saw the same humor in their situation that Varalen did. "Let us talk further over supper, then, by all means."

The old man, Eirnwin, cleared his throat. "We can have supper laid out momentarily, if Your Graces so please. But perhaps the Lady Margraine is still tired from her journey?"

She laughed. "Oh, nonsense. I'll just be happy to sit on something that isn't a horse."

As they followed King Kelken's party inside, Varalen drew close to the woman from the dungeons, but he didn't dare whisper anything to her, not with so many others so near. She held his gaze every time he caught hers, but other-wise she hardly seemed to notice him.

If she had fetched the stone for the marquise, did that mean that there was some value in it, or just that Lady Margraine was as eccentric as Elgar was? Or had she not especially meant to get her hands on it at all? Perhaps this mysteri-ous servant had taken it upon herself to steal something she knew her mistress's rival wanted, even without knowing herself what it was. Gods, if only Varalen had just kept her in that prison . . .

His shoulder grazed one of the king's retainers, a handsome fellow with a scar down his forehead. "Is everything all right?" the man asked, a sharp look in his blue eyes. His mouth stayed thin and flat, his expression opaque.

Varalen smiled, though the back of his neck prickled. "I'm well enough. How are *you*?"

The man grunted and looked away, and Varalen turned his own gaze ahead, fixing it on that familiar copper hair.

———

Kel had heard countless tales of royal banquets in days gone by, full of song and merriment and all manner of guests, with courses that seemed infinite in number and wine that flowed unceasingly. But there were far fewer nobles now than there had been in the days of Elesthene—or at any time before that, if the history books could be believed. The Margraines had never suffered anyone in Esthrades to be called lords or ladies save them alone, and Elgar had no nobles, only subordinates. As for Reglay, it was poor and small, and the only man of counsel his father had ever trusted within it was Eirnwin. So there was no great scroll to unfurl, no fantastic titles to announce: there was only Kel and Impera-tor Elgar and Lady Margraine, and the handful of intimates each had chosen to attend them. Kel had Lessa and Eirnwin, with Cadfael guarding the door; Lady Margraine had Gravis Ingret, who served as her captain of the guard, and a taciturn bodyguard named Seren. Elgar had only Lord Oswhent, who looked barely more at ease than he had when he'd arrived.

The food, too, was perhaps not so fine as he could have wished, but it had been all they could do to get the castle prepared in time. He'd had men bring-ing food stores from Second Hearth practically without pause since they'd ar-rived, and they'd bought up whatever the nearest villages could spare, but they'd still barely be able to offer every soldier even a meager meal. As for the banquet itself, the fact that they had venison at all was entirely due to the chance en-counter one of his men had had with a magnificent stag just the day before, and he couldn't help but think that the grapes looked rather scrawny. If his guests had wanted fine food, no doubt they could have stayed at home. But Kel knew everything a ruler did reflected back upon him in some way, and he wondered what the simple fare made them think of him.

Elgar paused over his plate, plucking idly at his beard. "Perhaps Lady Margraine would be so good as to test the food for us? You've naught to fear from it, if the stories are true."

She laughed. "It's no burden to me, but I'm afraid it wouldn't help you much. It seems a Margraine may survive a dish that might be the death of another— although if it's bad cooking you fear, I'm sure I'm as sensitive in that regard as any other, and I'll happily warn you against it."

"So it is true, then?"

Lady Margraine reached for a bunch of grapes. "Who knows? My ancestors were curiously unwilling to let the blood apples be studied, and who am I to scoff at so many years of tradition?" Kel was starting to think she scoffed at *every-thing*. Or perhaps she didn't scoff exactly, but everything that fell under her gaze seemed to amuse her in a way that had none of the innocence of simple mirth. "I suppose the only way to know for sure whether a Margraine can be poisoned is to poison one, but if that's your endeavor, we must unfortunately be at odds." She plucked a single grape from the bunch before her. "Well, if I do die, at least I'll have provided everyone here with a suitably rare spectacle, eh?"

Elgar did not smile, but he did finally start eating. "I suppose it is the prerogative of the young to talk so nonchalantly about dying."

She raised her eyebrows in mock surprise. "Is it? Then it's our good host who should lead the way, not I."

Kel shook his head. "My father passed too recently for that, I'm afraid." He could still remember the way his father's eyes had looked, as if there had never been anything behind them, anything human at all. Blood he had seen; blood he knew, though never in such quantities. But the eyes had been strange, and horrifying.

"Ah," Elgar said, on the heels of a sip of wine. "My apologies."

Kel couldn't say, *It's all right,* so he said nothing.

"I didn't much know my father," Elgar continued, half to himself, sloshing the wine around in his glass.

"And I knew mine far too well," Lady Margraine said, raising her own glass to him.

Instead of responding to that, Elgar turned his gaze to the wall behind her, where her bodyguard had been standing since the meal had begun. Kel had offered the woman a seat at the table, but she had not taken it, preferring to lean against the wall and watch the room, face blank and lips pressed together. If she'd spoken a word since she'd arrived, Kel hadn't heard it. "If you distrust the food," Elgar said, "then you should not have let your mistress taste of it, blood apples or no. If not, then eat; you'll hardly defend her on an empty stomach."

The words had been provocation, no doubt—hadn't Elgar said he didn't eat much himself?—but they had no effect; Seren glanced at him, as if acknowledging she had heard his words, then turned her gaze straight ahead once more. She said nothing. Out of the corner of his eye, Kel noticed that the marquise's captain had also turned, and was watching their interaction, a deep frown on his face.

Elgar raised his eyebrows, then turned to Lady Margraine. "Is she mute?" he asked, jerking his head at Seren.

She smiled. "Not at all. Just not so eager to waste words as you or I." She popped another grape into her mouth. "He is right, though, Seren—stop glowering and eat something."

Seren still said nothing, but she walked to the table and tore off a cluster of grapes, then returned to her post and began nonchalantly eating them.

The marquise curled her fingers idly around the stem of her glass. "More than that. Have some meat."

Seren inclined her head, but she did not look up, and she made no move toward the table. Even so, that seemed to be enough for Lady Margraine, who returned to her own meal. Captain Ingret continued watching them for some moments, but he seemed just about to turn away when Elgar spoke again. "She's an interesting one to trust your life to, Your Grace."

Seren ignored him as easily as before, leaving her mistress to respond to the lure. "Oh, Seren's interesting, to be sure. She would serve to counterbalance Gravis, even if she did nothing else."

Captain Ingret flinched, but did not speak. Elgar asked, "To balance . . . what?"

Lady Margraine devoted more care to her venison than to Elgar, but she answered the question. "Gravis, you see, is almost always boring. Seren is almost always interesting. Therefore, they balance each other out."

Elgar smiled wanly at that. "I should think you of all people would have no use for those who bore you at all."

"You *would* think that," she told him, taking luxurious pauses every few words to have another bite of meat, "and I can understand why. But boring people are often the best suited to handling boring things, and as much as it grieves me to admit it, even ruling a country can be boring in places."

"Boredom in a ruler generally bodes well," Lord Oswhent said, looking up only fleetingly from his own food. "It implies a stable realm."

Lady Margraine waved a dismissive hand at him; Seren, having finally finished her grapes, walked to the table and obediently carved herself a modest portion of venison. "Stable realms are all very well, but boredom, I assure you, can never bode well. There is no state I have sworn more zealously to avoid."

Lord Oswhent finally looked up in earnest. "Boredom is the worst fate you can imagine? You surprise me."

She laughed. "Well, I can hardly swear never to be dead, can I? Such are the risks we take when we assume power."

"Were you bored while your father ruled, Your Grace?" Elgar asked, his food lying forgotten on his plate.

She shrugged. "Not overmuch. I suppose he made enough bad decisions to keep things interesting." She turned to smirk at her captain. "Gravis was quite the awful prig in those days too—even worse than he is now. *He* wouldn't listen to a word I said—gods, I think even my father was more tractable."

Most of her words seemed to glide undetected right past Elgar's ears; he sat idly in his chair, sloshing his wine again, but never raising the cup to his lips to drink. Lord Oswhent stared at him curiously, his mouth a thin line. When Elgar finally spoke, his words were very slow, very deliberate: "Over the course of time," he said, "I happened to hear a rather interesting story about you and your father."

Captain Ingret frowned again, and this time even Seren's eyes narrowed. The marquise, however, tossed her hair just as easily as ever. "I've heard quite a few of those myself, though I wouldn't dare presume to say I've heard them all. Which one is it, that I fucked him or that I murdered him? I can assure you I did neither, but the stories grow more fantastical with each telling." She tore off another cluster of grapes, plucking each one almost contemplatively before eating it. "I heard one last winter about how my mother and I were the same person. I suppose it's because I look so much like her, though I believe resemblances between parents and their children are not uncommon. Either way, she, or I— we?—had struck some evil bargain in return for youth, such and so many virgins killed or something, so she and my father spread a rumor she'd died and instead she was me. That's the wisdom of the common folk for you: a woman with a pregnant belly becomes a coffin and an infant, and the natural conclusion is not *death in childbed* but *demonic transfiguration*." She rolled her eyes. "For the gods' sakes, who'd bargain with a demon just to become a baby again? At the very least, wouldn't you want to start with all your teeth?"

Alessa hid a smile behind her hand, and even Lord Oswhent let out a rueful chuckle. But Seren and Captain Ingret were still staring hard at Elgar, and he forged ahead as determinedly as ever, his words still quiet and slow, but ever relentless. "No," he said. "No, that's quite a story, Your Grace, but it's not the one I was thinking of. You must forgive me if it's inaccurate—Hallarnon is rather a ways from Esthrades, after all, and funny things can happen to information when it travels long distances. But they say that you were quite a difficult child to handle, even when you were very young. They say, indeed, that your lord father used to whip you for your disobedience—that you bear his scars on your back to this day. Is that true?"

The smile was wiped from the marquise's face as quickly and completely as mist from a pane of glass, and it was only then that Kel realized he'd never seen what she looked like without it. He understood, then, why her smile seemed beautiful but never pleasant: it might have been genuine, but there was nothing of warmth or gentleness in her eyes, only cold amusement. Without her smile, only her coldness remained, suddenly sharp and oppressive. She did not gape or stammer at Elgar; she merely *looked* at him, and if she were angry—she must have been angry—she did not give off any heat, only that persistent coldness, implacable enough to cut through stone.

Captain Ingret had shifted when Elgar spoke, dropping his hand to his sword; Seren had tensed, as if readying herself for something, but otherwise had not moved. Elgar ran his eyes over the three of them, taking his time in the growing silence, and what might have been a smile slipped across his mouth and disappeared. "It seems I've upset you," he said. "My apologies. By all means, forget I ever mentioned it."

"No," the marquise said, softly but distinctly, and if her eyes had been cold, her voice sent a chill up Kel's spine. "One ought never to waste a good question— isn't that right? So I will answer it." She drew her next breath in slowly, but she never took her eyes from Elgar's face. "My father did whip me, yes." Her fingers curled around the edge of the table, tightening against the wood. "But only once."

CHAPTER TWENTY-SEVEN

I s that all?" Elgar asked, folding his hands over his crossed knees. *That's not enough?* Varalen didn't say. "Yes, my lord."

Elgar pursed his lips, then relaxed them, then pursed them again. This was not precisely what Varalen had expected. To be sure, Elgar had never been especially demonstrative in his anger—he was not one to scream or throw things or fire off a slew of orders he would later regret—but he *was* a tyrant, and he usually acted like one. Failure was simply unacceptable, and if letting this Seren deliver that stone to Lady Margraine wasn't a failure, Varalen didn't know what was.

Elgar finally looked up almost mildly. "I'm half surprised you told me at all."

Varalen winced. "Yes, well, I thought it was preferable to what might happen if I didn't."

"And you're sure it was the same woman?"

"Oh, without a doubt. I'm not like to forget *her*."

Elgar raised his hands, tapped the fingertips together, folded them again. "Well," he said at last, "I don't suppose there's anything we need to do about it."

It was all Varalen could do not to gape like an idiot. "This isn't . . . er, a problem?"

"In some ways," Elgar said, "it's almost the reverse." And that was right, Varalen thought, because when he'd first confessed, he'd seen a flicker of what seemed like *relief* in Elgar's eyes, and he still couldn't imagine what it had been doing there.

"So it's . . . what, a benefit?"

"Not a benefit, but . . . it's one less thing to worry about, I suppose."

"But—" Varalen broke off, trying not to fidget, and collected his thoughts. "I thought you said that this stone you wanted had some sort of value or power or something. Wouldn't allowing Lady Margraine to have it be the very definition of a problem?"

Elgar nodded slowly. "Certainly, yes, because then she would be able to use it. But she hasn't used it, has she?"

"*Has* she?" Varalen asked. "How would we know?"

Elgar's laugh was grim. "Oh, we'd know." One hand curled into a fist, and he wrapped the fingers of the other hand around it. "Since she has not used it, I can conclude one of several things: it does not have the power I thought it did, or else she cannot figure out how to use it, or else she is unable to use it, or else she *will* not use it. No matter the specific reason, the result is the same. And without it to tip the scales, the balance of power is still in my favor. Much better to know where it is than to fear where it might be."

The stone was almost certainly of no value whatsoever, of course, but the idea that someone as clearly intelligent and practical as Lady Margraine concerned herself with it at all was troubling. "So you really want to do nothing?" *Please say yes,* he thought. *Say yes, and let's forget about it until your next superstition comes up.*

"I can't exactly steal it from her as things stand," Elgar said, "so yes, I plan to do nothing. But I do wonder what that strange servant of hers was doing in our dungeons—or in Valyanrend at all, for that matter. Perhaps the marquise merely knew I was searching for it, and sent her retainer to steal the information from me."

Was the damned thing truly that important? "I wish I knew that myself, my lord."

Elgar stroked his beard. "What's more, your information was good after all, wasn't it? That story was true—and how worth the telling."

Varalen picked at his nails, uncomfortable once more. "Well, we don't really know how much of it was true." He'd been the one who had first told Elgar that story. It was a strangely persistent rumor that had been floating around Esthrades for years, and more than one of his sources had passed some version of the tale on to him. There were few details that remained consistent across every version, but all the stories agreed that it had occurred on or around the marquise's tenth birthday.

On that day, so the story went, Arianrod Margraine, who had made a calling out of disobeying and exasperating her father, had angered him beyond all measure, beyond anything she had ever done before. None of the stories could agree on what it *was*, however: some said she had slandered him while he sat in judgment, others that she had turned the prisoners loose from his dungeons, still others that she had tried to sell the famed blood apples under his nose. But whatever it was, it had driven Caius Margraine into a fury not seen since his wife had died ten years before. (There were those who said, too, that his lordship was always in a foul mood on his daughter's birthdays, marking as they did the anniversary of his loss.) The young Arianrod was banished from her own festivities—that everyone could well remember, as there were many who had been there—and forced to await her father's judgment.

There were those who said he had called for his whip immediately, and others who claimed he had waited until the following morning, or even several days later, though that last seemed unlikely. But either way he had taken up the whip, and he had beaten his daughter so severely with it that she'd lain abed for almost a week while the servants fluttered about, wondering if she was going to die. She had pulled through in the end, but the wounds he had inflicted left scars that still remained—though Varalen wasn't sure how any of his sources knew *that*, as he was quite certain none of them had the ability to check.

But something still stranger had happened on the night he beat her, so the stories claimed. Caius Margraine *would* have whipped his daughter to death, but he had stopped—or, more precisely, she had stopped him. The idea had seemed strange to Varalen from the beginning, but everyone had agreed on that part, just as they had agreed, in the most basic sense, on *how*. She was normally careful, they said, but the ferocity of his assault had made her fear for her life.

So when she could withstand the pain no more, she had used her magic on her father.

The most popular story held that when the whip touched her back, it had turned into a giant tongue of flame, burning its way back up to Caius Margraine's fingers; another story transfigured it into a giant serpent, recoiling on the man who held it with its dripping fangs bared—only his diet of blood apples had saved him from its poison. Still others insisted that the whip had turned itself on him directly, wrapping itself around his throat and choking him within an inch of his life while his daughter looked on with that cold smile.

Whatever she had done, the story always concluded, Caius Margraine never took a whip to his daughter again. He never dared. And that was the final blow they dealt each other, the blow that sundered their household irrevocably: her vanity could not bear the sight of such ugly scars, and his pride could not forgive the indignity of having to fear a little girl.

Varalen propped his forehead against one finger, letting just the edge of the nail dig into his skin. "It was true enough to bother her, at the least. But you should be careful not to . . . set too much store by it."

"I wasn't aware I was setting *any* store by it," Elgar said, and laughed. "I'd thought I might score a hit with that stroke, but even I never thought she'd get so angry as all that. I'd scarcely have believed it—so much grief over an injury from so long ago, just because it marred her beauty." He rested his cheek on his knuckles. "I wish I knew what the scars looked like. They must be unsightly indeed, to wipe that persistent smirk off her face."

Varalen kept focusing on the point of his nail. "We don't know if there are any scars at all," he said, "and we don't know—"

"What, about the magic?" Elgar laughed again, softer. "I knew you'd say that."

"To be certain of such a thing just because of some peasants' story . . . You heard her at dinner: those people will believe anything. I can't even imagine what they whisper about you."

"Mm?" Elgar murmured, extending one long finger so it lay against his cheek. "And how do you know any of that isn't true, either?"

There was no dealing with him when he got into one of these moods. "Very well, my lord, but we can't just entertain any and all possibilities. As I have *said*, proceeding in fear of her supposed magic is giving her a gift we can ill afford. And I certainly hope that you didn't prod her like that just to try to get proof of that magic, because we *didn't* get any."

Elgar stood up smoothly, pacing the length of the table. "I assure you, Varalen, I *prodded* her just to see if it was possible to make her angry—nothing more.

As for her magic . . . I will not *fear,* but I will wait. You will have to be content with that."

————

Seren couldn't deny the slender thread of unease that worked its way through her, but she did her best to meet Gravis's gaze. "No one will pass through this door," she tried to assure him. "I can do my job well enough from here."

He frowned. "This castle is strange to us. She should not be in that room alone—she should not be in *any* of these rooms alone for any length of time."

He was right, of course, but there was nothing for it. "She ordered that we leave her alone," Seren said. "Even I was not to enter until she called."

"That does not mean we should—"

"It does," Seren said. "Should you enter, I am sure she would be more than simply displeased."

Gravis scowled at her, weighing her words, and finally turned on his heel. "I'm going to check the corridor. You stay here." As if she would do otherwise. If she was not to be permitted to defend Arianrod properly, the least she could do was stay here.

The moonlight filtered unevenly through the corridor. King Kelken had given them to understand that any amount of moonlight was unusual; Mist's Edge usually lived up to its name, and sometimes the fog would even drift in through the windows. The mist was thin tonight, though, and the moon had turned it a gentle silver, though that didn't ease the air of tension in the fortress in the slightest.

Arianrod had confined herself to her room immediately following dinner, and perhaps that was understandable, though Seren was uncomfortable with the idea. She had scarcely ever seen Arianrod as angry as that, but did she really want the room to herself just so she could rage? That seemed doubtful. Perhaps she only wanted some moments to compose herself, and then she would emerge, restored to her usual detached self again. So Seren tried to tell herself, anyway.

She peered down the corridor, trying to see where Gravis had got to. He seemed to have disappeared around the far corner; she couldn't even hear his footsteps anymore, or perhaps he was standing still. There was a vague chill in the air, not a breeze but a damp and persistent heaviness that somehow seeped through her clothes and made her arms prickle. She leaned just a little against the door, grateful to have wood at her back and not that cold, ancient stone. She could hear nothing from Arianrod's room, but that did more to unnerve than comfort her. A person in a room alone had no real cause to make noise, of course, but if she had just been allowed to stay with her . . .

She could not have said how long it was before she heard Gravis's slow footsteps returning, but it struck her that it had been too long. His face, once he'd rounded the corner again, was settled and still, but his brow was furrowed and his eyes determined.

He did not speak until he had drawn right up alongside her, and Seren did not ask him to. But when there were barely two inches of space between them, he murmured, "Switch places with me?"

"What?" She did not know why he was whispering, but it seemed wise to follow suit.

"Leave this to me, and go out into the hall—around the corner and along the corridor, where I was."

"What on earth for?"

He shook his head. "Just do it."

"Gravis—"

"Lady Margraine didn't say that *you* had to stay, did she? Just that her room had to be guarded. Well, I'll guard it. Go out into the far corridor." She frowned at him, but he just kept looking at her earnestly. "I can't," he said, in an even softer voice. "You'll do better than I will. Be on your guard, but *go*."

Gravis was not one for jokes or idle chatter, and he was not one to recommend risky or unnecessary actions. Seren drew her hand along her arm reflexively, feeling for her knife, but she finally peeled away from the door and allowed Gravis to take up his position in her place. "Only until I get back," she muttered.

He nodded, and she stepped away, walking as casually as she could down the corridor. She hadn't quite reached the intersection when she sensed another presence, and she moved more warily, preparing to dodge an incoming blow. But when she turned the corner, King Kelken's retainer had his sword sheathed, his hands resting calmly at his sides. It was the one with the handsome face and the sullen expression, the scar on his forehead clearly visible even in the low light.

"Sorry for being so abrupt," he said, in an even quieter voice than Gravis had used. "The captain suggested that you would be better at moving silently, and we'll need to."

It wasn't hard to move more silently than *Gravis,* who insisted on wearing full plate nearly everywhere he went, but it was admittedly one of Seren's talents. "Just where is it that we're going?" she asked.

His expression revealed nothing. "You'll see."

The man must have said something of significance to get Gravis to trust him, so Seren decided not to argue the point any further. "Lead the way."

Mist's Edge seemed even larger on the inside than it had looked from the outside, and it was all Seren could do to keep count of the turns they made. After leading her down more corridors than she would have thought possible, the man finally arrived at a ladder in an otherwise empty room, and she followed him up through a door in the ceiling. When he shut it behind her, she realized they were on the top floor of one of the smaller towers, with a low roof above their heads and a single window to her left. The view would surely have been impressive if it hadn't been choked by the mist, but she could see enough to tell that all the nearby ramparts were deserted.

"Care to explain why we're up here?" she asked him.

"Elgar doesn't want your mistress talking to the king," he said calmly. "I can understand why, but Kelken *does* want to talk to her, so we devoted ourselves to finding a way to get out of sight. Elgar might have his men darting about the halls, but he won't be able to get them anywhere near this tower."

"Does he really have them patrolling the halls?"

He nodded. "We've spotted a few. We can try to send them away, but they'll just keep creeping about as soon as we take our eyes off them."

Seren sighed. "Well, I suppose I can't blame him for not wanting his enemies to be alone together. What is it that King Kelken wishes for?"

"From your lady, nothing more than an hour or two of her time. He did promise her a look at the library, and he intends to make good on that promise—but he doesn't wish to have to show it off to Elgar as well."

That was probably wise, Seren thought. Either way, Arianrod would do much to spend time with those books, however briefly, and any potential danger would be no object to her. "When?" she asked.

The man leaned against the far wall. "Tomorrow night, we thought. We should be able to sneak you away from any prying glances, and the library's well guarded. I am confident we will be able to grant her some significant amount of time with the tomes."

"And will she be watched while she is there?"

"Of course. His Grace can't be too careful, I suppose."

What was he worried about, that Arianrod would try to steal one of his books? Well, Seren reflected, perhaps she would, but it wasn't as if he'd especially miss it. "I am sure she will agree to that," she told the scarred man. "Will you come to fetch us again?"

"I should be able to alert you or the captain once I'm close, yes, and I can lead you from there." His hand drifted absently to the hilt of his sword. "I don't sense any danger," he said, once he noticed her watching him. "Just an old habit."

She understood that well enough. "I will tell Lady Margraine what you have said." *As soon as she decides to admit people into her presence again,* she didn't add. "But I'd venture you can tell your lord that all will proceed as he expects."

He flinched, and Seren raised an eyebrow. "Have I spoken amiss?"

He hesitated. "No. It is only that he is not my lord."

Seren blinked. "And yet you serve—"

"I do not *serve* him. We are working in concert for the time being, but only for the time being." He shook his head. "A servant who really only does as he pleases is no true servant, is he?"

"And does it please you to run about on King Kelken's orders?"

He looked up sharply. "Does it please *you* to do the same on Lady Margraine's?"

She smiled at that. "Perhaps it does. But either way, *I* don't balk at being called a servant."

That deepened his frown, but he did not reply, only pushed himself away from the wall. "You'll want to follow me back down."

"What did your opponent look like?" Seren asked, and hardly knew why.

He'd been crouching to open the door, but he straightened again. "I'm sorry?"

"Whoever gave you that scar," she said. "What did you leave them with?"

At first she was almost certain he was not going to answer, but then he lifted a hand to his face, tracing the scar with one fingertip. That looked like an old habit too. "She would have to be the one to answer that," he said. "But if you're talking about wounds, I wasn't able to manage so much as a scratch."

"But she didn't kill you."

His jaw worked for a couple of moments, his mouth tensing and relaxing. "Perhaps she intended to," he said.

He turned without waiting for a response, prying the door open once again and slipping back down the ladder. Seren followed without pressing him further, and once they were back in the corridor, she did not detain him—if any of Elgar's roving spies caught them talking, all that caution would be for naught. Besides, she had been quite long enough away from her post.

Gravis did not argue when she returned to relieve him, just nodded and moved away from the door so she could stand before it. "All is well?" he asked.

"I should be asking you that."

He twitched his shoulders. "She will not admit anyone, but it has been quiet. I heard her move around once or twice, but nothing abrupt."

Seren did not like it at all. "What will you do now?"

"I ought to see to the men," he said, adding grimly, "what few we have. I don't expect our hosts mean us foul play, but Elgar would massacre the lot of us if he could only figure out how to do it, and he's a smart man. I wish she had not come here." He walked a step and turned. "Now you. He wanted nothing suspicious?"

Seren could almost have smiled. "Nothing suspicious, no, but better not to speak of it here."

Gravis nodded. It was strange how well they could get along, once everything else was set against them. "I can leave her to you?"

"As always," Seren said. He grunted at that, not quite acknowledging it, but he left.

The air was still cold, but not so cold as it had been atop the tower, and the wood was still warm where he had leaned against it. Seren fixed her eyes on the opposite wall, straining her ears for any hint of sound from the room behind her. Arianrod couldn't *still* be angry, surely? This wasn't like her at all.

There was finally a noise, but it was the softest rustle, like a bedsheet or the folds of a dress. What followed it was much more alarming: a half-stifled cry, not of surprise but of something like pain.

Seren gripped the door handle and turned it. "My lady?" She would wait only a moment for an answer, she told herself.

But Arianrod's laughter was unforced and only a little weak, and the tension in Seren's body eased. "You may as well come in," she called. "I expect you were about to break the door down anyway."

Seren slipped into the room immediately, pulling the door shut behind her. But what she saw only brought back the concern she'd just been able to shake off: Arianrod was sitting on the bed, one fist pressed against her heart, the fingers of the other hand gripping the footboard so tightly her knuckles had gone white. Her face was too pale and her eyes were too bright, and her breath came in short, shallow gasps, as if she couldn't quite catch it.

"What should I do?" Seren asked.

Arianrod eyed her lazily, but neither hand relaxed, and her breathing didn't steady. "There's nothing you *can* do, I'm afraid. Do try not to look so aghast, if you would."

"Are you ill?"

"In a manner of speaking, yes." She tried to laugh again, but it came out shaky and soon died away. "I have been foolish, that's all. I overexerted—" She gritted her teeth, and a shudder passed through her, lowering her head almost to her outstretched arm. "It is nothing," she insisted. "It will not last. There is no need to fret over me so."

"It will not get worse?" Seren asked.

"No."

"You know that for certain?"

"I do." Still she smiled. "I was often like this when I was a child. I learned myself better as I grew up, as we all do. It will pass. It always passes."

"So this has happened before?"

"I just said that, didn't I?"

Seren tried to think, but she could not recall ever seeing Arianrod in so much pain before, not without a readily discernible cause. "When has it happened?"

Arianrod sighed. "It only happens when I am not careful. I told you, it never lasts. It's none of your concern." Her voice did seem slightly stronger, or maybe it was just Seren's imagination. She even eased her grip on the footboard somewhat. After only a couple of deep breaths, she was able to let go of it entirely, and she reached down to loosen her shoes. "Seren, the best thing for me now is sleep. Make sure Elgar doesn't send an army in through the window; if anything even slightly less dire should occur, I wish to remain undisturbed." Without any further ceremony, she let her shoes fall to the floor and spread herself out on the bed. Her hands had finally relaxed, though her chest still trembled when she breathed.

Seren hesitated. "You're just going to—"

Arianrod's voice was muffled, the hand she waved halfhearted at best. "Seren, I am used to falling asleep in my *chair*. The lack of proper nightclothes will do me no harm, I assure you."

CHAPTER TWENTY-EIGHT

If his new crown caused him any discomfort, King Kelken the Fourth gave no sign of it. It seemed rather large for such a small boy, its golden tines sharp as spearpoints, but the old advisor had managed to put it on straight, and Varalen surprised himself by being unable to find anything comical in the image. He had never had the privilege of attending a coronation before, but he couldn't say he'd ever particularly wanted to, or that he'd found this one particularly impressive. It was the result that mattered: the king of Reglay had been newly minted, and Elgar and Lady Margraine, whether reluctantly or not, had lent the affair some amount of legitimacy by bearing witness to it. Then again, Varalen thought, it wasn't as if Elgar had had a reputation as a paragon of virtue before, so why should anyone be surprised if he moved to destroy a kingdom the moment its ruler had finished feasting him?

The pavilion King Kelken's men had built was more of a simple awning than anything else, and even that wasn't really necessary: you could barely see the sun, but it didn't look as if it was going to rain. The boy king, raised high in his seat of honor, was as painfully earnest as ever, his still-childish face oddly matured by that solemn, wistful look. Varalen did not think he had ever seen him smile.

On the other hand, Lady Margraine's good humor seemed fully restored. She smirked with new vivacity, and if she had rested ill, she hid it surpassingly well. When he had first seen her, Elgar had tried staring her down once or twice, as if expecting her to shrink from his gaze. But she had met his looks with such exquisite insolence that he soon averted *his* eyes, slumping into his seat with a frown. Seren still stood at her side, just slightly behind her chair, and Varalen found that he still couldn't look at her, not even now that Elgar knew all that had passed between them.

The young king had scant entertainment for his guests: "I had thought to have minstrels at least," he said, with another of those somber glances, "but the men tell me they have yet to arrive. I hope they haven't gotten into trouble along the way, but I am a little . . . relieved, I think. It just didn't seem right. I didn't have the heart for music, in the end." Either he was still too saddened over his father's death, or else the thought of granting any pleasure to a known enemy stung him. Perhaps it was both, and Varalen couldn't help but respect either. Dammit.

Had he not known better, he would have wondered if King Kelken was depressed, too caught up in the sickness of grief to pay much mind to what lay around him. But they could never have all been brought together like this by someone in the throes of despair. King Kelken knew what he was doing, whether or not he liked it. And he still had hope; even Varalen could tell that much.

In the absence of more joyful sport, they had been obliged to watch King Kelken's soldiers practice in the courtyard. It was a rather dreary affair to say the least: the damp, foggy air; the cold, imposing stone that rose up all around them; and only the grim mimicry of warfare for entertainment. Varalen would almost have donned motley and played the fool himself if it would've broken the tension that surrounded them.

"I *am* sorry," King Kelken said, for what must have been the fifth time. "Perhaps the bards will yet arrive, or perhaps—"

Elgar finally spoke, leaning slightly forward to meet Kelken's gaze. "Perhaps, Your Grace, since we are both fortunate enough to have so many men here, we might use them to make ourselves some sport? In keeping with the sober spirit of the occasion, of course, but you cannot be faulted for wanting a little excitement on a day that has brought so much to you."

King Kelken hesitated only a moment; Varalen waited for his eyes to flick to the old man who was his advisor, but they did not. "Excitement?" he mused.

"I'm afraid I don't know much about contests of arms—I couldn't ever join in, of course, so everyone usually tried to hide such things from me." He rubbed one swollen leg absently. "But if it will please you, then by all means. What did you have in mind?"

Elgar smiled, leaning farther forward still. "Well, I'm sure we couldn't set up a tourney on such short notice, but we might have a competitive match or two, don't you think? I know several soldiers of mine who'd be eager to show off, and I'm sure you have the same."

"I wouldn't know," King Kelken said thoughtfully. "I haven't asked them." He pondered a few moments more, then seemed to realize they were all still awaiting his answer. "Oh, but call whatever men you wish, of course. I'm sure we can come to some arrangement."

After he had sent a man to the northwest tower to summon more of his soldiers, Elgar looked to Lady Margraine. "Your Grace? Have you combatants to join our little game? I know you did not bring so many with you."

She smirked at him as cheerfully as ever. "I have enough, but I don't know that I want to wear them out in a pointless contest. They'll have real killing to do soon enough, I'm sure."

He stroked his beard. "My apologies. I forget women can be so squeamish about these things. You are not well used to the realities of the battlefield, as I recall."

"Why, I did not realize you were accustomed to take to the front lines. That is not what I have heard." She laughed. "Gravis is always telling me the same thing, you know—how I have only the *theory* of war, and none of the practice. I generally tell him I have to keep things sporting somehow."

Elgar's brow was furrowed. "Sporting?"

"I have only the theory of war, as you all say," the marquise said, leaning back lazily in her chair. "But I've been doing rather well for myself so far, wouldn't you say? I imagine if I were to master this practice of warfare that women know nothing about . . . well, then I'd really be a nuisance to you." She could not have missed the glower on Elgar's face, yet she barely looked at him. "I do wish you wouldn't group all women together like that, though; you're liable to give offense."

"How is it I've offended you, Your Grace?" Elgar nearly growled.

She waved a hand at him. "Oh, not *me,* of course. I was talking about Seren."

Her bodyguard was so stoic and so placid that Varalen doubted Elgar could've offended her if he spat in her face. "Seren is by far the best of my guards, and has been ever since she first came to me," the marquise continued. "Did you think I would choose anyone lesser to guard me personally? So she handles the practice of warfare, as it were, in my stead, woman or not."

Elgar eyed her skeptically. "She is really so very fine? She does not look like much."

Lady Margraine laughed. "How would you like her to look? They say Sebastian Valens was about as tall and as wide about the shoulders as any man, yet he was known as the greatest swordsman of his time."

"The greatest swordsman, but a rather bad bodyguard, as he killed the man he was sworn to protect," Varalen reminded her. "For your sake, I hope it's not a female Valens you're after, Your Grace."

She smiled—or perhaps it was more accurate to say she kept smiling—but said nothing.

"Ah," Elgar said as a line of dark-cloaked soldiers began streaming into the courtyard. "Here we are." He turned to King Kelken. "I hope you at least will indulge me in a bit of battle, Your Grace? The lady loves to boast of her favorite, but it seems she will not put her to the test."

"Oh, I shall if you like," Lady Margraine replied, with no more concern than if they were discussing the appropriate fashions for a midwinter ball. She looked up at the woman in her shadow. "Seren, it seems my word on your abilities will not satisfy the imperator. Go stand in the courtyard and await his pleasure."

Seren's expression had not changed while the marquise and Elgar were discussing her, and it did not now; she bowed to Lady Margraine and walked briskly to the center of the courtyard, as the soldiers standing there pulled back toward the walls to create a makeshift arena. Elgar ran his eyes very carefully across the ranks of the men he had summoned, nodding once or twice. Then he turned back to the marquise. "I wonder," he said slowly, "if you might go so far as to oblige me in another matter."

She raised her eyebrows, but the set of her mouth said she had guessed it already. "What might that be?"

Elgar pressed his fingertips together. "I only thought it might be best if we marked such an auspicious occasion with true blood sport, not merely the mockery of it."

At that, King Kelken's eyebrows lifted as well, and *his* expression showed nothing but alarm. "You can't mean—not to the death, surely?"

"Why not? Such displays were common in the past, and I am given to understand that in Lanvaldis, old King Eira marked even trivial events with mortal combat, right up until his death." Elgar turned to Varalen, and he felt himself tense at the unexpected attention. "Varalen, you spent quite some time in Lanvaldis, didn't you? Have I spoken correctly?"

"I . . . I never ventured anywhere near the Lanvaldian capital, my lord." *As you well know,* he didn't add. "But I did hear that such contests were popular in Araveil, yes." There was some movement in the corner of his eye that seemed out of place; Varalen turned his head, but by then all he could notice was that King Kelken's scarred retainer seemed to be scowling more deeply than usual.

Elgar spread his hands. "There, you see? It's traditional enough, and the lady and I would do you honor to risk our men for this day's sport. Provided you are amenable, of course," he added to the lady in question.

She shrugged, but she was considering it intently enough to frown. "Very well," she said slowly, "but only if whatever opponent you send against her wears no plate. Otherwise she might suffer a scratch or two, and I dislike for anything of mine to be damaged without sufficient cause."

Elgar smiled. "Confident, aren't you? Well, I'll not dispute those terms." To the king, he said, "And you, Your Grace? Have you further objections?"

King Kelken was silent for a long moment, his brow furrowed in thought. "The ones fighting are in service to the two of you, not to me," he finally said. "As long as they risk their lives freely, I suppose I should respect their decision." He set his jaw. "But my sister must have no part in this. She has no stomach for anything bloody."

"I rather suspected as much," Lady Margraine said. "By all means, let her amuse herself as she prefers."

"Of course," Elgar agreed, as the king nodded to his sister. She slipped away gratefully, and Varalen found he could not blame her. "Now let me see . . ." He examined the assembled soldiers thoroughly enough, but it did not take him long to come to a decision. "Colm." The man who stepped forward was tall and thickset, a bastard sword strapped to his side. True to the terms of the fight, he was wearing only leather, not plate, which suggested he was not among Elgar's elite. On the other hand, if Elgar knew him by name, he was no common soldier. Perhaps, as with more than a few of Elgar's men, he'd grown up too poor to buy armor and by now was too accustomed to fighting without it.

"Weapons?" Elgar asked the marquise.

She shrugged again. "Why not let them use what they have to hand? If you need another blade, I'm sure the king can provide one."

Elgar nodded. "You may use your own weapon, Colm." The man in question drew his sword from its sheath, holding it in both hands in preparation for a swing.

Seren raised her eyes to the marquise's; Lady Margraine considered a moment, then smiled. "Well, Seren, I don't want to make this *too* easy for you. Use the sword, unless you get into trouble."

Seren drew her own blade, and Lady Margraine looked to Elgar. "Will you give the signal to begin, or shall I?"

"Perhaps we had best let the king do it," Elgar said. "This is in honor of his coronation, after all."

King Kelken said nothing, just turned his attention back to the two combatants, staring hard at them as if he could predict the winner from their faces. Then he extended one hand, spreading the fingers wide. "Begin."

Colm leaped immediately forward, bringing his sword down in a stroke that could have split bone. Seren moved only partially out of the way, and his sword had hardly clanged against hers before he swung again, driving her back in a series of brutal strokes she seemed just barely to avoid each time. Eventually she drew near to the assembled soldiers, who tried their best to pull back so as not to seem to have interfered; Varalen thought belatedly that they ought to have marked a circle in the dirt. It turned out they needn't have worried: Seren dodged sideways instead of backward, and suddenly she was nearly behind Colm, aiming a swing at his shoulder that he only just managed to block. His superior strength and heavier blade forced her sword back just enough for him to turn himself about, and then he was on the offensive again, driving her before him in the other direction.

Varalen didn't know precisely what kind of performance he had expected from Seren, but it wasn't this. Colm might have been one of Elgar's chosen, but he was no Shinsei. If Seren was truly the best the marquise had, he couldn't say he was very impressed. She was agile, true, but she didn't seem able to dodge fast enough to put Colm on the defensive. More grievously, she was much weaker than he was, which meant that every time their blades clashed it was to her disadvantage. She would have to exert herself more just to stave him off, and eventually she would tire and become unable to block his strikes at all. Colm had clearly had the same thought, and he swung at her every chance he got, hardly giving her a moment to get her bearings. He drove her back and forth across the yard; each time she managed to dodge around him before he could box her in, but each time he regained the offensive and pushed her back once more.

Elgar was trying to keep his face impassive, but Varalen could see the smile tugging at the corner of his mouth. The marquise was smiling too, but it was the same smile she always wore, so it told him nothing. But as he looked closer he thought he could see something in her eyes, a flicker of heat that sparked against the coldness for the first time.

Then, by chance more than anything, he looked over at King Kelken, only to find him in conversation with the scarred man, whose narrowed eyes were following the fight closely. The king muttered something too soft for Varalen to hear, but his retainer shook his head at it. As he made his reply, he pointed at the combatants, and Varalen did his best to follow the man's finger, trying to see whatever it was he saw. The scarred man had pointed high, higher than the level of their swords, and Varalen had seen his lips move, directing his liege to *look at their . . .*

Brows, he realized suddenly, turning his own gaze there as well. *Look at their brows.*

Varalen obeyed that injunction, and what he saw didn't make sense. Colm's forehead was dripping with sweat, his damp hair plastered to his skin, but Seren's brow bore only a faint sheen, hardly worth the trouble to wipe away. But that couldn't be right. *She* ought to be tiring faster, and Colm's advantage should have been widening. Her dodges and counters ought to have been getting slower, and instead . . .

Instead Varalen cleared his mind of what *ought* to be happening and concentrated on what *was* happening. He watched Seren's movements closely, and he suddenly understood. The instant Colm initiated a stroke, Seren's eyes were already fixed on where it would land, but she waited until the last possible second before she moved out of the way. Even so, her maneuvers were fluid and assured, with not a trace of jerkiness or panic about them. She was not inept, he realized; she was holding back. To conserve her strength, she was doing only the bare minimum to keep from being struck, and Colm, spurred on by how narrowly she seemed to be escaping, was putting all his strength behind every swing. Seren had guessed what he thought of her, and how he'd try to defeat her, and he was so focused on the idea that he would inevitably wear her down that he hadn't yet noticed she was wearing *him* down.

Varalen leaned across to Elgar, lowering his voice as much as he could. "If Colm keeps wasting his strength like that, he's going to lose."

Elgar frowned, narrowing his eyes at the combatants, but Varalen couldn't tell if Elgar saw what he did. Either way, he called, "Colm, don't be so haphazard. Moderate your strokes, and watch for an opening."

Colm might well look confused; a minute ago Varalen himself would have thought that was terrible advice. But Elgar's men knew nothing if not how to obey, and he shifted and drew back, adopting a more defensive posture.

Lady Margraine laughed. "Oh, can we give instructions to our champions now? Then, Seren, I think you've entertained yourself enough. Aren't you supposed to be entertaining me?"

Varalen felt certain that the entire concept of *entertainment* was foreign to Seren, but she nodded nonetheless. And when Colm used that opportunity to strike at her, she executed a sidestep that was nothing like her previous ones; she moved so quickly that she seemed to have vanished from in front of him. Her own strike was almost too fast for Varalen's eyes to follow, and Colm only just drew back in time: the edge of her sword sliced a clean line across his cheek.

The marquise leaned forward, and there was no mistaking it now: she was watching the match with more than avid interest, her usual dispassion giving way to something else. Despite Elgar's instructions, the scratch panicked Colm enough to provoke another swing, hasty and poorly aimed; Seren sidestepped him again so smoothly that she didn't even seem to be in a hurry, but when she lashed out again, Colm caught her blade against his. She was unfazed, though, and quickly turned it; this time the edge slid along the side of his wrist, cutting deeper and letting the first drops of blood stain the dirt.

Colm's eyes were wide now, the first traces of fear beginning to show; Lady Margraine smiled as if she could taste it on the air, but Seren didn't react, only kept her eyes trained on her opponent.

In the next several exchanges, Seren landed a few more blows, but she only managed a couple of additional scratches and a slice to the leather at Colm's shoulder, tearing it without drawing blood from the skin beneath. He did not manage to hit her at all. Elgar's face was impassive throughout, his long fingers stroking his beard; King Kelken looked solemn as always, his scarred servant hardly less so. And Lady Margraine's eyes danced as she watched them, her fingers curled around the arms of her chair.

The decisive blow, when it came, looked almost casual: Seren half turned against one of Colm's particularly exhausted strokes, and her riposte sliced easily through the skin at his shoulder exposed by her previous tear. He fell to one knee, both hands wrapped around the hilt of his sword as he struggled to hold himself up. Seren paused for a single moment, though Varalen couldn't have said whether she was waiting to see if someone would order her to stop or if she just wanted to figure out the best angle from which to strike. He knew it couldn't have been out of pity, as there wasn't a trace of it on that face.

Whatever its cause, her stillness did not last. She gutted Colm as nonchalantly as if she were carving a roast, and he slumped to the ground with a wet squelch, blood spreading quickly from under him. Seren took no more notice of him, just cleaned her sword and sheathed it again. She turned back to the rest of them, and bowed once more. Even now she was only mildly sweating.

Elgar steepled his fingers. "Well, Your Grace, it seems I must congratulate you after all. I would give much for a woman of that one's talents."

"I allow her to act in my place," Lady Margraine said; her tone was lazy, but her eyes remained intent. "I regret to say *I* have no skills in weaponry—nor, I admit, did I ever have much of a taste for it. There's so much sweat and dirt involved, and swords just seem to slip from my hands. But Seren makes an art of it."

Elgar scowled, but no doubt he couldn't dispute it. Varalen certainly couldn't—Seren had moved with a precision he had rarely ever seen before. "It is just as well," Elgar said at last. "Your suitors would doubtless find abilities such as hers . . . unsettling, if you possessed them."

Lady Margraine laughed. "Perhaps you forget that I am the sole heir to the throne of Esthrades. My *suitors,* such as they are, are far too persistent to be put off by a bit of swordplay. I could probably be the demon some men claim I am and still have them begging for my favors. It does not mean I have to accept them."

Elgar raised his eyebrows. "But eventually you must, surely?"

She tilted her head. "Why must I? The fellows who seek me out are all so insipid; the best of them would bore me within a week. No, I prefer above all not to be bored. I'd choose a book over a suitor any day."

Elgar opened his mouth, but Varalen decided to interrupt before his master could say anything truly regrettable. "Well, either way, Your Grace, as the only one among the three of us, I think, who has ever *been* married—"

"Were you?" she asked, surprised. "And are you not married now?"

Varalen winced. "She died, Your Grace."

"Oh," she said. She did not look abashed, or pitying, or even mocking; she looked polite, and blank. "Well, I'm sorry to hear it."

"I never thought I'd care for marriage either," he continued, trying to think of nothing but the next line of his argument. "But love can change even the most cynical minds."

She waved away his words. "If *that's* so, I have even less to fear than I thought. It seems that I am incapable of love. So let that be the end to that question."

"The books you value so much are filled with tales of those who have said just such a thing, only to find themselves entirely mistaken."

"Quite so," she agreed, untroubled. "Perhaps I should not say so. But whether I say so or not, those who raised me amused themselves all my life by saying so, until it became quite tedious for me. Perhaps you ought to take it up with *them*, rather than with me."

Varalen had thought her impossibly cold after a day; if those who had had to live with her for years held such a worse opinion, he could not imagine what she must be like in her own halls. He responded with the only rejoinder he could think of: "If I may be so bold, Your Grace, it seems you do love one thing: you love the sound of your own voice quite unendurably."

She smiled widely, stretching like a cat. "Oh, I *do*. It's a dreadful weakness, I know. Perhaps if I were not quite so clever, I should not be quite so vain, but I suppose I'll never know."

"Unfortunately," Varalen said, trying not to stammer at her audacity, "we are all less clever than we believe ourselves to be."

She nodded. "The notion causes me much grief, I assure you. But then, we are generally cleverer than our enemies believe us to be, so at least there's that."

King Kelken cleared his throat, and they all started. Really, Varalen thought, that ability of his to slip from his guests' minds even when he was right in front of them was damned disconcerting. It didn't speak much to his majesty as a ruler, perhaps, but it might be useful for all that. He really would have to watch what he said around the boy. "I don't mean to interrupt you," Kelken continued, "but, well, she's been standing there for quite a while. She can retire now, can't she?"

Varalen had forgotten Seren entirely, and the hasty way Elgar's gaze flicked to her suggested he'd done the same; Lady Margraine's contented smile said she had not. "Retire? And leave me unattended? Surely not." To Seren, she added, "You don't have to stand out there, though—let others take the field, if they wish it."

Seren inclined her head, and returned to stand under the awning once more. As she passed him, Elgar said, "That was quite impressive, truly. How is it you became so accomplished at killing?"

Seren looked at him but did not speak. She seemed about to ignore him entirely when Lady Margraine glanced over her shoulder at her. "No, answer that."

"I practiced," Seren answered, without the barest hint of a delay.

"You practiced killing?"

"If you like." Her expression was as flat as her tone.

"For what reason?" Elgar asked.

"I thought it a useful skill to have," she answered, and though that sentence was as dry as any of Lady Margraine's, she did not give even the ghost of a smile.

"Fair enough." Elgar stroked his beard. "Then how did you come to Lady Margraine's service?"

"Voluntarily," Seren said. It was just like talking to her down in the dungeons had been—her answers were so terse that she had to know how infuriating they were, but her face betrayed no hint of humor, no irony, just that same stoic expression.

Elgar smiled. "I'll put it another way. *Why* did you come to Lady Margraine's service?" When she hesitated, he added, "Well, when a servant is asked such a thing in front of her master, I suppose the proper answer is because of her virtue and nobility, no?"

Seren looked to Lady Margraine, but she only smirked. "Oh, definitely answer that."

Seren turned back to Elgar. "No."

His eyebrows rose. "Indeed? Why, then?"

She paused a moment, as if gathering her thoughts. "To repay a debt," she said at last.

For only the second time since Varalen had known her, Lady Margraine looked displeased. There was none of the cold anger, though, that had gripped her the last time, just vague irritation; either it was not the answer she had been expecting, or else not the answer she would have preferred. Captain Ingret frowned as well, and leaned forward, as if this were news to him.

"A debt to the marquise?" Elgar asked.

"That's right."

"And when will this debt be discharged?"

"With my death," Seren said, with no less dispassion than before.

Varalen laughed, though the back of his neck was prickling. "That must be quite an obligation, then. I certainly wouldn't want to owe Her Grace anything if she demands such a rate of return."

Lady Margraine had no quip to make to that; she was still frowning, gazing vaguely off into the middle distance. Elgar peered at her for some moments, but then decided to leave her be, addressing King Kelken instead. "Well, Your Grace, the lady's champion has proven *her* skill—I suppose it falls to us to prove ours? Colm, sad to say, is no more"—wasn't *someone* going to remove the corpse, Varalen wondered?—"but I have many other men I believe will fare better—though I'm sure we needn't spill any more blood, unless you insist on it."

"I certainly don't," King Kelken said. He twitched his shoulders uncomfortably. "I . . . I haven't accustomed my men to things like this. I don't know how I should match them against you."

Elgar gestured at the scarred man, standing tall and stiff beside the king and avoiding all eyes. "This one here seems valorous enough. Why not have him try his hand?"

The old advisor caught his breath sharply, but it was too late: King Kelken had already turned to his retainer, raising his eyebrows quizzically. "Cadfael?"

The scarred man, if possible, looked even more uncomfortable, but his voice, when it came, was firm. "No."

The king said nothing, biting his lip. *He* was the one who looked apologetic, as if the roles of servant and master had been reversed. Elgar stared at this Cadfael in some surprise. "You refuse your master, sir?"

Cadfael turned his gaze on Elgar next, and it only gained in intensity. "I refuse to fight in mere idle displays of strength. I refuse to fight when there is no reason to."

Elgar's expression was mild, but his eyes were hard. "One might say that your master's bidding is reason enough."

"Aye," the man growled, his fingers clenching around the hilt of his sword. "That is the trouble with *masters*."

"If you despise masters so much," Elgar asked, "how is it you have come to have one?"

Cadfael said nothing, only gritted his teeth and turned his face away.

King Kelken seemed on the point of speaking, but Elgar's next words drowned him out. "I asked you a question, sir."

Cadfael looked at him again, and this time the anger in his eyes was plain. "I have no reason to answer. I have no *desire* to answer, *sir,* though I cannot stop you from asking, if it pleases you. Do as you like."

"Cadfael," the king said hurriedly, before Elgar could reply, "the imperator is my guest—"

"So he is," Cadfael agreed. "So he is. And so I respect him, in my way, as much as I am able. But I will not answer his questions, or anyone's, if I do not care to."

"And you call that respect?" Elgar asked.

Cadfael whirled on him. "I call it more than you deserve. I have no part in politics—I want nothing from *you,* but I've seen your work. Call yourself what you like, but I know what you are: a common butcher."

Varalen nearly reeled with panic, but Elgar, of all things, smiled. "Well, a butcher, perhaps. But I'd hardly say common."

At that point so many things happened so quickly that Varalen was hard-pressed to take them all in: Cadfael took two great strides toward Elgar, and every man of Elgar's in the courtyard reached for his blade; Cadfael drew his sword half out of its sheath, and as soon as the gleaming steel caught the light, Elgar flung himself so violently away from it that he lost his chair and fell sprawled upon the ground. His men all made abortive movements forward, but Seren was faster than all of them; she laid a hand on Cadfael's wrist, and his sword stopped where it was, half in his scabbard and half out of it.

"If you draw your sword now," Seren said calmly, "you will die for it. Are you content to die here, for this?"

Cadfael hesitated only a moment, all the breath going out of him in a deep sigh. Then he sheathed his blade, shook off her hand, and turned away. "No," he said. "I have something I must do first."

In the silence that followed, Elgar raised himself to his knees, then got slowly to his feet. He was not shaking; he did not even seem afraid. Why in the gods' name had he flung himself away like that? There had been something of reflex about the movement, of instinct, the way one flinches back from heat or shivers under the influence of cold. Lady Margraine had noticed it too, he was certain: she ought to have been pleased at Elgar's apparent cowardice, but instead her eyes were thoughtful, the fingers of one hand curling and uncurling slowly.

"Your Grace," Elgar said to King Kelken, brushing the dust from his clothes, "I must ask that that man be summarily put to justice."

Varalen had expected panic to show on the boy king's face, but he did not see it; Kelken looked as solemn as ever, and, in fact, oddly calm. "For what crime?" he asked.

"For the *crime*," Elgar snapped, "of attempting to kill me."

The king blinked. "Did he do that? I'm certainly not pleased with him for showing you such disrespect, but he didn't even draw his—"

"Only because *she* prevented him," Elgar said, with an almost sullen nod at Seren.

"No," she said. "I did not hold him with any force. He could easily have thrown me off if he had wished to."

King Kelken nodded. "I am sorry to disappoint you," he said to Elgar, "but I don't see how it's just for me to punish him. We are not in your lands; you are a guest here, like any other, not a ruler. He was discourteous toward you, but he did you no harm, and stopped of his own will. I wish it hadn't happened, but beyond that . . ."

Elgar scowled. "Are you truly saying you see no harm in keeping on a servant who would so flagrantly disobey your wishes?"

The king shook his head. "Cadfael is not my servant; he is my friend. I am sorry if that was not clear. The fault is mine, for not explaining things better." He touched his cheek. "With friends there are no orders, and as for going against my *wishes* . . . I may be angry with him, but that's where it ends."

"Whether you claim to be or not," Elgar said, "you are his *king*, and—"

"He isn't," Cadfael finally spoke up. "I am no Reglian."

Rather than respond to that, Elgar hesitated, his scowl fading to a thoughtful frown as he stared at Cadfael intently. "No," he said, very slowly. "I don't suppose you are. Might you, in fact, be from Lanvaldis?"

Cadfael started at that, and drew back warily. "That's right," he said, after several long moments of silence, and his voice was hoarse.

Elgar shrugged, and somehow that unnerved Varalen more than the most vehement gesture would have. "In your halls, Your Grace," he said to Kelken, "I cannot force you to see things my way. But might I inquire how long I shall have to contend with this . . . friend of yours in close quarters?"

Cadfael answered that. "Not long, I assure you. I will be gone at first light, and you have my word, I will not so much as approach you until then."

Elgar sighed. "I suppose I'll have to content myself with that." He took his seat again, pressing his palms together. "What an . . . edifying experience all this has been."

But Varalen knew his master would hardly be content to leave things there. He would have his revenge for this, one way or another.

CHAPTER TWENTY-NINE

Elgar had accepted his request to clear his head but had commanded him to return within the hour. Varalen supposed he should count himself lucky that his master trusted him at least that far, but it still didn't leave him with nearly as much time as he would have liked. He didn't have much of a chance anyway, of course—even if he did, by some miracle, manage to find Seren alone, why would she ever want to answer his questions?

After that little show in the courtyard, it was laughable to think of how hard he and Quentin had pushed to have her freed. *We argued she was harmless! Gods, that'll teach me to stick my neck out for an* innocent *again.* If he had just left well enough alone and kept her there . . . Well, there was no use thinking about it now.

He stumbled halfway down the next corridor and had to rest one hand against the wall to keep from falling. In that instant, while he stayed motionless and glanced aimlessly at the other end of the hall, where a perpendicular corridor formed a T shape as it crossed his own, he saw Captain Ingret come around the corner toward him, his strides swift and purposeful. He wore a sour expression, but Varalen had come to understand that he was seldom without one.

Though the captain's eyes flicked to him as he passed, he seemed about to leave him behind without comment. Varalen spoke up. "Are you in such a hurry to abandon your mistress, Captain?"

The man's voice was a tight, low growl, but that was normal too. "My presence was not required."

Varalen laughed. "What does that mean? Did she send you away?" Captain Ingret's expression didn't change, so he couldn't tell whether he'd guessed right or not. "I wonder if that isn't more of a relief to you than a disappointment."

The captain's face hardened; Varalen hadn't thought that was possible. "I might well ask *you* the meaning of *that.*"

Varalen shrugged. "It's simple enough. I merely suggested that you might not be so fond of your mistress as you could wish to be, that's all." He grinned. "It's a pity: she *is* fair, much as I've tried to find her otherwise. But perhaps you find her words more disagreeable than her face is agreeable, eh?"

"Her *face,*" Captain Ingret spat, "has only ever served to remind me of her mother, who was a thousand times more what a woman should be and who she does not deserve to resemble in any particular. Was that the answer you wished to hear, my *lord*? Now let me pass."

Varalen held up his hands. "I cannot block your way, I'm sure—I'm hardly a warrior. I have to earn my keep with my mind instead, so perhaps I can be forgiven for thinking too much."

"If you thought more, perhaps you would speak less."

"Aye, I'll admit the truth of that," Varalen said, wincing. "But my mouth's too used to the practice, I fear. Let me ask you just one more thing: If the lady dissatisfies you so, why is it you serve her?"

"Why do you serve your master?" the captain asked. He certainly liked turning questions back upon the asker, didn't he?

"Ah," Varalen said. "Well, as to that, the imperator can be . . . very persuasive." He tried to smile, but it felt wrong on his face, and he wasn't sure how it turned out.

Captain Ingret's expression softened slightly, turned inward. "So can she," he said, "but not in the way you mean." He nodded curtly and resumed his stride. "Good afternoon, Lord Oswhent."

I'm not a lord, Varalen wanted to call after him, but didn't; no doubt he'd pressed the man hard enough. Besides, his absence only increased Varalen's chances of getting to speak with Seren alone—not that that counted for much.

As he drew nearer to the Esthradians' rooms, he began to hear a voice, but it was soft, too low for him to make out the words. He could not exactly tell from the sound of it, but it had to be Lady Margraine's voice, as Seren would no doubt tire herself if she spoke so many words in a row. He edged closer and closer, not quite daring to peer around the corner, and finally the words came clearly: ". . . deliberately obtuse, or were you just clinging to that same outdated notion?"

Seren's voice was even softer, her tone very nearly like a normal person's. "I meant what I said. It was never my intention to lie."

"Yes, that's the problem," Lady Margraine said, sounding no more troubled than she ever was. "You *persist* in meaning it, past all attempts at correction. At this point I really ought to be cross with you, you know."

"If you are angry, I am sorry for it," Seren said. "But I cannot control what I believe any more than you can."

"Hmm. How should I take that, I wonder?"

Varalen shifted, leaning against the far wall instead of the near one and trying to crane his neck so he could see around the corner. They were facing each other, not him, and he pressed his back against the wall and stayed as quiet as he could, hoping to keep it that way.

The marquise walked sideways a couple of steps, not quite circling her retainer. "A debt? A *debt*? It merely gives you pleasure to believe such a thing exists. And as for your *death,* I am certain I never demanded something so melodramatic as that."

"I know you didn't—I know—" Seren dropped her gaze to the floor. Had she actually stammered? "But whether you admit it or not, you still—"

The marquise's smile did not waver, but though the movement of her arm was smooth and steady, it was also swift, cutting off whatever Seren had been about to say. She curled her fingers in the cloth at Seren's throat, and her thumb flicked up and outward, lifting Seren's chin so their eyes met once more. Her voice held none of the cold anger Varalen remembered so well, but it was not so languid as it was wont to be either. "Be very careful how you finish that. I still *what*?"

For a moment Seren just stood there, pressing her lips together, but then she opened her mouth—and halted, stiffening. Varalen did not realize she had seen him until Lady Margraine turned his way too, and by then it was too late to pretend he hadn't been eavesdropping.

They both stared at him, yet Lady Margraine, far from snatching her hand back, barely even slackened her grip. And Seren met his eyes coolly, her usual staid composure unblemished by even the slightest hint of embarrassment. "Well, Lord Oswhent," the marquise said, *still* smiling. "How unexpected. Is there something we can do for you?"

Varalen bowed as best he could; the gesture felt somehow off, somehow surreal. "I beg your pardon, Your Grace, but I was hoping I could have a word with your servant. It will not take long."

"That's a word with my servant *alone,* I take it?" Lady Margraine asked. "You don't imagine that's going to be an effective way to keep secrets from me, I hope?"

"It isn't a secret," Varalen said. "I just need to ask her something. I don't care whether you listen or not."

Lady Margraine finally released Seren's collar and faced him fully, tapping one fingertip against her chin. "You may ask her one question. If I tell her to answer you truthfully, she will. But if I allow that, then *I* get to ask *you* a question. That's fair, isn't it?"

What could she possibly have to ask him about? "That's fine," Varalen said.

"Very well." She nodded. "One question."

He turned to Seren. "Where is the stone?"

Seren shook her head, but it wasn't confusion or refusal. "There's no point in looking for it, or in trying to steal it back. It's gone."

"Gone?" Was Elgar right, then? "You mean it's been destroyed?"

She hesitated, then said, "For you, it is the same as if it had been destroyed. No one will ever see it again. Let that be the last word on it."

Lady Margraine was smirking serenely enough; *this* answer, at least, had pleased her. Varalen bowed again, stiffly. "If that is the truth, then I thank you for it."

"I cannot say that I never lie," Seren replied. "But I prefer to tell the truth, when I can help it."

He looked to the marquise. "And your question, Your Grace?"

She tilted her head. "Why *my lord*?"

Varalen tried not to look taken aback, and failed. "I beg your pardon?"

"You call me *Your Grace,* as do most foreigners, because that is how one addresses a monarch. But we Margraines are not monarchs." His confusion must have shown on his face, because she laughed. "We *are* monarchs, of course, in every way that matters, but we don't *claim* to be. So in Esthrades there exists no title higher than *my lady* or *my lord.*"

She leaned back against the wall. "But with Elgar, I am given to understand it is quite different. The title he has chosen to go along with *Imperator* is *Your Eminence,* is it not? And yet you call him only *my lord.* Why does he allow such a thing?"

Varalen could still remember that day well enough, though it felt as if ten years separated him from the man he'd been then. *I'm like to suffocate under all your ridiculous rules,* he had told Elgar. *I can barely remember them all, and there are always more. How much deference do you think you can wring out of a man whose son you've stolen? You know his fate. You* know *his condition. And yet you still think I have it in me to bear endless burdens, when my son could die tomorrow even if you spare him?*

He could not possibly tell Lady Margraine that, yet he doubted he'd be able to lie to her. Finally he smiled as best he could. "The answer to that . . . The answer to that is that even a little man can be pushed only so far," he said, "Your Grace."

"She didn't say destroyed?" Elgar asked for the third time. "Just gone?"

"Just gone." By this time Varalen was almost starting to get used to the lack of agitation, the almost-relief. Elgar was avid, but not especially anxious. If only the same could be said of him always.

He leaned back in his chair. "Well, close enough. It's as I told you, isn't it? The rogue piece is eliminated, but we still command the board."

"Something like that, my lord." If Elgar wasn't going to worry about a bloody magic *rock,* why in the world should he? Better to turn his master's mind to more practical matters. "Now, if I may . . ."

Elgar frowned. "You're going to ask me something irritating again, aren't you?"

He really ought to just keep his mouth shut. Why had he never learned to just keep his mouth shut? "My lord, if you told me you wished to give up your plans for the continent, no one would be happier than I. But as I doubt that's true—"

"You may well doubt it," Elgar said fiercely, sitting up, his right hand clenching into a fist. "What other dream have I ever had but Elesthene? Once, just once in our history, this land came under the sway of one man. That proves it *can* be done. I will fulfill his legacy or I will die trying."

"It proves," Varalen said, "that it is not meant to be. Vespasian Darrow held on to his empire for only a handful of months, and he . . . he had every advantage." According to all accounts, Darrow had been all the things Elgar was not: he was young and handsome and charismatic, beloved by nobles and commoners alike, even some of those who eventually decided to take up arms against the Citadel. Just not by his sworn knight, it seemed.

"Vespasian Darrow was betrayed," Elgar insisted. "That's all."

"That's *all*? My lord, have you forgotten that there was a *rebellion,* that the people rioted in the streets—"

"Stirred up by traitors. If Darrow had executed Radcliffe and Trevelyan when he'd had the chance, if he had only known Sebastian Valens for a faithless dog the first time he laid eyes on him, he never would have lost his grip on the empire."

That was debatable, but Varalen knew better than to debate it. "Either way, my lord, since you *are* still determined to pursue this goal, I must urge you again: take this castle back before it is too late."

Elgar turned his face aside, scuffing at the arm of the chair with his nails. "No."

"My lord—"

"*No.* That word, from me, should be enough, Varalen. Don't try me in this manner."

"I'm *trying* to *advise* you!" Varalen shouted, in a kind of hysteria. "That's what you wanted me to do, isn't it? And yet every time I try to turn you toward something that makes sense—"

"It does make sense." Elgar's voice was subdued, almost—gods, almost *contrite.* "Armed with only the information you have, you think that retaking Mist's Edge is the best choice. And you are right, so far as that goes. But I know more than you do, and if you knew what I know . . ." He trailed off, his jaw clenching. "This place is not meant for my possession."

"Because of the ghosts?" Varalen couldn't help asking.

Elgar smiled thinly. "I do not insist that ghosts exist. But neither do I insist, as you do, that they do not."

"But if it's ghosts you fear—"

"I fear a warning," Elgar said. "I fear a warning that was made to me in this very place."

Varalen frowned. "But you haven't ever been here before, have you?"

"I haven't," Elgar agreed. "But the warning was meant for me all the same. And before you roll your damned eyes and sigh at me . . . well, let me tell you a story, and then you can tell me what *you* would do, if you ever found yourself in a similar situation."

Varalen rubbed at his face. "A story? Well, as you like."

Elgar glanced suspiciously about him for a few moments, but finally he nodded, clasping his hands in front of him. "In the weeks before I abandoned Mist's Edge, I had about a hundred and fifty soldiers inside the castle at any given time. I sent somewhat more than a third of them to reinforce a garrison on the southern border, and I gave orders for them to remain there until further notice. This state of affairs continued for about a fortnight while I considered whether to send any more men to replace the ones I'd taken out of Mist's Edge. The castle didn't seem to me to be in any danger of being retaken—the Rayls had certainly been trying for long enough, after all—but a bit of caution might've been warranted, considering its strategic value. I ultimately decided to send more men, but before I could give the order, six sentries from Mist's Edge arrived in the capital. They informed me that none of my other soldiers had left the castle alive."

Varalen swallowed hard. He'd never heard the slightest whisper about this. "But what had happened to the rest of them?"

"I questioned the lot of them, not to say I found any of them especially coherent. They had all been on watch outside the walls, and they had returned from their rounds to find the gates lying open and three distinct piles of bodies in the courtyard."

Elgar winced, growing pale, though his eyes were intent. "The corpses in the first pile had been burned, charred a perfect black, though fire had touched no other part of Mist's Edge, and there were no traces of one ever having been built. In the second pile, not ten feet away, the bodies were frozen from the inside, blood like ice in their veins. And in the third pile . . . the third pile was not so much a pile of bodies as a collection of limbs and scraps, gashed with a thousand cuts, broken and twisted and torn. It was a scene of total, impossible devastation."

Elgar paused, drawing in a breath. "And in the center of the courtyard, cross-legged at the foot of the charred corpses, was a single man.

"He was Aurnian, perhaps no older than you. They said he wore a cloak the color of fresh blood, but the rest was all black, from his collar to his boot-heels. And there was something odd about his face: it was somehow *gray,* as if he were half a corpse himself. He stood up as they entered, and faced them calmly. 'I'm here to deliver a message,' he said. 'We are greatly displeased with your master.' The men were very insistent about that: he said *I* at the beginning, but after, ever after, it was *we.*"

Varalen was still trying to comprehend how such a series of deaths could take place at all, let alone what the motive behind it could have been. "Who did he mean by *we?*"

"He did not say, and my men were too distracted to ask. A couple made as if to apprehend him, but he merely smirked at the bodies behind him and asked if they were in such a hurry to join their companions. They didn't dare approach him again after that, and he was able to deliver his message more or less unopposed."

"And the message?" Varalen asked.

Elgar clenched his fingers on the arm of his chair. "I was to understand that *they* would not allow me to keep the castle, and required me to abandon it at once. 'It belongs to us now,' he said, 'and the dead. All who set foot in this castle without our leave will die, this we swear to you.'

"He said they assumed I would try to test them—that I would think, *Oh, what are fifty or a hundred men to me, when I have thousands?* But they needed me to understand that their quarrel was with *me,* and it was a very personal one. 'We considered attacking him directly, even if we had to seek him in the Citadel itself,' he said, 'but many people would die.' He stated this as a negative, yet the men claimed the idea did not seem all that unpleasant to him. 'Many, many people would die. So we have chosen to take our revenge in this way instead. But if he tries to take it back—if we find a single one of his men so much as *looking* at this castle—we will pursue him with everything we are. And you'll find, if our work here hasn't already convinced you, that we are not insignificant.'"

Elgar leaned back in his chair, pursing his lips. "Naturally, one of the men took that opportunity to ask something entirely beside the point: he inquired after what made this quarrel of theirs so very personal.

"'He killed our brother,' the man in the cloak replied. 'And in so doing he has made mortal enemies of us forever.'"

"*Did* you kill his brother?" Varalen had to ask.

Elgar shrugged. "Probably. I've killed enough people in the course of my life; I don't doubt many of them had brothers."

Killed them how? Varalen wondered. He had never seen him do it, never even seen him practicing. He wore a sword and a knife, but Varalen had never known him to so much as draw either of them; he'd always figured they were intended more for ceremony's sake than for any practical use. Was Elgar merely referring to the admittedly long list of people who had been killed on his orders? "Did this man say anything else?" he finally asked, just to say something.

Elgar shook his head. "Not that I could get out of the sentries, anyway. He delivered this message of his and then left, leaving them stunned and slack-jawed in his wake." He folded his hands. "Well? What would *you* do, Varalen, if a man like that issued such an ultimatum to you? Would you try to take back Mist's Edge, do you think?"

Varalen hesitated. "My lord, I can't really . . . believe such a thing—"

Elgar scoffed. "*Still* you insist on doubting everything? Nothing but magic could have killed those men in such a way."

"You never saw the bodies yourself, did you? There must be some explanation—"

"There is a very obvious explanation. You just don't want to see it."

Varalen ignored that; it was the same old argument, and in the meantime something else had occurred to him. "But, my lord, if you were so concerned about this, why on earth did you agree to come back to Mist's Edge in the first place? If you truly give credence to this strange man's threats, it's a wonder you aren't dead already. It's a wonder we all aren't."

"That's why I *had* to go," Elgar said. "I had to find out as much as I could before I invaded Reglay. It's been more than two years since that man delivered his message, and I had started . . . not to doubt, but to wonder. I wondered if this strange man and his *we* had really been living at Mist's Edge that whole time. And if they were somewhere else, how would they know if one of my men *did* so much as look at the castle? I wondered, but if I was wrong . . . I didn't want to risk it. And then that boy made his move." He stroked his beard. "He proved . . . not that they were never here, but that they're not here now. And if they were willing to let him steal their castle without so much as a squeak of protest, I wondered what they would do if *I* set foot within its walls—as a guest, of course. The bargain wasn't that I couldn't go to Mist's Edge, was it? It was that I couldn't try to take it back, and I'm not. If this man was lax enough to allow Kelken to take over again, and if Kelken wants to invite me here for dinner and a coronation, I expect that's within the rules."

It was still strange. How could Elgar be so paranoid about some things and so cavalier about others? "None of your men ever saw this apparition again?"

"None," Elgar agreed. "And he sent no more messages—or, if he did, I never received them. I might almost wonder if he ever existed in the first place."

"Are you so sure he did?" Varalen asked. "It couldn't have been . . . I don't know, some elaborate hoax? A plot by your men?"

Elgar actually laughed. "By *my* men? Gods no. My men couldn't half dream up something so intricate. They're all like you—they don't have any imagination."

CHAPTER THIRTY

Ritsu hadn't tried to kill them yet; Deinol could say that much for him. He hadn't tried much of anything, to be honest, and that included speaking. He'd expected the man to try to bolt as soon as they were out of sight of the village, or else, at the very least, to appeal for permission to bolt. But he'd just kept trotting faithfully along after them, without so much as asking where they were going.

He didn't speak to Deinol much, although Deinol could usually get him to answer direct questions, if cryptically. Seth seemed to have better luck, but even he was sometimes thwarted; Ritsu never openly disdained a question, but sometimes he frowned or said he didn't know, and sometimes he let whole sentences pass as if he hadn't realized they were directed at him.

Seth was the one who had asked him how old he was, and Ritsu had replied that he'd stopped counting years ago. "I'm sure I'm older than I look, though, because some people still call me *boy,* and I must be over twenty at least." And what kind of person simply stopped counting? Deinol wondered. He'd known people who never *knew,* sure, but none who used to keep track and simply gave it up one day.

Part of him had hoped Ritsu's strangeness would resolve itself as soon as they'd gotten away from his accusers, that they could find some starting point from which to understand him. But the man—even Deinol found it hard not to think of him as a boy—only seemed stranger the more he revealed about himself. Where on earth had he come from?

When he'd put that question to Ritsu, he had hesitated. "I was born in Aurnis, but I didn't come *here* from there. I left when it fell, and after that I went to many places." And *that* had smacked unpleasantly of Almasy, but where Almasy had felt slick, Ritsu seemed almost guileless, like a child or an idiot.

It didn't stop Seth from feeling the same way about Ritsu as he had about Almasy, of course. Around people in Sheath he had always been shy, but perhaps he felt responsible for Ritsu on account of this Sebastian fellow he was supposed to look like. (His attraction to Almasy was, and always would be, inexplicable.) Deinol could already tell they were going to get into a row once he proposed they'd taken Ritsu far enough and Seth protested that they couldn't just leave him *alone,* but he couldn't see how to avoid it. They weren't making this journey for their own pleasure, after all, and no doubt Ritsu didn't want to get involved in the search for Almasy any more than Deinol wanted him to.

When they stopped for water, Deinol unsheathed Ritsu's sword, which he'd been carrying with him since they'd left the village. Ritsu had surprised him yet again by not asking for it back, though perhaps he merely guessed Deinol wasn't about to trust him with it yet. Deinol took a few practice swings with it, listening to the blade whistle through the air. For size it looked like a common one-hander, though the grip was long enough to accommodate two hands, a not unusual modification. Not a *tsunshin,* then—had he been trained out of the Aurnian style? "Have you been using this blade long, Ritsu?" he asked.

Ritsu nodded. "For many years."

There was something about the sword that irked him; it just didn't feel right in his hands. Deinol swung it a couple more times. "You like it?"

"I am used to it."

Deinol certainly wasn't; he stumbled on the next swing, and frowned down at the blade. It wasn't that it was too light; he preferred his longsword, true, but he'd used one-handed swords before. So what was it?

On a whim, he took a swing at a nearby tree—and nearly yelled in pain as the blow connected, shivering down the blade and through his arm all the way to the shoulder.

"What on earth are you *doing?*" Seth asked. "You can't just bang his sword around like that."

Deinol's arm was inclined to agree, but at least now he knew what had bothered him about the sword. "This is weak steel," he said to Ritsu.

The man looked at him blankly. "What?"

"It's poorly made, I mean. Didn't you see how hard it shook when I struck that tree? It nearly leaped out of my hands. I didn't even swing it that hard."

"Oh," Ritsu said. "Well, that's odd."

"I'll say. You didn't notice?"

Ritsu touched his bottom lip. "It's the only sword I've used for some time, so perhaps I would not know the difference."

"But this . . ." Deinol cut the air with the sword again. It didn't even *sound* right. "You're a small man, so you can't be *that* strong, and with a sword like this . . . I don't understand how you wouldn't be overpowered every time."

Ritsu seemed to understand that, at least. "It's true I am small, but I'm stronger than I look. And I was taught to use speed, not power. Speed, technique, precision—that's what I was taught."

"Well, it seems to me you'd be faster and more precise with a better blade."

"Perhaps I should get one, then," Ritsu said mildly. "But as you don't even wish me to use this one . . ."

"Eh, aye, I guess the point's a bit moot." He sheathed the sword again, crouching by the river. "Where is it you're going, Ritsu?"

Ritsu had lowered his face to his cupped hands to drink, but he looked up at the question, water dripping from his chin. "Going? I didn't have a destination. I just didn't like staying in one place for too long. Perhaps . . ." He hesitated. "Perhaps eventually I'll find a place I would like to stay, and then I'll stay there."

"Weren't you looking for someone?" Seth asked, propping his chin on his hand. "You wanted to find someone, but you didn't know where to look?"

"Yes," Ritsu agreed. "I was told . . . hmm." He sat on the bank, a bemused expression passing over his face. "Who was it who told me? Was it my father? I think it may have been." He tapped his wet chin, staring off into the trees. "Yes, that feels right to me. My father told me once that whenever you are defeated, it is because the enemy swordsman knows something you do not." He laughed. "Yes, I remember now. I asked him what if the enemy swordsman knew he had an army at his back and you didn't, and he told me to stop trying to make a fool of myself. That was the way of things in Aurnis—the truest combat was single combat, that moment when you brought your whole being to bear on someone else's, when they became your whole world. And if you lost *then,* my father said, it was always because you did not know something, and your opponent did. It might simply be the best way to place your feet before a lunge, the way to counter your favorite stroke, but there was always *something,* always. You just had to find it."

"So does that mean you're looking for someone who defeated you?" Seth asked.

Ritsu frowned. "Not *looking,* because I don't know where to look. It just occurred to me that I wished we could meet again, that's all."

Deinol stretched out across from him. "Well, what do you know about him?"

"Nothing," Ritsu said.

"Come on. Surely not nothing at all? You must remember what he looked like, at least, or what sort of blade he used."

Ritsu nodded, very slowly. "Yes. I remember the blade. A *tsunshin,* like my father used—like I used to use, when I was younger."

"That narrows it down more than you might think," Seth offered. "Elgar killed so many of the *shinrian* when Aurnis fell, and since then the style's fallen out of favor."

Deinol wrinkled his nose. "Narrows it, sure, but unless the *shinrian* you fought was *Lucius,* I doubt we can help you." He paused. "It, er, wasn't Lucius, was it? Half-Aurnian, about my age, long black hair, nose even sharper than his chin? It wasn't, right? It can't have been."

Ritsu pressed his lips together, his fingers tightening in the grass. Deinol waited, but he said nothing. He hadn't seen anything like recognition or surprise in Ritsu's face, but then why was he so reluctant to answer?

"Look," Deinol said wearily, "I understand we just met, and there are some things you don't want to tell us, but if I have to travel around with you wondering if you want revenge on my friend—"

Ritsu looked up in surprise, holding his hands out in front of him. "No, no, not revenge, nothing like that. It was an honorable fight, and I'm just happy to be alive at all. I only wanted . . . to see if I could find it out. To see if I could learn whatever it was I didn't know. That's all." He bit his lip. "I don't think it's your friend, anyway. It may not be. It probably isn't."

Deinol opened his mouth to question him further, but stopped when Seth shook his head. "Let's hope not," he said instead. "I've caused him enough trouble already without unwittingly freeing one of his enemies."

CHAPTER THIRTY-ONE

The oaken table was not small, but the map covered it entirely, leaving the White Waste to dangle over its edge into empty air. Imperator Elgar paced on the far side of the room, stealing downward glances at the map every so often; Lady Margraine reclined on a cushioned chair, her fingers curled gently around a glass of wine. Kel felt restless himself, but his legs didn't agree, so he was seated as well, trying to keep from fidgeting.

All three of them had agreed it was best to remain alone together for the duration of their negotiations, but that didn't mean they had to like it. Without Eirnwin or Cadfael, or even Lessa, it was difficult to pretend he wasn't caught between two vipers, and doubtless Elgar found these terms too even for his taste.

Only Lady Margraine seemed content, but she was watching both of them carefully all the same.

Elgar spoke first. "I would venture we all want the same thing: peace, of any acceptable sort."

Lady Margraine laughed. "I'd wager we *do* all want the same thing: our kingdoms." She took a sip of wine. "The difference, of course, is that Kelken and I only want our own, and you would have them all."

Elgar inclined his head. "If you are determined to be so hostile from the very first—"

"There is no hope of our coming to terms? Do you think there is any regardless? We know what you will say, and you know *my* answer, at least."

"I wish to unite our sundered lands," Elgar said, holding up a hand. "I will not deny that. Valyanrend was once the crown jewel of an empire, and I will make it so again. But I am not so unreasonable as you think."

When neither one of them said anything, he continued, "I have no desire for a Council, as in the days of Elesthene, but neither can I be everywhere at once. I will need stewards to take the day-to-day matters of each region in hand when I cannot be present."

Lady Margraine laughed again, more harshly, shaking her head in disbelief. "Are you really proposing what I think you are?"

"My lady, if you understood warfare even as well as your father did, you would see that you have no chance. Why is it laughable in me to wish to spare your life, not to mention countless lives from both our armies?" He laid one hand against the edge of the table, his fingertips brushing the map. "You can still sit your throne—you can *both* still sit your thrones. Esthrades will become a province of the empire, just as it was in the beginning, and—"

"And Reglay can no longer be a *kingdom,* of course," Lady Margraine finished, "but names are only words, isn't that right? You will need, naturally, to give me a husband, someone you can trust to seize the reins of power from me, and the boy, once you take away his crown, will only be a boy, and thus unfit to rule an imperial province. You shall place another of your men above him—perhaps you'll marry him to the bastard sister for good measure—and assure Kelken that he can take over administration of the region once he comes of age. It wouldn't be unreasonable of you to hope he dies before that day comes, given his physical condition. Even if he does not, what power will he have to demand that which he has already given up?" She smiled. "Have I summed it up adequately?"

Imperator Elgar was unperturbed. "Any proposition may sound fair or foul when couched in the appropriate terms. Let me guess at what yours would be: I should leave Esthrades to you, when I could have it easily, simply because it is yours by *rights*? And what rights are those? Because your ancestor betrayed the masters he was sworn to serve and carved out a realm for himself by force?"

"Funny, I'd thought your own story was rather similar." She took another leisurely sip of wine. "At least *we* never had to fight our own people for power."

Elgar scoffed. "The Margraines were ever proud."

"You should read your history, sir. If you had, you would find that the Margraines were ever *eccentric*—hardly a generation passed without all the noble-blooded families in Valyanrend laughing at us for some reason or other. Why should the first Daven have taken as his reward a dilapidated ruin and a stand of apple trees? Why should the sixth Daven favor his daughter at a time when the Ninists taught us all to favor sons, and why should *she* fiddle with so many laws, wiping out centuries of tradition in favor of pithy arguments and long strings of numbers?" She leaned back in her chair. "I'm sure I needn't remind you that the dilapidated ruin and the apple trees remain, while Elesthene is long gone—along with the noble houses of our disdainful friends. We are entirely used to being called fools, yet we have a habit of outliving those who would name us so."

Far from being chastised, Elgar laughed. "It was never my intent to call you a fool. On the contrary, I have long held the hope that your knowledge might be of use to me, as mine might be to you."

She barely stirred, but her eyes narrowed, her posture suddenly straighter. "I can well believe you desire some part of my knowledge, but why on earth would I ever give it to you?"

"You *aren't* a fool, my lady, so don't play the part of one." He turned about, started pacing again. "It's no use to pretend you don't know what I'm speaking of; we both understand full well that we are perhaps the only people who can aid each other in this. We might accomplish together what we never could alone."

She shrugged, but her eyes were still fastened on him. "How do you know I never could?"

"I know you have met with no success thus far. I *know* you haven't, else you wouldn't have bothered to come here—you wouldn't have concerned yourself with a pointless parley at all. You would've been past all that. But you are not, and so you are here."

She frowned, contemplating her glass. To look at them, you'd think they'd forgotten they weren't alone in the room, but Kel knew they would not be speaking so obliquely but for his presence. What was Elgar getting at?

"We do have one wish in common," the marquise said at last. "I won't deny that. But it is not a goal we can pursue together."

"And why is that?"

"Because you have a greater desire, one that eclipses all others. The fact that you admire Elesthene at all . . ." She shook her head. "You clearly don't understand."

That made him scowl. "What does Elesthene have to do with anything?"

"Elesthene," Lady Margraine said, "was a land of brilliance and plenty—or so we are told to believe. But the truth is not even well hidden, despite the efforts of so many. Elesthene was a *dead* land—golden, certainly, but a corpse covered in gold will not smell any sweeter. As Elesthene grew, magic waned, until not a breath of power stirred the air from the Howling Gate to the cliffs south of Eldren Cael. And all the coin the Council ever held could not buy it back again." Her gaze grew distant, as if she could picture it. "Anyone who seeks to restore any part of *that* can only be my enemy."

Elgar sniffed. "To think they call *me* superstitious."

"It is not superstitious to read of the past and understand its lessons," Lady Margraine said, "but I don't expect you to own that. It doesn't matter. There is nothing I can do for you, nor you for me."

"Then why are you here?" Elgar snapped.

She raised her eyebrows. "Well, I'd *thought*—"

He laid his hands on the table. "I mean to say, why not show yourself *out*, if you're going to be so obstinate? Kelken still wants to treat with me, I think, so let me talk to him. Let me talk to him without you dripping poison into his ear."

She only laughed at that. "Of course, if you prefer. I wasn't finding this little exchange especially compelling anyway." She got to her feet, but laid her half-empty glass on the table before heading for the door. "I believe I will tour the castle again, Kelken," she said, right before opening it. "Perhaps the mist will lift for a moment and I'll actually be able to see something."

Kel saved his frown until after she had gone—Elgar had gotten rid of her far too easily, hadn't he? He'd thought she was the kind of person who enjoyed obstructing others just for the sake of it. Even if not, didn't good counsel dictate that leaving him and Elgar alone together was just what she *shouldn't* do?

Elgar, looking at the door, seemed to be having the same thought. "She's certainly arrogant enough, but at least she knows where she's not wanted," he said, before turning back to Kel. He finally took to his chair, pulling it close to the table. "Before I say anything else, answer me just one thing. Unless I am very much mistaken, you do not even want the throne of Reglay, do you? It certainly brings you no joy, that's plain enough."

Kel took a deep breath, but Elgar would be able to tell if he lied about something like this, wouldn't he? "It doesn't," he agreed, "and I don't. Everyone always told me I would have it one day, but it never seemed real to me—it doesn't seem real now." He looked down at his hands. "But my father wanted me to have it. That was his last wish—for me to have it. So I have to try."

"It is no fault in you to seek to be steadfast, or to carry on your father's hopes," Elgar said. "But a king is more than a son; the responsibility he bears his people must come first, before any common human attachment. If I must take Reglay by force, Kelken, then many of your people will die—people who need never be called to battle, who might be free to stay in their fields and their homes. They will die for nothing, because I will defeat you in the end. Or perhaps it is more accurate to say they will die for the sake of your father's wish." He folded his arms. "How many lives is that wish worth?"

What could he possibly say to that? "If I knew for sure that it would be better—"

"Neither one of us can know that," Elgar said. "But I imagine you fear for your own life, and for your sister's life. I understand that, but you must believe that I do not wish you dead. Arianrod Margraine would have you believe the worst of me, but that won't save you—either of you. As far as that woman goes, all she has are her throne and her pride, and I swear to you, I will strip her of both before my conquest ends." His eyes flashed, and Kel struggled not to wince. "But as far as you are concerned, I would rather be merciful, as much as it is in my power. I *would* rather have you rule for me than have to kill you and set someone else up in your place."

"Why?" Kel asked. "Why do you care what happens to me at all?"

Elgar smiled. "You won't believe for mercy's sake, I'm sure, or because of any admiration I might have for you. Fair enough. Let me explain, then, how *I* profit from keeping you alive: it gives me good standing in the eyes of the people. In my own city I become a conciliator, not a butcher, and here the people will be more likely to accept me without a fuss if I rule them through the one they believe has a right to the throne. If I thought you would make a poor adminis-trator where someone else in my employ would show some especial brilliance, that would be another matter. But men, I've found, are much the same one to the next."

"Maybe . . . maybe so," Kel said. It didn't sound any better out loud than it had in his mind.

Elgar sighed. "Well, never let it be said I wouldn't give you time to think it over. I promise you, if the letter bearing news of your surrender is put into my hand the very moment I am about to signal my men to march, I will send the lot of them home again with a cheerful heart. But as soon as I *have* marched, that will be the end of it—and the end of you, very shortly. I will also promise, however, that no matter what you choose, I will do all I can to spare your sister's life—she made no decision to resist me, after all."

Was Kel supposed to thank him for that? "I—I must think—"

"Yes, I expect you must," Elgar agreed. "But think quickly, Kelken, for your own sake."

He left Kel sitting there, staring at the map without truly seeing any part of it. He knew what a king would do in a situation like this—if he gave up his throne, he would cease to be a king. But what would a good man do? What was the *right* thing to do—for everyone, and for him?

He thought of what would happen to Reglay if Elgar decided to attack it, what would happen to him and Lessa. Was keeping the throne truly worth all that grief?

It wasn't. He knew it wasn't. But he could see no other way.

"This ancestor of yours was a proper magician, Kelken," Lady Margraine called over the balcony, her one-armed grip on the ladder so tenuous that Kel's own fingers clenched tight in sympathy. "Do you know the Ninists swore up and down that they'd burned every copy of *The Golden Future* in existence? The Council itself supported it—as they always did, the bastards. Where did he *find* this?" She flipped a few more pages with her free hand, heedless of how her body was leaning.

"Um," Kel said. "Do you think you should—"

"I've never even *heard* of this one," she continued; Kel wondered if she was even talking to him anymore. "*Old Lantian Wards* . . . that could be useful, but I suppose it's more likely a lot of nonsense . . . hmm."

The bookshelves curved along the walls of the library tower, stretching up two floors high. Even if he didn't need crutches, you couldn't have gotten Kel up on one of the rickety ladders for anything. Alessa and Seren and even Cadfael all seemed to feel the same way; they were staring up at Lady Margraine with the same vaguely panicked consternation Kel was sure was reflected on his own face.

She smiled suddenly. "Oh, *this* one I remember," she said, discarding the other books in favor of pulling out a thick, fragile tome with yellowing pages and a strained spine. "*One Hundred and One Dangerous Plants*. My old tutor and I could actually tolerate one another when we talked about this."

"Dangerous . . . plants?" Kel asked. "What's so special about that?"

"It was copied countless times during the days of the empire," she said, flicking through it absently. "Even today you can hardly swing a sword around without hitting one. In the empire they used to have entire academies dedicated to the pursuit of learning—which makes the long-standing tradition of book burning all the more bitterly ironic, of course—and this book was considered the absolute pinnacle of its kind. As a work of scholarship it's quite unmatched—the author must have dedicated decades to research. It isn't just about descriptions, symptoms, effects—every poison mentioned in this book has an antidote, and a good number of them were probably the author's own creations. And yet even though she—or he or they, I suppose—made such a mark in her field, she never put her name to the book, or else it got left out somehow in the copying. No one knows the author's true identity, though many have tried to find out." She smiled again. "You yourself have benefited a great deal from this book, without even having to read it."

Kel blinked. "Have I?"

"You treat your legs with snow's down, don't you? Before this book, it was known only as a deadly poison, but our mysterious author wrote extensively of its ability to reduce pain and combat inflammation. People used to use dusk nettles instead, and I'm given to understand some of the aftereffects were . . . unpleasant."

Kel wanted to ask her more about it, but Cadfael tapped his foot on the floor. "That's not what you're here for, is it?"

She would've paid a speck of lint on her sleeve more regard. "I half wonder what I am looking for. It doesn't seem like the king's illustrious ancestor cared much for organizing these. If only I had more time . . ." She closed her eyes a moment, leaning her head forward so it almost rested on the leather spines in front of her. "I'll just have to be more efficient, I suppose."

She'd gone nearly all the way around the second floor when she found the first book that made her pause. She didn't announce this one to them, though, just pulled it free and began to leaf through it as if she were alone in the room. Kel couldn't tell if she was pleased with what she found or not, but before too long she simply put it back and started scanning the rows of titles again. Once she was finished with the upper shelves, she descended to their level and continued reading the spines assembled there.

Lessa bit her lip and looked as if she wanted to say something helpful, but she evidently couldn't think of anything. Cadfael began to pace restlessly, and Seren just kept standing perfectly still, following the marquise with her eyes. "Ah," Lady Margraine finally said, pulling another book free. It puffed out a cloud of dust as she opened it, but she barely blinked. However, she didn't spend long on that book either, and then she pulled away from the shelves, frowning.

"Kelken," she said, "if I were free to enjoy these books at my leisure, you would find few more delighted by the prospect. However, since I am forced to engage with these texts in a businesslike manner, looking only to ends . . . I must admit it is somewhat disappointing."

"You didn't find what you were looking for, then?" Kel asked.

"I intend to keep looking," she said, "but I'm beginning to doubt it's here. I'm beginning to doubt it *can* be found in any of the past works of this world, even if I had all of them within my grasp." She shrugged. "No matter. I can always think of more things I wish to learn, and this library allows me to fill some of those gaps, at least." She started to turn toward the bookcases, but a sudden thought arrested her, and she turned back, that customary smirk tugging at her lips again. "While I'm thinking of it, there *is* a deal you and I might make with each other, provided it doesn't conflict with the one you made with Elgar."

Kel nearly jumped, tightening his grip on his crutches. "What?"

"I assume that was why he wished to speak to you alone, wasn't it? I won't ask what he said, but I doubt I need to. Never fear—what I would have of you is hardly as consequential as your throne."

Kel started to frown, and then thought better of it; he shouldn't do that before he'd even heard what she had to say. "What is it you'd want from me?" he asked.

She tapped her chin. "It wouldn't be here . . . it must all be at Second Hearth. Your father's papers—I understand this is a raw subject for you, but if you could go through your father's papers sooner rather than later, and save any letters you can find between him and King Jotun of Issamira, old King Eira of Lanvaldis, or my own father, Caius . . . I would be much obliged if you could send them to me."

Cadfael had started when he heard King Eira's name, and for several moments Kel allowed himself to wonder about that so he didn't have to wonder about how he was going to answer her. In the end, though, he asked what seemed to be the logical question: "And if I did . . . what would *you* do? Would you repay me for it?"

Lady Margraine shrugged. "That depends. What do you want?" He opened his mouth, but then she continued, "It's no use asking me for men, though—I can't spare any, and I mean it. If I could've chased Elgar off, I'd have done it already."

"I thought you'd say that." Kel sighed. "I may have to go to Issamira after all."

She raised an eyebrow at him. "It's up to you, of course, but I wouldn't recommend it."

That gave Kel pause. He, his father, and Eirnwin might have argued about methods, but they'd all been able to agree that getting help from Issamira was the only option open to them. "You *don't* think I should try an alliance with Issamira?" he asked, just to make sure he'd heard her right.

Lady Margraine shrugged again. "Well, no, I don't think that either, but that wasn't what we were talking about, strictly speaking. You were saying you planned to *go* to Issamira, and a worse plan than that I can hardly think of, unless you're planning to hold a sword out in front of you and trip."

"Is the journey there truly so perilous? I'd heard that the Gods' Curse is harsh, but once you've crossed it—"

She cut him off with a wave of her hand. "Oh, I don't expect the *journey* will be any great matter. It's once you've arrived that your problems will really begin." She was still looking through the book titles, but she hadn't taken any more out yet. "I wouldn't be standing in the Issamiri throne room right now for every scrap of gold in the whole country. And they're richer than Elgar over there—don't let him tell you otherwise." She half drew out another book, then shook her head and put it back. "You and I may be smaller and weaker, Kelken, but no one's about to challenge *our* right to the succession. A contested throne is a serious thing, and sooner or later it always becomes an ugly one; the fact that everyone seems so calm and reasonable now only means it'll be that much uglier later."

"But the throne *isn't* contested," Kel said. "Prince Landon is the oldest, then Adora, then Hephestion; everyone agrees on that. If Prince Landon's alive, he's the king; if he isn't, the crown goes to his sister."

"And if I were Princess Adora," Lady Margraine said, "it would have been just that simple. But Adora loves to make simple things complicated, and refuses to so much as close her fingers around the power that's been dropped into the palm of her hand. Princess Regent? She should be *queen,* for the gods' sakes, but instead she lets her widowed mother keep her pretenses to that title. Meanwhile, the Issamiri people have no great love for her, but they adore their prince, a dashing, empty-headed dandy who rides about brawling in the streets and chasing every pretty skirt. He's a fool, but even fools can occasionally see a thing once it's placed right in front of their eyes, and someone, sooner or later, will give him to understand that his sister has left the throne empty and his backside is every bit as royal as hers."

She smiled at him. "Now suppose you journey to Issamira. You will be faced with a choice. No one will tell you about it, but you must make it nevertheless. It is a choice between an intelligent coward and a charming fool. *They* won't ask you to choose, of course—if I know those two at all, they have yet to realize a choice exists. But even if you win their sympathy, neither of them will be able to help you in their current position. And the longer their stalemate continues, the more time the vultures around them have to draw up battle lines, to eat away at the neutral ground in between until nothing remains. If you are seen to be on the wrong side when a victor finally emerges . . ." She swept one finger sharply across a shelf, as if checking for dust. "No, if you take my advice, you won't venture there until they hold a coronation ceremony of their own, one way or another."

Kel tried not to look as despondent as he felt, but his crutches wobbled despite his best efforts. "Prince Landon wasn't a fool or a coward. Prince Landon was—"

"Ah yes, Prince Landon. The one person who might actually have been able to solve this mess—and so, naturally, he's nowhere to be found. I must admit, I never met the man myself, but my father thought he was nothing special, which by itself is almost a guarantee of greatness." She spread her hands. "*I'd* like to find him, but if the Issamiri elite can't turn him up, I doubt it's for lack of trying. If he doesn't want to be found, why go looking for him? If he's dead, then there's *definitely* no reason to look for him. And if he does want to be found, whoever's keeping him hidden must be a genius."

Kel gripped his crutches hard, forcing himself to meet her gaze. "Are you saying there's no hope for Reglay?"

She considered the question with total dispassion, but by now that didn't surprise him. "Little hope, but there's seldom none. Especially if you keep your wits about you. Now, are you going to let me look at that correspondence from Second Hearth or not?"

Kel took a deep breath, but he knew what he wanted to say. "If I give it to you, then I want to know too. Whatever you find out, no matter what it is."

She tilted her head. "And you trust me to tell you?"

He gave a shrug of his own. "I might find some of it out myself, I guess. And if I'm unimpressed by what you say, I can always stop sending you the letters."

"Mm," she agreed, but her attention was half diverted again, focused on the most recent tome she had drawn out. "I don't suppose it much matters if *you* know—it's Elgar I'm trying to outwit, and he's probably already found out more than I have."

"What makes you say that?"

"He conquered Lanvaldis, didn't he? That means he's almost certainly gone through all of Eira's papers himself. He can't get at the other pieces of it yet, though, so we'll have to hope he needs them."

"But you said your father was part of it as well, didn't you?" Kel asked. "Then you and Elgar are on equal ground."

"Unfortunately not." She replaced the book she'd been holding, but before she drew out another one, she added, "I did bring something with me, in the event I decided it was worth giving to you. You may as well have it."

The parchment she handed him had once been crumpled, but since then it had been smoothed out and neatly folded. He would have known the handwriting anywhere, and he laid the letter on a table so he could read it, gripping the edges of the table for balance. *"Caius,"* he said aloud, for Lessa's benefit, *"I beg that you will see sense—"*

"Always a hopeless proposition," Lady Margraine muttered.

"I beg that you will see sense, and cease this hopeless quarrel with Eira once and for all," Kel continued. *"He is closer to it than any of the rest of us, and your determination to make an eternal enemy of him only weakens your own position that much further. Draw a new border that you and he can find it within your pride to accept, and let us turn our attention to our true enemy, whose power waxes daily in the west. I do not know how far we can rely on Jotun in the future—I know he is of one mind with us, but his son, in whom he confides everything, has expressed his distaste for our plans in the most strident terms. Jotun is wont to be stubborn where his heir is concerned (a tendency, if you'll forgive my saying so, with which I am sure you are familiar), but in the end he sets great store by Landon's opinion, and the prince may yet sway him. And if he does, you and I must depend on Lanvaldis even more than before. I will entreat you once again: retract this foolish refusal to have dealings with Eira, and let us move forward together in this. Would you rather have to kiss Eira's hand or the point of Elgar's sword?"* When he had finished, he swallowed hard, and added, "It's from Father."

Before Lessa could make any reply, Lady Margraine said, "Well, it's clear the previous Kelken never shared any of this with you—maybe he didn't want to make Jotun's mistake. But it's a curious thing, isn't it? Wouldn't *you* like to know what this plan of theirs was?"

"I'm still not convinced that sharing anything with you would get me closer to the truth than just going through whatever letters my father kept on my own," Kel pointed out.

She closed the book she'd been flicking through, but she didn't replace it, just tucked it under her arm. "Whatever you find, I strongly doubt you'll be able to interpret it without my help. I *will* share my information with you, so long as you do the same."

"You said yourself I couldn't trust you," Kel said slowly.

"Oh, you certainly can't. But you don't have much choice. I'm sure your advisor is learned, but . . . well, let him try to solve it for you, if you like. Before long you'll send it to me regardless, and any scraps of knowledge I feed you will seem a marvel."

Kel didn't know what to say to that. "I will certainly look through my father's letters. I will have them brought up from Second Hearth."

She nodded. "You ought to look at them anyway. It's . . . an odd thing, I can tell you that from experience, but . . . well, you've already buried him, haven't you?"

"I did not bury my father," Kel said. "I closed my hand around all that was left of him, and gave him to the wind." He bit his lip. "And I let his murderer go unpunished."

She looked neither mocking nor sympathetic, just . . . blank, as if she could not understand his words or his feelings. She took out another book. "Well, you won't catch him now. The murderer, that is."

"No," Kel agreed. He had given that up, at least for the present.

"Hmm . . ." Lady Margraine might have mumbled something against the page of the book, but Kel couldn't make it out. She was turning the pages so rapidly, she couldn't possibly be reading them, and yet she nodded vaguely every so often regardless. Finally she snapped it shut. "I'll be taking this one, Kelken, with your permission."

Kel squinted at the cover: *Wardrenfell of . . .* something. Her arm was covering the rest. Anxiety prickled at the back of his neck, but he tried his best to tame it—it was just a book, wasn't it? It wasn't worth trying her ladyship's patience about it, not when she was being so strangely civil.

"Are you taking that one as well?" he asked, nodding at the one she'd tucked under her arm before.

She drew it out, brandishing it before him. "No. This one is for you." She must have realized it would be hard for him to hold on to it and keep his balance at once, because she relented slightly and laid it on the table next to the letter. "You should find chapters seven and twelve of exceptional interest."

Kel cocked his head. "You're . . . ordering me to read?"

"I am strongly advising it—even in a general sense, it's a good policy to follow. People who don't read tend to grow up like my father. But no, I don't much care whether you actually read it or not—it'll be your loss, not mine."

He nodded. "Fair enough. I'll take the book." This one was called *King Arvard and His Campaigns*—an ancestor, then.

Cadfael fidgeted. "Are we quite done here?"

"I'd be happy to spend another month here," Lady Margraine said, "but I know it is not to be. I'll have to content myself with this book alone."

"Can it really mean so much to you?" Kel couldn't help asking. It wasn't exactly polite, perhaps, but she seemed so indifferent to everything else.

He ought to have expected that she wouldn't take offense. "This world used to be very different, you know," she said, only half as if she were talking to him. "All the skeptics will tell you that questions of magic are only that, that there's no proof any of it ever existed. But books give the lie to that, as they do to so much else. It's not just spell books—more than a few ancient diaries survive, in which a fishwife takes her son to a healer, or a farmer is unimpressed by the tricks of a traveling mage who passed through his village. The skeptics will say that people were simply more gullible back then, but the truth is much simpler: magic was part of their lives, and they hardly blinked at it, no more than I am startled by the fire in my grate of an evening. And then magic went away." She shook her head. "I am not a particularly god-fearing individual, but even I have to admit there's a certain poetry to the concurrent fall of magic and the rise of our once-illustrious empire. And they ruined everything."

"But if magic was already gone by the time they—"

"Not magic, Kelken, *books*. They destroyed books by the thousands—perhaps by the hundreds of thousands. The Ninists hated any god that was not theirs, and so we know almost nothing of the religious traditions before the empire, only whatever scraps could be copied and saved by courageous dissenters. And as for the rest of them . . . perhaps they could not bear it, living in a world without magic and knowing that their ancestors had possessed it. Maybe they sought to destroy the books of magic because they were too painful. But it was not their right." She stroked the cover of the book she held. "The way the world is now, we're all cut off from where we came from—from who we are, and what we're capable of. But that just makes me that much more determined to find out."

They were all silent for a moment, and then Alessa said, "I don't know how much good it would do to rediscover a past we can never reclaim. But I can't fault you for wanting to find out."

"How do we know we can't reclaim it, if we hardly know what it is? Why did magic leave this world to begin with? We don't even know that much. The Ninists told a ridiculous story about a suggestible genius and a perfidious woman, and everyone just accepted it for hundreds of years." She fell silent, staring at the rows of books. "But I waste my breath. This is not the time or place to go into such matters." She walked to the center of the room, then suddenly turned back. "By the way, I do have one more piece of advice for you, before we part."

Kel bowed his head. "I'd be honored to accept it."

"You'd be *wise* to *obey* it." She jerked her chin at Lessa. "Hide the girl away better, or else don't treat her so well, at least in public."

Was that a joke or an insult? "What are you talking about?"

She sighed impatiently. "To the eyes of the world, that is your bastard sister, and you are expected to feel about her the way people generally feel about their bastard siblings. Therefore, when you dote on her the way you do, people mark it. You don't want them to mark it."

Kel gritted his teeth. "Why, because it'll look bad if I'm kind to her?"

"No, because when you *are* kind to her, so excessively and so publicly, you do your enemies the favor of pointing out your weakness. You tell them exactly how to hurt you. And unless that sweet sister of yours is hiding remarkable swordsmanship underneath that delicate veneer, you put her in quite a bit of danger."

He understood her, then, and his anger faded, but a kind of exasperation took its place. "All right," he said. "I see what you're saying well enough, but . . . everyone's got to love someone, and sometimes openly. Everyone shares that weakness, don't they?"

"I don't share it," she said. "And I'll bet Elgar doesn't either. There is no one in my family left, but even if there were, we cannot live as others do. Those in power do not have *friends,* not truly." She nodded at Cadfael. "This one is going to desert you for sure, and that is hardly out of the ordinary. That is why we tend to have servants, rather than friends."

"So Seren is not your friend?" Kel asked. The woman in question stood right in front of him, as unconcerned as ever. "Captain Ingret is not your friend?"

"I should hardly call either of them that, no."

"Then how can you trust them?"

She smiled. "*Captain Ingret* despises me, and it is for precisely that reason that I can trust him with . . . well, *almost* everything, and everything with which it is necessary to trust a man in his position. Seren I can trust because I know the reason why she serves me, and so long as that reason holds, she will not betray me. You will find as you grow, Kelken, that friendship is a very weak reason for trust, as it is for loyalty. That is why you must be stingy with your love, and extend it to as few people as possible—preferably none, but we all have our failings, I suppose."

"But you can't help it if you love someone," Kel said.

As cold as her smile always was, it was always amused; there was nothing kind about it, but nothing polite or forced, either. "Can you not? How unfortunate."

He dreamed of his sister, as he so often did. He dreamed of her, and they were training again, in the grounds behind the house—that stretch of beaten and dry earth their father had laughingly called the courtyard. He looked at her, hair tousled and falling in her face, her sword held out in front of her, quivering just a bit. *This isn't how I do it, Cadfael,* she said.

He ignored that, as he'd ignored every other protest, and swung at her again. She moved out of the way, and he frowned, swung again harder; his sword clanged against hers, and she staggered back, wincing.

And the third stroke would've killed you, he said. *Don't dodge—block. I told you to block.*

I know, she muttered, rolling her shoulder. *I heard you the first hundred times.*

You heard, but you didn't listen, he said. *Try it again. Plant your feet and* block.

Again he swung, and again she tried to move; this time he simply reached out and grabbed her wrist, pulling her back into place. *If I have to tie stones to your feet to keep them on the ground, I will do it.* Block my sword.

You're stronger than I am, she protested. *But I'm fast. That's how I'll be good, not by out-bludgeoning you.*

You are fast, he agreed; she was as quick as anyone he had ever seen, with a blade or without one. *But you can't dodge everything, and sometimes blocking puts you in a stronger position. I don't need to teach you how to dodge—you've taught yourself that well enough. But blocking has to become second nature; you have to move so quickly that your arm is faster than your mind. And you are* far *from that point. Again.*

No matter how much she strained or sweated, no matter how many bruises she bore, he never heard her complain about the training itself. He was always the one who finally said, "Let's stop here for today," and even when the sun had long since died away in the sky and she was panting as if her lungs would burst, a look of disappointment never failed to cross her face. It was not that she didn't want to work hard; she simply didn't want to do as he told her. But she did, in the end, or tried to. She always tried to, in the end.

You don't teach me anything truly impressive, she said, after several halfhearted blocks. *You're not Eira's best man because you* block *so well, are you?*

He frowned at her. *I am nothing of the sort to His Grace. Who told you that I was?*

Everyone says so.

I doubt that—

They do. They say they've seen you in the arena, and—

The arena, he said, *as I've told you many times, is no place for you—no place for you to be, and no place for you to think about.*

She looked troubled, then, her eyes dark and serious. *If it's so bad, then why do you fight there?*

If only he'd known the answer then. *Because His Grace wishes it,* he said, just as he had said at the time. And it was true, but he had not marked it, had not realized what it meant.

Sister, he said suddenly, because he remembered what she wished, *listen to me. You are talented; you know you are, and you will do much with it. But you must remember—*

Sister, she intoned, in a grave, deep voice, *you must remember to forswear fun wherever you find it, to engage with it, if you truly* must, *only as with a deadly foe.*

I don't mean to scold you always, he said. *I only want you to take care.*

A real hero doesn't take care.

Are you a hero, then? he asked her, holding her gaze until she looked away, blushing.

Well, she muttered, scuffing at the earth with her foot, *not now. But I want to be—or at least I want to try. Like the hero in your story.* She looked at him again, and smiled sheepishly. *I want to be like her, one day.*

Before he could say more, the dream pulled her away from him, and in her place was *that* woman, whose name he'd never learned but whose face he'd never forget. The dust-dry courtyard was gone, and in its place was the long grass of that meadow, crystalized in the morning frost. The wind whistled about his ears, just as it had that day, and her face was just the same. Sadness lurked behind her eyes, fathomless and unchanging, even in the face of all the fury she leveled at him.

Why did you not cut deeper? he might have said, but didn't. He wanted to know what she would say.

Do you cherish that face of yours? she asked.

No, he said.

Because you know what lies behind it? No one had ever asked that but her, over and over again in his dreams.

He opened his mouth to answer her, but the wind snatched away his voice. He would have pursued her, even if it meant being cut again, but suddenly there was a hand on his arm, pulling him sideways, pulling him out. He jerked awake, and found himself staring at Seren, the marquise's bodyguard.

"Sorry," she said, a trifle awkwardly. "I would not have woken you, but . . . the way you were perched on that window . . ."

Cadfael looked to his other side, and shrank back involuntarily from the drop. "Ah," he said, hoarse. "I . . . see. Thank you."

"It's all right," she said, and turned to leave.

He frowned. "Shouldn't you be guarding her? Lady Margraine?"

"That is what I'm attempting to do," she said. "Someone is skulking about these corridors who shouldn't be, so I turned the guard over to Gravis until I find him."

"I wish I could tell you for certain that no one passed this way," Cadfael said, "but the truth is, I probably wouldn't have noticed. I don't know what came over me; I was never this heavy a sleeper before."

She rubbed the side of her wrist. "I will be glad to quit this place."

Cadfael slipped off the windowsill. "If there is trouble, it's not from the king."

"I know that," she said. "I'm just surprised Elgar would dare in a place like this."

"Did you mean what you said to him?" he asked, before he could think better of it.

She only half turned to him. "Did I mean which thing I said to him?"

"After your duel, when you talked of your debt to Lady Margraine. Was that true?"

She took her time replying. "He asked me why I served her. That is the kind of question that has many answers. I gave him the one I did because I thought I should put it in a way he could understand. Obligation is a simple enough idea, so at the time it seemed best." She looked away. "Later I thought that perhaps my lady wished for him not to understand. Perhaps I should have given him a different answer."

"What answer?" he asked.

She shook her head. "Then I was commanded to reply, but now I am not. Leave it be." She frowned, looking back down the corridor. "He seems to have gotten away, or . . ." She did not finish the sentence, just peered into the dark.

"Shall I help you look?"

"No. I should return to Lady Margraine; perhaps I shall lure him back again."

"Are you truly at peace, serving her?" Cadfael asked. "Are you sure you won't regret it?"

Her smile was crooked, ironic. "What does it matter to you?"

"It does." He didn't trust himself to say more than that.

"Then don't be concerned. I might regret many things, but never that."

He reached for the hilt of his sword. "I was much like you, once."

Her smile cracked wider, almost as if she might have laughed. "That's funny. I was going to say I was once like you."

That puzzled him, and he chose his next words carefully. "I meant that I once used to believe following orders was enough."

"And I meant that I once felt I had no purpose, and suffered for it." She spread her fingers wide, staring down at her open hand. "I found my own answer, even if that answer troubles you."

"But you don't want to tell me."

"There is not enough time to tell you," she said, not unkindly. "The hour is late, and we both have other things that we must do. And I . . . I am not good at talking. I doubt I could explain it in the way I wish." She curled her fingers in toward her palm, not quite making a fist. "That scar," she said at last. "It has meaning for you. Why?"

He closed his eyes, just for a moment. "It was a gift."

"Then repay it," she said.

After she had gone, his sister crept once more into his dreams, though the woman who had marked him stayed away. Again he tried to teach her, to train her, as he always did. Through all his dreams he kept at it, as if one night it would be enough and she would stand before him again. Instead he woke alone, and leaned out of the window, the mist still thick in the dawn air. He drew his sword half out, and watched the gleaming metal pick out what scattered bits of sunlight there were.

With what cruelty, with what heartlessness did you strike her down? he thought. *I will find you. No matter how large this world is, no matter how much lies between us, I will draw you to me. I would clear out everything else, whole towns and cities like so much brushwood, if only it would lead me to you.*

It did not matter how many others Shinsei had killed, that day or any day: how many foes, how many men and women, how many children. It did not matter how long ago it had been or what else might have happened since. Cadfael would make him remember her, no matter what it took. He did not need to know how it had happened: he knew she had died bravely, as she had lived. But he would make her killer remember her. He would think of her, of how bravely she had died, and then he would feel his own life slipping away from him, and squeal like a coward as Cadfael lowered the blade to his throat.

CHAPTER THIRTY-TWO

An hour's ride out, the mist finally started to thin. Varalen tried to relax, but he hated riding with a passion he reserved for precious few things in life, and he'd never sat a horse that didn't seem to know that, somehow. This one, a brown-black mare every groom at the Citadel had assured him was as sweet as a newborn, had the advantage of being smaller than he was used to, but he couldn't say he felt much safer. Elgar, on the contrary, always rode as if he were entirely unaware he was doing it—Varalen was fairly certain some men devoted more concentration to walking.

He would have dearly loved to see the inside of a carriage, but Elgar had insisted on riding, and he *always* insisted that Varalen be denied any pleasures he'd forfeited for himself. Perhaps he merely thought that if they were somehow attacked, Varalen, in his bright red robes, was the one who would draw attention. If that was so, however, it wasn't exactly prudent of him to ride so close.

"Was there something you wished to discuss with me, my lord?" he asked at last.

Elgar looked up. "If I had something to discuss with you, Varalen, I wouldn't wait for you to issue me an invitation to do it. I do have orders for you, but you can hardly ride and carry them out at the same time."

Varalen shrugged. "You could at least tell me what they are; it'd pass the time, anyway."

"It's about the plan you proposed," Elgar said shortly. "I've decided it's time to execute it."

That certainly wasn't what he'd been expecting. If he'd thought staying on the horse had been difficult before . . . "M-my plan? My lord, are you sure—?"

"I wouldn't be telling you if I weren't. We've waited long enough. We won't find a better time than this."

"A better time than *now*? My lord, the reason we waited this long to begin with is because it's a very difficult thing to arrange—"

"Of course it is. If it were simple, I wouldn't need you, would I?" He tightened his grip on the reins. "You told me all was ready. You told me our little bird was ready to play his part whenever it was required of him."

"In theory, yes, but you know that he believes—I told you that he insisted on—"

Elgar waved a hand at him, barely bothering to hold on to the reins with the other, yet his horse seemed not to notice. "You can make him whatever promises you feel are necessary, Varalen. It isn't as if he'll be able to enforce them once he's played his part."

Well, that was true, but it hardly made Varalen feel more secure about it. He wasn't the one that was going to be put out if the scheme failed, though, was he? "Very well, my lord. I'll send a message on its way as soon as we reach the capital."

"You'll send a message on its way as soon as we make camp. Why wait until we've returned just to give it farther to travel?"

Gods, he was serious about this. Varalen prayed all was ready. "As you say, my lord."

"Good." He peered off into the trees. "What did you think of our enemies?"

He could see Arianrod Margraine as an enemy easily enough, but he still didn't like to picture King Kelken that way. *Boys become men all too soon,* he tried to remind himself. "The king was . . . not as I had imagined."

"Nor I," Elgar allowed. "He's braver than he has any right to be, yet for all that I don't think he's a fool." He twitched the reins. "The woman was just as I had pictured her, though."

Varalen shrugged, to hide the fact that he thought more of her than Elgar did. "Those suitors of hers must have quite a time of it."

"Mm, fools have always been able to find hope where none exists. Most people who say they've no use for marriage change their minds rather quickly after their first infatuation—isn't that your story?—but I wonder if she truly meant it."

As to *that,* Varalen had no idea, and the rumors from Stonespire hardly helped. He was used to wild stories, but he'd seldom had to deal with such a contradictory crop. One popular tale had it that, when her father was alive, she had used to invite the sons of his honored guests into her bed under his nose, while a different set of gossipmongers claimed that she preferred her own chambermaids. Still others insisted she was as frigid as the White Waste, incapable of being stirred to passion of any kind.

Varalen couldn't understand why so many people should care so much—it wasn't as if she was fucking *them,* after all—but sifting through rumors was part of his job. "I am beginning to think," he finally said, "that Arianrod Margraine never heard a story about herself she didn't find amusing, true or false. Perhaps that's why there are so many—other rulers would have their subjects' tongues out for telling any tales they didn't wish to hear."

"Well, one of those tales brought us a bit of amusement, at least." Elgar twitched the reins again, pulling slightly ahead. "There is one more thing you ought to know, for when you compose that letter—I've decided to give Nathaniel command of the men."

Varalen nearly fell off his damned horse. "*Wyles?* My lord, Wyles is captain of the city guard. That position, while respected, hardly qualifies him for—"

"You mean that he'd be leaving his post, I suppose," Elgar said, unperturbed; he knew that wasn't what Varalen had meant at all. "But I've found that captain of the guard is an easy enough post to fill, especially temporarily. And Nathaniel did ask for the assignment, after all."

Had they been discussing this behind Varalen's back? The way Elgar had always sent Wyles out of the room before speaking of it, he had thought . . . but no, Elgar must have told Wyles enough of the plan to pique his interest, at least. Worse, by sending him, Elgar made sure that, if the plan succeeded, it was Wyles who would get all the glory, while Varalen would no doubt be held responsible if it failed. "Did you truly . . . think that was best, my lord?" was all he could think of to say.

Elgar smiled, no doubt because he knew what Varalen was really thinking. "Don't look so concerned, Varalen. A talented thug is all that's really needed for that part of your plan, anyway." He peered over his horse's head at some far-off point in the distance. "Better think on your composition now. I'll expect that letter sent off at the earliest possible hour."

————

"What's a *wardrenfell*?" Kel asked, looking up from the table and across the library at Eirnwin.

Eirnwin frowned. "A *wardrenfell*, did you say? I'm not familiar with the term, but it sounds like Old Lantian. Why do you ask?"

"It was in the title of the book Lady Margraine took with her." And he had a suspicion about where else he might find it, but he had to wait for his men to arrive from Second Hearth for that. "You don't know what it means?"

"Well, Your Grace, I did study Old Lantian when I was younger, so let me see if I can guess. I know *wardren* is the possessive or adjective form of *ward*, which is the Old Lantian word for a spell, or sometimes for magic generally— you still see *wards* used in place of *spells* in certain treatises on magic. *Fell* means . . . 'gone awry,' or perhaps 'out of one's control.' There are some Hallerns who still call Stonespire Hall the Fellspire, especially in Valyanrend, but I wonder if they remember why. Most people assume it comes from the modern definition of *fell*, something evil or dangerous, but that's only half true. If the history books can be believed, it was Vespasian Darrow himself who coined the term: a pun of sorts, as the castle had both slipped from his control and become dangerous to him."

"So then a *wardrenfell* would be . . . a spell that's gone out of control?"

"That would be my guess. But words are sometimes more than the sum of their parts, I'm afraid." Eirnwin's brow furrowed. "Or no, that can't be right. *Wardren* is an *adjective*. A spell gone awry would be a *fellward*, not a *wardrenfell*. So if *wardren* is an adjective, does that make *fell* the noun? How would you translate that? The . . . loss of control of a spell? That just sounds like a different way of saying the same thing."

"But it has to mean something else, doesn't it? Or why would there be a separate word for it?" Kel rubbed his leg absently. "Either way, it must have meant something to Lady Margraine."

Eirnwin cleared his throat. "Do you really think it was wise to let her leave with that book?"

Kel shrugged. "It may not do us any good in the end, but I couldn't see how it could do any harm. If she shares what she learns, it could help us quite a bit, and we're not doing very well trying to figure it out on our own."

"And if she prefers not to share anything with us, Your Grace? If she uses what she learns to hurt you—"

"Why would she do that? We're allies, of a sort."

"Today you are, Your Grace."

"And we were when she was here, and when she gave me the hint about King Arvard." He tapped the edge of the book's cover with one finger.

Eirnwin pursed his lips, hesitating a bit before replying. "And what if she did not intend to help you with such advice, but only to mislead you?"

"I doubt *that*," Kel said. "What would she get out of doing that?"

"Is it necessary for her to get anything out of it?"

"I think so," Kel said, "yes."

"To put it a different way, Your Grace, some people—"

"Yes, I know what you're going to say: some people just like wreaking havoc for their own amusement. But I don't think she's like that—or even that Elgar is, for that matter. Elgar was . . . Elgar was surprisingly easy to understand, didn't you think? He was far more . . . almost *reasonable* than I'd ever expected him to be." He interlaced his fingers, resting them on the table in front of him. "With Elgar I can think, *What does he want?* and know the answer straightaway: he wants my land, and hers, and probably Issamira, too. That's no secret, and he hardly tries to make one of it. When I ask the same question of Lady Margraine, the answer doesn't come as easily. I don't know exactly what it would be, but I really don't think it's *my* destruction. She wouldn't care about that one way or the other."

"I think Kel's right, Eirnwin," Alessa called, and they both looked up to where she was pacing about the second floor, a book open on her outstretched arm. "She might be capricious, but she's not careless or foolish enough to ruin us for a lark, not when we could be helpful to her."

Eirnwin was still frowning, but he said nothing more, just dipped his head and glanced back down at his reading.

"You know," Kel said, as much to Alessa as to Eirnwin, "I was thinking about it—about whatever Elgar and Arianrod Margraine could possibly want in common. And the only thing I could think of is that they both want to find a way to bring magic back."

Eirnwin looked at him sharply, and Lessa peered over the edge of the balcony, nodding slowly. "Elgar, certainly," Eirnwin said, "but Lady Margraine, as well? She seemed more sensible than that."

"Why isn't it sensible?" Kel asked. "To hear her tell it, there are a lot of sound reasons to believe magic really did exist. And if it was here once, who's to say someone couldn't call it back again?"

Eirnwin sighed. "It's not for lack of trying that magic hasn't come back, Your Grace."

None of them really wanted to leave off what they were doing, so Eirnwin went to tell the cooks to have supper sent up to the library. "Is that much exertion good for you?" Kel asked Lessa, who was still pacing. The air at Mist's Edge was cold and damp, which couldn't possibly help her. She was coughing more than usual, but she hadn't had any serious attacks as of yet.

She smiled wearily at him. "I can't sit still."

"Are you afraid?"

"I'm frustrated." She leaned against the railing. "We know our enemy—that's more than most people can say. We *have* time, though we don't know how much. But I can't think of anything for us to *do*! So we just end up sitting here and doing nothing, just waiting for him to decide it's finally time to attack us."

"We're not doing *nothing*," Kel said. "We've been organizing our men, moving battalions about . . ." He had admittedly done most of that as Eirnwin had advised; his knowledge of battle strategy left much to be desired. In the end, though he'd never say it to Lessa, it mattered little. No matter how they arranged their soldiers, they simply didn't have enough of them. "But we've got to change the way the game is played—you're right. If we keep these rules in place, we're setting ourselves up to lose."

She sighed. "Did you find anything in that book Lady Margraine gave you?"

Kel stared down at it. A quick skimming of chapters seven and twelve had yielded nothing, and his more methodical second reading wasn't faring much better. "I don't know what about it she expected to help me. Chapter seven is basically a fat lot of praise about Arvard, how such and such things he said or did were witty or clever or brave—nice to know my ancestor was such an upstanding fellow, I suppose. And chapter twelve is just a record of some alterations he made to Mist's Edge: he reinforced this wall, extended it here, this other wall fell down halfway through and had to be redone . . . thrilling stuff, really." He shrugged, tapping the table for emphasis. "What, was she trying to be my schoolmaster?"

"I doubt that." Lessa had descended the stairs as he spoke, and now she stood by the table, tracing random patterns across the wood. "But even though it's not a lesson, I think it *is* a sort of test."

"In what way?"

Lessa followed the table's edge with her thumb. "Lady Margraine isn't kind, or generous. I don't think she would help anyone for its own sake, and you and she may end up being enemies one day. But on the other hand, the longer we can hold out against Elgar, the longer she has to make her own preparations to engage him. I think she saw the good to be had in helping you, but she was too capricious to just tell you what you needed to know." She tapped the page in front of him. "It's intelligence she values—didn't she say that? Or maybe I just guessed it. So it's a test of your intelligence—she left it up to that, the way some people leave things up to luck, or to the gods. She buried her advice somewhere in here, and if you're smart enough to figure it out, then she thinks you deserve to have it. If you *can't* figure it out . . . well, she'd probably just say it's nothing to her."

She was right; Kel was certain of it. "Well, I *will* figure it out," he said. "She's not the only one who can be smart."

"I know you will," Lessa said, and smiled at him. It faded quickly, though, and she glanced out the window at the mist-shrouded trees. "Are you very sad about Cadfael?"

Kel slumped a little lower in his chair. "I wish he would've stayed. I think we could've . . . helped each other, somehow. But it was his choice, and it's not as if I'm going to pine for him. We managed before he came, and we'll manage now." He looked at her closely. "You were never very fond of him, were you?"

She shook her head, but he wasn't quite sure what that meant. "I don't think he was a *bad* man, just . . . dangerous to have around. He was so focused on that one thing, and besides that there was just . . . nothing. I felt nothing else from him."

Kel fidgeted, but he wasn't about to correct her. Cadfael had cared only about his vengeance, and after that . . . he'd said himself he didn't care if he died, hadn't he? And Kel had thought at times that even his grudge against Shinsei was just an excuse to die, whatever he may have said to the contrary—that it was just a way of convincing himself that his death had accomplished something, instead of springing solely from his own weakness. "I wonder what it would take to make him happy again."

"Restore his sister to life," Lessa said immediately. "And neither one of us can do that, can we?"

No, Kel thought. Even magic couldn't conquer death—didn't the spell books agree on that? And even if it could, magic had deserted this world, hadn't it? When he was little, he'd read story after story about crippled mages. The poets seemed to like them—they probably thought it balanced out, magical ability and physical weakness. But Kel was just a cripple of the ordinary sort: his weakness was real, no matter what he did, so he had to try to make his strength real as well, in his mind and his heart and his will.

Would that be enough to protect Reglay? Well, probably not. But he wouldn't know until he tried, would he?

CHAPTER THIRTY-THREE

Thanks to Irjan, Morgan and Braddock had reached Issamira proper without incident, and their days afterward had proved similarly uneventful. Grass and living trees had started cropping up quickly once they'd reached the other side of the Curse, and the ground had turned the normal shade of brown—perhaps it had even gotten a bit *too* moist, as they'd had to squelch through more than one muddy patch of road on their way to the village where Nasser was holed up. The village itself appeared rather muddy too, the crooked wooden buildings packed too close together. It was bigger than Morgan would have expected, and that made her a little nervous. They'd been traveling for some time now, and she was about as used to being outside Valyanrend as she probably ever would be, but she was used to knowing the culture of a place, of being an insider rather than an outsider.

Braddock indicated a large and lopsided building that seemed to be the village's sad excuse for a tavern. "There. Nas's letter said he'd wait outside the tavern every day at sundown for as long as he could—whatever that means."

"At least we're right on time," Morgan said.

He nodded. "If he's here, he'll be close, but he'll be expecting Vash. I don't think that'll complicate things, but it might."

Morgan stayed by his side as he walked around the tavern, peering through the near-darkness at this loiterer and that. Most of them were drunk, on their way either homeward or into the nearest ditch. But finally Braddock stopped several yards from a man leaning against the tavern's far side. "Nas," he said, not even a question. "It's been some time."

The man turned to him unhurriedly, his eyebrows lifting as he smiled. "Well, this is unexpected! Perhaps the gods do hear us after all." Morgan herself had expected to see a man of an age with Braddock and Vash, but Nasser was easily fifteen or twenty years older, though he seemed no less spry for that. He was dark-skinned, like the people of Akozuchi to the southeast, but his lack of accent suggested he hadn't been born there. She was also surprised to see he dressed well for a mercenary—no bright colors or flashy ornaments, to be sure, but clean gray linen and new leather boots, with a dark blue coat stuffed under one arm that was doubtless too warm to wear in the southern heat. He wore his hair very short, with only the barest fuzz keeping him from baldness, and his stubble was considerably better maintained than Braddock's. Besides the coat, a small pack, and an ample quiver, over one shoulder he carried what seemed, even to Morgan's untrained eye, to be a very shoddy bow indeed.

Braddock smiled at the greeting, though it seemed to perplex him as much as it had Morgan. "What do the gods have to do with it?"

Nasser's smile only widened, showing off a set of perfect teeth. "Why, I was only just now thinking how, in my current troubles, an ox would suit me far better than a weasel, and here you are."

Braddock scratched the back of his neck sheepishly. "Well, it's not the gods that sent me, sorry to say." When Morgan and Nasser both kept looking at him expectantly, he started. "Oh. Ah, Nas, this is Morgan Imrick. She's, ah . . . well, she owns a tavern, but to sum it up, she's not there now, and so . . . here we are."

Nasser let the somewhat less than an explanation pass easily enough, and shook Morgan's hand firmly. "I see he hasn't become any more eloquent since I knew him. I'd offer my condolences, but I'm afraid they wouldn't be genuine—I confess to being rather fond of his clumsiness."

"I don't object to it myself," Morgan said. "Forgive me, but . . . what's this about a weasel and an ox?"

The mischievous glint in his eye reminded her of Roger. "They are my dear old friends, of course. Vash is the weasel because he's . . . not precisely a coward—I've seen him perform feats no true coward could stomach. But his courage doesn't come out until he really needs it, the way weasels can be tenacious when cornered. And Braddock is the ox because—"

"Oh, no, you needn't explain that part," Morgan said. "I found it entirely apt, I assure you."

"Yes," Braddock said, "well, now that we've all had a laugh at my expense, perhaps I could explain—"

"Ah," Nasser said. "Yes, please do. I assume your arrival in my time of need is not quite a coincidence?"

"Almost," Braddock said. "It was chance that I was with Vash when your message arrived, but I was the one who decided to head down your way when I realized he wouldn't. We tried to send a message ahead, but I don't think it reached you."

"It didn't," Nasser agreed. "The gods only know where it is now—and whoever carried it. I don't suppose it matters." He adjusted the bow on his shoulder. "You are prepared to help, then?"

"I'm prepared to try. Your letter wasn't exactly clear, so I didn't know how serious . . ." He trailed off, grimacing. "It's nothing to do with your family, is it?"

Nasser looked almost shocked. "No, no, thank the gods. Kira is still making rounds in southern Hallarnon, and my daughter . . . well, she's wherever it suits her to be, but not part of *my* trouble. I'm sorry if I worried you, but I did think I was only writing to Vash, and you know how he is. No, the heart of the matter is . . ." He scowled, gritting his teeth. "My bow's been stolen," he said at last.

Braddock nodded at the one he carried. "I was wondering about that, aye."

Nasser turned his head to regard it with the kind of glare reserved for only the foulest refuse. "This? I *bought* this crooked spawn of a gallows tree because I had to loose my arrows from *something,* but I can't be rid of it soon enough, I promise you."

Morgan squinted at it. "Did the other truly mean so much to you?"

Nasser looked to Braddock in disbelief. "Did it mean so *much* to me, the lady asks! With respect, Miss Imrick, I carved that bow myself out of the only straight-grained block of bowyer's mulberry I've ever seen in my life. It has been with me for nearly twenty years, through more fights than I can count, and never once disappointed me. It is simply not replaceable."

"It took me long enough to cure my kitchen boy of calling me Miss Imrick," Morgan said. "I don't think anyone else has ever tried, and I'm certainly not about to let you start. And I take your point—gods know I've heard Braddock moan about his ax enough times for me to understand the way some people can get about their weapons."

"What happened to your ax?" Nasser asked, with genuine concern.

Braddock gave a tragic sigh. "Been a bit busy since we parted, Nas, and, well, the end of it is, Morgan and I escaped a prison cell, but the ax didn't."

Nasser seemed more interested in the ax than the prison. Were all mercenaries like this? "Which one was it? Not the one you favored when we were in Reglay?"

"The very same."

Nasser shook his head sorrowfully, but Morgan broke in before he could start commending the damned thing to the gods. "Well, it wasn't as if that was the only ax you had, was it? What's wrong with the one you're using now?"

"There's nothing *wrong* with it, Morgan, it's just . . . a great pity I had to lose the other, that's all."

Morgan gave up. "Fine. My deepest condolences. Now, if we're going to talk about weapons, can we at least talk about the one that called us here?" To Nasser, she said, "Who is it that stole your bow, and how can we help you get it back?"

Nasser's brow furrowed. "*Bandits* stole it, and you can help me get it back by slitting their throats, bashing their heads in, or otherwise disposing of them."

"They stole it, but left you alive?" Braddock asked.

"We didn't meet on the road or in the field," Nasser said. "Well, strictly speaking we didn't properly meet at all. They attacked a tavern where I'd had rather a long night, and I'm ashamed to say that by the time I awoke, one of the fools was already laying hands on my bow—anyone who knows anything about them would see they don't make two like that in a million. I would have pursued him, but, well, he'd already taken my weapon. In the absence of truly life-threatening situations, I don't fight with my fists; I'm not that uncouth."

Braddock started to laugh. "Oh, Nas, you picked the wrong person to say that to."

Nasser stared at Morgan, his eyes wide. "Truly? Well, I suppose that explains why you don't carry a sword."

Morgan held up a hand. "It's not what you think; I'm not some brawl-hardened expert at it. You'd be surprised how many people don't know the right way to throw a punch, that's all." She cracked her knuckles absently. "So . . . how is it you plan to *find* this bandit who stole your bow, let alone kill him?"

Nasser leaned forward, his eyes intent; he'd clearly spent some time thinking through that very question. "I found out later that those bandits have become well known in this area—they've attacked nearly every inn, tavern, or settlement nearby. It's clear they're growing bolder by the day. But, well . . . have you heard of a place called Ibb's Rest?"

Morgan and Braddock exchanged a glance. "We have, actually," Morgan said. "That's one of those . . . traveler's havens, isn't it?"

Nasser nodded. "The Issamiri are very protective of whatever scraps of their pre-imperial religion they could save from the Ninists. Strictly speaking, *all* way-points on a journey are due proper reverence, but the traveler's havens especially so, since they cater to all equally. But the fact that these bandits are willing to strike inns to begin with means they are certainly not *religious* bandits, and thus it's only a matter of time before they pluck up the audacity to pillage Ibb's Rest." He folded his arms. "I intend to be waiting for them when they do."

That silenced both Morgan and Braddock for a bit, and they looked at each other, Braddock scuffing one foot in the dirt. "This traveler's haven . . . anyone can go there, anyone can stay there, and nobody pays so much as a copper for it, is that right?"

Nasser rubbed the back of his hand along his jaw. "Well, that's the idea, but a significant problem does present itself. One may stay at a traveler's haven without paying, but only if one is a *traveler* . . . so those who impose on its hosts' hospitality for too long tend to get unceremoniously turned out."

"So if we do go there, we have to hope these bandits show themselves somewhat quickly," Morgan finished.

"Aye, though there's nothing stopping us from making camp nearby if we do get turned out."

Braddock was still mulling it over. "These bandits," he said. "Just how many of them are you expecting?"

Nasser shrugged. "Hard to say. We'll be outnumbered, certainly, but we'll have surprise on our side, and I doubt we'll be the only patrons at Ibb's Rest fighting back."

Braddock still looked dubious. "With your own bow there's none can best you, Nas, but with that thing . . ."

"It's crooked as a demon root to be sure, but my skill remains," Nasser said. "I practiced enough with the damned thing; my shots won't suffer much."

"Morgan?" Braddock asked.

"I . . . doubt I'll be much help with the killing part," she admitted. "But if the bandits are loose in this area anyway, we might be attacked anywhere we go as it is. Why not make ready for them in this traveler's haven and take our stand where we'll be prepared?"

Braddock finally nodded. "All right. There you have it, Nas."

Nasser bowed jauntily. "And I thank you both for it." Then he laughed. "Don't look so gloomy, my dear ox. I'll fashion this adventure into a fine tale, you'll see. Even that stubborn daughter of mine will be impressed."

That made Braddock smile. "Do you really not know where she is? What exactly is she up to?"

"She sends her mother a letter every so often—I'll get the newest details from Kira when I return, scant as they will undoubtedly be. Beyond that, I know nothing, and will continue to know nothing until the next time she decides to drop in at home." He sighed. "When she was a child, she thought I could pull the very stars down from the sky. Now that she's a woman grown—barely— she thinks I am an old man with old ideas." Then he suddenly grinned. "She thought she could shoot better than me too, but our latest contest soon put an end to that. Even she had to admit my skill then. So it seems her father is still good for somewhat more than pitching into a shallow grave—until she's learned all my tricks, at least."

"Does she talk as much as you do?" Braddock asked.

Nasser laughed. "My friend, no one talks as much as I do."

"I know a swindling Sheather who could challenge you there," Morgan said.

Braddock groaned. "Let's hope to the gods *they* never meet."

———

Chandler's Assorted Goods was a small corner store a stone's throw from Iron's Den, whose owner seemed to have taken more care with the bright colors on the red-and-green-painted sign than with the haphazard attempts at patching the holes in the roof. It was also the third chandler's shop Marceline had visited in as many days, and compared to Webb's Waxen Wonders and Wares for Fire and Water (candles and soap, she assumed), she found the directness a little refreshing. She took a deep breath, tried uselessly to arrange her hair, and walked through the door as nonchalantly as she could manage.

The man behind the counter was pale and short, with small, watery blue eyes, but he looked genuinely kind when he smiled, and if he was smiling, he probably hadn't already assumed she was a thief. "Afternoon, miss."

"Ah—good afternoon," Marceline said, trying to speak the way Cerise would have. "I'm afraid I'm—not a customer, really, but . . . there's a young man who comes here, and I was wondering . . ."

She had thought it through as best she could, as well as she hoped Tom or Roger would have, and had come up with this: the leader of the resistance, Tom had heard, was some sort of amateur historian, a "book reader" who lived in Iron's Den. But Iron's Den was filled with tradesmen—blacksmiths, fletchers, tanners, and the like—and if this young man lived there, he was almost certainly either one of them or apprenticed to one of them. As such, he'd have to work his trade during the day, so if he read for any length of time, he'd have to do it at night. And if he read enough that he was famous for it, he'd have to go through candles like a sickle through wheat. The trouble was finding out where he got them—especially given that she hardly knew anything else about him.

But the chandler gave a deep sigh, shaking his head. "Another one? How does that boy find time for an honest day's work with all the heads he's busy turning?" He peered at her worriedly. "You look awfully young, you know, miss. Just what sort of overtures has our Mouse been making to you?"

Marceline started in spite of herself. "Mouse?"

The chandler laughed. "Oh, that's just a bit of fun the other boys had with him when he was small—folk in the neighborhood have been calling him that ever since. But I'm sure he's the one you mean: brown hair, couldn't grow a beard if he tried, fond of big words? And of course the beautiful eyes—gods know I've heard enough young women go on about *them*."

"Ah," Marceline said, nodding vaguely. "Yes, quite . . . quite so. Just like that."

"Thought so. Has he actually encouraged you, or are you just pining in secret? You wouldn't be the first, I'll tell you that much."

"Oh no, he doesn't know me," Marceline assured him. "I just . . . was curious about him."

"You and half a dozen others." He leaned forward. "Listen, miss, I'll tell you this for nothing: I've known Mouse since before he could see over this counter, and I'd do more than a little to help him, if he ever needed it. But that boy'll make some woman happy, for a while, and then he'll make her very *un*happy. He may be handsome, and he may speak like half a hundred books put together, but he prefers dreaming to working, and he always has. And I expect he always will."

And *this* was the leader of the resistance? Either Tom's rumors had vastly overestimated what that group had been up to, or the chandler didn't know this Mouse half as well as he thought he did. "I . . . see," she said, because she had to say something. "It's not as if— I mean, I just thought—"

"You've got a few years before you've got to be thinking about that anyway," he said. "There's no need to rush it."

"I believe I am older than I may appear," Marceline told him, as primly as she could, "but I thank you for the advice. I have . . . much to think about."

She did, but not about romance. Now she knew what to look for—even had a name, of sorts—but she suspected that had been the easy part. The real challenge would be finding out where this Mouse was hiding his resistance.

CHAPTER THIRTY-FOUR

The land, as far as Seth could tell, was generally more uneven in Esthrades, the gentle plains of Reglay replaced with abortive cliffs and sudden ravines. But where the grass of Reglay was usually scraggly and stiff, the dirt dry, here the grass was lush and springy, full of wildflowers and the odd oak or sycamore even on the rare occasions when you got out of the forest. The people tended to be a bit paler and fairer-haired, though Deinol said that was mostly due to all the northern refugees who'd been displaced when the Aurnians arrived from across the sea, from a home even they could no longer remember. They were still days away from the eastern sea, but sometimes Seth imagined he could sense it on the breeze anyway, though he'd admittedly never so much as seen any kind of ocean before. He asked Ritsu if *he'd* ever seen it, but Ritsu only said, "My father took me north to see the White Waste when I was very small, but I remember little save how cold it was. My fingers and the tip of my nose grew numb at night, and I cried. But I have never been to the eastern sea." He considered it. "They say it is not cold, so I wonder if I might like it."

Seth knew what Deinol was going to say about Ritsu—honestly, he was surprised he hadn't said it already. But even though he knew, and had known for days, he was still no closer to figuring out how he'd respond when Deinol finally *did* say it. He understood that they had to part ways with Ritsu eventually, but he just seemed so helpless—less experienced than Seth, in certain ways, though he could apparently wield a sword with deadly skill. Wouldn't he just get into trouble again on his own?

"Look sharp," Deinol said, pointing at a village that had just come into view now that the forest was thinning out. "Fancy a drink? We might even be able to garner some useful information this close to Stonespire."

"That sounds good," Seth said. Ritsu said nothing, as usual. When he said nothing, they'd learned to assume it was fine.

Deinol led the way into town, more cheerful than he'd been for the past several days, and he didn't slump even when he learned the place was too small to have a proper tavern. Was it the idea of being so close to Seren that put the extra bounce into his stride?

"Say there," he added to the farmer who told him the bad news, "do you get much gossip from Stonespire around here?"

The man squinted at him. "We get some. These days it's mostly speculation as to what her ladyship got up to out of Esthrades."

"Lady Margraine left Esthrades?" Deinol asked. "But she never does that."

"Aye, you don't have to tell me. But she did it this time, and all of a sudden, too. Went to Reglay on parley, or so they say, but it wasn't as if I was there." He rubbed his nose. "Hasn't been a quarter-court since her father—people liked 'em then, 'cause Lord Caius's judges tended to give better judgments than Lord Caius himself. But no one knew what kind of people *she'd* appoint."

"Well?" Deinol asked. "So what happened?"

The farmer laughed. "Nothing very interesting, and that's the best news if you ask me. Captain Ingret has good men, simple men, and it's largely them as handled it. In a pinch you want a mind like her ladyship's, I'm sure, but it's not as if she was gone for very long."

Deinol frowned at him. "Do you . . . do you like Lady Margraine?"

The man snorted. "*Like?* Do you like a hailstorm? Like's got nothing to do with it."

"But you . . . I'm sorry, I always thought that everyone, er, resented her."

"Like you Hallerns resent your jumped-up commoner?" The farmer laughed again. "I lived most of my life under her father's rule. For the change alone I'll not complain of her. Hell, if she murdered the man herself, I'd not hold it against her, foul crime though it be. Doubt even *she* could poison a fellow Margraine, though."

Deinol twitched his nose. "I never said I was a Hallern."

The man leaned on his spade. "Didn't have to. Hallerns always ask that." He wiped his brow, then scratched at his hairline. "My wife loves to say how she's not quite right, but even she nodded that proud head of hers when the marquise repealed the headless law."

Seth had heard that expression before, years ago—someone had mentioned it in front of Roger, and he had filled the Dragon's Head with half-drunken expostulations. "The headless law was . . . about thieves, wasn't it? The punishment for thieves?"

"Aye. Well, the bad headless law was, anyway—Caius's headless law. The punishment for thieves," the farmer said, "was death. Any thief, any theft, and your head rolled. No exceptions. Caius Margraine was mighty proud of himself for it, but anybody who still had a head could tell he'd lost his to think of it."

"Why?" Ritsu asked, tilting his own head.

Then Roger's words came back to him. "Because," Seth explained, "then wherever you have a thief, you also have a murderer. There will always be people who steal when they become desperate enough, no matter the penalty for it. And if your life is forfeit already, why wouldn't you commit any other crime to save yourself?"

"Too right," the farmer said, and sighed. "I think Lord Caius *did* understand, eventually, but the man was too damn proud to take it back if he did. *She* did it near as soon as she took the throne. Delighted in it, the wife said, as she always delighted in spiting him, but it's the end that matters, isn't it? Even if her ladyship *is* unnatural, if Lord Caius was natural, I much prefer her sort."

"Ah, the magic, is it?" Deinol asked, grinning. "We get those stories even in the capital. I think Elgar himself likes them—dark rituals are probably a better excuse for the loss of his men than simple incompetence."

The man scratched his chin. "Eh, the magic may be and it may not, and if the tales are to be believed, magic used to be the most natural thing in the world. No, it's her temperament the wife harps on. They say she's all ice and stone on the inside, not like a proper woman at all. But *I've* never seen her, and she's got no cause to be soft on my account—or anyone's, I guess, unless she gets married."

Seth cleared his throat. "Um, Deinol, weren't you going to ask about . . ."

"Ah, that's right!" Deinol rubbed his palms together. "Sorry about that; the conversation got clean away from me. I was wondering if you know much about one of the marquise's servants." They *thought* she was one of Lady Margraine's servants, anyway, but perhaps Deinol thought it was safer to start with that than with Seren's name.

"I might," the farmer said. "Is it one of the famous ones? Gravis Ingret is captain of the guard, and was under her father—he's been a member of the guard for almost thirty years now; everybody knows him. Glad to see him, too, even when Lord Caius was alive—a more reasonable man you're not likely to meet. On the other hand—"

"It's a woman we're seeking after," Deinol interrupted. "Seren Almasy, I believe, is her name."

The man's eyes narrowed. "Seren Almasy," he repeated. "Aye, that's her name all right. Seren Almasy, so they say, is her ladyship's butcher. *She's* only been around a couple of years, but word travels fast enough, and if it's to be believed, no one's ever happy to see *her*."

Deinol folded his arms. "So she is a killer, then."

"Oh, the finest. And fantastically efficient, or so I hear. Her ladyship wants to reason with a problem, she sends Captain Ingret; she wants to get *rid* of a problem, and it's Almasy's turn."

"I see." Deinol's mouth was grim, and it looked strange on him, warped and odd. "So if I wanted to see Almasy, I should go to Stonespire?"

"Nobody *wants* to see Almasy," the farmer said, "but normally that'd be right, aye. The marquise does send her off from time to time, but she always goes back again."

"That's good to know," Deinol said. "Thank you."

The farmer shrugged. "It's nothing to me. If you've got some quarrel with Almasy, though, it'd be wise to give it up."

Deinol grinned. "Oh, nothing like that," he lied. "I try not to quarrel with women, though they sometimes decide to quarrel with me." He cocked his head. "If there's no proper tavern in this place, do you mind telling me where there *is* one?"

The man pointed down the road. "Follow that southeast, and it won't take you two hours to reach it."

"Much obliged." He touched his sword. "Come on, Seth."

Seth walked silently along at his side, trying not to think about what he'd just heard. He knew Seren had killed people, of course—*Deinol* had certainly killed enough people—but there was something about what the farmer had said. . . .

"Pardon me," Ritsu said softly, at Deinol's elbow, "but I believe that man has some business with you."

Deinol whipped his head about. "What man?"

In answer, Ritsu nodded at a nearby stand of trees; a man was leaning against the closest one, looking at them intently.

"I don't know him," Deinol said. "What makes you say he has business with us?"

"He began to stare at you about halfway through your conversation with the other fellow," Ritsu said, "and he has not stopped since, though occasionally he blinks."

Deinol hesitated, frowning. "Well," he said at last, "perhaps we should see what he wants, then." He glanced at Seth. "Do you want to stay here?"

"Of course not," Seth said.

Deinol laughed. "Come on, then."

The man held up a hand as they approached, though Seth couldn't tell if he was greeting them or warning them not to get too close. Either way, Deinol slowed his pace, his own hand held out in front of him. "Afternoon," he said. "Was there something you wanted?"

The man sniffed. "Seemed to me like there was something *you* wanted. Or someone, more like."

"What, Seren Almasy?" Seth winced; Deinol was nothing if not direct. He doubted Lucius would have charged ahead so brazenly. "She a friend of yours?"

The man laughed. "Hardly. Is she yours?"

"Nothing near it, I promise you."

"But you've an interest in finding her even so," the man said.

"Aye, I told the other fellow as much." Deinol shrugged. "I've business to settle with her, that's all."

"You're not the only one, I can tell you that."

"Does that mean you've business with her as well?"

"Not I," the man said. "But I know those who do, and where you might find them."

Seth's gut gave a good twist at that, and he had to stop himself from clutching at Deinol's arm. Deinol himself looked far less surprised, let alone less reluctant, than he could have wished; he barely twitched at the man's pronouncement. "That sounds convenient."

"Hardly," the man said again, with another laugh. "I hear any man who wants to settle anything of note with Seren Almasy needs more than a little courage."

Deinol drew himself up. "Well, sir, you'll find I don't lack it. I still haven't heard a place, or a name."

The man hesitated, but only for a moment. "In Giltgrove you'll find the Russet—Inn of the Russet Hound, it properly is, but no one calls it that. You ask there for Horace Greenfield, might be you'll find someone who can help you."

"Someone I can help, you mean."

The man grinned. "Well, friends help friends alike, don't they?"

Seth swallowed hard. "Deinol—"

Deinol ignored him. "And what's in it for me if I do help?"

"Besides the satisfaction of knowing your business is concluded, you mean?" The man shrugged. "Have to ask the boys at the Russet about that one."

"Well," Deinol said. "Perhaps I will, then."

"And perhaps they'll take a shine to you," the man said, touching the brim of his hat. "Afternoon."

The three of them were entirely clear of the village before anyone spoke. Then: "Ritsu," Deinol said, so suddenly that Seth jumped, though Ritsu didn't, "you may as well know it now: we're looking for a very dangerous woman. I . . . doubt I could defeat her, if it came down to an even fight. But we've got to find her anyway."

Ritsu nodded. "All right."

Deinol sighed. "I'm telling you this . . . I'm telling you this because I assume you won't want to continue traveling with us if that means following the trail of a skilled killer. And, well, we've taken you far enough away from that village, and I've come to think you're . . . sensible enough. I won't object to your leaving, if that's what you want."

Ritsu stopped, tilting his head. "You won't object . . . to my leaving?"

"That's what I said. You're free to go. Here, you can even have the sword back, if you want it, though I still say you should get another one."

But Ritsu moved back a step, his brows drawing together. "You won't object to my leaving," he said again, "but . . . you would object to my staying?"

"Er," Deinol said. "You mean to say you wouldn't?"

Ritsu shrugged, but he was worrying at his bottom lip with his teeth. "I would . . . prefer to stay with you, if I could."

"Did you not hear what I said? We're seeking vengeance."

"I heard." But that clearly didn't trouble him.

Deinol threw up his hands. "So, what, you think you can just stand around staring like that while we're . . . well, to be fair, while we're probably being killed by Almasy before we even have time to negotiate, but still and all . . ."

"She won't *kill* us," Seth said. "She won't kill us unless she has to, and we're not going to kill her, so she doesn't have to."

Deinol laughed. "Well, maybe I'd like to kill her if I could, but I'm not stupid enough to bet on it."

This wasn't anything to laugh about. Not for the first time, Seth wished Lucius were with them. "You'd *like* to kill her? Deinol, you can't do that!"

"No, I probably can't. But as for *her* not wanting to kill us . . ." He scrubbed at his face. "Boy, were you not listening back there? She kills whoever Lady Margraine tells her to kill. It's like I *told* you, it's like I *told* Lucius—" He broke off guiltily at the mention of the name, and he and Seth looked away from each other, both probably hoping the same thing: that Lucius would ever forgive them for this. "I told you," Deinol tried again, "that killing's all of who she is. I told you that, but you didn't want to listen. Does she have to go beyond threats and *actually* slit your throat before you'll believe it?"

Seth kept his fingers well away from the itch at his neck, but he couldn't meet Deinol's gaze. He thought suddenly of the first time he'd ever seen Seren, of how she'd helped him escape their shared cell, disappointing as the ultimate results had been. She could have just left him there; he was none of her concern, and more of a hindrance than anything. But she hadn't done that.

"You weren't even talking to me," he said at last, still keeping his eyes away from Deinol's face. "You were talking to Ritsu. You were telling him how he wouldn't be able to just stand and watch if we ran into trouble with Seren. That's true," he added to Ritsu. "Even if we found her alone, which we probably won't, she's very skilled."

"But you don't want to kill her," Ritsu said slowly. "Isn't that right?"

Seth nodded, and he *did* look at Deinol then, daring him to contradict him.

"Then what is your business with her?" Ritsu asked.

Seth saw his own sheepishness reflected in Deinol's face, and he scratched the back of his neck, thinking it over. The most honest answer, he guessed, was that neither of them was exactly sure, but even Ritsu might think it was crazy to come all this way without knowing your own reason for doing it. So he thought about what else he could say that was true, and finally he found his answer. "It . . . It's like you said, Ritsu. I lost to her, and I want to know why. If there's something she knows that I should learn, then I want to know it too." *I know what happens to weak people,* Seren had said, but it had to be more than that. It had to be.

"I accept that," Ritsu said. "I hope you do find her, then."

Deinol shook his head in exasperation. "Now we share our motivations with *him*? Perhaps you and I are losing our grip on things, Seth."

Deinol slept easily enough that night, but Seth couldn't blame him—he'd been shouldering most of the watch in the evenings past. It suited him just fine, anyway; he'd been wanting to talk to Ritsu.

Their companion was hunched up under a tree, his arms wrapped around his knees. He was staring off into the depths of the forest, but Seth didn't think he was looking at anything in particular. "Are you really sure you want to stay with us?" he asked.

Ritsu nodded. "It's for the best."

Well, that didn't really explain anything. "Why is it best?"

Ritsu turned to look at him. "I feel as if . . . I've been able to think more clearly about things lately. I think it helps to have someone to talk them over with—like when I used to talk to Sebastian." His smile was melancholy. "Not my father, though—it was never easy to talk to my father."

Seth sat down next to him. "What was Sebastian like? If he looked like me, he can't have been Aurnian, right?"

"He wasn't," Ritsu agreed. "He had been born in Lanvaldis, but he lived in Reglay until he was ten. Then he came to Kaiferi with his father, and they settled down there. I could walk to his house from mine in less than a quarter of an hour." He pressed the pad of his thumb against his mouth. "Sebastian was— well, he acted more like your friend than like you, to be honest. He always wanted to be friends with everyone, but he could be proud. And they mocked him sometimes, because he was a foreigner and because they knew he shared a name with a villain in your people's history."

Seth nodded. "Sebastian Valens."

"Yes, that's the one. The reason there aren't knights anymore." He smiled. "The Sebastian I knew could never forgive his namesake for that. But we've never had knights, only *shinrian,* so he thought maybe he could be that instead. And that was all my father ever wanted for me to be, so we tried to help each other, to hone our skills together." His shoulders drooped. "But Sebastian had already learned to fight with a longsword back in Reglay, and you have to wield a *tsun-shin* to become a *shinrian.* He got his father to buy him one, and he was always practicing with it, but . . ." He sighed. "I used to think to myself that he would never be good enough to become a *shinrian,* but I never told him that. I knew that would hurt him more than anything else I could say."

Seth picked at the grass. "And did he ever become one?"

Ritsu slumped forward. "No. He never did." He squeezed his eyes shut. "And now Aurnis itself is gone. I don't think it means anything to be a *shinrian* anymore."

"Did *you* ever become one?" Seth asked.

Ritsu looked at him as if the question were strange. "No, I . . . I never even had a match. I was probably better than he was—I won more bouts against him than I lost—but I don't know that I was ever good enough to become a *shinrian* either."

"Oh," Seth said. "I thought the people from that village were impressed with your skills—I'm fairly certain they said something about it when we first met you." It was true he'd never seen Ritsu fight, though, and doubtless none of the villagers had either—all they'd had to go on was the body of the man Ritsu had killed.

Ritsu himself seemed troubled by Seth's words, and he hesitated before he answered. "I suppose . . . I suppose my skills have improved, since the days when I sparred with Sebastian. They must have."

They must have? What did that mean? "What happened to Sebastian?" he asked Ritsu. "Where is he now?"

If he had thought Ritsu seemed distressed before, it was nothing to how he looked now. He crumpled in on himself, dropping his chin to rest on his knees. "I don't want to think about that," he said, as close to stern as Seth had ever heard him.

Deinol would have asked, *Why not?* But Ritsu's tone had brooked no argument. "All right," Seth said. "Sorry." When Ritsu didn't say anything more, he added, "But if you don't want to be by yourself, then . . . after we find Seren, let's look for whatever it is you want. Whether it's Sebastian, or this swordsman who defeated you, or anything. You won't ever sort things out if you don't try, will you?"

Ritsu sat up straighter, tilting his head to one side. "Is that . . . all right?"

Seth sighed. "Well, it's all right with *me,* but I don't know what Deinol will say. If you help us with Seren, though, how can he say no? It's not as if we know what we're doing so very much more than you do."

It was dark, but he could still see Ritsu's smile clearly. He looked shyly hopeful, like a child reaching out to take a proffered gift. "That's . . . good," he said. "I think . . . I would like that."

CHAPTER THIRTY-FIVE

Stonespire Hall had been quiet all day—it was the seventh day, when the throne rested from its judgments, and for the marquise that meant retreating to her study with a tome or several, as it always did. But Gravis had been restless all morning, as if some task he'd left undone were niggling at the back of his mind, waiting to be remembered. Such moods were not entirely uncommon for him, but when it hadn't abated as noon approached, he gave up and went to look for Dent. They disagreed about more than a few matters, but Denton Halley, though a few years younger, had been a guard at Stonespire Hall even longer than Gravis had, and a steadfast friend through much of that time. There was no one living he trusted more, and he knew that Dent would take him seriously, no matter how nebulous his concerns.

It was odd not to find Dent waiting for him in the corridor behind the kitchens—they'd passed the time between their patrols there since they were young men together—and nearly as strange to find Almasy there instead, slicing up a blood apple with her favorite knife. She was standing, leaning against the wall—Gravis had long since learned that she preferred not to show her back to anyone if she could help it—and the knife moved so smoothly it hardly made a sound, biting into the apple as if sliding through water.

She annoyed him especially today, for reasons he could only half explain. "Don't you have some errand or other to get to?"

She barely looked up. "If I did, Gravis, I would be doing it, not idling here. But you know that."

He watched her slice off a few more pieces, chewing and swallowing each one before she made the next cut. She brought the knife perilously close to her lips every time she took a bite, but Gravis didn't doubt she could have done it with her eyes closed. He gritted his teeth. "Did you displace Dent?"

That surprised her. "Dent? I haven't seen him."

"It's his custom to wait for me here."

She shrugged. "Well, *I* didn't send him away. There's nothing stopping you from finding him, if you can't wait that long to share gossip."

"Some of us do prefer to rely on our friends, aye." He scowled. "I don't suppose you'd know about that, would you?"

Almasy took the question calmly. "No, I don't suppose I would. I don't think I've ever had a friend." If there was any regret in her words, Gravis couldn't find it.

"You have a creditor, though, I suppose," he said. "You never told me that before."

"That's right," Almasy said, and he thought she stabbed the apple with a bit more force. "I never told you, because I am not required to tell you whatever you may wish to know, simply because you ask it."

That reminded him of King Kelken's retainer, how he had scorned Elgar's questions back in the yard at Mist's Edge. But Almasy had answered him docilely enough, because Lady Margraine had told her to. For all her professed love of freedom, she always did whatever Lady Margraine told her to.

He shook his head. "You make no sense."

"I do not care whether you understand me, Gravis."

Dammit, he *would* make her concede something—"You're a hypocrite."

She *did* savage the apple with that cut; there was no doubt of it. "No more than you are."

"Than *I* am?"

"That's what I said." She looked up, then, pausing in her task to give him her full attention. "I've seen more men like you than I can count—as self-satisfied as you are blind, forever puffed up with the certainty that you are so very *righteous*. Your *justice,* as you call it, is as arbitrary as a lightning strike, but no one will ever make you see that. You will wallow in ignorance until you die, all the while thinking yourself the most enlightened of men."

Gravis was not even precisely angry at that, not yet. What had he said to bring all that out of her? "I was not speaking to you of justice."

"No, not at this moment. At this moment you were speaking of hypocrisy— but only of mine. When it comes to your own, you do not wish to hear of it. On the other hand, if we were to talk of the ways *I* am unjust, I am sure I would find you quite enthusiastic."

Gravis hesitated. "I cannot claim to know your private opinions on the matter," he said, "but as long as you follow Lady Margraine the way you have, agreeing to her every command . . . *She* cares nothing for justice, she admits that herself. How can you be her creature and be just?"

She smiled at that, that ever-sardonic smile. "I can't, of course. I never said I was. No one is truly just, Gravis—the very idea is only an illusion."

"That is a lie." The words came out more forcefully than he'd intended, but he had not spoken amiss. "Lord Caius cared for justice, if ever a monarch did— if ever a *man* did. I served him for more than twenty-five years—I *know* that to be true."

"Caius Margraine," Almasy spat, "was even more blind than you, and twice as self-righteous. I have seen more of the world than you ever will, and everywhere it is the same. The laws of men exist to protect the innocent—but what is an innocent? Peaceful subjects are innocent, until they protest. Children are innocent, but not if they steal." She shook her head. "It is a game, nothing more. Today your ruler grants you his protection, and tomorrow it is taken away because you dared to suffer, to starve, to ask too many questions. I have never, *never* seen anything that I would call justice."

His tongue felt clumsy in his mouth, but he could not let her go unanswered. "So if justice doesn't exist, you might as well serve someone who never tried to find it in the first place?"

"She makes it easy enough," Almasy said. "She does not fill my ears with hypocrisies or excuses. She tells me what were best done, and makes no apology for the nature of it." She glanced down at her knife. "And a weapon must be used, or it will rust. I would rather be of use here than anywhere else."

"You can't tell me that's all," Gravis insisted. "You can't. You get *something* out of this; I just have to find it. Just because you have no contract and no gold, that means nothing. You hide your own self-interest behind that mask of nonchalance, as if everything that happens is just the same to you, but I know better. She has some hold over you that you cannot break." He clenched his fist. "Do you have some score of your own to settle, some vengeance you cannot take without her help? Does she protect you from the consequences of some crime you committed wherever you came from? What *is* it, Almasy? Is it just her cunt?"

Almasy must have dropped the apple, but she moved so quickly that he did not even see it. Though her strength could not equal his, she slammed into him with such force that he staggered backward, hitting the opposite wall hard enough to wind him. He had wondered, many times, if it was possible to make Almasy not just irritated but truly angry. He need never ask that question again.

Her knife was pointed right at the center of his left eye, the hand that held it trembling. Gravis did not dare try to push her away; the slightest wrong movement could have her slitting his eye open far more easily than any apple. "You have just made two significant mistakes," Almasy said, sounding almost as breathless as he felt. "You have suggested, in my hearing, both that your mistress is a whore, and that I require one." Her fingers tightened against the knife's hilt. "I will not allow you to make either mistake again."

Gravis's only comfort was that the blade was pointed at his eye, and not at his throat. It was not, he admitted, so very reassuring. "You won't do me any harm," he said, and tried to believe it. "You know her ladyship prefers me alive."

"If she were here," Almasy said, "she would no doubt order me to stop. And I would, of course, obey." She paused. "She is not here."

"And when she finds out?"

Almasy was too angry to shrug with her usual nonchalance; her shoulder jerked stiffly, as if the muscle had convulsed. "Which of us do you think is easier replaced, Gravis, me or you?"

Before he could reply or she could continue, someone cleared his throat to Gravis's right, and he and Almasy both twitched, trying to look at the interloper without fully taking their eyes off each other. It was Kern, trying unsuccessfully to cloak his obvious alarm in a suitable amount of deference. "Ah—I don't mean to—ah—interrupt—but—you see—there's been a—"

Almasy finally relented, stepping back and letting her arm drop. Gravis stepped away from the wall, resisting the urge to rub his shoulder. Not in front of Kern.

The young man kept hovering uncertainly at his elbow, and Gravis turned to him, trying to keep any lingering irritation out of his voice. "What is it, Kern? There's no need to stand on ceremony."

"Ah, no, Captain, it's not that. It's—" He looked at Almasy, and Gravis suddenly understood his hesitation—she was the one he had to speak with. "Um, Almasy, you see . . . there's this." He handed her a folded parchment. "A messenger brought it to Stonespire, so I had it sent to her ladyship, but she just said to give it to you and have you take care of it. So . . ."

In the time it had taken him to stammer out those sentences, Almasy had already read the parchment once. She looked over it again while he lapsed into silence, and finally refolded it and nodded. "Very well. If she asks, you may tell her ladyship I have gone to see to it." She bent down to pick something up—the remains of her apple, Gravis realized. Then she turned on her heel without so much as a backward glance, and certainly without a sign that she viewed their conversation as in any way unfinished.

Kern swallowed, then spoke up. "Ah, good—good luck with the hunt," he called. Almasy gave no indication that she had heard.

"The hunt?" Gravis asked Kern, half distracted.

Kern shrugged. "What else is she ever called upon to do?"

"Then you don't know where she's going?"

"Ah, it's not for me to read her ladyship's letters, Captain. . . ."

"Is the messenger still here?"

"I'm afraid not." He hesitated. "Is everything all right?"

"Fine," Gravis lied. "I've one more question for you—have you seen Dent anywhere?"

"Guardsman Halley?" Kern frowned. "I've seen him, but . . ."

"Well?"

"He did not . . . look as if he wished to be disturbed. I think he was, well, put out about something. It stood out to me because—"

"Because Dent's never put out about something," Gravis finished. "I know."

It was impossible to lay hands on what precisely was not right, because *everything* was not right—everyone was acting strange. Almasy, who seemed made out of stone most days, had flown into a rage; Dent, the most cheerful man he'd ever known, was nursing some grudge; Kern, as far as he could tell, had done his best to treat Almasy with actual friendliness. . . . Even Lady Margraine, he realized, was acting oddly. She usually gave Almasy orders directly—what was so important up there in her study that she couldn't leave it for a handful of minutes?

Separately or together, these oddities portended ill; all his instincts were telling him that much. But how would the misfortune happen, and from where?

They found the Inn of the Russet Hound easily enough, though the young woman who pointed it out to them giggled as she did so—which, as Deinol said, did not inspire the greatest confidence as to what sort of place it was. The innkeeper giggled too, until they asked after Horace Greenfield. Then she pouted instead.

"Oh dear," she said, tilting her head so her curls dangled. "I'm afraid you've just missed them. Horace and the boys were here a couple of hours ago, but they've since cleared off. I'm as surprised as you must be—day before last he told me he'd be staying out the week."

Deinol frowned. "I see," he said. "Do you know where they went?"

She looked perplexed. "Why—home, I'm sure."

"Home?"

"Aye, you didn't think they all lived here, did you? Aren't you one of the boys?"

"We're . . . new acquaintances," Deinol said. "We don't know Horace, but we met a friend of his along the way who assured us we could, ah, join in."

It must have been the right thing to say, because her smile returned. "Always room for more, eh? Well, you'll not find a merrier band of revelers this side of Stonespire, I'll tell you that much. If their wives only knew what they got up to . . . but it's part of my job not to tell 'em, of course."

"Of course," Deinol agreed, smiling hesitantly. "But I'm no one's wife, so . . ."

She laughed. "You agreed to come on a revel without knowing the nature of it? You must be an easygoing sort indeed. It's only that there's no fun to be had in those tidy little towns in the shadow of Stonespire. It can be hard on some men, that's all. So every now and then they gather up here, where we're not quite so straitlaced, and they can do as they please."

"Well, I'm certainly used to doing as I please," Deinol said, "so I'm sorry I missed them. Will they not be back for some time?"

She nodded. "That's usually the way of it. They come all together, and when they leave, they all scatter back to their own little villages."

"I see." He considered it. "Would you happen to know any of these villages by name?"

"Well, sure. Saltmoor would be the nearest—not two hours to the east, through the forest. A couple of them live there—Symon and Jarrick, I think. The others are farther afield, back up north."

"And Saltmoor's on the path?"

"Aye, it's an easy walk." She smiled. "You *are* determined not to be left out, aren't you?"

"Oh, I'm always that," Deinol said, inclining his head to her. "Sorry for the bother."

Ritsu waited until they were back outside before he asked, "What manner of place was that?"

Deinol sighed. "If we had more time, Ritsu, I'd say it was the kind of place you might benefit from."

"Why don't we have time?" Seth asked, trying his best to sound nonchalant.

"Come on, you're not that thick, are you? We're going to follow these fellows to Saltmoor."

"Why?" Seth asked.

"To find out what they're up to, of course."

No, he *wasn't* that thick. "Not to help them?"

Deinol twitched his shoulders. "Depends what they *are* up to, doesn't it?"

Seth dug his nails into his palms, trying to gather his courage. "I think you know exactly what they're going to do. And if you try to help them, I'll—"

"You'll what? You'll stop me? And how do you plan to do that?" He scowled. "Why did you come all this way if you're just going to fight with me?"

"To keep you from doing something stupid. That's what I told you, isn't it?" He bit his lip. "And maybe there's nothing I can do, but for me to just stand and watch while you do something we both know is wrong—"

"It's not what you think, all right?" He broke off in exasperation, running a hand through his hair. "Look, I'm not *saying*—I'm not even saying I want to kill her. But what I want—what I do want is—"

"Is what?" Seth prompted.

Deinol took a deep breath. "I want to know. I want to know what that stone is, and why she stole it, and if she really gave it to the marquise, and what for. It ended up being all right for us, because Morgan and Braddock got free all the same. But she had no way of knowing that. So I want to know what was so important that it was worth their lives." He folded his arms. "Listen, Seth. Meeting with all those men at once might be dangerous for us, but there are only a couple of them in Saltmoor. If we can find out for sure whether they plan foul play, then . . . maybe we can warn her. Not that she'd *deserve* it, mind, but I can't just pretend I don't know what might happen to her."

"You mean—"

"Aye, you idiot. What did you think I meant?" He shook himself, as if trying to displace a fly. "You had the right of it, all right? She didn't kill you because—well, because she's fond of you, at least a little. And anyone who's fond of you can't be all bad." He ran a hand through his hair again, lips twisting in a one-sided smile. "So let's get going, shall we?"

———

Many towns in Esthrades had been named for the sea, even those that were many leagues removed from it. Seren could not smell salt water from within the town's borders, only leather, from the stalls of the tanners who'd taken up residence there. There was little of note to be found besides the shops and a tiny inn, but when Seren showed her letter to the innkeeper, the woman shook her head in puzzlement. "Armed resistance, milady? We've had none such—nothing more than a handful or two of bandits in living memory."

"I'm no milady," Seren said, without having to think about it. She skimmed the message's contents again, trying to think of what reason the woman might possibly have to lie. There were a few, but none that seemed likely. "Do you know the men who wrote this?"

"Symon Silk I know well—he's lived his whole life here. As for this other one . . . he's Tom Lately's . . . second cousin, I think? Came here about six months back."

"And nothing's been stolen?" Seren asked.

"Nothing, milady." It was probably no use trying to get the woman to stop calling her that, and it would have been highly inadvisable to explain who she actually was—thank the gods the people here seemed not to know. The absence of any visible weapons probably helped Seren blend in—her customary sword was primarily useful as a last resort and a distraction for her enemies, and she hadn't bothered to fetch it from her chambers after that obnoxious guard had handed her the message.

"No villagers killed?" she asked the innkeeper.

"Surely not. How would they hide something like that? I promise you, we've had nothing worse than drunkenness in a fortnight."

Seren frowned. "And if I asked others in the village, would they tell me the same tale?"

The woman smiled gently. "Do you disbelieve me? You can ask my husband, or anyone else in Saltmoor—save the madmen who wrote that letter, I suppose." She glanced at her kitchen boy, who'd been staring wide-eyed at Seren from behind her elbow. "Emmett, fetch your master back here, will you? He shouldn't have gone far." Emmett nodded and ran off without a word, and the woman turned back to Seren. "Milady, I'd say they were playing some prank, but if so, I don't know how they dared sign their names to it. Her ladyship's like to have their heads for it."

She certainly was, if it really was a jest, Seren thought. Out loud, she said, "Perhaps the prank was executed by someone else—and perhaps it was not so innocent. Perhaps someone wanted Silk and Lately to fall under her ladyship's ire."

The woman nodded slowly. "Aye, that seems more likely than the other, at least. But who would bear such hatred toward those two, and who would take such a risk? If they deny the letter . . ."

"Then the true culprit might well never be found," Seren finished. This was turning out to be more than a little headache, and much more of a job for Gravis than for her. She was no good at talking to people, let alone questioning them. Why had Arianrod seen fit to send her in the first place?

The man who entered next was the innkeeper's husband, if her relief upon seeing him was any indication. "John, have a look at this paper. This woman's come from the marquise, and she says they received this from Symon and that cousin of Tom's."

"Not Symon Silk?" John peered over her shoulder, then leaned back once he'd finished reading, his lips pressed together. "Well, that's right odd. What bloody bandits can he mean? The last thing I saw that remotely resembled a bandit was Hemp the last time he had more than five tankards in him."

Seren sighed. "Do you know where I can find these two men?"

John's frown deepened. "Well, that's just it—they're not here. They both took off toward some revel at Giltgrove, and I couldn't say when they'll be back. If you wish to wait—"

"No." This was getting ridiculous. "No, sir, if you and your wife assure me that there are, in fact, no such bandits as were described in this letter, then I must go to Giltgrove to demand an explanation of the ones who sent it. If I cannot find them there, I must return to her ladyship and inquire whether she wishes me to pursue them further, and what punishment they deserve. I am certain she would not wish me to wait here solely on the hope that they might decide to return." She turned to go. "Thank you for your help."

That was not the end of it, of course; she had to spend a good deal more time assuring them that Lady Margraine would not hold any part of the strange incident against them. With that done, and with her insistence that she did not wish to stay the night, not even on the house, she was free to go.

As she left, she heard the innkeeper say to her husband, "Did you send Emmett off somewhere?"

He sounded perplexed. "Emmett?"

"Aye, I sent him to find you. Did he not?"

"I never saw him. We must have passed each other on the road somewhere."

"Well, don't you think you should go find him?"

"What for? He'll find his own way back soon enough."

Seren reminded herself to hail the boy if she saw him, but she wasn't honestly sure she'd even remember his face.

As she left the inn, she looked around the village once more, to make sure she hadn't overlooked something. But there was nothing to see—just some thatched roofs, a few tanners working at their hides in front of their houses, and a shepherd driving his flock through. It was as peaceful a village as she'd ever seen;

she might almost have thought she'd been sent to the wrong place by mistake, but for the fact that the innkeeper had known the men who had written the letter. What on earth could they have been thinking?

She took the western path, with more than a little irritation: part of her wanted to just return to Arianrod, but Giltgrove wasn't far. She told herself she was leaving the horse behind because she suspected she'd ridden him a bit too hard from Stonespire, but the truth was probably that she preferred to walk—it was better to be on foot when you had to ponder something. And there was certainly a lot to ponder here, if very little to go on.

She'd proposed and discarded half a dozen theories before she'd gone two miles. She didn't hit upon the correct theory until she saw them, and by then an idiot could have figured it out.

She didn't know which were Symon Silk and Jarrick Lately; there were seven men, and they could have been any of that number. It was plain embarrassing that they'd been able to get so close to her before she noticed them—perhaps walking was *too* good for pondering, she reflected. They carried only swords— weak, cheap steel, but it was sharp enough to poke holes in her leathers, and that was all they needed.

"Well, well," one of them said—Silk, perhaps? "Looks like little Emmett earned his silver honestly. There's a dog come to Saltmoor after all."

Seren said nothing—she had no need to speak with them. She knew why they were there and what they intended. She only wished she'd lit upon it a quarter of an hour earlier, but that couldn't be helped now.

Their first and most grievous mistake was that they'd brought no dogs. Their second mistake was that they'd brought no bows. Their third mistake was that, judging by the first and second mistakes, they were most likely incompetents. But there were still seven of them, and seven against one was a heavily weighted proposition regardless of the circumstances.

Only once in her life she'd fought seven men together—well, seven men who knew she was there beforehand. That had been during her time across the sea, and she had led them on a lengthy chase through the gardens, picking them off one by one as they pursued her. Even then the wound she'd received had not been trivial, but those men had been much more talented than these—she doubted they'd killed much more than the errant rodent in their lives. But that wasn't the point. Surviving this at all was a doubtful enough undertaking as it was, and dispatching all her attackers in addition would take time she didn't have. She was not worth killing for her own sake; if anyone wanted her dead, it was only so it might leave Arianrod more vulnerable. And that meant something was going to happen at Stonespire—something might already be happening at Stonespire, and Arianrod didn't know.

She had to return at once. That, above all else, was what mattered.

The first few movements were easy: two strides forward, draw, and lunge, and by the time the man realized her knife had slashed open his gut, she'd already drawn it back again and then torn it across his throat. The sword slipped from his fingers, and as she pulled back a second time, she shoved his unresisting body into the man beside him, and ran.

She just had to get back to Saltmoor, she told herself. The villagers knew Arianrod had sent her, and this lot wouldn't dare try to kill her where so many people could see. All she had to do was get back to Saltmoor, get on her horse, and return to Stonespire as quickly as she could. She had some ground left to cover yet, but they wouldn't catch her—she was an experienced runner, and she knew how to move quietly in forests, and—

Her next step landed on what should have been solid ground, but instead her foot sank into the fallen leaves and *twisted*. Her momentum carried her forward and off her feet, and she hit the ground so hard that all the breath was knocked out of her. For the first few moments, all she could do was lie there, staring in confusion at the wobbly outlines of the trees.

CHAPTER THIRTY-SIX

They were, in Seth's admittedly hazy estimation, about halfway to Saltmoor when they heard the shouting. It had taken them longer than they would have liked: though there was a path, its meandering way through the forest was so confusing that they'd lost the thread of it several times and had to retrace their steps. The shouting didn't seem too far removed from the path—just off to the left a bit—and the three of them stopped and looked at each other, no doubt wanting to ask the same question.

"Well," Deinol said at last, "that doesn't sound . . . peaceful."

"Looters again?" Seth asked, but Deinol shrugged. "Do you think it's something worse?"

"Or something half as bad, just as like. Could just be drunken hunters or something." He hesitated. "So, are we going to go toward it or away from it?"

"I don't know," Seth said. "*Can* we get away from it?"

"I think that is very unlikely," Ritsu said, as neutrally as ever.

"Eh?" Deinol said. "Why?"

"Because we have not yet started to move," Ritsu said, "and they seem to be coming this way."

He was right: the shouting had mostly stopped, but there were footsteps coming closer. Deinol unbuckled Ritsu's sword belt and tossed it toward him. "I might as well give you this back; seems there's a good chance you'll be needing it."

But Ritsu did not put out his hand to catch the sword, just let it drop limply to the grass. He flinched from it as if it were a snake. "But . . . but if I take this, I . . ."

Deinol stared at him. "What's the bloody matter? It's not as if you haven't used it before. Didn't you want it back?"

Before Ritsu could answer, men emerged from between the trees—three of them, all with drawn swords in their hands. "Hey," one of them said, looking to the man in the middle. "Who's this lot, then?"

"Hell if I know," his companion answered. "Does it matter? They're not her, are they?"

The first man hesitated. "But, Horace, if they saw us—"

Deinol's eyes narrowed. "Horace? Not Horace Greenfield?"

That got the second man's attention. "I'm quite sure we haven't met."

"No," Deinol agreed, "and what I do know of you, I don't like."

"And what do you think you know, you—" He broke off, shaking his head, and turned to his companions. "We don't have time to banter with this lot. She's getting away." He tightened his grip on his sword. "Kill them and let's double back."

They didn't obey him right away, just stood there for a moment, staring. But Deinol didn't hesitate for an instant; the blow from his longsword landed between Horace Greenfield's shoulder and neck, crunching through bone. "Seth," he called as it connected, "run, you hear me? Let me and Ritsu take care of this."

After seeing what had happened to Greenfield, the other two men were no longer ambivalent, and rushed Deinol together. As he met their swords, he yelled, "You idiot, get out of here! I can't fight if I have to keep watch over you at the same time! Find someplace you can hide!"

There had to be something he could do, Seth thought, but another part of him knew Deinol couldn't keep his attention on the men he was fighting if he kept turning to call out to Seth. So he ran. It stuck in his throat to do it, but he ran into the trees.

He wasn't sure how far away he'd gotten or in which direction, and at first his heart was pounding so loudly in his ears that he couldn't hear anything over it. But eventually he slowed down, panting, and closed his eyes a moment, trying to concentrate. Finally he did hear something—a faint little scuffling, like an animal scrabbling among the leaves. He inched forward and sideways, trying to get a good view of what it was before he got too close. But then he caught sight of long hair in a very familiar shade of copper, and he let out the breath he'd been unconsciously holding, making his way over to her.

The scuffling, he soon found out, was the result of her trying to drag herself along the forest floor so she could catch hold of her knife, which was lying just out of reach. She seemed to be hindered by her leg, which was bent at such a strange angle it must surely be stuck. No matter how furiously she tugged at it, it wouldn't move.

She looked up at his approach, and bewilderment showed in her eyes for only a moment before she began to laugh. It was a bitter, sardonic laugh, with no mirth in it at all. "What a joke," she said. "Gods, what a fucking joke." She made one last grab at the knife and then gave up, sprawling on the ground with a sigh. "After all I did to get this far, *this* is how it's going to end." She laughed again. "How embarrassing."

Seth said nothing. First, he picked up the knife—it was bloody, so she must have already fought with the others—and set it down a safe distance away. Then he circled her, crouching by her feet. "What's wrong with your leg?" he asked. "It's stuck, isn't it?"

She blinked at him. "What?"

Seth buried his hands in the leaves, trying to find where her foot was, and finally closed his fingers around her ankle. "Aye, it's definitely stuck. There's some kind of . . ." He tried to clear the leaves away so he could get a better look. "Ah, that's it. You twisted it when you fell, didn't you? You've got to turn it a bit before you can pull it out."

Seren was still looking at him as if he'd said something mad. "What do you think you're doing?"

"Er . . . telling you how to get your leg free? Come on, help me turn it."

She obeyed, if slowly, twisting her ankle in compliance with the pressure from his fingers, and finally Seth judged that he could pull it out. "All right," he said, "I'm going to—"

Seren jerked her foot out of his hands before he could do anything at all— and then immediately winced. "See?" he said. "Was that really the best thing to do?"

"I'd already hurt it before you ever came along," she muttered, bending her leg so she could rub her ankle. She frowned. "Dammit."

She winced again when she stood up, but though her first few steps were shaky, she could still make them. Seth got to his feet too. "How bad is—"

"Quiet," she hissed, and then he could hear it too—multiple sets of footsteps coming toward them.

Seren darted over to her knife and snatched it up, then turned back to peer through the trees. Seth tried to hope that it could be Deinol and Ritsu, but he was almost certain it was three people, not two. But there was no way Horace Greenfield could have survived the cut Deinol had given him—did that mean there were three more people hanging about?

The answer to that question turned out to be yes: he didn't recognize any of the men who drew toward them. It was clear Seren did, however, and she tensed, clutching the knife tightly. She backed up a couple of steps, but she must have realized it would make no difference. So she stopped, holding her ground as they advanced, no doubt trying to surround her.

Then one of them noticed Seth. "Who's the boy, then?"

"He's of no concern to me," Seren replied.

It stung Seth, but only for a moment, and then he realized: if she'd acted like he was important to her in any way, they'd never let him live. But if they thought he was some oblivious stranger . . . well, they'd probably still kill him, but his chances were better.

None of the men responded—they were probably wary of taking their attention off Seren. She kept still as they closed in on her, and Seth tried to swallow the lump in his throat. Could she really take on all three of them at once? She'd been plenty fearsome when they were on the road together, true, but he still wasn't sure how hurt she was. She relied upon her agility to fight, and if she couldn't dodge and counter as quickly as she was used to . . .

The man in the middle and the one to the right both took another step forward, but the third man hesitated, picking his way over a root. Seren chose that instant to move. She feinted toward the man in the middle, then spun off to the left, lunging at the one on the outside instead. She caught him unprepared, and her thrust connected. But the other two men were already starting toward her, and there was no way she could turn to meet them in time.

Before he could even decide how best to hinder them, Seth had already thrown himself at the nearest man, jumping on his back and hanging about his neck. The man swore, trying to shake him off, but Seth held on as tightly as he could, hoping he could force the man to the ground.

He couldn't see much beyond the back of the man's neck, so he couldn't tell how Seren was faring; he thought the other men gave a muffled noise or two, but he didn't hear anything from her, which was probably either good or very, very bad. His own opponent twisted himself about, and Seth finally slipped to the side, clutching the man by the front instead. But there he was within reach of the man's arms, and his assailant battered at him and muttered curses, striking him so hard in the side it nearly knocked the breath out of him. His grip started to weaken, and he was just about to let go when the man suddenly stopped struggling. Seth stood up, releasing his hold, and the man slid away and to the ground, pierced by Seren's knife. The other two were already dead, bleeding fitfully on the forest floor.

"Thanks," Seth said, winded. He hunched over, trying to get his breath back. He couldn't see her face like that, though, so he craned his neck, pressing one hand against his aching side.

Perhaps it had been too much to hope for to see her smile back at him, but he certainly hadn't expected what he did see: she was staring at him wide-eyed, something almost like horror on her face. "Why did you do that?" she asked, gaping at him in the pauses between words. "Why on earth did you do that?"

"Well," Seth said, panting, "you'd have been—ah—in a right bit of trouble if I hadn't, wouldn't you?"

Her eyes only widened farther, and she shook her head, the knife hanging limp in her hand. "Do you—do you not understand?" she asked, hoarse. "Do you not see what you've done?"

Seth looked down, puzzled, and drew his hand away from his side, staring at the blood that coated it. "I— When did that . . ." He felt for the lip of the cut and blanched when he realized he could put his fingers—he could put his fingers right *inside,* where there was a great hole in him that hadn't been there before. The man had struck him all right, but not with his fist—he had hacked into Seth with the edge of his sword, tearing him open.

He looked to Seren for guidance, but her expression hadn't changed. "What's going to happen?" he asked her. "Is it—bad?"

She said nothing—perhaps she couldn't say anything. *I don't think she liked to lie,* Seth had told Roger, what seemed like a lifetime ago. She swallowed, clenched her fist around the knife, and looked at the ground.

Seth tried to take a step toward her, but he was overcome by a sudden wave of dizziness, and he staggered. Seren moved to steady him, her hands on his shoulders, and he felt the knife's hilt digging into the side of his neck. He searched her face. "What—what should I do?"

Her fingers fluttered against his shoulder blades. "I can— You should lie down. I must have something in here that can bind this up. . . ." She dropped one hand to her side, feeling for her satchel, but it wasn't there. Her eyes began to dart around the clearing instead, searching for it among the fallen leaves.

"Have you had to tend to your own injuries before? You have, haven't you?"

She swallowed hard again. "I have, but—I . . ." She shook her head. "I've never had a wound like that before."

All her years adventuring, and she'd never been hurt like this? He really had mucked it up, hadn't he?

Before he could say anything, Seren caught sight of her satchel. "There it is. If I ease you down, can you . . . ?"

They didn't have much of a choice; Seth couldn't stand on his own anymore. She helped him lie down, then brought the satchel over and rummaged through it. She finally pulled out a long strip of linen, and unfurled it, hesitating. "I've got to bind it up, but . . ."

Seth winced. "Is it really—going to do any good?"

She was quiet again. "What else can we do?" she said at last. "This is the only thing."

He nodded weakly, and she wrapped the cloth about his waist, while Seth gritted his teeth and tried to think about anything else but what was happening. The linen strip probably wasn't as long as it should have been, and eventually Seren was forced to tie it off. But his wound just kept bleeding, soaking the cloth right through.

Seren was as pale as if she'd lost the blood herself. "All right, so now . . ." Her jaw clenched. "You can't stand, can you? What if you leaned on my shoulder?"

They tried it, but the pain was so great as she started to raise him that Seth had to bite back a scream. "No," he gasped, "no, no, I can't, I can't, put me down."

She did as he asked, her hands shaking. "Saltmoor isn't far, and it might be they have someone there who'd know how to treat you. My foot . . ." She grimaced at it, out of frustration rather than pain. "It's nothing serious—in half a day I'll hardly notice it. But you can't wait that long. And I can't carry you, not . . . not with my foot like this."

Find Deinol, Seth thought, but his head was swimming. He moistened his lips. "If . . . maybe if Deinol . . . carried me—"

She frowned at that. "*He's* here? I guess he would be. And the other one?"

"Lucius? No, he's . . . It's Ritsu instead."

That was doubtless incomprehensible to her, but she gave no reaction. "There are more of them out there," she said. "If we call . . . we stand as much chance of bringing them down on us as of alerting your friend."

And even if Deinol *did* carry him the rest of the way to Saltmoor, would he even get that far? Bleeding like this . . . there couldn't be much left of him, could there? He groaned. "I'm so—I—I wish I could've told them." It was so easy to call their faces to mind—they were much clearer than the trees, than Seren's face above him. He knew it was his fault they'd all been scattered to the winds like this—if he hadn't been caught, and they'd never tried to rescue him . . . But if that hadn't happened, he'd never have met Seren, or Ritsu, either. And if he hadn't been here now, Seren would've had to face them all alone, with her foot stuck and without her knife. How could you tell what was a mistake, and what wasn't?

He hadn't realized Seren had slipped an arm behind his head until he felt her fingers tighten on his shoulder. She was looking off into the trees, her face turned away from him. "What on earth did you do it for?" she said again. "I could've—if you just hadn't—"

"Don't say that," Seth said. He reached for her other hand, and when he wrapped his fingers around it, hers stiffened, but she didn't pull away. "That makes it sound like—like I did it for nothing."

Deinol made certain Seth was well out of sight before turning his back to the place where he'd disappeared. It didn't take him half a dozen exchanges with the two louts in front of him to know he'd felled men thrice their ability, but there *were* two of them, and Lucius wasn't with him this time. Worse, they knew how to rely on each other: every time he broke one's guard, the other would step in until his friend had recovered. Deinol could create openings, but he never had enough time to take advantage of them, and he soon found himself being driven back, forced onto the defensive.

He spared what freedom he had to glance at Ritsu, but the fellow was still just *standing* there, gaping at his own sword as if he'd never seen it before. "But," he said again, "but if I pick this up . . ."

"You'd better fucking pick it up," Deinol snapped. "Do you want to die?" Before he could say any more, he was distracted by a slice that missed his cheek by a hair's breadth. He gathered his strength, swung at them as furiously as he could, but he could not get his opponents to give any ground.

If one of them would just break off from him to attack Ritsu, perhaps that would force him to defend himself. But they were smarter than that, and doubtless saw that their swords were best used to dispatch the one who *was* trying to kill them, not the one who might eventually decide to get around to it.

Deinol felt his arms tiring, and the first accompanying throb of fear. "Help me!" he screamed at Ritsu. "Help me, you idiot! What are you doing?"

Ritsu tensed at the noise, and finally reached out, grasping the sheath in one fist. His movements remained slow until his free hand closed around the hilt of his sword, but when he pulled it free, all his hesitation had gone.

Deinol turned with the other two men, watching Ritsu's blade. It was such an *ugly* sword, he couldn't help thinking—the metal was so dull, it couldn't give off the faintest shimmer of sunlight. Could Ritsu really wield it as well as those villagers had said?

His first charge was impressive, but one of the men quickly moved to block it, and Deinol winced, remembering how easily the sword had given when he'd struck it against the tree before. Yet when the swords clashed it was the stranger's blade that recoiled, and Ritsu who pressed his advantage forward, slashing first at the man's unprotected side and then at his neck. The first stroke sliced his arm off at the shoulder, and the second took off his head with such force that it went flying, hitting the ground with a wet splat.

His eyes flicking from Ritsu to Deinol and back again, the second man hesitated—but Ritsu didn't. There was something inhuman about the way he moved—he was amazingly fast, to be sure, but so were Lucius and Almasy. But where they had rigorous technique behind them, Ritsu had something almost bestial, like a wolf lunging at his prey out of pure instinct. He charged again at his second opponent, that useless sword bared—and cut him right in half, all the bloody way through.

Ritsu stood there, panting slightly, and Deinol stood watching him, as much at a loss as he could remember being. How had Ritsu learned to fight like that? How had it even been *possible* for him to fight like that, when Deinol had tested that sword's uselessness for himself?

Ritsu picked up the sword belt he'd discarded and buckled it back around his waist, sliding the sword into its sheath again with a visible shudder. He looked at the ground, where the pieces of the dead men lay, and shook his head violently. "No," he muttered, "no, no, no, I shouldn't have picked it up, I *shouldn't* have picked it up—"

Deinol grasped him by the shoulders, peering down into his eyes. "Ritsu. Hey. Ritsu, look at me." Ritsu did as he said, and he seemed to calm down as they stared at each other. Finally Deinol released him, stepping back. "Are you all right?" he asked—he hardly knew what to say. "Did something . . . happen?"

Ritsu closed his eyes, opened them again, flexed his fingers. "I should not have touched it. But I think I'll be all right."

What in all the hells was *wrong* with him? "Why would you get so upset over it? It's not as if they're the first men you've killed."

"No," Ritsu agreed. He paced a few steps around the bodies. "There were many others. I grew used to that part of it. Besides, these men . . . they intended much ill. I need not regret killing them."

Did that mean there were others he *did* need to regret killing? Deinol set the question aside; there wasn't time to worry about whatever passed for reasoning with Ritsu just now. "Did you see which way Seth went?" he asked. "I watched him go, but I got all turned around in the fighting. . . ."

"Hmm." Ritsu looked slowly about him. "Was it not in that direction?" He cocked his head. "We should not lose sight of the path, though."

That was, Deinol admitted, a good point. He'd never been outside a city until several weeks ago; he didn't want to imagine how long he'd be wandering if you turned him loose in the middle of a forest. "All right," he said. "You're sure Seth went that way? And can you remember that the path is *this* way?"

Ritsu shook his head. "I don't know; I merely think. As for finding our way back, you might mark the trees."

Deinol frowned. "That'll be loud, though. We don't know if there are more of those fellows wandering about; three seems rather a small number to kill Seren Almasy, especially three as sorry as that lot."

Ritsu shrugged. "What else would you have us do?"

That was another good point. Deinol sighed. "All right, tree marking it is." He aimed a slice at the nearest one, then marked every few trunks as they went, peering about for any sign of Seth.

But he didn't see a thing, and finally he decided to chance a call—they'd never find the boy otherwise. "Seth? Can you hear me?"

For several long moments there was no reply, and then someone said, "Here." It was Almasy's voice.

When Deinol saw him lying in Almasy's arms, at first he couldn't move or speak. Part of him would almost have welcomed misunderstanding, as a chance to let anger drown out everything else, but there could be no doubt of what had happened. The wound in his side was far too large to have come from a knife, and the bloody sword of one of the dead men lay in full view, slowly staining the fallen leaves. Even without all that, Almasy's face, which he'd never been able to read before, would have told him everything he needed to know.

She had not killed him, but Deinol might have said that he had died because of her. It was so tempting to lay it all at her feet, to say that everything that had happened since Hornoak had been her fault. But he knew whose fault this was; the certainty fell upon him like a heavy cloak, smothering and inescapable. There was only one man responsible for this.

Almasy looked up at him, her face bleak, but still with the ghost of that composure she seemed to prize so much. Her voice came slowly, and so softly that Deinol would have missed it if the forest had not been so still. "I'm so sorry," she said. "I'm so sorry."

He heard her words, but they provoked no response. He couldn't seem to attach any meaning to them, and they blew past him like dead leaves in the wind. "Give him back," he said, hardly understanding his own words. "Give him to me." And that was right—Seth shouldn't be with her. Seth was *his* boy, even before he'd been Morgan's. It was Deinol who'd found him first, thin as a rail, half starved and bleary-eyed but still gentle, still with that grateful smile he'd show at even the simplest things.

"Give him to me," he said again. "He belongs with me."

Perhaps Almasy nodded, and she started to raise Seth up, to put him into Deinol's arms—and then they both halted, turning to look at Ritsu.

He was standing there trembling, whining like a wounded animal as he stared at Seth, eyes wide and unblinking. "Sebastian," he whimpered. "Sebastian—"

Deinol did not precisely mean to do anything, but his anger, frustrated at being unable to latch on to Almasy, finally found a target. He lashed out with one fist—where had his sword gone? Had he dropped it?—catching Ritsu just below the temple. "He's not your fucking Sebastian, you fucking idiot! Will you stop your pathetic gibbering and act like a fucking man?"

Ritsu recoiled, touching his fingertips to the place where Deinol had hit him, along the ridge of bone between ear and eye. For several moments he just stared at Deinol, his eyes so strangely innocent and so openly betrayed that Deinol didn't want to meet them. One hand drifted down to the hilt of his sword, clutching at it as if it could protect him. And then he turned and ran, head down, into the depths of the woods.

Deinol felt a weight settle in his gut as he gazed after him, but what could he do now? It was Seth he had to see to, not some baffling stranger.

Almasy stirred, and he turned back to her. Her eyes were cast down, but the set of her mouth was firm. "I cannot stay here," she said. "If I don't get back . . ." She shook her head. "I have to go."

"I don't care where you go," Deinol said. "I've had too much to do with you already. Just give him to me."

This time she did shift Seth into Deinol's arms, and stood up. His blood had soaked into her clothes. She started to walk away, but Deinol called after her. "Almasy, tell me one thing."

She half turned to him, warily. "What?"

He hardly cared anymore, but he had to ask—otherwise what was the point of all this? "Why did you do it?" he said. "Why give it to her?"

She didn't look surprised, or ask who he was talking about—but then, she hadn't asked how they'd found her either, or what they'd intended. She didn't precisely look at him, but she did speak. "Because she asked me to."

"That's not an answer."

"Isn't it?" That crooked smile of hers was hardly even sardonic this time, just sad. "Because she is the only person who ever cared whether I lived or died." She glanced down at Seth, the first time Deinol had seen her actually look at him. "Except for him, I suppose."

CHAPTER THIRTY-SEVEN

Deinol carried him up the hill, to where the trees thinned out and there was only a single sycamore, a handful of still-green seeds scattered in its shade. He was so light in Deinol's arms that it was scarcely an effort, but that didn't matter—he'd have carried him the length of the Curse if he needed to. If it would have changed anything.

Getting the shovel had been the worst part—having to leave him there while he struggled the rest of the way to Saltmoor. He didn't want to lug Seth about where everyone in the village could see him, but he'd been terrified that something would get at him while he was gone, that some wolf would drag him off or some crow would start pecking at his eyes. He had made the journey there and back as quickly as he could, stopping only to pick up the sword he'd dropped before he followed the cut trees back to the path. He had thought they'd regard him with suspicion—what sort of man stumbled into a village asking desperately for a shovel?—but they hadn't even looked surprised. "Her ladyship's messenger told us you'd be coming," one of them said to him. "We're to give you whatever you need."

It took Deinol a moment to realize whom she meant. "A shovel," he repeated. "Just a shovel. That's all."

He had to look at Seth again when he first started digging, so he'd know how long and wide to make it. Even when he was sure it was deep enough, he kept digging for a while anyway, because once he stopped, he had to do the next part. He wore himself out eventually, and let the shovel drop. Then he knelt beside Seth in the shade of the tree, gathered him into his arms again. It occurred to him that perhaps he should've asked for something to use as a shroud—or didn't they do that out here? But he didn't want to go back again, and it wasn't as if the thing would actually protect Seth anyway.

He laid him down as gently as he could, then perched at the edge of the hole, wondering how he could bring himself to do the rest. How could you heap dirt on a friend's face? How could you leave him on a nameless hill in a strange land, while you walked away?

How had he ever allowed things to get this far? What had he been thinking? That he'd bring a defenseless boy along with him to chase down someone who had the skills to kill him and the disregard to actually do it, and . . . what, it would turn out all right somehow? He'd find Almasy, she'd miraculously refrain from killing him on sight, and he'd suddenly know what he wanted from her? No. It had never really been about her at all, had it? He'd been as much a captive to the word *adventure* as Roger ever was—that and the idea of accomplishing something without Lucius's help, of proving he didn't need him or anyone else to come to his rescue. He'd mucked *that* up in particular, hadn't he?

Gods, what would he *say* to Roger—how could he tell him about Seth? How could he tell Lucius, who had as good as ordered him not to go? How, above all, could he tell Morgan, who had given up her own freedom so Seth could escape?

What was he supposed to *do* now? What next step could there be after this?

He watched Seth's face, still and expressionless, his golden hair matted against the dirt. You were supposed to say something at times like this, he knew that. But how could he sum up Seth's life for him? Wouldn't that be as good as admitting it was over?

"Seth, I'm sorry." They were the same words Almasy had used. They still didn't seem to mean anything.

He stood up, finally, and picked up the shovel. He didn't set it down again until the hole was entirely filled in, the last handful of dirt packed into place. And then he sat under the tree, drew his knees to his chest, and did nothing for a very long time.

CHAPTER THIRTY-EIGHT

When it was up to him, Dent always chose to take his patrol through the orchard. It suited everyone: Lady Margraine could trust him not to eat or steal the apples, and Dent could do whatever pondering he had to do in peace, with only the birds and the rustling of leaves to disturb him. Sometimes he stayed there even when he had no post to man, calling back to the birds in their own tongues. But he was not whistling when Gravis found him there, when he could put it off no longer—his face was stern, his brows drawn together. Gravis's stomach churned at the sight of him—of all the men he ever wanted to fight with, Denton Halley was the last by far.

"Dent . . ." he started, and paused until he thought of the rest. "I hear you're in the grip of some displeasure."

Dent laughed, but Gravis had heard him laugh enough times to know this one was a pale imitation. "Did your little rat tell you that?"

Gravis blinked at the epithet—if Dent was talking about Kern, he didn't understand where it had come from. Kern was a handsome young man, with nothing of the rat in his face at all, and Gravis had only ever found him to be honest and direct. But whom else could Dent have meant, if not Kern?

"We've been friends for a long time," he said at last, deciding to ignore it. "If I've done something to make you angry with me—"

"Aye, Gravis, you have, all right?" Dent half turned away, wrinkling his nose as if the words were distasteful to him. "I'm sorry, but you have, and I can't help it."

"Then tell me how, so that I may amend it," Gravis said. "I am not so haughty yet that I will not stand to be corrected by my friends."

Dent grimaced. "You won't like it."

"No doubt. But tell me all the same."

Dent let out his breath in one big huff, pacing a circle beneath the trees. "The little rat is only part of it, but he's the best example. Why do you think he acts the way he does?"

"What way do you mean?"

"He's proud," Dent said, "and he's insolent. He's disrespectful."

Was he serious? "Are—are we talking about Kern?"

"Aye, who else?"

"But Kern is—he's always been the most polite and earnest—"

"Aye, to *you*, Gravis. But you are not his master, whatever he may think. You are a servant in these halls, just as he is, and nothing more."

"I have never claimed nor wished to be anything else," Gravis protested. He could not have said, before, how he had expected Dent to rebuke him, but he'd never have guessed it would be for a lack of forbearance.

"Then why do you not act like it? The things you say to her ladyship—"

"Dent, I don't always agree with her," Gravis said, holding out his hands. "If she'd wanted someone who never had an opinion of his own, she was free to have me replaced."

"It goes beyond that." He kept pacing his slow circles, his footsteps nearly noiseless in the grass. "No one ever said you had to love her, but when you treat her with contempt in front of your subordinates, you invite them to do the same, and it is *not their place*. It does not speak well of them, Gravis, or of you. She laughs at your censure because she does not care what you think of her, but *I* do. Ever since she was a child, you've had this . . . this antipathy toward her. It isn't natural."

"And has she been natural?" Gravis asked. "What about her was ever as a child should be? If she had shown her father but the love most men bear their dogs—"

"What, he wouldn't have opened up her back that day?" Gravis could not answer that. He remembered too well the scene that had awaited him when he'd returned to Stonespire, the sight of Lord Caius with that bloody whip tangled around his fingers. He had sat with it for hours, the servants said, until the dried blood had plastered it to his skin. "I buried my grudge against Lord Caius long ago," Dent continued. "You should do the same with her."

Have you buried it? Gravis wondered. *Have you really?* "Is that all?"

"No. Just the tip of it, I'm afraid." Dent sighed, scratching the back of his neck. "I looked over the recruitment lists."

That was yet another surprise. "The *recruitment* lists? What's wrong with them? I've met her ladyship's demands—I've *exceeded* her demands."

"Aye, that's just it." Dent's brow wrinkled in confusion. "I always knew you as a cautious fellow, Gravis—zealous, certainly, in your way, but cautious. But these new additions—nearly eighty on the city guard in the past month alone—"

The alarm that had been smoldering in Gravis all day suddenly sparked full into being, and it was all he could do not to yell *what?* at Dent like a slack-jawed imbecile. "Eighty . . . eighty city guardsmen would be—"

"Sorely helpful, I'm sure, but that's only if they can be trusted. I've looked over your records, Gravis, and I don't know these men. Maybe you do, and I trust you, I *do*, but these boys come to Stonespire from some two-cart village up north—some of them have never even *seen* a city. If you mean to bring eighty new faces here all at once, and even a third of them are like the rat—"

It was so strange. Panic was clamoring inside him fit to split his skull, yet his jaw stayed relaxed, his fingers loose at his sides. "I see," he heard himself say. "Well, I take your point. I'll review the Stonespire list—can't hurt to give it an additional looking-over. Perhaps I was a bit hasty with some of the appointments."

Dent smiled, but it didn't quite reach his eyes—had Gravis given something away after all? "A bit late for that, isn't it? Aren't they coming soon? You didn't mark it on the lists, but I've been hearing tomorrow or the day after."

Great gods. Gravis willed his face not to move. "Can it really be so soon? Time's quite gotten away from me, it seems. Now that I hear you say it, I—I wish I'd done it differently. . . ." He shook his head. "I can always send some of them back out to the nearby towns if I find they're not fit for the city. Either way, I *will* review them, with all thoroughness."

Dent finally gave a true smile. "I'd appreciate it if you would. I'd certainly be able to rest easier."

"Good." It was not good at all. "Now I must leave you, I'm afraid."

Dent was looking at him strangely, but he could hardly be blamed for that. "Gravis, is something amiss?"

"I don't believe so." Another lie. "I merely need to ask her ladyship something. Will you excuse me?"

Gods knew how he was able to extricate himself from the conversation without sprinting from the orchard, yet somehow he managed it. As soon as he was out of Dent's sight, he made immediately for the barracks. The grandiosely titled records room was little more than a large closet filled with bound sheaves of paper, but at least he had insisted it stay organized, and he had no trouble finding the record book that held the Stonespire lists.

Because Esthrades had no standing army, in times of peace it relied upon volunteers to the militia, and established guardsmen were sent all over the country to select and train would-be recruits. Their judgment was deemed sufficient where the defense of smaller villages was concerned, but city guardsmen had to be chosen by Gravis himself before they could be assigned to positions within Stonespire's walls. The result was an admittedly smaller group than they might otherwise have had, but smaller numbers were infinitely preferable to allowing anyone who wished it to call himself the purveyor of her ladyship's justice.

He turned to the most recent page, and saw immediately what had so concerned Dent. He had not exaggerated—Gravis counted seventy-eight names in the past four weeks alone. He was used to giving his consent to *half* that number—and he was not aware that he had done any differently in the recent past. In point of fact, what with the parley at Mist's Edge, he had been unable to evaluate new recruits, or to review the lists at all, and he had been worried he might end up short of his usual numbers. It seemed the opposite was true, but *how*?

It wasn't right, and no matter what he did, he couldn't seem to make it right. When could these names have been added, and who had added them? True, he did not always literally write the names in himself—after his evaluations were done, he was accustomed to hand off the names to some other guardsman or scribe to ink into the book. But no one would have simply signed on new men without consulting him. They might have asked Lady Margraine, he supposed, but why? Recruiting was the one task she had left entirely to his judgment, and there wasn't a soldier in Stonespire who wouldn't know that. No. Either he had found those men himself, which he hadn't, or else someone else had added them with his permission, which no one had asked for. Yet here were the names, standing starkly out against the parchment as if they were accusing him.

He ran through the list again and again, as if repeated checks might make the discrepancy that gnawed at him suddenly disappear. He stared at every name, trying fruitlessly to assign a face to each, to determine which he had approved and which he had no memory of. Finally he slammed the book shut almost in a fury and turned away from it. He knew what had happened. He knew. There was only one possibility, and one sure way to convince himself of it. He left the book alone and headed for the stairs. He had not lied to Dent about one thing: he *did* have a question for her ladyship.

He found Lady Margraine bent over her desk as usual, paging through whatever new tome had caught her fancy. Or maybe it was an old one; Gravis had no idea. He cleared his throat, not truly expecting it would actually get him sufficient attention; when Lady Margraine had her eye on a book, even the fury of the gods could not turn it aside.

Sure enough, she did not look at him. "Gravis, I am occupied at the moment. What?"

Gravis curled and uncurled his fingers, pondering the phrasing of his answer before he gave it. "I merely wanted to know if you expected Almasy to return shortly or not."

She drew her finger idly down the margin of the page. "Return from where?"

"From wherever it is you sent her."

"*I* didn't send Seren anywhere." She did look up, then, slightly. "Why, is she gone?"

Gravis hesitated; a clammy feeling settled in the pit of his stomach. "Well . . . perhaps not. I may have . . . misunderstood."

She waved him off. "You must have; it's not like her to go traveling for her own amusement. Seek her out if you like; someone must have seen her."

Gravis bowed, but it was not Almasy he left to seek.

He found Kern making his way down the western corridor, and hurried to catch up with him. "I need to speak to you," he said as they drew shoulder to shoulder. "At once."

Kern nodded, as amiable as ever, but then he bit his lip. "I do need to report to the wall, sir—it's my turn up there with Gregg until nightfall."

"That will be fine," Gravis said. "We can talk as well there."

When the very first Daven Margraine had laid claim to the land on which they now stood, there had been nothing on the hill but the blood apple orchard and the ancient tower that had given Stonespire Hall its name, and nothing in its shadow but the tiniest of villages. The new Lord Margraine had built his seat around the tower, using it as a backbone, but the hill was too small and too steep to accommodate the construction of any great castle. No doubt this had not seemed a problem at the time—Daven Margraine had only ever been intended to be a minor lord, Stonespire Hall a minor lord's seat. But though the city of Stonespire was free to grow as its successive line of rulers had expanded their influence further and further, the hall had remained largely the same— beautiful, in its way, but a castle of sand when compared with the fortresses at Mist's Edge and Eldren Cael, or Valyanrend's majestic Citadel.

There was one benefit to Stonespire's location, however—the hill was sheer on three sides, and you could only make your way to the gates up a wide but steep path cut into the fourth side. It was at the top of that path that the rampart they called "the wall" was built. Strictly speaking, it was three walls: one that slanted out from Stonespire's left side, one mirroring it on the opposite side, and one wall that connected them, running across the path to the hall. There was a portcullis in the middle, and a guard tower atop the ramparts at both points where the three walls converged, but the hall could boast no defenses more elaborate than that.

It was to one of the guard towers that Gravis led Kern, only to find Gregg already there. "You may retire," Gravis told him. "I have something to discuss with Kern, so I'll take your watch with him today. You may wait in the great hall until I send for you."

Dent would have questioned him, as would Kern. Gravis himself would have questioned it, if his superior had ordered such a thing. But Gravis had never known Gregg to question an order in all their years together, not unless he wanted to make sure he'd heard it right. He had, apparently, because he nodded, and marched back down off the wall.

Gravis watched him from the arrow slit, making sure he returned inside the hall instead of loitering about. Then, when he had decided they were about as alone as they could expect to be, he looked to Kern.

He looked to him, but he could not speak, and finally Kern himself spoke up. "Yes, what is it, Captain?" He gazed so guilelessly back at Gravis, eyes wide and quizzical, his eyebrows lifting gently.

Gravis felt his fingers shaking, and curled them inward, clenching his fists. The creak of metal seemed overloud, wrong when everything else was so still. "Explain to me what it is you have done," he said as firmly as he could.

Kern still looked at him blankly. "Captain, I—"

"There is no use telling me you do not know where Almasy has gone," Gravis said, cursing every hint of tremulousness he detected in his own voice. "I already know you were the one who sent her from Stonespire, and the marquise has no knowledge of it. So you are, in fact, the only one who knows where Almasy has gone. You will tell me where she is, and then you will tell me why you have sent her there."

There was nothing combative in Kern's face, nothing in his voice. "Or?"

"Or?" Gravis repeated, confused.

"Or what, sir?"

Gravis hesitated only a moment. "Or I will assume you no longer wish to serve me or her ladyship, and I will act accordingly."

"I will always wish to serve you, sir," Kern said, with every bit of the earnestness Gravis had always loved in him.

"Then answer my question," he said. "Where is Almasy, and why did you see fit to send her there?"

Kern's eyes flicked away for the first time, but he pulled them back again almost immediately. "Almasy has gone to Saltmoor, and I sent her there because that is where she belongs. She should never have been here."

"Am I to understand—" Gravis swallowed thickly "—that she will not be coming back from Saltmoor?"

"No," Kern agreed. "She will not, if the gods are good."

If the gods are good. Gravis could not tighten his fist any farther; the metal of his gauntlets would not allow it. "I would ask why you would send her ladyship's primary defender to her death, but I fear I already know the answer."

Kern looked at him intently. "Why do you fear, Captain? You need fear nothing."

I fear too much. He held one fist in the other so tightly that the metal groaned in protest. "What is it that will happen here? What will happen, while Almasy is not protecting her liege?"

"Justice," Kern said.

"Treason," Gravis corrected, forcing the word out from between clenched teeth.

"It is no treason. I would die before I committed any treason." He tilted his chin, setting his jaw defiantly. "Before the day is out, Captain, Esthrades will be free again, and ours."

How can it be free and ours at once? Gravis thought vaguely. "What are you saying?" he asked aloud. "Speak plainly."

"I am speaking plainly, Captain. You simply do not wish to understand." Kern met his gaze easily, his eyes a clear and piercing blue. "There will be no vulgar violence; you mustn't fear that. No harm will come to you, I'll make sure of it. Lord Oswhent assured me that all will be as I order it—all the men await my command."

Gravis fastened on to only two words. "Lord Oswhent?" The foppish man in the red robes that he'd met at Mist's Edge? *He* was behind this? "What have you to do with Lord Oswhent?"

"He provided the men," Kern said.

"The men." His voice was practically stifled, but he forced it out. "The men you added to my lists. *Elgar's* men."

Kern shook his head. "Our men. In the service of our freedom."

Oswhent would never give you men for such a purpose. "How many are there?" he said. "Tell me that."

Kern shrugged, but that wasn't uncertainty. "Fifty-three, by my last count. Word in the barracks is that they are expected soon—tomorrow or the day after, but you know how rumors are. No one will balk at their arriving today instead—and Gregg won't balk either, not when I tell him you wished me to let them in."

Great gods. "They are coming *today*?"

Kern's eyes remained steady. "Within the hour, Captain."

His head was going to burst; he could feel it. "They're coming to kill—"

"They're not going to *kill* her, Captain," Kern said calmly. "You know that. What would be the point in it? It would only cause chaos, and no one wants that."

"No," Gravis agreed, numbly. He could see what they wanted, all too clearly. As to what *Kern* wanted, he had far less of an idea than he could have wished. He thought himself in the right, that much was plain; his motives were not cowardly or mercenary. But there was no time to divine what they were; these men of Oswhent's, of *Elgar's*, would be coming any moment, and—

He tried to scour his brain for some answer, but the only image that came to his mind's eye was Lord Caius, bowed and broken on the day his wife had died. It was that man he had sworn to protect, but where could he find him now? *My lord,* he thought, *help me. What should I do?*

He looked through the arrow slit more out of helplessness than anything else. The portcullis was standing open: though this was the day the throne rested, they were in the habit of using the seventh day for delivering supplies to Stonespire. The lack of foot traffic from petitioners meant that goods could be transported more easily, but it still took some time—the stables were at the base of the hill, both because of size constraints at the summit and because it was damnably difficult to get a horse and rider up those steep steps, never mind a horse and cart. So all their suppliers pulled up their carts by the stables and carried their goods the rest of the way on foot; it was a process that easily took hours, but today it seemed they were nearly done.

There should have been nothing in all that to interest him, but his eyes fixed on a target immediately—Seren Almasy was staggering up the path to the hall. She looked terrible, haggard and weary, but she was, so far as he could tell, unharmed. He stared down at her, at the mysterious, solitary figure she always made, and he came to a decision at last.

"Captain?" Kern asked, and Gravis turned to him, smoothing his features into whatever semblance of composure he could muster.

"Yes," he said. "I heard you. She won't be killed."

"And you—"

"I know what I must do," Gravis told him, and there was no hesitation in his voice.

————

Lady Margraine was in her study—reading, just as he had left her. He stared at her a moment before he spoke. It was a strange feeling: for once he knew something she didn't, and she suspected nothing.

Finally he cleared his throat. "Almasy will be up to see you in a minute."

She barely looked up. "I hadn't asked for her presence, had I?"

"No," Gravis admitted.

"Then why is it necessary? All I said was that I hadn't sent her on any errand."

"I know that," Gravis said.

"Mm." She turned a page. "Was it your mistake, or another guardsman's? A servant's?"

"A guardsman's," Gravis said. "But mine as well, I suppose." He placed a hand on the hilt of his sword.

"Fair enough." She still wasn't looking at him. "If that's all you had to tell me, then you may go. I leave the discipline of your own soldiers to you—do whatever you see fit, or nothing."

"I have already done so," Gravis said.

"Oh?" She sounded, as ever, bored. "Then leave me to my reading."

"I cannot, my lady," Gravis said. "Not today."

She looked up, finally, as he had known she would. How strange to remember that she was, in truth, scarcely older than Kern, though her eyes seemed to hold the cunning of centuries. He had seen her on the day she was born, the day of Lord Caius's greatest loss. She had been a thing of bitterness to him then, a strange interloper who blinked quizzically and slept without fuss, as if oblivious to the grief she had caused. But he had pitied her then, because babes, so they said, were innocent, and he knew she would never know her mother. The bitterness remained, but he had stopped pitying her long ago.

"What is it you mean to say?" she asked, one hand pressed flat against the book but both eyes on him.

They were interrupted by Almasy, who opened the door just a sliver and slipped quickly through. She bowed to the marquise, though the look she gave Gravis was still wary.

"Were you able to pass unseen?" he asked.

She nodded. "To the best of my knowledge. I do wish you'd found a better way to warn me, but I suppose it couldn't be helped."

Lady Margraine had relaxed somewhat when Almasy had entered the room, but now she glanced between them, tensing once more. "Clearly you two know something I don't. When do you plan to tell me?" Then she frowned. "Seren, are you limping? How did that come about?"

"It's nothing," Almasy said, though she winced slightly as she turned her ankle. "It will heal soon enough."

"I did not ask you whether it was nothing, I asked you how you came by it."

Almasy acquiesced immediately, as she always did. "I was ambushed near Saltmoor, where I was sent on orders I had been led to believe were yours."

That was anger, finally, on the marquise's face. Gravis didn't see it often, but he'd seen it enough to recognize it. "And who gave you these orders?"

Almasy hesitated, and looked to Gravis. "Well, I . . . I don't precisely know. I assume it was—"

"My lady," Gravis broke in, "you will know all in time, but there is something I must tell you, immediately."

That got her attention. "Well?"

He swallowed hard. "There are more than fifty men within the city—men chosen by Elgar and Lord Oswhent. They were smuggled in—they were smuggled in by a traitor in the ranks of my guardsmen, and they are preparing to storm the hall and take you captive at any moment."

For a single instant Lady Margraine's eyes went wide—and then she began to laugh, curling her fingers around the back of her chair. "Gravis," she said, "choosing and maintaining the members of your guard was the *one* thing I gave you complete charge of, and you've mucked it up."

Gravis curled his fingers into a hard fist. "I am aware—"

"Oh, spare me your guilt; we don't have time for it. You are certain this traitor told the truth?"

"No," Gravis admitted, "but I suspect he did. Why would he bluff about such a thing? There's nothing he could stand to gain from it."

"That's true enough," she agreed. "Damn it all, how did he get them all in?"

"He added them to the recruitment lists," Gravis said. *Which no one but me will ever write in again,* he thought.

"It's brilliant, in its way," Lady Margraine said. "Even I have to admit that. It's far too brilliant to be Elgar's idea; that Oswhent must be the one behind it. I am the last of my line, and the only one who has the ghost of a claim to the throne of Esthrades. Without me, this realm can only fall into chaos and civil war. But if he can capture me, he captures the whole of Esthrades at one blow." She smiled. "Provided, of course, that he can *keep* me. But I think after Mist's Edge he became certain that I was the sort of person who'd do anything to spare my own life. And who knows? Perhaps I would."

Gravis shook his head. "Expounding on the reasoning behind his plan won't help us figure out how to thwart it."

She just kept smiling. "Normally I'd disagree, but in this instance there's no time." That was an understatement; they needed to come to a decision as close to *immediately* as possible.

Almasy's face was drawn and anxious, one hand tracing the curve of the opposite arm. "My lady, I am prepared to fight—"

"Yes, you're always prepared to fight, Seren," Lady Margraine said. "But as good as you are, you haven't a chance against fifty men."

"She need not fight even one man," Gravis pointed out. "They are expecting Kern to open the gate for them. We need only keep it barred—"

"And they'll scurry away like so many rats, and we will never find them. And I will have fifty more traitors in my city than I had before." She pressed her knuckles into the wood of her desk. "No. We cannot let them escape."

"Then let us open the gate and shut it behind them," Gravis said. "We will come to battle—"

"And they'll slaughter us." She laughed. "We don't have fifty fighting men of our own in the hall—we barely have half that. In the city itself we have hundreds, of course, but how are we to get them here? If we send for them too soon, they'll alert the rats that something is amiss; too late, and we'll be killed before they can arrive."

"We have the defensive position," Gravis insisted. "We can station archers—"

"And you're willing to bet all our lives on that, are you? How many men do you think we'll lose?"

"You are only telling me what we cannot do," Gravis growled. "What would you suggest? That we sit about at our leisure and wait for them to stroll in?"

Her smile was almost fond, and that put him more on guard than anything else had so far. "Perhaps," she said. "Perhaps that is the best way, after all."

Gravis opened and shut his mouth once before he could speak. "Are you—are you joking?"

"I'd say if I were joking you would know it, Gravis, but . . . well, the truth is you probably wouldn't." She shut her eyes a moment, thinking, and Gravis

realized how drawn her face looked, despite her apparent calmness. "I have decided," she finally said. "There is one way that is clearly best—a way to eliminate
their threat forever, without risking the lives of our men." She opened her eyes.
"I will take care of this myself."

Gravis balked, staring at her in stunned silence; Almasy looked hardly less
shocked. "What do you mean?" he asked. "Are you saying you wish to command the men?"

"I'm saying there will be no men, Gravis, because I will handle this. I will
handle it *alone*."

"My lady, if you think you can somehow persuade them to leave, I assure
you that even you—"

She smiled at him. "Do you think I wish to let traitors run free any more
than you do? *I* assure *you*, Gravis, they will all receive their just reward."

Gravis gritted his teeth. "My lady, you assure me of impossibilities."

"Not at all, Gravis. You will simply have to follow a command you have never
been able to follow before, and trust me."

He spread his hands helplessly. "You truly think—all by yourself—"

"Hmm, perhaps you do have a point there." She closed her eyes again, considering it. "No," she said. "Not quite by myself. Seren will stay with me, and
we shall await them in the great hall. The door will not be barred, and we shall
open the gate when they call—let them think they've taken us unawares." She
looked at him sharply, and she did not smile then, just made sure her eyes bored
into his. "As for you, Gravis, and all your men, and every last servant and hired
hand currently in this castle, let *no one else* enter the hall until I summon you.
No one, do you understand me?"

What could he say to such a command? Had she gone mad? He searched
her face, her demeanor, but she seemed the same as always. She was still pale,
and her mouth trembled just a bit, but a little fear, if that's what it was, was
certainly warranted at this point; he'd have been more worried if she had
seemed untroubled. But how could he simply let her persist in this, without
knowing what she planned?

He even wondered, for a moment, if she truly intended to surrender, and
simply didn't want any of them there to protest or witness it. But he could not
believe it. Few men loved their wives as ardently as Arianrod Margraine loved
her throne—she would not just give it up at the first signs of adversity. It was
impossible.

"My lady," he said, "I—"

"You are confused, Gravis," she said, "I know. However, it is not my responsibility or my inclination to enlighten you. It is *your* responsibility to see that

my orders are carried out, and I promise you it will go the worse for anyone who disobeys them."

"But, my lady, we are not to take up arms at *all*? We are to sit here cutting cards while traitors enter our halls? I will not abide such an order. I will *not*." He had prided himself, in some strange perverse way, on his obedience, even as he had prided himself on his defiance. His defiance allowed him to think that he did not just submit to her mindlessly, but his obedience was its own mark of honor, as if it proved she could not break him with her insolence, that he could bear the burden of his oath without flinching. This order, however, was one too far. How could he stand by while traitors marched up to Lord Caius's very throne?

Lady Margraine sighed. "Though your continued obstinacy is truly starting to wear on my patience, I doubt I have the time to argue with you. Very well. You may remain with me in the great hall, if that is truly your wish. But then you will do exactly as I tell you, and not a thing else. And if I hear the slightest word of protest, I will have you beheaded, and promote Dent to the captaincy that very instant."

CHAPTER THIRTY-NINE

Gravis curled his bare fingers into a fist, grimacing. He felt naked without his armor, but Lady Margraine had insisted upon its removal. "I doubt any of these traitors have seen your face before, Gravis," she had said, "but there's only one man who goes squeaking and clanking about Stonespire in full plate no matter the weather or time of day. We can't very well hide that Seren survived their plots—we may have women in the guard, but I am not accustomed to keep any so close about me. If they see you here in addition, they may grow skittish and turn their tails, and we cannot allow that. You must play the common guardsman for an afternoon."

The three of them were alone in the great hall, the doors closed but not barred, as her ladyship had instructed. Outside, the portcullis remained closed, but Gregg—reliable, obedient Gregg—had orders to raise it upon their enemies' arrival. They could only hope he would not be harmed, but it did not seem likely—for all the traitors knew, the other guardsmen thought they were new additions to the ranks. Why would they strike out at Gregg and betray the ruse so early?

Such thoughts gave him little comfort when he considered that Gregg knew nothing—they had thought it best not even to tell him to be on his guard, lest he give the game away. Gravis fidgeted, wringing his unarmored hands. Her ladyship was sitting on the throne, and she was reading. Almasy was standing at her right hand, stiff and straight as always, her eyes flicking from the marquise to the far doors and back. Finally she said, "My lady—"

Lady Margraine flattened her palm against the open book. "I know, Seren. I am collecting my thoughts. You will have your orders as soon as I have decided on them."

She was still pale, her smile faint and faded, with none of the usual confidence in her eyes. Was it truly fear he glimpsed there, Gravis wondered, or something else?

There was another brief silence, and then Almasy asked, "What are you reading?"

Gravis braced himself for a dry retort, but it seemed Almasy had the right of it—Lady Margraine's shoulders relaxed slightly, her voice steadying as she answered. "Tomar Gorrin's research on the War of the Valerian Succession, but I can't say I'm very impressed. Isthmus Gwyne's version is vastly superior—for one thing, Gorrin seems to have worshipped Eglantine so ardently that he leaves out all the best anecdotes from his life. It's an effort to make him seem more *serious,* I suppose, but whatever *for*?" She smiled. "Did you know that when the queen first raised him to a noble house, he wanted his words to be *Well, and What's Yours, Then?*" She didn't quite laugh, but her mouth twisted as if she was suppressing it. "The queen wouldn't hear of that, of course, so instead he proposed *No Hair in the Soup, Please.* Unsurprisingly, she wasn't any fonder of that one."

Gravis snorted in spite of himself. "Perhaps he wasn't as clever as the scholars would have us believe."

"Oh, I have no doubt he was, Gravis. Have you heard some of the drivel the other houses used? House Valerian itself was *Ancient and Pure*—I can't think of two more useless things to be. And then you had that butcher Ryvar Radcliffe, who chose a bloody sword and bloody words: *Blood Will Have Blood.* They say he wanted it to be *Let There Be Blood,* but it seems someone informed him that at that point he might as well have used *Stark Raving Mad* and had done with it." She scoffed, but then grew thoughtful again. "Even House Margraine had its own words, though after the public soured on the idea of noble houses, we made sure to push them into obscurity. *The Unclouded Eyes . . .* and that's not even a complete thought, is it? The unclouded eyes *what*? 'See better than clouded ones,' I suppose, but who doesn't know *that*?" She shook her head. "I think our ancestors had the right of it when they did away with such things, along with knights and Ninism and all the other trappings of Elesthene." But then she paused. "Except for *No Hair in the Soup*. That, I think, is true wisdom."

Gravis could not think of anything to say to that, and it seemed Almasy couldn't either, but at least the marquise's musings had returned a little color to her face. She finally turned to Almasy, clearly trying to make her smile seem as effortless as usual. "Seren, I'm afraid all I can do is repeat what I told you before: you must not move from my side, no matter what should happen. You must not fight them, even if they provoke you. Do you understand?"

Almasy frowned. "I understand well enough. That doesn't mean it sits well with me."

"But you will do it?"

Almasy looked singularly unhappy, but in the end she bowed her head. "If that is your command."

"Good." She curled her fingers around the wooden arm of the throne, then released it. "I shall take care of the rest."

Almasy raised her eyebrows. "The rest? But you are not having me do anything to begin with."

Lady Margraine tapped the wood. "And if everything goes well, you will not need to do anything. But they do say one should be prepared for the worst, don't they?"

Almasy said nothing. She kept her head bowed, and Gravis could not read the expression on her face.

Either Lady Margraine required no confirmation, or else she could read some meaning where Gravis could not. Either way, she did not look at Almasy again, only returned to the book on her lap and continued to read. Soon she was turning pages avidly, as absorbed in it as she'd ever been in her study.

And yet she was still so drawn, as subdued as Gravis had ever seen her. She took breath after shuddering breath, exhaling heavily as if hoping that would steady her, and her fingers shook ever so slightly on the arm of the throne when they were not engaged in page turning. Her gaze flicked up every so often, fixing on the far doors.

When he heard the groan as the portcullis was lifted, Gravis instinctively clutched at his sword. "You won't be needing that, Gravis," Lady Margraine said sharply. "I know you must be anxious, but I'd be gratified if you would keep your admittedly minor wits about you. If you throw yourself at them, you'll just get in the way." *In the way of what?* Gravis wanted to ask. But her ladyship was not one to bluff, and he figured he had already given her about as much insubordination as she could stomach. So he released the hilt of his sword, and tried his best to act like an ordinary soldier at his post, not one who was expecting any invaders.

The cowards entered as a mob, easily as many as Kern had told him. They strode down the hall shoulder to shoulder, swords and spears drawn and brandished, looking warily about them. They wanted to make sure they had taken the hall unawares, Gravis knew; the damned dogs would probably have flinched from even the whisper of a fair fight. They were rough, greedy-eyed men—none of Elgar's devout *here*, it seemed. Perhaps he needed only the shiftiest for such deceit.

He saw one of them, in a dented halfhelm that didn't obscure his rough stubble or heavy jaw, step a little forward as they marched—ready to take charge now that he'd seen there were only three people in the hall. The rest of them stayed in line, following his lead. Many of them kept their gazes warily trained on Almasy—they'd been right, then, to assume their guests would expect her to be dead.

By the time he'd closed in on the shallow steps leading to the throne, the man in the halfhelm must have realized the marquise had no intention of acknowledging his presence. No doubt this threw him a bit, but he was still smirking when he said, "Lady Margraine, is it? Nathaniel Wyles, of Hallarnon—at your service, as much as circumstances allow."

Lady Margraine looked up from her book with extreme and obvious reluctance. When she did, she betrayed no trace of emotion, just the usual cold amusement; this was perhaps the only time Gravis had been heartened to see it. "In Esthrades, the throne retires one day out of seven," she said, "so I will hear no grievances today. Thus, as you see, I was reading. Can you possibly think you have sufficient reason to interrupt me?"

This Nathaniel Wyles seemed to be the leader, at least as far as the talking was concerned. Gravis saw him balk at her words at first, but he quickly tried to hide it, attempting instead to match the lightness and unconcern of her tone. "Unfortunately, my lady," he said, "we do have a reason. You see, we've got to put you under our protection, at least until the throne is safe."

Lady Margraine turned a page idly. "I gave no orders to that end, nor would I ever consider doing so. I will keep the throne far safer than you lot ever could. So far you are not presenting a compelling argument for why I should leave off my reading to attend to you, and it's honestly not even that intriguing a book."

Wyles kept his calm, though the smirk was long gone; this scene must have gone quite differently in his imaginings. "My lady," he said, "there's quite a few of us, as you can see. And you . . . well, you've got yourself, and that woman of yours, and that fellow there, and that's it. So you see, whether you like it or not, we've taken this castle."

"I do have more guards inside the hall, you know," she replied. "Do you plan to leave those doors gaping open in the hopes that they'll see you, and make it a fairer fight? I'd never have guessed you were so honorable."

He looked askance at that, and called over his shoulder. "Shut them. And make sure they're barred." Several men at the back of the hall scurried to carry out his orders, and he turned back to Lady Margraine, trying his best to smooth away his frown. "My lady, you don't seem to understand the seriousness of your situation."

As if to underscore his point, she laughed at him. "Seriousness? I take few things seriously, and especially not arguments that are put to me by stupid people, thrown all out of order and made insipid with too many words. I grasped your meaning the moment you stepped in here: you have force of arms, you are within my walls, and you intend to take me captive. Be content with my understanding, sir, and leave the seriousness or lack of it to my own judgment."

Wyles jerked his head in a wary assent. "Can I take it, then, that that dog of yours will stand down, and not snap at our heels if we approach?" Gravis winced at the epithet. Kern had told them that. Kern had told them everything.

The twitch of Lady Margraine's eyebrow betrayed a twinge of irritation. "She will not harm you," she said. Almasy looked as if she wished to disagree, in deeds rather than in words, but she did not move.

Wyles smiled and took another step forward. "That's very good, my lady. Now"—his fingers tightened on his sword—"I think it'd be best if you retired to your chambers until we send for you. We'll give you an escort, of course."

If she had suffered that indignity, Gravis would not have been able to remain silent and still any longer, but her face made it clear that she had not entertained that notion for a moment. Instead she gazed at Wyles with utter contempt, somehow managing to look down her nose at him despite the fact that she was sitting and he was at his full height. "You really are determined, aren't you? How ridiculous." But her face was pale again, her breathing quickened, and suddenly Gravis knew where he had seen that expression before. In the aftermath of battle, when wounded soldiers were told they must either lose a limb to the knife or lose their lives to infection, there were those who did not scream or plead. There were those who grew pale, and nodded, and took deep, steadying breaths, closing their eyes or turning away, clenching their jaws and unclenching their trembling fingers, readying themselves for that loss in the only ways they knew how.

It was not fear. She was steeling herself for something.

Still, somehow, he waited, or perhaps he was just frozen. He waited, and he heard Wyles say, "The only ridiculousness here is yours, my lady. We will have you in your chambers, whether you walk there or whether my men carry you. Get up off that throne; you've no need to sit it anymore."

Lady Margraine shut the book that still remained on her lap, and tucked it carefully away at her side before looking at Wyles again. "You are an ant," she told him, almost pleasantly. "You are a weak, wretched, pathetic little worm. You are irrelevant. I could crush the lot of you with a single blow; I could level you like sand. And yet you think to drag me from my very throne, from the seat my ancestors have held for centuries, simply because there are rather a lot of you and you've got a tight grip on those little scraps of metal. It's . . . well, it's remarkable, really." She laughed, as if to herself. "The presumption of ants! Why did the scholars not write of *that*, I wonder?"

Gravis expected that would stir Wyles to anger, but he only shook his head, as if in disbelief. "My lady, I don't say my sword's the prettiest that's ever been forged, but as you're unarmed—"

"I have no *sword*," Lady Margraine corrected him, "but I am always armed."

He shrugged. "With what, your position? Your nobility?"

That made her eyebrow twitch again. "Of course not, you imbecile. With my *mind*."

Wyles laughed, but it was more relieved than mocking—Gravis wondered what he had expected her to say. "And you think that mind of yours'll save you, do you?"

"It's just about to, actually," the marquise said, as calm as could be.

"I would dearly love to see that, my lady."

"Oh, you'll see it," she said. "Set one foot upon those steps, and I swear to you, you will see it. Every man in this hall will see it, and then perhaps others like you will begin to know the fear they ought."

Wyles hesitated, as did all the men behind him. The marquise smirked as she watched them, awkward and fidgeting in their boots, avoiding one another's eyes. This was her power, Gravis thought—the same that even swayed him at times. They had her as defenseless as they could have hoped to, outnumbered and weaponless in an empty room, and *still* she could make them fear, with nothing more than her words and her confidence.

But it would not be enough; he had told her that, back in her study. He had told her she could not bluff her way out of this. And sure enough, Wyles gathered himself, tried to smile as confidently as she did. She saw it, and let one hand spill over the arm of the throne, her fingers unfurling toward him as if in invitation. The gesture was lazy, but her eyes were fixed on his face. "Come on," she said, and that smile was so wide it almost seemed hungry. "Show me what a man you are."

Wyles took one step, and then another. He had reached the base of the steps in moments, and he hesitated one last time before he placed his foot down on the bottom one, searching her face for whatever reaction he could find there.

Gravis expected Lady Margraine to smile, because she always smiled, especially when you expected her not to. But her smile had faded as Wyles had moved, and it did not spread across her face again: her lips stayed flat and thin, revealing nothing. She merely met his eyes, and waited. They held each other's gaze as he lowered his foot to the step, and then *he* smiled, into the silence that filled the hall as he stood there.

And then he flinched, and raised a hand to his chest.

In another moment he was on his knees, hunched over and grimacing with pain. And then the man behind him flinched.

By the time Nathaniel Wyles started to scream, Gravis was conscious of it, something that flowed like a wave toward the very back of the hall, surging faster and faster through the gathered men as it gained momentum. The ones at the very back turned to run, but they had no time to do more than take a few steps. And finally the first tongue of flame appeared, licking at Wyles as if from inside him. The flames spread so quickly, and yet they did not touch a thing in the hall that was not human, did not stain so much as the corner of a tapestry with ash. Only the men were burning.

Gravis turned to look at Almasy, but the shock on that usually stoic face was enough to tell him she hadn't expected this any more than he had. Yet for all her surprise, she did not so much as take a step back from the flames; she remained straight and stiff, unmoving from her place beside the throne. But Lady Margraine—

Lady Margraine staggered to her feet as if she did not know where she was, and for a moment Gravis thought she was startled. Then she took several halting, shaky steps, turned her face to the light, and he saw how pale and twisted with pain it was, heard the harsh rasp her voice made, as if every breath she drew tore at her lungs. She hunched over, one fist pressed against her heart, the other hand clutching absently at nothing. The screams were more muted now— the men were dying, or dead—and finally Lady Margraine managed to speak, though she sounded like nothing Gravis had ever heard.

"Seren," she said, her voice little more than a ragged gasp, "Seren, your arm— give me—hold—"

Hold me up, she was too proud to say, but Gravis saw the truth of it. She looked as if she might faint—she looked as if she might *expire.* Almasy, at her side, extended her arm, and Lady Margraine clutched at it as if it could keep her from drowning. Her nails were digging so hard into Almasy's arm that she must have felt it even through her clothing, but she gave no sign of pain, just made sure Lady Margraine didn't fall. When the marquise swayed on her feet, Almasy drew her other arm across her shoulders, and Lady Margraine shut her eyes, tilted backward as if she were going to swoon. She recovered, though, and stared at the last of the men.

Her laugh was so dry and weak that it crumbled to nothing nearly as soon as it left her throat, yet it chilled Gravis's blood all the same. "Look at that," she said, her voice still faint but undeniably triumphant. "Would you . . . *look* at that! It actually worked." She turned to Gravis. "How many of them . . . did your traitor say there were?"

Gravis's mind was reeling, but he heard himself answer her. "Fifty-three, my lady."

"Fifty . . . three." She was still laughing, her eyes fixed on the bodies before her. "Fifty-three . . . at a single stroke. Could even the greatest warriors boast as much?"

He knew this weakness, Gravis realized, though he had never seen it so severe. This was what they had thought illness when she was a child, that had left her exhausted and out of breath with no apparent cause. This was what she had brushed off as nothing, while the rest of them fretted and fussed and scratched their heads. And now he knew why.

"It's true," he said. "It's all true. You *are* a demon, or you made a deal with one. And all this time you told me—"

Perhaps she meant to laugh again; the noise she made was small and pained, but none the less contemptuous for that. "Don't be . . . ridiculous . . . Gravis. There's no such—no such *thing* . . . as demons. I told you that."

"But you—"

She shook her head. "Gravis, you always think so little of me, don't you? You think I needed to bargain and beg with some otherworldly creature? You think I needed . . . to *borrow* that power?" Her next laugh splintered as it left her throat, but somehow she sounded stronger. "It's *mine*. It's *always* been mine."

"You are not human, then," Gravis said. His hand was on the hilt of his sword, though he had not the faintest idea what he meant to do with it. Who on earth was his foe, at a time like this?

Lady Margraine took a halting step, staggered again as if under a new spell of dizziness, and clutched once more at Almasy's arm. She smiled at him, as self-satisfied as ever. "Oh, Gravis. In what living thing is magic more natural than in a human?"

CHAPTER FORTY

You should be abed, my lady," Seren said, shutting the door behind her. Arianrod did not answer that, nor turn to look at her. She was standing by the window, looking down at the orchard below. Though the sky had started to lighten, it was still too dark to see much. But the birds were calling as they fluttered about, no more than scraps of shadow between the trees. "They can be so noisy some days," Arianrod said.

"My lady," Seren said again, "in your condition—"

"I'm not an invalid." But she half stumbled as she turned away from the window, and leaned heavily on the sill. "I slept for hours," she insisted. "I hardly feel it anymore."

She was halfway across the room when she hesitated, swaying slightly on her feet. Seren caught her before she could stumble again; she felt so strange, as if her bones had gone as hollow as the birds'. "Damn it," Arianrod muttered, with a dry chuckle. "Well, at least more rest means more time before Gravis assaults me with the barrage of questions he is no doubt dying to ask me." She flopped back onto her bed, sinking into the pillows. "Speaking of Gravis, have he and the others returned yet?"

"Not that I know of, my lady," Seren said. "They did have . . . rather a lot of work to do."

Arianrod rolled her eyes. "*I* did the work. They're just cleaning up the mess."

That was, strictly speaking, true, but Seren wouldn't exactly enjoy the task of disposing of fifty-three charred bodies, all the same. "What happens if they're seen?"

"Oh, I expect they will be—and remarked upon, naturally. Members of the guard leading so many wagons out of the city at such a peculiar hour . . . yes, that would be strange. Who knows what rumors the common people will devise to explain it? I wouldn't dare try to guess—their ingenuity in these matters has amazed me far too many times already."

Seren took her time replying, trying to choose her words carefully. "You don't feel that they might . . . become upset, depending on which rumors they fasten on to?"

Arianrod just laughed. "Seren, if the common people are to be believed, I have, in somewhat more than three years of rule—a rule that began, let's not forget, when I murdered my father—conversed with the spirits of the dead, used forbidden sorcery to place curses upon my enemies, called upon the most preeminent scholars in the realm to devise novel methods of torture, and fed an unfortunate rentholder his own eyeballs because he disliked my new dress. If they truly wanted to become outraged at my lack of moral character, they've had plenty of opportunities."

"But if they think you've sent your soldiers to bury the bodies of innocents—"

"I thought you hated that word," Arianrod said, her smirk as keen as ever.

Seren bit her lip. "It doesn't mean anything to me. But to your people . . ."

"I take your point," Arianrod said, "but when *innocents* go missing, people tend to notice. I doubt Elgar's fifty-three were well known in Stonespire, or that they had savory reputations if they were. Once everyone realizes we haven't snatched any maidens or infants, they'll stop caring."

"And the soldiers themselves?"

Arianrod shrugged. "Gregg hasn't questioned an order in twenty years, and if Dent and the others have doubts, Gravis will put them to rest. He was always the one who distrusted me most, and he never made a secret of it. If *he* tells them that he can't offer them an explanation, but that he has no qualms about anything that happened, they'll accept that."

"Do you think he will tell them that?" Seren asked.

Arianrod propped her chin on her hand. "If you'd asked me three days ago, I wouldn't have believed it possible, but now I actually think he will. Perhaps the reality of what I'm capable of was less frightening for him than his fantasies of it—at least now he knows there were no demons involved, after all. Or perhaps he realizes how much I held myself back—how much damage I could have done, and how often, and didn't. I don't think *restraint* was something he ever attributed to me before."

Seren pressed her lips together, searching for the right words again. "Do you think . . . do you think you can really trust him with that secret?"

"By now I'm certain of it. If he were going to turn against me because of my magic, he'd have done it already."

"Perhaps he was afraid."

"Oh, don't worry about that, Seren. Gravis would never let fear hold him back from something he'd convinced himself he needed to do. He's not capable of it." She tilted her head, then reached up to brush a lock of hair back from her face. "Do you know why my father loved him so much?"

Seren scowled; Caius Margraine was not someone she liked to think on. "Because he agreed with him so much, I assume."

Arianrod laughed. "Not even close. In fact, it was for the opposite reason." She closed her eyes for a moment, then opened them again. "My father was always prone to rages, and when he was in the grip of one, what meager powers of judgment he had deserted him. What he did to me is proof enough of that, but on the day of my birth, when he saw my mother dead, he attempted to strangle the midwife, right there in the birthing chamber." She paused, perhaps waiting for a reaction, but when Seren said nothing, she continued. "He had his soldiers all about him, of course, but they weren't prepared to do anything; he was their lord, and they were sworn to his service, and so they just stood there, watching him do this thing. Well—they all but one stood there. A green recruit from out in the hills who'd been only two years in the castle guard—he was the only one to try to check my father's anger. He attacked him, actually, and tried to wrestle him to the ground. No true servant, he said, could stand by and watch his master dishonor himself."

"And that was Gravis?" Seren asked.

"That was Gravis. My father nearly killed him for getting in his way, but a few of the other men followed Gravis's lead, and eventually they subdued him. My father honored Gravis ever since." She sighed. "So you see, Gravis is incapable of any kind of prolonged deceit. He might badger me half to death during an argument, but if he ever became convinced I meant to do something he could not forgive, he would stop me or die in the attempt—almost definitely the latter, but I doubt it would make any difference to him. That's simply who he is."

She drifted into silence, and Seren moved to the window, peering down into the orchard as Arianrod had. The sky had grown lighter, and she could make out the blood apples hanging among the leaves. "You aren't going to ask me?" Arianrod said, so suddenly it took Seren a moment to make sense of her words. "About the magic?"

There was a question she wanted to ask, but she was afraid of how Arianrod might react if she did. "I could figure out enough," she said instead. "I know it isn't infinite. I know it hurts you, though I don't know why."

This silence was different—almost painfully heavy. Arianrod was staring at the ceiling, her jaw clenched tight. "Neither do I," she said at last. "And I have wished to know that as much as I ever wished to know anything."

Seren felt a shiver of unease, but she did her best to suppress it. "What do you mean?"

Arianrod still didn't look at her. She dropped her gaze to her hands instead, curling her fingers inward. "If this pain were merely the price every mage must pay, I would bear it gladly. But all the books I have read, all the research I have done—everything suggests that the mages of old could cast even the most complicated spells without any injury to themselves. Fatigue, certainly, occasionally to the point of exhaustion, but there is a world of difference between *fatigue* and what I suffer. This is not the way it is supposed to be. Something is wrong." She opened her hand again, staring at the lines of her palm. "At first I thought some weakness in my body was to blame. But I am *not* unduly weak— I've never been sickly in my life. It's something else."

Seren leaned back against the wall, trying to steady herself. "So when we were at Mist's Edge . . . you felt that pain because you had used magic?"

Arianrod made a face at that. "Yes, that was because I overexerted myself. I attempted to do something pointless, and therefore foolish—something I have tried many times before. It has never worked, and didn't then."

It was an effort for Seren to force her next words out without stammering. "And . . . before, when—when we met. That was also . . . that was magic?"

"Oh, you remembered that, did you?" Arianrod smiled. "Gods, I first came up with that spell when I was . . . seven? Eight? It was a favorite of mine when I was young—one of the first I devised that I could really be proud of."

"You could use magic when you were that young?" Seren asked. "When did you first realize you had it?"

Arianrod tapped her bottom lip. "Hmm, I wonder. There was never any great revelation for me—I think I always knew, in one way or another. At first I was just afraid I was wrong, that my childish certainty was no more than an elaborate game I was playing with myself. But I wasn't wrong."

She looked across the room, to where a lone candle was burning on her desk. "Here," she said. "Blow that out."

Seren crossed the room, and did as she'd asked. The sun had risen far enough that they were not plunged into darkness, and she could still make out Arianrod's face as she gazed at the slender wick. "For a true mage," she said, "a spell is not a painted circle or a string of arcane words. Those things, where they exist, are only crutches, for mages who are too weak to cast without them. They're like the tricks your tutor teaches you to remember your lessons; there's no need to memorize things when you simply *know* them." Then she fell silent, and stared at the candle again. She did not frown, or set her jaw, or stare unduly; she glanced at it quite casually, the way you might look out a window, or at a face you only thought you recognized. And the flame sparked itself into being again, enfolding the wick without so much as a sputter.

A smile spread across Arianrod's face, the most open expression of delight Seren had ever seen from her. "There," she breathed. "Just like that."

"And that doesn't hurt you?" Seren asked.

"That?" Arianrod laughed. "*That* is child's play. Perhaps if I lit a hundred candles at once, or continuously blew that one out and lit it again for an hour or so, I would start to feel it." But then her expression darkened, closed off slightly. "The problem is that I feel it at all—that a limit *exists* at all, where there should be none. There are things even the most talented mages have never been able to do, of course, but it wasn't due to any sort of weakness; the most impossible miracles were simply beyond them. But to have my true potential stifled like this . . . I must discover the reason for it. I must discover how it can be restored."

"It means so much to you?" Seren asked, before she could help herself. But perhaps it was the right thing to say, for Arianrod's expression opened up again.

"Of course," she said, but it wasn't dismissive, just contemplative. "Magic . . . Who could even hear the word and not desire it?" That same lock of hair had fallen back into her face again, and she twined it around her finger, smiling faintly. "Magic does not care for coin or blood or title; it cannot be bought, begged, stolen, or learned. You either have it or you don't. And if you *do* have it, what you make of it is entirely up to you."

Yet the thought of magic stirred no more covetousness in Seren than it ever had, only that same twinge of distrust. "Do you really think it's possible? That you could take away the pain?"

Arianrod didn't hesitate. "I'm sure of it. What I did to those men was the most powerful spell I have ever attempted, but even though it was a success, it was possible only through the most rigorous calculation. Like this, Seren, I can use magic only as if I were balancing an account, ever wary of spending too much. But there were people, once, for whom it was an art." She sat up with weary slowness, but her eyes were burning, as intent as they had ever been. "I have to find it. I *will* find it. I will have these damned shackles off, and then . . . what *couldn't* I do, if I were truly free? What could possibly stand in my way then?"

Seren could claim no eloquence at the best of times, but now her voice stuck in her throat, letting air fill her lungs only painfully. What could she possibly say or do, in the face of something Arianrod wanted so desperately, something Seren herself could barely understand?

After several moments of silence, Arianrod shrugged. "Well, so now you know. If you have some scruple against magic, our agreement, as ever, permits you to leave."

She did not know what to say, so she fell back on what she knew to be true. "It doesn't change anything," she said. "I am yours to command, as ever."

Arianrod lay back again, her sigh so soft that it was scarcely audible. "So you are," she said. "So you are." But then she glanced back at Seren. "You still haven't asked it."

"I—I haven't asked what?"

"Whatever it is you want to ask me."

Seren bit her lip. "You aren't going to like it."

"Then I am perfectly at liberty not to answer it. Ask."

That was a command, so Seren said, "I only . . . I don't understand. If you could do things like that—like what you did in the hall—why did you not simply erase them? The—the scars."

Arianrod looked away again, turning her eyes almost listlessly to the ceiling. "I told you, didn't I? I tried."

———

In another hour, Stonespire Hall would be opened to the public while Lady Margraine sat in judgment. All the bodies of Elgar's men had been successfully disposed of outside the walls, far enough away from any habitation that Gravis hoped they would never be found. He had pacified the ranks of his fellow guardsmen—though they were still, understandably, confused, they had agreed to accept his assurances about what had transpired the day before. But there was still one matter that needed seeing to before they were ready to open their doors.

Kern stood between Gravis and Dent, bound and chained with every possible precaution. There was a heavy bruise at his temple where Gravis had knocked him out when they were on the wall, but aside from that, he looked dignified enough, solemn and earnest, his gaze level.

Lady Margraine perched on her throne, still a bit pale in the face but otherwise sedate. They were the only people in the hall—Almasy would no doubt have preferred to be there, but she had stayed up the whole night through, and Lady Margraine had informed her that if she did not sleep until at least the afternoon, she would be tied down.

"Well, then." Lady Margraine propped her chin on her hand, glancing dismissively at Kern. "I have no strong feelings where this boy is concerned, so I'm willing to hear your opinions on the matter. There is, of course, Lady Gailin's proscription to consider, and I think we ought to follow it in this instance. The common people have no true knowledge that the throne was ever attacked. I think it best, to sustain their continued faith in the power of that throne, that they never be enlightened."

The first Lady Gailin Margraine, a far-distant ancestor, had decreed that murder, no matter how just, should never be a public spectacle or cause for celebration, and thus most Esthradian executions were carried out in private. If one of Lady Gailin's descendants wished to stage an execution in front of the people, he or she could dodge the proscription by claiming it was in the public's interest—its very sober and noncelebratory interest—to see justice done. But most of the rulers of Esthrades hewed quite close to the original decree, no doubt for the same reason Lady Gailin had made it in the first place—not, as was famed, for her ladyship's tender heart and distaste for bloodshed, but so that would-be martyrs were denied their stage.

"I agree," Dent said slowly, "that his execution should not be before the rest of Stonespire, but . . . perhaps your ladyship might wish to have it before the rest of the Stonespire *guard*."

She blinked at him. "Why would I wish to do that?"

Dent winced. "My lady, the treachery of this—begging your pardon—this whoreson fool has tainted the honor of every member of the guard. Allow us to see it restored together—and let his punishment turn aside any who'd seek to go a similar way."

Lady Margraine shrugged. "I have no objection to that. And you, Gravis? Do you agree?"

Gravis hesitated, searching for the right words. The request he had was impertinent, he knew, but he felt he had no choice but to make it. Finally he bowed, and then, so she would know he was serious, he knelt, keeping his eyes trained on the floor. He could not remember the last time he had knelt before her; perhaps he never had. The rest of them knew it, too, and there was silence throughout the room, as they waited for her or Gravis to speak.

"My lady," he said at last, "have I served you well in this matter?"

She pressed her lips together. "Well enough."

"Did I not reveal the traitor to you? Did I not apprehend him alive, that you might judge him for yourself?"

"You did." She shrugged again, but there was some discomfort in it, as if she were attempting to shake something off. "There's no need for this posturing, Gravis. What is it you wish to say?"

"I would beg"—the word was out before he considered it, and then he could not take it back—"a favor of you. Since this young man—this traitor—was among my men, since I found him and appointed him, and since it was I who uncovered his treachery . . . I ask that your ladyship render him into my care, for me to administer his justice, and me alone."

She frowned, but he could not tell if she was displeased or merely puzzled. "Your wish is . . . to be his executioner?"

"My wish is to administer his punishment with my own hands, yes," Gravis replied, "but I ask—I ask that I may do it alone."

She met his eyes for several long moments. Whatever she saw there must have satisfied her, for the tension went out of her face. "Very well, Gravis," she said. "If that is your request, I see fit to grant it. You did, as you say, discover the rat, after all." She turned to Dent. "Dent, assist Gravis with our young traitor until you have brought him down below. Then you may leave him with Gravis until judgment has been rendered."

Gravis tried not to wince; he would have preferred someone less perceptive than Dent to accompany him. For his part, Dent bowed his head wordlessly, then walked forward to take Kern by the arm. Gravis took the other, but before they could march Kern off down the hall, Lady Margraine held up a hand. "Wait." They did so, and she addressed her next words to Kern. "I suppose it is customary at times like this to ask if there is anything you'd like to say."

Kern lifted his chin. "There is. I wish it known that I regret none of what I did—I am only sorry that I failed, not that I tried."

"Had you succeeded," Lady Margraine said, "you would very quickly have become sorry that you tried. As you did not succeed, you are free to hold on to your dream of what success would have been, and need never look upon the reality." She waved them off. "He's yours, Gravis. Render your judgment as you wish."

The three of them remained in step with one another as they walked. Kern was unresisting, meekly following where they led him. Dent kept pace with Gravis, and looked calmly ahead; he did not speak. Gravis's vision was strained, focused too sharply on the space directly in front of him. He could not meet Dent's eyes.

Private executions within Stonespire Hall always took place in the dungeons, in spaces that had been bloodied so many times that one more mess hardly mattered. The room they came to was dark and low, fitting for what was meant to happen in it. Gravis pushed Kern in ahead of him, then hesitated in the doorway. He murmured back to Dent, still avoiding his gaze. "You can wait outside, if you like."

Dent shrugged, an answer that did not mean precisely yes or no, just that he understood. Gravis nodded, and shut the heavy door behind him, and then he was alone with Kern.

Gravis did not know where to begin at first, so he simply stood there and looked at him.

The boy did not speak, but he did not look away, either, just kept his chin level and his eyes calmly focused. He did not struggle against his bonds, and his lips were flat and composed. After several moments of Gravis's silence, he raised his eyebrows, but not insolently, only as if to say, *Did you not have something to tell me?*

Gravis did, but he could not get the words out as yet. Instead he said, "Why don't you tell me why you have done this thing."

"You have to ask that?" Kern said, and he truly looked surprised.

"I do," Gravis said. "I surely do, for I cannot understand it."

"Why, sir, I . . ." He pressed his lips together, considered his words, began again. "Sir, I love Esthrades. I loved Lord Caius, and I know he sits in glory among the gods."

I will be punished, Gravis, his lordship had said, before weakness and fever had taken away his lucidity. *The gods see all, and they will not spare me. Why should they? I have not deserved it.* But those words had not been spoken for Kern's ears, so Gravis said nothing, and simply nodded.

"I have no love for Elgar," Kern said, "but I have less for *her*. She spat on Lord Caius's legacy; she'll destroy it, if we continue to let her. I couldn't allow that to happen. I just couldn't." He shook his head. "Elgar needs to think he possesses this land, that's all. If he wins it this way, without waging a true war against us, he won't want to change things too drastically, for fear of angering the people. I had hoped—I had hoped I might persuade him to let you govern here. Lord Oswhent, at least, seemed amenable to the idea, and he has Elgar's ear. Who knows Esthrades the way you do? And the people love you. He would give you the command, and you would restore things to the way Lord Caius wanted them—to the way we both know is right." He set his jaw, looked Gravis in the eyes. "I know you love this land, sir. I know you do. You love it just as I do. In the service of your country, you could never give less than everything. You taught me that."

Gravis had intended his voice to come out steady and stern, yet the words he heard were melancholy, hesitant. "I do love Esthrades. I have loved it more than I could ever love another person, man or woman." He curled his fingers into a fist, the familiar feel of his armor a small comfort. "What makes you think her ladyship does not love it?"

Kern blinked at him. "What?"

"Let me put it another way," Gravis said. "You seem to think her a greater danger to Esthrades than Elgar. *He* would conquer this country by force and absorb it into his own, so whatever you think *her* capable of must be truly foul. I ask you, then: What is it she has done, to bring you to this opinion? What atrocity has she committed?"

The boy only stared at him, his eyes so earnest and astonished, so very blue.

Gravis sighed. "Much of the fault in this is mine, Kern, and I admit that freely. I gave you too much praise too soon; I was so certain you were following in my footsteps that I never once turned back to see if you had strayed. Perhaps worst of all, I never kept my personal dislike for her ladyship a secret from you, and it seems I should have. I will always regret that." He paused, clenching his fist again and releasing it. "I cannot blame you for sharing my dislike—indeed, perhaps mine even nurtured yours. But to allow that dislike to blind you to your responsibilities, to think for one instant that it gives you sufficient cause to betray your sworn liege—that is foolish and ignominious. It is unforgivable."

"Captain," Kern said, "if your service becomes merely a stone around your neck—"

"You are not released from your oath the moment you stop enjoying it," Gravis snapped. "If it were easy to keep your vows, you would not need to *swear*—to tie your honor to your service, so that, whatever you may think, you cannot put off one without the other. It is the virtue of a soldier to hold fast, not startle away like a sparrow at the first harsh word he hears or the first time his liege chooses not to follow his advice. You *hold fast*, no matter what comes. Even if it means nothing in the end."

"Even if it means dishonoring yourself?" Kern asked quietly.

Gravis shook his head. "If your liege had ever given you a command your conscience would not let you follow—as I am certain she has not—it would have been your duty to do everything you could to turn her from that path. If you could not, it would have been your duty to refuse to aid her in dishonoring herself, and to accept any punishment she wished to give you for your disobedience. It would *never*, in any situation or under any circumstance, be your duty to feign obedience while selling her to her enemies in secret, out of supposed loyalty to a man you never knew and could not possibly understand." He gritted his teeth. "In the midst of your contempt for her ladyship, did you somehow forget she is our lord's only daughter? Can you truly think he would ever wish harm or misfortune upon her, no matter what she might become?" *I will surely be punished, Gravis,* Lord Caius had said. *For every stroke I laid against my daughter's back, I will receive a thousand in the world beyond. And so it should be. I will deserve every one of them.* "Had you succeeded in your plan, Lord Caius himself would have returned to this world to snap your neck for committing such deeds in his name."

Kern's face had crumpled, as if he were going to cry. "I'm sorry," he whispered. "I . . . I am so sorry, sir. I never meant to disappoint you so."

"I know that," Gravis said. "And you are not truly the one I am most angry with. This was Lord Oswhent's plan—you told me that, did you not? And Lord Oswhent hoped, as you did, that I might join you."

Kern bowed his head. "That's right."

Gravis clenched his fist again, and this time his voice did not shake. "Then there is something I need this Lord Oswhent to understand. One thing, above all else. He is a smart man, I don't doubt, and he used that intelligence well. I don't blame him for trying to take the Esthradian throne for his master; that is his purpose, and without it Elgar would surely have no use for him. But he did something else." He met Kern's eyes. "He believed he knew what kind of a man I was. He believed I would abandon my oath for a chance at power, merely because my liege and I have our disagreements. Do you understand what that means?"

"Sir, I—"

Gravis's stomach roiled, but he suppressed it; his path was clear. "It means he took me for a man without honor. For that mistake I would gladly send him his head, if I could." His fingers tightened on the hilt of his sword. "Since I cannot, yours will have to do."

————

Once it was done, and once he had recovered his composure, he opened the door. But the hallway was empty; Dent was gone.

Gravis found him patrolling the orchard, walking among the shadows of the blood apple trees. He was whistling to the birds again, but he turned when he heard Gravis's footsteps. "Gravis?" he asked. "What's bothering you?"

"You didn't wait," Gravis said. He didn't know what else to say. "You didn't wait outside the door. You didn't make sure that justice was done."

"There was no need," Dent said calmly.

"No?"

"No," Dent said. "How many years have we served together? I know your heart, Gravis. Can you really think I would believe for a moment that you intended to deceive us?"

That was one weight off his heart, but it still felt so heavy. "I used to think myself a fair judge of men, and especially of the men under my command," he said. "I don't understand how I could have been so blind to the deceit in him. I was used to it from rulers, nobles, but I thought, a *soldier*—"

"You weren't wrong," Dent said. "Not completely. You looked for doubt, and you found none. You just didn't know that was because he'd already gone too far to the other side." He scratched his nose. "We all make mistakes, Gravis. You corrected this one, and everything turned out all right in the end, didn't it?"

"Not for him," Gravis said.

"And whose fault do you think that was? It was his own foolishness that drove him to treason, never doubt that."

Gravis looked down at the grass. "When Lord Caius still lived, I begged him to see her married. She was his heir, of course, but a husband could . . . soften her, I thought, or curb her stubbornness, at least." Dent was frowning, but that was an old disagreement, and one Gravis knew well. "Lord Caius always refused. 'My own father tried to marry me off,' he said, 'and I wouldn't have it either. My marriage may have brought me as much grief as joy, but I chose it for myself, and I would not change it. She has the right to choose her own misery as well, and I'll let no man compel her otherwise.'"

Dent laughed. "That sounds like him."

"After that," Gravis said, "I became convinced Esthrades was doomed. She showed about as much interest in marriage as butterflies do in beefsteak, and with her sitting the throne alone . . . I could scarcely imagine what orders I might hear then. When has she ever wanted to do anything but just as she likes? When has she ever shown the slightest bit of consideration for justice or compassion or honor? I imagined there was nothing she would not do if it would amuse her, and that we'd live to see the fields burn and the treasury run dry, the common folk spared or slaughtered at her whim."

He shook his head. "It never happened, of course. She rules . . . irreverently, infuriatingly, but *well*. Better—better than her father ever did, though it galls me to my soul to say so. And I . . . I still don't know *why*. Part of me still thinks I'll wake up one morning to burning fields." He looked at Dent. "How do you have such faith in her?"

Dent was looking away, through the soft morning light at the branches of the trees. "You're an old friend, Gravis, so I'll tell you the truth, as embarrassing as it is. I'd have to say it's the birds. More than anything else, I think it's because of the birds."

Gravis raised an eyebrow at him. "Is that some fable?"

"It's something that happened with her ladyship," Dent said. "Many, many years ago, when I was on patrol in this very orchard. She liked to come down and talk to me sometimes, when she was in the mood to talk to someone. And one day she came dragging a book near half as big as she was, while I was watching the birds. 'Denton,' she said—that was back when she used to insist on calling me Denton when my own mother never did, out of some caprice no one could ever determine—'do you know what I read today, Denton?' she said, and I told her I imagined it was a great many things, as she liked it so much. 'I read today,' she said, 'that a pinch of craehen's wort will kill an adult human in half an hour. Is that true?'

"I told her I couldn't swear to it myself, but I reckoned if her book said so, then it was true. 'But that's *all*?' she asked. I told her that people are very fragile creatures, when you get right down to it. Then she scrunched up her little face in that way she had, and she said, 'But *I* don't feel very fragile, and I'm a lot smaller than an adult.' 'Nobody ever feels it about themselves,' I said. 'You're your whole world, aren't you, and how could the world just cease to be one day?'

"So then she looked at the birds. She asked me, were the birds fragile? They certainly were, I said—much more delicate than the two of us. And she asked—" He swallowed. "She pointed to a sparrow, and asked if it would die if I shot it. 'I'm no expert with a bow,' I said, 'but if I *hit* it, then yes, I expect it would.' It would die *forever*, she asked? Yes, I said. Forever and a day.

"She thought about that for a moment, and then she said—she said, 'If I told you to shoot it, would you shoot it?' And what could I say to that, Gravis? She was mistress of Stonespire, and I told her as much, and that I'd do as she bade me, unless her father bade me otherwise. 'What about all the birds?' she asked. 'What if I told you to shoot *all* the birds in the orchard?' And I knew—I knew I had to say something.

"Trouble was, if anyone ever told her she *shouldn't* do a thing, that only ever made her more determined to do it—and woe betide the man who ever dared tell her she *couldn't* do it. So I took my time thinking about it, and I answered her in what seemed to me the best way.

"'Here's the thing, little mistress,' I said. 'I don't know how you feel about birds, but I like them. I like to hear them sing, to watch them flutter about when I take my rest here. It might be you like that too, and it might be you don't now, but you'll grow to like it in time. Or it might be you never do, and you never have any use for these fellows here. Now, I'm sworn to your service, and if you tell me to shoot them, I'll set aside my personal feelings and do as you say. But if I do that for you, and you find out this old orchard's too quiet without them, I won't be able to make them sing again, no matter how much I want to. So perhaps you'd be happiest if you thought on it awhile, and asked yourself if you might have a use for birdsong one day.'

"She screwed up her little face again, and she looked at the birds, and she looked at me, as if she were trying to figure out if I meant to trick her. But she gave me a nod, in the end. 'Very well,' she said, as prim and proper as you please. 'I will think on it.' And then she picked up that great book of hers and wandered off, and that was that."

Dent craned his neck, looking up at the crowded bustle of little wings about the trees. "It's been more than fifteen years since that day, Gravis, and those birds are still here. I guess I just have to tell myself that means something."

CHAPTER FORTY-ONE

"Shall we assume they're dead, then?" Elgar asked.

Varalen sighed. "Probably. I haven't heard a single word from Stonespire since I gave the order." He dug his thumb into the ridge of bone above one eye, trying to drive out the ache. "Who knows? Perhaps if we wait a bit longer, we'll receive tokens from the rest of them as well."

By the time the rider had arrived at the Citadel, the stink wafting off the head had grown so severe that Varalen had nearly retched when he opened the box. The note that accompanied it was simple enough, a scant two sentences long:

Lord Oswhent,
You may not recognize him—indeed, perhaps you never met him face-to-face—but this was Kern. Next time, I hope I may have the pleasure of your neck beneath my sword.

—Gravis Ingret

"Captain Ingret seems to have developed quite the grudge against you," Elgar said. "I wonder what the boy told him."

"Enough for him to know I was behind it, clearly," Varalen said. "And, by extension, that you were."

"Yes, but I'm not the one he's so angry at, am I?" Elgar traced the edge of the table with his fingertips. "I wonder that you ever thought it wise to allow the boy to try to turn him."

"*I* never thought anything of the sort, and you know it. *You* were the one who told me I should give the boy whatever assurances he needed to play his part, so I told him what he wanted to hear. That's all." He laughed weakly. "He was such a little fool—he really thought he could just flick Arianrod Margraine out of the way and set his precious captain up in her place, as you might pluck a single rose and leave the rest undisturbed. As for the captain, what I saw of him at Mist's Edge led me to believe there was a *chance* he might turn against his mistress—he clearly has no love for her. That was a mistake, obviously."

"And not the only one, either." Elgar stroked his knee. "I'd say it's a waste, but even a failed endeavor can prove worthwhile if it allows us to learn something."

"Well, *I* didn't learn anything," Varalen said. "Nothing besides rumors, anyway, and I even had less of *those* than usual. I had so many people inside that city, and now it's as if they've been pulled out by the roots." At least Wyles seemed to have perished with the rest of the men, though the news coming out of Stonespire had been worryingly vague about what precisely happened to them.

"You wagered too many of them," Elgar said.

Varalen shook his head. "What I don't understand is how she *did* it. My predictions weren't off, I'm sure of that. Our men should've outnumbered hers two to one, and they had the advantage of surprise, the difficulty of defending the hall once the walls have been breached. . . . I went over it again and again. I was as sure of that strategy as I've ever been of anything. I can't understand how she defeated them, and left no trace." He let his hand fall heavily to the table. "No matter how smart she is, if she hadn't detected what we'd been doing beforehand, she shouldn't have been able . . . Well, maybe that's it. Maybe she figured it out, and just pretended that she wasn't aware of it. But even so . . ." He trailed off, shaking his head again.

Elgar almost looked as if he were enjoying this. What had gotten into him these past few weeks? "You needn't worry so about it," he said. "It was an excellent strategy, and it ought to have worked under any normal circumstances. It's just a pity we couldn't use it at Mist's Edge or in Issamira."

He was right about that—Stonespire Hall had only ever been intended to be the seat of a minor lord, but Mist's Edge and Eldren Cael were military fortresses, even though a city had sprung up about the walls of the latter. The only way to get that many men inside *them* would be to pass them off as soldiers or servants, and that many traitors in close quarters were bound to raise suspicion. "Well, then." He sighed. "What will you have of me now? Is it time to turn to Reglay?"

"You're giving up so easily?"

Was Elgar baiting him? He had to be. "Nothing about this is *easy*, my lord, but this was my best plan, and I truly think—"

Elgar waved a hand at him. "Yes, yes, I know. You're right, of course; Reglay should be easy enough to snap up. I should even be able to give you the command without much worry."

Varalen pressed his knuckles into his forehead, hard enough to hurt. "If you are not pleased with my service, my lord, you are entirely at liberty to cut me loose."

Elgar smiled. "Oh, you don't want me to do that."

"Don't I?"

Elgar said nothing to that. He just waited, expectant, for the rest.

"At this point," Varalen said at last, "I am rather tired of being a constant disappointment. I am . . . rather tired in general. This may be as far as I can go. If it is not enough for you . . . well, you may do as you will, and perhaps I will prove to be too weary even to complain."

Elgar raised an eyebrow, his lips pursing slightly. "And what of your son? Can you go no further on his behalf, either?"

Varalen balled his hands into fists, tried to keep them steady atop his knees. "My son . . ." He could not allow himself to think of Ryam's face. "You know my son's condition. I have not tried to hide it from you, and I probably could not have done so even if I'd wished to. Whether you decide to show him mercy or not, he . . . he will not live long. He cannot live long, no matter what I do." He swallowed hard, trying ineffectually to dislodge the lump in his throat. "I believed that it was my duty as his father to lengthen his life as much as I could, whatever the cost. But for the sake of another fortnight, or a few more months . . . shall I surrender everything? Is it truly right to do so?" He laughed. "You don't care about my *moral* struggles, I'm sure; you only want to know if you can depend on me or not. The answer is I don't believe you can. I believe that I have had my fill of all this, and you must do whatever you will do about it."

Elgar *still* did not fly into a rage; he merely kept sitting there, and he almost smiled. "Normally," he said, "that would be acceptable, and I could give you the rest you seem to crave. But for now I am afraid I need you to go somewhat further. I am"—he did smile then—"somewhat hard on you, I know, but really you've served me quite well, and in the days ahead I must make full use of whatever resources I have at my disposal. That means I'll need you to keep working, and even to stretch your plans to loftier heights."

"Did you not hear me? I cannot continue, Elgar. I will not."

"Mm," Elgar said. "I have heard that before."

"And you'll hear it again, until it sticks."

"No doubt." He raised one hand, examining his palm. "Your plan for Stonespire truly wasn't a complete waste, you know."

Varalen sighed. "I know. You *learned* something."

"I did," Elgar said calmly. "I learned that, despite her vanity, Arianrod Margraine does quite well for herself when backed into a corner. And I learned I don't have to fear her as much as I'd . . . well, feared."

That brought Varalen up short. "You *don't* have to? Didn't you just say she'd exceeded your expectations?"

"Oh, I'd always allowed for the possibility of your plan's failure," Elgar said. "But you yourself told me that the marquise seems to have taken ill right around that time, didn't you? Or at least that's what your little rumormongers called it."

"That's . . . true," Varalen allowed, "but why does it matter?"

"I always suspected the extent of her abilities," Elgar said, "but I rather worried she'd outstripped me somehow—that she'd found a way around it, or perhaps never even had to live with it in the first place. But that isn't true. She is limited just as I am—no matter what, we have that in common."

Varalen looked at him blankly. "You have *what* in common?"

Elgar smiled, further lifting his raised hand, fingers spread and palm facing outward. "Why, this, of course."

At first a vague halo of light shimmered into existence around his fingers, and then it was flame, wrapped around his hand but not burning it, just hanging there, suspended.

"Gods preserve me," Varalen gasped, throwing himself so far backward that he upended his chair and spilled himself onto the floor. The impact knocked the breath from his lungs, and he lay there in a heap, gaping senselessly at the light that had enveloped Elgar's fingers.

Elgar laughed. "What, no rebuttal? No jokes for that, eh? I'm almost disappointed." When Varalen's mouth opened and closed again without any sound, Elgar lowered his hand, and the flames dispersed, dying down as if they had never been. "I rather thought you'd continue to assure me that such things don't exist."

Varalen raised himself onto one elbow; his other limbs were still a bit too shaken from his fall. "How did you—how—"

"Hmm," Elgar said. "Well, there's no such thing as magic, so I suppose it must have been some charlatan's trick. Perhaps I simply hid a flint up my sleeve and . . . No, that wouldn't work, would it? I wonder."

"You—you—" He coughed, finally managing to sit up. "You could always—do that?"

"Of course," Elgar said. "Since I was a boy."

"So you—you *knew*," Varalen said. "You knew about—about"—the word, which had always come so easily to him before, stuck in his throat now—"about *magic,* and you just let me think—"

"I always told you I knew magic existed," Elgar said. "You simply never believed me before."

"Damn right I didn't, because you never—"

"Because you thought I was a superstitious fool, and I knew you were a contemptuous one. I endured your scorn, Varalen, and your conceit, and your little moments of preening, because you were talented, and because I had no need for you to know the truth. But now, I think, some humility is called for."

Varalen's throat was dry, but he managed to steady himself. "Be all that as it may, I have just said I do not care what you do with me. What difference does it make whether you cut my head off with a sword or with some strange power? The result is the same, and the torments that can be visited on a man are finite."

"They are not," Elgar said, "but you mistake my meaning. We were speaking of your son, I believe?"

"And I have said—"

Elgar held up a hand, and Varalen flinched from it reflexively, even though the flames didn't return. "Yes, yes, I know what you said. Stop talking for once, Varalen, and *listen*. I will use short sentences. Your son is very ill, yes? Yes, deathly ill. And magic can be used for many things." He drew his dagger, the one Varalen had never seen out of its sheath, and closed the fingers of his free hand around Varalen's wrist. The cut he made was shallow, a diagonal line across Varalen's palm. Varalen barely felt it, but then Elgar pressed his thumb along the length of the wound. For a moment the pain was sharp, and then he felt nothing. And then Elgar drew his hand away, and he saw there was no cut—no blood on Elgar's fingers at all.

"Magic," Elgar said, "can do that as well."

And Varalen felt a fear he hadn't before—the fear of hoping for too much, for things that were impossible.

"I'll make you a deal, Varalen," Elgar said, leaning back in his chair. "So long as you remain in my service, I will keep your son alive. And on the day all my enemies are gone, and Elesthene is mine once more, your son's disease will disappear as well."

Varalen had just managed to recover his breath, only to lose it again. "You . . . you can do that?"

"I can." He crossed one leg over the other, brushing his fingers against the edge of the nearest map. "So. Do we have a deal?"

Varalen swallowed hard, and then again, searching for his voice. "Yes."

Elgar's eyes were fastened on his. "Yes *what*?"

He curled his fingers into a fist, then released it, dropping his gaze to the floor. "Yes, Your Eminence."

———

The letter was written in a crabbed, clumsy hand, the parchment full of ink-blots and an occasional crossed-out word or phrase. *"Kelken,"* Kel read, *"you quivering jelly, you assume all men share your lack of spine. Just because you cringe and snivel at the thought of Eira, it does not hold that I must therefore bend the knee to him. As for Jotun, I have no great love for him, and my daughter could rule more com—competently in her sleep than that precious heir of his, but the boy may have the right of it in this. If these* wardrenfell"—the word was crossed out three times before he'd managed to spell it correctly—*"are really as powerful as Eira says, we're much better off making sure that sack of bilgewater doesn't get his hands on any to start with, rather than hoping he'll only use them against Elgar. You hope that cooperating with him will earn you his favor, but just because you lick his asshole now, it doesn't mean he won't shove a sword up yours later. Do as you like, you tit, but don't expect me to change my plans on your account."*

Kel's face had grown a bit pink from reading all that aloud, and when he looked up, he saw that Lessa's had too. "So that's what her father was like."

Lessa tilted her head. "I'd say they couldn't be more different, but . . . well, they're both stubborn, aren't they? And they both have what I suppose you'd call a way with words. Just a . . . very different way."

Kel looked back down at the letter. "I'd love to call someone a sack of bilge-water."

"I'm sure you would, but I doubt it would do you any favors. And you're quite a bit less threatening than Caius Margraine, you know." She grinned at him, then turned back to the pile. "Are there any from her in there? There must be. It's been three years since her father died."

It was somehow odd to think of Arianrod Margraine corresponding with his father, but Lessa was right—if his father had kept letters from the time Lord Caius was still alive, he must've kept hers as well. He didn't seem to have put them in any sort of order, though, so Kel was just left to sift through stacks and stacks of paper. He chose a pile and started rifling through the letters it contained, looking for some handwriting quirk or turn of phrase that recalled Lady Margraine. The one he finally found caught his attention first for its brevity, and only second for her signature at the bottom. *I have found, Kelken,* she had written, in handwriting that was elegant but a bit irregular, each letter curling and looping into the next, *that it is never better not to know something. But since that is your answer, I have nothing to tell you either.*

"Hmm," Lessa said, when he read it to her. "I wonder what she wanted to know?"

"About the *wardrenfell,* probably," Kel said. "It seems like that's what they were all talking about. Too bad we're not any closer to knowing what it *is,* or even if they ever found it."

Lessa was staring at the letters. "Do you think she'd be surprised if she could see what he wrote about her?"

"Eh?"

She smiled sheepishly. "Sorry. I meant what Caius Margraine wrote about his daughter in that letter—something about her being more competent than Prince Landon?"

Kel picked up the letter again. *"My daughter could rule more competently in her sleep than that precious heir of his*—is that what you mean?"

"Right, exactly. It just surprised me, that's all. Didn't she seem to think he never thought much of her?"

"She said he never *listened* to her," Kel said, "but maybe that's not the same thing." His father had never listened to him, either, but he hadn't been any less determined to have Kel rule because of that.

"Oh, is that what she said? Maybe you're right." Lessa shrugged. "I just wondered what she'd think if she could read it."

"Well, we could send it to her, I suppose—aren't these the ones she asked for anyway?" Kel frowned at the pile. "They're not proving to be very useful, though."

Lessa followed his gaze. "Didn't they say Eira was the one most likely to get his hands on . . . I'm not sure if I should say *the wardrenfell* or *a wardrenfell*? Either way, if that's so, perhaps you should look for letters from Eira."

Kel did, and finally found one, a single sheet of parchment covered in thin, spidery script, cultured but somehow forbidding. The letters were thin and faded, as if the writer hadn't used enough ink. *"Kelken,"* he read, *"I must confess that matters have not progressed as I had wished. The soldier I sent to investigate reports of a* wardrenfell *near the border was one of my best, a man in whom I had every confidence. He returned, but worse than empty-handed. It seems the* wardrenfell *has inflicted upon him a most curious wound, one that has confounded every healer I sent to tend to him. The wound itself should not be mortal, but it will not heal, no matter how much time passes. I do not mean it has become infected—indeed, the healers say it is the cleanest wound they have ever seen. But stitch and bandage it as they may, it inevitably splits itself open anew, as fresh as the moment it was made. He has lost quite a bit of blood already, and at this rate he will surely die.*

"He told me what he could—it was meager and confused, but it was enough. Mark me, Kelken: though we sought to use the power of the wardrenfell *to defeat Elgar, I now believe that the danger posed by her is greater than any other we currently face—"*

Kel broke off, reading the last few lines again, then looked up at Lessa. Her startled face must have been a mirror image of his own. "Did he say—"

"Her," Lessa repeated. "The danger posed by *her*. Not *it*."

Kel sat back in his chair, letting the parchment flutter unimpeded to the desk. "A *wardrenfell* is a *person*," he said.

———

The other soldiers made quite a commotion when they saw him, but Shinsei had expected that. He kept his fingers tightly wrapped around the hilt of his sword, and gritted his teeth against the noise. "Tell my master I have returned," he said, in response to all their questions, "and ask him what he wishes of me." His master would not be pleased with him, he knew, and he had wondered many times if he even ought to return at all. But where else would he go? His master had always been patient with him, and Shinsei could only hope he would be so again.

He did not have to wait long before he was told his master would see him in his chambers. That was right—the others were all afraid of him, but his master was different. That made him feel a little better, and he climbed the steps without faltering.

His master was seated when Shinsei entered, as if in the middle of some task, though his hands were empty. He looked up, and though his face changed slightly, Shinsei could not read it. "Well," he said, with a quizzical lift of his eyebrows. "You took your time returning, didn't you?"

Shinsei bowed his head. "Forgive me. I . . . Things became more difficult than I could have guessed."

"That's putting it mildly." But there was no sharpness in his tone. He leaned back in his chair, crossed one leg over the other. "Tell me what happened, Shinsei."

"What happened." At first he could only repeat the words, but then he drew himself together, tried to put his memories in some semblance of order. "I went to the castle. To Second Hearth. I found the king, just like you told me to."

"And killed him, it seems," his master said. "But I told you to take care of the boy as well, did I not?"

"You did. But I—" He shook his head, trying to clear it. "The king tried to grapple with me, and told the boy to run. The boy's legs were bad, though, and I caught him. I—I would have killed him, but there was—" He shut his eyes, seeing it again. "There was this girl, and she—she had—"

His master caught his breath, and understanding dawned upon his face. "A girl with golden hair—the queen's bastard. Yes, I saw her." He sighed. "And this girl recalled the other in some way, did she?"

"The other." The girl in the snow, with her slender sword and clear, carrying voice. The girl who had called him a coward. And that was what he had seen in the eyes of the girl at Second Hearth. She had not spoken, not to him, but she had met his eyes. The reproach he had seen in hers was an echo of the anger he had seen in the other, anger that had burned so bright he wanted to cover his eyes, to crawl away to some dark place. "Why is it," he asked, as he had asked himself so many times, "that I am a coward?"

His master sighed again. "You are not a coward, Shinsei. You simply pay too much heed to the arguments of children."

His master was right, of course. His master was so much cleverer than he was. Shinsei hunched his shoulders, looking at the floor. "I'm sorry."

"Tell me what happened after that. Why did it take you so long to return?"

That was harder to remember. "I . . . After I saw that girl, I . . . wandered about. I don't think I properly knew myself. There was a man I killed—no, two men—or maybe . . ." He winced. "Maybe more than that."

If his master minded about the men, he did not show it. "But you eventually came to yourself again."

"Yes." After that he could remember more clearly. "I wondered about whether I should try to kill the boy again, but when I asked about him, they told me he was no longer at Second Hearth, that he keeps his court at Mist's Edge now. I didn't think I'd be able to get into Mist's Edge the way I did at Second Hearth, so . . . so I decided to come back, and wait for you to tell me what I should do."

"I see." His master pressed his fingertips together, tilting his head as he considered something. "You always tell me the truth, don't you, Shinsei?"

Shinsei nodded. "Of course."

"Then tell me this: Do you think I can trust you, if I send you far away again? Will you do what I ask of you? Or will you lose yourself again, like you did this time?"

Shinsei did always tell his master the truth, but this was a difficult question. He stroked the hilt of his sword, searching within himself for the answer. "I never wish to fail you," he said. "But it seems there are more and more things I don't understand. There are so many more things in the world than I could have guessed—I don't know if I can say for sure that one of them won't . . . make me strange." He shook his head. "I don't know why. I wish—I wish I could stop."

"If you truly wished that," his master said almost wearily, "then you *would* be able to stop. You torment yourself only because you think about things you shouldn't." He looked about to say more, but then he broke off with a vague click of his tongue. "Well, that's good enough. Let's stop there for now. You may return to your quarters—we will advance on Reglay soon enough, and I'll need you in the army when we march."

"I understand." He might have left it there, but more words sprang to his lips, bubbling forth with an urgency that almost frightened him. "I . . ." he started, almost stammering, "may I ask you one thing?"

His master frowned, but he said only, "What is it, Shinsei?"

Shinsei hesitated for a moment, but the question would not be denied. "Did I—did I ever know anyone named Sebastian?"

His master stayed very still for what seemed like a long time, and Shinsei could not read his face. "That name means nothing to me," he said at last.

"Oh," Shinsei said. "I see."

His master threaded his fingers together, still watching him closely. "Was that all you wanted to ask me?"

Shinsei nodded.

"Then you should get some rest."

Shinsei bowed, and left for his quarters. But he could not rid himself of the vision, despite what his master had said. There was an idea—a memory, perhaps—flickering faintly inside his mind, like a candle that would not go out.

In the vision, a young man had a hand on his arm, and was pulling him toward something. His hair was very pale. He was smiling. *Come on, Ritsu,* he said. *We'll be late if you keep dragging your feet like that.*

But, Sebastian, he said, *your father told you—*

Oh, my father's always telling me one thing or another. When'll we get the chance to see something like this again, eh?

That was all—try as he might, he could retrieve nothing more of it. But who was this Sebastian? And who, for that matter, was Ritsu?

CHAPTER FORTY-TWO

Cadfael put one foot in front of the other more out of stubbornness than anything else, distractedly watching his boots bite into the dust. He trudged forward as one who has dreamed his destination, barely more than an abstract idea somewhere beyond the horizon. His throat was dry, scratchy, as if lined with parchment, and sweat made the dust stick to his face and palms, despite the early morning chill. There was no blue in the sky that he could see, just oppressive clouds that reminded him uncomfortably of Mist's Edge.

The resolve he'd felt the day he left the castle had drained away the farther he got from it. The king had been understanding in every way; he had never tried to stop him, never offered any incentives to get him to stay. But Cadfael wondered, even so, if it had not been wrong of him to leave. The boy would need all the help he could get in the hard times to come, and what good was Cadfael doing anyone like this? Did he really have a hope of finding Shinsei?

He had been sure Elgar would not appear at Mist's Edge without his most trusted general, and yet he had. But if Shinsei was not with him, where could he be? What mission could be more important than protecting Elgar's life?

He wanted to strike something. Where would he even go next? Where could he search? He did not even know what Shinsei looked like; the man could pass by three inches from his face and he'd never suspect a thing. And the people who had ever seen him were few and far between; for someone as infamous as Shinsei undoubtedly was, he was remarkably elusive. Why was that? Cadfael wondered. Wouldn't such a legendary butcher relish the chance to strike fear into the hearts of all he met, simply through the force of his reputation?

The trees were starting to thin, and he could make out the shape of the hills beyond. He leaned against a nearby tree, calming his breathing so he could listen. He hadn't yet been able to determine the exact number of men following him; he guessed three, but it might well be four or five. He did not need to ask them who they were or why they were following him; he merely needed to decide how best to dispose of them. If the one creeping up on what he no doubt thought was Cadfael's blind spot could be encouraged to move just a few steps closer, Cadfael could have him at a stroke. But, truth be told, he didn't much care—this was the third time this had happened since he'd left Mist's Edge, and his patience was wearing thin.

"Awful morning," he said conversationally, and by the time the man had finished being startled, Cadfael's sword was already bare and in midswing. The man flung up his swordarm in a clumsy attempt at a block, so Cadfael cut it off for him, then swung again. This one caught the man right through the middle, tearing leather and flesh alike. Cadfael could tell he wouldn't be getting up again, but two more men were already bounding into view, weapons drawn. Cadfael thought there was a fourth somehow ahead of him, though he'd never sensed he was being passed. The last man seemed a ways off yet, though from the sound of it, he was hurrying to catch up. Better to finish with his fellows quickly, then.

The swordsmen were not wholly useless, but that did not save them: after only a handful of exchanges, Cadfael had cut the legs from under the first and beheaded the second. He made sure to give the former an additional cut afterward to end his suffering, but that was all the time he had—there was definitely a fourth man, and he was closing in fast. Cadfael darted behind a tree, hoping to conceal his position, and after several seconds he saw the last man. He was moving quickly, but starting to slow down a bit, perhaps because the sounds of battle had stopped. The fool hadn't even drawn his sword.

Cadfael charged from behind the tree, aiming his strike at the other man's heart, and the man's sword left its sheath so fast, Cadfael could barely see it. It met his in a beautiful, assured swing, driving him back a step that very nearly became a stumble.

The other man smiled. "You don't think it's a bit early in the morning for such fervent combat?"

"You seem apt enough," Cadfael grunted, and swung again.

The man blocked him again, just as smoothly as before—he had enough time to toss his long hair back from his face before his riposte, which Cadfael only just managed to block. He might not have been anything of a success in other areas, but swordplay was what he *knew,* and he couldn't remember the last time he'd been thwarted so easily. The other man, whose sword and build were a touch slighter than Cadfael's, relied more on his speed, so the closeness of the trees should've hampered him—but if it did, Cadfael saw no sign of it. His every movement was precise and surpassingly confident, and Cadfael had to struggle to keep his own strokes sure despite the rapidity of the other man's onslaught.

The man's eyebrows lifted curiously—was he impressed, or just surprised Cadfael wasn't dead yet? He was still smiling. "Well, look at that. It seems I'll have to try harder."

Cadfael saved his breath for his next swing, and his next. They moved about without a significant change in either's position, exchanging blows that never landed but were never countered by anything decisive. Cadfael's head was spinning, his palms sweating against the hilt of his sword. The other man slashed at him again and again, his dark hair streaming out behind him as he flew to meet Cadfael—that was what it seemed like, like his feet didn't even touch the ground between strides as he ran, as he spun and struck.

"Who *are* you?" he asked, as Cadfael's sword met his.

But Cadfael was not thinking of names, only of the movements he must perform, where the other man's blade would be in half an instant and the space his own would have to travel through to meet it, the space both swords would occupy after the parry. He understood, in some back corner of his mind, that the clang of metal was deafening. He barely heard it.

"You're *good,*" the other man said, in something like wonder. "You're one of the best I've ever fought with, do you know that?"

Cadfael thought he grunted, throwing his shoulder into the next swing but failing to stagger his opponent. The other man pivoted, and Cadfael nearly pitched forward, righting himself just in time to make the next block, though the force of the impact drove him to one knee.

"I'll ask you again," the other man said, eyes gleaming above him, bright as the blade of his sword. "Who are you?"

Cadfael struggled, managed to push up off his bent knee, forcing the other man back as he took his feet again. "Cadfael," he muttered, "is my name. A lot of good it'll do you."

"And is your name known?" the other man asked, slicing the air as he adjusted his grip on his sword. "Because I promise you, it will be."

Shouldn't the man who had been sent to kill him know his name? "It's known enough," he said, panting, "to make me wish it were known less. But most of those who used to know it are dead." Block, block, block—he wanted to dodge, but the man was so *fast*—

"I could say the same," the man said—nonchalantly enough, but Cadfael could see how he was sweating. "Do you mind if I ask what we're fighting over? Do you just want my coin, or can you possibly have some grudge against me?"

Cadfael nearly dropped his guard, recovering just in time to block again. "Is that some joke? I'm trying to kill you because you're trying to kill me."

"My friend, I'm not trying to kill you, I'm just trying to defend myself. If you recall, you were the one who came at me—I hadn't even drawn my sword."

No, Cadfael thought, *not that that seemed to hamper you much.* The lull in their battle gave him time to examine the man's sword more closely, and he felt a throb of pain as he realized its similarity to one he would never see again. It was a *tsunshin*—uncommon enough in these parts, to be certain. "Are you trying to tell me," he said, not dropping out of his stance but not advancing either, "that you aren't with those other men?"

The man backed up a few steps. "I am certainly saying that, as I don't even know which men you mean."

"They're dead," Cadfael said, twitching one shoulder toward where they lay. "Back there. They were Elgar's men."

"If they were trying to kill you," the man said, "then I doubt we have a quarrel." Cadfael must not have seemed convinced, because he backed up another step. "Look, I'll sheathe my sword first, see? I don't want to kill you, I swear it." He did as he said, holding his hands out in front of him.

He was young, maybe Cadfael's age or a bit younger, with features that weren't quite Aurnian—his gray eyes were too wide, his nose sharply pointed. His hair fell straight to the middle of his back, and he didn't even tie it— Cadfael had no idea how he'd kept it out of his eyes as they fought. Whatever he was, his sword was undoubtedly Aurnian; Cadfael didn't doubt the man could have it out again in less than an instant, but he backed off anyway, finally easing out of his stance.

The man smiled. "You have my thanks. I suppose I should apologize—that very nearly ended messily for at least one of us—but . . . well, you did draw first."

Cadfael didn't even know what to say. "I should . . . examine the others, then." He walked slowly back toward the bodies, keeping an eye on the man, who followed at a safe distance.

He searched the dead men, but he found nothing of note on them—not that he'd really been expecting to, as he doubted Elgar needed to send written instructions that said *kill him*. It was an easy enough command to understand, if not, in this instance, to follow.

The somewhat-Aurnian raised his eyebrows at the bodies. "Elgar isn't half angry with you, is he? What did you do to him?"

That was the question, wasn't it? He had made a grave move against Elgar at Mist's Edge, that was certain. But was that truly the only reason Elgar wanted him dead?

For what felt like the thousandth time, he thought back to Elgar's words at Mist's Edge. All Elgar had actually *said* was that he knew Cadfael for a Lanvald, but he could have deduced that in half a hundred ways. It didn't necessarily mean that he remembered Cadfael, or knew who he was. They had met only once before, and Cadfael was certain he'd been unrecognizable—his face had been bandaged, after all. He hadn't lied to this Aurnian, either—whatever fame he might have accrued under Eira was long gone. And yet, the way Elgar had looked at him . . .

"I insulted him, I believe," he said to the Aurnian. "He couldn't let that go, apparently." Was the man just going to follow him about? He sheathed his sword and folded his arms, waiting.

He didn't have to wait long. "If you're the type to insult Elgar," the man said, "maybe I can ask this of you: Where did he go? Village gossip puts him at Mist's Edge, but back in Valyanrend they say he wouldn't have so much as a single soldier occupy that castle for anything."

"He *was* there," Cadfael said, "but he must be gone by now—on his way back to Hallarnon, I assume, if he hasn't arrived already. Why, do you have business with him?"

The man's fingertips brushed the hilt of his sword. "Of a sort."

He reminded Cadfael of the way he himself spoke of Shinsei. "Has he wronged you in some way?"

The man shrugged. "He's wronged *you* for certain, hasn't he? What with sending his men to kill you."

Cadfael leaned against a nearby tree; he was still somewhat winded from the battle. "It doesn't change anything. I had no love for him before, so I had none to lose over this. If *you* hoped for some kind of revenge, though, you'd best turn back for Hallarnon—not that I imagine you'd have much luck there."

The man brushed his hair back from his face. "No, I wasn't after revenge— nothing so definite. I wouldn't mind a chance at him, but I've more pressing business at the moment." He shrugged again. "To be honest, I doubt I possess the conviction to make an earnest attempt on his life, despite all the pain I owe him. Perhaps I merely sought the novelty of his company, if it wouldn't take me too far out of my way."

"I doubt you would have found whatever you were looking for," Cadfael said. "He's an unremarkable man in just about every way."

The man laughed, but there was no mirth in it. "Yes. That's rather what I thought." He ran a hand through his hair. "It makes me wonder how he got to where he is, or why someone doesn't just stop him."

Cadfael's father had died before he could see Elgar's greatest victories, but he had always said the people of Hallarnon wanted someone steady and plain after Gerde Selte's wild caprices and the strain of Norverian's extravagant spending. And after the breathtaking array of tortures and punishments the pair of them had dreamed up, their subjects were certainly happy to bow to someone with a less morbid imagination. Elgar liked gold, but not so much as his former master had, and he used pain as a lesson, not as entertainment. King Eira had said that it was the war against Aurnis that made Elgar's name: Hallerns and Lanvalds alike still held grudges against the Aurnians for driving their grandfathers out of their lands a hundred years ago, and the Hallerns were only too glad to think of their leader as a great conqueror, never mind what he might be like at home.

But Cadfael himself had no opinion. Perhaps that was his problem: he had always had too few opinions. His sister had had opinions about everything. "It would be difficult to stop him now, I think," he said. "Perhaps it would have been easier, once."

"Perhaps," the man said. He sighed. "I'll tell you this much: never part from your friends. It's a damned hassle to find them again, and ten to one you won't."

Cadfael had no friends to speak of, though he couldn't help thinking of King Kelken. Most likely he would never see him again. "Either way," he said, "I wish you luck. Though with a swordarm like that, I doubt you'll need much of it."

The man laughed, and this one sounded genuine. "Oh, well, you nearly had me, for all that. I won't press you for details, but you're no common soldier, that's for certain."

That was exactly who he had been. As for who he was now, he wasn't sure. "I have told you my name."

"So you did—Cadfael, was it? I'll remember it. But it seems I haven't told you mine." He extended his hand, features smoothing into a slender smile. "Lucius. Lucius Aquila."

———

After three afternoons watching the comings and goings out of Chandler's Assorted Goods, the bright red and green of the sign seemed to Marceline a personal offense, and she was quite sure she never wanted to hear about candles ever again. She didn't want to risk asking the shopkeeper about Mouse again, but if he was as frequent a customer as he seemed to be, she figured he'd have to turn up at the shop before too long. But though she'd spotted a few young men, none had matched the chandler's description: beardless, brown-haired, and supposedly very handsome indeed.

She frowned as she caught sight of one she'd seen before—if he'd gone through his supply in only a couple of days, he really was a prodigious reader. But he didn't look any more like the shopkeeper's description than he had the other day: he was beardless, but his hair was black, and there wasn't anything handsome about him that Marceline could see. He was sallow, scowling like a child, and he certainly didn't have beautiful eyes.

Marceline rubbed her own eyes, which had done far too much work these past few days, and stretched with a weary yawn. And then she froze, because something very sharp was digging into the small of her back.

"Do me a favor and just stay still, all right?" someone said from behind her.

Marceline's limbs froze, but her head turned instinctively. She caught sight of a young woman, sleek and tanned, with short black hair and a lopsided smile. She grasped Marceline's shoulder with her free hand; the other was clearly holding some sort of weapon. "Gods, you *are* young, aren't you? I wonder if this isn't a little much, after all. But orders are orders, you know. Sorry."

Before Marceline had sufficient time to worry about just what her orders had been, another figure slipped into the shadows next to them—it was the black-haired young man with the unbeautiful eyes. "Aye, that's her—the little spy. Come on—grab her and let's get moving."

The woman looked dubious. "She's just a child, Rask. Perhaps there's been some mistake—"

"That's for Mouse to decide, not you." His scowl hardened. "People are going to notice if we don't move. We can discuss this when we get inside."

The woman's mouth twisted, but she nodded. Then she shifted her grip to Marceline's wrist and started dragging her away, moving through the streets at such a brisk pace that Marceline nearly stumbled trying to keep up with her. The man called Rask followed, keeping close behind them. When she tried to lash out with her free hand, the woman caught that one too, and paused, frowning down at her. "Don't do that. And don't draw attention. You want to get out of this alive, don't you?" All Marceline could do was gulp and nod, and all she could do afterward was keep pace, try to keep track of her surroundings, and hope fervently that she wasn't about to be murdered.

She wasn't sure what she'd been expecting, but the house the woman stopped at was just like any other. The first floor was made of stone, wider than it was long, with a second floor built of wood above it. The woman barely paused before its front door, and she certainly didn't loosen her grip on Marceline's wrist. With her free hand, she dug through the confusing flaps of her cloak and clothing and came up with a key. Once she'd unlocked the door, she kicked it unceremoniously open, dragging Marceline inside after her.

The house was sparsely decorated—if one could call it *decorated* at all—and at first Marceline thought it was deserted. But when the woman had dragged Marceline up the creaking wooden steps to the second floor, she came face-to-face with another woman at the top. Tall and dark-skinned, with long hair set in many thin braids that she'd tied off at her neck, she had a half-strung bow slung over one shoulder, though she lost interest in it when she saw them.

The woman holding Marceline smiled. "We've met with a bit of success, as you can see." She jerked her chin at the closed doorway. "Is Mouse in?"

"He's in." But the other woman was frowning. "We're capturing children now? Who ordered that?"

"I did," Rask spoke up from behind them. "But Mouse supported it, so you've no right to speak against it."

The woman with the bow regarded him calmly. "I intend to speak against it, to Mouse or anyone else. This might have been much better handled—though perhaps not by you."

The woman holding Marceline's arm interrupted before Rask could snap out a retort. "I have misgivings too, Naishe, but the thing's been done. Why not at least hear what Mouse plans to do about it?"

The woman with the bow considered it, then nodded. "I'll follow you." The woman holding Marceline shoved her way through the door, and the one with the bow followed, as Rask shut it behind them.

The man sprawled on a pile of threadbare cushions at the back of the room couldn't have been much older than the others. He had a thin, pretty face, with a small nose and pointed chin. His eyes were beautiful after all, large and gray, with an oddly wistful cast to them. He looked at the lot of them with only vague surprise, an easy smile crossing his lips. "That was fast. This is really the spy we've been searching for?"

"Well," the one holding Marceline said, "she's the one who's been looking for you. More than that I couldn't say."

The man with the gray eyes turned his gaze to her, but it was amiable, less searching than the woman with the bow's had been. "And who are you, then?"

That tied Marceline's tongue in knots—she didn't half want to say all about herself in front of *these* people, but she had to tell them something, didn't she? "I'm . . . a monkey," she said at last. "That's what everyone says."

She expected them to be cross with her, but the man with the gray eyes laughed as if she'd especially pleased him. "Is that so? Then I suppose it's not so strange for you to be looking for a mouse after all." Why wasn't it strange? Marceline wondered. But before she could ask him, he continued, "You may well already know where you are, but I'm told one should never dispense with politeness, even in the most trying of situations. So allow me to greet you . . . formally, as it were." He smiled. "Welcome to the resistance."

———

Braddock heaved a sigh and sat up, throwing one arm loosely about her shoulders. "Getting to be time, I'd wager. And Nasser doesn't half do a thing, so you can expect him to be here soon." He grinned crookedly. "Probably best for both of us to have pants on when he does."

"Eh, ruin my good mood, why don't you?" Morgan rolled off the side of the bed and dropped down next to the pile of clothes. She threw Braddock's shirt at him and picked up her own from underneath it. "You really think he knows what he's about with this?"

Braddock laughed. "Bit late for that now, isn't it? But aye, I think *he* does, at least." He scratched his cheek. "That is, I don't think you're in any danger over it—wouldn't have been so quick to agree if I did. The only thing I wonder about is whether those bandits will really be bold enough to attack this place."

"Hmm." Morgan glanced out the window into the courtyard. Ibb's Rest was a far nicer establishment than she'd ever expected, a slender, two-story building that curled across the plain in an almost-completed circle. The room they'd been given was pleasant enough, clean and cool, with plenty of sunlight. She was starting to understand why the Issamiri prized these places. "Temptation can make brave men out of even the most dedicated cowards," she said, turning back to Braddock. "I think Nasser was right—if Ibb's Rest itself wasn't enough of a jewel to lure them, these mysterious guests will be."

The innkeepers and servants at Ibb's Rest had been all aflutter with the news, and even some of the other guests had grown excited about it: it seemed that an exceedingly important person was coming to Ibb's Rest, and had sent a message ahead to make sure there would be room. Morgan hadn't been able to overhear precisely who was supposed to be coming, but since no one at Ibb's Rest actually had to pay to stay there, it had to be something more than wealth that set this visitor apart. However, as Nasser had pointed out, it certainly didn't mean the guest *wasn't* wealthy—the bandits would no doubt be counting on the reverse, in fact.

Nasser had also guessed right about another matter: if they did have to fight the bandits, they wouldn't be doing so alone. When Nasser had explained the potential danger Ibb's Rest was in and how he hoped to make a stand against the thieves if they attacked, he found the inn's proprietors only too willing to assist him. Ibb's Rest did have its own guards—seasoned men, although they didn't see much combat in their current location—and combined with Nasser and Braddock, they made a decent force. There were fewer than twenty of them, though, and for all they knew the bandits might have twice that number. "They might," Nasser had admitted, "but they might not, and they *definitely* don't know we're expecting them. Given the strengths of our position, chance is on our side."

Just then, the man himself knocked at their door. "Our mysterious guest is expected within the hour. It's time to move."

Morgan glanced at Braddock, but they were both as dressed as they needed to be. She opened the door. "We're ready. As much as we can be, anyway."

Braddock was still sitting on the edge of the bed. "Nas, where're they putting you?"

Nasser gave a vague frown. "Up on the roof. It's got quite the vantage, it's true, but I would've preferred to be closer."

"It'll do." Braddock jerked his chin at Morgan. "Take her up there with you. She's not going to want to stay out of it, and she'll be safer with you than down at the front with me."

"That suits me fine. An archer never scorns another pair of eyes." He smiled at her. "Any objections?"

She shook her head. "I've no eagerness to get within the reach of anyone's blades."

They parted outside the inn—Braddock went down the southern path with half the inn's guardsmen to await the bandits by the side of the road, and Morgan and Nasser climbed a ladder to the roof. The traveler's haven was built of stone, and the roof had stone panels strategically placed around its perimeter, tall enough to crouch behind.

"You'd still have more cover shooting from one of the second-story windows," Morgan said, sitting cross-legged behind one of the panels.

"I would," Nasser agreed, still standing, "but my range is superior from this height. And the ground is so flat that I can see as far as my eyesight allows." He grinned. "And that is no small distance, I assure you."

For her part, Morgan couldn't see half so well as she would've liked. "How far do you think they'll go down the road?"

He grimaced. "Too far for my tastes. I wish I could've gotten a position closer to them, but that's the problem with flat ground—no hills for me to stand on, and there are hardly any trees, either. This will have to do."

She looked up at him. "You can really shoot from this distance?"

He laughed. "And more, if I had to. Wait and see for yourself."

So wait she did, shivering slightly, though there was hardly any wind. Nasser drew an arrow from his quiver and nocked it, testing the bow. His scowl told her he found it as inadequate as ever, but it didn't seem to jar his confidence any.

What *did* stir him, finally, was the sound of shouting from the southern road—not from the spot where their men were waiting, mere shadows in the night, but from even farther away, too far for Morgan to make out.

Nasser swore under his breath. "I was afraid of this."

"What is it?" Morgan asked. "What's happened?"

He peered into the dark. "Their caution has outweighed their avarice. Rather than risk more on taking the whole pot, they have decided to seize the richest prize and be on their way."

It took Morgan only a moment to grasp his meaning: the bandits had every reason to believe there were many guests worth stealing from at Ibb's Rest, never mind the establishment itself. But this new guest was a jewel to make all the rest seem trivial—an exceptional mark in his own right, even if he was the only one they robbed. If they waited for him to get to Ibb's Rest, they'd have the advantage of having all their targets in the same place—but they'd have to fight through the inn's guards to get to him, and they had no way of knowing what room he'd be placed in. "They never intended to strike Ibb's Rest," she realized. "They're going to attack his party before he arrives."

Nasser smiled as if in spite of himself. "You're a quicker wit than the ox, aren't you? You've made just one error—they're not *going* to attack, they *are* attacking." He pointed straight ahead. "There. See the torches? That must be our guest's convoy."

Morgan blinked, but she could only see a faint flicker on the horizon—it could've been a torch or a bonfire for all she could tell. "I'll take your word for it," she said, and then looked down. "Our fellows must have seen it too—they're headed that way."

Nasser shook his head. "Even my arrows won't reach that far—not from here."

Morgan stood up. "Then let's close the distance."

He gave her another faint smile. "The ox would never forgive me if I let anything happen to you."

"And *I'd* never forgive me if *I* let anything happen to me," she replied. "So I'll make sure it doesn't."

They would have worn themselves out if they tried to sprint all that distance, but they moved as quickly as they could, always making for the flickering lights. They'd covered half the distance before they spotted a familiar figure racing toward them.

"Had your fill of battle already?" Nasser teased. "I never took you for a coward before."

"Hoping to find *you,* you idiot," Braddock said, panting. "Hurry up—we need your eyes. We're routing them, they're going to start running at any moment, and if you hope to get that bow back, you've got to start picking them off when they do."

Nasser raised his eyebrows. "Routing them so easily? What about our mysterious guest and his fellows?"

"That's just it," Braddock said, and he actually laughed. "Nas, I'd tell you, but we don't have the time, and either way you'd have to see this to believe it." He turned back toward the lights. "Come on."

They followed him, and bit by bit Morgan could pick out the combatants, guardsmen and bandits chasing one another about a battlefield littered with corpses and debris. Braddock had been right—the bandits were definitely having the worst of it. "Hold on," she said to him. "Aren't there more men here than we started w—"

"Get *back* here, you rats!" someone yelled, so fervently that Morgan couldn't help turning toward the voice. Two of the bandits were running across the field, and chasing them was a girl who couldn't have been much older than twenty, a slender sword sheathed at her hip. She closed the distance more quickly than Morgan could have believed, hardly slowing down as she leaped over a pile of bodies in her way.

The two men she was chasing had turned to face her, and Morgan heard Nasser suck in a sharp breath. "Draw your sword, girl," he muttered, nocking an arrow into place.

But Morgan was looking at the girl's sword, and remembering where she'd seen its like. She frowned. "Isn't that—"

The girl ripped her sword free of its sheath in a slash that cut down one of the men in front of her instantly. The second moved to attack her exposed side, but she wrapped her free hand around her sword hilt and moved fluidly into a second strike, driving him backward as their blades clanged. Again she cut across, scoring a shallow hit to his side, and again she used two hands to slash downward—this time the blow caught the side of his neck, half severing it.

"She fights like Lucius," Morgan finished.

Braddock shook his head. "Not quite—Lucius strikes with more discipline, and his footwork is different. But that's a *tsunshin,* to be sure, and she damn well knows how to use it."

The girl sheathed the blade and turned to survey the battlefield again, searching for more foes. Nasser was staring at her in confusion. "There are still more of them. Why did she put it away?"

She'd seen Lucius explain it to Seth once, holding his sword before the fire. *With one of your longswords,* he'd said, *you must begin with two movements—one to draw the sword from its sheath, and one to strike at your opponent. With a* tsun-shin, *the two are one and the same—the draw* is *the first cut, with no unnecessary motion. Depending on the techniques you prefer, starting with a sheathed sword might even be preferable to starting with a drawn one.*

Morgan only got as far as, "It's so she can—" before the girl struck again, this slash even faster than the one before it. Her opponent stood no chance. "It's so she can do that," she finished, as the girl sheathed her sword again.

"My lord!" she called. "My lord, where are you? There was one more about, did you see—"

An arrow thrummed past her ear, and then a second flew over her head. Each hit its mark with a satisfying thump, and the girl whirled toward them, star-tled. "There were two, actually," Nasser said, inclining his head to her. "Now there are none."

The girl followed the arrows' path with her eyes; she looked almost put out. "Oh," she said. "Sorry about that." Then she cupped her hands around her mouth. *"My lord—"*

"Wait, I said!" They all turned to see a young man about her age hobbling toward her, holding his side. There was some bulky object wrapped up in a torn cloak under his other arm, but it wasn't his sword—that was safely tucked into its sheath. "Gods be damned, Rhia, would you wait—one—second—"

She was at his side in an instant. "My lord, are you wounded?"

He waved her off. "No, no, of course not. Just a bit out of practice—all that damned bed rest . . ." He wrinkled his nose. "I wasn't entirely helpless, I'll have you know. I got two of them at least."

She looked unimpressed. "I think I managed ten."

He rolled his eyes. "Well, I beg your pardon if I don't have the damned statue built yet." They paused, and looked at each other—and then they started laugh-ing, as if they were children on a lark, not survivors standing on a battlefield.

They were not children any longer, though, however childhood might seem to cling to them. The girl, so pale and so blond she could only be a Lanvald, might well have been called pretty were it not for the youth standing next to her. *He* was as handsome as anyone Morgan had ever seen, his bronze skin per-fectly smooth and glowing beneath a layer of sweat, his brown hair, slightly bleached by the sun, curling into the suggestion of ringlets at the ends.

"Did you see it, though?" he asked the girl, when he could speak. "It all hap-pened just like I said, didn't it?"

"So it did, my lord." She clapped him on the shoulder. "They'll drink to you at Ibb's Rest tonight."

He straightened up, puffing out his chest. "That's right. They'll drink to *me,* because it was *my* idea. If *she'd* had her way, you and I would still be counting clouds at Eldren Cael while she debated a thousand different outcomes with anyone who would listen."

The girl pressed her lips together unhappily. "My lord, you know your sister was only concerned for your—"

"I know she was *concerned,* she's *always* concerned, because gods forbid I do anything on my own initiative! 'Oh, Feste, you're always putting Rhia to such *trouble.* Why can't you just *calm down* and do as you're *told*—'"

"My lord," the girl said, "you told us that your wound had fully healed, which, judging by the way you're hobbling right now, was certainly less than true. What do you think she's going to say when she finds out you put yourself in so much danger all for the sake of—"

"She's not going to say anything," the young man said, grinning, "because you're not going to tell her."

She bit her lip. "I—I hardly think—"

But he had already moved on, extricating the mysterious object from the cloak he'd wrapped around it. "Here, look what I pulled off one of our bandits! This is bowyer's mulberry, I'd swear to it. I once saw one like this in my—"

"It is bowyer's mulberry," Nasser said, stepping forward. "It's also mine." He extended his hand. "I'll have it back now, if you please."

The young man looked from the bow to Nasser and back again; there was surprise in his face, but no hostility. "Easy there, good fellow," he said, placing the bow in Nasser's outstretched hand. "No need to look so grim. I didn't know." He turned to the girl. "Who're this lot, then?"

"I don't know," she said. "The man whose bow you grabbed is a damned fine shot, though." To Nasser, she added, with a swift bow, "I don't think I properly thanked you for that either. My apologies."

If Nasser had heard, he gave no sign. The instant the young man put the bow into his hand, he had torn the replacement from his shoulder, thrown it to the ground, and spat into the dirt where it lay. Then he ran his hand along the length of the other, a broad grin spreading across his face. "There's my lovely," he murmured. "And not a scratch on her, either."

Braddock sighed. "Now, if only my—"

"Braddock," Morgan said, "if you say *one word* about that bloody ax, I *swear*—"

He held up his hands. "All right, all right! There're a couple of things I'd rather know about anyway." He rounded on the strangers. "You two. You're the guests we were expecting?"

They immediately looked guilty—like children once more, caught out in some mischief. The young man scratched the back of his neck. "Ah, right—forgot my manners again, it seems. I am Hephestion—er, Prince Hephestion would . . . not be incorrect of me to say."

Braddock frowned at him suspiciously. "That's not what you called yourself a minute ago."

The young man winced. "You heard that, did you? That's easy enough to explain, though my dignity won't thank you." He cleared his throat. "You see, when I was born, my brother still found long words rather difficult to say, and chose to shorten them by mysterious methods known only to him. Thus, without being consulted in the matter at all, I became Feste. My sister Adora, who has made it her life's endeavor to imitate our brother in every way possible—I swear she only came out of our mother's womb because he'd done it first—was only too happy to pick up the name. Unfortunately for me, it stuck, and my family has used it ever since."

That seemed to satisfy Braddock, if not humble him; he nodded at the girl. "And her?"

He smiled at her. "This is Rhia, our captain of the guard at Eldren Cael."

Nasser raised an eyebrow at that. "She's a bit young for that position, isn't she?"

The prince laughed. "You saw her fight just now, and you're saying that?"

But the girl—Rhia—ducked her head. "I'm sure I lack the experience I could wish—"

"Oh, nonsense," Hephestion said. "My sister's only a few years older than you, and nobody says *she's* too young to be queen, do they?" He waved at a nearby man carrying a torch. "Hey there, would you mind bringing some of that light this way?"

As the man hurried over, Nasser asked, "The additional men were yours, then?"

"They were," Hephestion said proudly. "We'd been hearing about those damned bandits all the way back in Eldren Cael—and Eldren Cael's got its fair share of bandits, let me tell you—so Rhia and I thought we'd do what we could to lure them out. It's the crown's duty to keep the roads safe for our people, after all." He took the torch from his servant, then nodded at him. "Go on ahead, if you like; we're doing quite well for ourselves here." The man bowed and complied, and Hephestion lifted the torch aloft. The light picked out the flecks of gold in his warm brown eyes, while his captain's glinted green. "We sent ahead to tell the keepers of Ibb's Rest of our plans, so if you didn't know of them, you must have chosen to help of your own accord. I must thank you for that—I hope you'll tell me if there's any way I can assist you."

Braddock was still looking at Rhia. "A Lanvald with an Aurnian sword in Issamira," he said slowly. "There's a story there, I'm sure."

Her eyes grew sad. "There is, but . . . I don't know that it's a very good one."

He hesitated, perhaps wary of overstepping, but Braddock had never been one for politeness. "Might I . . . see the blade?"

She hesitated too, but finally drew it forth, holding it out to him with both hands. The steel glimmered magnificently in the torchlight, as smooth and clear as mirrorglass; the edge looked sharp enough to cut the wind in two. "That's a beautiful sword," Braddock said with feeling, weighing it in his hands. "Is that vardrath steel?"

The girl couldn't have looked more pleased if she'd received the compliment herself. "You have a good eye," she said. "Yes, it is. It was my father's."

CHAPTER FORTY-THREE

Roger finished etching the third finger-sign next to the third tree branch of House Trevelyan, completing the pathway Morgan and Braddock had taken from the Citadel dungeon to the cave outside Valyanrend's walls. He was slowly sketching out quite a sizable map of the tunnels, but it was also worthwhile to mark the tunnels themselves, for any future wanderers as well as to help him remember. He took a moment to admire his handiwork in the light of the torch: a thief's finger-sign right beside the sigil of a man who had once been one of the most powerful people in the world. The sight made him oddly proud.

However, now that he knew the sigil's meaning, that mystery had taken him about as far as it could go. It meant the tunnels were old, certainly, if they had been in use since before the fall of Elesthene, but he doubted Trevelyan had known any more about them than Morgan and Braddock did. And that meant he had to devote himself to the second mystery, and figure out what it was that the ruby was reacting to down here.

Once or twice, on his travels through Sheath and beyond it, he'd felt the ruby warm in his pocket, but it had always been in crowded places where he feared taking it out to check. But he doubted he'd encounter anyone else down here, which made it his best chance to test the thing. He'd tried to test the emerald, too, but it remained stubbornly inert no matter what he did.

Yesterday he'd been down here for an hour, the ruby in one hand and the torch in the other, wandering the tunnels and looking for any changes. He'd finally found a tunnel mouth where the ruby would flicker slightly, but he'd been so tired by that point, he'd marked it to save for another day. Now that he'd marked everything else he'd discovered up to now, a final fail-safe against getting lost, he was ready to venture deeper into the tunnels than he ever had before.

He found where he'd left off yesterday, and sure enough, the ruby flickered as he made his way down the tunnel, as if there were a tiny flame inside it. It didn't seem to get any brighter as he walked, but it definitely wasn't any dimmer, and when he got to the next fork, he noticed it flared up a bit more down the right path than the left.

He put the ruby into his pocket for a moment so he could mark the wall, and set off again. The light wasn't very bright, but it was holding steady, with hardly any flickering this time. It was also quite warm, so that Roger fumbled for a handkerchief to wad up between it and his fingers. There was no telling how hot it was going to get, and he wasn't about to get burned for his curiosity.

It went on like that for three more turns—stop at a crossroads, check where the ruby was brighter, mark the path—before the ruby started to heat his hand even through the cloth. Warmth was radiating out from it, like firelight against his face, and it was getting too bright to look at for very long. Did that mean he was getting close?

He hit another crossroads, and started to check the left-hand path, but he hadn't taken three steps when the ruby shuddered in his hand, pulsing with intense light and heat. A sharp noise echoed off the walls as the gem's surface cracked, and Roger was so surprised, he dropped it without thinking. It hit the ground and bounced, rolling ahead of him down the tunnel, until suddenly—

Roger was flung against the wall, something whizzing past his face fast enough to hurt. He threw up a hand to protect his eyes, and promptly lost his balance. He hit the floor hard, dropping the torch, which fizzled out.

He lay there for what felt like an age, dazed and winded, the taste of blood in his mouth and bright spots dancing before his eyes. There was blood on his face, too, he realized, when he brought up a hand to trace the cut on his cheek. He fumbled in the dark for the torch, and struggled to light it again, to see if he could find the ruby.

The light revealed it was lying all around him, in half a hundred fragments, littering the tunnel, dead and dull. Roger walked to the nearest one and picked it up; it was jagged and sharp, the last remnants of heat quickly fading away. Could he have been mistaken? Could it possibly have been a fake, made only of glass?

But no, he knew the truth. It had been a pure gemstone, and something had exerted force enough to shatter it. And that something was here in these tunnels—for all he knew, it lay at the end of the one he was standing in now, somewhere down there in the dark.

Did he really want to find out what it was? Or wasn't it safer to flee these tunnels forever, and pretend he had never seen them?

"Well, that settles it," Arianrod said, slapping the letter down on her desk. "It's good to have at least one question definitively resolved, even if I had long suspected the answer."

Seren squinted at the letter, sliding it closer so she could read it. It was one of a bundle King Kelken had sent from Mist's Edge. "What does it confirm? You always knew magic existed—you didn't even have to look outside yourself for proof of it."

"I knew of the renewed existence of mages, yes—however imperfect that renewal might be. But *wardrenfell* are not mages, and the return of the one does not necessarily prove the return of the other."

"*Wardrenfell* aren't mages?" Seren repeated. "But this makes it sound like a *wardrenfell* is a person who can use magic. Is that . . . not what a mage is?"

Arianrod smiled. "I can use magic, Seren, because it is an essential part of my being, and could no more be extracted from me than could my heartbeat or the color of my eyes. It has always been this way, since the day that I was born. But just as a mage can only be born, a *wardrenfell* can only be created. They don't innately possess magic: it . . . comes to inhabit them at some later point, though the how and why of it are poorly understood. Just one more thing I'll have to figure out."

Seren was still looking over the letter. "All right, so you know *wardrenfell* exist. I assume that discovery has important implications for you?"

Arianrod reached over, pointing at a cluster of words. "This soldier of Eira's claimed he fought with this woman for an extended period, that her magic prevented him from ever getting close to her—that even when she had him at her mercy, she took her time deciding what to do with him. And this wound she inflicted on him, that remade itself over and over? That is no minor spell, Seren. Yet the man who fought her never observed that she grew tired or weak, that the use of all that magic ever harmed her in any way."

"So she . . . she doesn't suffer like you do," Seren realized. "She can use magic without pain?"

"That's what I think. And I think that is a gift common to all *wardrenfell*, not just this one."

That was certainly a crucial revelation, but part of Seren's mind couldn't fully focus on it, distracted by something in the way Arianrod had described the battle between the *wardrenfell* and Eira's soldier. She searched her memory until she finally found it: *I wasn't able to manage so much as a scratch.* That was what he had said, wasn't it? "Wait. That man who attended the king at Mist's Edge—the one with the scar on his face. We . . . had occasion to converse, and he told me his scar had been inflicted by a woman he believed had intended to kill him, a woman for whom he had been no match. We know he was from Lanvaldis, and though he denied being King Kelken's servant, he said he *had* been a servant, once. Do you think he could be . . . ?" But then she paused. "Oh, but I suppose . . . it sounds like this man of Eira's died, doesn't it?"

Arianrod looked thoughtful. "This was the last letter Eira ever sent to Kelken's father—or the last he could find, anyway. It must have been sent around the time of Lanvaldis's fall. Perhaps Eira himself did not live long enough to learn the fate of his wounded soldier." She smiled. "In fact, if the soldier really was that Cadfael, I might even know how he survived. A pity there's no way to test the theory, not now that he's disappeared."

"You don't want to try to find him?"

"That depends," Arianrod said. "Do you think he knows where this woman is now?"

Seren considered it, and shook her head. "I doubt it. I think he'd *like* to know, but that only makes me more certain that he doesn't."

"Then it isn't worth the time and resources it would take to find him. The details of his report to Eira are in the letter anyway."

Seren braced one hand on the desk, leaning against it. Though Arianrod seemed to have fully recovered from Elgar's attack, Seren still felt shaken, off balance somehow. She had been drawn from Stonespire so easily; she had panicked like a novice when she realized Arianrod was in danger. She couldn't stop lingering over those deficiencies, chastising herself for them in every idle moment.

She couldn't stop remembering that boy's face, no matter how much she wanted to.

She took a steadying breath. "What are you going to do, then?" she asked Arianrod. "What way forward do you see in all this?"

Arianrod leaned back in her chair, threading her fingers together. "We are a continent at war, Seren, so of course we are all scrambling to outmaneuver one another, searching for any advantage that might give us an edge. This woman would serve that purpose even if she were the only one of her kind, and I strongly suspect she is not. This research, at least, suggests that when *wardrenfell* do appear, they appear in groups." She tapped the cover of *Wardrenfell of Historical Distinction,* the book she had taken from the library at Mist's Edge. "I doubt we shall find half a hundred of them, but even several would not be insignificant, if they held this woman's share of power. Any country who could command their allegiance would possess a formidable asset, and that means no country can afford to ignore them. But for me and Elgar in particular, the stakes are even higher than that."

"Why in particular?"

Arianrod grinned at her. "Because we're the only two rulers I know of who are also mages."

"*Elgar* is a mage?" Seren asked. "Are you sure of that?"

"Oh, absolutely."

"So . . . so when you met him, you sensed—"

"No, it's nothing like that," Arianrod said. "It's not something you can detect in another person, like some kind of stain. But I am still certain of it, just as I'm sure he is certain of me." She reached for a blank sheet of parchment, and started scribbling what looked like a list. "For mages, Seren, *wardrenfell* present a further opportunity. If I can find them, if I can figure out how they are able to cast without pain . . . it may be I can deduce the nature of magic itself— where it comes from, why it exists. If I can learn that, I know I'll be able to figure out what causes my deficiency, and how it can be fixed. And if I can become the equal of the mages of old . . . well, defeating Elgar would be only the beginning of what I could do then." She brushed the quill against her cheek. "Of course, if Elgar makes contact with the *wardrenfell* before I do, he will gain the same opportunity. And if he is able to seize it, things will become very unpleasant for a great number of people, me in particular."

Seren shifted uneasily. "But if the *wardrenfell* remain elusive, and Elgar has no way of increasing his power . . . then our chances are better?"

Arianrod laughed. "Gods no, our chances are terrible. Half a glance at a map would convince even the dimmest peasant that we have no hope of defeating Elgar without aid. Our disadvantages are staggering . . . most would say insurmountable."

Seren hardly knew what she was supposed to say to that. "Yet you seem . . . content."

"Naturally." Looking over the parchment, she made one last entry and set the quill down. Her smile was as imperturbable as ever. "A genius needs an impossible task, Seren. What else would pose a sufficient challenge?"

———

Roger hated admitting failure almost as much as he hated any and all kinds of danger, so it was hardly a comfort to tell himself that doing the first had helped him avoid the second. His scrapes were minor, but he wanted to see to them, and without the ruby's guidance he had no idea how to navigate the tunnels anyway. That didn't mean he was admitting *defeat*—just a minor and extremely temporary setback. He had tested all the fragments of the ruby that he could find, and none of them reacted to the tunnels; it seemed whatever had been done to it had broken or run out when the ruby shattered. And that damned emerald was still as useless as ever; it had never reacted to anything but the ruby.

He lingered for a moment in the alley adjacent to the tunnel entrance—at the edge of Sheath, a stone's throw from the Fades. The sun had set while he had been on his investigation, but the growing dusk still left plenty of light to see by. He had intended just to catch his breath, to rub the dirt and blood from his face. But he went still when he heard a voice.

It was low, sibilant, most likely female. "Well, that was a disaster."

"It could hardly have been otherwise. The ward was too ancient—we are too far distant from the climate in which it was made. It was never going to hold." The second voice was rough with age, but not slurred or uncertain in the slightest—the words were perfectly enunciated, every syllable sharp as a knife.

Roger took a deep breath, and craned his head around the corner of the alleyway.

Even before they spoke again, it was easy to see which voice belonged to which figure. Standing straight as a pole in the middle of the street was an old woman, white-haired and lined with countless wrinkles, though she did not look frail. Gran had been keen and capable to the very hour of her death, and he suspected this woman was no different. Her eyes were piercing even at this distance, even though they aimed all their intensity not at Roger but at her companion.

The other woman recalled Gran too, in a strange way—though it was a version of her he had only imagined, never seen. It was Gran as she must have been when she was young, a master thief just coming into her own. This woman had that nimbleness, that agile grace; her movements were sweeping and precise as a dancer's, while the old crone stayed so still. And the woman's hair was not just any red; it was the *Halfen* red, the color such a perfect match that he almost wondered if he knew her, or if she was an offshoot of some family branch even Gran hadn't known about. She would have been more beautiful if she were not quite so thin: her limbs were long and spindly, her shoulder blades sharply defined. There was an unabashed hunger in her eyes.

She was displeased now, circling the crone restlessly. "It needn't be so significant. There are other ways—there are countless other ways. It could still turn out as we desire."

"No," the crone said calmly, the word as final as a slammed door. "He might find it, still—after *much* searching. But even if he does, what will he do with it?

He cannot see what needs to be seen. How will he know what he needs to know?" She sighed. "I know it is not in your nature to be patient, but if you would try—"

"You would speak to me of *patience*?" her companion hissed, fingers clawing at the air. "You would speak to *me* of patience? How long do you think I have been patient? How long have I been thwarted and cast aside, the province only of grasping cowards and two-bit schemers? How long has it been since I beheld a true *vision*?"

What bloody scheme was this? No common thief would dare to speak so arrogantly in the open street, yet this woman declaimed as if challenging the very air to defy her. Who was she, that he had no prior knowledge of her?

For the first time, he saw a hint of irony creep into the crone's expression. "Well, Imperator Elgar certainly has a vision, wouldn't you say?"

"An *old* vision," the younger woman spat, eyes flashing. "A vision we are *all* tired of, I not least of all." She scoffed. "Elesthene! That puddle of stagnant water! Is *that* what you want me to look forward to?"

"No one grieved more than I over the destruction wrought by Elesthene," the crone said, a slight edge to her voice. "I never claimed to be neutral in this matter. I merely wish to suggest that other avenues might prove more successful."

"Other avenues?" The younger woman's smirk was sharp and knowing; that reminded him of Gran, too. "Oh, not your pet? The little mage, who scratches at the smallest drop of blood and thinks she has found the vein?"

The crone pursed her lips. "No one is better suited for it."

"Better suited, perhaps, but there are many who are better *situated*. How is she to get to Valyanrend? She will come here only if she loses."

"We don't know that."

"Oh, we surely do. What other alternative can you discern, even with those far-seeing eyes of yours?" The younger woman leaped away from her companion, landed on the ball of her foot, and spun around. She extended her bony arm out straight, one long finger pointed into the crone's face. "Mark my words, Asariel," she said. "If your favorite should come to Valyanrend, she will die. She will die before she can ever discover its secret, or even begin to learn just how much her kind has forgotten." She relented slightly, dropping her hand. "It gives me no pleasure to tell you this, you understand. It is only that I above all know what it is to hope so ardently for so long, only to be crushed beneath the heel of circumstance."

If the crone had been at all affected by that dire pronouncement, she did not show it. "It is reality that crushes you most often, my old friend," she said. "We must both wait and see what it has in store for us this time."

As if by some unspoken agreement, they turned to walk down the street, away from Roger. But just before they rounded the corner, the younger woman glanced back over her shoulder, wearing that smirk again. "Evening, Roger," she said.

Roger jerked his head back into the shadows of the alleyway, his heart pounding absurdly. When had he ever . . . how had she known . . . ?

He was being ridiculous, he told himself. They were just an old crone and a skinny wisp of a woman, physically unimpressive even by his standards. What did he have to be afraid of?

He raced back into the street, following the route the two women had taken. But when he turned the corner, the road he saw was straight and wide and empty, only moonlight resting on the cobblestones.